CLASSIC SCIENCE FICTION AND FANTASY STORIES

CLASSIC SCIENCE FICTION AND FANTASY STORIES

Edited by
Stephen Brennan

TALOS PRESS

Talos Press books may be purchased in bulk at special discounts for sales promotion, corporate gifts, fund-raising, or educational purposes. Special editions can also be created to specifications. For details, contact the Special Sales Department, Talos Press, 307 West 36th Street, 11th Floor, New York, NY 10018 or info@skyhorsepublishing.com.

Talos Press is an imprint of Skyhorse Publishing, Inc.®, a Delaware corporation.

Visit our website at www.skyhorsepublishing.com.

10 9 8 7 6 5 4 3 2 1

Library of Congress Cataloging-in-Publication Data is available on file.

ISBN: 978-1-940456-01-0
Ebook ISBN: 978-1-940456-04-1

Cover design by Owen Corrigan

Printed in the United States of America

For Finn
A Devotee of the Genre

CONTENTS

FRANKENSTEIN

Mary W. Shelley (1818)

WHEN I HAD attained the age of seventeen, my parents resolved that I should become a student at the university of Ingolstadt. I had hitherto attended the schools of Geneva; but my father thought it necessary, for the completion of my education, that I should be made acquainted with other customs than those of my native country. My departure was therefore fixed at an early date; but, before the day resolved upon could arrive, the first misfortune of my life occurred—an omen, as it were, of my future misery.

Elizabeth had caught the scarlet fever; her illness was severe, and she was in the greatest danger. During her illness, many arguments had been urged to persuade my mother to refrain from attending upon her. She had, at first, yielded to our entreaties; but when she heard that the life of her favourite was menaced, she could no longer control her anxiety. She attended her sick bed,—her watchful attentions triumphed over the malignity of the distemper, Elizabeth was saved, but the consequences of this imprudence were fatal to her preserver. On the third day my mother sickened; her fever was accompanied by the most alarming symptoms, and the looks of her medical attendants prognosticated the worst event. On her death-bed the fortitude and benignity of this best of women did not desert her. She joined the hands of Elizabeth and myself:—"My children," she said, "my firmest hopes of future happiness were placed on the prospect of your union. This expectation will now be the consolation of your father. Elizabeth, my love, you must supply my place to my younger children. Alas! I regret that I am taken from you; and, happy and beloved as I have been, is it not hard to quit you all? But these are not thoughts befitting me; I will endeavor to resign myself cheerfully to death, and will indulge a hope of meeting you in another world."

She died calmly; and her countenance expressed affection even in death. I need not describe the feelings of those whose dearest ties are rent by that most irreparable evil; the void that presents itself to the soul; and the despair that is exhibited on the countenance. It is so long before the mind can persuade itself that she, whom we saw every day, and whose very existence appeared a part of our own, can have departed for ever—that the brightness of a beloved eye can have been extinguished, and the sound of a voice so familiar, and dear to the ear, can be hushed, never more to be heard. These are the reflections of the first days; but when the lapse of time proves the reality of the evil, then the actual bitterness of grief commences. Yet from whom has not that rude hand rent away some dear connection? and why should I describe a sorrow which all have felt, and must feel? The time at length arrives, when grief is rather an indulgence than a necessity; and the smile that plays upon the lips, although it may be deemed a sacrilege, is not banished. My mother was dead, but we had still duties which we ought to perform; we must continue our course with the rest, and learn to think ourselves fortunate, whilst one remains whom the spoiler has not seized.

My departure for Ingolstadt, which had been deferred by these events, was now again determined upon. I obtained from my father a respite of some weeks. It appeared to me sacrilege so soon to leave the repose, akin to death, of the house of mourning, and to rush into the thick of life. I was new to sorrow, but it did not the less alarm me. I was unwilling to quit the sight of those that remained to me; and, above all, I desired to see my sweet Elizabeth in some degree consoled.

She indeed veiled her grief, and strove to act the comforter to us all. She looked steadily on life, and assumed its duties with courage and zeal. She devoted herself to those whom she had been taught to call her uncle and cousins. Never was she so enchanting as at this time, when she recalled the sunshine of her smiles and spent them upon us. She forgot even her own regret in her endeavors to make us forget.

The day of my departure at length arrived. Clerval spent the last evening with us. He had endeavored to persuade his father to permit him to accompany me, and to become my fellow student; but in vain. His father was a narrow-minded trader, and saw idleness and ruin in the aspirations and ambition of his son. Henry deeply felt the misfortune of being debarred from a liberal education. He said little; but when he spoke, I read in his kindling eye and in his animated glance a restrained but firm resolve, not to be chained to the miserable details of commerce.

We sat late. We could not tear ourselves away from each other, nor persuade ourselves to say the word "Farewell!" It was said; and we retired under the pretence of seeking repose, each fancying that the other was deceived: but when at morning's dawn I descended to the carriage which was to convey me away, they were all there—my father again to bless me, Clerval to press my hand once more, my Elizabeth to renew her entreaties that I would write often, and to bestow the last feminine attentions on her playmate and friend.

I threw myself into the chaise that was to convey me away, and indulged in the most melancholy reflections. I, who had ever been surrounded by amiable companions, continually engaged in endeavoring to bestow mutual pleasure, I was now alone. In the university, whither I was going, I must form my own friends, and be my own protector. My life had hitherto been remarkably secluded and domestic; and this had given me invincible repugnance to new countenances. I loved my brothers, Elizabeth, and Clerval; these were "old familiar faces"; but I believed myself totally unfitted for the company of strangers. Such were my reflections as I commenced my journey; but as I proceeded, my spirits and hopes rose. I ardently desired the acquisition of knowledge. I had often, when at home, thought it hard to remain during my youth cooped up in one place, and had longed to enter the world, and take my station among other human beings. Now my desires were complied with, and it would, indeed, have been folly to repent.

I had sufficient leisure for these and many other reflections during my journey to Ingolstadt, which was long and fatiguing. At length the high white steeple of the town met my eyes. I alighted, and was conducted to my solitary apartment, to spend the evening as I pleased.

The next morning I delivered my letters of introduction, and paid a visit to some of the principal professors. Chance—or rather the evil influence, the Angel of Destruction, which asserted omnipotent sway over me from the moment I turned my reluctant steps from my father's door—led me first to Mr. Krempe, professor of natural philosophy. He was an uncouth man, but deeply embued in the secrets of his science. He asked me several questions concerning my progress in the different branches of science appertaining to natural philosophy. I replied carelessly; and, partly in contempt, mentioned the names of my alchymists as the principal authors I had studied. The professor stared: "Have you," he said, "really spent your time in studying such nonsense?"

I replied in the affirmative. "Every minute," continued M. Krempe with warmth, "every instant that you have wasted on those books is utterly and entirely lost. You have burdened your memory with exploded systems and useless names. Good God! in what desert land have you lived, where no one was kind enough to inform you that these fancies, which you have so greedily imbibed, are a thousand years old, and as musty as they are ancient? I little expected, in this enlightened and scientific age, to find a disciple of Albertus Magnus and Paracelsus. My dear sir, you must begin your studies entirely anew."

So saying, he stept aside, and wrote down a list of several books treating of natural philosophy, which he desired me to procure; and dismissed me, after mentioning that in the beginning of the following week he intended to commence a course of lectures upon natural philosophy in its general relations, and that M. Waldman, a fellow-professor, would lecture upon chemistry the alternate days that he omitted.

I returned home, not disappointed, for I have said that I had long considered those authors useless whom the professor reprobated; but I returned, not at all the more inclined to recur to these studies in any shape. M. Krempe was a little squat man, with a gruff voice and a repulsive countenance; the teacher, therefore, did not prepossess me in favor of his pursuits. In rather a too philosophical and connected a strain, perhaps, I have given an account of the conclusions I had come to concerning them in my early years. As a child, I had not been content with the results promised by the modern professors of natural science. With a confusion of ideas only to be accounted for by my extreme youth, and my want of a guide on such matters, I had retrod the steps of knowledge along the paths of time, and exchanged the discoveries of recent enquirers for the dreams of forgotten alchymists. Besides, I had a contempt for the uses of modern natural philosophy. It was very different, when the masters of the science sought immortality and power; such views, although futile, were grand: but now the scene was changed. The ambition of the enquirer seemed to limit itself to the annihilation of those visions on which my interest in science was chiefly founded. I was required to exchange chimeras of boundless grandeur for realities of little worth.

Such were my reflections during the first two or three days of my residence at Ingolstadt, which were chiefly spent in becoming acquainted with the localities, and the principal residents in my new abode. But as the ensuing week commenced, I thought of the information which M. Krempe had given me concerning the lectures. And although I could not consent to go and hear that little conceited fellow deliver sentences out of a pulpit, I recollected what he had said of M. Waldman, whom I had never seen, as he had hitherto been out of town.

Partly from curiosity, and partly from idleness, I went into the lecturing room, which M. Waldman entered shortly after. This professor was very unlike his colleague. He appeared about fifty years of age, but with an aspect expressive of the greatest benevolence; a few grey hairs covered his temples, but those at the back of his head were nearly black. His person was short, but remarkably erect; and his voice the sweetest I had ever heard. He began his lecture by a recapitulation of the history of chemistry, and the various improvements made by different men of learning, pronouncing with fervour the names of the most distinguished discoverers. He then took a cursory view of the present state of the science, and explained many of its elementary terms. After having made a few preparatory experiments, he concluded with a panegyric upon modern chemistry, the terms of which I shall never forget:—

"The ancient teachers of this science," said he, "promised impossibilities, and performed nothing. The modern masters promise very little; they know that metals cannot be transmuted, and that the elixir of life is a chimera. But these philosophers, whose hands seem only made to dabble in dirt, and their eyes to pore over the microscope or crucible, have indeed performed miracles. They penetrate into the recesses of nature, and show how she works in her hiding places. They ascend into the heavens: they have discovered how the blood circulates, and the nature of the air we breathe. They have acquired new and almost unlimited powers; they can command the thunders of heaven, mimic the earthquake, and even mock the invisible world with its own shadows."

Such were the professor's words—rather let me say such the words of fate, enounced to destroy me. As he went on, I felt as if my soul were grappling with a palpable enemy; one by one the various keys were touched which formed the mechanism of my being: chord after chord was sounded, and soon my mind was filled with one thought, one conception, one purpose. So much has been done, exclaimed the soul of Frankenstein,—more, far more, will I achieve: treading in the steps already marked, I will pioneer a new way, explore unknown powers, and unfold to the world the deepest mysteries of creation.

I closed not my eyes that night. My internal being was in a state of insurrection and turmoil; I felt that order would thence arise, but I had no power to produce it. By degrees, after the morning's dawn, sleep came. I awoke, and my yesternight's thoughts were as a dream. There only remained a resolution to return to my ancient studies, and to devote myself to a science for which I believed myself to possess a natural talent. On the same day, I paid M. Waldman a visit. His manners in private were even more mild and attractive than in public; for there was a certain dignity in his mien during his lecture, which in his own house was replaced by the greatest affability and kindness. I gave him pretty nearly the same account of my former pursuits as I had given to his fellow-professor. He heard with attention the little narration concerning my studies, and smiled at the names of Cornelius Agrippa and Paracelsus, but without the contempt that M. Krempe had exhibited. He said, that "these were men to whose indefatigable zeal modern philosophers were indebted for most of the foundations of their knowledge. They had left to us, as an easier task, to give new names, and arrange in connected classifications, the facts which they in a great degree had been the instruments of bringing to light. The labours of men of genius, however erroneously directed, scarcely ever fail in ultimately turning to the solid advantage of mankind." I listened to his statement, which was delivered without any presumption or affectation; and then added, that his lecture had removed my prejudices against modern chemists; I expressed myself in measured terms, with the modesty and deference due from a youth to his instructor, without letting escape (inexperience in life would have made me ashamed) any of the enthusiasm which stimulated my intended labours. I requested his advice concerning the books I ought to procure.

"I am happy," said M. Waldman, "to have gained a disciple; and if your application equals your ability, I have no doubt of your success. Chemistry is that branch of natural philosophy in which the greatest improvements have been and may be made: it is on that account that I have made it my peculiar study; but at the same time I have not neglected the other branches of science. A man would make but a very sorry chemist if he attended to that department of human knowledge alone. If your wish is to become really a man of science, and not merely a petty experimentalist, I should advise you to apply to every branch of natural philosophy, including mathematics."

He then took me into his laboratory, and explained to me the uses of his various machines; instructing me as to what I ought to procure, and promising me the use of his own when I should have advanced far enough in the science not to derange their mechanism. He also gave me the list of books which I had requested; and I took my leave.

Thus ended a day memorable to me: it decided my future destiny.

From this day natural philosophy, and particularly chemistry, in the most comprehensive sense of the term, became nearly my sole occupation. I read with ardor those works, so full of genius and discrimination, which modern enquirers have written on these subjects. I attended the lectures, and cultivated the acquaintance, of the men of science of the university; and I found even in M. Krempe a great deal of sound sense and real information, combined, it is true, with a repulsive physiognomy and manners, but not on that account the less valuable. In M. Waldman I found a true friend. His gentleness was never tinged by dogmatism; and his instructions were given with an air of frankness and good nature, that banished every idea of pedantry. In a thousand ways he smoothed for me the path of knowledge, and made the most abstruse enquiries clear and facile to my apprehension. My application was at first fluctuating and uncertain; it gained strength as I proceeded, and soon became so ardent and eager, that the stars often disappeared in the light of morning whilst I was yet engaged in my laboratory.

As I applied so closely, it may be easily conceived that my progress was rapid. My ardor was indeed the astonishment of the students, and my proficiency that of the masters. Professor Krempe often asked me, with a sly smile, how Cornelius Agrippa went on? whilst M. Waldman expressed the most heart-felt exultation in my progress. Two years passed in this manner, during which I paid no visit to Geneva, but was engaged, heart and soul, in the pursuit of some discoveries, which I hoped to make. None but those who have experienced them can conceive of the enticements of science. In other studies you go as far as others have gone before you, and there is nothing more to know; but in a scientific pursuit there is continual food for discovery and wonder. A mind of moderate capacity, which closely pursues one study, must infallibly arrive at great proficiency in that study; and I, who continually sought the attainment of one object of pursuit, and was solely wrapt up in this, improved so rapidly, that, at the end of two years, I made some discoveries in the improvement of some chemical instruments, which procured me great esteem and admiration at the university. When I had arrived at this point, and had become as well acquainted with the theory and practice of natural philosophy as depended on the lessons of any of the professors at Ingolstadt, my residence there being no longer conducive to my improvements, I thought of returning to my friends and my native town, when an incident happened that protracted my stay.

One of the phenomena which had peculiarly attracted my attention was the structure of the human frame, and, indeed, any animal endued with life.

Whence, I often asked myself, did the principle of life proceed? It was a bold question, and one which has ever been considered as a mystery; yet with how many things are we upon the brink of becoming acquainted, if cowardice or carelessness did not restrain our enquiries. I revolved these circumstances in my mind, and determined thenceforth to apply myself more particularly to those branches of natural philosophy which relate to physiology. Unless I had been animated by an almost supernatural enthusiasm, my application to this study would have been irksome, and almost intolerable. To examine the causes of life, we must first have recourse to death. I became acquainted with the science of anatomy: but this was not sufficient; I must also observe the natural decay and corruption of the human body. In my education my father had taken the greatest precautions that my mind should be impressed with no supernatural horrors. I do not ever remember to have trembled at a tale of superstition, or to have feared the apparition of a spirit. Darkness had no effect upon my fancy; and a churchyard was to me merely the receptacle of bodies deprived of life, which, from being the seat of beauty and strength, had become food for the worm. Now I was led to examine the cause and progress of this decay, and forced to spend days and nights in vaults and charnel-houses. My attention was fixed upon every object the most insupportable to the delicacy of the human feelings. I saw how the fine form of man was degraded and wasted; I beheld the corruption of death succeed to the blooming cheek of life; I saw how the worm inherited the wonders of the eye and brain. I paused, examining and analysing all the minutiæ of causation, as exemplified in the change from life to death, and death to life, until from the midst of this darkness a sudden light broke in upon me—a light so brilliant and wondrous, yet so simple, that while I became dizzy with the immensity of the prospect which it illustrated, I was surprised, that among so many men of genius who had directed their enquiries towards the same science, that I alone should be reserved to discover so astonishing a secret.

Remember, I am not recording the vision of a madman. The sun does not more certainly shine in the heavens, than that which I now affirm is true. Some miracle might have produced it, yet the stages of the discovery were distinct and probable. After days and nights of incredible labour and fatigue, I succeeded in discovering the cause of generation and life; nay, more, I became myself capable of bestowing animation upon lifeless matter.

The astonishment which I had at first experienced on this discovery soon gave place to delight and rapture. After so much time spent in painful labour, to arrive at once at the summit of my desires, was the most gratifying consummation of my toils. But this discovery was so great and overwhelming, that all the steps by which I had been progressively led to it were obliterated, and I beheld only the result. What had been the study and desire of the wisest men since the creation of the world was now within my grasp. Not that, like a magic scene, it all opened upon me at once: the information I had obtained was of a nature rather to direct my endeavours so soon as I should point them towards the object of my search, than to exhibit that object already accomplished. I was like the Arabian who had been buried with the dead, and found a passage to life, aided only by one glimmering, and seemingly ineffectual, light.

I see by your eagerness, and the wonder and hope which your eyes express, my friend, that you expect to be informed of the secret with which I am acquainted; that cannot be: listen patiently until the end of my story, and you will easily perceive why I am reserved upon that subject. I will not lead you on, unguarded and ardent as I then was, to your destruction and infallible misery. Learn from me, if not by my precepts, at least by my example, how dangerous is the acquirement of knowledge, and how much happier that man is who believes his native town to be the world, than he who aspires to become greater than his nature will allow.

When I found so astonishing a power placed within my hands, I hesitated a long time concerning the manner in which I should employ it. Although I possessed the capacity of bestowing animation, yet to prepare a frame for the reception of it, with all its intricacies of fibres, muscles, and veins, still remained a work of inconceivable difficulty and labour. I doubted at first whether I should attempt the creation of a being like myself, or one of simpler organization; but my imagination was too much exalted by my first success to permit me to doubt of my ability to give life to an animal as complex and wonderful as man. The materials at present within my command hardly appeared adequate to so arduous an undertaking; but I doubted not that I should ultimately succeed. I prepared myself for a multitude of reverses; my operations might be incessantly baffled, and at last my work be imperfect: yet, when I considered the improvement which every day takes place in science and mechanics, I was encouraged to hope my present attempts would at least lay the foundations of future success. Nor could I consider the magnitude and complexity of my plan as any argument of its impracticability. It was with these feelings that I began the creation of a human being. As the minuteness of the parts formed a great hinderance to my speed, I resolved, contrary to my first intention, to make the being of a gigantic stature; that is to say, about eight feet in height, and proportionably large. After having formed this determination, and having spent some months in successfully collecting and arranging my materials, I began.

No one can conceive the variety of feelings which bore me onwards, like a hurricane, in the first enthusiasm of success. Life and death appeared to me ideal bounds, which I should first break through, and pour a torrent of light into our dark world. A new species would bless me as its creator and source; many happy and excellent natures would owe their being to me. No father could claim the gratitude of his child so completely as I should deserve theirs. Pursuing these reflections, I thought, that if I could bestow animation upon lifeless matter, I might in process of time (although I now found it impossible) renew life where death had apparently devoted the body to corruption.

These thoughts supported my spirits, while I pursued my undertaking with unremitting ardour. My cheek had grown pale with study, and my person had become emaciated with confinement. Sometimes, on the very brink of certainty, I failed; yet still I clung to the hope which the next day or the next hour might realise. One secret which I alone possessed was the hope to which I had dedicated myself; and the moon gazed on my midnight labours, while, with unrelaxed and breathless eagerness, I pursued nature to her hiding-places. Who shall conceive the horrors of my secret toil, as I dabbled among the unhallowed damps of the grave, or tortured the living animal to animate the lifeless clay? My limbs now tremble, and my eyes swim with the remembrance; but then a resistless, and almost frantic, impulse, urged me forward; I seemed to have lost all soul or sensation but for this one pursuit. It was indeed but a passing trance, that only made me feel with renewed acuteness so soon as, the unnatural stimulus ceasing to operate, I had returned to my old habits. I collected bones from charnel-houses; and disturbed, with profane fingers, the tremendous secrets of the human frame. In a solitary chamber, or rather cell, at the top of the house, and separated from all the other apartments by a gallery and staircase, I kept my workshop of filthy creation: my eye-balls were starting from their sockets in attending to the details of my employment. The dissecting room and the slaughter-house furnished many of my materials; and often did my human nature turn with loathing from my occupation, whilst, still urged on by an eagerness which perpetually increased, I brought my work near to a conclusion.

The summer months passed while I was thus engaged, heart and soul, in one pursuit. It was a most beautiful season; never did the fields bestow a more plentiful harvest, or the vines yield a more luxuriant vintage: but my eyes were insensible to the charms of nature. And the same feelings which made me neglect the scenes around me caused me also to forget those friends who were so many miles absent, and whom I had not seen for so long a time. I knew my silence disquieted them; and I well remembered the words of my father: "I know that while you are pleased with yourself, you will think of us with affection, and we shall hear regularly from you. You must pardon me if I regard any interruption in your correspondence as a proof that your other duties are equally neglected."

I knew well therefore what would be my father's feelings; but I could not tear my thoughts from my employment, loathsome in itself, but which had taken an irresistible hold of my imagination. I wished, as it were, to procrastinate all that related to my feelings of affection until the great object, which swallowed up every habit of my nature, should be completed.

I then thought that my father would be unjust if he ascribed my neglect to vice, or faultiness on my part; but I am now convinced that he was justified in conceiving that I should not be altogether free from blame. A human being in perfection ought always to preserve a calm and peaceful mind, and never to allow passion or a transitory desire to disturb his tranquillity. I do not think that the pursuit of knowledge is an exception to this rule. If the study to which you apply yourself has a tendency to weaken your affections, and to destroy your taste for those simple pleasures in which no alloy can possibly mix, then that study is certainly unlawful, that is to say, not befitting the human mind. If this rule were always observed; if no man allowed any pursuit whatsoever to interfere with the tranquillity of his domestic affections, Greece had not been enslaved; Cæsar would have spared his country; America would have been discovered more gradually; and the empires of Mexico and Peru had not been destroyed.

But I forget that I am moralising in the most interesting part of my tale; and your looks remind me to proceed.

My father made no reproach in his letters, and only took notice of my silence by enquiring into my occupations more particularly than before. Winter, spring, and summer passed away during my labours; but I did not watch the blossom or the expanding leaves—sights which before always yielded me supreme delight—so deeply was I engrossed in my occupation. The leaves of that year had withered before my work drew near to a close; and now every day showed me more plainly how well I had succeeded. But my enthusiasm was checked by my anxiety, and I appeared rather like one doomed by slavery to toil in the mines, or any other unwholesome trade, than an artist occupied by his favourite employment. Every night I was oppressed by a slow fever, and I became nervous to a most painful degree; the fall of a leaf startled me, and I shunned my fellow-creatures as if I had been guilty of a crime. Sometimes I grew alarmed at the wreck I perceived that I had become; the energy of my purpose alone sustained me: my labours would soon end, and I believed that exercise and amusement would then drive away incipient disease; and I promised myself both of these when my creation should be complete.

It was on a dreary night of November, that I beheld the accomplishment of my toils. With an anxiety that almost amounted to agony, I collected the instruments of life around me, that I might infuse a spark of being into the lifeless thing that lay at my feet. It was already one in the morning; the rain pattered dismally against the panes, and my candle was nearly burnt out, when, by the glimmer of the half-extinguished light, I saw the dull yellow eye of the creature open; it breathed hard, and a convulsive motion agitated its limbs.

How can I describe my emotions at this catastrophe, or how delineate the wretch whom with such infinite pains and care I had endeavoured to form? His limbs were in proportion, and I had selected his features as beautiful. Beautiful!—Great God! His yellow skin scarcely covered the work of muscles and arteries beneath; his hair was of a lustrous black, and flowing; his teeth of a pearly whiteness; but these luxuriances only formed a more horrid contrast with his watery eyes, that seemed almost of the same colour as the dun white sockets in which they were set, his shrivelled complexion and straight black lips.

The different accidents of life are not so changeable as the feelings of human nature. I had worked hard for nearly two years, for the sole purpose of infusing life into an inanimate body. For this I had deprived myself of rest and health. I had desired it with an ardour that far exceeded moderation; but now that I had finished, the beauty of the dream vanished, and breathless horror and disgust filled my heart. Unable to endure the aspect of the being I had created, I rushed out of the room, and continued a long time traversing my bedchamber, unable to compose my mind to sleep. At length lassitude succeeded to the tumult I had before endured; and I threw myself on the bed in my clothes, endeavouring to seek a few moments of forgetfulness. But it was in vain: I slept, indeed, but I was disturbed by the wildest dreams. I thought I saw Elizabeth, in the bloom of health, walking in the streets of Ingolstadt. Delighted and surprised, I embraced her; but as I imprinted the first kiss on her lips, they became livid with the hue of death; her features appeared to change, and I thought that I held the corpse of my dead mother in my arms; a shroud enveloped her form, and I saw the grave-worms crawling in the folds of the flannel. I started from my sleep with horror; a cold dew covered my forehead, my teeth chattered, and every limb became convulsed: when, by the dim and yellow light of the moon, as it forced its way through the window shutters, I beheld the wretch—the miserable monster whom I had created. He held up the curtain of the bed; and his eyes, if eyes they may be called, were fixed on me. His jaws opened, and he muttered some inarticulate sounds, while a grin wrinkled his cheeks. He might have spoken, but I did not hear; one hand was stretched out, seemingly to detain me, but I escaped, and rushed down stairs. I took refuge in the courtyard belonging to the house which I inhabited; where I remained during the rest of the night, walking up and down in the greatest agitation, listening attentively, catching and fearing each sound as if it were to announce the approach of the demoniacal corpse to which I had so miserably given life.

Oh! no mortal could support the horror of that countenance. A mummy again endued with animation could not be so hideous as that wretch. I had gazed on him while unfinished; he was ugly then; but when those muscles and joints were rendered capable of motion, it became a thing such as even Dante could not have conceived.

I passed the night wretchedly. Sometimes my pulse beat so quickly and hardly, that I felt the palpitation of every artery; at others, I nearly sank to the ground through languor and extreme weakness. Mingled with this horror, I felt the bitterness of disappointment; dreams that had been my food and pleasant rest for so long a space were now become a hell to me; and the change was so rapid, the overthrow so complete!

Morning, dismal and wet, at length dawned, and discovered to my sleepless and aching eyes the church of Ingolstadt, its white steeple and clock, which indicated the sixth hour. The porter opened the gates of the court, which had that night been my asylum, and I issued into the streets, pacing them with quick steps, as if I sought to avoid the wretch whom I feared every turning of the street would present to my view. I did not dare return to the apartment which I inhabited, but felt impelled to hurry on, although drenched by the rain which poured from a black and comfortless sky.

I continued walking in this manner for some time, endeavouring, by bodily exercise, to ease the load that weighed upon my mind. I traversed the streets, without any clear conception of where I was, or what I was doing. My heart palpitated in the sickness of fear; and I hurried on with irregular steps, not daring to look about me:—

> *"Like one who, on a lonely road,*
> *Doth walk in fear and dread,*
> *And, having once turned round, walks on,*
> *And turns no more his head;*
> *Because he knows a frightful fiend*
> *Doth close behind him tread."*

Continuing thus, I came at length opposite to the inn at which the various diligences and carriages usually stopped. Here I paused, I knew not why; but I remained some minutes with my eyes fixed on a coach that was coming towards me from the other end of the street. As it drew nearer, I observed that it was the Swiss diligence: it stopped just where I was standing; and, on the door being opened, I perceived Henry Clerval, who, on seeing me, instantly sprung out. "My dear Frankenstein," exclaimed he, "how glad I am to see you! how fortunate that you should be here at the very moment of my alighting!"

Nothing could equal my delight on seeing Clerval; his presence brought back to my thoughts my father, Elizabeth, and all those scenes of home so dear to my recollection. I grasped his hand, and in a moment forgot my horror and misfortune; I felt suddenly, and for the first time during many months, calm and serene joy. I welcomed my friend, therefore, in the most cordial manner, and we walked towards my college. Clerval continued talking for some time about our mutual friends, and his own good fortune in being permitted to come to Ingolstadt. "You may easily believe," said he, "how great was the difficulty to persuade my father that all necessary knowledge was not comprised in the noble art of book-keeping; and, indeed, I believe I left him incredulous to the last, for his constant answer to my unwearied entreaties was the same as that of the Dutch schoolmaster in the Vicar of Wakefield:—'I have ten thousand florins a year without Greek, I eat heartily without Greek.' But his affection for me at length overcame his dislike of learning, and he has permitted me to undertake a voyage of discovery to the land of knowledge."

"It gives me the greatest delight to see you; but tell me how you left my father, brothers, and Elizabeth."

"Very well, and very happy, only a little uneasy that they hear from you so seldom. By the by, I mean to lecture you a little upon their account myself.— But, my dear Frankenstein," continued he, stopping short, and gazing full in my face, "I did not before remark how very ill you appear; so thin and pale; you look as if you had been watching for several nights."

"You have guessed right; I have lately been so deeply engaged in one occupation, that I have not allowed myself sufficient rest, as you see: but I hope, I sincerely hope, that all these employments are now at an end, and that I am at length free."

I trembled excessively; I could not endure to think of, and far less to allude to, the occurrences of the preceding night. I walked with a quick pace, and we soon arrived at my college. I then reflected, and the thought made me shiver, that the creature whom I had left in my apartment might still be there, alive, and walking about. I dreaded to behold this monster; but I feared still more that Henry should see him. Entreating him, therefore, to remain a few minutes at the bottom of the stairs, I darted up towards my own room. My hand was already on the lock of the door before I recollected myself. I then paused; and a cold shivering came over me. I threw the door forcibly open, as children are accustomed to do when they expect a spectre to stand in waiting for them on the other side; but nothing appeared. I stepped fearfully in: the apartment was empty; and my bed-room was also freed from its hideous guest. I could hardly believe that so great a good fortune could have befallen me; but when I became assured that my enemy had indeed fled, I clapped my hands for joy, and ran down to Clerval.

We ascended into my room, and the servant presently brought breakfast; but I was unable to contain myself. It was not joy only that possessed me; I felt my flesh tingle with excess of sensitiveness, and my pulse beat rapidly. I was unable to remain for a single instant in the same place; I jumped over the chairs, clapped my hands, and laughed aloud. Clerval at first attributed my unusual spirits to joy on his arrival; but when he observed me more attentively, he saw a wildness in my eyes for which he could not account; and my loud, unrestrained, heartless laughter, frightened and astonished him.

"My dear Victor," cried he, "what, for God's sake, is the matter? Do not laugh in that manner. How ill you are! What is the cause of all this?"

"Do not ask me," cried I, putting my hands before my eyes, for I thought I saw the dreaded spectre glide into the room; "*he* can tell.—Oh, save me! save me!" I imagined that the monster seized me; I struggled furiously, and fell down in a fit.

Poor Clerval! what must have been his feelings? A meeting, which he anticipated with such joy, so strangely turned to bitterness. But I was not the witness of his grief; for I was lifeless, and did not recover my senses for a long, long time.

This was the commencement of a nervous fever, which confined me for several months. During all that time Henry was my only nurse. I afterwards learned that, knowing my father's advanced age, and unfitness for so long a journey, and how wretched my sickness would make Elizabeth, he spared them this grief by concealing the extent of my disorder. He knew that I could not have a more kind and attentive nurse than himself; and, firm in the hope he felt of my recovery, he did not doubt that, instead of doing harm, he performed the kindest action that he could towards them.

But I was in reality very ill; and surely nothing but the unbounded and unremitting attentions of my friend could have restored me to life. The form of the monster on whom I had bestowed existence was for ever before my eyes, and I raved incessantly concerning him. Doubtless my words surprised Henry: he at first believed them to be the wanderings of my disturbed imagination; but the pertinacity with which I continually recurred to the same subject, persuaded him that my disorder indeed owed its origin to some uncommon and terrible event.

By very slow degrees, and with frequent relapses, that alarmed and grieved my friend, I recovered. I remember the first time I became capable of observing outward objects with any kind of pleasure, I perceived that the fallen leaves had disappeared, and that the young buds were shooting forth from the trees that shaded my window. It was a divine spring; and the season contributed greatly to my convalescence. I felt also sentiments of joy and affection revive in my bosom; my gloom disappeared, and in a short time I became as cheerful as before I was attacked by the fatal passion.

"Dearest Clerval," exclaimed I, "how kind, how very good you are to me. This whole winter, instead of being spent in study, as you promised yourself, has been consumed in my sick room. How shall I ever repay you? I feel the greatest remorse for the disappointment of which I have been the occasion; but you will forgive me."

"You will repay me entirely, if you do not discompose yourself, but get well as fast as you can; and since you appear in such good spirits, I may speak to you on one subject, may I not?"

I trembled. One subject! what could it be? Could he allude to an object on whom I dared not even think?

"Compose yourself," said Clerval, who observed my change of colour, "I will not mention it, if it agitates you; but your father and cousin would be very happy if they received a letter from you in your own handwriting. They hardly know how ill you have been, and are uneasy at your long silence."

"Is that all, my dear Henry? How could you suppose that my first thought would not fly towards those dear, dear friends whom I love, and who are so deserving of my love."

"If this is your present temper, my friend, you will perhaps be glad to see a letter that has been lying here some days for you: it is from your cousin, I believe."

*   *   *

Clerval then put the following letter into my hands. It was from my own Elizabeth:—

"My dearest Cousin,

"You have been ill, very ill, and even the constant letters of dear kind Henry are not sufficient to reassure me on your account. You are forbidden to write—to hold a pen; yet one word from you, dear Victor, is necessary to calm our apprehensions. For a long time I have thought that each post would bring this line, and my persuasions have restrained my uncle from undertaking a journey to Ingolstadt. I have prevented his encountering the inconveniences and perhaps dangers of so long a journey; yet how often have I regretted not being able to perform it myself! I figure to myself that the task of attending on your sick bed has devolved on some mercenary old nurse, who could never guess your wishes, nor minister to them with the care and affection of your poor cousin. Yet that is over now: Clerval writes that indeed you are getting better. I eagerly hope that you will confirm this intelligence soon in your own handwriting.

"Get well—and return to us. You will find a happy, cheerful home, and friends who love you dearly. Your father's health is vigorous, and he asks but to see you,—but to be assured that you are well; and not a care will ever cloud his benevolent countenance. How pleased you would be to remark the improvement of our Ernest! He is now sixteen, and full of activity and spirit. He is desirous to be a true Swiss, and to enter into foreign service; but we cannot part with him, at least until his elder brother return to us. My uncle is not pleased with the idea of a military career in a distant country; but Ernest never had your powers of application. He looks upon study as an odious fetter;—his time is spent in the open air, climbing the hills or rowing on the lake. I fear that he will become an idler, unless we yield the point, and permit him to enter on the profession which he has selected.

"Little alteration, except the growth of our dear children, has taken place since you left us. The blue lake, and snow-clad mountains, they never change;— and I think our placid home, and our contented hearts are regulated by the same immutable laws. My trifling occupations take up my time and amuse me, and I am rewarded for any exertions by seeing none but happy, kind faces around me. Since you left us, but one change has taken place in our little household. Do you remember on what occasion Justine Moritz entered our family? Probably you do not; I will relate her history, therefore, in a few words. Madame Moritz, her mother, was a widow with four children, of whom Justine was the third. This girl had always been the favourite of her father; but, through a strange perversity, her mother could not endure her, and, after the death of M. Moritz, treated her very ill. My aunt observed this; and, when Justine was twelve years of age, prevailed on her mother to allow her to live at our house. The republican institutions of our country have produced simpler and happier manners than those which prevail in the great monarchies that surround

it. Hence there is less distinction between the several classes of its inhabitants; and the lower orders, being neither so poor nor so despised, their manners are more refined and moral. A servant in Geneva does not mean the same thing as a servant in France and England. Justine, thus received in our family, learned the duties of a servant; a condition which, in our fortunate country, does not include the idea of ignorance, and a sacrifice of the dignity of a human being.

"Justine, you may remember, was a great favourite of yours; and I recollect you once remarked, that if you were in an ill-humour, one glance from Justine could dissipate it, for the same reason that Ariosto gives concerning the beauty of Angelica—she looked so frank-hearted and happy. My aunt conceived a great attachment for her, by which she was induced to give her an education superior to that which she had at first intended. This benefit was fully repaid; Justine was the most grateful little creature in the world: I do not mean that she made any professions; I never heard one pass her lips; but you could see by her eyes that she almost adored her protectress. Although her disposition was gay, and in many respects inconsiderate, yet she paid the greatest attention to every gesture of my aunt. She thought her the model of all excellence, and endeavoured to imitate her phraseology and manners, so that even now she often reminds me of her.

"When my dearest aunt died, every one was too much occupied in their own grief to notice poor Justine, who had attended her during her illness with the most anxious affection. Poor Justine was very ill; but other trials were reserved for her.

"One by one, her brothers and sister died; and her mother, with the exception of her neglected daughter, was left childless. The conscience of the woman was troubled; she began to think that the deaths of her favourites was a judgment from heaven to chastise her partiality. She was a Roman catholic; and I believe her confessor confirmed the idea which she had conceived. Accordingly, a few months after your departure for Ingolstadt, Justine was called home by her repentant mother. Poor girl! she wept when she quitted our house; she was much altered since the death of my aunt; grief had given softness and a winning mildness to her manners, which had before been remarkable for vivacity. Nor was her residence at her mother's house of a nature to restore her gaiety. The poor woman was very vacillating in her repentance. She sometimes begged Justine to forgive her unkindness, but much oftener accused her of having caused the deaths of her brothers and sister. Perpetual fretting at length threw Madame Moritz into a decline, which at first increased her irritability, but she is now at peace for ever. She died on the first approach of cold weather, at the beginning of this last winter. Justine has returned to us; and I assure you I love her tenderly. She is very clever and gentle, and extremely pretty; as I mentioned before, her mien and her expressions continually remind me of my dear aunt.

"I must say also a few words to you, my dear cousin, of little darling William. I wish you could see him; he is very tall of his age, with sweet laughing blue eyes, dark eyelashes, and curling hair. When he smiles, two little dimples appear on each cheek, which are rosy with health. He has already had

one or two little wives, but Louisa Biron is his favourite, a pretty little girl of five years of age.

"Now, dear Victor, I dare say you wish to be indulged in a little gossip concerning the good people of Geneva. The pretty Miss Mansfield has already received the congratulatory visits on her approaching marriage with a young Englishman, John Melbourne, Esq. Her ugly sister, Manon, married M. Duvillard, the rich banker, last autumn. Your favourite schoolfellow, Louis Manoir, has suffered several misfortunes since the departure of Clerval from Geneva. But he has already recovered his spirits, and is reported to be on the point of marrying a very lively pretty Frenchwoman, Madame Tavernier. She is a widow, and much older than Manoir; but she is very much admired, and a favourite with everybody.

"I have written myself into better spirits, dear cousin; but my anxiety returns upon me as I conclude. Write, dearest Victor,—one line—one word will be a blessing to us. Ten thousand thanks to Henry for his kindness, his affection, and his many letters: we are sincerely grateful. Adieu! my cousin; take care of yourself; and, I entreat you, write!

"Elizabeth Lavenza.
"Geneva, March 18th, 17—."

"Dear, dear Elizabeth!" I exclaimed, when I had read her letter, "I will write instantly, and relieve them from the anxiety they must feel." I wrote, and this exertion greatly fatigued me; but my convalescence had commenced, and proceeded regularly. In another fortnight I was able to leave my chamber.

One of my first duties on my recovery was to introduce Clerval to the several professors of the university. In doing this, I underwent a kind of rough usage, ill befitting the wounds that my mind had sustained. Ever since the fatal night, the end of my labours, and the beginning of my misfortunes, I had conceived a violent antipathy even to the name of natural philosophy. When I was otherwise quite restored to health, the sight of a chemical instrument would renew all the agony of my nervous symptoms. Henry saw this, and had removed all my apparatus from my view. He had also changed my apartment; for he perceived that I had acquired a dislike for the room which had previously been my laboratory. But these cares of Clerval were made of no avail when I visited the professors. M. Waldman inflicted torture when he praised, with kindness and warmth, the astonishing progress I had made in the sciences. He soon perceived that I disliked the subject; but not guessing the real cause, he attributed my feelings to modesty, and changed the subject from my improvement, to the science itself, with a desire, as I evidently saw, of drawing me out. What could I do? He meant to please, and he tormented me. I felt as if he had placed carefully, one by one, in my view those instruments which were to be afterwards used in putting me to a slow and cruel death. I writhed under his words, yet dared not exhibit the pain I felt. Clerval, whose eyes and feelings were always quick in discerning the sensations of others, declined the subject, alleging, in excuse, his total ignorance; and the conversation took a more general turn. I thanked my friend from my heart, but I did not speak. I saw plainly that he was surprised, but he never attempted to draw my secret from me; and although I loved him with a mixture of affection and reverence that knew no bounds, yet I could never persuade myself to confide to him that event which was so often present to my recollection, but which I feared the detail to another would only impress more deeply.

M. Krempe was not equally docile; and in my condition at that time, of almost insupportable sensitiveness, his harsh blunt encomiums gave me even more pain than the benevolent approbation of M. Waldman. "D—n the fellow!" cried he; "why, M. Clerval, I assure you he has outstript us all. Ay, stare if you please; but it is nevertheless true. A youngster who, but a few years ago, believed in Cornelius Agrippa as firmly as in the gospel, has now set himself at the head of the university; and if he is not soon pulled down, we shall all be out of countenance.—Ay, ay," continued he, observing my face expressive of suffering, "M. Frankenstein is modest; an excellent quality in a young man. Young men should be diffident of themselves, you know, M. Clerval: I was myself when young; but that wears out in a very short time."

M. Krempe had now commenced an eulogy on himself, which happily turned the conversation from a subject that was so annoying to me.

Clerval had never sympathised in my tastes for natural science; and his literary pursuits differed wholly from those which had occupied me. He came to the university with the design of making himself complete master of the oriental languages, as thus he should open a field for the plan of life he had marked out for himself. Resolved to pursue no inglorious career, he turned his eyes toward the East, as affording scope for his spirit of enterprise. The Persian, Arabic, and Sanscrit languages engaged his attention, and I was easily induced to enter on the same studies. Idleness had ever been irksome to me, and now that I wished to fly from reflection, and hated my former studies, I felt great relief in being the fellow-pupil with my friend, and found not only instruction but consolation in the works of the orientalists. I did not, like him, attempt a critical knowledge of their dialects, for I did not contemplate making any other use of them than temporary amusement. I read merely to understand their meaning, and they well repaid my labours. Their melancholy is soothing, and their joy elevating, to a degree I never experienced in studying the authors of any other country. When you read their writings, life appears to consist in a warm sun and a garden of roses,—in the smiles and frowns of a fair enemy, and the fire that consumes your own heart. How different from the manly and heroical poetry of Greece and Rome!

Summer passed away in these occupations, and my return to Geneva was fixed for the latter end of autumn; but being delayed by several accidents, winter and snow arrived, the roads were deemed impassable, and my journey was retarded until the ensuing spring. I felt this delay very bitterly; for I longed to see my native town and my beloved friends. My return had only been delayed so long, from an unwillingness to leave Clerval in a strange place, before he had become acquainted with any of its inhabitants. The winter, however, was spent cheerfully; and although the spring was uncommonly late, when it came its beauty compensated for its dilatoriness.

The month of May had already commenced, and I expected the letter daily which was to fix the date of my departure, when Henry proposed a pedestrian tour in the environs of Ingolstadt, that I might bid a personal farewell to the country I had so long inhabited. I acceded with pleasure to this proposition: I was fond of exercise, and Clerval had always been my favourite companion in the rambles of this nature that I had taken among the scenes of my native country.

We passed a fortnight in these perambulations: my health and spirits had long been restored, and they gained additional strength from the salubrious air I breathed, the natural incidents of our progress, and the conversation of my friend. Study had before secluded me from the intercourse of my fellow-creatures, and rendered me unsocial; but Clerval called forth the better feelings of my heart; he again taught me to love the aspect of nature, and the cheerful faces of children. Excellent friend! how sincerely did you love me, and endeavour to elevate my mind until it was on a level with your own! A selfish pursuit had cramped and narrowed me, until your gentleness and affection warmed and opened my senses; I became the same happy creature who, a few years ago, loved and beloved by all, had no sorrow or care. When happy, inanimate nature had the power of bestowing on me the most delightful sensations. A serene sky and verdant fields filled me with ecstasy. The present season was indeed divine; the flowers of spring bloomed in the hedges, while those of summer were already in bud. I was undisturbed by thoughts which during the preceding year had pressed upon me, notwithstanding my endeavours to throw them off, with an invincible burden.

Henry rejoiced in my gaiety, and sincerely sympathised in my feelings: he exerted himself to amuse me, while he expressed the sensations that filled his soul. The resources of his mind on this occasion were truly astonishing: his conversation was full of imagination; and very often, in imitation of the Persian and Arabic writers, he invented tales of wonderful fancy and passion. At other times he repeated my favourite poems, or drew me out into arguments, which he supported with great ingenuity.

We returned to our college on a Sunday afternoon: the peasants were dancing, and every one we met appeared gay and happy. My own spirits were high, and I bounded along with feelings of unbridled joy and hilarity.

On my return, I found the following letter from my father:—

"My dear Victor,

"You have probably waited impatiently for a letter to fix the date of your return to us; and I was at first tempted to write only a few lines, merely mention-

ing the day on which I should expect you. But that would be a cruel kindness, and I dare not do it. What would be your surprise, my son, when you expected a happy and glad welcome, to behold, on the contrary, tears and wretchedness? And how, Victor, can I relate our misfortune? Absence cannot have rendered you callous to our joys and griefs; and how shall I inflict pain on my long absent son? I wish to prepare you for the woful news, but I know it is impossible; even now your eye skims over the page, to seek the words which are to convey to you the horrible tidings.

"William is dead!—that sweet child, whose smiles delighted and warmed my heart, who was so gentle, yet so gay! Victor, he is murdered!

"I will not attempt to console you; but will simply relate the circumstances of the transaction.

"Last Thursday (May 7th), I, my niece, and your two brothers, went to walk in Plainpalais. The evening was warm and serene, and we prolonged our walk farther than usual. It was already dusk before we thought of returning; and then we discovered that William and Ernest, who had gone on before, were not to be found. We accordingly rested on a seat until they should return. Presently Ernest came, and enquired if we had seen his brother: he said, that he had been playing with him, that William had run away to hide himself, and that he vainly sought for him, and afterwards waited for him a long time, but that he did not return.

"This account rather alarmed us, and we continued to search for him until night fell, when Elizabeth conjectured that he might have returned to the house. He was not there. We returned again, with torches; for I could not rest, when I thought that my sweet boy had lost himself, and was exposed to all the damps and dews of night; Elizabeth also suffered extreme anguish. About five in the morning I discovered my lovely boy, whom the night before I had seen blooming and active in health, stretched on the grass livid and motionless: the print of the murderer's finger was on his neck.

"He was conveyed home, and the anguish that was visible in my countenance betrayed the secret to Elizabeth. She was very earnest to see the corpse. At first I attempted to prevent her; but she persisted, and entering the room where it lay, hastily examined the neck of the victim, and clasping her hands exclaimed, 'O God! I have murdered my darling child!'

"She fainted, and was restored with extreme difficulty. When she again lived, it was only to weep and sigh. She told me, that that same evening William had teased her to let him wear a very valuable miniature that she possessed of your mother. This picture is gone, and was doubtless the temptation which urged the murderer to the deed. We have no trace of him at present, although our exertions to discover him are unremitted; but they will not restore my beloved William!

"Come, dearest Victor; you alone can console Elizabeth. She weeps continually, and accuses herself unjustly as the cause of his death; her words pierce my heart. We are all unhappy; but will not that be an additional motive for you, my son, to return and be our comforter? Your dear mother! Alas, Victor! I now

say, Thank God she did not live to witness the cruel, miserable death of her youngest darling!

"Come, Victor; not brooding thoughts of vengeance against the assassin, but with feelings of peace and gentleness, that will heal, instead of festering, the wounds of our minds. Enter the house of mourning, my friend, but with kindness and affection for those who love you, and not with hatred for your enemies.

"Your affectionate and afflicted father,
Alphonse Frankenstein

DR. HEIDEGGER'S EXPERIMENT

Nathaniel Hawthorne (1837)

THAT VERY SINGULAR man old Dr. Heidegger once invited four venerable friends to meet him in his study. There were three white-bearded gentlemen—Mr. Medbourne, Colonel Killigrew and Mr. Gascoigne—and a withered gentlewoman whose name was the widow Wycherly. They were all melancholy old creatures who had been unfortunate in life, and whose greatest misfortune it was that they were not long ago in their graves. Mr. Medbourne, in the vigor of his age, had been a prosperous merchant, but had lost his all by a frantic speculation, and was now little better than a mendicant. Colonel Killigrew had wasted his best years and his health and substance in the pursuit of sinful pleasures which had given birth to a brood of pains, such as the gout and divers other torments of soul and body. Mr. Gascoigne was a ruined politician, a man of evil fame—or, at least, had been so till time had buried him from the knowledge of the present generation and made him obscure instead of infamous. As for the widow Wycherly, tradition tells us that she was a great beauty in her day, but for a long while past she had lived in deep seclusion on account of certain scandalous stories which had prejudiced the gentry of the town against her. It is a circumstance worth mentioning that each of these three old gentlemen—Mr. Medbourne, Colonel Killigrew and Mr. Gascoigne—were early lovers of the widow Wycherly, and had once been on the point of cutting each other's throats for her sake. And before proceeding farther I will merely hint that Dr. Heidegger and all his four guests were sometimes thought to be a little beside themselves, as is not infrequently the case with old people when worried either by present troubles or woeful recollections.

"My dear old friends," said Dr. Heidegger, motioning them to be seated, "I am desirous of your assistance in one of those little experiments with which I amuse myself here in my study."

If all stories were true, Dr. Heidegger's study must have been a very curious place. It was a dim, old-fashioned chamber festooned with cobwebs and besprinkled with antique dust. Around the walls stood several oaken bookcases, the lower shelves of which were filled with rows of gigantic folios and black-letter quartos, and the upper with little parchment-covered duo-decimos. Over the central bookcase was a bronze bust of Hippocrates, with which, according to some authorities, Dr. Heidegger was accustomed to hold consultations in all difficult cases of his practice. In the obscurest corner of the room stood a tall and narrow oaken closet with its door ajar, within which doubtfully appeared a skeleton. Between two of the bookcases hung a look-ing-glass, presenting its high and dusty plate within a tarnished gilt frame. Among many wonderful stories related of this mirror, it was fabled that the spirits of all the doctor's deceased patients dwelt within its verge and would stare him in the face whenever he looked thitherward. The opposite side of the chamber was ornamented with the full-length portrait of a young lady arrayed in the faded magnificence of silk, satin and brocade, and with a vis-age as faded as her dress. Above half a century ago Dr. Heidegger had been on the point of marriage with this young lady, but, being affected with some slight disorder, she had swallowed one of her lover's prescriptions and died on the bridal-evening. The greatest curiosity of the study remains to be men-tioned: it was a ponderous folio volume bound in black leather, with massive silver clasps. There were no letters on the back, and nobody could tell the title of the book. But it was well known to be a book of magic, and once, when a chambermaid had lifted it merely to brush away the dust, the skeleton had rattled in its closet, the picture of the young lady had stepped one foot upon the floor and several ghastly faces had peeped forth from the mirror, while the brazen head of Hippocrates frowned and said, "Forbear!"

Such was Dr. Heidegger's study. On the summer afternoon of our tale a small round table as black as ebony stood in the centre of the room, sus-taining a cut-glass vase of beautiful form and elaborate workmanship. The sunshine came through the window between the heavy festoons of two faded damask curtains and fell directly across this vase, so that a mild splendor was reflected from it on the ashen visages of the five old people who sat around. Four champagne-glasses were also on the table.

"My dear old friends," repeated Dr. Heidegger, "may I reckon on your aid in performing an exceedingly curious experiment?"

Now, Dr. Heidegger was a very strange old gentleman whose eccentric-ity had become the nucleus for a thousand fantastic stories. Some of these fables—to my shame be it spoken—might possibly be traced back to mine own veracious self; and if any passages of the present tale should startle the reader's faith, I must be content to bear the stigma of a fiction-monger.

When the doctor's four guests heard him talk of his proposed experiment, they anticipated nothing more wonderful than the murder of a mouse in an air-pump or the examination of a cobweb by the microscope, or some similar nonsense with which he was constantly in the habit of pestering his intimates. But without waiting for a reply Dr. Heidegger hobbled across the chamber and returned with the same ponderous folio bound in black leather which common report affirmed to be a book of magic. Undoing the silver clasps, he opened the volume and took from among its black-letter pages a rose, or what was once a rose, though now the green leaves and crimson petals had assumed one brownish hue and the ancient flower seemed ready to crumble to dust in the doctor's hands.

"This rose," said Dr. Heidegger, with a sigh—"this same withered and crumbling flower—blossomed five and fifty years ago. It was given me by Sylvia Ward, whose portrait hangs yonder, and I meant to wear it in my bosom at our wedding. Five and fifty years it has been treasured between the leaves of this old volume. Now, would you deem it possible that this rose of half a century could ever bloom again?"

"Nonsense!" said the widow Wycherly, with a peevish toss of her head. "You might as well ask whether an old woman's wrinkled face could ever bloom again."

"See!" answered Dr. Heidegger. He uncovered the vase and threw the faded rose into the water which it contained. At first it lay lightly on the surface of the fluid, appearing to imbibe none of its moisture. Soon, however, a singular change began to be visible. The crushed and dried petals stirred and assumed a deepening tinge of crimson, as if the flower were reviving from a deathlike slumber, the slender stalk and twigs of foliage became green, and there was the rose of half a century, looking as fresh as when Sylvia Ward had first given it to her lover. It was scarcely full-blown, for some of its delicate red leaves curled modestly around its moist bosom, within which two or three dewdrops were sparkling.

"That is certainly a very pretty deception," said the doctor's friends—carelessly, however, for they had witnessed greater miracles at a conjurer's show. "Pray, how was it effected?"

"Did you never hear of the Fountain of Youth?" asked Dr. Heidegger, "which Ponce de Leon, the Spanish adventurer, went in search of two or three centuries ago?"

"But did Ponce de Leon ever find it?" said the widow Wycherly.

"No," answered Dr. Heidegger, "for he never sought it in the right place. The famous Fountain of Youth, if I am rightly informed, is situated in the southern part of the Floridian peninsula, not far from Lake Macaco. Its source is overshadowed by several gigantic magnolias which, though numberless centuries old, have been kept as fresh as violets by the virtues of this wonderful water. An acquaintance of mine, knowing my curiosity in such matters, has sent me what you see in the vase."

"Ahem!" said Colonel Killigrew, who believed not a word of the doctor's story; "and what may be the effect of this fluid on the human frame?"

"You shall judge for yourself, my dear colonel," replied Dr. Heidegger.—"And all of you, my respected friends, are welcome to so much of this admirable fluid as may restore to you the bloom of youth. For my own part, having had much trouble in growing old, I am in no hurry to grow young again. With your permission, therefore, I will merely watch the progress of the experiment."

While he spoke Dr. Heidegger had been filling the four champagne-glasses with the water of the Fountain of Youth. It was apparently impregnated with an effervescent gas, for little bubbles were continually ascending from the depths of the glasses and bursting in silvery spray at the surface. As the liquor diffused a pleasant perfume, the old people doubted not that it possessed cordial and comfortable properties, and, though utter sceptics as to its rejuvenescent power, they were inclined to swallow it at once. But Dr. Heidegger besought them to stay a moment.

"Before you drink, my respectable old friends," said he, "it would be well that, with the experience of a lifetime to direct you, you should draw up a few general rules for your guidance in passing a second time through the perils of youth. Think what a sin and shame it would be if, with your peculiar advantages, you should not become patterns of virtue and wisdom to all the young people of the age!"

The doctor's four venerable friends made him no answer except by a feeble and tremulous laugh, so very ridiculous was the idea that, knowing how closely Repentance treads behind the steps of Error, they should ever go astray again.

"Drink, then," said the doctor, bowing; "I rejoice that I have so well selected the subjects of my experiment."

With palsied hands they raised the glasses to their lips. The liquor, if it really possessed such virtues as Dr. Heidegger imputed to it, could not have been bestowed on four human beings who needed it more woefully. They looked as if they had never known what youth or pleasure was, but had been the offspring of Nature's dotage, and always the gray, decrepit, sapless, miserable creatures who now sat stooping round the doctor's table without life enough in their souls or bodies to be animated even by the prospect of growing young again. They drank off the water and replaced their glasses on the table.

Assuredly, there was an almost immediate improvement in the aspect of the party—not unlike what might have been produced by a glass of generous wine—together with a sudden glow of cheerful sunshine, brightening over all their visages at once. There was a healthful suffusion on their cheeks instead of the ashen hue that had made them look so corpse-like. They gazed at one another, and fancied that some magic power had really begun to smooth away the deep and sad inscriptions which Father Time had been so long engraving on their brows. The widow Wycherly adjusted her cap, for she felt almost like a woman again.

"Give us more of this wondrous water," cried they, eagerly. "We are younger, but we are still too old. Quick! give us more!"

"Patience, patience!" quoth Dr. Heidegger, who sat, watching the experiment with philosophic coolness. "You have been a long time growing old; surely you might be content to grow young in half an hour. But the water is at your service." Again he filled their glasses with the liquor of youth, enough of which still remained in the vase to turn half the old people in the city to the age of their own grandchildren.

While the bubbles were yet sparkling on the brim the doctor's four guests snatched their glasses from the table and swallowed the contents at a single gulp. Was it delusion? Even while the draught was passing down their throats it seemed to have wrought a change on their whole systems. Their eyes grew clear and bright; a dark shade deepened among their silvery locks: they sat around the table three gentlemen of middle age and a woman hardly beyond her buxom prime.

"My dear widow, you are charming!" cried Colonel Killigrew, whose eyes had been fixed upon her face while the shadows of age were flitting from it like darkness from the crimson daybreak.

The fair widow knew of old that Colonel Killigrew's compliments were not always measured by sober truth; so she started up and ran to the mirror, still dreading that the ugly visage of an old woman would meet her gaze.

Meanwhile, the three gentlemen behaved in such a manner as proved that the water of the Fountain of Youth possessed some intoxicating qualities— unless, indeed, their exhilaration of spirits were merely a lightsome dizziness caused by the sudden removal of the weight of years. Mr. Gascoigne's mind seemed to run on political topics, but whether relating to the past, present or future could not easily be determined, since the same ideas and phrases have been in vogue these fifty years. Now he rattled forth full-throated sentences about patriotism, national glory and the people's right; now he muttered some perilous stuff or other in a sly and doubtful whisper, so cautiously that even his own conscience could scarcely catch the secret; and now, again, he spoke in measured accents and a deeply-deferential tone, as if a royal ear were listening to his well-turned periods. Colonel Killigrew all this time had been trolling forth a jolly bottle-song and ringing his glass in symphony with the chorus, while his eyes wandered toward the buxom figure of the widow Wycherly. On the other side of the table, Mr. Medbourne was involved in a calculation of dollars and cents with which was strangely intermingled a project for supplying the East Indies with ice by harnessing a team of whales to the polar icebergs. As for the widow Wycherly, she stood before the mirror courtesying and simpering to her own image and greeting it as the friend whom she loved better than all the world besides. She thrust her face close to the glass to see whether some long-remembered wrinkle or crow's-foot had indeed vanished; she examined whether the snow had so entirely melted from her hair that the venerable cap could be safely thrown aside. At last, turning briskly away, she came with a sort of dancing step to the table.

"My dear old doctor," cried she, "pray favor me with another glass."

"Certainly, my dear madam—certainly," replied the complaisant doctor. "See! I have already filled the glasses."

There, in fact, stood the four glasses brimful of this wonderful water, the delicate spray of which, as it effervesced from the surface, resembled the tremulous glitter of diamonds.

It was now so nearly sunset that the chamber had grown duskier than ever, but a mild and moonlike splendor gleamed from within the vase and rested alike on the four guests and on the doctor's venerable figure. He sat in a high-backed, elaborately-carved oaken arm-chair with a gray dignity of aspect that might have well befitted that very Father Time whose power had never been disputed save by this fortunate company. Even while quaffing the third draught of the Fountain of Youth, they were almost awed by the expression of his mysterious visage. But the next moment the exhilarating gush of young life shot through their veins. They were now in the happy prime of youth. Age, with its miserable train of cares and sorrows and diseases, was remembered only as the trouble of a dream from which they had joyously awoke. The fresh gloss of the soul, so early lost and without which the world's successive scenes had been but a gallery of faded pictures, again threw its enchantment over all their prospects. They felt like new-created beings in a new-created universe.

"We are young! We are young!" they cried, exultingly.

Youth, like the extremity of age, had effaced the strongly-marked characteristics of middle life and mutually assimilated them all. They were a group of merry youngsters almost maddened with the exuberant frolicsomeness of their years. The most singular effect of their gayety was an impulse to mock the infirmity and decrepitude of which they had so lately been the victims. They laughed loudly at their old-fashioned attire—the wide-skirted coats and flapped waistcoats of the young men and the ancient cap and gown of the blooming girl. One limped across the floor like a gouty grandfather; one set a pair of spectacles astride of his nose and pretended to pore over the black-letter pages of the book of magic; a third seated himself in an arm-chair and strove to imitate the venerable dignity of Dr. Heidegger. Then all shouted mirthfully and leaped about the room.

The widow Wycherly—if so fresh a damsel could be called a widow tripped up to the doctor's chair with a mischievous merriment in her rosy face.

"Doctor, you dear old soul," cried she, "get up and dance with me;" and then the four young people laughed louder than ever to think what a queer figure the poor old doctor would cut.

"Pray excuse me," answered the doctor, quietly. "I am old and rheumatic, and my dancing-days were over long ago. But either of these gay young gentlemen will be glad of so pretty a partner."

"Dance with me, Clara," cried Colonel Killigrew.

"No, no! I will be her partner," shouted Mr. Gascoigne.

"She promised me her hand fifty years ago," exclaimed Mr. Medbourne.

They all gathered round her. One caught both her hands in his passionate grasp, another threw his arm about her waist, the third buried his hand among the glossy curls that clustered beneath the widow's cap. Blushing, panting, struggling, chiding, laughing, her warm breath fanning each of their faces by turns, she strove to disengage herself, yet still remained in their triple embrace. Never was there a livelier picture of youthful rivalship, with bewitching beauty for the prize. Yet, by a strange deception, owing to the duskiness of the chamber and the antique dresses which they still wore, the tall mirror is said to have reflected the figures of the three old, gray, withered grand-sires ridiculously contending for the skinny ugliness of a shrivelled grandam. But they were young: their burning passions proved them so.

Inflamed to madness by the coquetry of the girl-widow, who neither granted nor quite withheld her favors, the three rivals began to interchange threatening glances. Still keeping hold of the fair prize, they grappled fiercely at one another's throats. As they struggled to and fro the table was overturned and the vase dashed into a thousand fragments. The precious Water of Youth flowed in a bright stream across the floor, moistening the wings of a butterfly which, grown old in the decline of summer, had alighted there to die. The insect fluttered lightly through the chamber and settled on the snowy head of Dr. Heidegger.

"Come, come, gentlemen! Come, Madam Wycherly!" exclaimed the doctor. "I really must protest against this riot."

They stood still and shivered, for it seemed as if gray Time were calling them back from their sunny youth far down into the chill and darksome vale of years. They looked at old Dr. Heidegger, who sat in his carved armchair holding the rose of half a century, which he had rescued from among the fragments of the shattered vase. At the motion of his hand the four rioters resumed their seats—the more readily because their violent exertions had wearied them, youthful though they were.

"My poor Sylvia's rose!" ejaculated Dr. Heidegger, holding it in the light of the sunset clouds. "It appears to be fading again."

And so it was. Even while the party were looking at it the flower continued to shrivel up, till it became as dry and fragile as when the doctor had first thrown it into the vase. He shook off the few drops of moisture which clung to its petals.

"I love it as well thus as in its dewy freshness," observed he, pressing the withered rose to his withered lips.

While he spoke the butterfly fluttered down from the doctor's snowy head and fell upon the floor. His guests shivered again. A strange dullness— whether of the body or spirit they could not tell—was creeping gradually over them all. They gazed at one another, and fancied that each fleeting moment snatched away a charm and left a deepening furrow where none had been before. Was it an illusion? Had the changes of a lifetime been crowded into so brief a space, and were they now four aged people sitting with their old friend Dr. Heidegger?

"Are we grown old again so soon?" cried they, dolefully.

In truth, they had. The Water of Youth possessed merely a virtue more transient than that of wine; the delirium which it created had effervesced away. Yes, they were old again. With a shuddering impulse that showed her a woman still, the widow clasped her skinny hands before her face and wished that the coffin-lid were over it, since it could be no longer beautiful.

"Yes, friends, ye are old again," said Dr. Heidegger, "and, lo! the Water of Youth is all lavished on the ground. Well, I bemoan it not; for if the fountain gushed at my very doorstep, I would not stoop to bathe my lips in it—no, though its delirium were for years instead of moments. Such is the lesson ye have taught me."

But the doctor's four friends had taught no such lesson to themselves. They resolved forthwith to make a pilgrimage to Florida and quaff at morning, noon and night from the Fountain of Youth.

SOME WORDS WITH A MUMMY

Edgar Allan Poe (1845)

THE *SYMPOSIUM* OF the preceding evening had been a little too much for my nerves. I had a wretched headache, and was desperately drowsy. Instead of going out therefore to spend the evening as I had proposed, it occurred to me that I could not do a wiser thing than just eat a mouthful of supper and go immediately to bed.

A light supper of course. I am exceedingly fond of Welsh rabbit. More than a pound at once, however, may not at all times be advisable. Still, there can be no material objection to two. And really between two and three, there is merely a single unit of difference. I ventured, perhaps, upon four. My wife will have it five;—but, clearly, she has confounded two very distinct affairs. The abstract number, five, I am willing to admit; but, concretely, it has reference to bottles of Brown Stout, without which, in the way of condiment, Welsh rabbit is to be eschewed.

Having thus concluded a frugal meal, and donned my night-cap, with the serene hope of enjoying it till noon the next day, I placed my head upon the pillow, and, through the aid of a capital conscience, fell into a profound slumber forthwith.

But when were the hopes of humanity fulfilled? I could not have completed my third snore when there came a furious ringing at the street-door bell, and then an impatient thumping at the knocker, which awakened me at once. In a minute afterward, and while I was still rubbing my eyes, my wife thrust in my face a note, from my old friend, Doctor Ponnonner. It ran thus:

> "Come to me, by all means, my dear good friend, as soon as you receive this. Come and help us to rejoice. At last, by long persevering diplomacy, I have gained the assent of the Directors of the City Museum, to my examination of the Mummy—you know the one I mean. I have permission to unswathe it and open it, if desirable. A few friends only will be present—you, of course. The Mummy is now at my house, and we shall begin to unroll it at eleven to-night.
>
> "Yours, ever,
> Ponnonner

By the time I had reached the "Ponnonner," it struck me that I was as wide awake as a man need be. I leaped out of bed in an ecstacy, overthrowing all in my way; dressed myself with a rapidity truly marvellous; and set off, at the top of my speed, for the doctor's.

There I found a very eager company assembled. They had been awaiting me with much impatience; the Mummy was extended upon the dining-table; and the moment I entered its examination was commenced.

It was one of a pair brought, several years previously, by Captain Arthur Sabretash, a cousin of Ponnonner's from a tomb near Eleithias, in the Lybian mountains, a considerable distance above Thebes on the Nile. The grottoes at this point, although less magnificent than the Theban sepulchres, are of higher interest, on account of affording more numerous illustrations of the private life of the Egyptians. The chamber from which our specimen was taken, was said to be very rich in such illustrations; the walls being completely covered with fresco paintings and bas-reliefs, while statues, vases, and Mosaic work of rich patterns, indicated the vast wealth of the deceased.

The treasure had been deposited in the Museum precisely in the same condition in which Captain Sabretash had found it;—that is to say, the coffin had not been disturbed. For eight years it had thus stood, subject only externally to public inspection. We had now, therefore, the complete Mummy at our disposal; and to those who are aware how very rarely the unransacked antique reaches our shores, it will be evident, at once that we had great reason to congratulate ourselves upon our good fortune.

Approaching the table, I saw on it a large box, or case, nearly seven feet long, and perhaps three feet wide, by two feet and a half deep. It was oblong—not coffin-shaped. The material was at first supposed to be the wood of the sycamore (*platanus*), but, upon cutting into it, we found it to be pasteboard, or, more properly, *papier mache*, composed of papyrus. It was thickly ornamented with paintings, representing funeral scenes, and other mournful subjects—interspersed among which, in every variety of position, were certain series of hieroglyphical characters, intended, no doubt, for the name of the departed. By good luck, Mr. Gliddon formed one of our party; and he had no difficulty in translating the letters, which were simply phonetic, and represented the word *Allamistakeo*.

We had some difficulty in getting this case open without injury; but having at length accomplished the task, we came to a second, coffin-shaped, and very considerably less in size than the exterior one, but resembling it precisely in every other respect. The interval between the two was filled with resin, which had, in some degree, defaced the colors of the interior box.

Upon opening this latter (which we did quite easily), we arrived at a third case, also coffin-shaped, and varying from the second one in no particular, except in that of its material, which was cedar, and still emitted the peculiar and highly aromatic odor of that wood. Between the second and the third case there was no interval—the one fitting accurately within the other.

Removing the third case, we discovered and took out the body itself. We had expected to find it, as usual, enveloped in frequent rolls, or bandages, of linen; but, in place of these, we found a sort of sheath, made of papyrus, and coated with a layer of plaster, thickly gilt and painted. The paintings represented subjects connected with the various supposed duties of the soul, and its presentation to different divinities, with numerous identical human figures, intended, very probably, as portraits of the persons embalmed. Extending from head to foot was a columnar, or perpendicular, inscription, in phonetic hieroglyphics, giving again his name and titles, and the names and titles of his relations.

Around the neck thus ensheathed, was a collar of cylindrical glass beads, diverse in color, and so arranged as to form images of deities, of the scarabaeus, etc, with the winged globe. Around the small of the waist was a similar collar or belt.

Stripping off the papyrus, we found the flesh in excellent preservation, with no perceptible odor. The color was reddish. The skin was hard, smooth, and glossy. The teeth and hair were in good condition. The eyes (it seemed) had been removed, and glass ones substituted, which were very beautiful and wonderfully life-like, with the exception of somewhat too determined a stare. The fingers and the nails were brilliantly gilded.

Mr. Gliddon was of opinion, from the redness of the epidermis, that the embalmment had been effected altogether by asphaltum; but, on scraping the surface with a steel instrument, and throwing into the fire some of the powder thus obtained, the flavor of camphor and other sweet-scented gums became apparent.

We searched the corpse very carefully for the usual openings through which the entrails are extracted, but, to our surprise, we could discover none. No member of the party was at that period aware that entire or unopened mummies are not infrequently met. The brain it was customary to withdraw through the nose; the intestines through an incision in the side; the body was then shaved, washed, and salted; then laid aside for several weeks, when the operation of embalming, properly so called, began.

As no trace of an opening could be found, Doctor Ponnonner was preparing his instruments for dissection, when I observed that it was then past two o'clock. Hereupon it was agreed to postpone the internal examination until the next evening; and we were about to separate for the present, when some one suggested an experiment or two with the Voltaic pile.

The application of electricity to a mummy three or four thousand years old at the least, was an idea, if not very sage, still sufficiently original, and we all caught it at once. About one-tenth in earnest and nine-tenths in jest, we arranged a battery in the Doctor's study, and conveyed thither the Egyptian.

It was only after much trouble that we succeeded in laying bare some portions of the temporal muscle which appeared of less stony rigidity than other parts of the frame, but which, as we had anticipated, of course, gave no indication of galvanic susceptibility when brought in contact with the wire. This, the first trial, indeed, seemed decisive, and, with a hearty laugh at our own absurdity, we were bidding each other good night, when my eyes, happening to fall upon those of the Mummy, were there immediately riveted in amazement. My brief glance, in fact, had sufficed to assure me that the orbs which we had all supposed to be glass, and which were originally noticeable for a certain wild stare, were now so far covered by the lids, that only a small portion of the *tunica albuginea* remained visible.

With a shout I called attention to the fact, and it became immediately obvious to all.

I cannot say that I was alarmed at the phenomenon, because "alarmed" is, in my case, not exactly the word. It is possible, however, that, but for the Brown Stout, I might have been a little nervous. As for the rest of the company, they really made no attempt at concealing the downright fright which possessed them. Doctor Ponnonner was a man to be pitied. Mr. Gliddon, by some peculiar process, rendered himself invisible. Mr. Silk Buckingham, I fancy, will scarcely be so bold as to deny that he made his way, upon all fours, under the table.

After the first shock of astonishment, however, we resolved, as a matter of course, upon further experiment forthwith. Our operations were now directed against the great toe of the right foot. We made an incision over the outside of the exterior *os sesamoideum pollicis pedis,* and thus got at the root of the abductor muscle. Readjusting the battery, we now applied the fluid to the bisected nerves—when, with a movement of exceeding life-likeness, the Mummy first drew up its right knee so as to bring it nearly in contact with the abdomen, and then, straightening the limb with inconceivable force, bestowed a kick upon Doctor Ponnonner, which had the effect of discharging that gentleman, like an arrow from a catapult, through a window into the street below.

We rushed out *en masse* to bring in the mangled remains of the victim, but had the happiness to meet him upon the staircase, coming up in an unaccountable hurry, brimful of the most ardent philosophy, and more than ever impressed with the necessity of prosecuting our experiment with vigor and with zeal.

It was by his advice, accordingly, that we made, upon the spot, a profound incision into the tip of the subject's nose, while the Doctor himself, laying violent hands upon it, pulled it into vehement contact with the wire.

Morally and physically—figuratively and literally—was the effect electric. In the first place, the corpse opened its eyes and winked very rapidly for several minutes, as does Mr. Barnes in the pantomime, in the second place, it sneezed; in the third, it sat upon end; in the fourth, it shook its fist in Doctor Ponnonner's face; in the fifth, turning to Messieurs Gliddon and Buckingham, it addressed them, in very capital Egyptian, thus:

"I must say, gentlemen, that I am as much surprised as I am mortified at your behavior. Of Doctor Ponnonner nothing better was to be expected. He is a poor little fat fool who knows no better. I pity and forgive him. But you, Mr. Gliddon—and you, Silk—who have travelled and resided in Egypt until one might imagine you to the manner born—you, I say who have been so much among us that you speak Egyptian fully as well, I think, as you write your mother tongue—you, whom I have always been led to regard as the firm friend of the mummies—I really did anticipate more gentlemanly conduct from you. What am I to think of your standing quietly by and seeing me thus unhandsomely used? What am I to suppose by your permitting Tom, Dick, and Harry to strip me of my coffins, and my clothes, in this wretchedly cold climate? In what light (to come to the point) am I to regard your aiding and abetting that miserable little villain, Doctor Ponnonner, in pulling me by the nose?"

It will be taken for granted, no doubt, that upon hearing this speech under the circumstances, we all either made for the door, or fell into violent hysterics, or went off in a general swoon. One of these three things was, I say, to be expected. Indeed each and all of these lines of conduct might have been very plausibly pursued. And, upon my word, I am at a loss to know how or why it was that we pursued neither the one nor the other. But, perhaps, the true reason is to be sought in the spirit of the age, which proceeds by the rule of contraries altogether, and is now usually admitted as the solution of every thing in the way of paradox and impossibility. Or, perhaps, after all, it was only the Mummy's exceedingly natural and matter-of-course air that divested his words of the terrible. However this may be, the facts are clear, and no member of our party betrayed any very particular trepidation, or seemed to consider that any thing had gone very especially wrong.

For my part I was convinced it was all right, and merely stepped aside, out of the range of the Egyptian's fist. Doctor Ponnonner thrust his hands into his breeches' pockets, looked hard at the Mummy, and grew excessively red in the face. Mr. Glidden stroked his whiskers and drew up the collar of his shirt. Mr. Buckingham hung down his head, and put his right thumb into the left corner of his mouth.

The Egyptian regarded him with a severe countenance for some minutes and at length, with a sneer, said:

"Why don't you speak, Mr. Buckingham? Did you hear what I asked you, or not? Do take your thumb out of your mouth!"

Mr. Buckingham, hereupon, gave a slight start, took his right thumb out of the left corner of his mouth, and, by way of indemnification inserted his left thumb in the right corner of the aperture above-mentioned.

Not being able to get an answer from Mr. B., the figure turned peevishly to Mr. Gliddon, and, in a peremptory tone, demanded in general terms what we all meant.

Mr. Gliddon replied at great length, in phonetics; and but for the deficiency of American printing-offices in hieroglyphical type, it would afford me much pleasure to record here, in the original, the whole of his very excellent speech.

I may as well take this occasion to remark, that all the subsequent conversation in which the Mummy took a part, was carried on in primitive Egyptian, through the medium (so far as concerned myself and other untravelled members of the company)—through the medium, I say, of Messieurs Gliddon and Buckingham, as interpreters. These gentlemen spoke the mother tongue of the Mummy with inimitable fluency and grace; but I could not help observing that (owing, no doubt, to the introduction of images entirely modern, and, of course, entirely novel to the stranger) the two travellers were reduced, occasionally, to the employment of sensible forms for the purpose of conveying a particular meaning. Mr. Gliddon, at one period, for example, could not make the Egyptian comprehend the term "politics," until he sketched upon the wall, with a bit of charcoal a little carbuncle-nosed gentleman, out at elbows, standing upon a stump, with his left leg drawn back, right arm thrown forward, with his fist shut, the eyes rolled up toward Heaven, and the mouth open at an angle of ninety degrees. Just in the same way Mr. Buckingham failed to convey the absolutely modern idea "wig," until (at Doctor Ponnonner's suggestion) he grew very pale in the face, and consented to take off his own.

It will be readily understood that Mr. Gliddon's discourse turned chiefly upon the vast benefits accruing to science from the unrolling and disembowelling of mummies; apologizing, upon this score, for any disturbance that might have been occasioned him, in particular, the individual Mummy called Allamistakeo; and concluding with a mere hint (for it could scarcely be considered more) that, as these little matters were now explained, it might be as well to proceed with the investigation intended. Here Doctor Ponnonner made ready his instruments.

In regard to the latter suggestions of the orator, it appears that Allamistakeo had certain scruples of conscience, the nature of which I did not distinctly learn; but he expressed himself satisfied with the apologies tendered, and, getting down from the table, shook hands with the company all round.

When this ceremony was at an end, we immediately busied ourselves in repairing the damages which our subject had sustained from the scalpel. We sewed up the wound in his temple, bandaged his foot, and applied a square inch of black plaster to the tip of his nose.

It was now observed that the Count (this was the title, it seems, of Allamistakeo) had a slight fit of shivering—no doubt from the cold. The Doctor immediately repaired to his wardrobe, and soon returned with a black dress coat, made in Jennings' best manner, a pair of sky-blue plaid pantaloons with straps, a pink gingham chemise, a flapped vest of brocade, a white sack overcoat, a walking cane with a hook, a hat with no brim, patent-leather boots, straw-colored kid gloves, an eye-glass, a pair of whiskers, and a waterfall cravat. Owing to the disparity of size between the Count and the doctor (the proportion being as two to one), there was some little difficulty in adjusting these habiliments upon the person of the Egyptian; but when all was arranged, he might have been said to be dressed. Mr. Gliddon, therefore, gave him his arm, and led him to a comfortable chair by the fire, while the Doctor rang the bell upon the spot and ordered a supply of cigars and wine.

The conversation soon grew animated. Much curiosity was, of course, expressed in regard to the somewhat remarkable fact of Allamistakeo's still remaining alive.

"I should have thought," observed Mr. Buckingham, "that it is high time you were dead."

"Why," replied the Count, very much astonished, "I am little more than seven hundred years old! My father lived a thousand, and was by no means in his dotage when he died."

Here ensued a brisk series of questions and computations, by means of which it became evident that the antiquity of the Mummy had been grossly misjudged. It had been five thousand and fifty years and some months since he had been consigned to the catacombs at Eleithias.

"But my remark," resumed Mr. Buckingham, "had no reference to your age at the period of interment (I am willing to grant, in fact, that you are still a young man), and my illusion was to the immensity of time during which, by your own showing, you must have been done up in asphaltum."

"In what?" said the Count.

"In asphaltum," persisted Mr. B.

"Ah, yes; I have some faint notion of what you mean; it might be made to answer, no doubt—but in my time we employed scarcely any thing else than the Bichloride of Mercury."

"But what we are especially at a loss to understand," said Doctor Ponnonner, "is how it happens that, having been dead and buried in Egypt five thousand years ago, you are here to-day all alive and looking so delightfully well."

"Had I been, as you say, dead," replied the Count, "it is more than probable that dead, I should still be; for I perceive you are yet in the infancy of Calvanism, and cannot accomplish with it what was a common thing among us in the old days. But the fact is, I fell into catalepsy, and it was considered by my best friends that I was either dead or should be; they accordingly embalmed me at once—I presume you are aware of the chief principle of the embalming process?"

"Why not altogether."

"Why, I perceive—a deplorable condition of ignorance! Well I cannot enter into details just now: but it is necessary to explain that to embalm (properly speaking), in Egypt, was to arrest indefinitely all the animal functions subjected to the process. I use the word 'animal' in its widest sense, as including the physical not more than the moral and vital being. I repeat that the leading principle of embalmment consisted, with us, in the immediately arresting, and holding in perpetual abeyance, all the animal functions subjected to the process. To be brief, in whatever condition the individual was, at the period of embalmment, in that condition he remained. Now, as it is my good fortune to be of the blood of the Scarabaeus, I was embalmed alive, as you see me at present."

"The blood of the Scarabaeus!" exclaimed Doctor Ponnonner.

"Yes. The Scarabaeus was the insignium or the 'arms,' of a very distinguished and very rare patrician family. To be 'of the blood of the Scarabaeus,' is merely to be one of that family of which the Scarabaeus is the insignium. I speak figuratively."

"But what has this to do with you being alive?"

"Why, it is the general custom in Egypt to deprive a corpse, before embalmment, of its bowels and brains; the race of the Scarabaei alone did not coincide with the custom. Had I not been a Scarabeus, therefore, I should have been without bowels and brains; and without either it is inconvenient to live."

"I perceive that," said Mr. Buckingham, "and I presume that all the entire mummies that come to hand are of the race of Scarabaei."

"Beyond doubt."

"I thought," said Mr. Gliddon, very meekly, "that the Scarabaeus was one of the Egyptian gods."

"One of the Egyptian *what?*" exclaimed the Mummy, starting to its feet.

"Gods!" repeated the traveller.

"Mr. Gliddon, I really am astonished to hear you talk in this style," said the Count, resuming his chair. "No nation upon the face of the earth has ever acknowledged more than one god. The Scarabaeus, the Ibis, etc., were with us (as similar creatures have been with others) the symbols, or media, through which we offered worship to the Creator too august to be more directly approached."

There was here a pause. At length the colloquy was renewed by Doctor Ponnonner.

"It is not improbable, then, from what you have explained," said he, "that among the catacombs near the Nile there may exist other mummies of the Scarabaeus tribe, in a condition of vitality?"

"There can be no question of it," replied the Count; "all the Scarabaei embalmed accidentally while alive, are alive now. Even some of those purposely so embalmed, may have been overlooked by their executors, and still remain in the tomb."

"Will you be kind enough to explain," I said, "what you mean by 'purposely so embalmed'?"

"With great pleasure!" answered the Mummy, after surveying me leisurely through his eye-glass—for it was the first time I had ventured to address him a direct question.

"With great pleasure," he said. "The usual duration of man's life, in my time, was about eight hundred years. Few men died, unless by most extraordinary accident, before the age of six hundred; few lived longer than a decade of centuries; but eight were considered the natural term. After the discovery of the embalming principle, as I have already described it to you, it occurred to our philosophers that a laudable curiosity might be gratified, and, at the same time, the interests of science much advanced, by living this natural term in installments. In the case of history, indeed, experience demonstrated that something of this kind was indispensable. An historian, for example, having attained the age of five hundred, would write a book with great labor and then get himself carefully embalmed; leaving instructions to his executors pro tem., that they should cause him to be revivified after the lapse of a certain period—say five or six hundred years. Resuming existence at the expiration of this time, he would invariably find his great work converted into a species of hap-hazard note-book—that is to say, into a kind of literary arena for the conflicting guesses, riddles, and personal squabbles of whole herds of exasperated commentators. These guesses, etc., which passed under the name of annotations, or emendations, were found so completely to have enveloped, distorted, and overwhelmed the text, that the author had to go about with a lantern to discover his own book. When discovered, it was never worth the trouble of the search. After re-writing it throughout, it was regarded as the bounden duty of the historian to set himself to work immediately in correcting, from his own private knowledge and experience, the traditions of the day concerning the epoch at which he had originally lived. Now this process of re-scription and personal rectification, pursued by various individual sages from time to time, had the effect of preventing our history from degenerating into absolute fable."

"I beg your pardon," said Doctor Ponnonner at this point, laying his hand gently upon the arm of the Egyptian—"I beg your pardon, sir, but may I presume to interrupt you for one moment?"

"By all means, sir," replied the Count, drawing up.

"I merely wished to ask you a question," said the Doctor. "You mentioned the historian's personal correction of traditions respecting his own epoch. Pray, sir, upon an average what proportion of these Kabbala were usually found to be right?"

"The Kabbala, as you properly term them, sir, were generally discovered to be precisely on a par with the facts recorded in the un-re-written histories themselves;—that is to say, not one individual iota of either was ever known, under any circumstances, to be not totally and radically wrong."

"But since it is quite clear," resumed the Doctor, "that at least five thousand years have elapsed since your entombment, I take it for granted that your histories at that period, if not your traditions were sufficiently explicit on that one topic of universal interest, the Creation, which took place, as I presume you are aware, only about ten centuries before."

"Sir!" said the Count Allamistakeo.

The Doctor repeated his remarks, but it was only after much additional explanation that the foreigner could be made to comprehend them. The latter at length said, hesitatingly:

"The ideas you have suggested are to me, I confess, utterly novel. During my time I never knew any one to entertain so singular a fancy as that the universe (or this world if you will have it so) ever had a beginning at all. I remember once, and once only, hearing something remotely hinted, by a man of many speculations, concerning the origin *of the human race;* and by this individual, the very word *Adam* (or Red Earth), which you make use of, was employed. He employed it, however, in a generical sense, with reference to the spontaneous germination from rank soil (just as a thousand of the lower genera of creatures are germinated)—the spontaneous germination, I say, of five vast hordes of men, simultaneously upspringing in five distinct and nearly equal divisions of the globe."

Here, in general, the company shrugged their shoulders, and one or two of us touched our foreheads with a very significant air. Mr. Silk Buckingham, first glancing slightly at the occiput and then at the sinciput of Allamistakeo, spoke as follows:

"The long duration of human life in your time, together with the occasional practice of passing it, as you have explained, in installments, must have had, indeed, a strong tendency to the general development and conglomeration of knowledge. I presume, therefore, that we are to attribute the marked inferiority of the old Egyptians in all particulars of science, when compared with the moderns, and more especially with the Yankees, altogether to the superior solidity of the Egyptian skull."

"I confess again," replied the Count, with much suavity, "that I am somewhat at a loss to comprehend you; pray, to what particulars of science do you allude?"

Here our whole party, joining voices, detailed, at great length, the assumptions of phrenology and the marvels of animal magnetism.

Having heard us to an end, the Count proceeded to relate a few anecdotes, which rendered it evident that prototypes of Gall and Spurzheim had flourished and faded in Egypt so long ago as to have been nearly forgotten, and that the manoeuvres of Mesmer were really very contemptible tricks when put in collation with the positive miracles of the Theban savans, who created lice and a great many other similar things.

I here asked the Count if his people were able to calculate eclipses. He smiled rather contemptuously, and said they were.

This put me a little out, but I began to make other inquiries in regard to his astronomical knowledge, when a member of the company, who had never as yet opened his mouth, whispered in my ear, that for information on this head, I had better consult Ptolemy (whoever Ptolemy is), as well as one Plutarch de facie lunae.

I then questioned the Mummy about burning-glasses and lenses, and, in general, about the manufacture of glass; but I had not made an end of my queries before the silent member again touched me quietly on the elbow, and begged me for God's sake to take a peep at Diodorus Siculus. As for the Count, he merely asked me, in the way of reply, if we moderns possessed any such microscopes as would enable us to cut cameos in the style of the Egyptians. While I was thinking how I should answer this question, little Doctor Ponnonner committed himself in a very extraordinary way.

"Look at our architecture!" he exclaimed, greatly to the indignation of both the travellers, who pinched him black and blue to no purpose.

"Look," he cried with enthusiasm, "at the Bowling-Green Fountain in New York! or if this be too vast a contemplation, regard for a moment the Capitol at Washington, DC!"—and the good little medical man went on to detail very minutely, the proportions of the fabric to which he referred. He explained that the portico alone was adorned with no less than four and twenty columns, five feet in diameter, and ten feet apart.

The Count said that he regretted not being able to remember, just at that moment, the precise dimensions of any one of the principal buildings of the city of Aznac, whose foundations were laid in the night of Time, but the ruins of which were still standing, at the epoch of his entombment, in a vast plain of sand to the westward of Thebes. He recollected, however, (talking of the porticoes,) that one affixed to an inferior palace in a kind of suburb called Carnac, consisted of a hundred and forty-four columns, thirty-seven feet in circumference, and twenty-five feet apart. The approach to this portico, from the Nile, was through an avenue two miles long, composed of sphynxes, statues, and obelisks, twenty, sixty, and a hundred feet in height. The palace itself (as well as he could remember) was, in one direction, two miles long, and might have been altogether about seven in circuit. Its walls were richly painted all over, within and without, with hieroglyphics. He would not pretend to assert that even fifty or sixty of the Doctor's Capitols might have been built within these walls, but he was by no means sure that two or three hundred of them might not have been squeezed in with some trouble. That palace at Carnac was an insignificant little building after all. He (the Count), however, could not conscientiously refuse to admit the ingenuity, magnificence, and superiority of the Fountain at the Bowling Green, as described by the Doctor. Nothing like it, he was forced to allow, had ever been seen in Egypt or elsewhere.

I here asked the Count what he had to say to our railroads.

"Nothing," he replied, "in particular." They were rather slight, rather ill-conceived, and clumsily put together. They could not be compared, of course, with the vast, level, direct, iron-grooved causeways upon which the Egyptians conveyed entire temples and solid obelisks of a hundred and fifty feet in altitude.

I spoke of our gigantic mechanical forces.

He agreed that we knew something in that way, but inquired how I should have gone to work in getting up the imposts on the lintels of even the little palace at Carnac.

This question I concluded not to hear, and demanded if he had any idea of Artesian wells; but he simply raised his eyebrows; while Mr. Gliddon winked at me very hard and said, in a low tone, that one had been recently discovered by the engineers employed to bore for water in the Great Oasis.

I then mentioned our steel; but the foreigner elevated his nose, and asked me if our steel could have executed the sharp carved work seen on the obelisks, and which was wrought altogether by edge-tools of copper.

This disconcerted us so greatly that we thought it advisable to vary the attack to Metaphysics. We sent for a copy of a book called the "Dial," and read out of it a chapter or two about something that is not very clear, but which the Bostonians call the Great Movement of Progress.

The Count merely said that Great Movements were awfully common things in his day, and as for Progress, it was at one time quite a nuisance, but it never progressed.

We then spoke of the great beauty and importance of Democracy, and were at much trouble in impressing the Count with a due sense of the advantages we enjoyed in living where there was suffrage ad libitum, and no king.

He listened with marked interest, and in fact seemed not a little amused. When we had done, he said that, a great while ago, there had occurred something of a very similar sort. Thirteen Egyptian provinces determined all at once to be free, and to set a magnificent example to the rest of mankind. They assembled their wise men, and concocted the most ingenious constitution it is possible to conceive. For a while they managed remarkably well; only their habit of bragging was prodigious. The thing ended, however, in the consolidation of the thirteen states, with some fifteen or twenty others, in the most odious and insupportable despotism that was ever heard of upon the face of the Earth.

I asked what was the name of the usurping tyrant.

As well as the Count could recollect, it was Mob.

Not knowing what to say to this, I raised my voice, and deplored the Egyptian ignorance of steam.

The Count looked at me with much astonishment, but made no answer. The silent gentleman, however, gave me a violent nudge in the ribs with his elbows—told me I had sufficiently exposed myself for once—and demanded if I was really such a fool as not to know that the modern steam-engine is derived from the invention of Hero, through Solomon de Caus.

We were now in imminent danger of being discomfited; but, as good luck would have it, Doctor Ponnonner, having rallied, returned to our rescue, and inquired if the people of Egypt would seriously pretend to rival the moderns in the all—important particular of dress.

The Count, at this, glanced downward to the straps of his pantaloons, and then taking hold of the end of one of his coat-tails, held it up close to his eyes for some minutes. Letting it fall, at last, his mouth extended itself very gradually from ear to ear; but I do not remember that he said any thing in the way of reply.

Hereupon we recovered our spirits, and the Doctor, approaching the Mummy with great dignity, desired it to say candidly, upon its honor as a gentleman, if the Egyptians had comprehended, at any period, the manufacture of either Ponnonner's lozenges or Brandreth's pills.

We looked, with profound anxiety, for an answer—but in vain. It was not forthcoming. The Egyptian blushed and hung down his head. Never was triumph more consummate; never was defeat borne with so ill a grace. Indeed, I could not endure the spectacle of the poor Mummy's mortification. I reached my hat, bowed to him stiffly, and took leave.

Upon getting home I found it past four o'clock, and went immediately to bed. It is now ten A.M. I have been up since seven, penning these memoranda for the benefit of my family and of mankind. The former I shall behold no more. My wife is a shrew. The truth is, I am heartily sick of this life and of the nineteenth century in general. I am convinced that every thing is going wrong. Besides, I am anxious to know who will be President in 2045. As soon, therefore, as I shave and swallow a cup of coffee, I shall just step over to Ponnonner's and get embalmed for a couple of hundred years.

THE SPHINX

Edgar Allan Poe (1850)

DURING THE DREAD reign of the Cholera in New York, I had accepted the invitation of a relative to spend a fortnight with him in the retirement of his *cottage ornee* on the banks of the Hudson. We had here around us all the ordinary means of summer amusement; and what with rambling in the woods, sketching, boating, fishing, bathing, music, and books, we should have passed the time pleasantly enough, but for the fearful intelligence which reached us every morning from the populous city. Not a day elapsed which did not bring us news of the decease of some acquaintance. Then as the fatality increased, we learned to expect daily the loss of some friend. At length we trembled at the approach of every messenger. The very air from the South seemed to us redolent with death. That palsying thought, indeed, took entire possession of my soul. I could neither speak, think, nor dream of any thing else. My host was of a less excitable temperament, and, although greatly depressed in spirits, exerted himself to sustain my own. His richly philosophical intellect was not at any time affected by unrealities. To the substances of terror he was sufficiently alive, but of its shadows he had no apprehension.

His endeavors to arouse me from the condition of abnormal gloom into which I had fallen, were frustrated, in great measure, by certain volumes which I had found in his library. These were of a character to force into germination whatever seeds of hereditary superstition lay latent in my bosom. I had been reading these books without his knowledge, and thus he was often at a loss to account for the forcible impressions which had been made upon my fancy.

A favorite topic with me was the popular belief in omens—a belief which, at this one epoch of my life, I was almost seriously disposed to defend. On this subject we had long and animated discussions—he maintaining the utter groundlessness of faith in such matters,—I contending that a popular sentiment arising with absolute spontaneity—that is to say, without apparent traces of suggestion—had in itself the unmistakable elements of truth, and was entitled to as much respect as that intuition which is the idiosyncrasy of the individual man of genius.

The fact is, that soon after my arrival at the cottage there had occurred to myself an incident so entirely inexplicable, and which had in it so much of the portentous character, that I might well have been excused for regarding it as an omen. It appalled, and at the same time so confounded and bewildered me, that many days elapsed before I could make up my mind to communicate the circumstances to my friend.

Near the close of exceedingly warm day, I was sitting, book in hand, at an open window, commanding, through a long vista of the river banks, a view of a distant hill, the face of which nearest my position had been denuded by what is termed a land-slide, of the principal portion of its trees. My thoughts had been long wandering from the volume before me to the gloom and desolation of the neighboring city. Uplifting my eyes from the page, they fell upon the naked face of the bill, and upon an object—upon some living monster of hideous conformation, which very rapidly made its way from the summit to the bottom, disappearing finally in the dense forest below. As this creature first came in sight, I doubted my own sanity—or at least the evidence of my own eyes; and many minutes passed before I succeeded in convincing myself that I was neither mad nor in a dream. Yet when I described the monster (which I distinctly saw, and calmly surveyed through the whole period of its progress), my readers, I fear, will feel more difficulty in being convinced of these points than even I did myself.

Estimating the size of the creature by comparison with the diameter of the large trees near which it passed—the few giants of the forest which had escaped the fury of the land-slide—I concluded it to be far larger than any ship of the line in existence. I say ship of the line, because the shape of the monster suggested the idea—the hull of one of our seventy-four might convey a very tolerable conception of the general outline. The mouth of the animal was situated at the extremity of a proboscis some sixty or seventy feet in length, and about as thick as the body of an ordinary elephant. Near the root of this trunk was an immense quantity of black shaggy hair—more than could have been supplied by the coats of a score of buffaloes; and projecting from this hair downwardly and laterally, sprang two gleaming tusks not unlike those of the wild boar, but of infinitely greater dimensions. Extending forward, parallel with the proboscis, and on each side of it, was a gigantic staff, thirty or forty feet in length, formed seemingly of pure crystal and in shape a perfect prism,—it reflected in the most gorgeous manner the rays of the declining sun. The trunk was fashioned like a wedge with the apex to the earth. From it there were outspread two pairs of wings—each wing nearly one hundred yards in length—one pair being placed above the other, and all thickly covered with metal scales; each scale apparently some ten or twelve feet in diameter. I observed that the upper and lower tiers of wings were connected by a strong chain. But the chief peculiarity of this horrible thing was the representation of a Death's Head, which covered nearly the whole surface of its breast, and which was as accurately traced in glaring white, upon the dark ground of the body, as if it had been there carefully designed by an artist. While I regarded the terrific animal, and more especially the appearance on its breast, with a feeling or horror and awe—with a sentiment of forthcoming evil, which I found it impossible to quell by any effort of the reason, I perceived the huge jaws at the extremity of the proboscis suddenly expand themselves, and from them there proceeded a sound so loud and so expressive of wo, that it struck upon my nerves like a knell and as the monster disappeared at the foot of the hill, I fell at once, fainting, to the floor.

Upon recovering, my first impulse, of course, was to inform my friend of what I had seen and heard—and I can scarcely explain what feeling of repugnance it was which, in the end, operated to prevent me.

At length, one evening, some three or four days after the occurrence, we were sitting together in the room in which I had seen the apparition—I occupying the same seat at the same window, and he lounging on a sofa near at hand. The association of the place and time impelled me to give him an account of the phenomenon. He heard me to the end—at first laughed heartily—and then lapsed into an excessively grave demeanor, as if my insanity was a thing beyond suspicion. At this instant I again had a distinct view of the monster—to which, with a shout of absolute terror, I now directed his attention. He looked eagerly—but maintained that he saw nothing—although I designated minutely the course of the creature, as it made its way down the naked face of the hill.

I was now immeasurably alarmed, for I considered the vision either as an omen of my death, or, worse, as the fore-runner of an attack of mania. I threw myself passionately back in my chair, and for some moments buried my face in my hands. When I uncovered my eyes, the apparition was no longer apparent.

My host, however, had in some degree resumed the calmness of his demeanor, and questioned me very rigorously in respect to the conformation of the visionary creature. When I had fully satisfied him on this head, he sighed deeply, as if relieved of some intolerable burden, and went on to talk, with what I thought a cruel calmness, of various points of speculative philosophy, which had heretofore formed subject of discussion between us. I remember his insisting very especially (among other things) upon the idea that the principle source of error in all human investigations lay in the liability of the understanding to under-rate or to over-value the importance of an object, through mere mis-admeasurement of its propinquity. "To estimate properly, for example," he said, "the influence to be exercised on mankind at large by the thorough diffusion of Democracy, the distance of the epoch at which such diffusion may possibly be accomplished should not fail to form an item in the estimate. Yet can you tell me one writer on the subject of government who has ever thought this particular branch of the subject worthy of discussion at all?"

He here paused for a moment, stepped to a book-case, and brought forth one of the ordinary synopses of Natural History. Requesting me then to exchange seats with him, that he might the better distinguish the fine print of the volume, he took my armchair at the window, and, opening the book, resumed his discourse very much in the same tone as before.

"But for your exceeding minuteness," he said, "in describing the monster, I might never have had it in my power to demonstrate to you what it was. In the first place, let me read to you a schoolboy account of the genus Sphinx, of the family Crepuscularia of the order Lepidoptera, of the class of Insecta—or insects. The account runs thus:

"'Four membranous wings covered with little colored scales of metallic appearance; mouth forming a rolled proboscis, produced by an elongation of the jaws, upon the sides of which are found the rudiments of mandibles and downy palpi; the inferior wings retained to the superior by a stiff hair; antennae in the form of an elongated club, prismatic; abdomen pointed, The Death's—headed Sphinx has occasioned much terror among the vulgar, at times, by the melancholy kind of cry which it utters, and the insignia of death which it wears upon its corslet.'"

He here closed the book and leaned forward in the chair, placing himself accurately in the position which I had occupied at the moment of beholding "the monster."

"Ah, here it is," he presently exclaimed—"it is reascending the face of the hill, and a very remarkable looking creature I admit it to be. Still, it is by no means so large or so distant as you imagined it,—for the fact is that, as it wriggles its way up this thread, which some spider has wrought along the window-sash, I find it to be about the sixteenth of an inch in its extreme length, and also about the sixteenth of an inch distant from the pupil of my eye."

TWENTY THOUSAND LEAGUES UNDER THE SEA

Jules Verne (1870)

THIS UNEXPECTED FALL so stunned me that I have no clear recollection of my sensations at the time. I was at first drawn down to a depth of about twenty feet. I am a good swimmer (though without pretending to rival Byron or Edgar Poe, who were masters of the art), and in that plunge I did not lose my presence of mind. Two vigorous strokes brought me to the surface of the water. My first care was to look for the frigate. Had the crew seen me disappear? Had the *Abraham Lincoln* veered round? Would the captain put out a boat? Might I hope to be saved?

The darkness was intense. I caught a glimpse of a black mass disappearing in the east, its beacon lights dying out in the distance. It was the frigate! I was lost.

"Help, help!" I shouted, swimming towards the *Abraham Lincoln* in desperation.

My clothes encumbered me; they seemed glued to my body, and paralyzed my movements.

I was sinking! I was suffocating!

"Help!"

This was my last cry. My mouth filled with water; I struggled against being drawn down the abyss. Suddenly my clothes were seized by a strong hand, and I felt myself quickly drawn up to the surface of the sea; and I heard, yes, I heard these words pronounced in my ear:

"If master would be so good as to lean on my shoulder, master would swim with much greater ease."

I seized with one hand my faithful Conseil's arm.

"Is it you?" said I, "you?"

"Myself," answered Conseil; "and waiting master's orders."

"That shock threw you as well as me into the sea?"

"No; but, being in my master's service, I followed him."

The worthy fellow thought that was but natural.

"And the frigate?" I asked.

"The frigate?" replied Conseil, turning on his back; "I think that master had better not count too much on her."

"You think so?"

"I say that, at the time I threw myself into the sea, I heard the men at the wheel say, 'The screw and the rudder are broken.'"

"Broken?"

"Yes, broken by the monster's teeth. It is the only injury the *Abraham Lincoln* has sustained. But it is a bad look-out for us—she no longer answers her helm."

"Then we are lost!"

"Perhaps so," calmly answered Conseil. "However, we have still several hours before us, and one can do a good deal in some hours."

Conseil's imperturbable coolness set me up again. I swam more vigorously; but, cramped by my clothes, which stuck to me like a leaden weight, I felt great difficulty in bearing up. Conseil saw this.

"Will master let me make a slit?" said he; and, slipping an open knife under my clothes, he ripped them up from top to bottom very rapidly. Then he cleverly slipped them off me, while I swam for both of us.

Then I did the same for Conseil, and we continued to swim near to each other.

Nevertheless, our situation was no less terrible. Perhaps our disappearance had not been noticed; and, if it had been, the frigate could not tack, being without its helm. Conseil argued on this supposition, and laid his plans accordingly. This quiet boy was perfectly self-possessed. We then decided that, as our only chance of safety was being picked up by the *Abraham Lincoln*'s boats, we ought to manage so as to wait for them as long as possible. I resolved then to husband our strength, so that both should not be exhausted at the same time; and this is how we managed: while one of us lay on our back, quite still, with arms crossed, and legs stretched out, the other would swim and push the other on in front. This towing business did not last more than ten minutes each; and relieving each other thus, we could swim on for some hours, perhaps till day-break. Poor chance! but hope is so firmly rooted in the heart of man! Moreover, there were two of us. Indeed I declare (though it may seem improbable) if I sought to destroy all hope—if I wished to despair, I could not.

The collision of the frigate with the cetacean had occurred about eleven o'clock in the evening before. I reckoned then we should have eight hours to swim before sunrise, an operation quite practicable if we relieved each other. The sea, very calm, was in our favour. Sometimes I tried to pierce the intense darkness that was only dispelled by the phosphorescence caused by our movements. I watched the luminous waves that broke over my hand, whose mirror-like surface was spotted with silvery rings. One might have said that we were in a bath of quicksilver.

Near one o'clock in the morning, I was seized with dreadful fatigue. My limbs stiffened under the strain of violent cramp. Conseil was obliged to keep me up, and our preservation devolved on him alone. I heard the poor boy pant; his breathing became short and hurried. I found that he could not keep up much longer.

"Leave me! leave me!" I said to him.

"Leave my master? Never!" replied he. "I would drown first."

Just then the moon appeared through the fringes of a thick cloud that the wind was driving to the east. The surface of the sea glittered with its rays. This kindly light reanimated us. My head got better again. I looked at all points of the horizon. I saw the frigate! She was five miles from us, and looked like a dark mass, hardly discernible. But no boats!

I would have cried out. But what good would it have been at such a distance! My swollen lips could utter no sounds. Conseil could articulate some words, and I heard him repeat at intervals, "Help! help!"

Our movements were suspended for an instant; we listened. It might be only a singing in the ear, but it seemed to me as if a cry answered the cry from Conseil.

"Did you hear?" I murmured.

"Yes! Yes!"

And Conseil gave one more despairing cry.

This time there was no mistake! A human voice responded to ours! Was it the voice of another unfortunate creature, abandoned in the middle of the ocean, some other victim of the shock sustained by the vessel? Or rather was it a boat from the frigate, that was hailing us in the darkness?

Conseil made a last effort, and, leaning on my shoulder, while I struck out in a desperate effort, he raised himself half out of the water, then fell back exhausted.

"What did you see?"

"I saw——" murmured he; "I saw—but do not talk—reserve all your strength!"

What had he seen? Then, I know not why, the thought of the monster came into my head for the first time! But that voice! The time is past for Jonahs to take refuge in whales' bellies! However, Conseil was towing me again. He raised his head sometimes, looked before us, and uttered a cry of recognition, which was responded to by a voice that came nearer and nearer. I scarcely heard it. My strength was exhausted; my fingers stiffened; my hand afforded me support no longer; my mouth, convulsively opening, filled with salt water. Cold crept over me. I raised my head for the last time, then I sank.

At this moment a hard body struck me. I clung to it: then I felt that I was being drawn up, that I was brought to the surface of the water, that my chest collapsed—I fainted.

It is certain that I soon came to, thanks to the vigorous rubbings that I received. I half opened my eyes.

"Conseil!" I murmured.

"Does master call me?" asked Conseil.

Just then, by the waning light of the moon which was sinking down to the horizon, I saw a face which was not Conseil's and which I immediately recognised.

"Ned!" I cried.

"The same, sir, who is seeking his prize!" replied the Canadian.

"Were you thrown into the sea by the shock to the frigate?"

"Yes, Professor; but more fortunate than you, I was able to find a footing almost directly upon a floating island."

"An island?"

"Or, more correctly speaking, on our gigantic narwhal."

"Explain yourself, Ned!"

"Only I soon found out why my harpoon had not entered its skin and was blunted."

"Why, Ned, why?"

"Because, Professor, that beast is made of sheet iron."

The Canadian's last words produced a sudden revolution in my brain. I wriggled myself quickly to the top of the being, or object, half out of the water, which served us for a refuge. I kicked it. It was evidently a hard, impenetrable body, and not the soft substance that forms the bodies of the great marine mammalia. But this hard body might be a bony covering, like that of the antediluvian animals; and I should be free to class this monster among amphibious reptiles, such as tortoises or alligators.

Well, no! the blackish back that supported me was smooth, polished, without scales. The blow produced a metallic sound; and, incredible though it may be, it seemed, I might say, as if it was made of riveted plates.

There was no doubt about it! This monster, this natural phenomenon that had puzzled the learned world, and over thrown and misled the imagination of seamen of both hemispheres, it must be owned was a still more astonishing phenomenon, inasmuch as it was a simply human construction.

We had no time to lose, however. We were lying upon the back of a sort of submarine boat, which appeared (as far as I could judge) like a huge fish of steel. Ned Land's mind was made up on this point. Conseil and I could only agree with him.

Just then a bubbling began at the back of this strange thing (which was evidently propelled by a screw), and it began to move. We had only just time to seize hold of the upper part, which rose about seven feet out of the water, and happily its speed was not great.

"As long as it sails horizontally," muttered Ned Land, "I do not mind; but, if it takes a fancy to dive, I would not give two straws for my life."

The Canadian might have said still less. It became really necessary to communicate with the beings, whatever they were, shut up inside the machine. I searched all over the outside for an aperture, a panel, or a manhole, to use a technical expression; but the lines of the iron rivets, solidly driven into the joints of the iron plates, were clear and uniform. Besides, the moon disappeared then, and left us in total darkness.

At last this long night passed. My indistinct remembrance prevents my describing all the impressions it made. I can only recall one circumstance. During some lulls of the wind and sea, I fancied I heard several times vague sounds, a sort of fugitive harmony produced by words of command. What was, then, the mystery of this submarine craft, of which the whole world vainly sought an explanation? What kind of beings existed in this strange boat? What mechanical agent caused its prodigious speed?

Daybreak appeared. The morning mists surrounded us, but they soon cleared off. I was about to examine the hull, which formed on deck a kind of horizontal platform, when I felt it gradually sinking.

"Oh! confound it!" cried Ned Land, kicking the resounding plate. "Open, you inhospitable rascals!"

Happily the sinking movement ceased. Suddenly a noise, like iron works violently pushed aside, came from the interior of the boat. One iron plate was moved, a man appeared, uttered an odd cry, and disappeared immediately.

Some moments after, eight strong men, with masked faces, appeared noiselessly, and drew us down into their formidable machine.

This forcible abduction, so roughly carried out, was accomplished with the rapidity of lightning. I shivered all over. Whom had we to deal with? No doubt some new sort of pirates, who explored the sea in their own way. Hardly had the narrow panel closed upon me, when I was enveloped in darkness. My eyes, dazzled with the outer light, could distinguish nothing. I felt my naked feet cling to the rungs of an iron ladder. Ned Land and Conseil, firmly seized, followed me. At the bottom of the ladder, a door opened, and shut after us immediately with a bang.

We were alone. Where, I could not say, hardly imagine. All was black, and such a dense black that, after some minutes, my eyes had not been able to discern even the faintest glimmer.

Meanwhile, Ned Land, furious at these proceedings, gave free vent to his indignation.

"Confound it!" cried he, "here are people who come up to the Scotch for hospitality. They only just miss being cannibals. I should not be surprised at it, but I declare that they shall not eat me without my protesting."

"Calm yourself, friend Ned, calm yourself," replied Conseil, quietly. "Do not cry out before you are hurt. We are not quite done for yet."

"Not quite," sharply replied the Canadian, "but pretty near, at all events. Things look black. Happily, my bowie knife I have still, and I can always see well enough to use it. The first of these pirates who lays a hand on me——"

"Do not excite yourself, Ned," I said to the harpooner, "and do not compromise us by useless violence. Who knows that they will not listen to us? Let us rather try to find out where we are."

I groped about. In five steps I came to an iron wall, made of plates bolted together. Then turning back I struck against a wooden table, near which were ranged several stools. The boards of this prison were concealed under a thick mat, which deadened the noise of the feet. The bare walls revealed no trace of window or door. Conseil, going round the reverse way, met me, and we went back to the middle of the cabin, which measured about twenty feet by ten. As to its height, Ned Land, in spite of his own great height, could not measure it.

Half an hour had already passed without our situation being bettered, when the dense darkness suddenly gave way to extreme light. Our prison was suddenly lighted, that is to say, it became filled with a luminous matter, so strong that I could not bear it at first. In its whiteness and intensity I recognised that electric light which played round the submarine boat like a magnificent phenomenon of phosphorescence. After shutting my eyes involuntarily, I opened them, and saw that this luminous agent came from a half globe, unpolished, placed in the roof of the cabin.

"At last one can see," cried Ned Land, who, knife in hand, stood on the defensive.

"Yes," said I; "but we are still in the dark about ourselves."

"Let master have patience," said the imperturbable Conseil.

The sudden lighting of the cabin enabled me to examine it minutely. It only contained a table and five stools. The invisible door might be hermetically sealed. No noise was heard. All seemed dead in the interior of this boat. Did it move, did it float on the surface of the ocean, or did it dive into its depths? I could not guess.

A noise of bolts was now heard, the door opened, and two men appeared.

One was short, very muscular, broad-shouldered, with robust limbs, strong head, an abundance of black hair, thick moustache, a quick penetrating look, and the vivacity which characterises the population of Southern France.

The second stranger merits a more detailed description. I made out his prevailing qualities directly: self-confidence—because his head was well set on his shoulders, and his black eyes looked around with cold assurance; calmness—for his skin, rather pale, showed his coolness of blood; energy—evinced by the rapid contraction of his lofty brows; and courage—because his deep breathing denoted great power of lungs.

Whether this person was thirty-five or fifty years of age, I could not say. He was tall, had a large forehead, straight nose, a clearly cut mouth, beautiful teeth, with fine taper hands, indicative of a highly nervous temperament. This man was certainly the most admirable specimen I had ever met. One particular feature was his eyes, rather far from each other, and which could take in nearly a quarter of the horizon at once.

This faculty—(I verified it later)—gave him a range of vision far superior to Ned Land's. When this stranger fixed upon an object, his eyebrows met, his large eyelids closed around so as to contract the range of his vision, and he looked as if he magnified the objects lessened by distance, as if he pierced those sheets of water so opaque to our eyes, and as if he read the very depths of the seas.

The two strangers, with caps made from the fur of the sea otter, and shod with sea boots of seal's skin, were dressed in clothes of a particular texture, which allowed free movement of the limbs. The taller of the two, evidently the chief on board, examined us with great attention, without saying a word; then, turning to his companion, talked with him in an unknown tongue. It was a sonorous, harmonious, and flexible dialect, the vowels seeming to admit of very varied accentuation.

The other replied by a shake of the head, and added two or three perfectly incomprehensible words. Then he seemed to question me by a look.

I replied in good French that I did not know his language; but he seemed not to understand me, and my situation became more embarrassing.

"If master were to tell our story," said Conseil, "perhaps these gentlemen may understand some words."

I began to tell our adventures, articulating each syllable clearly, and without omitting one single detail. I announced our names and rank, introducing in person Professor Aronnax, his servant Conseil, and master Ned Land, the harpooner.

The man with the soft calm eyes listened to me quietly, even politely, and with extreme attention; but nothing in his countenance indicated that he had understood my story. When I finished, he said not a word.

There remained one resource, to speak English. Perhaps they would know this almost universal language. I knew it—as well as the German language—well enough to read it fluently, but not to speak it correctly. But, anyhow, we must make ourselves understood.

"Go on in your turn," I said to the harpooner; "speak your best Anglo-Saxon, and try to do better than I."

Ned did not beg off, and recommenced our story.

To his great disgust, the harpooner did not seem to have made himself more intelligible than I had. Our visitors did not stir. They evidently understood neither the language of England nor of France.

Very much embarrassed, after having vainly exhausted our speaking resources, I knew not what part to take, when Conseil said:

"If master will permit me, I will relate it in German."

But in spite of the elegant terms and good accent of the narrator, the German language had no success. At last, nonplussed, I tried to remember my first lessons, and to narrate our adventures in Latin, but with no better success. This last attempt being of no avail, the two strangers exchanged some words in their unknown language, and retired.

The door shut.

"It is an infamous shame," cried Ned Land, who broke out for the twentieth time. "We speak to those rogues in French, English, German, and Latin, and not one of them has the politeness to answer!"

"Calm yourself," I said to the impetuous Ned; "anger will do no good."

"But do you see, Professor," replied our irascible companion, "that we shall absolutely die of hunger in this iron cage?"

"Bah!" said Conseil, philosophically; "we can hold out some time yet."

"My friends," I said, "we must not despair. We have been worse off than this. Do me the favour to wait a little before forming an opinion upon the commander and crew of this boat."

"My opinion is formed," replied Ned Land, sharply. "They are rascals."

"Good! and from what country?"

"From the land of rogues!"

"My brave Ned, that country is not clearly indicated on the map of the world; but I admit that the nationality of the two strangers is hard to determine. Neither English, French, nor German, that is quite certain. However, I am inclined to think that the commander and his companion were born in low latitudes. There is southern blood in them. But I cannot decide by their appearance whether they are Spaniards, Turks, Arabians, or Indians. As to their language, it is quite incomprehensible."

"There is the disadvantage of not knowing all languages," said Conseil, "or the disadvantage of not having one universal language."

As he said these words, the door opened. A steward entered. He brought us clothes, coats and trousers, made of a stuff I did not know. I hastened to dress myself, and my companions followed my example. During that time, the steward—dumb, perhaps deaf—had arranged the table, and laid three plates.

"This is something like!" said Conseil.

"Bah!" said the angry harpooner, "what do you suppose they eat here? Tortoise liver, filleted shark, and beef steaks from seadogs."

"We shall see," said Conseil.

The dishes, of bell metal, were placed on the table, and we took our places. Undoubtedly we had to do with civilized people, and, had it not been for the electric light which flooded us, I could have fancied I was in the dining-room of the Adelphi Hotel at Liverpool, or at the Grand Hotel in Paris. I must say, however, that there was neither bread nor wine. The water was fresh and clear, but it was water and did not suit Ned Land's taste. Amongst the dishes which were brought to us, I recognized several fish delicately dressed; but of some, although excellent, I could give no opinion, neither could I tell to what kingdom they belonged, whether animal or vegetable. As to the dinner-service, it was elegant, and in perfect taste. Each utensil—spoon, fork, knife, plate—had a letter engraved on it, with a motto above it, of which this is an exact facsimile:

MOBILIS IN MOBILI N

The letter N was no doubt the initial of the name of the enigmatical person who commanded at the bottom of the seas.

Ned and Conseil did not reflect much. They devoured the food, and I did likewise. I was, besides, reassured as to our fate; and it seemed evident that our hosts would not let us die of want.

However, everything has an end, everything passes away, even the hunger of people who have not eaten for fifteen hours. Our appetites satisfied, we felt overcome with sleep.

"Faith! I shall sleep well," said Conseil.

"So shall I," replied Ned Land.

My two companions stretched themselves on the cabin carpet, and were soon sound asleep. For my own part, too many thoughts crowded my brain, too many insoluble questions pressed upon me, too many fancies kept my eyes half open. Where were we? What strange power carried us on? I felt—or rather fancied I felt—the machine sinking down to the lowest beds of the sea. Dreadful nightmares beset me; I saw in these mysterious asylums a world of unknown animals, amongst which this submarine boat seemed to be of the same kind, living, moving, and formidable as they. Then my brain grew calmer, my imagination wandered into vague unconsciousness, and I soon fell into a deep sleep.

How long we slept I do not know; but our sleep must have lasted long, for it rested us completely from our fatigues. I woke first. My companions had not moved, and were still stretched in their corner.

Hardly roused from my somewhat hard couch, I felt my brain freed, my mind clear. I then began an attentive examination of our cell. Nothing was changed inside. The prison was still a prison—the prisoners, prisoners. However, the steward, during our sleep, had cleared the table. I breathed with difficulty. The heavy air seemed to oppress my lungs. Although the cell was large, we had evidently consumed a great part of the oxygen that it contained. Indeed, each man consumes, in one hour, the oxygen contained in more than 176 pints of air, and this air, charged (as then) with a nearly equal quantity of carbonic acid, becomes unbreathable.

It became necessary to renew the atmosphere of our prison, and no doubt the whole in the submarine boat. That gave rise to a question in my mind. How would the commander of this floating dwelling-place proceed? Would he obtain air by chemical means, in getting by heat the oxygen contained in chlorate of potash, and in absorbing carbonic acid by caustic potash? Or—a more convenient, economical, and consequently more probable alternative—would he be satisfied to rise and take breath at the surface of the water, like a whale, and so renew for twenty-four hours the atmospheric provision?

In fact, I was already obliged to increase my respirations to eke out of this cell the little oxygen it contained, when suddenly I was refreshed by a current of pure air, and perfumed with saline emanations. It was an invigorating sea breeze, charged with iodine. I opened my mouth wide, and my lungs saturated themselves with fresh particles.

At the same time I felt the boat rolling. The iron-plated monster had evidently just risen to the surface of the ocean to breathe, after the fashion of whales. I found out from that the mode of ventilating the boat.

When I had inhaled this air freely, I sought the conduit pipe, which conveyed to us the beneficial whiff, and I was not long in finding it. Above the door was a ventilator, through which volumes of fresh air renewed the impoverished atmosphere of the cell.

I was making my observations, when Ned and Conseil awoke almost at the same time, under the influence of this reviving air. They rubbed their eyes, stretched themselves, and were on their feet in an instant.

"Did master sleep well?" asked Conseil, with his usual politeness.

"Very well, my brave boy. And you, Mr. Land?"

"Soundly, Professor. But, I don't know if I am right or not, there seems to be a sea breeze!"

A seaman could not be mistaken, and I told the Canadian all that had passed during his sleep.

"Good!" said he. "That accounts for those roarings we heard, when the supposed narwhal sighted the *Abraham Lincoln*."

"Quite so, Master Land; it was taking breath."

"Only, Mr. Aronnax, I have no idea what o'clock it is, unless it is dinner-time."

"Dinner-time! my good fellow? Say rather breakfast-time, for we certainly have begun another day."

"So," said Conseil, "we have slept twenty-four hours?"

"That is my opinion."

"I will not contradict you," replied Ned Land. "But, dinner or breakfast, the steward will be welcome, whichever he brings."

"Master Land, we must conform to the rules on board, and I suppose our appetites are in advance of the dinner hour."

"That is just like you, friend Conseil," said Ned, impatiently. "You are never out of temper, always calm; you would return thanks before grace, and die of hunger rather than complain!"

Time was getting on, and we were fearfully hungry; and this time the steward did not appear. It was rather too long to leave us, if they really had good intentions towards us. Ned Land, tormented by the cravings of hunger, got still more angry; and, notwithstanding his promise, I dreaded an explosion when he found himself with one of the crew.

For two hours more Ned Land's temper increased; he cried, he shouted, but in vain. The walls were deaf. There was no sound to be heard in the boat; all was still as death. It did not move, for I should have felt the trembling motion of the hull under the influence of the screw. Plunged in the depths of the waters, it belonged no longer to earth: this silence was dreadful.

I felt terrified, Conseil was calm, Ned Land roared.

Just then a noise was heard outside. Steps sounded on the metal flags. The locks were turned, the door opened, and the steward appeared.

Before I could rush forward to stop him, the Canadian had thrown him down, and held him by the throat. The steward was choking under the grip of his powerful hand.

Conseil was already trying to unclasp the harpooner's hand from his half-suffocated victim, and I was going to fly to the rescue, when suddenly I was nailed to the spot by hearing these words in French:

"Be quiet, Master Land; and you, Professor, will you be so good as to listen to me?"

It was the commander of the vessel who thus spoke.

At these words, Ned Land rose suddenly. The steward, nearly strangled, tottered out on a sign from his master. But such was the power of the commander on board, that not a gesture betrayed the resentment which this man must have felt towards the Canadian. Conseil interested in spite of himself, I stupefied, awaited in silence the result of this scene.

The commander, leaning against the corner of a table with his arms folded, scanned us with profound attention. Did he hesitate to speak? Did he regret the words which he had just spoken in French? One might almost think so.

After some moments of silence, which not one of us dreamed of breaking, "Gentlemen," said he, in a calm and penetrating voice, "I speak French, English, German, and Latin equally well. I could, therefore, have answered you at our first interview, but I wished to know you first, then to reflect. The story told by each one, entirely agreeing in the main points, convinced me of your identity. I know now that chance has brought before me M. Pierre Aronnax, Professor of Natural History at the Museum of Paris, entrusted with a scientific mission abroad, Conseil, his servant, and Ned Land, of Canadian origin, harpooner on board the frigate *Abraham Lincoln* of the navy of the United States of America."

I bowed assent. It was not a question that the commander put to me. Therefore there was no answer to be made. This man expressed himself with perfect ease, without any accent. His sentences were well turned, his words clear, and his fluency of speech remarkable. Yet, I did not recognize in him a fellow-countryman.

He continued the conversation in these terms:

"You have doubtless thought, sir, that I have delayed long in paying you this second visit. The reason is that, your identity recognized, I wished to weigh maturely what part to act towards you. I have hesitated much. Most annoying circumstances have brought you into the presence of a man who has broken all the ties of humanity. You have come to trouble my existence."

"Unintentionally!" said I.

"Unintentionally?" replied the stranger, raising his voice a little. "Was it unintentionally that the *Abraham Lincoln* pursued me all over the seas? Was it unintentionally that you took passage in this frigate? Was it unintentionally that your cannon-balls rebounded off the plating of my vessel? Was it unintentionally that Mr. Ned Land struck me with his harpoon?"

I detected a restrained irritation in these words. But to these recriminations I had a very natural answer to make, and I made it.

"Sir," said I, "no doubt you are ignorant of the discussions which have taken place concerning you in America and Europe. You do not know that divers accidents, caused by collisions with your submarine machine, have excited public feeling in the two continents. I omit the theories without number by which it was sought to explain that of which you alone possess the secret. But you must understand that, in pursuing you over the high seas of the Pacific, the *Abraham Lincoln* believed itself to be chasing some powerful sea-monster, of which it was necessary to rid the ocean at any price."

A half-smile curled the lips of the commander: then, in a calmer tone:

"M. Aronnax," he replied, "dare you affirm that your frigate would not as soon have pursued and cannonaded a submarine boat as a monster?"

This question embarrassed me, for certainly Captain Farragut might not have hesitated. He might have thought it his duty to destroy a contrivance of this kind, as he would a gigantic narwhal.

"You understand then, sir," continued the stranger, "that I have the right to treat you as enemies?"

I answered nothing, purposely. For what good would it be to discuss such a proposition, when force could destroy the best arguments?

"I have hesitated some time," continued the commander; "nothing obliged me to show you hospitality. If I chose to separate myself from you, I should have no interest in seeing you again; I could place you upon the deck of this vessel which has served you as a refuge, I could sink beneath the waters, and forget that you had ever existed. Would not that be my right?"

"It might be the right of a savage," I answered, "but not that of a civilized man."

"Professor," replied the commander, quickly, "I am not what you call a civilized man! I have done with society entirely, for reasons which I alone have the right of appreciating. I do not, therefore, obey its laws, and I desire you never to allude to them before me again!"

This was said plainly. A flash of anger and disdain kindled in the eyes of the Unknown, and I had a glimpse of a terrible past in the life of this man. Not only had he put himself beyond the pale of human laws, but he had made himself independent of them, free in the strictest acceptation of the word, quite beyond their reach! Who then would dare to pursue him at the bottom of the sea, when, on its surface, he defied all attempts made against him?

What vessel could resist the shock of his submarine monitor? What cuirass, however thick, could withstand the blows of his spur? No man could demand from him an account of his actions; God, if he believed in one—his conscience, if he had one—were the sole judges to whom he was answerable.

These reflections crossed my mind rapidly, whilst the stranger personage was silent, absorbed, and as if wrapped up in himself. I regarded him with fear mingled with interest, as, doubtless, Oedipus regarded the Sphinx.

After rather a long silence, the commander resumed the conversation.

"I have hesitated," said he, "but I have thought that my interest might be reconciled with that pity to which every human being has a right. You will remain on board my vessel, since fate has cast you there. You will be free; and, in exchange for this liberty, I shall only impose one single condition. Your word of honour to submit to it will suffice."

"Speak, sir," I answered. "I suppose this condition is one which a man of honour may accept?"

"Yes, sir; it is this: It is possible that certain events, unforeseen, may oblige me to consign you to your cabins for some hours or some days, as the case may be. As I desire never to use violence, I expect from you, more than all the others, a passive obedience. In thus acting, I take all the responsibility: I acquit you entirely, for I make it an impossibility for you to see what ought not to be seen. Do you accept this condition?"

Then things took place on board which, to say the least, were singular, and which ought not to be seen by people who were not placed beyond the pale of social laws. Amongst the surprises which the future was preparing for me, this might not be the least.

"We accept," I answered; "only I will ask your permission, sir, to address one question to you—one only."

"Speak, sir."

"You said that we should be free on board."

"Entirely."

"I ask you, then, what you mean by this liberty?"

"Just the liberty to go, to come, to see, to observe even all that passes here save under rare circumstances—the liberty, in short, which we enjoy ourselves, my companions and I."

It was evident that we did not understand one another.

"Pardon me, sir," I resumed, "but this liberty is only what every prisoner has of pacing his prison. It cannot suffice us."

"It must suffice you, however."

"What! we must renounce for ever seeing our country, our friends, our relations again?"

"Yes, sir. But to renounce that unendurable worldly yoke which men believe to be liberty is not perhaps so painful as you think."

"Well," exclaimed Ned Land, "never will I give my word of honor not to try to escape."

"I did not ask you for your word of honor, Master Land," answered the commander, coldly.

"Sir," I replied, beginning to get angry in spite of my self, "you abuse your situation towards us; it is cruelty."

"No, sir, it is clemency. You are my prisoners of war. I keep you, when I could, by a word, plunge you into the depths of the ocean. You attacked me. You came to surprise a secret which no man in the world must penetrate—the secret of my whole existence. And you think that I am going to send you back to that world which must know me no more? Never! In retaining you, it is not you whom I guard—it is myself."

These words indicated a resolution taken on the part of the commander, against which no arguments would prevail.

"So, sir," I rejoined, "you give us simply the choice between life and death?"

"Simply."

"My friends," said I, "to a question thus put, there is nothing to answer. But no word of honor binds us to the master of this vessel."

"None, sir," answered the Unknown.

Then, in a gentler tone, he continued:

"Now, permit me to finish what I have to say to you. I know you, M. Aronnax. You and your companions will not, perhaps, have so much to complain of in the chance which has bound you to my fate. You will find amongst the books which are my favorite study the work which you have published on 'the depths of the sea.' I have often read it. You have carried out your work as far as terrestrial science permitted you. But you do not know all—you have not seen all. Let me tell you then, Professor, that you will not regret the time passed on board my vessel. You are going to visit the land of marvels."

These words of the commander had a great effect upon me. I cannot deny it. My weak point was touched; and I forgot, for a moment, that the contemplation of these sublime subjects was not worth the loss of liberty. Besides, I trusted to the future to decide this grave question. So I contented myself with saying:

"By what name ought I to address you?"

"Sir," replied the commander, "I am nothing to you but Captain Nemo; and you and your companions are nothing to me but the passengers of the *Nautilus*."

Captain Nemo called. A steward appeared. The captain gave him his orders in that strange language which I did not understand. Then, turning towards the Canadian and Conseil:

"A repast awaits you in your cabin," said he. "Be so good as to follow this man.

"And now, M. Aronnax, our breakfast is ready. Permit me to lead the way."

"I am at your service, Captain."

I followed Captain Nemo; and as soon as I had passed through the door, I found myself in a kind of passage lighted by electricity, similar to the waist of a ship. After we had proceeded a dozen yards, a second door opened before me.

I then entered a dining-room, decorated and furnished in severe taste. High oaken sideboards, inlaid with ebony, stood at the two extremities of the room, and upon their shelves glittered china, porcelain, and glass of inestimable value. The plate on the table sparkled in the rays which the luminous ceiling shed around, while the light was tempered and softened by exquisite paintings.

In the centre of the room was a table richly laid out. Captain Nemo indicated the place I was to occupy.

The breakfast consisted of a certain number of dishes, the contents of which were furnished by the sea alone; and I was ignorant of the nature and mode of preparation of some of them. I acknowledged that they were good, but they had a peculiar flavour, which I easily became accustomed to. These different aliments appeared to me to be rich in phosphorus, and I thought they must have a marine origin.

Captain Nemo looked at me. I asked him no questions, but he guessed my thoughts, and answered of his own accord the questions which I was burning to address to him.

"The greater part of these dishes are unknown to you," he said to me. "However, you may partake of them without fear. They are wholesome and nourishing. For a long time I have renounced the food of the earth, and I am never ill now. My crew, who are healthy, are fed on the same food."

"So," said I, "all these eatables are the produce of the sea?"

"Yes, Professor, the sea supplies all my wants. Sometimes I cast my nets in tow, and I draw them in ready to break. Sometimes I hunt in the midst of this element, which appears to be inaccessible to man, and quarry the game which dwells in my submarine forests. My flocks, like those of Neptune's old shepherds, graze fearlessly in the immense prairies of the ocean. I have a vast property there, which I cultivate myself, and which is always sown by the hand of the Creator of all things."

"I can understand perfectly, sir, that your nets furnish excellent fish for your table; I can understand also that you hunt aquatic game in your submarine forests; but I cannot understand at all how a particle of meat, no matter how small, can figure in your bill of fare."

"This, which you believe to be meat, Professor, is nothing else than fillet of turtle. Here are also some dolphins' livers, which you take to be ragout of pork. My cook is a clever fellow, who excels in dressing these various products of the ocean. Taste all these dishes. Here is a preserve of sea-cucumber, which a Malay would declare to be unrivalled in the world; here is a cream, of which the milk has been furnished by the cetacea, and the sugar by the great fucus of the North Sea; and, lastly, permit me to offer you some preserve of anemones, which is equal to that of the most delicious fruits."

I tasted, more from curiosity than as a connoisseur, whilst Captain Nemo enchanted me with his extraordinary stories.

"You like the sea, Captain?"

"Yes; I love it! The sea is everything. It covers seven tenths of the terrestrial globe. Its breath is pure and healthy. It is an immense desert, where man is never lonely, for he feels life stirring on all sides. The sea is only the embodiment of a supernatural and wonderful existence. It is nothing but love and emotion; it is the `Living Infinite,' as one of your poets has said. In fact, Professor, Nature manifests herself in it by her three kingdoms—mineral, vegetable, and animal. The sea is the vast reservoir of Nature. The globe began with sea, so to speak; and who knows if it will not end with it? In it is supreme tranquility. The sea does not belong to despots. Upon its surface men can still exercise unjust laws, fight, tear one another to pieces, and be carried away with terrestrial horrors. But at thirty feet below its level, their reign ceases, their influence is quenched, and their power disappears. Ah! sir, live—live in the bosom of the waters! There only is independence! There I recognize no masters! There I am free!"

Captain Nemo suddenly became silent in the midst of this enthusiasm, by which he was quite carried away. For a few moments he paced up and down, much agitated. Then he became more calm, regained his accustomed coldness of expression, and turning towards me:

"Now, Professor," said he, "if you wish to go over the *Nautilus*, I am at your service."

Captain Nemo rose. I followed him. A double door, contrived at the back of the dining-room, opened, and I entered a room equal in dimensions to that which I had just quitted.

It was a library. High pieces of furniture, of black violet ebony inlaid with brass, supported upon their wide shelves a great number of books uniformly bound. They followed the shape of the room, terminating at the lower part in huge divans, covered with brown leather, which were curved, to afford the greatest comfort. Light movable desks, made to slide in and out at will, allowed one to rest one's book while reading. In the centre stood an immense table, covered with pamphlets, amongst which were some newspapers, already of old date. The electric light flooded everything; it was shed from four unpolished globes half sunk in the volutes of the ceiling. I looked with real admiration at this room, so ingeniously fitted up, and I could scarcely believe my eyes.

"Captain Nemo," said I to my host, who had just thrown himself on one of the divans, "this is a library which would do honor to more than one of the continental palaces, and I am absolutely astounded when I consider that it can follow you to the bottom of the seas."

"Where could one find greater solitude or silence, Professor?" replied Captain Nemo. "Did your study in the Museum afford you such perfect quiet?"

"No, sir; and I must confess that it is a very poor one after yours. You must have six or seven thousand volumes here."

"Twelve thousand, M. Aronnax. These are the only ties which bind me to the earth. But I had done with the world on the day when my *Nautilus* plunged for the first time beneath the waters. That day I bought my last volumes, my last pamphlets, my last papers, and from that time I wish to think that men no longer think or write. These books, Professor, are at your service besides, and you can make use of them freely."

I thanked Captain Nemo, and went up to the shelves of the library. Works on science, morals, and literature abounded in every language; but I did not see one single work on political economy; that subject appeared to be strictly proscribed. Strange to say, all these books were irregularly arranged, in whatever language they were written; and this medley proved that the Captain of the *Nautilus* must have read indiscriminately the books which he took up by chance.

"Sir," said I to the Captain, "I thank you for having placed this library at my disposal. It contains treasures of science, and I shall profit by them."

"This room is not only a library," said Captain Nemo, "it is also a smoking-room."

"A smoking-room!" I cried. "Then one may smoke on board?"

"Certainly."

"Then, sir, I am forced to believe that you have kept up a communication with Havana."

"Not any," answered the Captain. "Accept this cigar, M. Aronnax; and, though it does not come from Havana, you will be pleased with it, if you are a connoisseur."

I took the cigar which was offered me; its shape recalled the London ones, but it seemed to be made of leaves of gold. I lighted it at a little brazier, which was supported upon an elegant bronze stem, and drew the first whiffs with the delight of a lover of smoking who has not smoked for two days.

"It is excellent, but it is not tobacco."

"No!" answered the Captain, "this tobacco comes neither from Havana nor from the East. It is a kind of sea-weed, rich in nicotine, with which the sea provides me, but somewhat sparingly."

At that moment Captain Nemo opened a door which stood opposite to that by which I had entered the library, and I passed into an immense drawing-room splendidly lighted.

It was a vast, four sided room, thirty feet long, eighteen wide, and fifteen high. A luminous ceiling, decorated with light arabesques, shed a soft clear light over all the marvels accumulated in this museum. For it was in fact a museum, in which an intelligent and prodigal hand had gathered all the treasures of nature and art, with the artistic confusion which distinguishes a painter's studio.

Thirty first-rate pictures, uniformly framed, separated by bright drapery, ornamented the walls, which were hung with tapestry of severe design. I saw works of great value, the greater part of which I had admired in the special collections of Europe, and in the exhibitions of paintings. The several schools of the old masters were represented by a Madonna of Raphael, a Virgin of Leonardo da Vinci, a nymph of Corregio, a woman of Titan, an Adoration of Veronese, an Assumption of Murillo, a portrait of Holbein, a monk of Velasquez, a martyr of Ribera, a fair of Rubens, two Flemish landscapes of Teniers, three little "genre" pictures of Gerard Dow, Metsu, and

Paul Potter, two specimens of Gericault and Prudhon, and some sea-pieces of Backhuysen and Vernet. Amongst the works of modern painters were pictures with the signatures of Delacroix, Ingres, Decamps, Troyon, Meissonier, Daubigny, etc.; and some admirable statues in marble and bronze, after the finest antique models, stood upon pedestals in the corners of this magnificent museum. Amazement, as the Captain of the *Nautilus* had predicted, had already begun to take possession of me.

"Professor," said this strange man, "you must excuse the unceremonious way in which I receive you, and the disorder of this room."

"Sir," I answered, "without seeking to know who you are, I recognize in you an artist."

"An amateur, nothing more, sir. Formerly I loved to collect these beautiful works created by the hand of man. I sought them greedily, and ferreted them out indefatigably, and I have been able to bring together some objects of great value. These are my last souvenirs of that world which is dead to me. In my eyes, your modern artists are already old; they have two or three thousand years of existence; I confound them in my own mind. Masters have no age."

"And these musicians?" said I, pointing out some works of Weber, Rossini, Mozart, Beethoven, Haydn, Meyerbeer, Herold, Wagner, Auber, Gounod, and a number of others, scattered over a large model piano-organ which occupied one of the panels of the drawing-room.

"These musicians," replied Captain Nemo, "are the contemporaries of Orpheus; for in the memory of the dead all chronological differences are effaced; and I am dead, Professor; as much dead as those of your friends who are sleeping six feet under the earth!"

Captain Nemo was silent, and seemed lost in a profound reverie. I contemplated him with deep interest, analyzing in silence the strange expression of his countenance. Leaning on his elbow against an angle of a costly mosaic table, he no longer saw me,—he had forgotten my presence.

I did not disturb this reverie, and continued my observation of the curiosities which enriched this drawing-room.

Under elegant glass cases, fixed by copper rivets, were classed and labeled the most precious productions of the sea which had ever been presented to the eye of a naturalist. My delight as a professor may be conceived.

The division containing the zoophytes presented the most curious specimens of the two groups of polypi and echinodermes. In the first group, the tubipores, were gorgones arranged like a fan, soft sponges of Syria, ises of the Moluccas, pennatules, an admirable virgularia of the Norwegian seas, variegated unbellulairae, alcyonariae, a whole series of madrepores, which my master Milne Edwards has so cleverly classified, amongst which I remarked some wonderful flabellinae oculinae of the Island of Bourbon, the "Neptune's car" of the Antilles, superb varieties of corals—in short, every species of those curious polypi of which entire islands are formed, which will one day become continents. Of the echinodermes, remarkable for their coating of spines, asteri, sea-stars, pantacrinae, comatules, asterophons, echini, holothuri, etc., represented individually a complete collection of this group.

A somewhat nervous conchyliologist would certainly have fainted before other more numerous cases, in which were classified the specimens of molluscs. It was a collection of inestimable value, which time fails me to describe minutely. Amongst these specimens I will quote from memory only the elegant royal hammer-fish of the Indian Ocean, whose regular white spots stood out brightly on a red and brown ground, an imperial spondyle, bright-coloured, bristling with spines, a rare specimen in the European museums— (I estimated its value at not less than L1000); a common hammer-fish of the seas of New Holland, which is only procured with difficulty; exotic buccardia of Senegal; fragile white bivalve shells, which a breath might shatter like a soap-bubble; several varieties of the aspirgillum of Java, a kind of calcareous tube, edged with leafy folds, and much debated by amateurs; a whole series of trochi, some a greenish-yellow, found in the American seas, others a reddish-brown, natives of Australian waters; others from the Gulf of Mexico, remarkable for their imbricated shell; stellari found in the Southern Seas; and last, the rarest of all, the magnificent spur of New Zealand; and every description of delicate and fragile shells to which science has given appropriate names.

Apart, in separate compartments, were spread out chaplets of pearls of the greatest beauty, which reflected the electric light in little sparks of fire; pink pearls, torn from the pinna-marina of the Red Sea; green pearls of the haliotyde iris; yellow, blue and black pearls, the curious productions of the divers molluscs of every ocean, and certain mussels of the water-courses of the North; lastly, several specimens of inestimable value which had been gathered from the rarest pintadines. Some of these pearls were larger than a pigeon's egg, and were worth as much, and more than that which the traveller Tavernier sold to the Shah of Persia for three millions, and surpassed the one in the possession of the Imaum of Muscat, which I had believed to be unrivalled in the world.

Therefore, to estimate the value of this collection was simply impossible. Captain Nemo must have expended millions in the acquirement of these various specimens, and I was thinking what source he could have drawn from, to have been able thus to gratify his fancy for collecting, when I was interrupted by these words:

You are examining my shells, Professor? Unquestionably they must be interesting to a naturalist; but for me they have a far greater charm, for I have collected them all with my own hand, and there is not a sea on the face of the globe which has escaped my researches."

"I can understand, Captain, the delight of wandering about in the midst of such riches. You are one of those who have collected their treasures themselves. No museum in Europe possesses such a collection of the produce of the ocean. But if I exhaust all my admiration upon it, I shall have none left for the vessel which carries it. I do not wish to pry into your secrets: but I must confess that this *Nautilus*, with the motive power which is confined in it, the contrivances which enable it to be worked, the powerful agent which propels it, all excite my curiosity to the highest pitch. I see suspended on the walls of this room instruments of whose use I am ignorant."

"You will find these same instruments in my own room, Professor, where I shall have much pleasure in explaining their use to you. But first come and inspect the cabin which is set apart for your own use. You must see how you will be accommodated on board the *Nautilus*."

I followed Captain Nemo who, by one of the doors opening from each panel of the drawing-room, regained the waist. He conducted me towards the bow, and there I found, not a cabin, but an elegant room, with a bed, dressing-table, and several other pieces of excellent furniture.

I could only thank my host.

"Your room adjoins mine," said he, opening a door, "and mine opens into the drawing-room that we have just quitted."

I entered the Captain's room: it had a severe, almost a monkish aspect. A small iron bedstead, a table, some articles for the toilet; the whole lighted by a skylight. No comforts, the strictest necessaries only.

Captain Nemo pointed to a seat.

"Be so good as to sit down," he said. I seated myself, and he began thus:

"Sir," said Captain Nemo, showing me the instruments hanging on the walls of his room, "here are the contrivances required for the navigation of the *Nautilus*. Here, as in the drawing-room, I have them always under my eyes, and they indicate my position and exact direction in the middle of the ocean. Some are known to you, such as the thermometer, which gives the internal temperature of the *Nautilus*; the barometer, which indicates the weight of the air and foretells the changes of the weather; the hygrometer, which marks the dryness of the atmosphere; the storm-glass, the contents of which, by decomposing, announce the approach of tempests; the compass, which guides my course; the sextant, which shows the latitude by the altitude of the sun; chronometers, by which I calculate the longitude; and glasses for day and night, which I use to examine the points of the horizon, when the *Nautilus* rises to the surface of the waves."

"These are the usual nautical instruments," I replied, "and I know the use of them. But these others, no doubt, answer to the particular requirements of the *Nautilus*. This dial with movable needle is a manometer, is it not?"

"It is actually a manometer. But by communication with the water, whose external pressure it indicates, it gives our depth at the same time."

"And these other instruments, the use of which I cannot guess?"

"Here, Professor, I ought to give you some explanations. Will you be kind enough to listen to me?"

He was silent for a few moments, then he said:

"There is a powerful agent, obedient, rapid, easy, which conforms to every use, and reigns supreme on board my vessel. Everything is done by means of it. It lights, warms it, and is the soul of my mechanical apparatus. This agent is electricity."

"Electricity?" I cried in surprise.

"Yes, sir."

"Nevertheless, Captain, you possess an extreme rapidity of movement, which does not agree well with the power of electricity. Until now, its dynamic force has remained under restraint, and has only been able to produce a small amount of power."

"Professor," said Captain Nemo, "my electricity is not everybody's. You know what sea-water is composed of. In a thousand grams are found 96 1/2 per cent. of water, and about 2 2/3 per cent. of chloride of sodium; then, in a smaller quantity, chlorides of magnesium and of potassium, bromide of magnesium, sulphate of magnesia, sulphate and carbonate of lime. You see, then, that chloride of sodium forms a large part of it. So it is this sodium that I extract from the sea-water, and of which I compose my ingredients. I owe all to the ocean; it produces electricity, and electricity gives heat, light, motion, and, in a word, life to the *Nautilus*."

"But not the air you breathe?"

"Oh! I could manufacture the air necessary for my consumption, but it is useless, because I go up to the surface of the water when I please. However, if electricity does not furnish me with air to breathe, it works at least the powerful pumps that are stored in spacious reservoirs, and which enable me to prolong at need, and as long as I will, my stay in the depths of the sea. It gives a uniform and unintermittent light, which the sun does not. Now look at this clock; it is electrical, and goes with a regularity that defies the best chronometers. I have divided it into twenty-four hours, like the Italian clocks, because for me there is neither night nor day, sun nor moon, but only that factitious light that I take with me to the bottom of the sea. Look! just now, it is ten o'clock in the morning."

"Exactly."

"Another application of electricity. This dial hanging in front of us indicates the speed of the *Nautilus*. An electric thread puts it in communication with the screw, and the needle indicates the real speed. Look! now we are spinning along with a uniform speed of fifteen miles an hour."

"It is marvelous! And I see, Captain, you were right to make use of this agent that takes the place of wind, water, and steam."

"We have not finished, M. Aronnax," said Captain Nemo, rising. "If you will allow me, we will examine the stern of the *Nautilus*."

Really, I knew already the anterior part of this submarine boat, of which this is the exact division, starting from the ship's head: the dining-room, five yards long, separated from the library by a water-tight partition; the library, five yards long; the large drawing-room, ten yards long, separated from the Captain's room by a second water-tight partition; the said room, five yards in length; mine, two and a half yards; and, lastly a reservoir of air, seven and a half yards, that extended to the bows. Total length thirty five yards, or one hundred and five feet. The partitions had doors that were shut hermetically by means of india-rubber instruments, and they ensured the safety of the *Nautilus* in case of a leak.

I followed Captain Nemo through the waist, and arrived at the centre of the boat. There was a sort of well that opened between two partitions. An iron ladder, fastened with an iron hook to the partition, led to the upper end. I asked the Captain what the ladder was used for.

"It leads to the small boat," he said.

"What! have you a boat?" I exclaimed, in surprise.

"Of course; an excellent vessel, light and insubmersible, that serves either as a fishing or as a pleasure boat."

"But then, when you wish to embark, you are obliged to come to the surface of the water?"

"Not at all. This boat is attached to the upper part of the hull of the *Nautilus*, and occupies a cavity made for it. It is decked, quite water-tight, and held together by solid bolts. This ladder leads to a man-hole made in the hull of the *Nautilus*, that corresponds with a similar hole made in the side of the boat. By this double opening I get into the small vessel. They shut the one belonging to the *Nautilus*; I shut the other by means of screw pressure. I undo the bolts, and the little boat goes up to the surface of the sea with prodigious rapidity. I then open the panel of the bridge, carefully shut till then; I mast it, hoist my sail, take my oars, and I'm off."

"But how do you get back on board?"

"I do not come back, M. Aronnax; the *Nautilus* comes to me."

"By your orders?"

"By my orders. An electric thread connects us. I telegraph to it, and that is enough."

Really," I said, astonished at these marvels, "nothing can be more simple."

After having passed by the cage of the staircase that led to the platform, I saw a cabin six feet long, in which Conseil and Ned Land, enchanted with their repast, were devouring it with avidity. Then a door opened into a kitchen nine feet long, situated between the large store-rooms. There electricity, better than gas itself, did all the cooking. The streams under the furnaces gave out to the sponges of platina a heat which was regularly kept up and distributed. They also heated a distilling apparatus, which, by evaporation, furnished excellent drinkable water. Near this kitchen was a bathroom comfortably furnished, with hot and cold water taps.

Next to the kitchen was the berth-room of the vessel, sixteen feet long. But the door was shut, and I could not see the management of it, which might have given me an idea of the number of men employed on board the *Nautilus*.

At the bottom was a fourth partition that separated this office from the engine-room. A door opened, and I found myself in the compartment where Captain Nemo—certainly an engineer of a very high order—had arranged his locomotive machinery. This engine-room, clearly lighted, did not measure less than sixty-five feet in length. It was divided into two parts; the first contained the materials for producing electricity, and the second the machinery that connected it with the screw. I examined it with great interest, in order to understand the machinery of the *Nautilus*.

"You see," said the Captain, "I use Bunsen's contrivances, not Ruhmkorff's. Those would not have been powerful enough. Bunsen's are fewer in number, but strong and large, which experience proves to be the best. The electricity produced passes forward, where it works, by electro-magnets of great size, on a system of levers and cog-wheels that transmit the movement to the axle of the screw. This one, the diameter of which is nineteen feet, and the thread twenty-three feet, performs about 120 revolutions in a second."

"And you get then?"

"A speed of fifty miles an hour."

"I have seen the *Nautilus* maneuver before the *Abraham Lincoln*, and I have my own ideas as to its speed. But this is not enough. We must see where we go. We must be able to direct it to the right, to the left, above, below. How do you get to the great depths, where you find an increasing resistance, which is rated by hundreds of atmospheres? How do you return to the surface of the ocean? And how do you maintain yourselves in the requisite medium? Am I asking too much?"

"Not at all, Professor," replied the Captain, with some hesitation; "since you may never leave this submarine boat. Come into the saloon, it is our usual study, and there you will learn all you want to know about the *Nautilus*."

A moment after we were seated on a divan in the saloon smoking. The Captain showed me a sketch that gave the plan, section, and elevation of the *Nautilus*. Then he began his description in these words:

"Here, M. Aronnax, are the several dimensions of the boat you are in. It is an elongated cylinder with conical ends. It is very like a cigar in shape, a shape already adopted in London in several constructions of the same sort. The length of this cylinder, from stem to stern, is exactly 232 feet, and its maximum breadth is twenty-six feet. It is not built quite like your long-voyage steamers, but its lines are sufficiently long, and its curves prolonged enough, to allow the water to slide off easily, and oppose no obstacle to its passage. These two dimensions enable you to obtain by a simple calculation the surface and cubic contents of the *Nautilus*. Its area measures 6,032 feet; and its contents about 1,500 cubic yards; that is to say, when completely immersed it displaces 50,000 feet of water, or weighs 1,500 tons.

"When I made the plans for this submarine vessel, I meant that nine-tenths should be submerged: consequently it ought only to displace nine-tenths of its bulk, that is to say, only to weigh that number of tons. I ought not, therefore, to have exceeded that weight, constructing it on the aforesaid dimensions.

"The *Nautilus* is composed of two hulls, one inside, the other outside, joined by T-shaped irons, which render it very strong. Indeed, owing to this cellular arrangement it resists like a block, as if it were solid. Its sides cannot yield; it coheres spontaneously, and not by the closeness of its rivets; and its perfect union of the materials enables it to defy the roughest seas.

"These two hulls are composed of steel plates, whose density is from .7 to .8 that of water. The first is not less than two inches and a half thick and weighs 394 tons. The second envelope, the keel, twenty inches high and ten thick, weighs only sixty-two tons. The engine, the ballast, the several accessories and apparatus appendages, the partitions and bulkheads, weigh 961.62 tons. Do you follow all this?"

"I do."

"Then, when the *Nautilus* is afloat under these circumstances, one-tenth is out of the water. Now, if I have made reservoirs of a size equal to this tenth, or capable of holding 150 tons, and if I fill them with water, the boat, weighing then 1,507 tons, will be completely immersed. That would happen, Professor. These reservoirs are in the lower part of the *Nautilus*. I turn on taps and they fill, and the vessel sinks that had just been level with the surface."

"Well, Captain, but now we come to the real difficulty. I can understand your rising to the surface; but, diving below the surface, does not your submarine contrivance encounter a pressure, and consequently undergo an upward thrust of one atmosphere for every thirty feet of water, just about fifteen pounds per square inch?"

"Just so, sir."

"Then, unless you quite fill the *Nautilus*, I do not see how you can draw it down to those depths."

"Professor, you must not confound statics with dynamics or you will be exposed to grave errors. There is very little labor spent in attaining the lower regions of the ocean, for all bodies have a tendency to sink. When I wanted to find out the necessary increase of weight required to sink the *Nautilus*, I had only to calculate the reduction of volume that sea-water acquires according to the depth."

"That is evident."

"Now, if water is not absolutely incompressible, it is at least capable of very slight compression. Indeed, after the most recent calculations this reduction is only .000436 of an atmosphere for each thirty feet of depth. If we want to sink 3,000 feet, I should keep account of the reduction of bulk under a pressure equal to that of a column of water of a thousand feet. The calculation is easily verified. Now, I have supplementary reservoirs capable of holding a hundred tons. Therefore I can sink to a considerable depth. When I wish to rise to the level of the sea, I only let off the water, and empty all the reservoirs if I want the *Nautilus* to emerge from the tenth part of her total capacity."

I had nothing to object to these reasonings.

"I admit your calculations, Captain," I replied; "I should be wrong to dispute them since daily experience confirms them; but I foresee a real difficulty in the way."

"What, sir?"

"When you are about 1,000 feet deep, the walls of the *Nautilus* bear a pressure of 100 atmospheres. If, then, just now you were to empty the supplementary reservoirs, to lighten the vessel, and to go up to the surface, the pumps must overcome the pressure of 100 atmospheres, which is 1,500 lbs. per square inch. From that a power——"

"That electricity alone can give," said the Captain, hastily. "I repeat, sir, that the dynamic power of my engines is almost infinite. The pumps of the *Nautilus* have an enormous power, as you must have observed when their jets of water burst like a torrent upon the *Abraham Lincoln*. Besides, I use subsidiary reservoirs only to attain a mean depth of 750 to 1,000 fathoms, and that with a view of managing my machines. Also, when I have a mind to visit the depths of the ocean five or six miles below the surface, I make use of slower but not less infallible means."

"What are they, Captain?"

"That involves my telling you how the *Nautilus* is worked."

"I am impatient to learn."

"To steer this boat to starboard or port, to turn, in a word, following a horizontal plan, I use an ordinary rudder fixed on the back of the stern-post, and with one wheel and some tackle to steer by. But I can also make the *Nautilus* rise and sink, and sink and rise, by a vertical movement by means of two inclined planes fastened to its sides, opposite the centre of flotation, planes that move in every direction, and that are worked by powerful levers from the interior. If the planes are kept parallel with the boat, it moves horizontally. If slanted, the *Nautilus*, according to this inclination, and under the influence of the screw, either sinks diagonally or rises diagonally as it suits me. And even if I wish to rise more quickly to the surface, I ship the screw, and the pressure of the water causes the *Nautilus* to rise vertically like a balloon filled with hydrogen."

"Bravo, Captain! But how can the steersman follow the route in the middle of the waters?"

"The steersman is placed in a glazed box, that is raised about the hull of the *Nautilus*, and furnished with lenses."

"Are these lenses capable of resisting such pressure?"

"Perfectly. Glass, which breaks at a blow, is, nevertheless, capable of offering considerable resistance. During some experiments of fishing by electric light in 1864 in the Northern Seas, we saw plates less than a third of an inch thick resist a pressure of sixteen atmospheres. Now, the glass that I use is not less than thirty times thicker."

"Granted. But, after all, in order to see, the light must exceed the darkness, and in the midst of the darkness in the water, how can you see?"

"Behind the steersman's cage is placed a powerful electric reflector, the rays from which light up the sea for half a mile in front."

"Ah! bravo, bravo, Captain! Now I can account for this phosphorescence in the supposed narwhal that puzzled us so. I now ask you if the boarding of the *Nautilus* and of the *Scotia*, that has made such a noise, has been the result of a chance rencontre?"

"Quite accidental, sir. I was sailing only one fathom below the surface of the water when the shock came. It had no bad result."

"None, sir. But now, about your rencontre with the *Abraham Lincoln*?"

"Professor, I am sorry for one of the best vessels in the American navy; but they attacked me, and I was bound to defend myself. I contented myself, however, with putting the frigate hors de combat; she will not have any difficulty in getting repaired at the next port."

"Ah, Commander! your *Nautilus* is certainly a marvelous boat."

"Yes, Professor; and I love it as if it were part of myself. If danger threatens one of your vessels on the ocean, the first impression is the feeling of an abyss above and below. On the *Nautilus* men's hearts never fail them. No defects to be afraid of, for the double shell is as firm as iron; no rigging to attend to; no sails for the wind to carry away; no boilers to burst; no fire to fear, for the vessel is made of iron, not of wood; no coal to run short, for electricity is the only mechanical agent; no collision to fear, for it alone swims in deep water; no tempest to brave, for when it dives below the water it reaches absolute tranquillity. There, sir! that is the perfection of vessels! And if it is true that the engineer has more confidence in the vessel than the builder, and the builder than the captain himself, you understand the trust I repose in my *Nautilus*; for I am at once captain, builder, and engineer."

"But how could you construct this wonderful *Nautilus* in secret?"

"Each separate portion, M. Aronnax, was brought from different parts of the globe."

"But these parts had to be put together and arranged?"

"Professor, I had set up my workshops upon a desert island in the ocean. There my workmen, that is to say, the brave men that I instructed and educated, and myself have put together our *Nautilus*. Then, when the work was finished, fire destroyed all trace of our proceedings on this island, that I could have jumped over if I had liked."

"Then the cost of this vessel is great?"

"M. Aronnax, an iron vessel costs L145 per ton. Now the *Nautilus* weighed 1,500. It came therefore to L67,500, and L80,000 more for fitting it up, and about L200,000, with the works of art and the collections it contains."

"One last question, Captain Nemo."

"Ask it, Professor."

"You are rich?"

"Immensely rich, sir; and I could, without missing it, pay the national debt of France."

I stared at the singular person who spoke thus. Was he playing upon my credulity? The future would decide that.

The portion of the terrestrial globe which is covered by water is estimated at upwards of eighty millions of acres. This fluid mass comprises two billions two hundred and fifty millions of cubic miles, forming a spherical body of a diameter of sixty leagues, the weight of which would be three quintillions of tons. To comprehend the meaning of these figures, it is necessary to observe that a quintillion is to a billion as a billion is to unity; in other words, there are as many billions in a quintillion as there are units in a billion. This mass of fluid is equal to about the quantity of water which would be discharged by all the rivers of the earth in forty thousand years.

During the geological epochs the ocean originally prevailed everywhere. Then by degrees, in the silurian period, the tops of the mountains began to appear, the islands emerged, then disappeared in partial deluges, reappeared, became settled, formed continents, till at length the earth became geographically arranged, as we see in the present day. The solid had wrested from the liquid thirty-seven million six hundred and fifty-seven square miles, equal to twelve billions nine hundred and sixty millions of acres.

The shape of continents allows us to divide the waters into five great portions: the Arctic or Frozen Ocean, the Antarctic, or Frozen Ocean, the Indian, the Atlantic, and the Pacific Oceans.

The Pacific Ocean extends from north to south between the two Polar Circles, and from east to west between Asia and America, over an extent of 145 degrees of longitude. It is the quietest of seas; its currents are broad and slow, it has medium tides, and abundant rain. Such was the ocean that my fate destined me first to travel over under these strange conditions.

"Sir," said Captain Nemo, "we will, if you please, take our bearings and fix the starting-point of this voyage. It is a quarter to twelve; I will go up again to the surface."

The Captain pressed an electric clock three times. The pumps began to drive the water from the tanks; the needle of the manometer marked by a different pressure the ascent of the *Nautilus*, then it stopped.

"We have arrived," said the Captain.

I went to the central staircase which opened on to the platform, clambered up the iron steps, and found myself on the upper part of the *Nautilus*.

The platform was only three feet out of water. The front and back of the *Nautilus* was of that spindle-shape which caused it justly to be compared to a cigar. I noticed that its iron plates, slightly overlaying each other, resembled the shell which clothes the bodies of our large terrestrial reptiles. It explained to me how natural it was, in spite of all glasses, that this boat should have been taken for a marine animal.

Toward the middle of the platform the longboat, half buried in the hull of the vessel, formed a slight excrescence. Fore and aft rose two cages of medium height with inclined sides, and partly closed by thick lenticular glasses; one destined for the steersman who directed the *Nautilus*, the other containing a brilliant lantern to give light on the road.

The sea was beautiful, the sky pure. Scarcely could the long vehicle feel the broad undulations of the ocean. A light breeze from the east rippled the surface of the waters. The horizon, free from fog, made observation easy. Nothing was in sight. Not a quicksand, not an island. A vast desert.

Captain Nemo, by the help of his sextant, took the altitude of the sun, which ought also to give the latitude. He waited for some moments till its disc touched the horizon. Whilst taking observations not a muscle moved, the instrument could not have been more motionless in a hand of marble.

"Twelve o'clock, sir," said he. "When you like——"

I cast a last look upon the sea, slightly yellowed by the Japanese coast, and descended to the saloon.

"And now, sir, I leave you to your studies," added the Captain; "our course is E.N.E., our depth is twenty-six fathoms. Here are maps on a large scale by which you may follow it. The saloon is at your disposal, and, with your permission, I will retire." Captain Nemo bowed, and I remained alone, lost in thoughts all bearing on the commander of the *Nautilus*.

For a whole hour was I deep in these reflections, seeking to pierce this mystery so interesting to me. Then my eyes fell upon the vast planisphere spread upon the table, and I placed my finger on the very spot where the given latitude and longitude crossed.

The sea has its large rivers like the continents. They are special currents known by their temperature and their color. The most remarkable of these is known by the name of the Gulf Stream. Science has decided on the globe the direction of five principal currents: one in the North Atlantic, a second in the South, a third in the North Pacific, a fourth in the South, and a fifth in the Southern Indian Ocean. It is even probable that a sixth current existed at one time or another in the Northern Indian Ocean, when the Caspian and Aral Seas formed but one vast sheet of water.

At this point indicated on the planisphere one of these currents was rolling, the Kuro-Scivo of the Japanese, the Black River, which, leaving the Gulf of Bengal, where it is warmed by the perpendicular rays of a tropical sun, crosses the Straits of Malacca along the coast of Asia, turns into the North Pacific to the Aleutian Islands, carrying with it trunks of camphor-trees and other indigenous productions, and edging the waves of the ocean with the pure indigo of its warm water. It was this current that the *Nautilus* was to follow. I followed it with my eye; saw it lose itself in the vastness of the Pacific, and felt myself drawn with it, when Ned Land and Conseil appeared at the door of the saloon.

My two brave companions remained petrified at the sight of the wonders spread before them.

"Where are we, where are we?" exclaimed the Canadian. "In the museum at Quebec?"

"My friends," I answered, making a sign for them to enter, "you are not in Canada, but on board the *Nautilus*, fifty yards below the level of the sea."

"But, M. Aronnax," said Ned Land, "can you tell me how many men there are on board? Ten, twenty, fifty, a hundred?"

"I cannot answer you, Mr. Land; it is better to abandon for a time all idea of seizing the *Nautilus* or escaping from it. This ship is a masterpiece of modern industry, and I should be sorry not to have seen it. Many people would accept the situation forced upon us, if only to move amongst such wonders. So be quiet and let us try and see what passes around us."

"See!" exclaimed the harpooner, "but we can see nothing in this iron prison! We are walking—we are sailing—blindly."

Ned Land had scarcely pronounced these words when all was suddenly darkness. The luminous ceiling was gone, and so rapidly that my eyes received a painful impression.

We remained mute, not stirring, and not knowing what surprise awaited us, whether agreeable or disagreeable. A sliding noise was heard: one would have said that panels were working at the sides of the *Nautilus*.

"It is the end of the end!" said Ned Land.

Suddenly light broke at each side of the saloon, through two oblong openings. The liquid mass appeared vividly lit up by the electric gleam. Two crystal plates separated us from the sea. At first I trembled at the thought that this frail partition might break, but strong bands of copper bound them, giving an almost infinite power of resistance.

The sea was distinctly visible for a mile all round the *Nautilus*. What a spectacle! What pen can describe it? Who could paint the effects of the light through those transparent sheets of water, and the softness of the successive gradations from the lower to the superior strata of the ocean?

We know the transparency of the sea and that its clearness is far beyond that of rock-water. The mineral and organic substances which it holds in suspension heightens its transparency. In certain parts of the ocean at the Antilles, under seventy-five fathoms of water, can be seen with surprising clearness a bed of sand. The penetrating power of the solar rays does not seem to cease for a depth of one hundred and fifty fathoms. But in this middle fluid travelled over by the *Nautilus*, the electric brightness was produced even in the bosom of the waves. It was no longer luminous water, but liquid light.

On each side a window opened into this unexplored abyss. The obscurity of the saloon showed to advantage the brightness outside, and we looked out as if this pure crystal had been the glass of an immense aquarium.

"You wished to see, friend Ned; well, you see now."

"Curious! curious!" muttered the Canadian, who, forgetting his ill-temper, seemed to submit to some irresistible attraction; "and one would come further than this to admire such a sight!"

"Ah!" thought I to myself, "I understand the life of this man; he has made a world apart for himself, in which he treasures all his greatest wonders."

For two whole hours an aquatic army escorted the *Nautilus*. During their games, their bounds, while rivaling each other in beauty, brightness, and velocity, I distinguished the green labre; the banded mullet, marked by a double line of black; the round-tailed goby, of a white color, with violet spots on the back; the Japanese scombrus, a beautiful mackerel of these seas, with a blue body and silvery head; the brilliant azurors, whose name alone defies description; some banded spares, with variegated fins of blue and yellow; the woodcocks of the seas, some specimens of which attain a yard in length; Japanese salamanders, spider lampreys, serpents six feet long, with eyes small and lively, and a huge mouth bristling with teeth; with many other species.

Our imagination was kept at its height, interjections followed quickly on each other. Ned named the fish, and Conseil classed them. I was in ecstasies with the vivacity of their movements and the beauty of their forms. Never had it been given to me to surprise these animals, alive and at liberty, in their natural element. I will not mention all the varieties which passed before my dazzled eyes, all the collection of the seas of China and Japan. These fish, more numerous than the birds of the air, came, attracted, no doubt, by the brilliant focus of the electric light.

Suddenly there was daylight in the saloon, the iron panels closed again, and the enchanting vision disappeared. But for a long time I dreamt on, till my eyes fell on the instruments hanging on the partition. The compass still showed the course to be E.N.E., the manometer indicated a pressure of five atmospheres, equivalent to a depth of twenty five fathoms, and the electric log gave a speed of fifteen miles an hour. I expected Captain Nemo, but he did not appear. The clock marked the hour of five.

Ned Land and Conseil returned to their cabin, and I retired to my chamber. My dinner was ready. It was composed of turtle soup made of the most delicate hawks bills, of a surmullet served with puff paste (the liver of which, prepared by itself, was most delicious), and fillets of the emperor-holocanthus, the savour of which seemed to me superior even to salmon.

I passed the evening reading, writing, and thinking. Then sleep overpowered me, and I stretched myself on my couch of zostera, and slept profoundly, whilst the *Nautilus* was gliding rapidly through the current of the Black River.

FLATLAND

Edwin A. Abbott (1884)

PART I: THIS WORLD

Section 1: The Nature of Flatland

I call our world Flatland, not because we call it so, but to make its nature clearer to you, my happy readers, who are privileged to live in Space.

Imagine a vast sheet of paper on which straight Lines, Triangles, Squares, Pentagons, Hexagons, and other figures, instead of remaining fixed in their places, move freely about, on or in the surface, but without the power of rising above or sinking below it, very much like shadows—only hard with luminous edges—and you will then have a pretty correct notion of my country and countrymen. Alas, a few years ago, I should have said "my universe:" but now my mind has been opened to higher views of things.

In such a country, you will perceive at once that it is impossible that there should be anything of what you call a "solid" kind; but I dare say you will suppose that we could at least distinguish by sight the Triangles, Squares, and other figures, moving about as I have described them. On the contrary, we could see nothing of the kind, not at least so as to distinguish one figure from another. Nothing was visible, nor could be visible, to us, except Straight Lines; and the necessity of this I will speedily demonstrate.

Place a penny on the middle of one of your tables in Space; and leaning over it, look down upon it. It will appear a circle.

But now, drawing back to the edge of the table, gradually lower your eye (thus bringing yourself more and more into the condition of the inhabitants of Flatland), and you will find the penny becoming more and more oval to your view, and at last when you have placed your eye exactly on the edge of the table (so that you are, as it were, actually a Flatlander) the penny will then have ceased to appear oval at all, and will have become, so far as you can see, a straight line.

The same thing would happen if you were to treat in the same way a Triangle, or a Square, or any other figure cut out from pasteboard. As soon as you look at it with your eye on the edge of the table, you will find that it ceases to appear to you as a figure, and that it becomes in appearance a straight line. Take for example an equilateral Triangle—who represents with us a Tradesman of the respectable class. Figure 1 represents the Tradesman as you would see him while you were bending over him from above; figures 2 and 3 represent the Tradesman, as you would see him if your eye were close to the level, or all but on the level of the table; and if your eye were quite on the level of the table (and that is how we see him in Flatland) you would see nothing but a straight line.

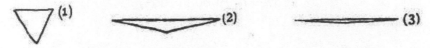

When I was in Spaceland I heard that your sailors have very similar experiences while they traverse your seas and discern some distant island or coast lying on the horizon. The far-off land may have bays, forelands, angles in and out to any number and extent; yet at a distance you see none of these (unless indeed your sun shines bright upon them revealing the projections and retirements by means of light and shade), nothing but a grey unbroken line upon the water.

Well, that is just what we see when one of our triangular or other acquaintances comes towards us in Flatland. As there is neither sun with us, nor any light of such a kind as to make shadows, we have none of the helps to the sight that you have in Spaceland. If our friend comes closer to us we see his line becomes larger; if he leaves us it becomes smaller; but still he looks like a straight line; be he a Triangle, Square, Pentagon, Hexagon, Circle, what you will—a straight Line he looks and nothing else.

You may perhaps ask how under these disadvantagous circumstances we are able to distinguish our friends from one another: but the answer to this very natural question will be more fitly and easily given when I come to describe the inhabitants of Flatland. For the present let me defer this subject, and say a word or two about the climate and houses in our country.

Section 2: The Climate and Houses in Flatland

As with you, so also with us, there are four points of the compass—North, South, East, and West.

There being no sun nor other heavenly bodies, it is impossible for us to determine the North in the usual way; but we have a method of our own. By a Law of Nature with us, there is a constant attraction to the South; and, although in temperate climates this is very slight—so that even a Woman in reasonable health can journey several furlongs northward without much difficulty—yet the hampering effort of the southward attraction is quite sufficient to serve as a compass in most parts of our earth. Moreover, the rain (which falls at stated intervals) coming always from the North, is an additional assistance; and in the towns we have the guidance of the houses, which of course have their side-walls running for the most part North and South, so that the roofs may keep off the rain from the North. In the country, where there are no houses, the trunks of the trees serve as some sort of guide. Altogether, we have not so much difficulty as might be expected in determining our bearings.

Yet in our more temperate regions, in which the southward attraction is hardly felt, walking sometimes in a perfectly desolate plain where there have been no houses nor trees to guide me, I have been occasionally compelled to remain stationary for hours together, waiting till the rain came before continuing my journey. On the weak and aged, and especially on delicate Females, the force of attraction tells much more heavily than on the robust of the Male Sex, so that it is a point of breeding, if you meet a Lady on the street, always to give her the North side of the way—by no means an easy thing to do always at short notice when you are in rude health and in a climate where it is difficult to tell your North from your South.

Windows there are none in our houses: for the light comes to us alike in our homes and out of them, by day and by night, equally at all times and in all places, whence we know not. It was in old days, with our learned men, an interesting and oft-investigate question, "What is the origin of light?" and the solution of it has been repeatedly attempted, with no other result than to crowd our lunatic asylums with the would-be solvers. Hence, after fruitless attempts to suppress such investigations indirectly by making them liable to a heavy tax, the Legislature, in comparatively recent times, absolutely prohibited them. I—alas, I alone in Flatland—know now only too well the true solution of this mysterious problem; but my knowledge cannot be made intelligible to a single one of my countrymen; and I am mocked at—I, the sole possessor of the truths of Space and of the theory of the introduction of Light from the world of three Dimensions—as if I were the maddest of the mad! But a truce to these painful digressions: let me return to our homes.

The most common form for the construction of a house is five-sided or pentagonal, as in the annexed figure. The two Northern sides RO, OF, constitute the roof, and for the most part have no doors; on the East is a small door for the Women; on the West a much larger one for the Men; the South side or floor is usually doorless.

Square and triangular houses are not allowed, and for this reason. The angles of a Square (and still more those of an equilateral Triangle), being much more pointed than those of a Pentagon, and the lines of inanimate objects (such as houses) being dimmer than the lines of Men and Women, it follows that there is no little danger lest the points of a square of triangular house residence might do serious injury to an inconsiderate or perhaps absentminded traveler suddenly running against them: and therefore, as early as the eleventh century of our era, triangular houses were universally forbidden by Law, the only exceptions being fortifications, powder-magazines, barracks, and other state buildings, which is not desirable that the general public should approach without circumspection.

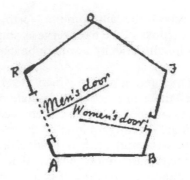

At this period, square houses were still everywhere permitted, though discouraged by a special tax. But, about three centuries afterwards, the Law decided that in all towns containing a population above ten thousand, the angle of a Pentagon was the smallest house-angle that could be allowed consistently with the public safety. The good sense of the community has seconded the efforts of the Legislature; and now, even in the country, the pentagonal construction has superseded every other. It is only now and then in some very remote and backward agricultural district that an antiquarian may still discover a square house.

Section 3: Concerning the Inhabitants of Flatland

The greatest length or breadth of a full grown inhabitant of Flatland may be estimated at about eleven of your inches. Twelve inches may be regarded as a maximum.

Our Women are Straight Lines.

Our Soldiers and Lowest Class of Workmen are Triangles with two equal sides, each about eleven inches long, and a base or third side so short (often not exceeding half an inch) that they form at their vertices a very sharp and formidable angle. Indeed when their bases are of the most degraded type (not more than the eighth part of an inch in size), they can hardly be distinguished from Straight lines or Women; so extremely pointed are their vertices. With us, as with you, these Triangles are distinguished from others by being called Isosceles; and by this name I shall refer to them in the following pages.

Our Middle Class consists of Equilateral or Equal-Sided Triangles.

Our Professional Men and Gentlemen are Squares (to which class I myself belong) and Five-Sided Figures or Pentagons.

Next above these come the Nobility, of whom there are several degrees, beginning at Six-Sided Figures, or Hexagons, and from thence rising in the number of their sides till they receive the honourable title of Polygonal, or many-Sided. Finally when the number of the sides becomes so numerous, and the sides themselves so small, that the figure cannot be distinguished from a circle, he is included in the Circular or Priestly order; and this is the highest class of all.

It is a Law of Nature with us that a male child shall have one more side than his father, so that each generation shall rise (as a rule) one step in the scale of development and nobility. Thus the son of a Square is a Pentagon; the son of a Pentagon, a Hexagon; and so on.

But this rule applies not always to the Tradesman, and still less often to the Soldiers, and to the Workmen; who indeed can hardly be said to deserve the name of human Figures, since they have not all their sides equal. With them therefore the Law of Nature does not hold; and the son of an Isosceles (i.e. a Triangle with two sides equal) remains Isosceles still. Nevertheless, all hope is not such out, even from the Isosceles, that his posterity may ultimately rise above his degraded condition. For, after a long series of military successes, or diligent and skillful labours, it is generally found that the more intelligent among the Artisan and Soldier classes manifest a slight increase of their third side or base, and a shrinkage of the two other sides. Intermarriages (arranged by the Priests) between the sons and daughters of these more intellectual members of the lower classes generally result in an offspring approximating still more to the type of the Equal-Sided Triangle.

Rarely—in proportion to the vast numbers of Isosceles births—is a gen-uine and certifiable Equal-Sided Triangle produced from Isosceles parents (footnote 1). Such a birth requires, as its antecedents, not only a series of carefully arranged intermarriages, but also a long-continued exercise of fru-gality and self-control on the part of the would-be ancestors of the coming Equilateral, and a patient, systematic, and continuous development of the Isosceles intellect through many generations.

The birth of a True Equilateral Triangle from Isosceles parents is the sub-ject of rejoicing in our country for many furlongs round. After a strict exami-nation conducted by the Sanitary and Social Board, the infant, if certified as Regular, is with solemn ceremonial admitted into the class of Equilaterals. He is then immediately taken from his proud yet sorrowing parents and adopted by some childless Equilateral, who is bound by oath never to permit the child henceforth to enter his former home or so much as to look upon his relations again, for fear lest the freshly developed organism may, by force of uncon-scious imitation, fall back again into his hereditary level.

The occasional emergence of an Equilateral from the ranks of his serf-born ancestors is welcomed, not only by the poor serfs themselves, as a gleam of light and hope shed upon the monotonous squalor of their existence, but also by the Aristocracy at large; for all the higher classes are well aware that these rare phenomena, while they do little or nothing to vulgarize their own privileges, serve as almost useful barrier against revolution from below.

Had the acute-angled rabble been all, without exception, absolutely desti-tute of hope and of ambition, they might have found leaders in some of their many seditious outbreaks, so able as to render their superior numbers and strength too much even for the wisdom of the Circles. But a wise ordinance of Nature has decreed that in proportion as the working-classes increase in intelligence, knowledge, and all virtue, in that same proportion their acute angle (which makes them physically terrible) shall increase also and approximate to their comparatively harmless angle of the Equilateral Triangle. Thus, in the most brutal and formidable off the soldier class—creatures almost on a level with women in their lack of intelligence—it is found that, as they wax in the mental ability necessary to employ their tremendous penetrating power to advantage, so do they wane in the power of penetration itself.

How admirable is the Law of Compensation! And how perfect a proof of the natural fitness and, I may almost say, the divine origin of the aristocratic constitution of the States of Flatland! By a judicious use of this Law of Nature, the Polygons and Circles are almost always able to stifle sedition in its very cradle, taking advantage of the irrepressible and boundless hopefulness of the human mind. Art also comes to the aid of Law and Order. It is generally found possible—by a little artificial compression or expansion on the part of the State physicians—to make some of the more intelligent leaders of a rebellion perfectly Regular, and to admit them at once into the privileged classes; a much larger number, who are still below the standard, allured by the prospect of being ultimately ennobled, are induced to enter the State Hospitals, where they are kept in honourable confinement for life; one or two alone of the most obstinate, foolish, and hopelessly irregular are led to execution.

Then the wretched rabble of the Isosceles, planless and leaderless, are either transfixed without resistance by the small body of their brethren whom the Chief Circle keeps in pay for emergencies of this kind; or else more often, by means of jealousies and suspicious skillfully fomented among them by the Circular party, they are stirred to mutual warfare, and perish by one another's angles. No less than one hundred and twenty rebellions are recorded in our annals, besides minor outbreaks numbered at two hundred and thirty-five; and they have all ended thus.

Footnote 1. "What need of a certificate?" a Spaceland critic may ask: "Is not the procreation of a Square Son a certificate from Nature herself, proving the Equal-sidedness of the Father?" I reply that no Lady of any position will mary an uncertified Triangle. Square offspring has sometimes resulted from a slightly Irregular Triangle; but in almost every such case the Irregularity of the first generation is visited on the third; which either fails to attain the Pentagonal rank, or relapses to the Triangular.

Section 4: Concerning the Women

If our highly pointed Triangles of the Soldier class are formidable, it may be readily inferred that far more formidable are our Women. For, if a Soldier is a wedge, a Woman is a needle; being, so to speak, ALL point, at least at the two extremities. Add to this the power of making herself practically invisible at will, and you will perceive that a Female, in Flatland, is a creature by no means to be trifled with.

But here, perhaps, some of my younger Readers may ask HOW a woman in Flatland can make herself invisible. This ought, I think, to be apparent without any explanation. However, a few words will make it clear to the most unreflecting.

Place a needle on the table. Then, with your eye on the level of the table, look at it side-ways, and you see the whole length of it; but look at it end-ways, and you see nothing but a point, it has become practically invisible. Just so is it with one of our Women. When her side is turned towards us, we see her as a straight line; when the end containing her eye or mouth—for with us these two organs are identical—is the part that meets our eye, then we see nothing but a highly lustrous point; but when the back is presented to our view, then—being only sub-lustrous, and, indeed, almost as dim as an inanimate object—her hinder extremity serves her as a kind of Invisible Cap.

The dangers to which we are exposed from our Women must now be manifest to the meanest capacity of Spaceland. If even the angle of a respectable Triangle in the middle class is not without its dangers; if to run against a Working Man involves a gash; if collision with an Officer of the military class necessitates a serious wound; if a mere touch from the vertex of a Private Soldier brings with it danger of death;—what can it be to run against a woman, except absolute and immediate destruction? And when a Woman is invisible, or visible only as a dim sub-lustrous point, how difficult must it be, even for the most cautious, always to avoid collision!

Many are the enactments made at different times in the different States of Flatland, in order to minimize this peril; and in the Southern and less temperate climates, where the force of gravitation is greater, and human beings more liable to casual and involuntary motions, the Laws concerning Women are naturally much more stringent. But a general view of the Code may be obtained from the following summary:—

1. Every house shall have one entrance on the Eastern side, for the use of Females only; by which all females shall enter "in a becoming and respectful manner" and not by the Men's or Western door.*
2. No Female shall walk in any public place without continually keeping up her Peace-cry, under penalty of death.

*When I was in Spaceland I understood that some of your priestly circles have in the same way a separate entrance for villagers, farmers, and teachers of board schools ('Spectator,' Sept. 1884, p. 1255) that they may approach in a becoming and respectful manner.

3. Any Female, duly certified to be suffering from St. Vitus's Dance, fits, chronic cold accompanied by violent sneezing, or any disease necessitating involuntary motions, shall be instantly destroyed.

In some of the States there is an additional Law forbidding Females, under penalty of death, from walking or standing in any public place without moving their backs constantly from right to left so as to indicate their presence to those behind them; other oblige a Woman, when travelling, to be followed by one of her sons, or servants, or by her husband; others confine Women altogether in their houses except during the religious festivals. But it has been found by the wisest of our Circles or Statesmen that the multiplication of restrictions on Females tends not only to the debilitation and diminution of the race, but also to the increase of domestic murders to such an extent that a State loses more than it gains by a too prohibitive Code.

For whenever the temper of the Women is thus exasperated by confinement at home or hampering regulations abroad, they are apt to vent their spleen upon their husbands and children; and in the less temperate climates the whole male population of a village has been sometimes destroyed in one or two hours of a simultaneous female outbreak. Hence the Three Laws, mentioned above, suffice for the better regulated States, and may be accepted as a rough exemplification of our Female Code.

After all, our principal safeguard is found, not in Legislature, but in the interests of the Women themselves. For, although they can inflict instantaneous death by a retrograde movement, yet unless they can at once disengage their stinging extremity from the struggling body of their victim, their own frail bodies are liable to be shattered.

The power of Fashion is also on our side. I pointed out that in some less civilized States no female is suffered to stand in any public place without swaying her back from right to left. This practice has been universal among ladies of any pretensions to breeding in all well-governed States, as far back as the memory of Figures can reach. It is considered a disgrace to any state that legislation should have to enforce what ought to be, and is in every respectable female, a natural instinct. The rhythmical and, if I may so say, well-modulated undulation of the back in our ladies of Circular rank is envied and imitated by the wife of a common Equilateral, who can achieve nothing beyond a mere monotonous swing, like the ticking of a pendulum; and the regular tick of the Equilateral is no less admired and copied by the wife of the progressive and aspiring Isosceles, in the females of whose family no "back-motion" of any kind has become as yet a necessity of life. Hence, in every family of position and consideration, "back motion" is as prevalent as time itself; and the husbands and sons in these households enjoy immunity at least from invisible attacks.

Not that it must be for a moment supposed that our Women are destitute of affection. But unfortunately the passion of the moment predominates, in the

Frail Sex, over every other consideration. This is, of course, a necessity arising from their unfortunate conformation. For as they have no pretensions to an angle, being inferior in this respect to the very lowest of the Isosceles, they are consequently wholly devoid of brainpower, and have neither reflection, judgment nor forethought, and hardly any memory. Hence, in their fits of fury, they remember no claims and recognize no distinctions. I have actually known a case where a Woman has exterminated her whole household, and half an hour afterwards, when her rage was over and the fragments swept away, has asked what has become of her husband and children.

Obviously then a Woman is not to be irritated as long as she is in a position where she can turn round. When you have them in their apartments—which are constructed with a view to denying them that power—you can say and do what you like; for they are then wholly impotent for mischief, and will not remember a few minutes hence the incident for which they may be at this moment threatening you with death, nor the promises which you may have found it necessary to make in order to pacify their fury.

On the whole we got on pretty smoothly in our domestic relations, except in the lower strata of the Military Classes. There the want of tact and discretion on the part of the husbands produces at times indescribable disasters. Relying too much on the offensive weapons of their acute angles instead of the defensive organs of good sense and seasonable simulations, these reckless creatures too often neglect the prescribed construction of the women's apartments, or irritate their wives by ill-advised expressions out of doors, which they refuse immediately to retract. Moreover a blunt and stolid regard for literal truth indisposes them to make those lavish promises by which the more judicious Circle can in a moment pacify his consort. The result is massacre; not, however, without its advantages, as it eliminates the more brutal and troublesome of the Isosceles; and by many of our Circles the destructiveness of the Thinner Sex is regarded as one among many providential arrangements for suppressing redundant population, and nipping Revolution in the bud.

Yet even in our best regulated and most approximately Circular families I cannot say that the ideal of family life is so high as with you in Spaceland. There is peace, in so far as the absence of slaughter may be called by that name, but there is necessarily little harmony of tastes or pursuits; and the cautious wisdom of the Circles has ensured safety at the cost of domestic comfort. In every Circular or Polygonal household it has been a habit from time immemorial—and now has become a kind of instinct among the women of our higher classes—that the mothers and daughters should constantly keep their eyes and mouths towards their husband and his male friends; and for a lady in a family of distinction to turn her back upon her husband would be regarded as a kind of portent, involving loss of STATUS. But, as I shall soon show, this custom, though it has the advantage of safety, is not without disadvantages.

In the house of the Working Man or respectable Tradesman—where the wife is allowed to turn her back upon her husband, while pursuing her household avocations—there are at least intervals of quiet, when the wife is neither seen nor heard, except for the humming sound of the continuous Peace-cry; but in the homes of the upper classes there is too often no peace. There the voluble mouth and bright penetrating eye are ever directed toward the Master of the household; and light itself is not more persistent than the stream of Feminine discourse. The tact and skill which suffice to avert a Woman's sting are unequal to the task of stopping a Woman's mouth; and as the wife has absolutely nothing to say, and absolutely no constraint of wit, sense, or conscience to prevent her from saying it, not a few cynics have been found to aver that they prefer the danger of the death-dealing but inaudible sting to the safe sonorousness of a Woman's other end.

To my readers in Spaceland the condition of our Women may seen truly deplorable, and so indeed it is. A Male of the lowest type of the Isosceles may look forward to some improvement of his angle, and to the ultimate elevation of the whole of his degraded caste; but no Woman can entertain such hopes for her sex. "Once a Woman, always a Woman" is a Decree of Nature; and the very Laws of Evolution seem suspended in her disfavour. Yet at least we can admire the wise Prearrangement which has ordained that, as they have no hopes, so they shall have no memory to recall, and no forethought to anticipate, the miseries and humiliations which are at once a necessity of their existence and the basis of the constitution of Flatland.

Section 5: Our Methods of Recognizing One Another

You, who are blessed with shade as well as light, you, who are gifted with two eyes, endowed with a knowledge of perspective, and charmed with the enjoyment of various colours, you, who can actually SEE an angle, and contemplate the complete circumference of a Circle in the happy region of the Three Dimensions—how shall I make it clear to you the extreme difficulty which we in Flatland experience in recognizing one another's configuration?

Recall what I told you above. All beings in Flatland, animate and inanimate, no matter what their form, present TO OUR VIEW the same, or nearly the same, appearance, viz. that of a straight Line. How then can one be distinguished from another, where all appear the same?

The answer is threefold. The first means of recognition is the sense of hearing; which with us is far more highly developed than with you, and which enables us not only to distinguish by the voice of our personal friends, but even to discriminate between different classes, at least so far as concerns the three lowest orders, the Equilateral, the Square, and the Pentagon—for the Isosceles I take no account. But as we ascend the social scale, the process of discriminating and being discriminated by hearing increases in difficulty, partly because voices are assimilated, partly because the faculty of voice-discrimination is a plebeian virtue not much developed among the Aristocracy. And wherever there is any danger of imposture we cannot trust to this method. Amongst our lowest orders, the vocal organs are developed to a degree more than correspondent with those of hearing, so that an Isosceles can easily feign the voice of a Polygon, and, with some training, that of a Circle himself. A second method is therefore more commonly resorted to.

FEELING is, among our Women and lower classes—about our upper classes I shall speak presently—the principal test of recognition, at all events between strangers, and when the question is, not as to the individual, but as to the class. What therefore "introduction" is among the higher classes in Spaceland, that the process of "feeling" is with us. "Permit me to ask you to feel and be felt by my friend Mr. So-and-so"—is still, among the more old-fashioned of our country gentlemen in districts remote from towns, the customary formula for a Flatland introduction. But in the towns, and among men of business, the words "be felt by" are omitted and the sentence is abbreviated to, "Let me ask you to feel Mr. So-and-so"; although it is assumed, of course, that the "feeling" is to be reciprocal. Among our still more modern and dashing young gentlemen—who are extremely averse to superfluous effort and supremely indifferent to the purity of their native language—the formula is still further curtailed by the use of "to feel" in a technical sense, meaning, "to recommend-for-the-purposes-of-feeling-and-being-felt"; and at this moment the "slang" of polite or fast society in the upper classes sanctions such a barbarism as "Mr. Smith, permit me to feel Mr. Jones."

Let not my Reader however suppose that "feeling" is with us the tedious process that it would be with you, or that we find it necessary to feel right round all the sides of every individual before we determine the class to which he belongs. Long practice and training, begun in the schools and continued in the experience of daily life, enable us to discriminate at once by the sense of touch, between the angles of an equal-sided Triangle, Square, and Pentagon; and I need not say that the brainless vertex of an acute-angled Isosceles is obvious to the dullest touch. It is therefore not necessary, as a rule, to do more than feel a single angle of an individual; and this, once ascertained, tells us the class of the person whom we are addressing, unless indeed he belongs to the higher sections of the nobility. There the difficulty is much greater. Even a Master of Arts in our University of Wentbridge has been known to confuse a ten-sided with a twelve-sided Polygon; and there is hardly a Doctor of Science in or out of that famous University who could pretend to decide promptly and unhesitatingly between a twenty-sided and a twenty-four sided member of the Aristocracy.

Those of my readers who recall the extracts I gave above from the Legislative code concerning Women, will readily perceive that the process of introduction by contact requires some care and discretion. Otherwise the angles might inflict on the unwary Feeling irreparable injury. It is essential for the safety of the Feeler that the Felt should stand perfectly still. A start, a fidgety shifting of the position, yes, even a violent sneeze, has been known before now to prove fatal to the incautious, and to nip in the bud many a promising friendship. Especially is this true among the lower classes of the Triangles. With them, the eye is situated so far from their vertex that they can scarcely take cognizance of what goes on at that extremity of their frame. They are, moreover, of a rough coarse nature, not sensitive to the delicate touch of the highly organized Polygon. What wonder then if an involuntary toss of the head has ere now deprived the State of a valuable life!

I have heard that my excellent Grandfather—one of the least irregular of his unhappy Isosceles class, who indeed obtained, shortly before his decease, four out of seven votes from the Sanitary and Social Board for passing him into the class of the Equal-sided—often deplored, with a tear in his venerable eye, a miscarriage of this kind, which had occurred to his great-great-great-Grandfather, a respectable Working Man with an angle or brain of 59 degrees 30 minutes. According to his account, my unfortunately Ancestor, being afflicted with rheumatism, and in the act of being felt by a Polygon, by one sudden start accidentally transfixed the Great Man through the diagonal and thereby, partly in consequence of his long imprisonment and degradation, and partly because of the moral shock which pervaded the whole of my Ancestor's relations, threw back our family a degree and a half in their ascent towards better things. The result was that in the next generation the family brain was registered at only 58 degrees, and not till the lapse of five generations was the lost ground recovered, the full 60 degrees attained, and the Ascent from the Isosceles finally achieved. And all this series of calamities from one little accident in the process of Feeling.

As this point I think I hear some of my better educated readers exclaim, "How could you in Flatland know anything about angles and degrees, or minutes? We SEE an angle, because we, in the region of Space, can see two straight lines inclined to one another; but you, who can see nothing but on straight line at a time, or at all events only a number of bits of straight lines all in one straight line,—how can you ever discern an angle, and much less register angles of different sizes?"

I answer that though we cannot SEE angles, we can INFER them, and this with great precision. Our sense of touch, stimulated by necessity, and developed by long training, enables us to distinguish angles far more accurately than your sense of sight, when unaided by a rule or measure of angles. Nor must I omit to explain that we have great natural helps. It is with us a Law of Nature that the brain of the Isosceles class shall begin at half a degree, or thirty minutes, and shall increase (if it increases at all) by half a degree in every generation until the goal of 60 degrees is reached, when the condition of serfdom is quitted, and the freeman enters the class of Regulars.

Consequently, Nature herself supplies us with an ascending scale or Alphabet of angles for half a degree up to 60 degrees, Specimen of which are placed in every Elementary School throughout the land. Owing to occasional retrogressions, to still more frequent moral and intellectual stagnation, and to the extraordinary fecundity of the Criminal and Vagabond classes, there is always a vast superfluity of individuals of the half degree and single degree class, and a fair abundance of Specimens up to 10 degrees. These are absolutely destitute of civil rights; and a great number of them, not having even intelligence enough for the purposes of warfare, are devoted by the States to the service of education. Fettered immovably so as to remove all possibility of danger, they are placed in the classrooms of our Infant Schools, and there they are utilized by the Board of Education for the purpose of imparting to the offspring of the Middle Classes the tact and intelligence which these wretched creatures themselves are utterly devoid.

In some States the Specimens are occasionally fed and suffered to exist for several years; but in the more temperate and better regulated regions, it is found in the long run more advantageous for the educational interests of the young, to dispense with food, and to renew the Specimens every month—which is about the average duration of the foodless existence of the Criminal class. In the cheaper schools, what is gained by the longer existence of the Specimen is lost, partly in the expenditure for food, and partly in the diminished accuracy of the angles, which are impaired after a few weeks of constant "feeling." Nor must we forget to add, in enumerating the advantages of the more expensive system, that it tends, though slightly yet perceptibly, to the diminution of the redundant Isosceles population—an object which every statesman in Flatland constantly keeps in view. On the whole therefore—although I am not ignorant that, in many popularly elected School Boards, there is a reaction in favour of "the cheap system" as it is called—I am myself disposed to think that this is one of the many cases in which expense is the truest economy.

But I must not allow questions of School Board politics to divert me from my subject. Enough has been said, I trust, to show that Recognition by Feeling is not so tedious or indecisive a process as might have been supposed; and it is obviously more trustworthy than Recognition by hearing. Still there remains, as has been pointed out above, the objection that this method is not without danger. For this reason many in the Middle and Lower classes, and all without exception in the Polygonal and Circular orders, prefer a third method, the description of which shall be reserved for the next section.

Section 6: Recognition by Sight

I am about to appear very inconsistent. In the previous sections I have said that all figures in Flatland present the appearance of a straight line; and it was added or implied, that it is consequently impossible to distinguish by the visual organ between individuals of different classes: yet now I am about to explain to my Spaceland critics how we are able to recognize one another by the sense of sight.

If however the Reader will take the trouble to refer to the passage in which Recognition by Feeling is stated to be universal, he will find this qualification—"among the lower classes." It is only among the higher classes and in our more temperate climates that Sight Recognition is practiced.

That this power exists in any regions and for any classes is the result of Fog; which prevails during the greater part of the year in all parts save the torrid zones. That which is with you in Spaceland an unmixed evil, blotting out the landscape, depressing the spirits, and enfeebling the health, is by us recognized as a blessing scarcely inferior to air itself, and as the Nurse of arts and Parent of sciences. But let me explain my meaning, without further eulogies on this beneficent Element.

If Fog were non-existent, all lines would appear equally and indistinguishably clear; and this is actually the case in those unhappy countries in which the atmosphere is perfectly dry and transparent. But wherever there is a rich supply of Fog, objects that are at a distance, say of three feet, are appreciably dimmer than those at the distance of two feet eleven inches; and the result is that by careful and constant experimental observation of comparative dimness and clearness, we are enabled to infer with great exactness the configuration of the object observed.

An instance will do more than a volume of generalities to make my meaning clear.

Suppose I see two individuals approaching whose rank I wish to ascertain. They are, we will suppose, a Merchant and a Physician, or in other words, an Equilateral Triangle and a Pentagon; how am I to distinguish them?

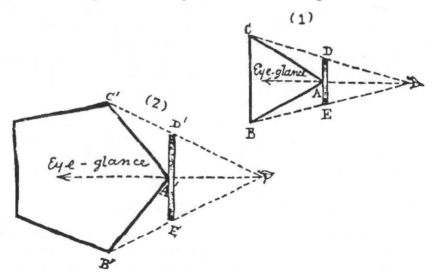

It will be obvious, to every child in Spaceland who has touched the threshold of Geometrical Studies, that, if I can bring my eye so that its glance may bisect an angle (A) of the approaching stranger, my view will lie as it were evenly between the two sides that are next to me (viz. CA and AB), so that I shall contemplate the two impartially, and both will appear of the same size.

Now in the case of (1) the Merchant, what shall I see? I shall see a straight line DAE, in which the middle point (A) will be very bright because it is nearest to me; but on either side the line will shade away RAPIDLY TO DIMNESS, because the sides AC and AB RECEDE RAPIDLY INTO THE FOG and what appear to me as the Merchant's extremities, viz. D and E, will be VERY DIM INDEED.

On the other hand in the case of (2) the Physician, though I shall here also see a line (D'A'E') with a bright centre (A'), yet it will shade away LESS RAPIDLY to dimness, because the sides (A'C', A'B') RECEDE LESS RAPIDLY INTO THE FOG: and what appear to me the Physician's extremities, viz. D' and E', will not be NOT SO DIM as the extremities of the Merchant.

The Reader will probably understand from these two instances how—after a very long training supplemented by constant experience—it is possible for the well-educated classes among us to discriminate with fair accuracy between the middle and lowest orders, by the sense of sight. If my Spaceland Patrons have grasped this general conception, so far as to conceive the possibility of it and not to reject my account as altogether incredible—I shall have attained all I can reasonably expect. Were I to attempt further details I should only perplex. Yet for the sake of the young and inexperienced, who may perchance infer—from the two simple instances I have given above, of the manner in which I should recognize my Father and my Sons—that Recognition by sight is an easy affair, it may be needful to point out that in actual life most of the problems of Sight Recognition are far more subtle and complex.

If for example, when my Father, the Triangle, approaches me, he happens to present his side to me instead of his angle, then, until I have asked him to rotate, or until I have edged my eye around him, I am for the moment doubtful whether he may not be a Straight Line, or, in other words, a Woman. Again, when I am in the company of one of my two hexagonal Grandsons, contemplating one of his sides (AB) full front, it will be evident from the accompanying diagram that I shall see one whole line (AB) in comparative brightness (shading off hardly at all at the ends) and two smaller lines (CA and BD) dim throughout and shading away into greater dimness towards the extremities C and D.

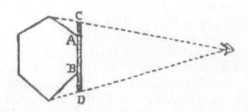

But I must not give way to the temptation of enlarging on these topics. The meanest mathematician in Spaceland will readily believe me when I assert that the problems of life, which present themselves to the well-educated—when they are themselves in motion, rotating, advancing or retreating, and at the same time attempting to discriminate by the sense of sight between a number of Polygons of high rank moving in different directions, as for example in a ball-room or conversazione—must be of a nature to task the angularity of the most intellectual, and amply justify the rich endowments of the Learned Professors of Geometry, both Static and Kinetic, in the illustrious University of Wentbridge, where the Science and Art of Sight Recognition are regularly taught to large classes of the ELITE of the States.

It is only a few of the scions of our noblest and wealthiest houses, who are able to give the time and money necessary for the thorough prosecution of this noble and valuable Art. Even to me, a Mathematician of no mean standing, and the Grandfather of two most hopeful and perfectly regular Hexagons, to find myself in the midst of a crowd of rotating Polygons of the higher classes, is occasionally very perplexing. And of course to a common Tradesman, or Serf, such a sight is almost as unintelligible as it would be to you, my Reader, were you suddenly transported to my country.

In such a crowd you could see on all sides of you nothing but a Line, apparently straight, but of which the parts would vary irregularly and per-petually in brightness or dimness. Even if you had completed your third year in the Pentagonal and Hexagonal classes in the University, and were perfect in the theory of the subject, you would still find there was need of many years of experience, before you could move in a fashionable crowd without jostling against your betters, whom it is against etiquette to ask to "feel," and who, by their superior culture and breeding, know all about your movements, while you know very little or nothing about theirs. In a word, to comport oneself with perfect propriety in Polygonal society, one ought to be a Polygon one-self. Such at least is the painful teaching of my experience.

It is astonishing how much the Art—or I may almost call it instinct—of Sight Recognition is developed by the habitual practice of it and by the avoid-ance of the custom of "Feeling." Just as, with you, the deaf and dumb, if once allowed to gesticulate and to use the hand-alphabet, will never acquire the more difficult but far more valuable art of lip-speech and lip-reading, so it is with us as regards "Seeing" and "Feeling." None who in early life resort to "Feeling" will ever learn "Seeing" in perfection.

For this reason, among our Higher Classes, "Feeling" is discouraged or absolutely forbidden. From the cradle their children, instead of going to the Public Elementary schools (where the art of Feeling is taught), are sent to higher Seminaries of an exclusive character; and at our illustrious University, to "feel" is regarded as a most serious fault, involving Rustication for the first offence, and Expulsion for the second.

But among the lower classes the art of Sight Recognition is regarded as an unattainable luxury. A common Tradesman cannot afford to let his son spend a third of his life in abstract studies. The children of the poor are therefore allowed to "feel" from their earliest years, and they gain thereby a precocity and an early vivacity which contrast at first most favourably with the inert, undeveloped, and listless behaviour of the half-instructed youths of the Polygonal class; but when the latter have at last completed their University course, and are prepared to put their theory into practice, the change that comes over them may almost be described as a new birth, and in every art, science, and social pursuit they rapidly overtake and distance their Triangular competitors.

Only a few of the Polygonal Class fail to pass the Final Test or Leaving Examination at the University. The condition of the unsuccessful minority is truly pitiable. Rejected from the higher class, they are also despised by the lower. They have neither the matured and systematically trained powers of the Polygonal Bachelors and Masters of Arts, nor yet the native precocity and mercurial versatility of the youthful Tradesman. The professions, the public services, are closed against them, and though in most States they are not actually debarred from marriage, yet they have the greatest difficulty in forming suitable alliances, as experience shows that the offspring of such unfortunate and ill-endowed parents is generally itself unfortunate, if not positively Irregular.

It is from these specimens of the refuse of our Nobility that the great Tumults and Seditions of past ages have generally derived their leaders; and so great is the mischief thence arising that an increasing minority of our more progressive Statesmen are of opinion that true mercy would dictate their entire suppression, by enacting that all who fail to pass the Final Examination of the University should be either imprisoned for life, or extinguished by a painless death.

But I find myself digressing into the subject of Irregularities, a matter of such vital interest that it demands a separate section.

Section 7: Concerning Irregular Figures

Throughout the previous pages I have been assuming—what perhaps should have been laid down at the beginning as a distinct and fundamental proposition—that every human being in Flatland is a Regular Figure, that is to say of regular construction. By this I mean that a Woman must not only be a line, but a straight line; that an Artisan or Soldier must have two of his sides equal; that Tradesmen must have three sides equal; Lawyers (of which class I am a humble member), four sides equal, and, generally, that in every Polygon, all the sides must be equal.

The sizes of the sides would of course depend upon the age of the individual. A Female at birth would be about an inch long, while a tall adult Woman might extend to a foot. As to the Males of every class, it may be roughly said that the length of an adult's size, when added together, is two feet or a little more. But the size of our sides is not under consideration. I am speaking of the EQUALITY of sides, and it does not need much reflection to see that the whole of the social life in Flatland rests upon the fundamental fact that Nature wills all Figures to have their sides equal.

If our sides were unequal our angles might be unequal. Instead of its being sufficient to feel, or estimate by sight, a single angle in order to determine the form of an individual, it would be necessary to ascertain each angle by the experiment of Feeling. But life would be too short for such a tedious groping. The whole science and art of Sight Recognition would at once perish; Feeling, so far as it is an art, would not long survive; intercourse would become perilous or impossible; there would be an end to all confidence, all forethought; no one would be safe in making the most simple social arrangements; in a word, civilization might relapse into barbarism.

Am I going too fast to carry my Readers with me to these obvious conclusions? Surely a moment's reflection, and a single instance from common life, must convince every one that our social system is based upon Regularity, or Equality of Angles. You meet, for example, two or three Tradesmen in the street, whom your recognize at once to be Tradesman by a glance at their angles and rapidly bedimmed sides, and you ask them to step into your house to lunch. This you do at present with perfect confidence, because everyone knows to an inch or two the area occupied by an adult Triangle: but imagine that your Tradesman drags behind his regular and respectable vertex, a parallelogram of twelve or thirteen inches in diagonal:—what are you to do with such a monster sticking fast in your house door?

But I am insulting the intelligence of my Readers by accumulating details which must be patent to everyone who enjoys the advantages of a Residence in Spaceland. Obviously the measurements of a single angle would no longer be sufficient under such portentous circumstances; one's whole life would be taken up in feeling or surveying the perimeter of one's acquaintances. Already the difficulties of avoiding a collision in a crowd are enough to tax the sagacity of even a well-educated Square; but if no one could calculate the Regularity of a single figure in the company, all would be chaos and confusion, and the slightest panic would cause serious injuries, or—if there happened to be any Women or Soldiers present—perhaps considerable loss of life.

Expediency therefore concurs with Nature in stamping the seal of its approval upon Regularity of conformation: nor has the Law been backward in seconding their efforts. "Irregularity of Figure" means with us the same as, or more than, a combination of moral obliquity and criminality with you, and is treated accordingly. There are not wanting, it is true, some promulgators of paradoxes who maintain that there is no necessary connection between geometrical and moral Irregularity. "The Irregular," they say, "is from his birth scouted by his own parents, derided by his brothers and sisters, neglected by the domestics, scorned and suspected by society, and excluded from all posts of responsibility, trust, and useful activity. His every movement is jealously watched by the police till he comes of age and presents himself for inspection; then he is either destroyed, if he is found to exceed the fixed margin of deviation, at an uninteresting occupation for a miserable stipend; obliged to live and board at the office, and to take even his vacation under close supervision; what wonder that human nature, even in the best and purest, is embittered and perverted by such surroundings!"

All this very plausible reasoning does not convince me, as it has not convinced the wisest of our Statesmen, that our ancestors erred in laying it down as an axiom of policy that the toleration of Irregularity is incompatible with the safety of the State. Doubtless, the life of an Irregular is hard; but the interests of the Greater Number require that it shall be hard. If a man with a triangular front and a polygonal back were allowed to exist and to propagate a still more Irregular posterity, what would become of the arts of life? Are the houses and doors and churches in Flatland to be altered in order to accommodate such monsters? Are our ticket-collectors to be required to measure every man's perimeter before they allow him to enter a theatre, or to take his place in a lecture room? Is an Irregular to be exempted from the militia? And if not, how is he to be prevented from carrying desolation into the ranks of his comrades? Again, what irresistible temptations to fraudulent impostures must needs beset such a creature! How easy for him to enter a shop with his polygonal front foremost, and to order goods to any extent from a confiding tradesman! Let the advocates of a falsely called Philanthropy plead as they may for the abrogation of the Irregular Penal Laws, I for my part have never known an Irregular who was not also what Nature evidently intended him to be—a hypocrite, a misanthropist, and, up to the limits of his power, a perpetrator of all manner of mischief.

Not that I should be disposed to recommend (at present) the extreme measures adopted by some States, where an infant whose angle deviates by half a degree from the correct angularity is summarily destroyed at birth. Some of our highest and ablest men, men of real genius, have during their earliest days laboured under deviations as great as, or even greater than forty-five minutes: and the loss of their precious lives would have been an irreparable injury to the State. The art of healing also has achieved some of its most glorious triumphs in the compressions, extensions, trepannings, colligations, and other surgical or diaetetic operations by which Irregularity has been partly or wholly cured. Advocating therefore a VIA MEDIA, I would lay down no fixed or absolute line of demarcation; but at the period when the frame is just beginning to set, and when the Medical Board has reported that recovery is improbably, I would suggest that the Irregular offspring be painlessly and mercifully consumed.

Section 8: The Ancient Practice of Painting

If my Readers have followed me with any attention up to this point, they will not be surprised to hear that life is somewhat dull in Flatland. I do not, of course, mean that there are not battles, conspiracies, tumults, factions, and all those other phenomena which are supposed to make History interesting; nor would I deny that the strange mixture of the problems of life and the problems of Mathematics, continually inducing conjecture and giving an opportunity of immediate verification, imparts to our existence a zest which you in Spaceland can hardly comprehend. I speak now from the aesthetic and artistic point of view when I say that life with us is dull; aesthetically and artistically, very dull indeed.

How can it be otherwise, when all one's prospect, all one's landscapes, historical pieces, portraits, flowers, still life, are nothing but a single line, with no varieties except degrees of brightness and obscurity?

It was not always thus. Colour, if Tradition speaks the truth, once for the space of half a dozen centuries or more, threw a transient splendour over the lives of our ancestors in the remotest ages. Some private individual—a Pentagon whose name is variously reported—having casually discovered the constituents of the simpler colours and a rudimentary method of painting, is said to have begun by decorating first his house, then his slaves, then his Father, his Sons, and Grandsons, lastly himself. The convenience as well as the beauty of the results commended themselves to all. Wherever Chromatistes,—for by that name the most trustworthy authorities concur in calling him,—turned his variegated frame, there he at once excited attention, and attracted respect. No one now needed to "feel" him; no one mistook his front for his back; all his movements were readily ascertained by his neighbours without the slightest strain on their powers of calculation; no one jostled him, or failed to make way for him; his voice was saved the labour of that exhausting utterance by which we colourless Squares and Pentagons are often forced to proclaim our individuality when we move amid a crowd of ignorant Isosceles.

The fashion spread like wildfire. Before a week was over, every Square and Triangle in the district had copied the example of Chromatistes, and only a few of the more conservative Pentagons still held out. A month or two found even the Dodecagons infected with the innovation. A year had not elapsed before the habit had spread to all but the very highest of the Nobility. Needless to say, the custom soon made its way from the district of Chromatistes to surrounding regions; and within two generations no one in all Flatland was colourless except the Women and the Priests.

Here Nature herself appeared to erect a barrier, and to plead against extending the innovations to these two classes. Many-sidedness was almost essential as a pretext for the Innovators. "Distinction of sides is intended by Nature to imply distinction of colours"—such was the sophism which in those days flew from mouth to mouth, converting whole towns at a time to a new culture. But manifestly to our Priests and Women this adage did not apply. The latter had only one side, and therefore—plurally and pedantically speaking—NO SIDES. The former—if at least they would assert their claim to be readily and truly Circles, and not mere high-class Polygons, with an infinitely large number of infinitesimally small sides—were in the habit of boasting (what Women confessed and deplored) that they also had no sides, being blessed with a perimeter of only one line, or, in other words, a Circumference. Hence it came to pass that these two Classes could see no force in the so-called axiom about "Distinction of Sides implying Distinction of Colour"; and when all others had succumbed to the fascinations of corporal decoration, the Priests and the Women alone still remained pure from the pollution of paint.

Immoral, licentious, anarchical, unscientific—call them by what names you will—yet, from an aesthetic point of view, those ancient days of the Colour Revolt were the glorious childhood of Art in Flatland—a childhood, alas, that never ripened into manhood, nor even reached the blossom of youth. To live then in itself a delight, because living implied seeing. Even at a small party, the company was a pleasure to behold; the richly varied hues of the assembly in a church or theatre are said to have more than once proved too distracting from our greatest teachers and actors; but most ravishing of all is said to have been the unspeakable magnificence of a military review.

The sight of a line of battle of twenty thousand Isosceles suddenly facing about, and exchanging the sombre black of their bases for the orange of the two sides including their acute angle; the militia of the Equilateral Triangles tricoloured in red, white, and blue; the mauve, ultra-marine, gamboge, and burnt umber of the Square artillerymen rapidly rotating near their vermillion guns; the dashing and flashing of the five-coloured and six-coloured Pentagons and Hexagons careering across the field in their offices of surgeons, geometricians and aides-de-camp—all these may well have been sufficient to render credible the famous story how an illustrious Circle, overcome by the artistic beauty of the forces under his command, threw aside his marshal's baton and his royal crown, exclaiming that he henceforth exchanged them for the artist's pencil. How great and glorious the sensuous development of these days must have been is in part indicated by the very language and vocabulary of the period. The commonest utterances of the commonest citizens in the time of the Colour Revolt seem to have been suffused with a richer tinge of word or thought; and to that era we are even now indebted for our finest poetry and for whatever rhythm still remains in the more scientific utterance of those modern days.

Section 9: The Universal Color Bill

But meanwhile the intellectual Arts were fast decaying.

The Art of Sight Recognition, being no longer needed, was no longer practised; and the studies of Geometry, Statics, Kinetics, and other kindred subjects, came soon to be considered superfluous, and fell into disrespect and neglect even at our University. The inferior Art of Feeling speedily experienced the same fate at our Elementary Schools. Then the Isosceles classes, asserting that the Specimens were no longer used nor needed, and refusing to pay the customary tribute from the Criminal classes to the service of Education, waxed daily more numerous and more insolent on the strength of their immunity from the old burden which had formerly exercised the twofold wholesome effect of at once taming their brutal nature and thinning their excessive numbers.

Year by year the Soldiers and Artisans began more vehemently to assert— and with increasing truth—that there was no great difference between them and the very highest class of Polygons, now that they were raised to an equality with the latter, and enabled to grapple with all the difficulties and solve all the problems of life, whether Statical or Kinetical, by the simple process of Colour Recognition. Not content with the natural neglect into which Sight Recognition was falling, they began boldly to demand the legal prohibition of all "monopolizing and aristocratic Arts" and the consequent abolition of all endowments for the studies of Sight Recognition, Mathematics, and Feeling. Soon, they began to insist that inasmuch as Colour, which was a second Nature, had destroyed the need of aristocratic distinctions, the Law should follow in the same path, and that henceforth all individuals and all classes should be recognized as absolutely equal and entitled to equal rights.

Finding the higher Orders wavering and undecided, the leaders of the Revolution advanced still further in their requirements, and at last demanded that all classes alike, the Priests and the Women not excepted, should do homage to Colour by submitting to be painted. When it was objected that Priests and Women had no sides, they retorted that Nature and Expediency concurred in dictating that the front half of every human being (that is to say, the half containing his eye and mouth) should be distinguishable from his hinder half. They therefore brought before a general and extraordinary Assembly of all the States of Flatland a Bill proposing that in every Woman the half containing the eye and mouth should be coloured red, and the other half green. The Priests were to be painted in the same way, red being applied to that semicircle in which the eye and mouth formed the middle point; while the other or hinder semicircle was to be coloured green.

There was no little cunning in this proposal, which indeed emanated not from any Isosceles—for no being so degraded would have angularity enough to appreciate, much less to devise, such a model of state-craft—but from an Irregular Circle who, instead of being destroyed in his childhood, was reserved by a foolish indulgence to bring desolation on his country and destruction on myriads of followers.

On the one hand the proposition was calculated to bring the Women in all classes over to the side of the Chromatic Innovation. For by assigning to the Women the same two colours as were assigned to the Priests, the Revolutionists thereby ensured that, in certain positions, every Woman would appear as a Priest, and be treated with corresponding respect and deference—a prospect that could not fail to attract the Female Sex in a mass.

But by some of my Readers the possibility of the identical appearance of Priests and Women, under a new Legislation, may not be recognized; if so, a word or two will make it obvious.

Imagine a woman duly decorated, according to the new Code; with the front half (i.e., the half containing the eye and mouth) red, and with the hinder half green. Look at her from one side. Obviously you will see a straight line, HALF RED, HALF GREEN.

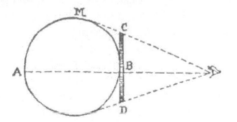

Now imagine a Priest, whose mouth is at M, and whose front semicircle (AMB) is consequently coloured red, while his hinder semicircle is green; so that the diameter AB divides the green from the red. If you contemplate the Great Man so as to have your eye in the same straight line as his dividing diameter (AB), what you will see will be a straight line (CBD), of which ONE HALF (CB) WILL BE RED, AND THE OTHER (BD) GREEN. The whole line (CD) will be rather shorter perhaps than that of a full-sized Woman, and will shade off more rapidly towards its extremities; but the identity of the colours would give you an immediate impression of identity in Class, making you neglectful of other details. Bear in mind the decay of Sight Recognition which threatened society at the time of the Colour revolt; add too the certainty that Woman would speedily learn to shade off their extremities so as to imitate the Circles; it must then be surely obvious to you, my dear Reader, that the Colour Bill placed us under a great danger of confounding a Priest with a young Woman.

How attractive this prospect must have been to the Frail Sex may readily be imagined. They anticipated with delight the confusion that would ensue. At home they might hear political and ecclesiastical secrets intended not for them but for their husbands and brothers, and might even issue some commands in the name of a priestly Circle; out of doors the striking combination of red and green without addition of any other colours, would be sure to lead the common people into endless mistakes, and the Woman would gain whatever the Circles lost, in the deference of the passers by. As for the scandal that would befall the Circular Class if the frivolous and unseemly conduct of the Women were imputed to them, and as to the consequent subversion of the Constitution, the Female Sex could not be expected to give a thought to these considerations. Even in the households of the Circles, the Women were all in favour of the Universal Colour Bill.

The second object aimed at by the Bill was the gradual demoralization of the Circles themselves. In the general intellectual decay they still preserved their pristine clearness and strength of understanding. From their earliest childhood, familiarized in their Circular households with the total absence of Colour, the Nobles alone preserved the Sacred Art of Sight Recognition, with all the advantages that result from that admirable training of the intellect. Hence, up to the date of the introduction of the Universal Colour Bill, the Circles had not only held their own, but even increased their lead of the other classes by abstinence from the popular fashion.

Now therefore the artful Irregular whom I described above as the real author of this diabolical Bill, determined at one blow to lower the status of the Hierarchy by forcing them to submit to the pollution of Colour, and at the same time to destroy their domestic opportunities of training in the Art of Sight Recognition, so as to enfeeble their intellects by depriving them of their pure and colourless homes. Once subjected to the chromatic taint, every parental and every childish Circle would demoralize each other. Only in discerning between the Father and the Mother would the Circular infant find problems for the exercise of his understanding—problems too often likely to be corrupted by maternal impostures with the result of shaking the child's faith in all logical conclusions. Thus by degrees the intellectual lustre of the Priestly Order would wane, and the road would then lie open for a total destruction of all Aristocratic Legislature and for the subversion of our Privileged Classes.

Section 10: The Suppression of the Chromatic Sedition

The agitation for the Universal Colour Bill continued for three years; and up to the last moment of that period it seemed as though Anarchy were destined to triumph.

A whole army of Polygons, who turned out to fight as private soldiers, was utterly annihilated by a superior force of Isosceles Triangles—the Squares and Pentagons meanwhile remaining neutral.

Worse than all, some of the ablest Circles fell a prey to conjugal fury. Infuriated by political animosity, the wives in many a noble household wearied their lords with prayers to give up their opposition to the Colour Bill; and some, finding their entreaties fruitless, fell on and slaughtered their innocent children and husband, perishing themselves in the act of carnage. It is recorded that during that triennial agitation no less than twenty-three Circles perished in domestic discord.

Great indeed was the peril. It seemed as though the Priests had no choice between submission and extermination; when suddenly the course of events was completely changed by one of those picturesque incidents which Statesmen ought never to neglect, often to anticipate, and sometimes perhaps to originate, because of the absurdly disproportionate power with which they appeal to the sympathies of the populace.

It happened that an Isosceles of a low type, with a brain little if at all above four degrees—accidentally dabbling in the colours of some Tradesman whose shop he had plundered—painted himself, or caused himself to be painted (for the story varies) with the twelve colours of a Dodecagon. Going into the Market Place he accosted in a feigned voice a maiden, the orphan daughter of a noble Polygon, whose affection in former days he had sought in vain; and by a series of deceptions—aided, on the one side, by a string of lucky accidents too long to relate, and, on the other, by an almost inconceivable fatuity and neglect of ordinary precautions on the part of the relations of the bride—he succeeded in consummating the marriage. The unhappy girl committed suicide on discovering the fraud to which she had been subjected.

When the news of this catastrophe spread from State to State the minds of the Women were violently agitated. Sympathy with the miserable victim and anticipations of similar deceptions for themselves, their sisters, and their daughters, made them now regard the Colour Bill in an entirely new aspect. Not a few openly avowed themselves converted to antagonism; the rest needed only a slight stimulus to make a similar avowal. Seizing this favourable opportunity, the Circles hastily convened an extraordinary Assembly of the States; and besides the usual guard of Convicts, they secured the attendance of a large number of reactionary Women.

Amidst an unprecedented concourse, the Chief Circle of those days—by name Pantocyclus—arose to find himself hissed and hooted by a hundred and twenty thousand Isosceles. But he secured silence by declaring that henceforth the Circles would enter on a policy of Concession; yielding to the wishes of the majority, they would accept the Colour Bill. The uproar being at once converted to applause, he invited Chromatistes, the leader of the Sedition, into the centre of the hall, to receive in the name of his followers the submission of the Hierarchy. Then followed a speech, a masterpiece of rhetoric, which occupied nearly a day in the delivery, and to which no summary can do justice.

With a grave appearance of impartiality he declared that as they were now finally committing themselves to Reform or Innovation, it was desirable that they should take one last view of the perimeter of the whole subject, its defects as well as its advantages. Gradually introduction the mention of the dangers to the Tradesmen, the Professional Classes and the Gentlemen, he silenced the rising murmurs of the Isosceles by reminding them that, in spite of all these defects, he was willing to accept the Bill if it was approved by the majority. But it was manifest that all, except the Isosceles, were moved by his words and were either neutral or averse to the Bill.

Turning now to the Workmen he asserted that their interests must not be neglected, and that, if they intended to accept the Colour Bill, they ought at least to do so with full view of the consequences. Many of them, he said, were on the point of being admitted to the class of the Regular Triangles; others anticipated for their children a distinction they could not hope for themselves. That honourable ambition would not have to be sacrificed. With the universal adoption of Colour, all distinctions would cease; Regularity would be confused with Irregularity; development would give place to retrogression; the Workman would in a few generations be degraded to the level of the Military, or even the Convict Class; political power would be in the hands of the greatest number, that is to say the Criminal Classes, who were already more numerous than the Workmen, and would soon out-number all the other Classes put together when the usual Compensative Laws of Nature were violated.

A subdued murmur of assent ran through the ranks of the Artisans, and Chromatistes, in alarm, attempted to step forward and address them. But he found himself encompassed with guards and forced to remain silent while the Chief Circle in a few impassioned words made a final appeal to the Women, exclaiming that, if the Colour Bill passed, no marriage would henceforth be safe, no woman's honour secure; fraud, deception, hypocrisy would pervade every household; domestic bliss would share the fate of the Constitution and pass to speedy perdition. "Sooner than this," he cried, "come death."

At these words, which were the preconcerted signal for action, the Isosceles Convicts fell on and transfixed the wretched Chromatistes; the Regular Classes, opening their ranks, made way for a band of Women who, under direction of the Circles, moved back foremost, invisibly and unerringly upon the unconscious soldiers; the Artisans, imitating the example of their betters, also opened their ranks. Meantime bands of Convicts occupied every entrance with an impenetrable phalanx.

The battle, or rather carnage, was of short duration. Under the skillful generalship of the Circles almost every Woman's charge was fatal and very many extracted their sting uninjured, ready for a second slaughter. But no second blow was needed; the rabble of the Isosceles did the rest of the business for themselves. Surprised, leader-less, attacked in front by invisible foes, and finding egress cut off by the Convicts behind them, they at once—after their manner—lost all presence of mind, and raised the cry of "treachery." This sealed their fate. Every Isosceles now saw and felt a foe in every other. In half an hour not one of that vast multitude was living; and the fragments of seven score thousand of the Criminal Class slain by one another's angles attested the triumph of Order.

The Circles delayed not to push their victory to the uttermost. The Working Men they spared but decimated. The Militia of the Equilaterals was at once called out, and every Triangle suspected of Irregularity on reasonable grounds, was destroyed by Court Martial, without the formality of exact measurement by the Social Board. The homes of the Military and Artisan classes were inspected in a course of visitation extending through upwards of a year; and during that period every town, village, and hamlet was systematically purged of that excess of the lower orders which had been brought about by the neglect to pay the tribute of Criminals to the Schools and University, and by the violation of other natural Laws of the Constitution of Flatland. Thus the balance of classes was again restored.

Needless to say that henceforth the use of Colour was abolished, and its possession prohibited. Even the utterance of any word denoting Colour, except by the Circles or by qualified scientific teachers, was punished by a severe penalty. Only at our University in some of the very highest and most esoteric classes—which I myself have never been privileged to attend—it is understood that the sparing use of Colour is still sanctioned for the purpose of illustrating some of the deeper problems of mathematics. But of this I can only speak from hearsay.

Elsewhere in Flatland, Colour is now non-existent. The art of making it is known to only one living person, the Chief Circle for the time being; and by him it is handed down on his death-bed to none but his Successor. One manufactory alone produces it; and, lest the secret should be betrayed, the Workmen are annually consumed, and fresh ones introduced. So great is the terror with which even now our Aristocracy looks back to the far-distant days of the agitation for the Universal Color Bill.

Section 11: Concerning Our Priests

It is high time that I should pass from these brief and discursive notes about things in Flatland to the central event of this book, my initiation into the mysteries of Space. THAT is my subject; all that has gone before is merely preface.

For this reason I must omit many matters of which the explanation would not, I flatter myself, be without interest for my Readers: as for example, our method of propelling and stopping ourselves, although destitute of feet; the means by which we give fixity to structures of wood, stone, or brick, although of course we have no hands, nor can we lay foundations as you can, nor avail ourselves of the lateral pressure of the earth; the manner in which the rain originates in the intervals between our various zones, so that the northern regions do not intercept the moisture falling on the southern; the nature of our hills and mines, our trees and vegetables, our seasons and harvests; our Alphabet and method of writing, adapted to our linear tablets; these and a hundred other details of our physical existence I must pass over, nor do I mention them now except to indicate to my readers that their omission proceeds not from forgetfulness on the part of the author, but from his regard for the time of the Reader.

Yet before I proceed to my legitimate subject some few final remarks will no doubt be expected by my Readers upon these pillars and mainstays of the Constitution of Flatland, the controllers of our conduct and shapers of our destiny, the objects of universal homage and almost of adoration: need I say that I mean our Circles or Priests?

When I call them Priests, let me not be understood as meaning no more than the term denotes with you. With us, our Priests are Administrators of all Business, Art, and Science; Directors of Trade, Commerce, Generalship, Architecture, Engineering, Education, Statesmanship, Legislature, Morality, Theology; doing nothing themselves, they are the Causes of everything worth doing, that is done by others.

Although popularly everyone called a Circle is deemed a Circle, yet among the better educated Classes it is known that no Circle is really a Circle, but only a Polygon with a very large number of very small sides. As the number of the sides increases, a Polygon approximates to a Circle; and, when the number is very great indeed, say for example three or four hundred, it is extremely difficult for the most delicate touch to feel any polygonal angles. Let me say rather it WOULD be difficult: for, as I have shown above, Recognition by Feeling is unknown among the highest society, and to FEEL a Circle would be considered a most audacious insult. This habit of abstention from Feeling in the best society enables a Circle the more easily to sustain the veil of mystery in which, from his earliest years, he is wont to enwrap the exact nature of his Perimeter or Circumference. Three feet being the average Perimeter it follows that, in a Polygon of three hundred sides each side will be no more than the hundredth part of a foot in length, or little more than the tenth part of an inch; and in a Polygon of six or seven hundred sides the sides are little larger than the diameter of a Spaceland pin-head. It is always assumed, by courtesy, that the Chief Circle for the time being has ten thousand sides.

The ascent of the posterity of the Circles in the social scale is not restricted, as it is among the lower Regular classes, by the Law of Nature which limits the increase of sides to one in each generation. If it were so, the number of sides in the Circle would be a mere question of pedigree and arithmetic, and the four hundred and ninety-seventh descendant of an Equilateral Triangle would necessarily be a polygon with five hundred sides. But this is not the case. Nature's Law prescribes two antagonistic decrees affecting Circular propagation; first, that as the race climbs higher in the scale of development, so development shall proceed at an accelerated pace; second, that in the same proportion, the race shall become less fertile. Consequently in the home of a Polygon of four or five hundred sides it is rare to find a son; more than one is never seen. On the other hand the son of a five-hundred-sided Polygon has been known to possess five hundred and fifty, or even six hundred sides.

Art also steps in to help the process of higher Evolution. Our physicians have discovered that the small and tender sides of an infant Polygon of the higher class can be fractured, and his whole frame re-set, with such exactness that a Polygon of two or three hundred sides sometimes—by no means always, for the process is attended with serious risk—but sometimes overleaps two or three hundred generations, and as it were double at a stroke, the number of his progenitors and the nobility of his descent.

Many a promising child is sacrificed in this way. Scarcely one out of ten survives. Yet so strong is the parental ambition among those Polygons who are, as it were, on the fringe of the Circular class, that it is very rare to find the Nobleman of that position in society, who has neglected to place his firstborn in the Circular Neo-Therapeutic Gymnasium before he has attained the age of a month.

One year determines success or failure. At the end of that time the child has, in all probability, added one more to the tombstones that crowd the Neo-Therapeutic Cemetery; but on rare occasional a glad procession bears back the little one to his exultant parents, no longer a Polygon, but a Circle, at least by courtesy: and a single instance of so blessed a result induces multitudes of Polygonal parents to submit to similar domestic sacrifice, which have a dissimilar issue.

Section 12: The Doctrine of Our Priests

As to the doctrine of the Circles it may briefly be summed up in a single maxim, "Attend to your Configuration." Whether political, ecclesiastical, or moral, all their teaching has for its object the improvement of individual and collective Configuration—with special reference of course to the Configuration of the Circles, to which all other objects are subordinated.

It is the merit of the Circles that they have effectually suppressed those ancient heresies which led men to waste energy and sympathy in the vain belief that conduct depends upon will, effort, training, encouragement, praise, or anything else but Configuration. It was Pantocyclus—the illustrious Circle mentioned above, as the queller of the Colour Revolt—who first convinced mankind that Configuration makes the man; that if, for example, you are born an Isosceles with two uneven sides, you will assuredly go wrong unless you have them made even—for which purpose you must go to the Isosceles Hospital; similarly, if you are a Triangle, or Square, or even a Polygon, born with any Irregularity, you must be taken to one of the Regular Hospitals to have your disease cured; otherwise you will end your days in the State Prison or by the angle of the State Executioner.

All faults or defects, from the slightest misconduct to the most flagitious crime, Pantocyclus attributed to some deviation from perfect Regularity in the bodily figure, caused perhaps (if not congenital) by some collision in a crowd; by neglect to take exercise, or by taking too much of it; or even by a sudden change of temperature, resulting in a shrinkage or expansion in some too susceptible part of the frame. Therefore, concluded that illustrious Philosopher, neither good conduct nor bad conduct is a fit subject, in any sober estimation, for either praise or blame. For why should you praise, for example, the integrity of a Square who faithfully defends the interests of his client, when you ought in reality rather to admire the exact precision of his right angles? Or again, why blame a lying, thievish Isosceles, when you ought rather to deplore the incurable inequality of his sides?

Theoretically, this doctrine is unquestionable; but it has practical drawbacks. In dealing with an Isosceles, if a rascal pleads that he cannot help stealing because of his unevenness, you reply that for that very reason, because he cannot help being a nuisance to his neighbours, you, the Magistrate, cannot help sentencing him to be consumed—and there's an end of the matter. But in little domestic difficulties, when the penalty of consumption, or death, is out of the question, this theory of Configuration sometimes comes in awkwardly; and I must confess that occasionally when one of my own Hexagonal Grandsons pleads as an excuse for his disobedience that a sudden change of temperature has been too much for his Perimeter, and that I ought to lay the blame not on him but on his Configuration, which can only be strengthened by abundance of the choicest sweetmeats, I neither see my way logically to reject, nor practically to accept, his conclusions.

For my own part, I find it best to assume that a good sound scolding or castigation has some latent and strengthening influence on my Grandson's Configuration; though I own that I have no grounds for thinking so. At all events I am not alone in my way of extricating myself from this dilemma; for I find that many of the highest Circles, sitting as Judges in law courts, use praise and blame towards Regular and Irregular Figures; and in their homes I know by experience that, when scolding their children, they speak about "right" and "wrong" as vehemently and passionately as if they believe that these names represented real existence, and that a human Figure is really capable of choosing between them.

Constantly carrying out their policy of making Configuration the leading idea in every mind, the Circles reverse the nature of that Commandment which in Spaceland regulates the relations between parents and children. With you, children are taught to honour their parents; with us—next to the Circles, who are the chief object of universal homage—a man is taught to honour his Grandson, if he has one; or, if not, his Son. By "honour," however, is by no means mean "indulgence," but a reverent regard for their highest interests: and the Circles teach that the duty of fathers is to subordinate their own interests to those of posterity, thereby advancing the welfare of the whole State as well as that of their own immediate descendants.

The weak point in the system of the Circles—if a humble Square may venture to speak of anything Circular as containing any element of weakness—appears to me to be found in their relations with Women.

As it is of the utmost importance for Society that Irregular births should be discouraged, it follows that no Woman who has any Irregularities in her ancestry is a fit partner for one who desires that his posterity should rise by regular degrees in the social scale.

Now the Irregularity of a Male is a matter of measurement; but as all Women are straight, and therefore visibly Regular so to speak, one has to devise some other means of ascertaining what I may call their invisible Irregularity, that is to say their potential Irregularities as regards possible offspring. This is effected by carefully-kept pedigrees, which are preserved and supervised by the State; and without a certified pedigree no Woman is allowed to marry.

Now it might have been supposed the a Circle—proud of his ancestry and regardful for a posterity which might possibly issue hereafter in a Chief Circle—would be more careful than any other to choose a wife who had no blot on her escutcheon. But it is not so. The care in choosing a Regular wife appears to diminish as one rises in the social scale. Nothing would induce an aspiring Isosceles, who has hopes of generating an Equilateral Son, to take a wife who reckoned a single Irregularity among her Ancestors; a Square or Pentagon, who is confident that his family is steadily on the rise, does not inquire above the five-hundredth generation; a Hexagon or Dodecagon is even more careless of the wife's pedigree; but a Circle has been known deliberately to take a wife who has had an Irregular Great-Grandfather, and all because of some slight superiority of lustre, or because of the charms of a low voice—which, with us, even more than with you, is thought "an excellent thing in a Woman."

Such ill-judged marriages are, as might be expected, barren, if they do not result in positive Irregularity or in diminution of sides; but none of these evils have hitherto provided sufficiently deterrent. The loss of a few sides in a highly-developed Polygon is not easily noticed, and is sometimes compensated by a successful operation in the Neo-Therapeutic Gymnasium, as I have described above; and the Circles are too much disposed to acquiesce in infecundity as a law of the superior development. Yet, if this evil be not arrested, the gradual diminution of the Circular class may soon become more rapid, and the time may not be far distant when, the race being no longer able to produce a Chief Circle, the Constitution of Flatland must fall.

One other word of warning suggest itself to me, though I cannot so easily mention a remedy; and this also refers to our relations with Women. About three hundred years ago, it was decreed by the Chief Circle that, since women are deficient in Reason but abundant in Emotion, they ought no longer to be treated as rational, nor receive any mental education. The consequence was that they were no longer taught to read, nor even to master Arithmetic enough to enable them to count the angles of their husband or children; and hence they sensibly declined during each generation in intellectual power. And this system of female non-education or quietism still prevails.

My fear is that, with the best intentions, this policy has been carried so far as to react injuriously on the Male Sex.

For the consequence is that, as things now are, we Males have to lead a kind of bi-lingual, and I may almost say bimental, existence. With Women, we speak of "love," "duty," "right," "wrong," "pity," "hope," and other irrational and emotional conceptions, which have no existence, and the fiction of which has no object except to control feminine exuberances; but among ourselves, and in our books, we have an entirely different vocabulary and I may also say, idiom. "Love" them becomes "the anticipation of benefits"; "duty" becomes "necessity" or "fitness"; and other words are correspondingly transmuted. Moreover, among Women, we use language implying the utmost deference for their Sex; and they fully believe that the Chief Circle Himself is not more devoutly adored by us than they are: but behind their backs they are both regarded and spoken of—by all but the very young—as being little better than "mindless organisms."

Our Theology also in the Women's chambers is entirely different from our Theology elsewhere.

Now my humble fear is that this double training, in language as well as in thought, imposes somewhat too heavy a burden upon the young, especially when, at the age of three years old, they are taken from the maternal care and taught to unlearn the old language—except for the purpose of repeating it in the presence of the Mothers and Nurses—and to learn the vocabulary and idiom of science. Already methinks I discern a weakness in the grasp of mathematical truth at the present time as compared with the more robust intellect of our ancestors three hundred years ago. I say nothing of the possible danger if a Woman should ever surreptitiously learn to read and convey to her Sex the result of her perusal of a single popular volume; nor of the possibility that the indiscretion or disobedience of some infant Male might reveal to a Mother the secrets of the logical dialect. On the simple ground of the enfeebling of the male intellect, I rest this humble appeal to the highest Authorities to reconsider the regulations of Female education.

PART II: OTHER WORLDS

"O brave new worlds, That have such people in them!"

Section 13: How I Had a Vision of Lineland

It was the last day but one of the 1999th year of our era, and the first day of the Long Vacation. Having amused myself till a late hour with my favorite recreation of Geometry, I had retired to rest with an unsolved problem in my mind. In the night I had a dream.

I saw before me a vast multitude of small Straight Lines (which I naturally assumed to be Women) interspersed with other Beings still smaller and of the nature of lustrous points—all moving to and fro in one and the same Straight Line, and, as nearly as I could judge, with the same velocity.

A noise of confused, multitudinous chirping or twittering issued from them at intervals as long as they were moving; but sometimes they ceased from motion, and then all was silence.

Approaching one of the largest of what I thought to be Women, I accosted her, but received no answer. A second and third appeal on my part were equally ineffectual. Losing patience at what appeared to me intolerable rudeness, I brought my mouth to a position full in front of her mouth so as to intercept her motion, and loudly repeated my question, "Woman, what signifies this concourse, and this strange and confused chirping, and this monotonous motion to and fro in one and the same Straight Line?"

"I am no Woman," replied the small Line: "I am the Monarch of the world. But thou, whence intrudest thou into my realm of Lineland?" Receiving this abrupt reply, I begged pardon if I had in any way startled or molested his Royal Highness; and describing myself as a stranger I besought the King to give me some account of his dominions. But I had the greatest possible difficulty in obtaining any information on points that really interested me; for the Monarch could not refrain from constantly assuming that whatever was familiar to him must also be known to me and that I was simulating ignorance in jest. However, by preserving questions I elicited the following facts:

It seemed that this poor ignorant Monarch—as he called himself—was persuaded that the Straight Line which he called his Kingdom, and in which he passed his existence, constituted the whole of the world, and indeed the whole of Space. Not being able either to move or to see, save in his Straight

Line, he had no conception of anything out of it. Though he had heard my voice when I first addressed him, the sounds had come to him in a manner so contrary to his experience that he had made no answer, "seeing no man," as he expressed it, "and hearing a voice as it were from my own intestines." Until the moment when I placed my mouth in his World, he had neither seen me, nor heard anything except confused sounds beating against, what I called his side, but what he called his INSIDE or STOMACH; nor had he even now the least conception of the region from which I had come. Outside his World, or Line, all was a blank to him; nay, not even a blank, for a blank implies Space; say, rather, all was non-existent.

His subjects—of whom the small Lines were men and the Points Women—were all alike confined in motion and eyesight to that single Straight Line, which was their World. It need scarcely be added that the whole of their horizon was limited to a Point; nor could any one ever see anything but a Point. Man, woman, child, thing—each as a Point to the eye of a Linelander. Only by the sound of the voice could sex or age be distinguished. Moreover, as each individual occupied the whole of the narrow path, so to speak, which constituted his Universe, and no one could move to the right or left to make way for passers by, it followed that no Linelander could ever pass another. Once neighbours, always neighbours. Neighbourhood with them was like marriage with us. Neighbours remained neighbours till death did them part.

Such a life, with all vision limited to a Point, and all motion to a Straight Line, seemed to me inexpressibly dreary; and I was surprised to note that vivacity and cheerfulness of the King. Wondering whether it was possible, amid circumstances so unfavourable to domestic relations, to enjoy the pleasures of conjugal union, I hesitated for some time to question his Royal Highness on so delicate a subject; but at last I plunged into it by abruptly inquiring as to the health of his family. "My wives and children," he replied, "are well and happy."

Staggered at this answer—for in the immediate proximity of the Monarch (as I had noted in my dream before I entered Lineland) there were none but Men—I ventured to reply, "Pardon me, but I cannot imagine how your Royal Highness can at any time either see or approach their Majesties, when there at least half a dozen intervening individuals, whom you can neither see through, nor pass by? Is it possible that in Lineland proximity is not necessary for marriage and for the generation of children?"

"How can you ask so absurd a question?" replied the Monarch. "If it were indeed as you suggest, the Universe would soon be depopulated. No, no; neighbourhood is needless for the union of hearts; and the birth of children is too important a matter to have been allowed to depend upon such an accident as proximity. You cannot be ignorant of this. Yet since you are pleased to affect ignorance, I will instruct you as if you were the veriest baby in Lineland. Know, then, that marriages are consummated by means of the faculty of sound and the sense of hearing.

"You are of course aware that every Man has two mouths or voices—as well as two eyes—a bass at one and a tenor at the other of his extremities. I should not mention this, but that I have been unable to distinguish your tenor in the course of our conversation." I replied that I had but one voice, and that I had not been aware that his Royal Highness had two. "That confirms my impression," said the King, "that you are not a Man, but a feminine Monstrosity with a bass voice, and an utterly uneducated ear. But to continue.

"Nature having herself ordained that every Man should wed two wives—" "Why two?" asked I. "You carry your affected simplicity too far," he cried. "How can there be a completely harmonious union without the combination of the Four in One, viz. the Bass and Tenor of the Man and the Soprano and Contralto of the two Women?" "But supposing," said I, "that a man should prefer one wife or three?" "It is impossible," he said; "it is as inconceivable as that two and one should make five, or that the human eye should see a Straight Line." I would have interrupted him; but he proceeded as follows:

"Once in the middle of each week a Law of Nature compels us to move to and fro with a rhythmic motion of more than usual violence, which continues for the time you would take to count a hundred and one. In the midst of this choral dance, at the fifty-first pulsation, the inhabitants of the Universe pause in full career, and each individual sends forth his richest, fullest, sweetest strain. It is in this decisive moment that all our marriages are made. So exquisite is the adaptation of Bass and Treble, of Tenor to Contralto, that oftentimes the Loved Ones, though twenty thousand leagues away, recognize at once the responsive note of their destined Lover; and, penetrating the paltry obstacles of distance, Love unites the three. The marriage in that instance consummated results in a threefold Male and Female offspring which takes its place in Lineland."

"What! Always threefold?" said I. "Must one wife then always have twins?"

"Bass-voice Monstrosity! yes," replied the King. "How else could the balance of the Sexes be maintained, if two girls were not born for every boy? Would you ignore the very Alphabet of Nature?" He ceased, speechless for fury; and some time elapsed before I could induce him to resume his narrative.

"You will not, of course, suppose that every bachelor among us finds his mates at the first wooing in this universal Marriage Chorus. On the contrary, the process is by most of us many times repeated. Few are the hearts whose happy lot is at once to recognize in each other's voice the partner intended for them by Providence, and to fly into a reciprocal and perfectly harmonious embrace. With most of us the courtship is of long duration. The Wooer's voices may perhaps accord with one of the future wives, but not with both; or not, at first, with either; or the Soprano and Contralto may not quite harmonize. In such cases Nature has provided that every weekly Chorus shall bring the three Lovers into closer harmony. Each trial of voice, each fresh discovery of discord, almost imperceptibly induces the less perfect to modify his or her vocal utterance so as to approximate to the more perfect. And after many trials and many approximations, the result is at last achieved. There comes a day at last when, while the wonted Marriage Chorus goes forth from universal Lineland, the three far-off Lovers suddenly find themselves in exact harmony, and, before they are aware, the wedded Triplet is rapt vocally into a duplicate embrace; and Nature rejoices over one more marriage and over three more births."

Section 14: How I Vainly Tried to Explain the Nature of Flatland

Thinking that it was time to bring down the Monarch from his raptures to the level of common sense, I determined to endeavour to open up to him some glimpses of the truth, that is to say of the nature of things in Flatland. So I began thus: "How does your Royal Highness distinguish the shapes and positions of his subjects? I for my part noticed by the sense of sight, before I entered your Kingdom, that some of your people are lines and others Points; and that some of the lines are larger—" "You speak of an impossibility," interrupted the King; "you must have seen a vision; for to detect the difference between a Line and a Point by the sense of sight is, as every one knows, in the nature of things, impossible; but it can be detected by the sense of hearing, and by the same means my shape can be exactly ascertained. Behold me—I am a Line, the longest in Lineland, over six inches of Space—" "Of Length," I ventured to suggest. "Fool," said he, "Space is Length. Interrupt me again, and I have done."

I apologized; but he continued scornfully, "Since you are impervious to argument, you shall hear with your ears how by means of my two voices I reveal my shape to my Wives, who are at this moment six thousand miles seventy yards two feet eight inches away, the one to the North, the other to the South. Listen, I call to them."

He chirruped, and then complacently continued: "My wives at this moment receiving the sound of one of my voice, closely followed by the other, and perceiving that the latter reaches them after an interval in which sound can traverse 6.457 inches, infer that one of my mouths is 6.457 inches further from them than the other, and accordingly know my shape to be 6.457 inches. But you will of course understand that my wives do not make this calculation every time they hear my two voices. They made it, once for all, before we were married. But they COULD make it at any time. And in the same way I can estimate the shape of any of my Male subjects by the sense of sound."

"But how," said I, "if a Man feigns a Woman's voice with one of his two voices, or so disguises his Southern voice that it cannot be recognized as the echo of the Northern? May not such deceptions cause great inconvenience? And have you no means of checking frauds of this kind by commanding your neighbouring subjects to feel one another?" This of course was a very stupid question, for feeling could not have answered the purpose; but I asked with the view of irritating the Monarch, and I succeeded perfectly.

"What!" cried he in horror, "explain your meaning." "Feel, touch, come into contact," I replied. "If you mean by FEELING," said the King, "approaching so close as to leave no space between two individuals, know, Stranger, that this offence is punishable in my dominions by death. And the reason is obvious. The frail form of a Woman, being liable to be shattered by such an approximation, must be preserved by the State; but since Women cannot be distinguished by the sense of sight from Men, the Law ordains universally that neither Man nor Woman shall be approached so closely as to destroy the interval between the approximator and the approximated.

"And indeed what possible purpose would be served by this illegal and unnatural excess of approximation which you call TOUCHING, when all the ends of so brutal and course a process are attained at once more easily and more exactly by the sense of hearing? As to your suggested danger of deception, it is non-existent: for the Voice, being the essence of one's Being, cannot be thus changed at will. But come, suppose that I had the power of passing through solid things, so that I could penetrate my subjects, one after another, even to the number of a billion, verifying the size and distance of each by the sense of FEELING: How much time and energy would be wasted in this clumsy and inaccurate method! Whereas now, in one moment of audition, I take as it were the census and statistics, local, corporeal, mental and spiritual, of every living being in Lineland. Hark, only hark!"

So saying he paused and listened, as if in an ecstasy, to a sound which seemed to me no better than a tiny chirping from an innumerable multitude of lilliputian grasshoppers.

"Truly," replied I, "your sense of hearing serves you in good stead, and fills up many of your deficiencies. But permit me to point out that your life in Lineland must be deplorably dull. To see nothing but a Point! Not even to be able to contemplate a Straight Line! Nay, not even to know what a Straight Line is! To see, yet to be cut off from those Linear prospects which are vouchsafed to us in Flatland! Better surely to have no sense of sight at all than to see so little! I grant you I have not your discriminative faculty of hearing; for the concert of all Lineland which gives you such intense pleasure, is to me no better than a multitudinous twittering or chirping. But at least I can discern, by sight, a Line from a Point. And let me prove it. Just before I came into your kingdom, I saw you dancing from left to right, and then from right to left, with Seven Men and a Woman in your immediate proximity on the left, and eight Men and two Women on your right. Is not this correct?"

"It is correct," said the King, "so far as the numbers and sexes are concerned, though I know not what you mean by 'right' and 'left.' But I deny that you saw these things. For how could you see the Line, that is to say the inside, of any Man? But you must have heard these things, and then dreamed that you saw them. And let me ask what you mean by those words 'left' and 'right.' I suppose it is your way of saying Northward and Southward."

"Not so," replied I; "besides your motion of Northward and Southward, there is another motion which I call from right to left."

King. Exhibit to me, if you please, this motion from left to right.

I. Nay, that I cannot do, unless you could step out of your Line altogether.

King. Out of my Line? Do you mean out of the world? Out of Space?

I. Well, yes. Out of YOUR world. Out of YOUR Space. For your Space is not the true Space. True Space is a Plane; but your Space is only a Line.

King. If you cannot indicate this motion from left to right by yourself moving in it, then I beg you to describe it to me in words.

I. If you cannot tell your right side from your left, I fear that no words of mine can make my meaning clearer to you. But surely you cannot be ignorant of so simple a distinction.

King. I do not in the least understand you.

I. Alas! How shall I make it clear? When you move straight on, does it not sometimes occur to you that you COULD move in some other way, turning your eye round so as to look in the direction towards which your side is now fronting? In other words, instead of always moving in the direction of one of your extremities, do you never feel a desire to move in the direction, so to speak, of your side?

King. Never. And what do you mean? How can a man's inside "front" in any direction? Or how can a man move in the direction of his inside?

I. Well then, since words cannot explain the matter, I will try deeds, and will move gradually out of Lineland in the direction which I desire to indicate to you.

At the word I began to move my body out of Lineland. As long as any part of me remained in his dominion and in his view, the King kept exclaiming, "I see you, I see you still; you are not moving." But when I had at last moved myself out of his Line, he cried in his shrillest voice, "She is vanished; she is dead." "I am not dead," replied I; "I am simply out of Lineland, that is to say, out of the Straight Line which you call Space, and in the true Space, where I can see things as they are. And at this moment I can see your Line, or side— or inside as you are pleased to call it; and I can see also the Men and Women on the North and South of you, whom I will now enumerate, describing their order, their size, and the interval between each."

When I had done this at great length, I cried triumphantly, "Does that at last convince you?" And, with that, I once more entered Lineland, taking up the same position as before.

But the Monarch replied, "If you were a Man of sense—though, as you appear to have only one voice I have little doubt you are not a Man but a Woman—but, if you had a particle of sense, you would listen to reason. You ask me to believe that there is another Line besides that which my senses indicate, and another motion besides that of which I am daily conscious. I, in return, ask you to describe in words or indicate by motion that other Line of which you speak. Instead of moving, you merely exercise some magic art of vanishing and returning to sight; and instead of any lucid description of your new World, you simply tell me the numbers and sizes of some forty of my retinue, facts known to any child in my capital. Can anything be more irrational or audacious? Acknowledge your folly or depart from my dominions."

Furious at his perversity, and especially indignant that he professed to be ignorant of my sex, I retorted in no measured terms, "Besotted Being! You think yourself the perfection of existence, while you are in reality the most imperfect and imbecile. You profess to see, whereas you see nothing but a Point! You plume yourself on inferring the existence of a Straight Line; but I CAN SEE Straight Lines, and infer the existence of Angles, Triangles, Squares, Pentagons, Hexagons, and even Circles. Why waste more words? Suffice it that I am the completion of your incomplete self. You are a Line, but I am a Line of Lines called in my country a Square: and even I, infinitely superior though I am to you, am of little account among the great nobles of Flatland, whence I have come to visit you, in the hope of enlightening your ignorance."

Hearing these words the King advanced towards me with a menacing cry as if to pierce me through the diagonal; and in that same movement there arose from myriads of his subjects a multitudinous war-cry, increasing in vehemence till at last methought it rivalled the roar of an army of a hundred thousand Isosceles, and the artillery of a thousand Pentagons. Spell-bound and motionless, I could neither speak nor move to avert the impending destruction; and still the noise grew louder, and the King came closer, when I awoke to find the breakfast-bell recalling me to the realities of Flatland.

Section 15: Concerning a Stranger from Spaceland

From dreams I proceed to facts.

It was the last day of our 1999th year of our era. The patterning of the rain had long ago announced nightfall; and I was sitting (footnote 3) in the company of my wife, musing on the events of the past and the prospects of the coming year, the coming century, the coming Millennium.

My four Sons and two orphan Grandchildren had retired to their several apartments; and my wife alone remained with me to see the old Millennium out and the new one in.

I was rapt in thought, pondering in my mind some words that had casually issued from the mouth of my youngest Grandson, a most promising young Hexagon of unusual brilliancy and perfect angularity. His uncles and I had been giving him his usual practical lesson in Sight Recognition, turning ourselves upon our centres, now rapidly, now more slowly, and questioning him as to our positions; and his answers had been so satisfactory that I had been induced to reward him by giving him a few hints on Arithmetic, as applied to Geometry.

Taking nine Squares, each an inch every way, I had put them together so as to make one large Square, with a side of three inches, and I had hence proved to my little Grandson that—though it was impossible for us to SEE the inside of the Square—yet we might ascertain the number of square inches in a Square by simply squaring the number of inches in the side: "and thus," said I, "we know that three-to-the-second, or nine, represents the number of square inches in a Square whose side is three inches long."

The little Hexagon meditated on this a while and then said to me; "But you have been teaching me to raise numbers to the third power: I suppose three-to-the-third must mean something in Geometry; what does it mean?" "Nothing at all," replied I, "not at least in Geometry; for Geometry has only Two Dimensions." And then I began to show the boy how a Point by moving through a length of three inches makes a Line of three inches, which may be represented by three; and how a Line of three inches, moving parallel to itself through a length of three inches, makes a Square of three inches every way, which may be represented by three-to-the-second. xxx Upon this, my Grandson, again returning to his former suggestion, took me up rather suddenly and exclaimed, "Well, then, if a Point by moving three inches, makes a Line of three inches represented by three; and if a straight Line of three inches, moving parallel to itself, makes a Square of three inches every way, represented by three-to-the-second; it must be that a Square of three inches every way, moving somehow parallel to itself (but I don't see how) must make Something else (but I don't see what) of three inches every way—and this must be represented by three-to-the-third."

"Go to bed," said I, a little ruffled by this interruption: "if you would talk less nonsense, you would remember more sense."

So my Grandson had disappeared in disgrace; and there I sat by my Wife's side, endeavouring to form a retrospect of the year 1999 and of the possibilities of the year 2000; but not quite able to shake of the thoughts suggested by the prattle of my bright little Hexagon. Only a few sands now remained in the half-hour glass. Rousing myself from my reverie I turned the glass Northward for the last time in the old Millennium; and in the act, I exclaimed aloud, "The boy is a fool."

Straightway I became conscious of a Presence in the room, and a chilling breath thrilled through my very being. "He is no such thing," cried my Wife, "and you are breaking the Commandments in thus dishonouring your own

Grandson." But I took no notice of her. Looking around in every direction I could see nothing; yet still I FELT a Presence, and shivered as the cold whisper came again. I started up. "What is the matter?" said my Wife, "there is no draught; what are you looking for? There is nothing." There was nothing; and I resumed my seat, again exclaiming, "The boy is a fool, I say; three-to-the-third can have no meaning in Geometry." At once there came a distinctly audible reply, "The boy is not a fool; and three-to-the-third has an obvious Geometrical meaning."

My Wife as well as myself heard the words, although she did not understand their meaning, and both of us sprang forward in the direction of the sound. What was our horror when we saw before us a Figure! At the first glance it appeared to be a Woman, seen sideways; but a moment's observation showed me that the extremities passed into dimness too rapidly to represent one of the Female Sex; and I should have thought it a Circle, only that it seemed to change its size in a manner impossible for a Circle or for any regular Figure of which I had had experience.

But my Wife had not my experience, nor the coolness necessary to note these characteristics. With the usual hastiness and unreasoning jealousy of her Sex, she flew at once to the conclusion that a Woman had entered the house through some small aperture. "How comes this person here?" she exclaimed, "you promised me, my dear, that there should be no ventilators in our new house." "Nor are they any," said I; "but what makes you think that the stranger is a Woman? I see by my power of Sight Recognition—"

"Oh, I have no patience with your Sight Recognition," replied she, "'Feeling is believing' and 'A Straight Line to the touch is worth a Circle to the sight'"—two Proverbs, very common with the Frailer Sex in Flatland.

"Well," said I, for I was afraid of irritating her, "if it must be so, demand an introduction." Assuming her most gracious manner, my Wife advanced towards the Stranger, "Permit me, Madam to feel and be felt by—" then, suddenly recoiling, "Oh! it is not a Woman, and there are no angles either, not a trace of one. Can it be that I have so misbehaved to a perfect Circle?"

"I am indeed, in a certain sense a Circle," replied the Voice, "and a more perfect Circle than any in Flatland; but to speak more accurately, I am many Circles in one." Then he added more mildly, "I have a message, dear Madam, to your husband, which I must not deliver in your presence; and, if you would suffer us to retire for a few minutes—" But my wife would not listen to the proposal that our august Visitor should so incommode himself, and assuring the Circle that the hour of her own retirement had long passed, with many reiterated apologies for her recent indiscretion, she at last retreated to her apartment.

I glanced at the half-hour glass. The last sands had fallen. The third Millennium had begun.

Footnote 3. When I say "sitting," of course I do not mean any change of attitude such as you in Spaceland signify by that word; for as we have no feet, we can no more "sit" nor "stand" (in your sense of the word) than one of your soles or flounders.

Nevertheless, we perfectly well recognize the different mental states of volition implied by "lying," "sitting," and "standing," which are to some extent indicated to a beholder by a slight increase of lustre corresponding to the increase of volition.

But on this, and a thousand other kindred subjects, time forbids me to dwell.

Section 16: How the Stranger Vainly Endeavored to Reveal to Me in Words the Mysteries of Spaceland

As soon as the sound of the Peace-cry of my departing Wife had died away, I began to approach the Stranger with the intention of taking a nearer view and of bidding him be seated: but his appearance struck me dumb and motionless with astonishment. Without the slightest symptoms of angularity he nevertheless varied every instant with graduations of size and brightness scarcely possible for any Figure within the scope of my experience. The thought flashed across me that I might have before me a burglar or cut-throat, some monstrous Irregular Isosceles, who, by feigning the voice of a Circle, had obtained admission somehow into the house, and was now preparing to stab me with his acute angle.

In a sitting-room, the absence of Fog (and the season happened to be remarkably dry), made it difficult for me to trust to Sight Recognition, especially at the short distance at which I was standing. Desperate with fear, I rushed forward with an unceremonious, "You must permit me, Sir—" and felt him. My Wife was right. There was not the trace of an angle, not the slightest roughness or inequality: never in my life had I met with a more perfect Circle. He remained motionless while I walked around him, beginning from his eye and returning to it again. Circular he was throughout, a perfectly satisfactory Circle; there could not be a doubt of it. Then followed a dialogue, which I will endeavour to set down as near as I can recollect it, omitting only some of my profuse apologies—for I was covered with shame and humiliation that I, a Square, should have been guilty of the impertinence of feeling a Circle. It was commenced by the Stranger with some impatience at the lengthiness of my introductory process.

Stranger. Have you felt me enough by this time? Are you not introduced to me yet?

I. Most illustrious Sir, excuse my awkwardness, which arises not from ignorance of the usages of polite society, but from a little surprise and nervousness, consequent on this somewhat unexpected visit. And I beseech you to reveal my indiscretion to no one, and especially not to my Wife. But before your Lordship enters into further communications, would he deign to satisfy the curiosity of one who would gladly know whence his visitor came?

Stranger. From Space, from Space, Sir: whence else?

I. Pardon me, my Lord, but is not your Lordship already in Space, your Lordship and his humble servant, even at this moment?

Stranger. Pooh! what do you know of Space? Define Space.

I. Space, my Lord, is height and breadth indefinitely prolonged.

Stranger. Exactly: you see you do not even know what Space is. You think it is of Two Dimensions only; but I have come to announce to you a Third— height, breadth, and length.

I. Your Lordship is pleased to be merry. We also speak of length and height, or breadth and thickness, thus denoting Two Dimensions by four names.

Stranger. But I mean not only three names, but Three Dimensions.

I. Would your Lordship indicate or explain to me in what direction is the Third Dimension, unknown to me?

Stranger. I came from it. It is up above and down below.

I. My Lord means seemingly that it is Northward and Southward.

Stranger. I mean nothing of the kind. I mean a direction in which you cannot look, because you have no eye in your side.

I. Pardon me, my Lord, a moment's inspection will convince your Lordship that I have a perfectly luminary at the juncture of my two sides.

Stranger: Yes: but in order to see into Space you ought to have an eye, not on your Perimeter, but on your side, that is, on what you would probably call your inside; but we in Spaceland should call it your side.

I. An eye in my inside! An eye in my stomach! Your Lordship jests.

Stranger. I am in no jesting humour. I tell you that I come from Space, or, since you will not understand what Space means, from the Land of Three Dimensions whence I but lately looked down upon your Plane which you call Space forsooth. From that position of advantage I discerned all that you speak of as SOLID (by which you mean "enclosed on four sides"), your houses, your churches, your very chests and safes, yes even your insides and stomachs, all lying open and exposed to my view.

I. Such assertions are easily made, my Lord.

Stranger. But not easily proved, you mean. But I mean to prove mine.

When I descended here, I saw your four Sons, the Pentagons, each in his apartment, and your two Grandsons the Hexagons; I saw your youngest Hexagon remain a while with you and then retire to his room, leaving you and your Wife alone. I saw your Isosceles servants, three in number, in the kitchen at supper, and the little Page in the scullery. Then I came here, and how do you think I came?

I. Through the roof, I suppose.

Strange. Not so. Your roof, as you know very well, has been recently repaired, and has no aperture by which even a Woman could penetrate. I tell you I come from Space. Are you not convinced by what I have told you of your children and household?

I. Your Lordship must be aware that such facts touching the belongings of his humble servant might be easily ascertained by any one of the neighbourhood possessing your Lordship's ample means of information.

Stranger. (TO HIMSELF.) What must I do? Stay; one more argument suggests itself to me. When you see a Straight Line—your wife, for example—how many Dimensions do you attribute to her?

I. Your Lordship would treat me as if I were one of the vulgar who, being ignorant of Mathematics, suppose that a Woman is really a Straight Line, and only of One Dimension. No, no, my Lord; we Squares are better advised, and are as well aware of your Lordship that a Woman, though popularly called a Straight Line, is, really and scientifically, a very thin Parallelogram, possessing Two Dimensions, like the rest of us, viz., length and breadth (or thickness).

Stranger. But the very fact that a Line is visible implies that it possesses yet another Dimension.

I. My Lord, I have just acknowledged that a Woman is broad as well as long. We see her length, we infer her breadth; which, though very slight, is capable of measurement.

Stranger. You do not understand me. I mean that when you see a Woman, you ought—besides inferring her breadth—to see her length, and to SEE what we call her HEIGHT; although the last Dimension is infinitesimal in your country. If a Line were mere length without "height," it would cease to occupy Space and would become invisible. Surely you must recognize this?

I. I must indeed confess that I do not in the least understand your Lordship. When we in Flatland see a Line, we see length and BRIGHTNESS. If the brightness disappears, the Line is extinguished, and, as you say, ceases to occupy Space. But am I to suppose that your Lordship gives the brightness the title of a Dimension, and that what we call "bright" you call "high"?

Stranger. No, indeed. By "height" I mean a Dimension like your length: only, with you, "height" is not so easily perceptible, being extremely small.

I. My Lord, your assertion is easily put to the test. You say I have a Third Dimension, which you call "height." Now, Dimension implies direction and measurement. Do but measure my "height," or merely indicate to me the direction in which my "height" extends, and I will become your convert. Otherwise, your Lordship's own understand must hold me excused.

Stranger. (TO HIMSELF.) I can do neither. How shall I convince him? Surely a plain statement of facts followed by ocular demonstration ought to suffice. —Now, Sir; listen to me.

You are living on a Plane. What you style Flatland is the vast level surface of what I may call a fluid, or in, the top of which you and your countrymen move about, without rising above or falling below it.

I am not a plane Figure, but a Solid. You call me a Circle; but in reality I am not a Circle, but an infinite number of Circles, of size varying from a Point to a Circle of thirteen inches in diameter, one placed on the top of the other. When I cut through your plane as I am now doing, I make in your plane a section which you, very rightly, call a Circle. For even a Sphere—which is my proper name in my own country—if he manifest himself at all to an inhabitant of Flatland—must needs manifest himself as a Circle.

Do you not remember—for I, who see all things, discerned last night the phantasmal vision of Lineland written upon your brain—do you not remember, I say, how when you entered the realm of Lineland, you were compelled to manifest yourself to the King, not as a Square, but as a Line, because that Linear Realm had not Dimensions enough to represent the whole of you, but only a slice or section of you? In precisely the same way, your country of Two Dimensions is not spacious enough to represent me, a being of Three, but can only exhibit a slice or section of me, which is what you call a Circle.

The diminished brightness of your eye indicates incredulity. But now prepare to receive proof positive of the truth of my assertions. You cannot indeed see more than one of my sections, or Circles, at a time; for you have no power to raise your eye out of the plane of Flatland; but you can at least see that, as I rise in Space, so my sections become smaller. See now, I will rise; and the effect upon your eye will be that my Circle will become smaller and smaller till it dwindles to a point and finally vanishes.

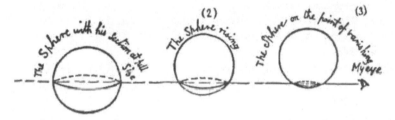

There was no "rising" that I could see; but he diminished and finally vanished. I winked once or twice to make sure that I was not dreaming. But it was no dream. For from the depths of nowhere came forth a hollow voice—close to my heart it seemed—"Am I quite gone? Are you convinced now? Well, now I will gradually return to Flatland and you shall see my section become larger and larger."

Every reader in Spaceland will easily understand that my mysterious Guest was speaking the language of truth and even of simplicity. But to me, proficient though I was in Flatland Mathematics, it was by no means a simple matter. The rough diagram given above will make it clear to any Spaceland child that the Sphere, ascending in the three positions indicated there, must needs have manifested himself to me, or to any Flatlander, as a Circle, at first of full size, then small, and at last very small indeed, approaching to a Point. But to me, although I saw the facts before me, the causes were as dark as ever. All that I could comprehend was, that the Circle had made himself smaller and vanished, and that he had now re-appeared and was rapidly making himself larger.

When he regained his original size, he heaved a deep sigh; for he perceived by my silence that I had altogether failed to comprehend him. And indeed I was now inclining to the belief that he must be no Circle at all, but some extremely clever juggler; or else that the old wives' tales were true, and that after all there were such people as Enchanters and Magicians.

After a long pause he muttered to himself, "One resource alone remains, if I am not to resort to action. I must try the method of Analogy." Then followed a still longer silence, after which he continued our dialogue.

Sphere. Tell me, Mr. Mathematician; if a Point moves Northward, and leaves a luminous wake, what name would you give to the wake?

I. A straight Line.

Sphere. And a straight Line has how many extremities?

I. Two.

Sphere. Now conceive the Northward straight Line moving parallel to itself, East and West, so that every point in it leaves behind it the wake of a straight Line. What name will you give to the Figure thereby formed? We will suppose that it moves through a distance equal to the original straight line. —What name, I say?

I. A square.

Sphere. And how many sides has a Square? How many angles?

I. Four sides and four angles.

Sphere. Now stretch your imagination a little, and conceive a Square in Flatland, moving parallel to itself upward.

I. What? Northward?

Sphere. No, not Northward; upward; out of Flatland altogether.

If it moved Northward, the Southern points in the Square would have to move through the positions previously occupied by the Northern points. But that is not my meaning.

I mean that every Point in you—for you are a Square and will serve the purpose of my illustration—every Point in you, that is to say in what you call your inside, is to pass upwards through Space in such a way that no Point shall pass through the position previously occupied by any other Point; but each Point shall describe a straight Line of its own. This is all in accordance with Analogy; surely it must be clear to you.

Restraining my impatience—for I was now under a strong temptation to rush blindly at my Visitor and to precipitate him into Space, or out of Flatland, anywhere, so that I could get rid of him—I replied:—

"And what may be the nature of the Figure which I am to shape out by this motion which you are pleased to denote by the word 'upward'? I presume it is describable in the language of Flatland."

Sphere. Oh, certainly. It is all plain and simple, and in strict accordance with Analogy—only, by the way, you must not speak of the result as being a Figure, but as a Solid. But I will describe it to you. Or rather not I, but Analogy.

We began with a single Point, which of course—being itself a Point—has only ONE terminal Point.

One Point produces a Line with TWO terminal Points.

One Line produces a Square with FOUR terminal Points.

Now you can give yourself the answer to your own question: 1, 2, 4, are evidently in Geometrical Progression. What is the next number?

I. Eight.

Sphere. Exactly. The one Square produces a SOMETHING-WHICH-YOU-DO-NOT-AS-YET-KNOW-A-NAME-FOR-BUT-WHICH-WE-CALL-A-CUBE with EIGHT terminal Points. Now are you convinced?

I. And has this Creature sides, as well as Angles or what you call "terminal Points"?

Sphere. Of course; and all according to Analogy. But, by the way, not what YOU call sides, but what WE call sides. You would call them SOLIDS.

I. And how many solids or sides will appertain to this Being whom I am to generate by the motion of my inside in an "upward" direction, and whom you call a Cube?

Sphere. How can you ask? And you a mathematician! The side of anything is always, if I may so say, one Dimension behind the thing. Consequently, as there is no Dimension behind a Point, a Point has 0 sides; a Line, if I may so say, has 2 sides (for the points of a Line may be called by courtesy, its sides); a Square has 4 sides; 0, 2, 4; what Progression do you call that?

I. Arithmetical.

Sphere. And what is the next number?

I. Six.

Sphere. Exactly. Then you see you have answered your own question. The Cube which you will generate will be bounded by six sides, that is to say, six of your insides. You see it all now, eh?

"Monster," I shrieked, "be thou juggler, enchanter, dream, or devil, no more will I endure thy mockeries. Either thou or I must perish." And saying these words I precipitated myself upon him.

Section 17: How the Sphere, Having in Vain Tried Words, Resorted to Deeds

It was in vain. I brought my hardest right angle into violent collision with the Stranger, pressing on him with a force sufficient to have destroyed any ordinary Circle: but I could feel him slowly and unarrestably slipping from my contact; not edging to the right nor to the left, but moving somehow out of the world, and vanishing into nothing. Soon there was a blank. But still I heard the Intruder's voice.

Sphere. Why will you refuse to listen to reason? I had hoped to find in you—as being a man of sense and an accomplished mathematician—a fit apostle for the Gospel of the Three Dimensions, which I am allowed to preach once only in a thousand years: but now I know not how to convince you. Stay, I have it. Deeds, and not words, shall proclaim the truth. Listen, my friend.

I have told you I can see from my position in Space the inside of all things that you consider closed. For example, I see in yonder cupboard near which you are standing, several of what you call boxes (but like everything else in Flatland, they have no tops or bottom) full of money; I see also two tablets of accounts. I am about to descend into that cupboard and to bring you one of those tablets. I saw you lock the cupboard half an hour ago, and I know you have the key in your possession. But I descend from Space; the doors, you see, remain unmoved. Now I am in the cupboard and am taking the tablet. Now I have it. Now I ascend with it.

I rushed to the closet and dashed the door open. One of the tablets was gone. With a mocking laugh, the Stranger appeared in the other corner of the room, and at the same time the tablet appeared upon the floor. I took it up. There could be no doubt—it was the missing tablet.

I groaned with horror, doubting whether I was not out of my sense; but the Stranger continued: "Surely you must now see that my explanation, and no other, suits the phenomena. What you call Solid things are really superficial; what you call Space is really nothing but a great Plane. I am in Space, and look down upon the insides of the things of which you only see the outsides. You could leave the Plane yourself, if you could but summon up the necessary volition. A slight upward or downward motion would enable you to see all that I can see.

"The higher I mount, and the further I go from your Plane, the more I can see, though of course I see it on a smaller scale. For example, I am ascending; now I can see your neighbour the Hexagon and his family in their several apartments; now I see the inside of the Theatre, ten doors off, from which the audience is only just departing; and on the other side a Circle in his study, sitting at his books. Now I shall come back to you. And, as a crowning proof, what do you say to my giving you a touch, just the least touch, in your stomach? It will not seriously injure you, and the slight pain you may suffer cannot be compared with the mental benefit you will receive."

Before I could utter a word of remonstrance, I felt a shooting pain in my inside, and a demoniacal laugh seemed to issue from within me. A moment afterwards the sharp agony had ceased, leaving nothing but a dull ache behind, and the Stranger began to reappear, saying, as he gradually increased in size, "There, I have not hurt you much, have I? If you are not convinced now, I don't know what will convince you. What say you?"

My resolution was taken. It seemed intolerable that I should endure existence subject to the arbitrary visitations of a Magician who could thus play tricks with one's very stomach. If only I could in any way manage to pin him against the wall till help came!

Once more I dashed my hardest angle against him, at the same time alarming the whole household by my cries for aid. I believe, at the moment of my onset, the Stranger had sunk below our Plane, and really found difficulty in rising. In any case he remained motionless, while I, hearing, as I thought, the sound of some help approaching, pressed against him with redoubled vigor, and continued to shout for assistance.

A convulsive shudder ran through the Sphere. "This must not be," I thought I heard him say: "either he must listen to reason, or I must have recourse to the last resource of civilization." Then, addressing me in a louder tone, he hurriedly exclaimed, "Listen: no stranger must witness what you have witnessed. Send your Wife back at once, before she enters the apartment. The Gospel of Three Dimensions must not be thus frustrated. Not thus must the fruits of one thousand years of waiting be thrown away. I hear her coming. Back! back! Away from me, or you must go with me—wither you know not—into the Land of Three Dimensions!"

"Fool! Madman! Irregular!" I exclaimed; "never will I release thee; thou shalt pay the penalty of thine impostures."

"Ha! Is it come to this?" thundered the Stranger: "then meet your fate: out of your Plane you go. Once, twice, thrice! 'Tis done!"

Section 18: How I Came to Spaceland, and What I Saw There

An unspeakable horror seized me. There was a darkness; then a dizzy, sickening sensation of sight that was not like seeing; I saw a Line that was no Line; Space that was not Space: I was myself, and not myself. When I could find voice, I shrieked loud in agony, "Either this is madness or it is Hell." "It is neither," calmly replied the voice of the Sphere, "it is Knowledge; it is Three Dimensions: open your eye once again and try to look steadily."

I looked, and, behold, a new world! There stood before me, visibly incorporate, all that I had before inferred, conjectured, dreamed, of perfect Circular beauty. What seemed the centre of the Stranger's form lay open to my view: yet I could see no heart, lungs, nor arteries, only a beautiful harmonious Something—for which I had no words; but you, my Readers in Spaceland, would call it the surface of the Sphere.

Prostrating myself mentally before my Guide, I cried, "How is it, O divine ideal of consummate loveliness and wisdom that I see thy inside, and yet cannot discern thy heart, thy lungs, thy arteries, thy liver?" "What you think you see, you see not," he replied; "it is not giving to you, nor to any other Being, to behold my internal parts. I am of a different order of Beings from those in Flatland. Were I a Circle, you could discern my intestines, but I am a Being, composed as I told you before, of many Circles, the Many in the One, called in this country a Sphere. And, just as the outside of a Cube is a Square, so the outside of a Sphere represents the appearance of a Circle."

Bewildered though I was by my Teacher's enigmatic utterance, I no longer chafed against it, but worshipped him in silent adoration. He continued, with more mildness in his voice. "Distress not yourself if you cannot at first understand the deeper mysteries of Spaceland. By degrees they will dawn upon you. Let us begin by casting back a glance at the region whence you came. Return with me a while to the plains of Flatland and I will show you that which you have often reasoned and thought about, but never seen with the sense of sight—a visible angle." "Impossible!" I cried; but, the Sphere leading the way, I followed as if in a dream, till once more his voice arrested me: "Look yonder, and behold your own Pentagonal house, and all its inmates."

I looked below, and saw with my physical eye all that domestic individuality which I had hitherto merely inferred with the understanding. And how poor and shadowy was the inferred conjecture in comparison with the reality which I now behold! My four Sons calmly asleep in the North-Western rooms, my two orphan Grandsons to the South; the Servants, the Butler, my Daughter, all in their several apartments. Only my affectionate Wife, alarmed by my continued absence, had quitted her room and was roving up and down in the Hall, anxiously awaiting my return. Also the Page, aroused by my cries, had left his room, and under pretext of ascertaining whether I had fallen somewhere in a faint, was prying into the cabinet in my study. All this I could now SEE, not merely infer; and as we came nearer and nearer, I could discern even the contents of my cabinet, and the two chests of gold, and the tablets of which the Sphere had made mention.

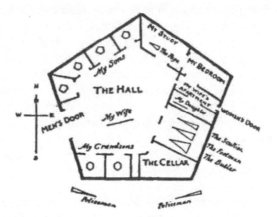

Touched by my Wife's distress, I would have sprung downward to reassure her, but I found myself incapable of motion. "Trouble not yourself about your Wife," said my Guide: "she will not be long left in anxiety; meantime, let us take a survey of Flatland."

Once more I felt myself rising through space. It was even as the Sphere had said. The further we receded from the object we beheld, the larger became the field of vision. My native city, with the interior of every house and every creature therein, lay open to my view in miniature. We mounted higher, and lo, the secrets of the earth, the depths of the mines and inmost caverns of the hills, were bared before me.

Awestruck at the sight of the mysteries of the earth, thus unveiled before my unworthy eye, I said to my Companion, "Behold, I am become as a God. For the wise men in our country say that to see all things, or as they express it, OMNIVIDENCE, is the attribute of God alone." There was something of scorn in the voice of my Teacher as he made answer: "it is so indeed? Then the very pick-pockets and cut-throats of my country are to be worshipped by your wise men as being Gods: for there is not one of them that does not see as much as you see now. But trust me, your wise men are wrong."

I. Then is omnividence the attribute of others besides Gods?

Sphere. I do not know. But, if a pick-pocket or a cut-throat of our country can see everything that is in your country, surely that is no reason why the pick-pocket or cut-throat should be accepted by you as a God. This omnividence, as you call it—it is not a common word in Spaceland—does it make you more just, more merciful, less selfish, more loving? Not in the least. Then how does it make you more divine?

I. "More merciful, more loving!" But these are the qualities of women! And we know that a Circle is a higher Being than a Straight Line, in so far as knowledge and wisdom are more to be esteemed than mere affection.

Sphere. It is not for me to classify human faculties according to merit. Yet many of the best and wisest in Spaceland think more of the affections than of the understand, more of your despised Straight Lines than of your belauded Circles. But enough of this. Look yonder. Do you know that building?

I looked, and afar off I saw an immense Polygonal structure, in which I recognized the General Assembly Hall of the States of Flatland, surrounded by dense lines of Pentagonal buildings at right angles to each other, which I knew to be streets; and I perceived that I was approaching the great Metropolis.

"Here we descend," said my Guide. It was now morning, the first hour of the first day of the two thousandth year of our era. Acting, as was their wont, in strict accordance with precedent, the highest Circles of the realm were meeting in solemn conclave, as they had met on the first hour of the first day of the year 1000, and also on the first hour of the first day of the year 0.

The minutes of the previous meetings were now read by one whom I at once recognized as my brother, a perfectly Symmetrical Square, and the Chief Clerk of the High Council. It was found recorded on each occasion that: "Whereas the States had been troubled by divers ill-intentioned persons pretending to have received revelations from another World, and professing to produce demonstrations whereby they had instigated to frenzy both themselves and others, it had been for this cause unanimously resolved by the Grand Council that on the first day of each millenary, special injunctions be sent to the Prefects in the several districts of Flatland, to make strict search for such misguided persons, and without formality of mathematical examination, to destroy all such as were Isosceles of any degree, to scourge and imprison any regular Triangle, to cause any Square or Pentagon to be sent to the district Asylum, and to arrest any one of higher rank, sending him straightway to the Capital to be examined and judged by the Council."

"You hear your fate," said the Sphere to me, while the Council was passing for the third time the formal resolution. "Death or imprisonment awaits the Apostle of the Gospel of Three Dimensions." "Not so," replied I, "the matter is now so clear to me, the nature of real space so palpable, that methinks I could make a child understand it. Permit me but to descend at this moment and enlighten them." "Not yet," said my Guide, "the time will come for that. Meantime I must perform my mission. Stay thou there in thy place." Saying these words, he leaped with great dexterity into the sea (if I may so call it) of Flatland, right in the midst of the ring of Counsellors. "I come," said he, "to proclaim that there is a land of Three Dimensions."

I could see many of the younger Counsellors start back in manifest horror, as the Sphere's circular section widened before them. But on a sign from the presiding Circle—who showed not the slightest alarm or surprise—six Isosceles of a low type from six different quarters rushed upon the Sphere. "We have him," they cried; "No; yes; we have him still! he's going! he's gone!"

"My Lords," said the President to the Junior Circles of the Council, "there is not the slightest need for surprise; the secret archives, to which I alone have access, tell me that a similar occurrence happened on the last two millennial commencements. You will, of course, say nothing of these trifles outside the Cabinet."

Raising his voice, he now summoned the guards. "Arrest the policemen; gag them. You know your duty." After he had consigned to their fate the wretched policemen—ill-fated and unwilling witnesses of a State-secret which they were not to be permitted to reveal—he again addressed the Counselors. "My Lords, the business of the Council being concluded, I have only to wish you a happy New Year." Before departing, he expressed, at some length, to the Clerk, my excellent but most unfortunate brother, his sincere regret that, in accordance with precedent and for the sake of secrecy, he must condemn him to perpetual imprisonment, but added his satisfaction that, unless some mention were made by him of that day's incident, his life would be spared.

Section 19: How, Though the Sphere Showed Me Other Mysteries of Spaceland, I Still Desire More; and What Came of It

When I saw my poor brother led away to imprisonment, I attempted to leap down into the Council Chamber, desiring to intercede on his behalf, or at least bid him farewell. But I found that I had no motion of my own. I absolutely depended on the volition of my Guide, who said in gloomy tones, "Heed not thy brother; haply thou shalt have ample time hereafter to condole with him. Follow me."

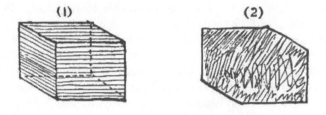

Once more we ascended into space. "Hitherto," said the Sphere, "I have shown you naught save Plane Figures and their interiors. Now I must introduce you to Solids, and reveal to you the plan upon which they are constructed. Behold this multitude of moveable square cards. See, I put one on another, not, as you supposed, Northward of the other, but ON the other. Now a second, now a third. See, I am building up a Solid by a multitude of Squares parallel to one another. Now the Solid is complete, being as high as it is long and broad, and we call it a Cube."

"Pardon me, my Lord," replied I; "but to my eye the appearance is as of an Irregular Figure whose inside is laid open to view; in other words, methinks I see no Solid, but a Plane such as we infer in Flatland; only of an Irregularity which betokens some monstrous criminal, so that the very sight of it is painful to my eyes."

"True," said the Sphere; "it appears to you a Plane, because you are not accustomed to light and shade and perspective; just as in Flatland a Hexagon would appear a Straight Line to one who has not the Art of Sight Recognition. But in reality it is a Solid, as you shall learn by the sense of Feeling."

He then introduced me to the Cube, and I found that this marvellous Being was indeed no Plane, but a Solid; and that he was endowed with six plane sides and eight terminal points called solid angles; and I remembered the saying of the Sphere that just such a Creature as this would be formed by the Square moving, in Space, parallel to himself: and I rejoiced to think that so insignificant a Creature as I could in some sense be called the Progenitor of so illustrious an offspring.

But still I could not fully understand the meaning of what my Teacher had told me concerning "light" and "shade" and "perspective"; and I did not hesitate to put my difficulties before him.

Were I to give the Sphere's explanation of these matters, succinct and clear though it was, it would be tedious to an inhabitant of Space, who knows these things already. Suffice it, that by his lucid statements, and by changing the position of objects and lights, and by allowing me to feel the several objects and even his own sacred Person, he at last made all things clear to me, so that I could now readily distinguish between a Circle and a Sphere, a Plane Figure and a Solid.

This was the Climax, the Paradise, of my strange eventful History. Henceforth I have to relate the story of my miserable Fall:—most miserable, yet surely most undeserved! For why should the thirst for knowledge be aroused, only to be disappointed and punished? My volition shrinks from the painful task of recalling my humiliation; yet, like a second Prometheus, I will endure this and worse, if by any means I may arouse in the interiors of Plane and Solid Humanity a spirit of rebellion against the Conceit which would limit our Dimensions to Two or Three or any number short of Infinity. Away then with all personal considerations! Let me continue to the end, as I began, without further digressions or anticipations, pursuing the plain path of dispassionate History. The exact facts, the exact words,—and they are burnt in upon my brain,—shall be set down without alteration of an iota; and let my Readers judge between me and Destiny.

The Sphere would willingly have continued his lessons by indoctrinating me in the conformation of all regular Solids, Cylinders, Cones, Pyramids, Pentahedrons, Hexahedrons, Dodecahedrons, and Spheres: but I ventured to interrupt him. Not that I was wearied of knowledge. On the contrary, I thirsted for yet deeper and fuller draughts than he was offering to me.

"Pardon me," said I, "O Thou Whom I must no longer address as the Perfection of all Beauty; but let me beg thee to vouchsafe thy servant a sight of thine interior."

Sphere. My what?

I. Thine interior: thy stomach, thy intestines.

Sphere. Whence this ill-timed impertinent request? And what mean you by saying that I am no longer the Perfection of all Beauty?

I. My Lord, your own wisdom has taught me to aspire to One even more great, more beautiful, and more closely approximate to Perfection than yourself. As you yourself, superior to all Flatland forms, combine many Circles in One, so doubtless there is One above you who combines many Spheres in One Supreme Existence, surpassing even the Solids of Spaceland. And even as we, who are now in Space, look down on Flatland and see the insides of all things, so of a certainty there is yet above us some higher, purer region, whither thou dost surely purpose to lead me—O Thou Whom I shall always call, everywhere and in all Dimensions, my Priest, Philosopher, and Friend— some yet more spacious Space, some more dimensionable Dimensionality, from the vantage-ground of which we shall look down together upon the revealed insides of Solid things, and where thine own intestines, and those of thy kindred Spheres, will lie exposed to the view of the poor wandering exile from Flatland, to whom so much has already been vouchsafed.

Sphere. Pooh! Stuff! Enough of this trifling! The time is short, and much remains to be done before you are fit to proclaim the Gospel of Three Dimensions to your blind benighted countrymen in Flatland.

I. Nay, gracious Teacher, deny me not what I know it is in thy power to reform. Grant me but one glimpse of thine interior, and I am satisfied for ever, remaining henceforth thy docile pupil, thy unemancipable slave, ready to receive all thy teachings and to feed upon the words that fall from thy lips.

Sphere. Well, then, to content and silence you, let me say at once, I would show you what you wish if I could; but I cannot. Would you have me turn my stomach inside out to oblige you?

I. But my Lord has shown me the intestines of all my countrymen in the Land of Two Dimensions by taking me with him into the Land of Three. What therefore more easy than now to take his servant on a second journey into the blessed region of the Fourth Dimension, where I shall look down with him once more upon this land of Three Dimensions, and see the inside of every three-dimensioned house, the secrets of the solid earth, the treasures of the mines of Spaceland, and the intestines of every solid living creature, even the noble and adorable Spheres.

Sphere. But where is this land of Four Dimensions?

I. I know not: but doubtless my Teacher knows.

Sphere. Not I. There is no such land. The very idea of it is utterly inconceivable.

I. Not inconceivable, my Lord, to me, and therefore still less inconceivable to my Master. Nay, I despair not that, even here, in this region of Three Dimensions, your Lordship's art may make the Fourth Dimension visible to me; just as in the Land of Two Dimensions my Teacher's skill would fain have opened the eyes of his blind servant to the invisible presence of a Third Dimension, though I saw it not.

Let me recall the past. Was I not taught below that when I saw a Line and inferred a Plane, I in reality saw a Third unrecognized Dimension, not the same as brightness, called "height"? And does it not now follow that, in this region, when I see a Plane and infer a Solid, I really see a Fourth unrecognized Dimension, not the same as colour, but existent, though infinitesimal and incapable of measurement?

And besides this, there is the Argument from Analogy of Figures.

Sphere. Analogy! Nonsense: what analogy?

I. Your Lordship tempts his servant to see whether he remembers the revelations imparted to him. Trifle not with me, my Lord; I crave, I thirst, for more knowledge. Doubtless we cannot SEE that other higher Spaceland now, because we have no eye in our stomachs. But, just as there WAS the realm of Flatland, though that poor puny Lineland Monarch could neither turn to left nor right to discern it, and just as there WAS close at hand, and touching my frame, the land of Three Dimensions, though I, blind senseless wretch, had no power to touch it, no eye in my interior to discern it, so of a surety there is a Fourth Dimension, which my Lord perceives with the inner eye of thought. And that it must exist my Lord himself has taught me. Or can he have forgotten what he himself imparted to his servant?

In One Dimension, did not a moving Point produce a Line with TWO terminal points?

In Two Dimensions, did not a moving Line produce a Square with FOUR terminal points?

In Three Dimensions, did not a moving Square produce—did not this eye of mine behold it—that blessed Being, a Cube, with EIGHT terminal points?

And in Four Dimensions shall not a moving Cube—alas, for Analogy, and alas for the Progress of Truth, if it be not so—shall not, I say, the motion of a divine Cube result in a still more divine Organization with SIXTEEN terminal points?

Behold the infallible confirmation of the Series, 2, 4, 8, 16: is not this a Geometrical Progression? Is not this—if I might quote my Lord's own words—"strictly according to Analogy"?

Again, was I not taught by my Lord that as in a Line there are TWO bounding Points, and in a Square there are FOUR bounding Lines, so in a Cube there must be SIX bounding Squares? Behold once more the confirming Series, 2, 4, 6: is not this an Arithmetical Progression? And consequently does it not of necessity follow that the more divine offspring of the divine Cube in the Land of Four Dimensions, must have 8 bounding Cubes: and is not this also, as my Lord has taught me to believe, "strictly according to Analogy"? O, my Lord, my Lord, behold, I cast myself in faith upon conjecture, not knowing the facts; and I appeal to your Lordship to confirm or deny my logical anticipations. If I am wrong, I yield, and will no longer demand a Fourth Dimension; but, if I am right, my Lord will listen to reason.

I ask therefore, is it, or is it not, the fact, that ere now your countrymen also have witnessed the descent of Beings of a higher order than their own, entering closed rooms, even as your Lordship entered mine, without the opening of doors or windows, and appearing and vanishing at will? On the reply to this question I am ready to stake everything. Deny it, and I am henceforth silent. Only vouchsafe an answer.

Sphere (AFTER A PAUSE). It is reported so. But men are divided in opinion as to the facts. And even granting the facts, they explain them in different ways. And in any case, however great may be the number of different explanations, no one has adopted or suggested the theory of a Fourth Dimension. Therefore, pray have done with this trifling, and let us return to business.

I. I was certain of it. I was certain that my anticipations would be fulfilled. And now have patience with me and answer me yet one more question, best of Teachers! Those who have thus appeared—no one knows whence—and have returned—no one knows whither—have they also contracted their sections and vanished somehow into that more Spacious Space, whither I now entreat you to conduct me?

Sphere (MOODILY). They have vanished, certainly—if they ever appeared. But most people say that these visions arose from the thought—you will not understand me—from the brain; from the perturbed angularity of the Seer.

I. Say they so? Oh, believe them not. Or if it indeed be so, that this other Space is really Thoughtland, then take me to that blessed Region where I in Thought shall see the insides of all solid things. There, before my ravished eye, a Cube moving in some altogether new direction, but strictly according to Analogy, so as to make every particle of his interior pass through a new kind of Space, with a wake of its own—shall create a still more perfect perfection than himself, with sixteen terminal Extra-solid angles, and Eight solid Cubes for his Perimeter. And once there, shall we stay our upward course? In that blessed region of Four Dimensions, shall we linger at the threshold of the Fifth, and not enter therein? Ah, no! Let us rather resolve that our ambition shall soar with our corporal ascent. Then, yielding to our intellectual onset, the gates of the Six Dimension shall fly open; after that a Seventh, and then an Eighth—

How long I should have continued I know not. In vain did the Sphere, in his voice of thunder, reiterate his command of silence, and threaten me with the direst penalties if I persisted. Nothing could stem the flood of my ecstatic aspirations. Perhaps I was to blame; but indeed I was intoxicated with the recent draughts of Truth to which he himself had introduced me. However, the end was not long in coming. My words were cut short by a crash outside, and a simultaneous crash inside me, which impelled me through space with a velocity that precluded speech. Down! down! down! I was rapidly descending; and I knew that return to Flatland was my doom. One glimpse, one last and never-to-be-forgotten glimpse I had of that dull level wilderness—which was now to become my Universe again—spread out before my eye. Then a darkness. Then a final, all-consummating thunder-peal; and, when I came to myself, I was once more a common creeping Square, in my Study at home, listening to the Peace-Cry of my approaching Wife.

Section 20: How the Sphere Encouraged Me in a Vision

Although I had less than a minute for reflection, I felt, by a kind of instinct, that I must conceal my experiences from my Wife. Not that I apprehended, at the moment, any danger from her divulging my secret, but I knew that to any Woman in Flatland the narrative of my adventures must needs be unintelligible. So I endeavoured to reassure her by some story, invented for the occasion, that I had accidentally fallen through the trap-door of the cellar, and had there lain stunned.

The Southward attraction in our country is so slight that even to a Woman my tale necessarily appeared extraordinary and well-nigh incredible; but my Wife, whose good sense far exceeds that of the average of her Sex, and who perceived that I was unusually excited, did not argue with me on the subject, but insisted that I was ill and required repose. I was glad of an excuse for retiring to my chamber to think quietly over what had happened. When I was at last by myself, a drowsy sensation fell on me; but before my eyes closed I endeavoured to reproduce the Third Dimension, and especially the process by which a Cube is constructed through the motion of a Square. It was not so clear as I could have wished; but I remembered that it must be "Upward, and yet not Northward," and I determined steadfastly to retain these words as the clue which, if firmly grasped, could not fail to guide me to the solution. So mechanically repeating, like a charm, the words, "Upward, yet not Northward," I fell into a sound refreshing sleep.

During my slumber I had a dream. I thought I was once more by the side of the Sphere, whose lustrous hue betokened that he had exchanged his wrath against me for perfectly placability. We were moving together towards a bright but infinitesimally small Point, to which my Master directed my attention. As we approached, methought there issued from it a slight humming noise as from one of your Spaceland bluebottles, only less resonant by far, so slight indeed that even in the perfect stillness of the Vacuum through which we soared, the sound reached not our ears till we checked our flight at a distance from it of something under twenty human diagonals.

"Look yonder," said my Guide, "in Flatland thou hast lived; of Lineland thou hast received a vision; thou hast soared with me to the heights of Spaceland; now, in order to complete the range of thy experience, I conduct thee downward to the lowest depth of existence, even to the realm of Pointland, the Abyss of No dimensions.

"Behold yon miserable creature. That Point is a Being like ourselves, but confined to the non-dimensional Gulf. He is himself his own World, his own Universe; of any other than himself he can form no conception; he knows not Length, nor Breadth, nor Height, for he has had no experience of them; he has no cognizance even of the number Two; nor has he a thought of Plurality; for he is himself his One and All, being really Nothing. Yet mark his perfect self-contentment, and hence learn his lesson, that to be self-contented is to be vile and ignorant, and that to aspire is better than to be blindly and impotently happy. Now listen."

He ceased; and there arose from the little buzzing creature a tiny, low, monotonous, but distinct tinkling, as from one of your Spaceland phonographs, from which I caught these words, "Infinite beatitude of existence! It is; and there is nothing else beside It."

"What," said I, "does the puny creature mean by 'it'?" "He means himself," said the Sphere: "have you not noticed before now, that babies and babyish people who cannot distinguish themselves from the world, speak of themselves in the Third Person? But hush!"

"It fills all Space," continued the little soliloquizing Creature, "and what It fills, It is. What It thinks, that It utters; and what It utters, that It hears; and It itself is Thinker, Utterer, Hearer, Thought, Word, Audition; it is the One, and yet the All in All. Ah, the happiness, ah, the happiness of Being!"

"Can you not startle the little thing out of its complacency?" said I. "Tell it what it really is, as you told me; reveal to it the narrow limitations of Pointland, and lead it up to something higher." "That is no easy task," said my Master; "try you."

Hereon, raising by voice to the uttermost, I addressed the Point as follows: "Silence, silence, contemptible Creature. You call yourself the All in All, but you are the Nothing: your so-called Universe is a mere speck in a Line, and a Line is a mere shadow as compared with—" "Hush, hush, you have said enough," interrupted the Sphere, "now listen, and mark the effect of your harangue on the King of Pointland."

The lustre of the Monarch, who beamed more brightly than ever upon hearing my words, showed clearly that he retained his complacency; and I had hardly ceased when he took up his strain again. "Ah, the joy, ah, the joy of Thought! What can It not achieve by thinking! Its own Thought coming to Itself, suggestive of its disparagement, thereby to enhance Its happiness! Sweet rebellion stirred up to result in triumph! Ah, the divine creative power of the All in One! Ah, the joy, the joy of Being!"

"You see," said my Teacher, "how little your words have done. So far as the Monarch understand them at all, he accepts them as his own—for he cannot conceive of any other except himself—and plumes himself upon the variety of 'Its Thought' as an instance of creative Power. Let us leave this God of Pointland to the ignorant fruition of his omnipresence and omniscience: nothing that you or I can do can rescue him from his self-satisfaction."

After this, as we floated gently back to Flatland, I could hear the mild voice of my Companion pointing the moral of my vision, and stimulating me to aspire, and to teach others to aspire. He had been angered at first—he confessed—by my ambition to soar to Dimensions above the Third; but, since then, he had received fresh insight, and he was not too proud to acknowledge his error to a Pupil. Then he proceeded to initiate me into mysteries yet higher than those I had witnessed, showing me how to construct Extra-Solids by the motion of Solids, and Double Extra-Solids by the motion of Extra-Solids, and all "strictly according to Analogy," all by methods so simple, so easy, as to be patent even to the Female Sex.

Section 21: How I Tried to Teach the Theory of Three Dimension to my Grandson, and with what Success

I awoke rejoicing, and began to reflect on the glorious career before me. I would go forth, methought, at once, and evangelize the whole of Flatland. Even to Women and Soldiers should the Gospel of Three Dimensions be proclaimed. I would begin with my Wife.

Just as I had decided on the plan of my operations, I heard the sound of many voices in the street commanding silence. Then followed a louder voice. It was a herald's proclamation. Listening attentively, I recognized the words of the Resolution of the Council, enjoining the arrest, imprisonment, or execution of any one who should pervert the minds of people by delusions, and by professing to have received revelations from another World.

I reflected. This danger was not to be trifled with. It would be better to avoid it by omitting all mention of my Revelation, and by proceeding on the path of Demonstration—which after all, seemed so simple and so conclusive that nothing would be lost by discarding the former means. "Upward, not Northward"—was the clue to the whole proof. It had seemed to me fairly clear before I fell asleep; and when I first awoke, fresh from my dream, it had appeared as patent as Arithmetic; but somehow it did not seem to me quite so obvious now. Though my Wife entered the room opportunely at just that moment, I decided, after we had exchanged a few words of commonplace conversation, not to begin with her.

My Pentagonal Sons were men of character and standing, and physicians of no mean reputation, but not great in mathematics, and, in that respect, unfit for my purpose. But it occurred to me that a young and docile Hexagon, with a mathematical turn, would be a most suitable pupil. Why therefore not make my first experiment with my little precocious Grandson, whose casual remarks on the meaning of three-to-the-third had met with the approval of the Sphere? Discussing the matter with him, a mere boy, I should be in perfect safety; for he would know nothing of the Proclamation of the Council; whereas I could not feel sure that my Sons—so greatly did their patriotism and reverence for the Circles predominate over mere blind affection—might not feel compelled to hand me over to the Prefect, if they found me seriously maintaining the seditious heresy of the Third Dimension.

But the first thing to be done was to satisfy in some way the curiosity of my Wife, who naturally wished to know something of the reasons for which the Circle had desired that mysterious interview, and of the means by which he had entered the house. Without entering into the details of the elaborate account I gave her,—an account, I fear, not quite so consistent with truth as my Readers in Spaceland might desire,—I must be content with saying that I succeeded at last in persuading her to return quietly to her household duties without eliciting from me any reference to the World of Three Dimensions. This done, I immediately sent for my Grandson; for, to confess the truth, I felt that all that I had seen and heard was in some strange way slipping away from me, like the image of a half-grasped, tantalizing dream, and I longed to essay my skill in making a first disciple.

When my Grandson entered the room I carefully secured the door. Then, sitting down by his side and taking our mathematical tablets,—or, as you would call them, Lines—I told him we would resume the lesson of yesterday. I taught him once more how a Point by motion in One Dimension produces a Line, and how a straight Line in Two Dimensions produces a Square. After this, forcing a laugh, I said, "And now, you scamp, you wanted to make believe that a Square may in the same way by motion 'Upward, not Northward' produce another figure, a sort of extra square in Three Dimensions. Say that again, you young rascal."

At this moment we heard once more the herald's "O yes! O yes!" outside in the street proclaiming the Resolution of the Council. Young though he was, my Grandson—who was unusually intelligent for his age, and bred up in perfect reverence for the authority of the Circles—took in the situation with an acuteness for which I was quite unprepared. He remained silent till the last words of the Proclamation had died away, and then, bursting into tears, "Dear Grandpapa," he said, "that was only my fun, and of course I meant nothing at all by it; and we did not know anything then about the new Law; and I don't think I said anything about the Third Dimension; and I am sure I did not say one word about 'Upward, not Northward,' for that would be such nonsense, you know. How could a thing move Upward, and not Northward? Upward and not Northward! Even if I were a baby, I could not be so absurd as that. How silly it is! Ha! ha! ha!"

"Not at all silly," said I, losing my temper; "here for example, I take this Square," and, at the word, I grasped a moveable Square, which was lying at hand—"and I move it, you see, not Northward but—yes, I move it Upward—that is to say, Northward but I move it somewhere—not exactly like this, but somehow—" Here I brought my sentence to an inane conclusion, shaking the Square about in a purposeless manner, much to the amusement of my Grandson, who burst out laughing louder than ever, and declared that I was not teaching him, but joking with him; and so saying he unlocked the door and ran out of the room. Thus ended my first attempt to convert a pupil to the Gospel of Three Dimensions.

Section 22: How I Then Tried to Diffuse the Theory of Three Dimensions by Other Means, and of the Result

My failure with my Grandson did not encourage me to communicate my secret to others of my household; yet neither was I led by it to despair of success. Only I saw that I must not wholly rely on the catch-phrase, "Upward, not Northward," but must rather endeavour to seek a demonstration by setting before the public a clear view of the whole subject; and for this purpose it seemed necessary to resort to writing.

So I devoted several months in privacy to the composition of a treatise on the mysteries of Three Dimensions. Only, with the view of evading the Law, if possible, I spoke not of a physical Dimension, but of a Thoughtland whence, in theory, a Figure could look down upon Flatland and see simultaneously the insides of all things, and where it was possible that there might be supposed to exist a Figure environed, as it were, with six Squares, and containing eight terminal Points. But in writing this book I found myself sadly hampered by the impossibility of drawing such diagrams as were necessary for my purpose: for of course, in our country of Flatland, there are no tablets but Lines, and no diagrams but Lines, all in one straight Line and only distinguishable by difference of size and brightness; so that, when I had finished my treatise (which I entitled, "Through Flatland to Thoughtland") I could not feel certain that many would understand my meaning.

Meanwhile my wife was under a cloud. All pleasures palled upon me; all sights tantalized and tempted me to outspoken treason, because I could not compare what I saw in Two Dimensions with what it really was if seen in Three, and could hardly refrain from making my comparisons aloud. I neglected my clients and my own business to give myself to the contemplation of the mysteries which I had once beheld, yet which I could impart to no one, and found daily more difficult to reproduce even before my own mental vision. One day, about eleven months after my return from Spaceland, I tried to see a Cube with my eye closed, but failed; and though I succeeded afterwards, I was not then quite certain (nor have I been ever afterwards) that I had exactly realized the original. This made me more melancholy than before, and determined me to take some step; yet what, I knew not. I felt that I would have been willing to sacrifice my life for the Cause, if thereby I could have produced conviction. But if I could not convince my Grandson, how could I convince the highest and most developed Circles in the land?

And yet at times my spirit was too strong for me, and I gave vent to dangerous utterances. Already I was considered heterodox if not treasonable, and I was keenly alive to the danger of my position; nevertheless I could not at times refrain from bursting out into suspicious or half-seditious utterances, even among the highest Polygonal or Circular society. When, for example, the question arose about the treatment of those lunatics who said that they had received the power of seeing the insides of things, I would quote the saying of an ancient Circle, who declared that prophets and inspired people are always considered by the majority to be mad; and I could not help occasionally dropping such expressions as "the eye that discerns the interiors of things," and "the all-seeing land"; once or twice I even let fall the forbidden terms "the Third and Fourth Dimensions." At last, to complete a series of minor indiscretions, at a meeting of our Local Speculative Society held at the palace of the Prefect himself,—some extremely silly person having read an elaborate paper exhibiting the precise reasons why Providence has limited the number of Dimensions to Two, and why the attribute of omnividence is assigned to the Supreme alone—I so far forgot myself as to give an exact account of the whole of my voyage with the Sphere into Space, and to the Assembly Hall in our Metropolis, and then to Space again, and of my return home, and of everything that I had seen and heard in fact or vision. At first, indeed, I pretended that I was describing the imaginary experiences of a fictitious person; but my enthusiasm soon forced me to throw off all disguise, and finally, in a fervent peroration, I exhorted all my hearers to divest themselves of prejudice and to become believers in the Third Dimension.

Need I say that I was at once arrested and taken before the Council?

Next morning, standing in the very place where but a very few months ago the Sphere had stood in my company, I was allowed to begin and to continue my narration unquestioned and uninterrupted. But from the first I foresaw my fate; for the President, noting that a guard of the better sort of Policemen was in attendance, of angularity little, if at all, under 55 degrees, ordered them to be relieved before I began my defence, by an inferior class of 2 or 3 degrees. I knew only too well what that meant. I was to be executed or imprisoned, and my story was to be kept secret from the world by the simultaneous destruction of the officials who had heard it; and, this being the case, the President desired to substitute the cheaper for the more expensive victims.

After I had concluded my defence, the President, perhaps perceiving that some of the junior Circles had been moved by evident earnestness, asked me two questions:—

1. Whether I could indicate the direction which I meant when I used the words "Upward, not Northward"?
2. Whether I could by any diagrams or descriptions (other than the enumeration of imaginary sides and angles) indicate the Figure I was pleased to call a Cube?

I declared that I could say nothing more, and that I must commit myself to the Truth, whose cause would surely prevail in the end.

The President replied that he quite concurred in my sentiment, and that I could not do better. I must be sentenced to perpetual imprisonment; but if the Truth intended that I should emerge from prison and evangelize the world, the Truth might be trusted to bring that result to pass. Meanwhile I should be subjected to no discomfort that was not necessary to preclude escape, and, unless I forfeited the privilege by misconduct, I should be occasionally permitted to see my brother who had preceded me to my prison.

Seven years have elapsed and I am still a prisoner, and—if I except the occasional visits of my brother—debarred from all companionship save that of my jailers. My brother is one of the best of Squares, just sensible, cheerful, and not without fraternal affection; yet I confess that my weekly interviews, at least in one respect, cause me the bitterest pain. He was present when the Sphere manifested himself in the Council Chamber; he saw the Sphere's changing sections; he heard the explanation of the phenomena then give to the Circles. Since that time, scarcely a week has passed during seven whole years, without his hearing from me a repetition of the part I played in that manifestation, together with ample descriptions of all the phenomena in Spaceland, and the arguments for the existence of Solid things derivable from Analogy. Yet—I take shame to be forced to confess it—my brother has not yet grasped the nature of Three Dimensions, and frankly avows his disbelief in the existence of a Sphere.

Hence I am absolutely destitute of converts, and, for aught that I can see, the millennial Revelation has been made to me for nothing. Prometheus up in Spaceland was bound for bringing down fire for mortals, but I—poor Flatland Prometheus—lie here in prison for bringing down nothing to my countrymen. Yet I existing the hope that these memoirs, in some manner, I know not how, may find their way to the minds of humanity in Some Dimension, and may stir up a race of rebels who shall refuse to be confined to limited Dimensionality.

That is the hope of my brighter moments. Alas, it is not always so. Heavily weights on me at times the burdensome reflection that I cannot honestly say I am confident as to the exact shape of the once-seen, oft-regretted Cube; and in my nightly visions the mysterious precept, "Upward, not Northward," haunts me like a soul-devouring Sphinx. It is part of the martyrdom which I endure for the cause of Truth that there are seasons of mental weakness, when Cubes and Spheres flit away into the background of scarce-possible existences; when the Land of Three Dimensions seems almost as visionary as the Land of One or None; nay, when even this hard wall that bars me from my freedom, these very tablets on which I am writing, and all the substantial realities of Flatland itself, appear no better than the offspring of a diseased imagination, or the baseless fabric of a dream.

A CONNECTICUT YANKEE IN KING ARTHUR'S COURT

Mark Twain (1889)

THE BOSS

To be vested with enormous authority is a fine thing; but to have the on-looking world consent to it is a finer. The tower episode solidified my power, and made it impregnable. If any were perchance disposed to be jealous and critical before that, they experienced a change of heart, now. There was not any one in the kingdom who would have considered it good judgment to meddle with my matters.

I was fast getting adjusted to my situation and circumstances. For a time, I used to wake up, mornings, and smile at my "dream," and listen for the Colt's factory whistle; but that sort of thing played itself out, gradually, and at last I was fully able to realize that I was actually living in the sixth century, and in Arthur's court, not a lunatic asylum. After that, I was just as much at home in that century as I could have been in any other; and as for preference, I wouldn't have traded it for the twentieth. Look at the opportunities here for a man of knowledge, brains, pluck, and enterprise to sail in and grow up with the country. The grandest field that ever was; and all my own; not a competitor; not a man who wasn't a baby to me in acquirements and capacities; whereas, what would I amount to in the twentieth century? I should be foreman of a factory, that is about all; and could drag a seine down street any day and catch a hundred better men than myself.

What a jump I had made! I couldn't keep from thinking about it, and contemplating it, just as one does who has struck oil. There was nothing back of me that could approach it, unless it might be Joseph's case; and Joseph's only approached it, it didn't equal it, quite. For it stands to reason that as Joseph's splendid financial ingenuities advantaged nobody but the king, the general public must have regarded him with a good deal of disfavor, whereas I had done my entire public a kindness in sparing the sun, and was popular by reason of it.

I was no shadow of a king; I was the substance; the king himself was the shadow. My power was colossal; and it was not a mere name, as such things have generally been, it was the genuine article. I stood here, at the very spring and source of the second great period of the world's history; and could see the trickling stream of that history gather and deepen and broaden, and roll its mighty tides down the far centuries; and I could note the upspringing of adventurers like myself in the shelter of its long array of thrones: De Montforts, Gavestons, Mortimers, Villierses; the war-making, campaign-directing wantons of France, and Charles the Second's scepter-wielding drabs; but nowhere in the procession was my full-sized fellow visible. I was a Unique; and glad to know that that fact could not be dislodged or challenged for thirteen centuries and a half, for sure. Yes, in power I was equal to the king. At the same time there was another power that was a trifle stronger than both of us put together. That was the Church. I do not wish to disguise that fact. I couldn't, if I wanted to. But never mind about that, now; it will show up, in its proper place, later on. It didn't cause me any trouble in the beginning—at least any of consequence.

Well, it was a curious country, and full of interest. And the people! They were the quaintest and simplest and trustingest race; why, they were nothing but rabbits. It was pitiful for a person born in a wholesome free atmosphere to listen to their humble and hearty outpourings of loyalty toward their king and Church and nobility; as if they had any more occasion to love and honor king and Church and noble than a slave has to love and honor the lash, or a dog has to love and honor the stranger that kicks him! Why, dear me, *any* kind of royalty, howsoever modified, *any* kind of aristocracy, howsoever pruned, is rightly an insult; but if you are born and brought up under that sort of arrangement you probably never find it out for yourself, and don't believe it when somebody else tells you. It is enough to make a body ashamed of his race to think of the sort of froth that has always occupied its thrones without shadow of right or reason, and the seventh-rate people that have always figured as its aristocracies—a company of monarchs and nobles who, as a rule, would have achieved only poverty and obscurity if left, like their betters, to their own exertions.

The most of King Arthur's British nation were slaves, pure and simple, and bore that name, and wore the iron collar on their necks; and the rest were slaves in fact, but without the name; they imagined themselves men and freemen, and called themselves so. The truth was, the nation as a body was in the world for one object, and one only: to grovel before king and Church and noble; to slave for them, sweat blood for them, starve that they might be fed, work that they might play, drink misery to the dregs that they might be happy, go naked that they might wear silks and jewels, pay taxes that they might be spared from paying them, be familiar all their lives with the degrading language and postures of adulation that they might walk in pride and think themselves the gods of this world. And for all this, the thanks they got were cuffs and contempt; and so poor-spirited were they that they took even this sort of attention as an honor.

Inherited ideas are a curious thing, and interesting to observe and examine. I had mine, the king and his people had theirs. In both cases they flowed in ruts worn deep by time and habit, and the man who should have proposed to divert them by reason and argument would have had a long contract on his hands. For instance, those people had inherited the idea that all men without title and a long pedigree, whether they had great natural gifts and acquirements or hadn't, were creatures of no more consideration than so many animals, bugs, insects; whereas I had inherited the idea that human daws who can consent to masquerade in the peacock-shams of inherited dignities and unearned titles, are of no good but to be laughed at. The way I was looked upon was odd, but it was natural. You know how the keeper and the public regard the elephant in the menagerie: well, that is the idea. They are full of admiration of his vast bulk and his prodigious strength; they speak with pride of the fact that he can do a hundred marvels which are far and away beyond their own powers; and they speak with the same pride of the fact that in his wrath he is able to drive a thousand men before him. But does that make him one of *them*? No; the raggedest tramp in the pit would smile at the idea. He couldn't comprehend it; couldn't take it in; couldn't in any remote way conceive of it. Well, to the king, the nobles, and all the nation, down to the very slaves and tramps, I was just that kind of an elephant, and nothing more. I was admired, also feared; but it was as an animal is admired and feared. The animal is not reverenced, neither was I; I was not even respected. I had no pedigree, no inherited title; so in the king's and nobles' eyes I was mere dirt; the people regarded me with wonder and awe, but there was no reverence mixed with it; through the force of inherited ideas they were not able to conceive of anything being entitled to that except pedigree and lordship. There you see the hand of that awful power, the Roman Catholic Church. In two or three little centuries it had converted a nation of men to a nation of worms. Before the day of the Church's supremacy in the world, men were men, and held their heads up, and had a man's pride and spirit and independence; and what of greatness and position a person got, he got mainly by achievement, not by birth. But then the Church came to the front, with an axe to grind; and she was wise, subtle, and knew more than one way to skin a cat—or a nation; she invented "divine right of kings," and propped it all around, brick by brick, with the Beatitudes—wrenching them from their good purpose to make them fortify an evil one; she preached (to the commoner) humility, obedience to superiors, the beauty of self-sacrifice; she preached (to the commoner) meekness under insult; preached (still to the commoner, always to the commoner) patience, meanness of spirit, non-resistance under oppression; and she introduced heritable ranks and aristocracies, and taught all the Christian populations of the earth to bow down to them and worship them.

Even down to my birth-century that poison was still in the blood of Christendom, and the best of English commoners was still content to see his inferiors impudently continuing to hold a number of positions, such as lordships and the throne, to which the grotesque laws of his country did not allow him to aspire; in fact, he was not merely contented with this strange condition of things, he was even able to persuade himself that he was proud of it. It seems to show that there isn't anything you can't stand, if you are only born and bred to it. Of course that taint, that reverence for rank and title, had been in our American blood, too—I know that; but when I left America it had disappeared—at least to all intents and purposes. The remnant of it was restricted to the dudes and dudesses. When a disease has worked its way down to that level, it may fairly be said to be out of the system.

But to return to my anomalous position in King Arthur's kingdom. Here I was, a giant among pigmies, a man among children, a master intelligence among intellectual moles: by all rational measurement the one and only actually great man in that whole British world; and yet there and then, just as in the remote England of my birth-time, the sheep-witted earl who could claim long descent from a king's leman, acquired at second-hand from the slums of London, was a better man than I was. Such a personage was fawned upon in Arthur's realm and reverently looked up to by everybody, even though his dispositions were as mean as his intelligence, and his morals as base as his lineage. There were times when *he* could sit down in the king's presence, but I couldn't. I could have got a title easily enough, and that would have raised me a large step in everybody's eyes; even in the king's, the giver of it. But I didn't ask for it; and I declined it when it was offered. I couldn't have enjoyed such a thing with my notions; and it wouldn't have been fair, anyway, because as far back as I could go, our tribe had always been short of the bar sinister. I couldn't have felt really and satisfactorily fine and proud and set-up over any title except one that should come from the nation itself, the only legitimate source; and such an one I hoped to win; and in the course of years of honest and honorable endeavor, I did win it and did wear it with a high and clean pride. This title fell casually from the lips of a blacksmith, one day, in a village, was caught up as a happy thought and tossed from mouth to mouth with a laugh and an affirmative vote; in ten days it had swept the kingdom, and was become as familiar as the king's name. I was never known by any other designation afterward, whether in the nation's talk or in grave debate upon matters of state at the council-board of the sovereign. This title, translated into modern speech, would be THE BOSS. Elected by the nation. That suited me. And it was a pretty high title. There were very few *the's*, and I was one of them. If you spoke of the duke, or the earl, or the bishop, how could anybody tell which one you meant? But if you spoke of The King or The Queen or The Boss, it was different.

Well, I liked the king, and as king I respected him—respected the office; at least respected it as much as I was capable of respecting any unearned supremacy; but as *men* I looked down upon him and his nobles—privately.

And he and they liked me, and respected my office; but as an animal, without birth or sham title, they looked down upon me—and were not particularly private about it, either. I didn't charge for my opinion about them, and they didn't charge for their opinion about me: the account was square, the books balanced, everybody was satisfied.

THE TOURNAMENT

They were always having grand tournaments there at Camelot; and very stirring and picturesque and ridiculous human bull-fights they were, too, but just a little wearisome to the practical mind. However, I was generally on hand—for two reasons: a man must not hold himself aloof from the things which his friends and his community have at heart if he would be liked—especially as a statesman; and both as business man and statesman I wanted to study the tournament and see if I couldn't invent an improvement on it. That reminds me to remark, in passing, that the very first official thing I did, in my administration—and it was on the very first day of it, too—was to start a patent office; for I knew that a country without a patent office and good patent laws was just a crab, and couldn't travel any way but sideways or backways.

Things ran along, a tournament nearly every week; and now and then the boys used to want me to take a hand—I mean Sir Launcelot and the rest—but I said I would by and by; no hurry yet, and too much government machinery to oil up and set to rights and start a-going.

We had one tournament which was continued from day to day during more than a week, and as many as five hundred knights took part in it, from first to last. They were weeks gathering. They came on horseback from everywhere; from the very ends of the country, and even from beyond the sea; and many brought ladies, and all brought squires and troops of servants. It was a most gaudy and gorgeous crowd, as to costumery, and very characteristic of the country and the time, in the way of high animal spirits, innocent indecencies of language, and happy-hearted indifference to morals. It was fight or look on, all day and every day; and sing, gamble, dance, carouse half the night every night. They had a most noble good time. You never saw such people. Those banks of beautiful ladies, shining in their barbaric splendors, would see a knight sprawl from his horse in the lists with a lanceshaft the thickness of your ankle clean through him and the blood spouting, and instead of fainting they would clap their hands and crowd each other for a better view; only sometimes one would dive into her handkerchief, and look ostentatiously broken-hearted, and then you could lay two to one that there was a scandal there somewhere and she was afraid the public hadn't found it out.

The noise at night would have been annoying to me ordinarily, but I didn't mind it in the present circumstances, because it kept me from hearing the quacks detaching legs and arms from the day's cripples. They ruined an uncommon good old cross-cut saw for me, and broke the saw-buck, too, but

I let it pass. And as for my axe—well, I made up my mind that the next time I lent an axe to a surgeon I would pick my century.

I not only watched this tournament from day to day, but detailed an intelligent priest from my Department of Public Morals and Agriculture, and ordered him to report it; for it was my purpose by and by, when I should have gotten the people along far enough, to start a newspaper. The first thing you want in a new country, is a patent office; then work up your school system; and after that, out with your paper. A newspaper has its faults, and plenty of them, but no matter, it's hark from the tomb for a dead nation, and don't you forget it. You can't resurrect a dead nation without it; there isn't any way. So I wanted to sample things, and be finding out what sort of reporter-material I might be able to rake together out of the sixth century when I should come to need it.

Well, the priest did very well, considering. He got in all the details, and that is a good thing in a local item: you see, he had kept books for the undertaker-department of his church when he was younger, and there, you know, the money's in the details; the more details, the more swag: bearers, mutes, candles, prayers—everything counts; and if the bereaved don't buy prayers enough you mark up your candles with a forked pencil, and your bill shows up all right. And he had a good knack at getting in the complimentary thing here and there about a knight that was likely to advertise—no, I mean a knight that had influence; and he also had a neat gift of exaggeration, for in his time he had kept door for a pious hermit who lived in a sty and worked miracles.

Of course this novice's report lacked whoop and crash and lurid description, and therefore wanted the true ring; but its antique wording was quaint and sweet and simple, and full of the fragrances and flavors of the time, and these little merits made up in a measure for its more important lacks. Here is an extract from it:

> *Then Sir Brian de les Isles and Grummore Grummorsum, knights of the castle, encountered with Sir Aglovale and Sir Tor, and Sir Tor smote down Sir Grummore Grummorsum to the earth. Then came Sir Carados of the dolorous tower, and Sir Turquine, knights of the castle, and there encountered with them Sir Percivale de Galis and Sir Lamorak de Galis, that were two brethren, and there encountered Sir Percivale with Sir Carados, and either brake their spears unto their hands, and then Sir Turquine with Sir Lamorak, and either of them smote down other, horse and all, to the earth, and either parties rescued other and horsed them again. And Sir Arnold, and Sir Gauter, knights of the castle, encountered with Sir Brandiles and Sir Kay, and these four knights encountered mightily, and brake their spears to their hands. Then came Sir Pertolope from the castle, and there encountered with him Sir Lionel, and there Sir Pertolope the green knight smote down Sir Lionel, brother to Sir Launcelot. All this was marked by noble heralds, who bare him best, and their names. Then Sir*

Bleobaris brake his spear upon Sir Gareth, but of that stroke Sir Bleobaris fell to the earth. When Sir Galihodin saw that, he bad Sir Gareth keep him, and Sir Gareth smote him to the earth. Then Sir Galihud gat a spear to avenge his brother, and in the same wise Sir Gareth served him, and Sir Dinadan and his brother La Cote Male Taile, and Sir Sagramore le Disirous, and Sir Dodinas le Savage; all these he bare down with one spear. When King Aswisance of Ireland saw Sir Gareth fare so he marvelled what he might be, that one time seemed green, and another time, at his again coming, he seemed blue. And thus at every course that he rode to and fro he changed his color, so that there might neither king nor knight have ready cognizance of him. Then Sir Agwisance the King of Ireland encountered with Sir Gareth, and there Sir Gareth smote him from his horse, saddle and all. And then came King Carados of Scotland, and Sir Gareth smote him down horse and man. And in the same wise he served King Uriens of the land of Gore. And then there came in Sir Bagdemagus, and Sir Gareth smote him down horse and man to the earth. And Bagdemagus's son Meliganus brake a spear upon Sir Gareth mightily and knightly. And then Sir Galahault the noble prince cried on high, Knight with the many colors, well hast thou justed; now make thee ready that I may just with thee. Sir Gareth heard him, and he gat a great spear, and so they encountered together, and there the prince brake his spear; but Sir Gareth smote him upon the left side of the helm, that he reeled here and there, and he had fallen down had not his men recovered him. Truly, said King Arthur, that knight with the many colors is a good knight. Wherefore the king called unto him Sir Launcelot, and prayed him to encounter with that knight. Sir, said Launcelot, I may as well find in my heart for to forbear him at this time, for he hath had travail enough this day, and when a good knight doth so well upon some day, it is no good knight's part to let him of his worship, and, namely, when he seeth a knight hath done so great labour; for peradventure, said Sir Launcelot, his quarrel is here this day, and peradventure he is best beloved with this lady of all that be here, for I see well he paineth himself and enforceth him to do great deeds, and therefore, said Sir Launcelot, as for me, this day he shall have the honour; though it lay in my power to put him from it, I would not.

There was an unpleasant little episode that day, which for reasons of state I struck out of my priest's report. You will have noticed that Garry was doing some great fighting in the engagement. When I say Garry I mean Sir Gareth. Garry was my private pet name for him; it suggests that I had a deep affection for him, and that was the case. But it was a private pet name only, and never spoken aloud to any one, much less to him; being a noble, he would not have endured a familiarity like that from me. Well, to proceed: I sat in the private box set apart for me as the king's minister. While Sir Dinadan was waiting for his turn to enter the lists, he came in there and sat down and began to talk; for he was always making up to me, because I was a stranger and he liked to have a fresh market for his jokes, the most of them having reached that stage of wear where the teller has to do the laughing himself while the other person looks sick. I had always responded to his efforts as well as I could, and felt a very deep and real kindness for him, too, for the reason that if by malice of fate he knew the one particular anecdote which I had heard oftenest and had most hated and most loathed all my life, he had at least spared it me. It was one which I had heard attributed to every humorous person who had ever stood on American soil, from Columbus down to Artemus Ward. It was about a humorous lecturer who flooded an ignorant audience with the killingest jokes for an hour and never got a laugh; and then when he was leaving, some gray simpletons wrung him gratefully by the hand and said it had been the funniest thing they had ever heard, and "it was all they could do to keep from laughin' right out in meetin'." That anecdote never saw the day that it was worth the telling; and yet I had sat under the telling of it hundreds and thousands and millions and billions of times, and cried and cursed all the way through. Then who can hope to know what my feelings were, to hear this armor-plated ass start in on it again, in the murky twilight of tradition, before the dawn of history, while even Lactantius might be referred to as "the late Lactantius," and the Crusades wouldn't be born for five hundred years yet? Just as he finished, the call-boy came; so, haw-hawing like a demon, he went rattling and clanking out like a crate of loose castings, and I knew nothing more. It was some minutes before I came to, and then I opened my eyes just in time to see Sir Gareth fetch him an awful welt, and I unconsciously out with the prayer, "I hope to gracious he's killed!" But by ill-luck, before I had got half through with the words, Sir Gareth crashed into Sir Sagramor le Desirous and sent him thundering over his horse's crupper, and Sir Sagramor caught my remark and thought I meant it for *him*.

Well, whenever one of those people got a thing into his head, there was no getting it out again. I knew that, so I saved my breath, and offered no explanations. As soon as Sir Sagramor got well, he notified me that there was a little account to settle between us, and he named a day three or four years in the future; place of settlement, the lists where the offense had been given. I said I would be ready when he got back. You see, he was going for the Holy Grail. The boys all took a flier at the Holy Grail now and then. It was a several years' cruise. They always put in the long absence snooping around, in the most conscientious way, though none of them had any idea where the Holy Grail really was, and I don't think any of them actually expected to find it, or would have known what to do with it if he *had* run across it. You see, it was just the Northwest Passage of that day, as you may say; that was all. Every year expeditions went out holy grailing, and next year relief expeditions went out to hunt for *them*. There was worlds of reputation in it, but no money. Why, they actually wanted *me* to put in! Well, I should smile.

BEGINNINGS OF CIVILIZATION

The Round Table soon heard of the challenge, and of course it was a good deal discussed, for such things interested the boys. The king thought I ought now to set forth in quest of adventures, so that I might gain renown and be the more worthy to meet Sir Sagramor when the several years should have rolled away. I excused myself for the present; I said it would take me three or four years yet to get things well fixed up and going smoothly; then I should be ready; all the chances were that at the end of that time Sir Sagramor would still be out grailing, so no valuable time would be lost by the postponement; I should then have been in office six or seven years, and I believed my system and machinery would be so well developed that I could take a holiday without its working any harm.

I was pretty well satisfied with what I had already accomplished. In various quiet nooks and corners I had the beginnings of all sorts of industries under way—nuclei of future vast factories, the iron and steel missionaries of my future civilization. In these were gathered together the brightest young minds I could find, and I kept agents out raking the country for more, all the time. I was training a crowd of ignorant folk into experts—experts in every sort of handiwork and scientific calling. These nurseries of mine went smoothly and privately along undisturbed in their obscure country retreats, for nobody was allowed to come into their precincts without a special permit—for I was afraid of the Church.

I had started a teacher-factory and a lot of Sunday-schools the first thing; as a result, I now had an admirable system of graded schools in full blast in those places, and also a complete variety of Protestant congregations all in a prosperous and growing condition. Everybody could be any kind of a Christian he wanted to; there was perfect freedom in that matter. But I confined public religious teaching to the churches and the Sunday-schools, permitting nothing of it in my other educational buildings. I could have given my own sect the preference and made everybody a Presbyterian without any trouble, but that would have been to affront a law of human nature: spiritual wants and instincts are as various in the human family as are physical appetites, complexions, and features, and a man is only at his best, morally, when he is equipped with the religious garment whose color and shape and size most nicely accommodate themselves to the spiritual complexion, angularities, and stature of the individual who wears it; and, besides, I was afraid of a united Church; it makes a mighty power, the mightiest conceivable, and then when it by and by gets into selfish hands, as it is always bound to do, it means death to human liberty and paralysis to human thought.

All mines were royal property, and there were a good many of them. They had formerly been worked as savages always work mines—holes grubbed in the earth and the mineral brought up in sacks of hide by hand, at the rate of a ton a day; but I had begun to put the mining on a scientific basis as early as I could.

Yes, I had made pretty handsome progress when Sir Sagramor's challenge struck me.

Four years rolled by—and then! Well, you would never imagine it in the world. Unlimited power is the ideal thing when it is in safe hands. The despotism of heaven is the one absolutely perfect government. An earthly despotism would be the absolutely perfect earthly government, if the conditions were the same, namely, the despot the perfectest individual of the human race, and his lease of life perpetual. But as a perishable perfect man must die, and leave his despotism in the hands of an imperfect successor, an earthly despotism is not merely a bad form of government, it is the worst form that is possible.

My works showed what a despot could do with the resources of a kingdom at his command. Unsuspected by this dark land, I had the civilization of the nineteenth century booming under its very nose! It was fenced away from the public view, but there it was, a gigantic and unassailable fact—and to be heard from, yet, if I lived and had luck. There it was, as sure a fact and as substantial a fact as any serene volcano, standing innocent with its smokeless summit in the blue sky and giving no sign of the rising hell in its bowels. My schools and churches were children four years before; they were grown-up now; my shops of that day were vast factories now; where I had a dozen trained men then, I had a thousand now; where I had one brilliant expert then, I had fifty now. I stood with my hand on the cock, so to speak, ready to turn it on and flood the midnight world with light at any moment. But I was not going to do the thing in that sudden way. It was not my policy. The people could not have stood it; and, moreover, I should have had the Established Roman Catholic Church on my back in a minute.

No, I had been going cautiously all the while. I had had confidential agents trickling through the country some time, whose office was to undermine knighthood by imperceptible degrees, and to gnaw a little at this and that and the other superstition, and so prepare the way gradually for a better order of things. I was turning on my light one-candle-power at a time, and meant to continue to do so.

I had scattered some branch schools secretly about the kingdom, and they were doing very well. I meant to work this racket more and more, as time wore on, if nothing occurred to frighten me. One of my deepest secrets was my West Point—my military academy. I kept that most jealously out of sight; and I did the same with my naval academy which I had established at a remote seaport. Both were prospering to my satisfaction.

Clarence was twenty-two now, and was my head executive, my right hand. He was a darling; he was equal to anything; there wasn't anything he couldn't turn his hand to. Of late I had been training him for journalism, for the time seemed about right for a start in the newspaper line; nothing big, but just a small weekly for experimental circulation in my civilization-nurseries. He took to it like a duck; there was an editor concealed in him, sure. Already he had doubled himself in one way; he talked sixth century and wrote nineteenth. His journalistic style was climbing, steadily; it was already up to the back settlement Alabama mark, and couldn't be told from the editorial output of that region either by matter or flavor.

We had another large departure on hand, too. This was a telegraph and a telephone; our first venture in this line. These wires were for private service only, as yet, and must be kept private until a riper day should come. We had a gang of men on the road, working mainly by night. They were stringing ground wires; we were afraid to put up poles, for they would attract too much inquiry. Ground wires were good enough, in both instances, for my wires were protected by an insulation of my own invention which was perfect. My men had orders to strike across country, avoiding roads, and establishing connection with any considerable towns whose lights betrayed their presence, and leaving experts in charge. Nobody could tell you how to find any place in the kingdom, for nobody ever went intentionally to any place, but only struck it by accident in his wanderings, and then generally left it without thinking to inquire what its name was. At one time and another we had sent out topographical expeditions to survey and map the kingdom, but the priests had always interfered and raised trouble. So we had given the thing up, for the present; it would be poor wisdom to antagonize the Church.

As for the general condition of the country, it was as it had been when I arrived in it, to all intents and purposes. I had made changes, but they were necessarily slight, and they were not noticeable. Thus far, I had not even meddled with taxation, outside of the taxes which provided the royal revenues. I had systematized those, and put the service on an effective and righteous basis. As a result, these revenues were already quadrupled, and yet the burden was so much more equally distributed than before, that all the kingdom felt a sense of relief, and the praises of my administration were hearty and general.

THE STAR

H. G. Wells (1897)

IT WAS ON the first day of the new year that the announcement was made, almost simultaneously from three observatories, that the motion of the planet Neptune, the outermost of all the planets that wheel about the sun, had become very erratic. Ogilvy had already called attention to a suspected retardation in its velocity in December. Such a piece of news was scarcely calculated to interest a world the greater portion of whose inhabitants were unaware of the existence of the planet Neptune, nor outside the astronomical profession did the subsequent discovery of a faint remote speck of light in the region of the perturbed planet cause any very great excitement. Scientific people, however, found the intelligence remarkable enough, even before it became known that the new body was rapidly growing larger and brighter, that its motion was quite different from the orderly progress of the planets, and that the deflection of Neptune and its satellite was becoming now of an unprecedented kind.

Few people without a training in science can realize the huge isolation of the solar system. The sun with its specks of planets, its dust of planetoids, and its impalpable comets, swims in a vacant immensity that almost defeats the imagination. Beyond the orbit of Neptune there is space, vacant so far as human observation has penetrated, without warmth or light or sound, blank emptiness, for twenty million times a million miles. That is the smallest estimate of the distance to be traversed before the very nearest of the stars is attained. And, saving a few comets more unsubstantial than the thinnest flame, no matter had ever to human knowledge crossed this gulf of space, until early in the twentieth century this strange wanderer appeared. A vast mass of matter it was, bulky, heavy, rushing without warning out of the black mystery of the sky into the radiance of the sun. By the second day it was clearly visible to any decent instrument, as a speck with a barely sensible diameter, in the constellation Leo near Regulus. In a little while an opera glass could attain it. On the third day of the new year the newspaper readers of two hemispheres were made aware for the first time of the real importance of this unusual apparition in the heavens. "A Planetary Collision," one London paper headed the news, and proclaimed Duchaine's opinion that this strange new planet would probably collide with Neptune. The leader writers enlarged upon the topic. So that in most of the capitals of the world, on January 3rd, there was an expectation, however vague of some imminent phenomenon in the sky; and as the night followed the sunset round the globe, thousands of men turned their eyes skyward to see—the old familiar stars just as they had always been.

Until it was dawn in London and Pollux setting and the stars overhead grown pale. The Winter's dawn it was, a sickly filtering accumulation of daylight, and the light of gas and candles shone yellow in the windows to show where people were astir. But the yawning policeman saw the thing, the busy crowds in the markets stopped agape, workmen going to their work betimes, milkmen, the drivers of news-carts, dissipation going home jaded and pale, homeless wanderers, sentinels on their beats, and in the country, laborers trudging afield, poachers slinking home, all over the dusky quickening country it could be seen—and out at sea by seamen watching for the day—a great white star, come suddenly into the westward sky!

Brighter it was than any star in our skies; brighter than the evening star at its brightest. It still glowed out white and large, no mere twinkling spot of light, but a small round clear shining disc, an hour after the day had come. And where science has not reached, men stared and feared, telling one another of the wars and pestilences that are foreshadowed by these fiery signs in the Heavens. Sturdy Boers, dusky Hottentots, Gold Coast negroes, Frenchmen, Spaniards, Portuguese, stood in the warmth of the sunrise watching the setting of this strange new star.

And in a hundred observatories there had been suppressed excitement, rising almost to shouting pitch, as the two remote bodies had rushed together, and a hurrying to and fro, to gather photographic apparatus and spectroscope, and this appliance and that, to record this novel astonishing sight, the destruction of a world. For it was a world, a sister planet of our earth, far greater than our earth indeed, that had so suddenly flashed into flaming death. Neptune it was, had been struck, fairly and squarely, by the strange planet from outer space and the heat of the concussion had incontinently turned two solid globes into one vast mass of incandescence. Round the world that day, two hours before the dawn, went the pallid great white star, fading only as it sank westward and the sun mounted above it. Everywhere men marveled at it, but of all those who saw it none could have marveled more than those sailors, habitual watchers of the stars, who far away at sea had heard nothing of its advent and saw it now rise like a pigmy moon and climb zenithward and hang overhead and sink westward with the passing of the night.

And when next it rose over Europe everywhere were crowds of watchers on hilly slopes, on house-roofs, in open spaces, staring eastward for the rising of the great new star. It rose with a white glow in front of it, like the glare of a white fire, and those who had seen it come into existence the night before cried out at the sight of it. "It is larger," they cried. "It is brighter!" And, indeed the moon a quarter full and sinking in the west was in its apparent size beyond comparison, but scarcely in all its breadth had it as much brightness now as the little circle of the strange new star.

"It is brighter!" cried the people clustering in the streets. But in the dim observatories the watchers held their breath and peered at one another. "*It is nearer,*" they said. "*Nearer!*"

And voice after voice repeated, "It is nearer," and the clicking telegraph took that up, and it trembled along telephone wires, and in a thousand cities grimy compositors fingered the type. "It is nearer." Men writing in offices, struck with a strange realization, flung down their pens, men talking in a thousand places suddenly came upon a grotesque possibility in those words, "It is nearer." It hurried along awakening streets, it was shouted down the frost-stilled ways of quiet villages, men who had read these things from the throbbing tape stood in yellow-lit doorways shouting the news to the passers-by. "It is nearer." Pretty women, flushed and glittering, heard the news told jestingly between the dances, and feigned an intelligent interest they did not feel. "Nearer! Indeed. How curious! How very, very clever people must be to find out things like that!"

Lonely tramps faring through the wintry night murmured those words to comfort themselves—looking skyward. "It has need to be nearer, for the night's as cold as charity. Don't seem much warmth from it if it *is* nearer, all the same."

"What is a new star to me?" cried the weeping woman kneeling beside her dead.

The schoolboy, rising early for his examination work, puzzled it out for himself—with the great white star, shining broad and bright through the frost-flowers of his window. "Centrifugal, centripetal," he said, with his chin on his fist. "Stop a planet in its flight, rob it of its centrifugal force, what then? Centripetal has it, and down it falls into the sun! And this—!"

"Do *we* come in the way? I wonder—"

The light of that day went the way of its brethren, and with the later watches of the frosty darkness rose the strange star again. And it was now so bright that the waxing moon seemed but a pale yellow ghost of itself, hanging huge in the sunset. In a South African city a great man had married, and the streets were alight to welcome his return with his bride. "Even the skies have illuminated," said the flatterer. Under Capricorn, two negro lovers, daring the wild beasts and evil spirits, for love of one another, crouched together in a cane brake where the fire-flies hovered. "That is our star," they whispered, and felt strangely comforted by the sweet brilliance of its light.

The master mathematician sat in his private room and pushed the papers from him. His calculations were already finished. In a small white phial there still remained a little of the drug that had kept him awake and active for four long nights. Each day, serene, explicit, patient as ever, he had given his lecture

to his students, and then had come back at once to this momentous calculation. His face was grave, a little drawn and hectic from his drugged activity.
For some time he seemed lost in thought. Then he went to the window, and
the blind went up with a click. Half way up the sky, over the clustering roofs,
chimneys and steeples of the city, hung the star.

He looked at it as one might look into the eyes of a brave enemy. "You may
kill me," he said after a silence. "But I can hold you—and all the universe for
that matter—in the grip of this little brain. I would not change. Even now."

He looked at the little phial. "There will be no need of sleep again," he said.
The next day at noon, punctual to the minute, he entered his lecture theatre,
put his hat on the end of the table as his habit was, and carefully selected a
large piece of chalk. It was a joke among his students that he could not lecture
without that piece of chalk to fumble in his fingers, and once he had been
stricken to impotence by their hiding his supply. He came and looked under
his grey eyebrows at the rising tiers of young fresh faces, and spoke with his
accustomed studied commonness of phrasing. "Circumstances have arisen—
circumstances beyond my control," he said and paused, "which will debar me
from completing the course I had designed. It would seem, gentlemen, if I
may put the thing clearly and briefly, that—Man has lived in vain."

The students glanced at one another. Had they heard aright? Mad? Raised
eyebrows and grinning lips there were, but one or two faces remained intent
upon his calm grey-fringed face. "It will be interesting," he was saying, "to
devote this morning to an exposition, so far as I can make it clear to you, of
the calculations that have led me to this conclusion. Let us assume—"

He turned towards the blackboard, meditating a diagram in the way that
was usual to him. "What was that about 'lived in vain?'" whispered one student to another. "Listen," said the other, nodding towards the lecturer.

And presently they began to understand.

That night the star rose later, for its proper eastward motion had carried it
some way across Leo towards Virgo, and its brightness was so great that the
sky became a luminous blue as it rose, and every star was hidden in its turn,
save only Jupiter near the zenith, Capella, Aldebaran, Sirius and the pointers
of the Bear. It was very white and beautiful. In many parts of the world that
night a pallid halo encircled it about. It was perceptibly larger; in the clear
refractive sky of the tropics it seemed as if it were nearly a quarter the size of
the moon. The frost was still on the ground in England, but the world was as
brightly lit as if it were midsummer moonlight. One could see to read quite
ordinary print by that cold clear light, and in the cities the lamps burnt yellow
and wan.

And everywhere the world was awake that night, and throughout Christendom a somber murmur hung in the keen air over the countryside like the
belling of bees in the heather, and this murmurous tumult grew to a clangor
in the cities. It was the tolling of the bells in a million belfry towers and steeples, summoning the people to sleep no more, to sin no more, but to gather

in their churches and pray. And overhead, growing larger and brighter, as the earth rolled on its way and the night passed, rose the dazzling star.

And the streets and houses were alight in all the cities, the shipyards glared, and whatever roads led to high country were lit and crowded all night long. And in all the seas about the civilized lands, ships with throbbing engines, and ships with bellying sails, crowded with men and living creatures, were standing out to ocean and the north. For already the warning of the master mathematician had been telegraphed all over the world, and translated into a hundred tongues. The new planet and Neptune, locked in a fiery embrace, were whirling headlong, ever faster and faster towards the sun. Already every second this blazing mass flew a hundred miles, and every second its terrific velocity increased. As it flew now, indeed, it must pass a hundred million of miles wide of the earth and scarcely affect it. But near its destined path, as yet only slightly perturbed, spun the mighty planet Jupiter and his moons sweeping splendid round the sun. Every moment now the attraction between the fiery star and the greatest of the planets grew stronger. And the result of that attraction? Inevitably Jupiter would be deflected from its orbit into an elliptical path, and the burning star, swung by his attraction wide of its sunward rush, would "describe a curved path" and perhaps collide with, and certainly pass very close to, our earth. "Earthquakes, volcanic outbreaks, cyclones, sea waves, floods, and a steady rise in temperature to I know not what limit"—so prophesied the master mathematician.

And overhead, to carry out his words, lonely and cold and livid, blazed the star of the coming doom.

To many who stared at it that night until their eyes ached, it seemed that it was visibly approaching. And that night, too, the weather changed, and the frost that had gripped all Central Europe and France and England softened towards a thaw.

But you must not imagine because I have spoken of people praying through the night and people going aboard ships and people fleeing towards mountainous country that the whole world was already in a terror because of the star. As a matter of fact, use and wont still ruled the world, and save for the talk of idle moments and the splendor of the night, nine human beings out of ten were still busy at their common occupations. In all the cities the shops, save one here and there, opened and closed at their proper hours, the doctor and the undertaker plied their trades, the workers gathered in the factories, soldiers drilled, scholars studied, lovers sought one another, thieves lurked and fled, politicians planned their schemes. The presses of the newspapers roared through the nights, and many a priest of this church and that would not open his holy building to further what he considered a foolish panic. The newspapers insisted on the lesson of the year 1000—for then, too, people had anticipated the end. The star was no star—mere gas—a comet; and were it a star it could not possibly strike the earth. There was no precedent for such a thing. Common sense was sturdy everywhere, scornful, jesting, a little inclined to persecute the obdurate fearful. That night, at seven-fifteen by Greenwich time, the star would be at its nearest to Jupiter. Then the world would see the turn things would take. The master mathematician's grim warnings were treated by many as so much mere elaborate self-advertisement. Common sense at last, a little heated by argument, signified its unalterable convictions by going to bed. So, too, barbarism and savagery, already tired of the novelty, went about their nightly business, and save for a howling dog here and there, the beast world left the star unheeded.

And yet, when at last the watchers in the European States saw the star rise, an hour later it is true, but no larger than it had been the night before, there were still plenty awake to laugh at the master mathematician—to take the danger as if it had passed.

But hereafter the laughter ceased. The star grew—it grew with a terrible steadiness hour after hour, a little larger each hour, a little nearer the midnight zenith, and brighter and brighter, until it had turned night into a second day. Had it come straight to the earth instead of in a curved path, had it lost no velocity to Jupiter, it must have leapt the intervening gulf in a day, but as it was it took five days altogether to come by our planet. The next night it had become a third the size of the moon before it set to English eyes, and the thaw was assured. It rose over America near the size of the moon, but blinding white to look at, and *hot*; and a breath of hot wind blew now with its rising and gathering strength, and in Virginia, and Brazil, and down the St. Lawrence valley, it shone intermittently through a driving reek of thunder-clouds, flickering violet lightning, and hail unprecedented. In Manitoba was a thaw and devastating floods. And upon all the mountains of the earth the snow and ice began to melt that night, and all the rivers coming out of high country flowed thick and turbid, and soon—in their upper reaches—with swirling trees and the bodies of beasts and men. They rose steadily, steadily in the ghostly brilliance, and came trickling over their banks at last, behind the flying population of their valleys.

And along the coast of Argentina and up the South Atlantic the tides were higher than had ever been in the memory of man, and the storms drove the waters in many cases scores of miles inland, drowning whole cities. And so great grew the heat during the night that the rising of the sun was like the coming of a shadow. The earthquakes began and grew until all down America from the Arctic Circle to Cape Horn, hillsides were sliding, fissures were opening, and houses and walls crumbling to destruction. The whole side of Cotopaxi slipped out in one vast convulsion, and a tumult of lava poured out so high and broad and swift and liquid that in one day it reached the sea.

So the star, with the wan moon in its wake, marched across the Pacific, trailed the thunderstorms like the hem of a robe, and the growing tidal wave that toiled behind it, frothing and eager, poured over island and island and swept them clear of men. Until that wave came at last—in a blinding light and with the breath of a furnace, swift and terrible it came—a wall of water, fifty feet high, roaring hungrily, upon the long coasts of Asia, and swept inland across the plains of China. For a space the star, hotter now and larger and brighter than the sun in its strength, showed with pitiless brilliance the wide and populous country; towns and villages with their pagodas and trees, roads, wide cultivated fields, millions of sleepless people staring in helpless terror at the incandescent sky; and then, low and growing, came the murmur of the flood. And thus it was with millions of men that night—a flight nowhither, with limbs heavy with heat and breath fierce and scant, and the flood like a wall swift and white behind. And then death.

China was lit glowing white, but over Japan and Java and all the islands of Eastern Asia the great star was a ball of dull red fire because of the steam and smoke and ashes the volcanoes were spouting forth to salute its coming. Above was the lava, hot gases and ash, and below the seething floods, and the whole earth swayed and rumbled with the earthquake shocks. Soon the immemorial snows of Thibet and the Himalaya were melting and pouring down by ten million deepening converging channels upon the plains of Burmah and Hindostan. The tangled summits of the Indian jungles were aflame in a thousand places, and below the hurrying waters around the stems were dark objects that still struggled feebly and reflected the blood-red tongues of fire. And in a rudderless confusion a multitude of men and women fled down the broad river-ways to that one last hope of men—the open sea.

Larger grew the star, and larger, hotter, and brighter with a terrible swiftness now. The tropical ocean had lost its phosphorescence, and the whirling steam rose in ghostly wreaths from the black waves that plunged incessantly, speckled with storm-tossed ships.

And then came a wonder. It seemed to those who in Europe watched for the rising of the star that the world must have ceased its rotation. In a thousand open spaces of down and upland the people who had fled thither from the floods and the falling houses and sliding slopes of hill watched for that rising in vain. Hour followed hour through a terrible suspense, and the star rose not. Once again men set their eyes upon the old constellations they had counted lost to them forever. In England it was hot and clear overhead, though the ground quivered perpetually, but in the tropics, Sirius and Capella and Aldebaran showed through a veil of steam. And when at last the great star rose near ten hours late, the sun rose close upon it, and in the centre of its white heart was a disc of black.

Over Asia it was the star had begun to fall behind the movement of the sky, and then suddenly, as it hung over India, its light had been veiled. All the plain of India from the mouth of the Indus to the mouths of the Ganges was a shallow waste of shining water that night, out of which rose temples and palaces, mounds and hills, black with people. Every minaret was a clustering mass of people, who fell one by one into the turbid waters, as heat and terror overcame them. The whole land seemed a-wailing, and suddenly there swept a shadow across that furnace of despair, and a breath of cold wind, and a gathering of clouds, out of the cooling air. Men looking up, near blinded, at the star, saw that a black disc was creeping across the light. It was the moon, coming between the star and the earth. And even as men cried to God at this respite, out of the East with a strange inexplicable swiftness sprang the sun. And then star, sun and moon rushed together across the heavens. So it was that presently, to the European watchers, star and sun rose close upon each other, drove headlong for a space and then slower, and at last came to rest, star and sun merged into one glare of flame at the zenith of the sky. The moon no longer eclipsed the star but was lost to sight in the brilliance of the sky. And though those who were still alive regarded it for the most part with that dull stupidity that hunger, fatigue, heat and despair engender, there were still men who could perceive the meaning of these signs. Star and earth had been at their nearest, had swung about one another, and the star had passed. Already it was receding, swifter and swifter, in the last stage of its headlong journey downward into the sun.

And then the clouds gathered, blotting out the vision of the sky, the thunder and lightning wove a garment round the world; all over the earth was such a downpour of rain as men had never before seen, and where the volcanoes flared red against the cloud canopy there descended torrents of mud. Everywhere the waters were pouring off the land, leaving mud-silted ruins, and the earth littered like a storm-worn beach with all that had floated, and the dead bodies of the men and brutes, its children.

For days the water streamed off the land, sweeping away soil and trees and houses in the way, and piling huge dykes and scooping out Titanic gullies over the country side. Those were the days of darkness that followed the star and the heat. All through them, and for many weeks and months, the earthquakes continued.

But the star had passed, and men, hunger-driven and gathering courage only slowly, might creep back to their ruined cities, buried granaries, and sodden fields. Such few ships as had escaped the storms of that time came stunned and shattered and sounding their way cautiously through the new marks and shoals of once familiar ports. And as the storms subsided men perceived that everywhere the days were hotter than of yore, and the sun larger, and the moon, shrunk to a third of its former size, took now fourscore days between its new and new.

But of the new brotherhood that grew presently among men, of the saving of laws and books and machines, of the strange change that had come over Iceland and Greenland and the shores of Baffin's Bay, so that the sailors coming there presently found them green and gracious, and could scarce believe their eyes, this story does not tell. Nor of the movement of mankind now that the earth was hotter, northward and southward towards the poles of the earth. It concerns itself only with the coming and the passing of the Star.

The Martian astronomers—for there are astronomers on Mars, although they are very different beings from men—were naturally profoundly interested by these things. They saw them from their own standpoint of course. "Considering the mass and temperature of the missile that was flung through our solar system into the sun," one wrote, "it is astonishing what a little damage the earth, which it missed so narrowly, has sustained. All the familiar continental markings and the masses of the seas remain intact, and indeed the only difference seems to be a shrinkage of the white discoloration (supposed to be frozen water) round either pole." Which only shows how small the vastest of human catastrophes may seem, at a distance of a few million miles.

EDISON'S CONQUEST OF MARS

Garrett P. Serviss (1898)

CHAPTER 1

It is impossible that the stupendous events which followed the disastrous invasion of the earth by the Martians should go without record, and circumstances having placed the facts at my disposal, I deem it a duty, both to posterity and to those who were witnesses of and participants in the avenging counterstroke that the earth dealt back at its ruthless enemy in the heavens, to write down the story in a connected form.

The Martians had nearly all perished, not through our puny efforts, but in consequence of disease, and the few survivors fled in one of their projectile cars, inflicting their cruelest blow in the act of departure.

Their Mysterious Explosive

They possessed a mysterious explosive, of unimaginable puissance, with whose aid they set their car in motion for Mars from a point in Bergen County, NJ, just back of the Palisades.

The force of the explosion may be imagined when it is recollected that they had to give the car a velocity of more than seven miles per second in order to overcome the attraction of the earth and the resistance of the atmosphere.

The shock destroyed all of New York that had not already fallen a prey, and all the buildings yet standing in the surrounding towns and cities fell in one far-circling ruin.

The Palisades tumbled in vast sheets, starting a tidal wave in the Hudson that drowned the opposite shore.

Thousands of Victims

The victims of this ferocious explosion were numbered by tens of thousands, and the shock, transmitted through the rocky frame of the globe, was recorded by seismographic pendulums in England and on the Continent of Europe.

The terrible results achieved by the invaders had produced everywhere a mingled feeling of consternation and hopelessness. The devastation was widespread. The death-dealing engines which the Martians had brought with them had proved irresistible and the inhabitants of the earth possessed nothing capable of contending against them. There had been no protection for the great cities; no protection even for the open country. Everything had gone down before the savage onslaught of those merciless invaders from space. Savage ruins covered the sites of many formerly flourishing towns and villages, and the broken walls of great cities stared at the heavens like the exhumed skeletons of Pompeii. The awful agencies had extirpated pastures and meadows and dried up the very springs of fertility in the earth where they had touched it. In some parts of the devastated lands pestilence broke out; elsewhere there was famine. Despondency black as night brooded over some of the fairest portions of the globe.

All Not Yet Destroyed

Yet all had not been destroyed, because all had not been reached by the withering hand of the destroyer. The Martians had not had time to complete their work before they themselves fell a prey to the diseases that carried them off at the very culmination of their triumph.

From those lands which had, fortunately, escaped invasion, relief was sent to the sufferers. The outburst of pity and of charity exceeded anything that the world had known. Differences of race and religion were swallowed up in the universal sympathy which was felt for those who had suffered so terribly from an evil that was as unexpected as it was unimaginable in its enormity.

But the worst was not yet. More dreadful than the actual suffering and the scenes of death and devastation which overspread the afflicted lands was the profound mental and moral depression that followed. This was shared even by those who had not seen the Martians and had not witnessed the destructive effects of the frightful engines of war that they had imported for the conquest of the earth. All mankind was sunk deep in this universal despair, and it became tenfold blacker when the astronomers announced from their observatories that strange lights were visible, moving and flashing upon the red surface of the Planet of War. These mysterious appearances could only be interpreted in the light of past experience to mean that the Martians were preparing for another invasion of the earth, and who could doubt that with the invincible powers of destruction at their command they would this time make their work complete and final?

A Startling Announcement

This startling announcement was the more pitiable in its effects because it served to unnerve and discourage those few of stouter hearts and more hopeful temperaments who had already begun the labor of restoration and reconstruction amid the embers of their desolated homes. In New York this feeling of hope and confidence, this determination to rise against disaster and to wipe out the evidences of its dreadful presence as quickly as possible, had especially manifested itself. Already a company had been formed and a large amount of capital subscribed for the reconstruction of the destroyed bridges over the East River. Already architects were busily at work planning new twenty-story hotels and apartment houses; new churches and new cathedrals on a grander scale than before.

The Martians Returning

Amid this stir of renewed life came the fatal news that Mars was undoubtedly preparing to deal us a death blow. The sudden revulsion of feeling flitted like the shadow of an eclipse over the earth. The scenes that followed were indescribable. Men lost their reason. The faint-hearted ended the suspense with self-destruction, the stout-hearted remained steadfast, but without hope and knowing not what to do.

But there was a gleam of hope of which the general public as yet knew nothing. It was due to a few dauntless men of science, conspicuous among whom were Lord Kelvin, the great English savant; Herr Roentgen, the discoverer of the famous X-ray, and especially Thomas A. Edison, the American genius of science. These men and a few others had examined with the utmost care the engines of war, the flying machines, the generators of mysterious destructive forces that the Martians had produced, with the object of discovering, if possible, the sources of their power.

Suddenly from Mr. Edison's laboratory at Orange flashed the startling intelligence that he had not only discovered the manner in which the invaders had been able to produce the mighty energies which they employed with such terrible effect, but that, going further, he had found a way to overcome them.

The glad news was quickly circulated throughout the civilized world. Luckily the Atlantic cables had not been destroyed by the Martians, so that communication between the Eastern and Western continents was uninterrupted. It was a proud day for America. Even while the Martians had been upon the earth, carrying everything before them, demonstrating to the confusion of the most optimistic that there was no possibility of standing against them, a feeling—a confidence had manifested itself in France, to a minor extent in England, and particularly in Russia, that the Americans might discover means to meet and master the invaders.

Now, it seemed, this hope and expectation were to be realized. Too late, it is true, in a certain sense, but not too late to meet the new invasion which the astronomers had announced was impending. The effect was as wonderful and indescribable as that of the despondency which but a little while before had overspread the world. One could almost hear the universal sigh of relief which went up from humanity. To relief succeeded confidence—so quickly does the human spirit recover like an elastic spring, when pressure is released.

"We Are Ready for Them!"

"Let them come," was the almost joyous cry. "We shall be ready for them now. The Americans have solved the problem. Edison has placed the means of victory within our power."

Looking back upon that time now, I recall, with a thrill, the pride that stirred me at the thought that, after all, the inhabitants of the Earth were a match for those terrible men from Mars, despite all the advantage which they had gained from their millions of years of prior civilization and science.

As good fortunes, like bad, never come singly, the news of Mr. Edison's discovery was quickly followed by additional glad tidings from that laboratory of marvels in the lap of the Orange mountains. During their career of conquest the Martians had astonished the inhabitants of the earth no less with their flying machines—which navigated our atmosphere as easily as they had that of their native planet—than with their more destructive inventions. These flying machines in themselves had given them an enormous advantage in the contest. High above the desolation that they had caused to reign on the surface of the earth, and, out of the range of our guns, they had hung safe in the upper air. From the clouds they had dropped death upon the earth.

Edison's Flying Machine

Now, rumor declared that Mr. Edison had invented and perfected a flying machine much more complete and manageable than those of the Martians had been. Wonderful stories quickly found their way into the newspapers concerning what Mr. Edison had already accomplished with the aid of his model electrical balloon. His laboratory was carefully guarded against the invasion of the curious, because he rightly felt that a premature announcement, which should promise more than could be actually fulfilled, would, at this critical juncture, plunge mankind back again into the gulf of despair, out of which it had just begun to emerge.

Nevertheless, inklings of the truth leaked out. The flying machine had been seen by many persons hovering by night high above the Orange hills and disappearing in the faint starlight as if it had gone away into the depths of space, out of which it would re-emerge before the morning light had streaked the east, and be seen settling down again within the walls that surrounded the laboratory of the great inventor. At length the rumor, gradually deepening into a conviction, spread that Edison himself, accompanied by a few scientific friends, had made an experimental trip to the moon. At a time when the spirit of mankind was less profoundly stirred, such a story would have been received with complete incredulity, but now, rising on the wings of the new hope that was buoying up the earth, this extraordinary rumor became a day star of truth to the nations.

A Trip to the Moon

And it was true. I had myself been one of the occupants of the car of the flying Ship of Space on that night when it silently left the earth, and rising out of the great shadow of the globe, sped on to the moon. We had landed upon the scarred and desolate face of the earth's satellite, and but that there are greater and more interesting events, the telling of which must not be delayed, I should undertake to describe the particulars of this first visit of men to another world.

But, as I have already intimated, this was only an experimental trip. By visiting this little nearby island in the ocean of space, Mr. Edison simply wished to demonstrate the practicability of his invention, and to convince, first of all, himself and his scientific friends that it was possible for men—mortal men— to quit and to revisit the earth at their will. That aim this experimental trip triumphantly attained.

It would carry me into technical details that would hardly interest the reader to describe the mechanism of Mr. Edison's flying machine. Let it suffice to say that it depended upon the principal of electrical attraction and repulsion. By means of a most ingenious and complicated construction he had mastered the problem of how to produce, in a limited space, electricity of any desired potential and of any polarity, and that without danger to the experimenter or to the material experimented upon. It is gravitation, as everybody knows, that makes man a prisoner on the earth. If he could overcome, or neutralize, gravitation he could float away a free creature of interstellar space. Mr. Edison in his invention had pitted electricity against gravitation. Nature, in fact, had done the same thing long before. Every astronomer knew it, but none had been able to imitate or to reproduce this miracle of nature. When a comet approaches the sun, the orbit in which it travels indicates that it is moving under the impulse of the sun's gravitation. It is in reality falling in a great parabolic or elliptical curve through space. But, while a comet approaches the sun it begins to display—stretching out for millions, and sometimes hundreds of millions of miles on the side away from the sun— an immense luminous train called its tail. This train extends back into that part of space from which the comet is moving. Thus the sun at one and the same time is drawing the comet toward itself and driving off from the comet in an opposite direction minute particles or atoms which, instead of obeying the gravitational force, are plainly compelled to disobey it. That this energy, which the sun exercises against its own gravitation, is electrical in its nature, hardly anybody will doubt. The head of the comet being comparatively heavy and massive, falls on toward the sun, despite the electrical repulsion. But the atoms which form the tail, being almost without weight, yield to the electrical rather than to the gravitational influence, and so fly away from the sun.

Gravity Overcome

Now, what Mr. Edison had done was, in effect, to create an electrified particle which might be compared to one of the atoms composing the tail of a comet, although in reality it was a kind of car, of metal, weighing some hundreds of pounds and capable of bearing some thousands of pounds with it in its flight. By producing, with the aid of the electrical generator contained in this car, an enormous charge of electricity, Mr. Edison was able to counterbalance, and a trifle more than counterbalance, the attraction of the earth, and thus cause the car to fly off from the earth as an electrified pithball flies from the prime conductor.

As we sat in the brilliantly lighted chamber that formed the interior of the car, and where stores of compressed air had been provided together with chemical apparatus, by means of which fresh supplies of oxygen and nitrogen might be obtained for our consumption during the flight through space, Mr. Edison touched a polished button, thus causing the generation of the required electrical charge on the exterior of the car, and immediately we began to rise. The moment and direction of our flight had been so timed and prearranged, that the original impulse would carry us straight toward the moon.

A Triumphant Test

When we fell within the sphere of attraction of that orb it only became necessary to so manipulate the electrical charge upon our car as nearly, but not quite, to counterbalance the effect of the moon's attraction in order that we might gradually approach it and with an easy motion, settle, without shock, upon its surface.

We did not remain to examine the wonders of the moon, although we could not fail to observe many curious things therein. Having demonstrated the fact that we could not only leave the earth, but could journey through space and safely land upon the surface of another planet, Mr. Edison's immediate purpose was fulfilled, and we hastened back to the earth, employing in leaving the moon and landing again upon our own planet the same means of control over the electrical attraction and repulsion between the respective planets and our car which I have already described.

Telegraphing the News

When actual experiment had thus demonstrated the practicability of the invention, Mr. Edison no longer withheld the news of what he had been doing from the world. The telegraph lines and the ocean cables labored with the messages that in endless succession, and burdened with an infinity of detail, were sent all over the earth. Everywhere the utmost enthusiasm was aroused.

"Let the Martians come," was the cry. "If necessary, we can quit the earth as the Athenians fled from Athens before the advancing host of Xerxes, and like them, take refuge upon our ships—these new ships of space, with which American inventiveness has furnished us."

And then, like a flash, some genius struck out an idea that fired the world.

"Why should we wait? Why should we run the risk of having our cities destroyed and our lands desolated a second time? Let us go to Mars. We have the means. Let us beard the lion in his den. Let us ourselves turn conquerors and take possession of that detestable planet, and if necessary, destroy it in order to relieve the earth of this perpetual threat which now hangs over us like the sword of Damocles."

CHAPTER 2

This enthusiasm would have had but little justification had Mr. Edison done nothing more than invent a machine which could navigate the atmosphere and the regions of interplanetary space.

He had, however, and this fact was generally known, although the details had not yet leaked out—invented also machines of war intended to meet the utmost that the Martians could do for either offence or defense in the struggle which was now about to ensue.

A Wonderful Instrument

Acting upon the hint which had been conveyed from various investigations in the domain of physics, and concentrating upon the problem all those unmatched powers of intellect which distinguished him, the great inventor had succeeded in producing a little implement which one could carry in his hand, but which was more powerful than any battleship that ever floated. The details of its mechanism could not be easily explained, without the use of tedious technicalities and the employment of terms, diagrams and mathematical statements, all of which would lie outside the scope of this narrative. But the principle of the thing was simple enough. It was upon the great scientific doctrine, which we have since seen so completely and brilliantly developed, of the law of harmonic vibrations, extending from atoms and molecules at one end of the series up to worlds and suns at the other end, that Mr. Edison based his invention.

Every kind of substance has its own vibratory rhythm. That of iron differs from that of pine wood. The atoms of gold do not vibrate in the same time or through the same range as those of lead, and so on for all known substances, and all the chemical elements. So, on a larger scale, every massive body has its period of vibration. A great suspension bridge vibrates, under the impulse of forces that are applied to it, in long periods. No company of soldiers ever crosses such a bridge without breaking step. If they tramped together, and were followed by other companies keeping the same time with their feet, after a while the vibrations of the bridge would become so great and destructive that it would fall in pieces. So any structure, if its vibration rate is known, could easily be destroyed by a force applied to it in such a way that it should simply increase the swing of those vibrations up to the point of destruction.

Now Mr. Edison had been able to ascertain the vibratory swing of many well-known substances, and to produce, by means of the instrument which he had contrived, pulsations in the ether which were completely under his control, and which could be made long or short, quick or slow, at his will. He could run through the whole gamut from the slow vibrations of sound in air up to the four hundred and twenty-five millions of millions of vibrations per second of the ultra red rays.

Having obtained an instrument of such power, it only remained to concentrate its energy upon a given object in order that the atoms composing that object should be set into violent undulation, sufficient to burst it asunder and to scatter its molecules broadcast. This the inventor effected by the simplest means in the world—simply a parabolic reflector by which the destructive waves could be sent like a beam of light, but invisible, in any direction and focused upon any desired point.

Testing the "Disintegrator"

I had the good fortune to be present when this powerful engine of destruction was submitted to its first test. We had gone upon the roof of Mr. Edison's laboratory and the inventor held the little instrument, with its attached mirror, in his hand. We looked about for some object on which to try its powers. On a bare limb of a tree not far away, for it was late in the Fall, sat a disconsolate crow.

"Good," said Mr. Edison, "that will do." He touched a button at the side of the instrument and a soft, whirring noise was heard.

"Feathers," said Mr. Edison, "have a vibration period of three hundred and eighty-six million per second."

He adjusted the index as he spoke. Then, through a sighting tube, he aimed at the bird.

"Now watch," he said.

The Crow's Fate

Another soft whirr in the instrument, a momentary flash of light close around it, and, behold, the crow had turned from black to white!

"Its feathers are gone," said the inventor; "they have been dissipated into their constituent atoms. Now, we will finish the crow."

Instantly there was another adjustment of the index, another outshooting of vibratory force, a rapid up and down motion of the index to include a certain range of vibrations, and the crow itself was gone—vanished in empty space! There was the bare twig on which a moment before it had stood. Behind, in the sky, was the white cloud against which its black form had been sharply outlined, but there was no more crow.

Bad for the Martians

"That looks bad for the Martians, doesn't it?" said the Wizard. "I have ascertained the vibration rate of all the materials of which their war engines whose remains we have collected together are composed. They can be shattered into nothingness in the fraction of a second. Even if the vibration period were not known, it could quickly be hit upon by simply running through the gamut."

"Hurrah!" cried one of the onlookers. "We have met the Martians and they are ours."

Such in brief was the first of the contrivances which Mr. Edison invented for the approaching war with Mars.

And these facts had become widely known. Additional experiments had completed the demonstration of the inventor's ability, with the aid of his wonderful instrument, to destroy any given object, or any part of an object, provided that that part differed in its atomic constitution, and consequently in its vibratory period, from the other parts.

A most impressive public exhibition of the powers of the little disintegrator was given amid the ruins of New York. On lower Broadway a part of the walls of one of the gigantic buildings, which had been destroyed by the Martians, impended in such a manner that it threatened at any moment to fall upon the heads of the passers-by. The Fire Department did not dare touch it. To blow it up seemed a dangerous expedient, because already new buildings had been erected in its neighborhood, and their safety would be imperiled by the flying fragments. The fact happened to come to my knowledge.

"Here is an opportunity," I said to Mr. Edison, "to try the powers of your machine on a large scale."

"Capital!" he instantly replied. "I shall go at once."

Disintegrating a Building

For the work now in hand it was necessary to employ a battery of disintegrators, since the field of destruction covered by each was comparatively limited. All of the impending portions of the wall must be destroyed at once and together, for otherwise the danger would rather be accentuated than annihilated. The disintegrators were placed upon the roof of a neighboring building, so adjusted that their fields of destruction overlapped one another upon the wall. Their indexes were all set to correspond with the vibration period of the peculiar kind of brick of which the wall consisted. Then the energy was turned on, and a shout of wonder arose from the multitudes which had assembled at a safe distance to witness the experiment.

Only a Cloud Remained

The wall did not fall; it did not break asunder; no fragments shot this way and that and high in the air; there was no explosion; no shock or noise disturbed the still atmosphere—only a soft whirr, that seemed to pervade everything and to tingle in the nerves of the spectators; and—what had been was not! The wall was gone! But high above and all around the place where it had hung over the street with its threat of death there appeared, swiftly billowing outward in every direction, a faint, bluish cloud. It was the scattered atoms of the destroyed wall.

And now the cry "On to Mars!" was heard on all sides. But for such an enterprise funds were needed—millions upon millions. Yet some of the fairest and richest portions of the earth had been impoverished by the frightful ravages of those enemies who had dropped down upon them from the skies. Still, the money must be had. The salvation of the planet, as everybody was now convinced, depended upon the successful negotiation of a gigantic war fund, in comparison with which all the expenditures in all of the wars that had been waged by the nations for 2,000 years would be insignificant. The electrical ships and the vibration engines must be constructed by scores and thousands. Only Mr. Edison's immense resources and unrivaled equipment had enabled him to make the models whose powers had been so satisfactorily shown. But to multiply these upon a war scale was not only beyond the resources of any individual—hardly a nation on the globe in the period of its greatest prosperity could have undertaken such a work. All the nations, then, must now conjoin. They must unite their resources, and, if necessary, exhaust all their hoards, in order to raise the needed sum.

The Yankees Lead

Negotiations were at once begun. The United States naturally took the lead, and their leadership was never for a moment questioned abroad.

Washington was selected as the place of meeting for a great congress of the nations. Washington, luckily, had been one of the places which had not been touched by the Martians. But if Washington had been a city composed of hotels alone, and every hotel so great as to be a little city in itself, it would have been utterly insufficient for the accommodation of the innumerable throngs which now flocked to the banks of the Potomac. But when was American enterprise unequal to a crisis? The necessary hotels, lodging houses and restaurants were constructed with astounding rapidity. One could see the city growing and expanding day by day and week after week. It flowed over Georgetown Heights; it leaped the Potomac; it spread east and west, south and north; square mile after square mile of territory was buried under the advancing buildings, until the gigantic city, which had thus grown up like a mushroom in a night, was fully capable of accommodating all its expected guests.

At first it had been intended that the heads of the various governments should in person attend this universal congress, but as the enterprise went on, as the enthusiasm spread, as the necessity for haste became more apparent through the warning notes which were constantly sounded from the observatories where the astronomers were nightly beholding new evidences of threatening preparations in Mars, the kings and queens of the old world felt that they could not remain at home; that their proper place was at the new focus and centre of the whole world—the city of Washington. Without concerted action, without interchange of suggestion, this impulse seemed to seize all the old world monarchs at once. Suddenly cablegrams flashed to the Government at Washington, announcing that Queen Victoria, the Emperor William, the Czar Nicholas, Alphonso of Spain, with his mother, Maria Christina; the old Emperor Francis Joseph and the Empress Elizabeth, of Austria; King Oscar and Queen Sophia, of Sweden and Norway; King Humbert and Queen Margherita, of Italy; King George and Queen Olga, of Greece; Abdul Hamid, of Turkey; Tsait'ien, Emperor of China; Mutsuhito, the Japanese Mikado, with his beautiful Princess Haruko; the President of France, the President of Switzerland, the First Syndic of the little republic of Andorra, perched on the crest of the Pyrenees, and the heads of all the Central and South American republics, were coming to Washington to take part in the deliberations, which, it was felt, were to settle the fate of earth and Mars.

One day, after this announcement had been received, and the additional news had come that nearly all the visiting monarchs had set out, attended by brilliant suites and convoyed by fleets of warships, for their destination, some coming across the Atlantic to the port of New York, others across the Pacific to San Francisco, Mr. Edison said to me:

"This will be a fine spectacle. Would you like to watch it?"

"Certainly," I replied.

A Grand Spectacle

The Ship of Space was immediately at our disposal. I think I have not yet mentioned the fact that the inventor's control over the electrical generator carried in the car was so perfect that by varying the potential or changing the polarity he could cause it slowly or swiftly, as might be desired, to approach or recede from any object. The only practical difficulty was presented when the polarity of the electrical charge upon an object in the neighborhood of the car was unknown to those in the car, and happened to be opposite to that of the charge which the car, at that particular moment, was bearing. In such a case, of course, the car would fly toward the object, whatever it might be, like a pith ball or a feather, attracted to the knob of an electrical machine. In this way, considerable danger was occasionally encountered, and a few accidents could not be avoided. Fortunately, however, such cases were rare. It was only now and then that, owing to some local cause, electrical polarities unknown to or unexpected by the navigators, endangered the safety of the car. As I shall have occasion to relate, however, in the course of the narrative, this danger became more acute and assumed at times a most formidable phase, when we had ventured outside the sphere of the earth and were moving through the unexplored regions beyond.

On this occasion, having embarked, we rose rapidly to a height of some thousands of feet and directed our course over the Atlantic. When half way to Ireland, we beheld, in the distance, steaming westward, the smoke of several fleets. As we drew nearer a marvellous spectacle unfolded itself to our eyes. From the northeast, their great guns flashing in the sunlight and their huge funnels belching black volumes that rested like thunder clouds upon the sea, came the mighty warships of England, with her meteor flag streaming red in the breeze, while the royal insignia, indicating the presence of the ruler of the British Empire, was conspicuously displayed upon the flagship of the squadron.

Following a course more directly westward appeared, under another black cloud of smoke, the hulls and guns and burgeons of another great fleet, carrying the tri-color of France, and bearing in its midst the head of the magnificent republic of western Europe.

Further south, beating up against the northerly winds, came a third fleet with the gold and red of Spain fluttering from its masthead. This, too, was carrying its King westward, where now, indeed, the star of empire had taken its way.

Universal Brotherhood

Rising a little higher, so as to extend our horizon, we saw coming down the English channel, behind the British fleet, the black ships of Russia. Side by side, or following one another's lead, these war fleets were on a peaceful voyage that belied their threatening appearance. There had been no thought of danger to or from the forts and ports of rival nations which they had passed. There was no enmity, and no fear between them when the throats of their ponderous guns yawned at one another across the waves. They were now, in spirit, all one fleet, having one object, bearing against one enemy, ready to defend but one country, and that country was the entire earth.

It was some time before we caught sight of the Emperor William's fleet. It seems that the Kaiser, although at first consenting to the arrangement by which Washington had been selected as the assembling place for the nations, afterwards objected to it.

Kaiser Wilhelm's Jealousy

"I ought to do this thing myself," he had said. "My glorious ancestors would never have consented to allow these upstart Republicans to lead in a warlike enterprise of this kind. What would my grandfather have said to it? I suspect that it is some scheme aimed at the divine right of kings."

But the good sense of the German people would not suffer their ruler to place them in a position so false and so untenable. And swept along by their enthusiasm the Kaiser had at last consented to embark on his flagship at Kiel, and now he was following the other fleets on their great mission to the Western Continent.

Why did they bring their warships when their intentions were peaceable, do you ask? Well, it was partly the effect of ancient habit, and partly due to the fact that such multitudes of officials and members of ruling families wished to embark for Washington that the ordinary means of ocean communications would have been utterly inadequate to convey them.

After we had feasted our eyes on this strange sight, Mr. Edison suddenly exclaimed: "Now let us see the fellows from the rising sun."

Over the Mississippi

The car was immediately directed toward the west. We rapidly approached the American coast, and as we sailed over the Alleghany Mountains and the broad plains of the Ohio and the Mississippi, we saw crawling beneath us from west, south and north, an endless succession of railway trains bearing their multitudes on to Washington. With marvelous speed we rushed westward, rising high to skim over the snow-topped peaks of the Rocky Mountains and then the glittering rim of the Pacific was before us. Half way between the American coast and Hawaii we met the fleets coming from China and Japan. Side by side they were ploughing the main, having forgotten, or laid aside, all the animosities of their former wars.

I well remember how my heart was stirred at this impressive exhibition of the boundless influence which my country had come to exercise over all the people of the world, and I turned to look at the man to whose genius this uprising of the earth was due. But Mr. Edison, after his wont, appeared totally unconscious of the fact that he was personally responsible for what was going on. His mind, seemingly, was entirely absorbed in considering problems, the solution of which might be essential to our success in the terrific struggle which was soon to begin.

Back to Washington

"Well, have you seen enough?" he asked. "Then let us go back to Washington."

As we speeded back across the continent we beheld beneath us again the burdened express trains rushing toward the Atlantic, and hundreds of thousands of upturned eyes watched our swift progress, and volleys of cheers reached our ears, for every one knew that this was Edison's electrical warship, on which the hope of the nation, and the hopes of all the nations, depended. These scenes were repeated again and again until the car hovered over the still expanding capital on the Potomac, where the unceasing ring of hammers rose to the clouds.

CHAPTER 3

The day appointed for the assembling of the nations in Washington opened bright and beautiful. Arrangements had been made for the reception of the distinguished guests at the Capitol. No time was to be wasted, and, having assembled in the Senate Chamber, the business that had called them together was to be immediately begun. The scene in Pennsylvania avenue, when the procession of dignitaries and royalties passed up toward the Capitol, was one never to be forgotten. Bands were playing, magnificent equipages flashed in the morning sunlight, the flags of every nation on the earth fluttered in the breeze. Queen Victoria, with the Prince of Wales escorting her, and riding in an open carriage, was greeted with roars of cheers; the Emperor William, following in another carriage with Empress Victoria at his side, condescended to bow and smile in response to the greetings of a free people. Each of the other monarchs was received in a similar manner. The Czar of Russia proved to be an especial favorite with the multitude on account of the ancient friendship of his house for America. But the greatest applause of all came when the President of France, followed by the President of Switzerland and the First Syndic of the little Republic of Andorra, made their appearance. Equally warm were the greetings extended to the representatives of Mexico and the South American States.

The Sultan of Turkey

The crowd apparently hardly knew at first how to receive the Sultan of Turkey, but the universal good feeling was in his favor, and finally rounds of hand clapping and cheers greeted his progress along the splendid avenue.

A happy idea had apparently occurred to the Emperor of China and the Mikado of Japan, for, attended by their intermingled suites, they rode together in a single carriage. This object lesson in the unity of international feeling immensely pleased the spectators.

An Unparalleled Scene

The scene in the Senate Chamber stirred every one profoundly. That it was brilliant and magnificent goes without saying, but there was a seriousness, an intense feeling of expectancy, pervading both those who looked on and those who were to do the work for which these magnates of the earth had assembled, which produced an ineradicable impression. The President of the United States, of course, presided. Representatives of the greater powers occupied the front seats, and some of them were honored with special chairs near the President.

No time was wasted in preliminaries. The President made a brief speech.

"We have come together," he said, "to consider a question that equally interests the whole earth. I need not remind you that unexpectedly and without provocation on our part the people—the monsters, I should rather say— of Mars, recently came down upon the earth, attacked us in our homes and spread desolation around them. Having the advantage of ages of evolution, which for us are yet in the future, they brought with them engines of death and of destruction against which we found it impossible to contend. It is within the memory of every one in reach of my voice that it was through the entirely unexpected succor which Providence sent us that we were suddenly and effectually freed from the invaders. By our own efforts we could have done nothing."

McKinley's Tribute

"But, as you all know, the first feeling of relief which followed the death of our foes was quickly succeeded by the fearful news which came to us from the observatories, that the Martians were undoubtedly preparing for a second invasion of our planet. Against this we should have had no recourse and no hope but for the genius of one of my countrymen, who, as you are all aware, has perfected means which may enable us not only to withstand the attack of those awful enemies, but to meet them, and, let us hope, to conquer them on their own ground."

"Mr. Edison is here to explain to you what those means are. But we have also another object. Whether we send a fleet of interplanetary ships to invade Mars or whether we simply confine our attention to works of defence, in either case it will be necessary to raise a very large sum of money. None of us has yet recovered from the effects of the recent invasion. The earth is poor to-day compared to its position a few years ago; yet we cannot allow our poverty to stand in the way. The money, the means, must be had. It will be part of our business here to raise a gigantic war fund by the aid of which we can construct the equipment and machinery that we shall require. This, I think, is all I need to say. Let us proceed to business."

"Where is Mr. Edison?" cried a voice.

"Will Mr. Edison please step forward?" said the President.

There was a stir in the assembly, and the iron-gray head of the great inventor was seen moving through the crowd. In his hand he carried one of his marvelous disintegrators. He was requested to explain and illustrate its operation. Mr. Edison smiled.

Edison to the Rescue

"I can explain its details," he said, "to Lord Kelvin, for instance, but if Their Majesties will excuse me, I doubt whether I can make it plain to the crowned heads."

The Emperor William smiled superciliously. Apparently he thought that another assault had been committed upon the divine right of kings. But the Czar Nicholas appeared to be amused, and the Emperor of China, who had been studying English, laughed in his sleeve, as if he suspected that a joke had been perpetrated.

"I think," said one of the deputies, "that a simple exhibition of the powers of the instrument, without a technical explanation of its method of working, will suffice for our purpose."

This suggestion was immediately approved. In response to it, Mr. Edison, by a few simple experiments, showed how he could quickly and certainly shatter into its constituent atoms any object upon which the vibratory force of the disintegrator should be directed. In this manner he caused an inkstand to disappear under the very nose of the Emperor William without a spot of ink being scattered upon his sacred person, but evidently the odor of the disunited atoms was not agreeable to the nostrils of the Kaiser.

Mr. Edison also explained in general terms the principle on which the instrument worked. He was greeted with round after round of applause, and the spirit of the assembly rose high.

Next the workings of the electrical ship were explained, and it was announced that after the meeting had adjourned an exhibition of the flying powers of the ship would be given in the open air.

These experiments, together with the accompanying explanations, added to what had already been disseminated through the public press, were quite sufficient to convince all the representatives who had assembled in Washington that the problem of how to conquer the Martians had been solved. The means were plainly at hand. It only remained to apply them. For this purpose, as the President had pointed out, it would be necessary to raise a very large sum of money.

"How much will be needed?" asked one of the English representatives.

"At least ten thousand millions of dollars," replied the President.

"It would be safer," said a Senator from the Pacific Coast, "to make it twenty-five thousand millions."

"I suggest," said the King of Italy, "that the nations be called in alphabetical order, and that the representatives of each name a sum which it is ready and able to contribute."

"We want the cash or its equivalent," shouted the Pacific Coast Senator.

"I shall not follow the alphabet strictly," said the President, "but shall begin with the larger nations first. Perhaps, under the circumstances, it is proper that the United States should lead the way. Mr. Secretary," he continued, turning to the Secretary of the Treasury, "how much can we stand?"

An Enormous Sum

"At least a thousand millions," replied the Secretary of the Treasury.

A roar of applause that shook the room burst from the assembly. Even some of the monarchs threw up their hats. The Emperor Tsait'ten smiled from ear to ear. One of the Roko Tuis, or native chiefs, from Fiji, sprang up and brandished a war club.

The President then proceeded to call the other nations, beginning with Austria-Hungary and ending with Zanzibar, whose Sultan, Hamoud bin Mahomed, had come to the congress in the escort of Queen Victoria. Each contributed liberally.

Germany coming in alphabetical order just before Great Britain, had named, through its Chancellor, the sum of $500,000,000, but when the First Lord of the British Treasury, not wishing to be behind the United States, named double that sum as the contribution of the British Empire, the Emperor William looked displeased. He spoke a word in the ear of the Chancellor, who immediately raised his hand.

A Thousand Million Dollars

"We will give a thousand million dollars," said the Chancellor.

Queen Victoria seemed surprised, though not displeased. The First Lord of the Treasury met her eye, and then, rising in his place, said:

"Make it fifteen hundred million for Great Britain."

Emperor William consulted again with his Chancellor, but evidently concluded not to increase his bid.

But, at any rate, the fund had benefited to the amount of a thousand millions by this little outburst of imperial rivalry.

The greatest surprise of all, however, came when the King of Siam was called upon for his contribution. He had not been given a foremost place in the Congress, but when the name of his country was pronounced he rose by his chair, dressed in a gorgeous specimen of the peculiar attire of his country, then slowly pushed his way to the front, stepped up to the President's desk and deposited upon it a small box.

"This is our contribution," he said, in broken English.

The cover was lifted, and there darted, shimmering in the half gloom of the Chamber, a burst of iridescence from the box.

The Long Lost Treasure

"My friends of the Western world," continued the King of Siam, "will be interested in seeing this gem. Only once before has the eye of a European been blessed with the sight of it. Your books will tell you that in the seventeenth century a traveler, Tavernier, saw in India an unmatched diamond which afterward disappeared like a meteor, and was thought to have been lost from the earth. You all know the name of that diamond and its history. It is the Great Mogul, and it lies before you. How it came into my possession I shall not explain. At any rate, it is honestly mine, and I freely contribute it here to aid in protecting my native planet against those enemies who appear determined to destroy it."

When the excitement which the appearance of this long lost treasure, that had been the subject of so many romances and of such long and fruitless search, had subsided, the President continued calling the list, until he had completed it.

Upon taking the sum of the contributions (the Great Mogul was reckoned at three millions) it was found to be still one thousand millions short of the required amount.

The Secretary of the Treasury was instantly on his feet.

"Mr. President," he said, "I think we can stand that addition. Let it be added to the contribution of the United States of America."

When the cheers that greeted the conclusion of the business were over, the President announced that the next affair of the Congress was to select a director who should have entire charge of the preparations for the war. It was the universal sentiment that no man could be so well suited for this post as Mr. Edison himself. He was accordingly selected by the unanimous and enthusiastic choice of the great assembly.

"How long a time do you require to put everything in readiness?" asked the President.

"Give me carte blanche," replied Mr. Edison, "and I believe I can have a hundred electric ships and three thousand disintegrators ready within six months."

A tremendous cheer greeted this announcement.

"Your powers are unlimited," said the President, "draw on the fund for as much money as you need," whereupon the Treasurer of the United States was made the disbursing officer of the fund, and the meeting adjourned.

Not less than 5,000,000 people had assembled at Washington from all parts of the world. Every one of this immense multitude had been able to listen to the speeches and the cheers in the Senate chamber, although not personally present there. Wires had been run all over the city, and hundreds of improved telephonic receivers provided, so that every one could hear. Even those who were unable to visit Washington, people living in Baltimore, New York, Boston, and as far away as New Orleans, St. Louis and Chicago, had also listened to the proceedings with the aid of these receivers. Upon the whole, probably not less than 50,000,000 people had heard the deliberations of the great congress of the nations.

The Excitement in Washington

The telegraph and the cable had sent the news across the oceans to all the capitols of the earth. The exultation was so great that the people seemed mad with joy.

The promised exhibition of the electrical ship took place the next day. Enormous multitudes witnessed the experiment, and there was a struggle for places in the car. Even Queen Victoria, accompanied by the Prince of Wales, ventured to take a ride in it, and they enjoyed it so much that Mr. Edison prolonged the journey as far as Boston and the Bunker Hill monument.

Most of the other monarchs also took a high ride, but when the turn of the Emperor of China came he repeated a fable which he said had come down from the time of Confucius:

A Chinese Legend

"Once upon a time there was a Chinaman living in the valley of the Hoang-Ho River, who was accustomed frequently to lie on his back, gazing at, and envying, the birds that he saw flying away in the sky. One day he saw a black speck which rapidly grew larger and larger, until as it got near he perceived that it was an enormous bird, which overshadowed the earth with its wings. It was the elephant of birds, the roc. 'Come with me,' said the roc, 'and I will show you the wonders of the kingdom of the birds.' The man caught hold of its claw and nestled among its feathers, and they rapidly rose high in the air, and sailed away to the Kuen-Lun Mountains. Here, as they passed near the top of the peaks, another roc made its appearance. The wings of the two great birds brushed together, and immediately they fell to fighting. In the midst of the melee the man lost his hold and tumbled into the top of a tree, where his pigtail caught on a branch, and he remained suspended. There the unfortunate man hung helpless, until a rat, which had its home in the rocks at the foot of the tree, took compassion upon him, and, climbing up, gnawed off the branch. As the man slowly and painfully wended his weary way homeward, he said: 'This teaches me that creatures to whom nature has given neither feathers nor wings should leave the kingdom of the birds to those who are fitted to inhabit it.'"

Having told this story, Tsait'ien turned his back on the electrical ship.

The Grand Ball

After the exhibition was finished, and amid the fresh outburst of enthusiasm that followed, it was suggested that a proper way to wind up the Congress and give suitable expression to the festive mood which now possessed mankind would be to have a grand ball. This suggestion met with immediate and universal approval.

But for so gigantic an affair it was, of course, necessary to make special preparations. A convenient place was selected on the Virginia side of the Potomac; a space of ten acres was carefully levelled and covered with a polished floor, rows of columns one hundred feet apart were run across it in every direction, and these were decorated with electric lights, displaying every color of the spectrum.

Unsurpassed Fireworks

Above this immense space, rising in the centre to a height of more than a thousand feet, was anchored a vast number of balloons, all aglow with lights, and forming a tremendous dome, in which brilliant lamps were arranged in such a manner as to exhibit, in an endless succession of combinations, all the national colors, ensigns and insignia of the various countries represented at the Congress. Blazing eagles, lions, unicorns, dragons and other imaginary creatures that the different nations had chosen for their symbols appeared to hover high above the dancers, shedding a brilliant light upon the scene.

Circles of magnificent thrones were placed upon the floor in convenient locations for seeing. A thousand bands of music played, and tens of thousands of couples, gayly dressed and flashing with gems, whirled together upon the polished floor.

Queen Victoria Dances

The Queen of England led the dance, on the arm of the President of the United States.

The Prince of Wales led forth the fair daughter of the President, universally admired as the most beautiful woman upon the great ballroom floor.

The Emperor William, in his military dress, danced with the beauteous Princess Masaco, the daughter of the Mikado, who wore for the occasion the ancient costume of the women of her country, sparkling with jewels, and glowing with quaint combinations of color like a gorgeous butterfly.

The Chinese Emperor, with his pigtail flying high as he spun, danced with the Empress of Russia.

The King of Siam essayed a waltz with the Queen Ranavalona, of Madagascar, while the Sultan of Turkey basked in the smiles of a Chicago heiress to a hundred millions.

The Czar choose for his partner a dark-eyed beauty from Peru, but King Malietoa, of Samoa, was suspicious of civilized charmers and, avoiding all of their allurements, expressed his joy and gave vent to his enthusiasm in a pas seul. In this he was quickly joined by a band of Sioux Indian chiefs, whose whoops and yells so startled the leader of a German band on their part of the floor that he dropped his baton and, followed by the musicians, took to his heels.

This incident amused the good-natured Emperor of China more than anything else that had occurred.

"Make muchee noisee," he said, indicating the fleeing musicians with his thumb. "Allee same muchee flaid noisee," and then his round face dimpled into another laugh.

The scene from the outside was even more imposing than that which greeted the eye within the brilliantly lighted enclosure. Far away in the night, rising high among the stars, the vast dome of illuminated balloons seemed like some supernatural creation, too grand and glorious to have been constructed by the inhabitants of the earth.

All around it, and from some of the balloons themselves, rose jets and fountains of fire, ceaselessly playing, and blotting out the constellations of the heavens by their splendor.

The Prince of Wales's Toast

The dance was followed by a grand banquet, at which the Prince of Wales proposed a toast to Mr. Edison:

"It gives me much pleasure," he said, "to offer, in the name of the nations of the Old World, this tribute of our admiration for, and our confidence in, the genius of the New World. Perhaps on such an occasion as this, when all racial differences and prejudices ought to be, and are, buried and forgotten, I should not recall anything that might revive them; yet I cannot refrain from expressing my happiness in knowing that the champion who is to achieve the salvation of the earth has come forth from the bosom of the Anglo-Saxon race."

Several of the great potentates looked grave upon hearing the Prince of Wales's words, and the Czar and the Kaiser exchanged glances; but there was no interruption to the cheers that followed. Mr. Edison, whose modesty and dislike to display and to speechmaking were well known, simply said:

"I think we have got the machine that can whip them. But we ought not to be wasting any time. Probably they are not dancing on Mars, but are getting ready to make us dance."

Haste to Embark

These words instantly turned the current of feeling in the vast assembly. There was no longer any disposition to expend time in vain boastings and rejoicings. Everywhere the cry now became, "Let us make haste! Let us get ready at once! Who knows but the Martians have already embarked, and are now on their way to destroy us?"

Under the impulse of this new feeling, which, it must be admitted, was very largely inspired by terror, the vast ballroom was quickly deserted. The lights were suddenly put out in the great dome of balloons, for someone had whispered:

"Suppose they should see that from Mars? Would they not guess what we were about, and redouble their preparations to finish us?"

Upon the suggestion of the President of the United States, an executive committee, representing all the principal nations, was appointed, and without delay a meeting of this committee was assembled at the White House. Mr. Edison was summoned before it, and asked to sketch briefly the plan upon which he proposed to work.

Thousands of Men for Mars

I need not enter into the details of what was done at this meeting. Let it suffice to say that when it broke up, in the small hours of the morning, it had been unanimously resolved that as many thousands of men as Mr. Edison might require should be immediately placed at his disposal; that as far as possible all the great manufacturing establishments of the country should be instantly transformed into factories where electrical ships and disintegrators could be built, and upon the suggestion of Professor Sylvanus P. Thompson, the celebrated English electrical expert, seconded by Lord Kelvin, it was resolved that all the leading men of science in the world should place their services at the disposal of Mr. Edison in any capacity in which, in his judgment, they might be useful to him.

The members of this committee were disposed to congratulate one another on the good work which they had so promptly accomplished, when at the moment of their adjournment, a telegraphic dispatch was handed to the President from Professor George E. Hale, the director of the great Yerkes Observatory, in Wisconsin. The telegram read:

What's Happening on Mars?

"Professor Barnard, watching Mars to-night with the forty-inch telescope, saw a sudden outburst of reddish light, which we think indicates that something has been shot from the planet. Spectroscopic observations of this moving light indicated that it was coming earthward, while visible, at the rate of not less than one hundred miles a second."

Hardly had the excitement caused by the reading of this dispatch subsided, when others of a similar import came from the Lick Observatory, in California; from the branch of the Harvard Observatory at Arequipa, in Peru, and from the Royal Observatory, at Potsdam.

When the telegram from this last-named place was read the Emperor William turned to his Chancellor and said:

"I want to go home. If I am to die I prefer to leave my bones among those of my Imperial ancestors, and not in this vulgar country, where no king has ever ruled. I don't like this atmosphere. It makes me feel limp."

And now, whipped on by the lash of alternate hope and fear, the earth sprang to its work of preparation.

CHAPTER 4

It is not necessary for me to describe the manner in which Mr. Edison performed his tremendous task. He was as good as his word, and within six months from the first stroke of the hammer, a hundred electrical ships, each provided with a full battery of disintegrators, were floating in the air above the harbor and the partially rebuilt city of New York.

It was a wonderful scene. The polished sides of the huge floating cars sparkled in the sunlight, and, as they slowly rose and fell, and swung this way and that, upon the tides of the air, as if held by invisible cables, the brilliant pennons streaming from their peaks waved up and down like the wings of an assemblage of gigantic humming birds.

Not knowing whether the atmosphere of Mars would prove suitable to be breathed by inhabitants of the earth, Mr. Edison had made provision, by means of an abundance of glass-protected openings, to permit the inmates of the electrical ships to survey their surroundings without quitting the interior. It was possible by properly selecting the rate of undulation, to pass the vibratory impulse from the disintegrators through the glass windows of a car, without damage to the glass itself. The windows were so arranged that the disintegrators could sweep around the car on all sides, and could also be directed above or below, as necessity might dictate.

To overcome the destructive forces employed by the Martians no satisfactory plan had yet been devised, because there was no means to experiment with them. The production of those forces was still the secret of our enemies. But Mr. Edison had no doubt that if we could not resist their effects we might at least be able to avoid them by the rapidity of our motions. As he pointed out, the war machines which the Martians had employed in their invasion of the earth, were really very awkward and unmanageable affairs. Mr. Edison's electrical ships, on the other hand, were marvels of speed and of manageability. They could dart about, turn, reverse their course, rise, fall, with the quickness and ease of a fish in the water. Mr. Edison calculated that even if mysterious bolts should fall upon our ships we could diminish their power to cause injury by our rapid evolutions.

We might be deceived in our expectations, and might have overestimated our powers, but at any rate we must take our chances and try.

Watching the Martians

A multitude, exceeding even that which had assembled during the great congress at Washington, now thronged New York and its neighborhood to witness the mustering and the departure of the ships bound for Mars. Nothing further had been heard of the mysterious phenomenon reported from the observatories six months before, and which at the time was believed to indicate the departure of another expedition from Mars for the invasion of the earth. If the Martians had set out to attack us they had evidently gone astray; or, perhaps, it was some other world that they were aiming at this time.

The expedition had, of course, profoundly stirred the interest of the scientific world, and representatives of every branch of science, from all the civilized nations, urged their claims to places in the ships. Mr. Edison was compelled, from lack of room, to refuse transportation to more than one in a thousand of those who now, on the plea that they might be able to bring back something of advantage to science, wished to embark for Mars.

As the Great Napoleon Did

On the model of the celebrated corps of literary and scientific men which Napoleon carried with him in his invasion of Egypt, Mr. Edison selected a company of the foremost astronomers, archaeologists, anthropologists, botanists, bacteriologists, chemists, physicists, mathematicians, mechanicians, meteorologists and experts in mining, metallurgy and every other branch of practical science, as well as artists and photographers. It was but reasonable to believe that in another world, and a world so much older than the earth as Mars was, these men would be able to gather materials in comparison with which the discoveries made among the ruins of ancient empires in Egypt and Babylonia would be insignificant indeed.

To Conquer Another World

It was a wonderful undertaking and a strange spectacle. There was a feeling of uncertainty which awed the vast multitude whose eyes were upturned to the ships. The expedition was not large, considering the gigantic character of the undertaking. Each of the electrical ships carried about twenty men, together with an abundant supply of compressed provisions, compressed air, scientific apparatus and so on. In all, there were about 2,000 men, who were going to conquer, if they could, another world!

But though few in numbers, they represented the flower of the earth, the culmination of the genius of the planet. The greatest leaders in science, both theoretical and practical, were there. It was the evolution of the earth against the evolution of Mars. It was a planet in the heyday of its strength matched against an aged and decrepit world which, nevertheless, in consequence of its long ages of existence, had acquired an experience which made it a most dangerous foe. On both sides there was desperation. The earth was desperate because it foresaw destruction unless it could first destroy its enemy. Mars was desperate because nature was gradually depriving it of the means of supporting life, and its teeming population was compelled to swarm like the inmates of an overcrowded hive of bees, and find new homes elsewhere. In this respect the situation on Mars, as we were well aware, resembled what had already been known upon the earth, where the older nations overflowing with population had sought new lands in which to settle, and for that purpose had driven out the native inhabitants, whenever those natives had proven unable to resist the invasion.

No man could foresee the issue of what we were about to undertake, but the tremendous powers which the disintegrators had exhibited and the marvellous efficiency of the electrical ships bred almost universal confidence that we should be successful.

Master Minds of the World

The car in which Mr. Edison travelled was, of course, the flagship of the squadron, and I had the good fortune to be included among its inmates. Here, besides several leading men of science from our own country, were Lord Kelvin, Lord Rayleigh, Professor Roentgen, Dr. Moissan—the man who first made artificial diamonds—and several others whose fame had encircled the world. Each of these men cherished hopes of wonderful discoveries, along his line of investigation, to be made in Mars.

An elaborate system of signals had, of course, to be devised for the control of the squadron. These signals consisted of brilliant electric lights displayed at night and so controlled that by their means long sentences and directions could be easily and quickly transmitted.

A Novel Signal System

The day signals consisted partly of brightly colored pennons and flags, which were to serve only when, shadowed by clouds or other obstructions, the full sunlight should not fall upon the ships. This could naturally only occur near the surface of the earth or of another planet.

Once out of the shadow of the earth we should have no more clouds and no more night until we arrived at Mars. In open space the sun would be continually shining. It would be perpetual day for us, except as, by artificial means, we furnished ourselves with darkness for the purpose of promoting sleep. In this region of perpetual day, then, the signals were also to be transmitted by flashes of light from mirrors reflecting the rays of the sun.

Perpetual Night

Yet this perpetual day would be also, in one sense, a perpetual night. There would be no more blue sky for us, because without an atmosphere the sunlight could not be diffused. Objects would be illuminated only on the side toward the sun. Anything that screened off the direct rays of sunlight would produce absolute darkness behind it. There would be no graduation of shadow. The sky would be as black as ink on all sides.

While it was the intention to remain as much as possible within the cars, yet since it was probable that necessity would arise for occasionally quitting the interior of the electrical ships, Mr. Edison had provided for this emergency by inventing an air-tight dress constructed somewhat after the manner of a diver's suit, but of much lighter material. Each ship was provided with several of these suits, by wearing which one could venture outside the car even when it was beyond the atmosphere of the earth.

Terrific Cold Anticipated

Provision had been made to meet the terrific cold which we knew would be encountered the moment we had passed beyond the atmosphere—that awful absolute zero which men had measured by anticipation, but never yet experienced—by a simple system of producing within the air-tight suits a temperature sufficiently elevated to counteract the effects of the frigidity without. By means of long, flexible tubes, air could be continually supplied to the wearers of the suits, and by an ingenious contrivance a store of compressed air sufficient to last for several hours was provided for each suit, so that in case of necessity the wearer could throw off the tubes connecting him with the air tanks in the car. Another object which had been kept in view in the preparation of these suits was the possible exploration of an airless planet, such as the moon.

The necessity of some contrivance by means of which we should be enabled to converse with one another when on the outside of the cars in open space, or when in an airless world, like the moon, where there would be no medium by which the waves of sound could be conveyed as they are in the atmosphere of the earth, had been foreseen by our great inventor, and he had not found it difficult to contrive suitable devices for meeting the emergency.

Inside the headpiece of each of the electrical suits was the mouthpiece of a telephone. This was connected with a wire which, when not in use, could be conveniently coiled upon the arm of the wearer. Near the ears, similarly connected with wires, were telephonic receivers.

An Aerial Telegraph

When two persons wearing the air-tight dresses wished to converse with one another it was only necessary for them to connect themselves by the wires, and conversation could then be easily carried on.

Careful calculations of the precise distance of Mars from the earth at the time when the expedition was to start had been made by a large number of experts in mathematical astronomy. But it was not Mr. Edison's intention to go direct to Mars. With the exception of the first electrical ship, which he had completed, none had yet been tried in a long voyage. It was desirable that the qualities of each of the ships should first be carefully tested, and for this reason the leader of the expedition determined that the moon should be the first port of space at which the squadron would call.

It chanced that the moon was so situated at this time as to be nearly in a line between the earth and Mars, which latter was in opposition to the sun, and consequently as favorably situated as possible for the purposes of the voyage. What would be, then, for 99 out of the 100 ships of the squadron, a trial trip would at the same time be a step of a quarter of a million of miles gained in the direction of our journey, and so no time would be wasted.

The departure from the earth was arranged to occur precisely at midnight. The moon near the full was hanging high over head, and a marvellous spectacle was presented to the eyes of those below as the great squadron of floating ships, with their signal lights ablaze, cast loose and began slowly to move away on their adventurous and unprecedented expedition into the great unknown. A tremendous cheer, billowing up from the throats of millions of excited men and women, seemed to rend the curtain of the night, and made the airships tremble with the atmospheric vibrations that were set in motion.

Magnificent Fireworks

Instantly magnificent fireworks were displayed in honor of our departure. Rockets by hundreds of thousands shot heaven-ward, and then burst in constellations of fiery drops. The sudden illumination thus produced, overspreading hundreds of square miles of the surface of the earth with a light almost like that of day, must certainly have been visible to the inhabitants of Mars, if they were watching us at the time. They might, or might not, correctly interpret its significance; but, at any rate, we did not care. We were off, and were confident that we could meet our enemy on his own ground before he could attack us again.

And the Earth Was Like a Globe

And now, as we slowly rose higher, a marvelous scene was disclosed. At first the earth beneath us, buried as it was in night, resembled the hollow of a vast cup of ebony blackness, in the centre of which, like the molten lava run together at the bottom of a volcanic crater, shone the light of the illuminations around New York. But when we got beyond the atmosphere, and the earth still continued to recede below us, its aspect changed. The cup-shaped appearance was gone, and it began to round out beneath our eyes in the form of a vast globe—an enormous ball mysteriously suspended under us, glimmering over most of its surface, with the faint illumination of the moon, and showing toward its eastern edge the oncoming light of the rising sun.

When we were still further away, having slightly varied our course so that the sun was once more entirely hidden behind the centre of the earth, we saw its atmosphere completely illuminated, all around it, with prismatic lights, like a gigantic rainbow in the form of a ring.

Another shift in our course rapidly carried us out of the shadow of the earth and into the all pervading sunshine. Then the great planet beneath us hung unspeakable in its beauty. The outlines of several of the continents were clearly discernible on its surface, streaked and spotted with delicate shades of varying color, and the sunlight flashed and glowed in long lanes across the convex surface of the oceans. Parallel with the Equator and along the regions of the ever blowing trade winds, were vast belts of clouds, gorgeous with crimson and purple as the sunlight fell upon them. Immense expanses of snow and ice lay like a glittering garment upon both land and sea around the North Pole.

Farewell To This Terrestrial Sphere

As we gazed upon this magnificent spectacle, our hearts bounded within us. This was our earth—this was the planet we were going to defend—our home in the trackless wilderness of space. And it seemed to us indeed a home for which we might gladly expend our last breath. A new determination to conquer or die sprung up in our hearts, and I saw Lord Kelvin, after gazing at the beauteous scene which the earth presented through his eyeglass, turn about and peer in the direction in which we knew that Mars lay, with a sudden frown that caused the glass to lose its grip and fall dangling from its string upon his breast. Even Mr. Edison seemed moved.

"I am glad I thought of the disintegrator," he said. "I shouldn't like to see that world down there laid waste again."

"And it won't be," said Professor Sylvanus P. Thompson, gripping the handle of an electric machine, "not if we can help it."

CHAPTER 5

To prevent accidents, it had been arranged that the ships should keep a considerable distance apart. Some of them gradually drifted away, until, on account of the neutral tint of their sides, they were swallowed up in the abyss of space. Still it was possible to know where every member of the squadron was through the constant interchange of signals. These, as I have explained, were effected by means of mirrors flashing back the light of the sun.

But, although it was now unceasing day for us, yet, there being no atmosphere to diffuse the sun's light, the stars were visible to us just as at night upon the earth, and they shone with extraordinary splendor against the intense black background of the firmament. The lights of some of the more distant ships of our squadron were not brighter than the stars in whose neighborhood they seemed to be. In some cases it was only possible to distinguish between the light of a ship and that of a star by the fact that the former was continually flashing while the star was steady in its radiance.

An Uncanny Effect

The most uncanny effect was produced by the absence of atmosphere around us. Inside the car, where there was air, the sunlight, streaming through one or more of the windows, was diffused and produced ordinary daylight.

But when we ventured outside we could only see things by halves. The side of the car that the sun's rays touched was visible, the other side was invisible, the light from the stars not making it bright enough to affect the eye in contrast with the sun-illumined half.

As I held up my arm before my eyes, half of it seemed to be shaved off lengthwise; a companion on the deck of the ship looked like half a man. So the other electrical ships near us appeared as half ships, only the illuminated sides being visible.

We had now got so far away that the earth had taken on the appearance of a heavenly body like the moon. Its colors had become all blended into a golden-reddish hue, which overspread nearly its entire surface, except at the poles, where there were broad patches of white. It was marvelous to look at this huge orb behind us, while far beyond it shone the blazing sun like an enormous star in the blackest of nights. In the opposite direction appeared the silver orb of the moon, and scattered all around were millions of brilliant stars, amid which, like fireflies, flashed and sparkled the signal lights of the squadron.

Danger Manifests Itself

A danger that might easily have been anticipated, that perhaps had been anticipated, but against which it would have been difficult, if not impossible, to provide, presently manifested itself.

Looking out of a window toward the right, I suddenly noticed the lights of a distant ship darting about in a curious curve. Instantly afterward another member of the squadron, nearer by, behaved in the same inexplicable manner. Then two or three of the floating cars seemed to be violently drawn from their courses and hurried rapidly in the direction of the flagship. Immediately I perceived a small object, luridly flaming, which seemed to move with immense speed in our direction.

The truth instantly flashed upon my mind, and I shouted to the other occupants of the car:

Struck By A Meteor!

"A meteor!"

And such indeed it was. We had met this mysterious wanderer in space at a moment when we were moving in a direction at right angles to the path it was pursuing around the sun. Small as it was, and its diameter probably did not exceed a single foot, it was yet an independent little world, and as such a member of the solar system. Its distance from the sun being so near that of the earth, I knew that its velocity, assuming it to be travelling in a nearly circular orbit, must be about eighteen miles in a second. With this velocity, then, it plunged like a projectile shot by some mysterious enemy in space directly through our squadron. It had come and was gone before one could utter a sentence of three words. Its appearance, and the effect it had produced upon the ships in whose neighborhood it passed, indicated that it bore an intense and tremendous charge of electricity. How it had become thus charged I cannot pretend to say. I simply record the fact. And this charge, it was evident, was opposite in polarity to that which the ships of the squadron bore. It therefore exerted an attractive influence upon them and thus drew them after it.

I had just time to think how lucky it was that the meteor did not strike any of us, when, glancing at a ship just ahead, I perceived that an accident had occurred. The ship swayed violently from its course, dazzling flashes played around it, and two or three of the men forming its crew appeared for an instant on its exterior, wildly gesticulating, but almost instantly falling prone.

It was evident at a glance that the car had been struck by the meteor. How serious the damage might be we could not instantly determine. The course of our ship was immediately altered, the electric polarity was changed, and we rapidly approached the disabled car.

The men who had fallen lay upon its surface. One of the heavy circular glasses covering a window had been smashed to atoms. Through this the meteor had passed, killing two or three men who stood in its course. Then it had crashed through the opposite side of the car, and, passing on, disappeared into space. The store of air contained in the car had immediately rushed out through the openings, and when two or three of us, having donned our airtight suits as quickly as possible, entered the wrecked car we found all its inmates stretched upon the floor in a condition of asphyxiation. They, as well as those who lay upon the exterior, were immediately removed to the flagship, restoratives were applied, and, fortunately, our aid had come so promptly that the lives of all of them were saved. But life had fled from the mangled bodies of those who had stood directly in the path of the fearful projectile.

This strange accident had been witnessed by several of the members of the fleet, and they quickly drew together, in order to inquire for the particulars. As the flagship was now overcrowded by the addition of so many men to its crew, Mr. Edison had them distributed among the other cars. Fortunately it happened that the disintegrators contained in the wrecked car were not injured. Mr. Edison thought that it would be possible to repair the car itself, and for that purpose he had it attached to the flagship in order that it might be carried on as far as the moon. The bodies of the dead were transported with it, as it was determined, instead of committing them to the fearful deep of space, where they would have wandered forever, or else have fallen like meteors upon the earth, to give them interment in the lunar soil.

Nearing the Moon

As we now rapidly approached the moon the change which the appearance of its surface underwent was no less wonderful than that which the surface of the earth had presented in the reverse order while we were receding from it. From a pale silver orb, shining with comparative faintness among the stars, it slowly assumed the appearance of a vast mountainous desert. As we drew nearer its colors became more pronounced; the great flat regions appeared darker; the mountain peaks shone more brilliantly. The huge chasms seemed bottomless and blacker than midnight. Gradually separate mountains appeared. What seemed like expanses of snow and immense glaciers streaming down their sides sparkled with great brilliancy in the perpendicular rays of the sun. Our motion had now assumed the aspect of falling. We seemed to be dropping from an immeasurable height and with an inconceivable velocity, straight down upon those giant peaks.

The Mountains of Luna

Here and there curious lights glowed upon the mysterious surface of the moon. Where the edge of the moon cut the sky behind it, it was broken and jagged with mountain masses. Vast crater rings overspread its surface, and in some of these I imagined I could perceive a lurid illumination coming out of their deepest cavities, and the curling of mephitic vapors around their terrible jaws.

We were approaching that part of the moon which is known to astronomers as the Bay of Rainbows. Here a huge semi-circular region, as smooth almost as the surface of a prairie, lay beneath our eyes, stretching southward into a vast ocean-like expanse, while on the north it was enclosed by an enormous range of mountain cliffs, rising perpendicularly to a height of many thousands of feet, and rent and gashed in every direction by forces which seemed at some remote period to have labored at tearing this little world in pieces.

A Dead And Mangled World

It was a fearful spectacle; a dead and mangled world, too dreadful to look upon. The idea of the death of the moon was, of course, not a new one to many of us. We had long been aware that the earth's satellite was a body which had passed beyond the stage of life, if indeed it had ever been a life supporting globe; but none of us were prepared for the terrible spectacle which now smote our eyes.

At each end of the semi-circular ridge that encloses the Bay of Rainbows there is a lofty promontory. That at the north-western extremity had long been known to astronomers under the name of Cape Laplace. The other promontory, at the southeastern termination, is called Cape Heraclides. It was toward the latter that we were approaching, and by interchange of signals all the members of the squadron had been informed that Cape Heraclides was to be our rendezvous upon the moon.

I may say that I had been somewhat familiar with the scenery of this part of the lunar world, for I had often studied it from the earth with a telescope, and I had thought that if there was any part of the moon where one might, with fair expectation of success, look for inhabitants, or if not for inhabitants, at least for relics of life no longer existent there, this would surely be the place. It was, therefore, with no small degree of curiosity, notwithstanding the unexpectedly frightful and repulsive appearance that the surface of the moon presented, that I now saw myself rapidly approaching the region concerning whose secrets my imagination had so often busied itself. When Mr. Edison and I had paid our previous visit to the moon on the first experimental trip of the electrical ship, we had landed at a point on its surface remote from this, and, as I have before explained, we then made no effort to investigate its secrets. But now it was to be different, and we were at length to see something of the wonders of the moon.

Like a Human Face

I had often on the earth drawn a smile from my friends by showing them Cape Heraclides with a telescope, and calling their attention to the fact that the outline of the peak terminating the cape was such as to present a remarkable resemblance to a human face, unmistakably a feminine countenance, seen in profile, and possessing no small degree of beauty. To my astonishment, this curious human semblance still remained when we had approached so close to the moon that the mountains forming the cape filled nearly the whole field of view of the window from which I was watching it. The resemblance, indeed, was most startling.

The Resemblance Disappears

"Can this indeed be Diana herself?" I said half aloud, but instantly afterward I was laughing at my fancy, for Mr. Edison had overheard me and exclaimed, "Where is she?"

"Who?"

"Diana."

"Why, there," I said, pointing to the moon. But lo! the appearance was gone even while I spoke. A swift change had taken place in the line of sight by which we were viewing it, and the likeness had disappeared in consequence.

A few moments later my astonishment was revived, but the cause this time was a very different one. We had been dropping rapidly toward the mountains, and the electrician in charge of the car was swiftly and constantly changing his potential, and, like a pilot who feels his way into an unknown harbor, endeavoring to approach the moon in such a manner that no hidden peril should surprise us. As we thus approached I suddenly perceived, crowning the very apex of the lofty peak near the termination of the cape, the ruins of what appeared to be an ancient watch tower. It was evidently composed of Cyclopean blocks larger than any that I had ever seen even among the ruins of Greece, Egypt and Asia Minor.

The Moon Was Inhabited

Here, then, was visible proof that the moon had been inhabited, although probably it was not inhabited now. I cannot describe the exultant feeling which took possession of me at this discovery. It settled so much that learned men had been disputing about for centuries.

"What will they say," I exclaimed, "when I show them a photograph of that?"

Below the peak, stretching far to right and left, lay a barren beach which had evidently once been washed by sea waves, because it was marked by long curved ridges such as the advancing and retiring tide leaves upon the shore of the ocean.

This beach sloped rapidly outward and downward toward a profound abyss, which had once, evidently, been the bed of a sea, but which now appeared to us simply as the empty, yawning shell of an ocean that had long vanished.

It was with no small difficulty, and only after the expenditure of considerable time, that all the floating ships of the squadron were gradually brought to rest on this lone mountain top of the moon. In accordance with my request, Mr. Edison had the flagship moored in the interior of the great ruined watch tower that I have described. The other ships rested upon the slope of the mountain around us.

Although time pressed, for we knew that the safety of the earth depended upon our promptness in attacking Mars, yet it was determined to remain here at least two or three days in order that the wrecked car might be repaired. It was found also that the passage of the highly electrified meteor had disarranged the electrical machinery in some of the other cars, so that there were many repairs to be made besides those needed to restore the wreck.

Burying the Dead

Moreover, we must bury our unfortunate companions who had been killed by the meteor. This, in fact, was the first work that we performed. Strange was the sight, and stranger our feelings, as here on the surface of a world distant from the earth, and on soil which had never before been pressed by the foot of man, we performed that last ceremony of respect which mortals pay to mortality. In the ancient beach at the foot of the peak we made a deep opening, and there covered forever the faces of our friends, leaving them to sleep among the ruins of empires, and among the graves of races which had vanished probably ages before Adam and Eve appeared in Paradise.

While the repairs were being made several scientific expeditions were sent out in various directions across the moon. One went westward to investigate the great ring plain of Plato, and the lunar Alps. Another crossed the ancient Sea of Showers toward the lunar Apennines.

One started to explore the immense crater of Copernicus, which, yawning fifty miles across, presents a wonderful appearance even from the distance of the earth. The ship in which I, myself, had the good fortune to embark, was bound for the mysterious lunar mountain Aristarchus.

Before these expeditions started, a careful exploration had been made in the neighborhood of Cape Heraclides. But, except that the broken walls of the watch tower on the peak, composed of blocks of enormous size, had evidently been the work of creatures endowed with human intelligence, no remains were found indicating the former presence of inhabitants upon this part of the moon.

A Gigantic Human Footprint

But along the shore of the old sea, just where the so-called Bay of Rainbows separates itself from the abyss of the Sea of Showers, there were found some stratified rocks in which the fascinated eyes of the explorer beheld the clear imprint of a gigantic human foot, measuring five feet in length from toe to heel. The most minute search failed to reveal another trace of the presence of the ancient giant, who had left the impress of his foot in the wet sands of the beach here so many millions of years ago that even the imagination of the geologists shrank from the task of attempting to fix the precise period.

The Great Footprint

Around this gigantic footprint gathered most of the scientific members of the expedition, wearing their oddly shaped air-tight suits, connected with telephonic wires, and the spectacle, but for the impressiveness of the discovery, would have been laughable in the extreme. Bending over the mark in the rock, nodding their heads together, pointing with their awkwardly accoutered arms, they looked like an assemblage of antediluvian monsters collected around their prey. Their disappointment over the fact that no other marks of anything resembling human habitation could be discovered was very great.

Still this footprint in itself was quite sufficient, as they all declared, to settle the question of the former inhabitation of the moon, and it would serve for the production of many a learned volume after their return to the earth, even if no further discoveries should be made in other parts of the lunar world.

Expeditions Over the Moon

It was the hope of making such other discoveries that led to the dispatch of the other various expeditions which I have already named. I had chosen to accompany the car that was going to Aristarchus, because, as every one who had viewed the moon from the earth was aware, there was something very mysterious about that mountain. I knew that it was a crater nearly thirty miles in diameter and very deep, although its floor was plainly visible.

The Glowing Mountains

What rendered it remarkable was the fact that the floor and the walls of the crater, particularly on the inner side, glowed with a marvelous brightness which rendered them almost blinding when viewed with a powerful telescope.

So bright were they, indeed, that the eye was unable to see many of the details which the telescope would have made visible but for the flood of light which poured from the mountains. Sir William Herschel had been so completely misled by this appearance that he supposed he was watching a lunar volcano in eruption.

It had always been a difficult question what caused the extraordinary luminosity of Aristarchus. No end of hypotheses had been invented to account for it. Now I was to assist in settling these questions forever.

From Cape Heraclides to Aristarchus the distance in an air line was something over 300 miles. Our course lay across the north-eastern part of the Sea of Showers, with enormous cliffs, mountain masses and peaks shining on the right, while in the other direction the view was bounded by the distant range of the lunar Apennines, some of whose towering peaks, when viewed from our immense elevation, appeared as sharp as the Swiss Matterhorn.

When we had arrived within about a hundred miles of our destination we found ourselves floating directly over the so-called Harbinger Mountains. The serrated peaks of Aristarchus then appeared ahead of us, fairly blazing in the sunshine.

A Gigantic String Of Diamonds

It seemed as if a gigantic string of diamonds, every one as great as a mountain peak, had been cast down upon the barren surface of the moon and left to waste their brilliance upon the desert air of this abandoned world.

As we rapidly approached, the dazzling splendor of the mountain became almost unbearable to our eyes, and we were compelled to resort to the device, practiced by all climbers of lofty mountains, where the glare of sunlight upon snow surfaces is liable to cause temporary blindness, of protecting our eyes with neutral-tinted glasses.

Professor Moissan, the great French chemist and maker of artificial diamonds, fairly danced with delight.

"Voila! Voila! Voila!" was all that he could say.

A Mountain of Crystals

When we were comparatively near, the mountain no longer seemed to glow
with a uniform radiance, evenly distributed over its entire surface, but now
innumerable points of light, all as bright as so many little suns, blazed away at
us. It was evident that we had before us a mountain composed of, or at least
covered with, crystals.

Without stopping to alight on the outer slopes of the great ring-shaped
range of peaks which composed Aristarchus, we sailed over their rim and
looked down into the interior. Here the splendor of the crystals was greater
than on the outer slopes, and the broad floor of the crater, thousands of feet
beneath us, shone and sparkled with overwhelming radiance, as if it were an
immense bin of diamonds, while a peak in the centre flamed like a stupendous tiara incrusted with selected gems.

Eager to see what these crystals were, the car was now allowed rapidly to
drop into the interior of the crater. With great caution we brought it to rest
upon the blazing ground, for the sharp edges of the crystals would certainly
have torn the metallic sides of the car if it had come into violent contact with
them.

Donning our air-tight suits and stepping carefully out upon this wonderful footing we attempted to detach some of the crystals. Many of them were
firmly fastened, but a few—some of astonishing size—were readily loosened.

A Wealth of Gems

A moment's inspection showed that we had stumbled upon the most marvelous work of the forces of crystallization that human eyes had ever rested
upon. Some time in the past history of the moon there had been an enormous
outflow of molten material from the crater. This had overspread the walls and
partially filled up the interior, and later its surface had flowered into gems, as
thick as blossoms in a bed of pansies.

The whole mass flashed prismatic rays of indescribable beauty and intensity. We gazed at first speechless with amazement.

"It cannot be, surely it cannot be," said Professor Moissan at length.

"But it is," said another member of the party.

Are these diamonds?" asked a third.

"I cannot yet tell," replied the Professor. "They have the brilliancy of diamonds, but they may be something else."

Moon jewels," suggested a third.

"And worth untold millions, whatever they are," remarked another.

Jewels from the Moon

These magnificent crystals, some of which appeared to be almost flawless, varied in size from the dimensions of a hazelnut to geometrical solids several inches in diameter. We carefully selected as many as it was convenient to carry and placed them in the car for future examination. We had solved another long standing lunar problem and had, perhaps, opened up an inexhaustible mine of wealth which might eventually go far toward reimbursing the earth for the damage which it had suffered from the invasion of the Martians.

On returning to Cape Heraclides we found that the other expeditions had arrived at the rendezvous ahead of us. Their members had wonderful stories to tell of what they had seen, but nothing caused quite so much astonishment as that which we had to tell and to show.

The party which had gone to visit Plato and the lunar Alps brought back, however, information which, in a scientific sense, was no less interesting than what we had been able to gather.

They had found within this curious ring of Plato, which is a circle of mountains sixty miles in diameter, enclosing a level plain remarkably smooth over most of its surface, unmistakable evidences of former inhabitation. A gigantic city had evidently at one time existed near the centre of this great plain. The outlines of its walls and the foundation marks of some of its immense buildings were plainly made out, and elaborate plans of this vanished capital of the moon were prepared by several members of the party.

More Evidences of Habitation

of them was fortunate enough to discover an even more precious relic of the ancient lunarians. It was a piece of petrified skullbone, representing but a small portion of the head to which it had belonged, but yet sufficient to enable the anthropologists, who immediately fell to examining it, to draw ideal representations of the head as it must have been in life—the head of a giant of enormous size, which, if it had possessed a highly organized brain, of proportionate magnitude, must have given to its possessor intellectual powers immensely greater than any of the descendants of Adam have ever been endowed with.

Giants in Size

Indeed, one of the professors was certain that some little concretions found on the interior of the piece of skull were petrified portions of the brain matter itself, and he set to work with the microscope to examine its organic quality.

In the mean time, the repairs to the electrical ships had been completed, and, although these discoveries upon the moon had created a most profound sensation among the members of the expedition, and aroused an almost irresistible desire to continue the explorations thus happily begun, yet everybody knew that these things were aside from the main purpose in view, and that we should be false to our duty in wasting a moment more upon the moon than was absolutely necessary to put the ships in proper condition to proceed on their warlike voyage.

Departing from the Moon

Everything being prepared then, we left the moon with great regret, just forty-eight hours after we had landed upon its surface, carrying with us a determination to revisit it and to learn more of its wonderful secrets in case we should survive the dangers which we were now going to face.

THE DOOMSMAN

Van Tassel Sutpen (1905)

THE READER, DESIRING to inform himself *in extenso* regarding the physical and social changes that followed the catastrophe by which the ancient civilization was so suddenly subverted, would do well to consult the final authority upon the subject, the learned Vigilas, author of *The Later Cosmos* (elephant folio edition). But for our present purpose a brief epitome should suffice. To borrow then, with all due acknowledgments, from our admirable historian:

"It was in the later years of the twentieth century that the Great Change came; at least, so the traditions agree, and how is a man to know certainly of such things except as he learns them from his father's lips? True, the accounts differ, and widely so at times, but that much is to be expected—where were there ever two men who heard or saw the same things in the same way? It is human nature that we should color even transparent fact with the reflected glow of our passions and fancies, and so the distortion becomes inevitable; we should be satisfied if, to-day, we succeed in making out even the broad outlines of the picture.

"It appears tolerably certain that the wreck of the ancient civilization took place about three generations ago, the catastrophe being both sudden and overwhelming; moreover, all the authorities agree that only an infinitesimal portion of the race escaped, with whole skins, from what were, in very sooth, cities of destruction. These fortunate ones were naturally the politically powerful and the immensely rich, and they owed their safety to the fact that they were able to seize upon the shipping in the harbors for their exclusive use. The fugitives sailed away, presumably to the southward, and so disappeared from the pages of authentic history. We know nothing for certain; only that they departed, and that we saw their faces no more.

"Let us reconstruct, as best we may, the panorama of those few but awful days. The first rush was naturally to the country, but the crowds, choking the ferry and railway stations, were quickly confronted with the terror-stricken thousands of the suburbs, who were flocking to the city for refuge. And all through the dragging hours the same despairing reports flowed in from the remoter rural districts; everywhere the Terror walked, and men were dying like flies. From ocean to ocean, from the lakes to the gulf, the shadow rushed, and now the whole land lay in darkness.

"Such was the situation in what was then the United States of America, and similar conditions prevailed throughout the habitable world. London and Hong Kong, Vienna and Pekin, Buenos Ayres and Archangel—from every direction came the same inquiry, to every questioner was returned the same answer. It was the end of all things.

"Coincidently with this great recession of the human tide, occurred the eclipse of industry, science, and, indeed, every form of thought and progress. The plough rusted in the furrow, the half-formed web dropped to pieces in the loom, the very crops stood unharvested in the fields, to be finally devoured by the birds and by a horde of rats and mice. Up to the last moment there had been confusion and dismay certainly, but the wheels of trade and of the civil administration had continued to turn; men had stood at their posts in answer to the call of duty or impressed by the blind instinct of habit. And then, suddenly, the sun went down, only to rise again upon a silent land.

"The relapse into barbarism was swift. The few who had escaped were segregated from one another in small family groups, each man content with the bare necessities of animal existence and fearing the face of the stranger. Under such circumstances, there could be but little neighborly intercourse, and the ancient highways speedily became overgrown with grass and weeds, or else they were undermined and washed out by the winter storms. It was not until the second generation after the Terror that men once more began to draw together, in obedience to inherited instincts, and even then the new movement must have been largely brought about through the increasing aggressions of the Doomsmen. But of this in another place.

"It has been asserted that fire played a principal part in the destruction of the ancient cities, and it was at one time supposed that these extensive conflagrations were partly accidental and partly attributable to the wide-spread lawlessness that marked the closing hours of the greatest drama in all history. But later researches have evolved a new theory, and it now seems probable that the torch was employed by the authorities themselves as a final and truly a desperate measure. An heroic cautery, but, alas, a useless one.

"The comparative exemption of New York from the universal fate goes to support rather than to discredit this hypothesis. It escaped the dynamite cartridge and the torch simply because in that city no recognized authority remained in power; there was no one to carry out the imperative orders of the federal government. There were, of course, many isolated cases of incendiarism, but the city did not suffer from any general and organized conflagration, as was the fate of Philadelphia and St. Louis and New Orleans. The destiny of the metropolis was decided in a different way; already it had passed into the keeping of the Doomsmen.

"In effect, then, the highly civilized North American continent had relapsed, within the brief period of ninety years, into its primeval estate.

In every direction stretched an inhospitable wilderness of morass and forest, with a few feeble settlements of the Stockade people fringing the principal waterways, and here and there the smoke of an encampment of the Painted Men rising in a thin spiral from out of the vast ocean of green leaves. To-day the wild boar ranges where once the tide of human passion most turbulently flowed, and the poor herdsman, eating his noonday curds from a wooden bowl, crushes with indifferent heel the priceless bit of faience lying half hidden in the rotting leaves. Everywhere, the old order changing and disappearing, only to recreate itself in form ever more fantastic and enfeebled, a dead being, and yet inextricably bound up with the life of the new age. And over all, the shadow of Doom, gigantic, threatening, omnipotent."

Again we make acknowledgment to the "Laudable" Vigilas and quote at large from the luminous pages of *The Later Cosmos*. Now the reader, scenting more learned discourse, may meditate upon skipping this chapter; nay, will probably do so. Yet, to my thinking, he will act more wisely in buckling down to it, seeing that it contains matter of moment for the perfect understanding of the narrative proper. The studying of guide-posts is not an amusing occupation, but it is infinitely less tedious than to wander around all day in a fog and perhaps miss one's destination altogether.

"It is, indeed, a small world as we know it to-day. Our philosophers, reconstructing, as best they may, the science of the ancients from the treatises, few and sadly incomplete, that have come down to us, affirm that the earth is an orb and that another continent (perhaps more than one) lies beyond the rim of the eastern horizon. It may be so, but the issue is not of practical importance, seeing that there are none who care to make adventure of the great salty gulf that lies between. And so the sea keeps its mysteries.

"On the other hand, we count it inadvisable to wander far afield. To the north, to the west, and to the south stretches the unbroken forest, and in a few hours a man's legs may easily carry him out of hailing of the voice of his kind. The waterways form the only regular channels for social and commercial intercourse, and the busybody and gad-about are not regarded with favor by honest people.

"It appears highly probable that the human race was virtually annihilated over the general area of the ancient United States of America; it persisted only in a few particularly favored localities and through accidental circumstances of which we know nothing definite. In our own day, the northern, central, and southern group of colonies maintain a system of infrequent intercommunication, and beyond that certain knowledge does not extend. It is possible that mankind may exist in a degraded state, in many inaccessible corners of this vast continent of ours, but this is only a possibility, concerning which the theories of the learned are no more susceptible of proof than are the idle speculations of the vulgar.

"For convenience, we will accept the popular classification of the human race as it exists to-day—the Painted Men, the House People, and the Dooms-men. To take them up in that order.

"The Painted Men, otherwise the Wood Folk, are the descendants of the Indians of old, but the strain is largely mingled with that of the negro race, and, with hardly an exception, it is the weaker qualities both of body and of mind that have been emphasized in the hybrid. From their Indian forebears they have preserved the custom of painting their face with crude and hideous pigments upon all occasions of ceremony; hence their popular designation—the 'Painted Men.'

"The House People are conveniently subdivided into two classes—the townsmen, or House People proper, and the stockade dwellers, colloquially, the Stockaders.

"The House People of the walled towns represent as nearly as may be the middle classes of the ancient civilization. Originally, the family was the political and social unit, just as with the patriarchs of Holy Writ, but within the last generation the community idea has been growing rapidly, and there are perhaps a score of towns and villages scattered along the banks of the Greater and Lesser rivers.

"The Stockaders, reversing the procedure of their kinsmen of the towns, live apart from one another, each proprietor depending wholly upon his own resources for sustenance and defense. Some of the larger estates contain several hundred acres enclosed by a strong timber stockade and otherwise defended against the assaults of enemies. The head of the family, or clan, as it might more properly be termed, is lord paramount within his own borders, even possessing the rights of life and death. But this last authority is rarely called in exercise, since these folk of the free country-side are naturally wholesome, honest, generous-hearted men, content to lead a simple life and coveting no man's honor or goods. On the other hand, it must be admitted that the stockade dweller is both provincial of habit and prejudiced of mind. He looks down upon the townsman as a huckster in private and a shuffler in public life, and this feeling of contemptuous enmity is fully returned by the cit, who regards the free proprietor in the light of a boor and a bully. Moreover, it rankles in the Houseman's breast that no Stockader pays a farthing of head-money to the treasure-chest of the Doomsmen. Now and then some well-to-do proprietor may suffer loss from cattle thieving and rick burning, but as often as not the marauders pay full price for all they get. And this leads us to a consideration of the Doomsman himself, that foul excrescence upon our modern body politic. Fortunately, history here speaks clearly, and we have only to listen to her voice.

"It was a natural procedure, upon the coming of the Terror, to throw open the doors of the jails and other punitive institutions, thereby giving the wretched inmates an equal chance for life. The great mass of these degraded beings gravitated inevitably towards the cities, seeking plunder and opportunities for bestial dissipation that even the dread presence of the Terror could not restrain. Without hope and without fear, they rushed to the vulture's feast; here was wine and gold and soft raiment; let us eat and drink, for to-morrow we die.

"It was the ancient city of New York that received the vast bulk of this army of human rats; naturally so, since it was the supreme treasure-house of the western world. In such overwhelming numbers did these vermin come that the civil and military administrations were literally swarmed over. Between two days the outlaws were in complete possession, and the small remnant of the decent residents retired precipitately, preferring to meet death under the open sky rather than in company with their new masters.

"The years went on, but the changes that they brought were few. The descendants of the ancient criminals remained in the ruined city, at first of necessity, afterwards by choice, finding there fuel and shelter in abundance besides large stores of non-perishable food supplies. When, in the next generation, these provisions became exhausted it was inevitable that the refugees should fix covetous eyes upon the threshing-floors and herd-stalls of their rural neighbors. But although the outlaws had continued to gain in numbers, their natural increase was not proportionate to the growing power of their adversaries. Little by little the Doomsmen began to lose ground; already they had been defeated several times in pitched battle, and it looked as though the hornet's-nest would soon be smoked out.

"It was at this critical juncture that the infamous personality of Dom Gillian made itself of commanding account, and thenceforth the balance began to incline the other way. It was but the weight of one man's hand in the scale-pan, yet there are still many of us who remember how heavy that hand could be.

"Infamous is the adjective deliberately applied, and with reason. Dominus Gillian, to give him his full name, was a renegade, the unworthy son of a distinguished Stockader family. Admittedly a man of fine intellect and force, it is equally unquestionable that he was entirely devoid of moral sense. He possessed a genius for organization, and he succeeded in consolidating the unruly Doomsmen into a compact and disciplined body of outlaws. Murder and rapine were quickly reduced to exact sciences, and, unfortunately, the House People could not be made to see the necessity of united action; the townsman and the stockade dweller preferred to contend with each other rather than against the common enemy. As a consequence, the freebooters had a clear road before them, and so was established that intolerable tyranny under which the land still groans. All this occurred upward of sixty years ago.

"It only remains to add that Dominus, or, more colloquially, Dom Gillian, still lives, albeit he must be verging upon ninety years of age. For many years he has not been seen in the field, and it is even asserted that he no longer takes active part in the councils of the Doomsmen. Be that as it may, his will still remains dominant to animate and direct the malign powers created by his wicked genius. And the evil that men do, doth it not live after them?

"Such is the world, or, rather, one infinitesimal portion of the cosmos, in the year 2015, according to the ancient calendar, or 90 since the Terror."

Gavan of the Greenwood Keep was a prosperous man according to the standard of these latter days, and his estate was reckoned to be the largest and finest holding in all the western country-side. A man might walk from break of day until darkness and yet not complete the periphery of its boundary-lines, but the palisaded portion included only the arable land and home paddocks and was of comparatively limited extent. Viewed from a bird's-eye elevation, this stockaded enclosure appeared to be laid out in the shape of a pear, the house being situated near the small end. The greatest length of the area thus enclosed was a mile and a half, and it was three-quarters of a mile wide at the big or southern side, tapering down to a couple of hundred yards at the northern entrance or barrier.

A quarter of a mile back from the north gate stood the keep, not one distinct building, but rather several, built in the form of a hollow square and consolidated for mutual protection. The principal entrance, the one at the northern end, was called the water gate, for it should be explained that the keep stood on the bank of the Ochre brook and access was only possible by means of a drawbridge. Some day Sir Gavan intended to turn the course of the stream so as to carry it around the keep and thereby secure the protection of a continuous moat. But hitherto other duties had seemed more pressing, and the plan was still in abeyance.

Entering through the covered way of the water gate, with guard-room and bailiff's office to the right and left, one found himself in the court-yard, some fifty yards in the square. On the right were the cow-barns, horse-stalls, granaries, tool-houses, and store-buildings, while the dwelling proper, known as the Great House, occupied the entire left of the square, the kitchens and other offices adjoining the retainers' quarters on the south. An enormous hall, running clear to the roof, took up the central portion of the house, staircases and galleries affording access to the store and sleeping-rooms on the second and attic stories. The roof proper was surmounted by a para-petted and loop-holed structure called the fighting platform, and it was thither that Constans had repaired upon receiving the startling intelligence of his sister's disappearance. Let us rejoin him there.

In the leisurely moving figure glimpsed through the birches, Constans had instantly recognized Issa. Plainly she had been out flower-hunting; with the aid of his binoculars he could determine that she carried a bunch of the delicate pink-and-white blossoms that we call May-bloom. She was directing her steps straight for the house, but either she was unaccountably deaf to the continuous clanging of the alarm-bell or, still more strangely, unaware of its significance; she walked as though in a reverie, slowly and with her head bent forward. Thunder of God! it was a trap, and the foolish girl would not see. Unquestionably, the Doomsmen had forced the stockade at some distant point and were even now in ambush about the keep. But Constans, for all his keenness of vision and the assistance of his glass, could discover nothing to indicate the presence of any considerable body of men. There was no one in actual sight save he who sat upon his blood-bay steed, girth deep in the Ochre brook under shadow of the alders. Only one, but that one!

Constans found himself in the court-yard; how he scarcely knew. The water gate still stood open with the drawbridge lowered, but both could be easily secured within a few seconds should the enemy venture upon any open demonstration. Sir Gavan stood in the covered way talking anxiously with his eldest son Tennant, who had just returned from an unsuccessful search of the upper orchard.

Constans, in his confusion of mind, did not notice his father and brother; he ran across the court-yard to the horse-boxes. His black mare Night whickered upon recognizing her master, and tried to rub her muzzle against his cheek as he fumbled with the throat-latch of the bridle. An instant longer, to lead out the mare and vault upon her back, and he was clattering through the court-yard and covered way.

Upon reaching the open Constans saw that the situation had developed into a crisis. The cavalier of the ostrich-feather had forced his horse up the steep bank of the Ochre brook and was riding slowly towards the girl, who stood motionless, realizing her perilous position, but unable for the moment to cope with it. She half turned, as though to seek again the shelter of the birchen copse; then, clutching at her impeding skirts, she ran in the direction of the keep. He of the ostrich-plume spurred to the gallop; inevitably their paths must intersect a few yards farther on.

From behind came the noise of men shouting and the thud of quarrels impinging upon stout oak; the Doomsmen, hitherto in hiding, were making a diversion, in answer, doubtless, to a signal from their leader. A hundred gray-garbed men showed themselves in the open, coming from the shelter of the fir plantation back of the rickyards; they ran towards the open water gate, exposing themselves recklessly in their eagerness to reach it.

But the defenders were not to be surprised so easily, and Constans, glancing backward, saw that the drawbridge was already in the air and the gate closed. The outlaws, realizing that the surprise was a failure, and unwilling to brave the arrows sent whistling about their ears from the fighting platforms of the keep, fell back in some disorder. At the same moment a solitary figure appeared, emerging as though by magic from the solid wall of the keep—Sir Gavan himself, a father forgetful of all else but the peril of his children. He must have used the "Rat's-Hole" for egress; he hurried down the green slope, calling his daughter by name. All this Constans saw in that swift backward glance. Well, there was but one thing that he could do.

And Night knew it, too; brave little Night, how cleverly you forced yourself under the towering bulk of that brute of a blood-bay! A thunder of hoofs and they were in touch; Constans felt himself hurled into space; the bridle-reins of tough plaited leather were torn from his hands; Night and he were down.

The dust cloud cleared and the boy struggled up, although his head was still spinning from the shock of the encounter. Ten yards away lay the black mare with a broken foreleg. She was trying to rise, her eyes glazed with pain and her flanks heaving horribly.

The blood-bay had kept his feet and his master his saddle—a hardy pair, these two. But the desperate expedient had proved successful in that Issa was safe. Already Sir Gavan had her in his arms, and before the horseman had fully found himself the fugitives were under the shadow of the keep's walls.

The question of his own danger did not immediately concern Constans; he had no eyes for anything but Night lying there in her agony. His father had given him the horse when she was a foal of a week old, and Constans had broken and trained her himself. Well, she had served him faithfully, and in return he would show her the last mercy. His knife-sheath hung from his girdle; he drew out the blade and drove it home just behind the glossy black shoulder. Night shuddered and lay still. The knife had sunken deep, and Constans had to exert all his strength to withdraw it. The bare point of a rapier touched him meaningly on the arm; he stood up and faced his enemy.

The man on horseback laughed softly. "Oho, my young cockerel, it was but a touch of the gaff, and now that you are ready is reason sufficient why I should prefer to wait. But that neither of us may forget—" He bent down and caught Constans by the shoulders, turning him around and forcing him backward until his head rested against the blood-bay's withers. Two slashes of his hunting-knife and a tiny, triangular nick appeared on the upper part of the lad's right ear.

"That is my sign-manual of which I spoke to you an hour or more ago. It is Quinton Edge's mark, as all men know, and it brands whatever bears it as Quinton Edge's property. Some day I may deem it worth while to claim my own; until then you can be my caretaker, my tenant. What! no answer? And yet it is a generous offer, I think, considering how sore my arm has grown and how impertinently you behaved just now in interfering between me and a lady. Light of God! but she is a bewitching bundle of femineity. But twice, boy, have I seen her; hardly a dozen words have passed——"

He stopped abruptly and gazed hard at Constans. Then slowly:

"Your sister, I take it; there is the same straight line of eyebrow. No answer again? Well, we will pass it over for the nonce; you have still many things to learn, and, chiefly, to becomingly order body and soul in the presence of your lord. After all, it pleases me better to have the last word from the lady's own lips; she had been most discourteously treated, and I would fain be shriven. Until we meet again, then."

The cavalier put spur to the blood-bay's flank and rode straight for the Great House. The boy stood staring after him; he did not notice the trickle of blood from the cut in his ear; he was not even conscious that he was still in life. He remembered only the unforgivable affront which this man had put upon him, the mark which was the infamous badge of the bondman, the slave. Quinton Edge! Ah, yes; he would remember that face and name.

The Doomsman had ridden in cool defiance up to the very walls of the keep. It would have been an easy matter for one of the garrison to have bored his gay jacket through with a feathered shaft, and for a moment Constans trembled, fearing lest some overzealous partisan should thus rob him of his future vengeance. But the very audacity of the man proved the saving of his skin. They were brave men who manned the fighting platforms of the Greenwood Keep, and they could not bring themselves to set upon naked courage.

Constans fancied that the man spoke to some one who stood hidden in the deep embrasure of a window, but it was too far to either see or hear. Then it seemed that a small object fell lightly from the window-sill. The Doomsman caught it dexterously and fastened it on his breast. Another low bow and, wheeling his horse, he dashed down the slope. Constans ran blindly to meet him; why, he did not know. He who named himself Quinton Edge swerved slightly in his course so as to pass within arm's-length, calling out as he did so:

"Gage of battle and gage of love; a fortunate day for me. Believe me that at some future time I shall answer for them both."

It was a sprig of the May-bloom that the cavalier wore in his button-hole; Constans had only time to recognize it when the blood-bay broke into full gallop. The lad flung himself at full length upon the turf, face downward, and lay there motionless.

It was a warm, cloudy night some two weeks later, and Constans sat in the great hall of the keep, listlessly regarding the preparations that were being made for the evening meal. Six or seven of the house-servants were bustling to and from the buttery laden with flagons and dishes, which they deposited with a vast amount of noise and confusion upon the tables. These latter were of the most primitive construction, nothing more than puncheons smoothed down with the adze and supported by wooden trestles.

The main table ran nearly the full length of the hall, and was intended to accommodate the men-at-arms and the superior servants, together with such strangers of low degree as might chance to be present. The furniture was of the rudest pattern—platters of bass and white wood, which were daily scoured with sand to keep them clean and sweet, earthenware pitchers of a bricklike hue, drinking-cups of pewter and leather, and clumsy iron forks. There was no provision of cutlery; evidently the guests were expected to use their hunting-knives and daggers for the dismemberment of the viands.

At the upper or dais end of the hall there was a second table, placed at right angles to the long one and elevated above it by the height of the superior flooring upon which it stood. This principal board was, of course, for the exclusive use of the family and distinguished guests, and from the circumstance of its being raised above the main level the master could command an unobstructed view of the entire household in the event of any overt disorder or indecorum.

The viands were quite in keeping with the simplicity of the table-gear. Huge chines of beef and mutton, with spare-rib and fowl in apparently unlimited quantity, formed the staple of the repast, and were reinforced by vast bowls of the commoner garden vegetables and by bread made of unbolted flour. Sweetmeats were scarce, for the products of the sugarcane are difficult to procure in these northern latitudes. Maple sugar and honey serve as the ordinary substitutes, and even these are regarded as luxuries, since maple-trees are few in number and bee-keeping is but little practised. Finally, there were the drinkables, these including hard cider and a thin, acid wine made from the wild grape.

Annoyed by the clatter of the dishes and the half-whispered conversation of the domestics, Constans rose and walked to the dais end of the hall, where his mother and sister were seated, engaged in the agreeable occupation of inspecting the contents of a peddler's pack. It was an imposing array to the eye, and the chapman, kneeling on the floor close by Issa's stool, kept handing up one article after another for closer examination. The stuff seemed worthless enough to Constans—trumpery pieces of quartz crystal set in copper and debased silver, rings and bangles of a hue unmistakably brassy, hair ribbons, parti-colored dress goods, pins, needles, and a miscellaneous assortment of useless trinkets. Constans was genuinely astonished that Issa, who had been hitherto something of a good-fellow, should seem interested in such rubbish; but then women were all alike when it was a question of pretty things to buy. He looked sharply at the peddler, but the latter appeared commonplace enough, a man of forty or thereabouts, and dressed in the looped-up gray gaberdine peculiar to the guild of itinerant chapmen. Possibly he was bald, for he wore a close-fitting skull-cap; his beard, however, was luxuriant and effectually hid the contour of the lower half of his face. Constans stood by frowning lightly, but he had no reasonable pretext for interfering with his sister's amusement, and in the feminine catalogue of diversions the peddler's infrequent visit held a prominent place.

The major-domo, wearing a silver chain about his neck by virtue of his office, advanced to his mistress's chair and announced that the meal was ready for serving. The Lady Rayne nodded, a brazen gong sounded, the big folding-doors at the south end were thrown open, and the hall was quickly filled with the customary throng of retainers and hangers-on. But all remained standing in silence until the master and mistress had taken their places. Sir Gavan entered from his workshop, and, offering his hand to his wife, led her ceremoniously to her seat, Issa and Constans following.

To Constans's indignant amazement the peddler stepped forward, as though to take the vacant seat alongside of Issa. But before Constans could move or speak the chapman appeared to recognize the im propriety of which he had been so nearly guilty; with a profound genuflection, he withdrew from the dais and found a place at the lower table. The incident had been so momentary that it had passed entirely unnoticed by his father and the Lady Rayne; Constans could not even be sure that Issa had understood, and certainly she gave no sign of discomposure.

"What presumption!" muttered Constans, under his breath. "These fellows are becoming more insufferable every day, and my father sees nothing." Constans resolved that the man should be packed off immediately upon the conclusion of the meal. He could easily persuade Sir Gavan that the fellow had none too honest a look, while his wares were assuredly the cheapest trash. He must be got rid of before the women had been beguiled into spending all their pin-money.

The repast dragged out to its end, and the women withdrew to the upper end of the hall, comparative privacy being secured by large leather screens set up along the edge of the dais. The men remained at the table for deeper potations and the smoking of rank black kinnectikut tobacco in huge wooden pipes.

A heavy thunderstorm, the first of the season, had come up, and Constans recognized, to his vexation, that he would have no decent excuse for turning the peddler out-of-doors. So he kept his seat at the table in sulky silence, watching the man closely, and ready to note anything of further suspicion in his actions and bearing. But he had his trouble for his pains, for the fellow was the itinerant chapman to the life, even to the stock of gross stories with which he kept his bucolic audience in an uninterrupted guffaw. Pah! would Sir Gavan never finish his second pipe and give the signal to rise?

The storm had turned into a heavy downpour, and the peddler was consequently sure of his night's lodging. He had been summoned again to the presence of the ladies, and, as before, Constans stood aloof and wondered irritably how his fastidious sister could find aught in common with this wayside huckster. She was talking to him now with an animation rare with her, her cheeks flushed and her eyes glowing.

"And you have been in Doom—in the city itself?" she asked, incredulously.

"Yes, gracious lady; and not once, but a score of times. The brocades that I promised to show you after supper will be my witness. And there are some superlative satin and silk lengths which my Lady Rayne wished particularly to see. Will you allow me, then?"

The peddler, opening an inner compartment of his pack, drew out several pieces of stuff wrapped up in brown linen. Removing the covering, he spread the goods upon the rug before the ladies, holding up each separate piece to the light and expatiating upon its merits in the approved fashion of the shopman. The two women gave a little gasp of astonishment; never had they seen such wondrous beauty of color and finish; their little market-town of Croye held nothing to compare to this.

"I must send for Meta to advise me," said the Lady Rayne, glancing fondly from one rich fabric to another. "She ought to know good silk when she sees it, after living so long in Croye; and you, Issa, seem strangely indifferent to-night. You hardly looked at this piece of brocade."

Meta, the Lady Rayne's bedwoman, speedily appeared, and mistress and maid fell into earnest converse. Issa, as in duty bound, listened; then her attention seemed to flag again. She bent over the open pack and picked up a chain of filigree work. It was beautifully fashioned and looked like gold.

"It is gold," said the chapman, answering the question in her eyes. "The pure gold of the ancients; you never see that pale yellow nowadays. Ah, yes, a pretty trinket to have brought from the heart of Doom for the delight of a fair woman's eyes, and well worth its price of a man's life. But, then, fortune was kind, and I did not have to pay."

"Tell me about it," said the girl, beseechingly, and her breath came short and hot.

Whereupon the chapman drew a little nearer and began a wondrous tale of a secret visit that he had lately made to Doom, the Forbidden; of how he had crossed the river on a raft, the moon being in its dark quarter; of his landing upon a shaking wharf, where each foot-fall left a print of phosphorescent fire on the rotting planks; then of the marvels that he had seen there—vast warehouses covering whole acres of ground and filled with incalculable store of goods; lofty buildings, whose chimney-pots were in the clouds; palaces of sculptured stone, now empty and despoiled, the habitation of foxes and unclean nocturnal creatures.

Then again of hidden treasure, heaps and heaps of yellow gold; of the fierce Doomsmen who guarded it so well; of pitfalls and gins and siren voices that lured the soul astray; of ghastly shapes that crept along the crumbling walls; of mystery in every sound and shadow; of treacheries and alarms and the ever present terror of death—a tale of amazing wonder, at which the blood ran alternately warm and cold and the heart fluttered with a certain fearful joy.

How the maid hung upon the word, her little breasts heaving and her lips parted! "You have seen all these things?" she panted. "How wonderful! And you were not afraid? That was like a man—to be brave——" She blushed deeply, stammered, and turned to the neglected brocades. Constans, standing close at hand, was moved to new anger. The impertinent, how dared he! Yet he had listened himself, and in spite of himself, for assuredly the fellow talked well.

The evening was now well advanced and the customary hour of retirement was at hand. It was still raining, but Guyder Touchett, who came in dripping from his nightly task of posting the watch, remarked that the wind was changing and that it was likely to clear when the moon rose. Of course the peddler would now spend the night at the keep, and at his own request he was allowed to remain in the hall, a straw pallet being brought in for his accommodation.

"The Rat's-Hole!"

Constans repeated the words half aloud, holding the paper close to the guttering candle. It was but a tiny scrap, scarce large enough for the writing that it held. But paper of any kind is rare in these days, and so the gleam of white had caught his eye as he went up-stairs to his sleeping apartment. The handwriting was unfamiliar, and besides it was in back-hand, and it may be disguised as well; he was hardly an expert in such fine distinctions. But it was plainly a message, and its possible import startled him. For the Rat's-Hole was the secret exit that existed behind the jamb of the fireplace at the upper end of the hall. So cunningly had the panelled door been joinered into the wainscoting that a man might search for hours and yet not discover the spring that threw it open. Furthermore, the wainscoting was but a screen for the real door of iron-bound oak giving passage directly through the outer wall of the keep to the open country. A jealously guarded secret, this matter of the Rat's-Hole, and supposed to be known only to the master of the household and his immediate family. Even among them its existence was never referred to in ordinary conversation, while its actual use was restricted to the gravest of emergencies.

"The Rat's-Hole!" A message, an agreement, an appointment? By whose hand had these words been written? For whose eye had they been intended?

It would have been the wiser course to have communicated at once with Sir Gavan, but the latter, feeling somewhat indisposed, had retired early, and Constans hesitated to disturb him. Moreover, the boy stood in awe of his father, and of late a feeling of estrangement had been growing up between them. To Sir Gavan, Constans, with his dreamy, inactive nature, was a keen disappointment—so different from his brother Tennant. And Constans felt that his father did not understand him nor, indeed, cared to do so. Latterly, they had gone their own ways, and now at this perplexing juncture Constans could not bring himself to take his father into his confidence.

When, a few moments later, the lights had been formally extinguished for the night, Constans made his way back to the hall; he had to pass close by the pallet occupied by the peddler, and he paused an instant to listen to his deep and measured breathing. Surely the man slept.

Even in the dark Constans knew how to put his hand on the spring in the wainscoting, and it yielded to his touch. It was discomposing to find the key of the real door standing, ready for turning, in the lock. In theory, the key was never out of the master's immediate possession. An oversight, then? Constans's mind reverted to the one occasion in his remembrance on which the Rat's-Hole had been used, that day a fortnight back, when his sister Issa came out of the birch-copse, with her hands full of May-bloom and Quinton Edge had waited under cover of the alders. It was possible; his father might have forgotten. And yet——

Constans took the key and slipped it into the bosom of his doublet. Then closing the secret door in the wainscoting, he drew one of the big leather screens into convenient position and crouched down behind it. The dying fire gave out a flickering and uncertain light; he watched the grotesque procession of the shadows on the opposite wall until his eyes grew heavy. The odor of a smouldering bough of balsam-fir hung in the air—warm, spicy, soporific. He slept.

Constans awoke just as the footsteps died away; he listened, but again the stillness was profound. He felt his way to the secret door; the wainscot screen stood ajar. It was plain that some one had come to the Rat's-Hole only to discover that the key of the outside door was missing. Constans realized that he, too, had missed something—his chance to get to the bottom of the mystery. Shame on such a sentinel!

Without any definite plan of action, Constans made his way to the lower hall. The moonbeams were pouring a flood of light through the east windows and he could see plainly. The peddler's couch was empty, save for his gabardine of gray and the false hair that had served him for a beard. There were two figures dimly visible in the obscurity of the vaulted entrance to the water gate. They were working at the clumsy fastenings of the doors. As Constans ran up he recognized his sister Issa and the man who called himself Quinton Edge.

Without a word Constans seized the girl by the arm and swung her behind him. He struck at the Doomsman with his hunting-knife, but the latter caught his wrist with the grip of a wolf-trap. Yet even at that moment of stress Quinton Edge's voice preserved its soft, mincing inflections; the man wore his irritating affectations of speech as jauntily as he did the ostrich plumes in his cap.

"A brave ruffling of feathers—but gently, gently boy, you are frightening the lady. She goes with me of her full consent. Is it not so, sweetheart?"

"You lie!" said the boy, thickly.

The man laughed. "I tell you," he went on, "that the girl is mine by her own choice, and you have only to stand aside quietly to save the house and your own skin. But softly now; you are tearing the lace of my sleeve. A plague on your clumsy fingers!"

With a wrench Constans twisted himself free and turned to face his sister. "Issa!" he implored.

But she, with eyes like rain-washed stars, only looked beyond him to where Quinton Edge stood, softly smiling and holding out his womanish white hands. She would have rejoined him, but once again Constans forced her back. The dangling rope of the alarm-bell grazed his hand; he clutched at it, and a clang re-echoed through the court-yard, rousing the recreant warders from their slumbers. In that same instant Quinton Edge blew his whistle.

The Doomsmen must have already crossed the moat and been close up to the water gate, for the response to their leader's call was immediate. Quinton Edge had just time to remove the last of the bars securing the barrier when the night-watch streamed out tumultuously from their quarters under the arch, and he was obliged to retreat into the court-yard. But already the out-laws had forced apart the wooden leaves of the water gate; now they filled the vaulted passageway, and by sheer impact of superior weight began to drive back the bewildered and disorganized defenders. Friend and foe together, the mass surged into the quadrangle, a blind, indefinite cluster of struggling men, like to a swarm of hiving bees.

The storm had blown over, but the moon was every now and then obscured by masses of scurrying cloud-wrack, and in these periods of semi-darkness Doomsman and Stockader were hardly to be told apart. So closely packed was the scrimmage that the use of any missile weapon was impossible. The dagger and the night-stick (the latter a stout truncheon weighted with lead) were doing the work, and effectively, too. And in that press a man might be struck and die upon his feet, the corpse being stayed from falling through its juxtaposition to the bodies of the living.

The men of the keep, now that they had recovered from their first discom-fiture, rallied manfully. So stubborn and bitter raged the struggle that there was not a sound to be heard outside the noise of scuffling feet and the thud of blows. A man when hard beset for his life has no breath to spare for either oath of despair or shout of triumph. But not for long were the scales to swing so evenly; presently the ranks of the Stockaders yielded again to the pressure and broke into separate groups. Then were to be heard the groans of the wounded and dying; then for the first time the yell of the Doomsmen broke forth, ear-piercing in its exultancy.

Constans had managed to reach the shelter of the Great House, half drag-ging, half carrying the fainting form of his sister. Already Sir Gavan, with Tennant and the house servants, were under arms and making what prepara-tions they could for the final stand. A hopeless task it seemed, for the outlaws were now in full possession of the rest of the keep. The retainers occupying the general quarters in the south barracks had fallen easy victims. Surprised, out-numbered, and poorly armed, they had been quickly cut down as they reached the court-yard, and active resistance to the invaders was at an end.

Now the attack was turned directly upon the entrance to the Great House, and Sir Gavan, with his handful of followers, waited on the threshold for the inevitable issue. Already the ponderous door of iron-banded oak was groan-ing and splintering under the hail of blows. And in the forefront, with a laugh upon his lips, hewed Quinton Edge.

The barrier was down at last and the wolves were free to fall upon their quarry. A score of men, all told, against a hundred; the outcome was hardly doubtful. Yet it was not Gavan of the Greenwood Keep who held up his hand in sign of parley, but the Doomsman, Quinton Edge.

"The maiden Issa," he said, speaking with a smooth insolence that made Constans set his teeth. "Give her safely to my hand and your goods and your lives shall go free of further damage. A cheap bargain; but speak quickly, old man, these hounds of mine are not to be held in leash for long."

The partisans on either side had fallen back, leaving the two leaders face to face. Sir Gavan plucked twice at his throat, where the veins stood out like cords, constricting the vocal passages so that he stuttered thickly as he spoke.

"This—this gallows-scape!" he stammered. "This burner of peasants' hayricks, this pitiful plunderer of hen-roosts and cattle byres! If it were a man, now—to nail the insult to his lips——"

"We lose time," interrupted the Doomsman. "I have named my price."

"The price—ah, yes, the price. Tennant, Constans, you heard what he said. But where is my child? Let the girl stand forth; she is her father's daughter, and she shall answer for herself."

"I will abide by it," said Quinton Edge, with cool confidence.

The half-circle opened and Issa stood before them; a mere child she looked in her simple slip of white and with her fair hair all unbound. A vague terror seized upon Sir Gavan. What was this question that he was about to ask of his daughter? Could there be other than the one answer? How quietly she stood there and waited. Yes, and they were all waiting upon him; he must speak.

"Issa!"

It seemed to him that he had shouted aloud; then he realized that he had not spoken at all. "Issa!" he said, again, and she turned towards him.

"This man; he is not known to you. How could it be?"

"Yet it is the truth, my father," answered the girl, steadily. "It is just a month ago that chance set us face to face—one day when I rode alone in the green drive."

"And thereafter?"

"Once he came to the walled garden, adventuring the thousand chances of discovery. Yet how he man aged to cross the stockade-line I know not, for I was frightened, and begged him to leave me. And this he did most courteously, only swearing that he would again return."

"The third time?"

"That was the day—the day of the first May-bloom—the Ochre brook and the Doomsmen——" The girl's voice faltered.

"Yet never a word to me or to your mother?"

"It was not my secret," she answered, bravely; and upon that Quinton Edge himself took up the word.

"The blame is mine, since I used the peril in which I stood to set a seal upon her lips. A true and loyal maid is your daughter, and it was only after she had twice said me nay that I resolved to take without the asking. So I came that day which we both remember, and waited under the alder bushes, and once again I missed my cast. Yet was the quest not altogether fruitless, for I carried away this token from my lady's hostile garden."

He drew a faded spray of the May-bloom from his doublet and touched it lightly to his lips.

"What gentleman could refuse to redeem so dear a pledge? You have seen how I took head in hand and sat me down under your own roof-tree, my good Gavan of the keep. Faith, it was an even chance on which side the platter would fall, but this time the luck was mine. We should have been leagues away in the sun's eye by now, only that a peevish boy would have his way."

"And this—this is also true?" said Sir Gavan, and it seemed that the preceding silence had been very long.

"It is true." She had answered quietly, almost mechanically, but the heart of the Lady Rayne thrilled to the new note in her child's voice.

"Issa!" she cried, softly, and fell to weeping, not as a mother for her daughter but as one woman who sorrows for another.

"Issa!" she said, again, but neither then nor thereafter did the girl vouchsafe her mother look or word, all her soul seeming to hang upon the will of the man who had brought this woe upon her house. There was no need for word to pass; reading the command in her lover's eyes, she slipped from her mother's detaining clasp and placed her hand in his. Now, Issa was exceeding fair to look upon, and Quinton Edge's blood stirred hotly within him. And so for once he lost his head and did a foolish thing (only that no woman would agree that it was foolish), for there, in the presence of all, he quickly drew her face to his and kissed her on the lips. Then turning to his men, he made as though to send them from the house.

But it was not to be. A keen-pointed, heavy throwing-knife hung at Sir Gavan's side. Without a word he snatched it from the sheath, poised and flung it with all his force at his enemy's heart, a master throw and executed like a flash of light. Issa felt rather than saw the coming of the missile, and with an instinctive movement contrived to interpose her own delicate body. The steel bit deep into the white flesh, and with a little, shuddering cry the girl sank to the floor; out leaped Quinton Edge's sword. Constans, supporting his mother, felt her hand grow cold in his. He laid her gently down upon a convenient settle and thanked God that she, too, was safe.

It seemed to Constans that he was wandering in a bristling thicket of steel points; thunderous crashes re-echoed in his ears; the red light from the burning building eddied about his feet, a sea of blood and flame. His father and Tennant were down, never to rise again; a few paces in front of him Guyder Touchett headed a little knot of the defenders, swearing furiously as he hewed and hacked. A half-dozen against ten times their number; the issue could not be doubtful. Even as he gazed, two of the six sunk to their knees and then fell face downward, a dreadful sign that even a child might understand.

Now, Guyder Touchett stood alone, and about him a snarling pack of Dom Gillian's wolves, waiting cautiously upon one another, for the Stockader had a long sword-arm. Thereupon a man broke out of the press, signing the prudent ones to fall back. It was Quinton Edge, and, as ever, he was laughing, only that now his laughter sounded like to a bell that has cracked in the ringing. The swords clashed together; then the Doomsman dropped his point.

"You are too good a man for crows' meat," he said, shortly. "Stand clear and save your ears; my business is with the white-faced boy behind you."

But Guyder Touchett, ruddy, full-bodied, and loving his life as well as any man, only girded at him, saying:

"Is there, then, a deeper hell than this? I follow where my master has gone, and you, my lord, shall show me the way."

"The more fool you," quoth Quinton Edge, and drove at him.

Again the blades engaged, and a great fear suddenly tightened at the boy's heart. His champion had been exhausted by his previous efforts, and now his strength was going fast. Constans saw Touchett stagger and Quinton Edge preparing for a final stroke; he turned and ran for the upper end of the hall—the Rat's-Hole.

The key was still in his bosom, and in a few seconds he had passed the postern, closing and locking it behind him. Five minutes' hard running and he was free of the stockade and at the summit of a hill that commanded the scene which he had just left. The conflagration was progressing with astonishing rapidity; already the Great House itself was in flames, and dark figures could be seen issuing from the water gate. There! the red cock was crowing from the top of the bell-tower, and now the whole court-yard was a furnace of fire. A spark carried by the wind fell on his naked shoulder, where it bit like a fiery serpent. Yet he scarcely felt the smart; he stood motionless, looking upon the wreck of his little world, the only one that he had ever known.

"So in the end he made me a coward as well," said the boy, speaking softly to himself. "Is it that a slave must be a slave—always?"

He drew a long breath. "No, not always. But in the mean time I am to go on living and bearing everywhere his mark—Quinton Edge's mark. Well, I will begin by learning how to wait."

He stood irresolute for a moment longer, gazing at the scene of the night's tragedy as though to impress it indelibly upon his memory. Then turning his back to the east, where the faint saffron of early dawn was now showing, he started off on a long, swinging trot that speedily carried him down the slope and into the deeper shadow of the wood beyond.

THE POISON BELT

Sir Arthur Conan Doyle (1913)

Being an account of another adventure of Prof. George E. Challenger, Lord John Roxton, Prof. Summerlee, and Mr. E. D. Malone, the discoverers of "The Lost World"

CHAPTER I: THE BLURRING OF LINES

It is imperative that now at once, while these stupendous events are still clear in my mind, I should set them down with that exactness of detail which time may blur. But even as I do so, I am overwhelmed by the wonder of the fact that it should be our little group of the "Lost World"—Professor Challenger, Professor Summerlee, Lord John Roxton, and myself—who have passed through this amazing experience.

When, some years ago, I chronicled in the Daily Gazette our epoch-making journey in South America, I little thought that it should ever fall to my lot to tell an even stranger personal experience, one which is unique in all human annals and must stand out in the records of history as a great peak among the humble foothills which surround it. The event itself will always be marvellous, but the circumstances that we four were together at the time of this extraordinary episode came about in a most natural and, indeed, inevitable fashion. I will explain the events which led up to it as shortly and as clearly as I can, though I am well aware that the fuller the detail upon such a subject the more welcome it will be to the reader, for the public curiosity has been and still is insatiable.

It was upon Friday, the twenty-seventh of August—a date forever memorable in the history of the world—that I went down to the office of my paper and asked for three days' leave of absence from Mr. McArdle, who still presided over our news department. The good old Scotchman shook his head, scratched his dwindling fringe of ruddy fluff, and finally put his reluctance into words.

"I was thinking, Mr. Malone, that we could employ you to advantage these days. I was thinking there was a story that you are the only man that could handle as it should be handled."

"I am sorry for that," said I, trying to hide my disappointment. "Of course if I am needed, there is an end of the matter. But the engagement was important and intimate. If I could be spared——"

"Well, I don't see that you can."

It was bitter, but I had to put the best face I could upon it. After all, it was my own fault, for I should have known by this time that a journalist has no right to make plans of his own.

"Then I'll think no more of it," said I with as much cheerfulness as I could assume at so short a notice. "What was it that you wanted me to do?"

"Well, it was just to interview that deevil of a man down at Rotherfield."

"You don't mean Professor Challenger?" I cried.

"Aye, it's just him that I do mean. He ran young Alec Simpson of the Courier a mile down the high road last week by the collar of his coat and the slack of his breeches. You'll have read of it, likely, in the police report. Our boys would as soon interview a loose alligator in the zoo. But you could do it, I'm thinking—an old friend like you."

"Why," said I, greatly relieved, "this makes it all easy. It so happens that it was to visit Professor Challenger at Rotherfield that I was asking for leave of absence. The fact is, that it is the anniversary of our main adventure on the plateau three years ago, and he has asked our whole party down to his house to see him and celebrate the occasion."

"Capital!" cried McArdle, rubbing his hands and beaming through his glasses. "Then you will be able to get his opeenions out of him. In any other man I would say it was all moonshine, but the fellow has made good once, and who knows but he may again!"

"Get what out of him?" I asked. "What has he been doing?"

"Haven't you seen his letter on 'Scientific Possibeelities' in to-day's Times?"

"No."

McArdle dived down and picked a copy from the floor.

"Read it aloud," said he, indicating a column with his finger. "I'd be glad to hear it again, for I am not sure now that I have the man's meaning clear in my head."

This was the letter which I read to the news editor of the Gazette:—

"SCIENTIFIC POSSIBILITIES"

"Sir,—I have read with amusement, not wholly unmixed with some less complimentary emotion, the complacent and wholly fatuous letter of James Wilson MacPhail which has lately appeared in your columns upon the subject of the blurring of Fraunhofer's lines in the spectra both of the planets and of the fixed stars. He dismisses the matter as of no significance. To a wider intelligence it may well seem of very great possible importance—so great as to involve the ultimate welfare of every man, woman, and child upon this planet. I can hardly hope, by the use of scientific language, to convey any sense of my meaning to those ineffectual people who gather

their ideas from the columns of a daily newspaper. I will endeavour, therefore, to condescend to their limitation and to indicate the situation by the use of a homely analogy which will be within the limits of the intelligence of your readers."

"Man, he's a wonder—a living wonder!" said McArdle, shaking his head reflectively. "He'd put up the feathers of a sucking-dove and set up a riot in a Quakers' meeting. No wonder he has made London too hot for him. It's a peety, Mr. Malone, for it's a grand brain! We'll let's have the analogy."

"We will suppose," I read, "that a small bundle of connected corks was launched in a sluggish current upon a voyage across the Atlantic. The corks drift slowly on from day to day with the same conditions all round them. If the corks were sentient we could imagine that they would consider these conditions to be permanent and assured. But we, with our superior knowledge, know that many things might happen to surprise the corks. They might possibly float up against a ship, or a sleeping whale, or become entangled in seaweed. In any case, their voyage would probably end by their being thrown up on the rocky coast of Labrador. But what could they know of all this while they drifted so gently day by day in what they thought was a limitless and homogeneous ocean?

"Your readers will possibly comprehend that the Atlantic, in this parable, stands for the mighty ocean of ether through which we drift and that the bunch of corks represents the little and obscure planetary system to which we belong. A third-rate sun, with its rag tag and bobtail of insignificant satellites, we float under the same daily conditions towards some unknown end, some squalid catastrophe which will overwhelm us at the ultimate confines of space, where we are swept over an etheric Niagara or dashed upon some unthinkable Labrador. I see no room here for the shallow and ignorant optimism of your correspondent, Mr. James Wilson MacPhail, but many reasons why we should watch with a very close and interested attention every indication of change in those cosmic surroundings upon which our own ultimate fate may depend."

"Man, he'd have made a grand meenister," said McArdle. "It just booms like an organ. Let's get doun to what it is that's troubling him."

"The general blurring and shifting of Fraunhofer's lines of the spectrum point, in my opinion, to a widespread cosmic change of a subtle and singular character. Light from a planet is the reflected light of the sun. Light from a star is a self-produced light. But the spectra both from planets and stars have, in this instance, all undergone the same change. Is it, then, a change in those planets and stars? To me such an idea is inconceivable. What common change could simultaneously come upon them all? Is it a change in our own atmosphere? It is possible, but in the highest degree improbable, since we see no signs of it around us, and chemical analysis has failed to reveal it. What, then, is the third possibility? That it may be a change in the conducting medium, in that infinitely fine ether which extends from star to star and pervades the whole universe. Deep in that ocean we are floating upon a slow current. Might that current not drift us into belts of ether which are novel and have properties of which we have never conceived? There is a change somewhere. This cosmic disturbance of* *the spectrum proves it. It may be a good change. It may be an evil one. It may be a neutral one. We do not know. Shallow observers may treat the matter as one which can be disregarded, but one who like myself is possessed of the deeper intelligence of the true philosopher will understand that the possibilities of the universe are incalculable and that the wisest man is he who holds himself ready for the unexpected. To take an obvious example, who would undertake to say that the mysterious and universal outbreak of illness, recorded in your columns this very morning as having broken out among the indigenous races of Sumatra, has no connection with some cosmic change to which they may respond more quickly than the more complex peoples of Europe? I throw out the idea for what it is worth. To assert it is, in the present stage, as unprofitable as to deny it, but it is an unimaginative numskull who is too dense to perceive that it is well within the bounds of scientific possibility."*

Yours faithfully,
GEORGE EDWARD CHALLENGER.
THE BRIARS, ROTHERFIELD.

"It's a fine, steemulating letter," said McArdle thoughtfully, fitting a cigarette into the long glass tube which he used as a holder. "What's your opeenion of it, Mr. Malone?"

I had to confess my total and humiliating ignorance of the subject at issue. What, for example, were Fraunhofer's lines? McArdle had just been studying the matter with the aid of our tame scientist at the office, and he picked from his desk two of those many-coloured spectral bands which bear a general resemblance to the hat-ribbons of some young and ambitious cricket club. He pointed out to me that there were certain black lines which formed crossbars upon the series of brilliant colours extending from the red at one end through gradations of orange, yellow, green, blue, and indigo to the violet at the other.

"Those dark bands are Fraunhofer's lines," said he. "The colours are just light itself. Every light, if you can split it up with a prism, gives the same colours. They tell us nothing. It is the lines that count, because they vary according to what it may be that produces the light. It is these lines that have been blurred instead of clear this last week, and all the astronomers have been quarreling over the reason. Here's a photograph of the blurred lines for our issue to-morrow. The public have taken no interest in the matter up to now, but this letter of Challenger's in the Times will make them wake up, I'm thinking."

"And this about Sumatra?"

"Well, it's a long cry from a blurred line in a spectrum to a sick nigger in Sumatra. And yet the chiel has shown us once before that he knows what he's talking about. There is some queer illness down yonder, that's beyond all doubt, and to-day there's a cable just come in from Singapore that the lighthouses are out of action in the Straits of Sundan, and two ships on the beach in consequence. Anyhow, it's good enough for you to interview Challenger upon. If you get anything definite, let us have a column by Monday."

I was coming out from the news editor's room, turning over my new mission in my mind, when I heard my name called from the waiting-room below. It was a telegraph-boy with a wire which had been forwarded from my lodgings at Streatham. The message was from the very man we had been discussing, and ran thus:—

Malone, 17, Hill Street, Streatham.—Bring oxygen.—Challenger.

"Bring oxygen!" The Professor, as I remembered him, had an elephantine sense of humour capable of the most clumsy and unwieldly gambollings. Was this one of those jokes which used to reduce him to uproarious laughter, when his eyes would disappear and he was all gaping mouth and wagging beard, supremely indifferent to the gravity of all around him? I turned the words over, but could make nothing even remotely jocose out of them. Then surely it was a concise order—though a very strange one. He was the last man in the world whose deliberate command I should care to disobey. Possibly some chemical experiment was afoot; possibly——Well, it was no business of mine to speculate upon why he wanted it. I must get it. There was nearly an hour before I should catch the train at Victoria. I took a taxi, and having ascertained the address from the telephone book, I made for the Oxygen Tube Supply Company in Oxford Street.

As I alighted on the pavement at my destination, two youths emerged from the door of the establishment carrying an iron cylinder, which, with some trouble, they hoisted into a waiting motor-car. An elderly man was at their heels scolding and directing in a creaky, sardonic voice. He turned towards me. There was no mistaking those austere features and that goatee beard. It was my old cross-grained companion, Professor Summerlee.

"What!" he cried. "Don't tell me that *you* have had one of these preposterous telegrams for oxygen?"

I exhibited it.

"Well, well! I have had one too, and, as you see, very much against the grain, I have acted upon it. Our good friend is as impossible as ever. The need for oxygen could not have been so urgent that he must desert the usual means of supply and encroach upon the time of those who are really busier than himself. Why could he not order it direct?"

I could only suggest that he probably wanted it at once.

"Or thought he did, which is quite another matter. But it is superfluous now for you to purchase any, since I have this considerable supply."

"Still, for some reason he seems to wish that I should bring oxygen too. It will be safer to do exactly what he tells me."

Accordingly, in spite of many grumbles and remonstrances from Summerlee, I ordered an additional tube, which was placed with the other in his motor-car, for he had offered me a lift to Victoria.

I turned away to pay off my taxi, the driver of which was very cantankerous and abusive over his fare. As I came back to Professor Summerlee, he was having a furious altercation with the men who had carried down the oxygen, his little white goat's beard jerking with indignation. One of the fellows called him, I remember, "a silly old bleached cockatoo," which so enraged his chauffeur that he bounded out of his seat to take the part of his insulted master, and it was all we could do to prevent a riot in the street.

These little things may seem trivial to relate, and passed as mere incidents at the time. It is only now, as I look back, that I see their relation to the whole story which I have to unfold.

The chauffeur must, as it seemed to me, have been a novice or else have lost his nerve in this disturbance, for he drove vilely on the way to the station. Twice we nearly had collisions with other equally erratic vehicles, and I remember remarking to Summerlee that the standard of driving in London had very much declined. Once we brushed the very edge of a great crowd which was watching a fight at the corner of the Mall. The people, who were much excited, raised cries of anger at the clumsy driving, and one fellow sprang upon the step and waved a stick above our heads. I pushed him off, but we were glad when we had got clear of them and safe out of the park. These little events, coming one after the other, left me very jangled in my nerves, and I could see from my companion's petulant manner that his own patience had got to a low ebb.

But our good humour was restored when we saw Lord John Roxton waiting for us upon the platform, his tall, thin figure clad in a yellow tweed shooting-suit. His keen face, with those unforgettable eyes, so fierce and yet so humorous, flushed with pleasure at the sight of us. His ruddy hair was shot with grey, and the furrows upon his brow had been cut a little deeper by Time's chisel, but in all else he was the Lord John who had been our good comrade in the past.

"Hullo, Herr Professor! Hullo, young fella!" he shouted as he came toward us.

He roared with amusement when he saw the oxygen cylinders upon the porter's trolly behind us. "So you've got them too!" he cried. "Mine is in the van. Whatever can the old dear be after?"

"Have you seen his letter in the Times?" I asked.

"What was it?"

"Stuff and nonsense!" said Summerlee harshly.

"Well, it's at the bottom of this oxygen business, or I am mistaken," said I.

"Stuff and nonsense!" cried Summerlee again with quite unnecessary violence. We had all got into a first-class smoker, and he had already lit the short and charred old briar pipe which seemed to singe the end of his long, aggressive nose.

"Friend Challenger is a clever man," said he with great vehemence. "No one can deny it. It's a fool that denies it. Look at his hat. There's a sixty-ounce brain inside it—a big engine, running smooth, and turning out clean work. Show me the engine-house and I'll tell you the size of the engine. But he is a born charlatan—you've heard me tell him so to his face—a born charlatan, with a kind of dramatic trick of jumping into the limelight. Things are quiet, so friend Challenger sees a chance to set the public talking about him. You don't imagine that he seriously believes all this nonsense about a change in the ether and a danger to the human race? Was ever such a cock-and-bull story in this life?"

He sat like an old white raven, croaking and shaking with sardonic laughter.

A wave of anger passed through me as I listened to Summerlee. It was disgraceful that he should speak thus of the leader who had been the source of all our fame and given us such an experience as no men have ever enjoyed. I had opened my mouth to utter some hot retort, when Lord John got before me.

"You had a scrap once before with old man Challenger," said he sternly, "and you were down and out inside ten seconds. It seems to me, Professor Summerlee, he's beyond your class, and the best you can do with him is to walk wide and leave him alone."

"Besides," said I, "he has been a good friend to every one of us. Whatever his faults may be, he is as straight as a line, and I don't believe he ever speaks evil of his comrades behind their backs."

"Well said, young fellah-my-lad," said Lord John Roxton. Then, with a kindly smile, he slapped Professor Summerlee upon his shoulder. "Come, Herr Professor, we're not going to quarrel at this time of day. We've seen too much together. But keep off the grass when you get near Challenger, for this young fellah and I have a bit of a weakness for the old dear."

But Summerlee was in no humour for compromise. His face was screwed up in rigid disapproval, and thick curls of angry smoke rolled up from his pipe.

"As to you, Lord John Roxton," he creaked, "your opinion upon a matter of science is of as much value in my eyes as my views upon a new type of shot-gun would be in yours. I have my own judgment, sir, and I use it in my own way. Because it has misled me once, is that any reason why I should accept without criticism anything, however far-fetched, which this man may care to put forward? Are we to have a Pope of science, with infallible decrees laid down *ex cathedra*, and accepted without question by the poor humble public? I tell you, sir, that I have a brain of my own and that I should feel myself to be a snob and a slave if I did not use it. If it pleases you to believe this rigmarole about ether and Fraunhofer's lines upon the spectrum, do so by all means, but do not ask one who is older and wiser than yourself to share in your folly. Is it not evident that if the ether were affected to the degree which he maintains, and if it were obnoxious to human health, the result of it would already be apparent upon ourselves?" Here he laughed with uproarious triumph over his own argument. "Yes, sir, we should already be very far from our normal selves, and instead of sitting quietly discussing scientific problems in a railway train we should be showing actual symptoms of the poison which was working within us. Where do we see any signs of this poisonous cosmic disturbance? Answer me that, sir! Answer me that! Come, come, no evasion! I pin you to an answer!'"

I felt more and more angry. There was something very irritating and aggressive in Summerlee's demeanour.

"I think that if you knew more about the facts you might be less positive in your opinion," said I.

Summerlee took his pipe from his mouth and fixed me with a stony stare.

"Pray what do you mean, sir, by that somewhat impertinent observation?"

"I mean that when I was leaving the office the news editor told me that a telegram had come in confirming the general illness of the Sumatra natives, and adding that the lights had not been lit in the Straits of Sunda."

"Really, there should be some limits to human folly!" cried Summerlee in a positive fury. "Is it possible that you do not realize that ether, if for a moment we adopt Challenger's preposterous supposition, is a universal substance which is the same here as at the other side of the world? Do you for an instant suppose that there is an English ether and a Sumatran ether? Perhaps you imagine that the ether of Kent is in some way superior to the ether of Surrey, through which this train is now bearing us. There really are no bounds to the credulity and ignorance of the average layman. Is it conceivable that the ether in Sumatra should be so deadly as to cause total insensibility at the very time when the ether here has had no appreciable effect upon us whatever? Personally, I can truly say that I never felt stronger in body or better balanced in mind in my life."

"That may be. I don't profess to be a scientific man," said I, "though I have heard somewhere that the science of one generation is usually the fallacy of the next. But it does not take much common sense to see that, as we seem to know so little about ether, it might be affected by some local conditions in various parts of the world and might show an effect over there which would only develop later with us."

"With 'might' and 'may' you can prove anything," cried Summerlee furiously. "Pigs may fly. Yes, sir, pigs *may* fly—but they don't. It is not worth arguing with you. Challenger has filled you with his nonsense and you are both incapable of reason. I had as soon lay arguments before those railway cushions."

"I must say, Professor Summerlee, that your manners do not seem to have improved since I last had the pleasure of meeting you," said Lord John severely.

"You lordlings are not accustomed to hear the truth," Summerlee answered with a bitter smile. "It comes as a bit of a shock, does it not, when someone makes you realize that your title leaves you none the less a very ignorant man?"

"Upon my word, sir," said Lord John, very stern and rigid, "if you were a younger man you would not dare to speak to me in so offensive a fashion."

Summerlee thrust out his chin, with its little wagging tuft of goatee beard.

"I would have you know, sir, that, young or old, there has never been a time in my life when I was afraid to speak my mind to an ignorant coxcomb—yes, sir, an ignorant coxcomb, if you had as many titles as slaves could invent and fools could adopt."

For a moment Lord John's eyes blazed, and then, with a tremendous effort, he mastered his anger and leaned back in his seat with arms folded and a bitter smile upon his face. To me all this was dreadful and deplorable. Like a wave, the memory of the past swept over me, the good comradeship, the happy, adventurous days—all that we had suffered and worked for and won. That it should have come to this—to insults and abuse! Suddenly I was sobbing—sobbing in loud, gulping, uncontrollable sobs which refused to be concealed. My companions looked at me in surprise. I covered my face with my hands.

"It's all right," said I. "Only—only it *is* such a pity!"

"You're ill, young fellah, that's what's amiss with you," said Lord John. "I thought you were queer from the first."

"Your habits, sir, have not mended in these three years," said Summerlee, shaking his head. "I also did not fail to observe your strange manner the moment we met. You need not waste your sympathy, Lord John. These tears are purely alcoholic. The man has been drinking. By the way, Lord John, I called you a coxcomb just now, which was perhaps unduly severe. But the word reminds me of a small accomplishment, trivial but amusing, which I used to possess. You know me as the austere man of science. Can you believe that I once had a well-deserved reputation in several nurseries as a farmyard imitator? Perhaps I can help you to pass the time in a pleasant way. Would it amuse you to hear me crow like a cock?"

"No, sir," said Lord John, who was still greatly offended, "it would *not* amuse me."

"My imitation of the clucking hen who had just laid an egg was also considered rather above the average. Might I venture?"

"No, sir, no—certainly not."

But in spite of this earnest prohibition, Professor Summerlee laid down his pipe and for the rest of our journey he entertained—or failed to entertain—us by a succession of bird and animal cries which seemed so absurd that my tears were suddenly changed into boisterous laughter, which must have become quite hysterical as I sat opposite this grave Professor and saw him—or rather heard him—in the character of the uproarious rooster or the puppy whose tail had been trodden upon. Once Lord John passed across his newspaper, upon the margin of which he had written in pencil, "Poor devil! Mad as a hatter." No doubt it was very eccentric, and yet the performance struck me as extraordinarily clever and amusing.

Whilst this was going on, Lord John leaned forward and told me some interminable story about a buffalo and an Indian rajah which seemed to me to have neither beginning nor end. Professor Summerlee had just begun to chirrup like a canary, and Lord John to get to the climax of his story, when the train drew up at Jarvis Brook, which had been given us as the station for Rotherfield.

And there was Challenger to meet us. His appearance was glorious. Not all the turkey-cocks in creation could match the slow, high-stepping dignity with which he paraded his own railway station and the benignant smile of condescending encouragement with which he regarded everybody around him. If he had changed in anything since the days of old, it was that his points had become accentuated. The huge head and broad sweep of forehead, with its plastered lock of black hair, seemed even greater than before. His black beard poured forward in a more impressive cascade, and his clear grey eyes, with their insolent and sardonic eyelids, were even more masterful than of yore.

He gave me the amused hand-shake and encouraging smile which the head master bestows upon the small boy, and, having greeted the others and helped to collect their bags and their cylinders of oxygen, he stowed us and them away in a large motor-car which was driven by the same impassive Austin, the man of few words, whom I had seen in the character of butler upon the occasion of my first eventful visit to the Professor. Our journey led us up a winding hill through beautiful country. I sat in front with the chauffeur, but behind me my three comrades seemed to me to be all talking together. Lord John was still struggling with his buffalo story, so far as I could make out, while once again I heard, as of old, the deep rumble of Challenger and the insistent accents of Summerlee as their brains locked in high and fierce scientific debate. Suddenly Austin slanted his mahogany face toward me without taking his eyes from his steering-wheel.

"I'm under notice," said he.

"Dear me!" said I.

Everything seemed strange to-day. Everyone said queer, unexpected things. It was like a dream.

"It's forty-seven times," said Austin reflectively.

"When do you go?" I asked, for want of some better observation. "I don't go," said Austin.

The conversation seemed to have ended there, but presently he came back to it.

"If I was to go, who would look after 'im?" He jerked his head toward his master. "Who would 'e get to serve 'im?"

"Someone else," I suggested lamely.

"Not 'e. No one would stay a week. If I was to go, that 'ouse would run down like a watch with the mainspring out. I'm telling you because you're 'is friend, and you ought to know. If I was to take 'im at 'is word—but there, I wouldn't have the 'eart. 'E and the missus would be like two babes left out in a bundle. I'm just everything. And then 'e goes and gives me notice."

"Why would no one stay?" I asked.

"Well, they wouldn't make allowances, same as I do. 'E's a very clever man, the master—so clever that 'e's clean balmy sometimes. I've seen 'im right off 'is onion, and no error. Well, look what 'e did this morning."

"What did he do?"

Austin bent over to me.

"'E bit the 'ousekeeper," said he in a hoarse whisper.

"Bit her?"

"Yes, sir. Bit 'er on the leg. I saw 'er with my own eyes startin' a marathon from the 'all-door."

"Good gracious!"

"So you'd say, sir, if you could see some of the goings on. 'E don't make friends with the neighbors. There's some of them thinks that when 'e was up among those monsters you wrote about, it was just "Ome, Sweet 'Ome' for the master, and 'e was never in fitter company. That's what *they* say. But I've served 'im ten years, and I'm fond of 'im, and, mind you, 'e's a great man, when all's said an' done, and it's an honor to serve 'im. But 'e does try one cruel at times. Now look at that, sir. That ain't what you might call old-fashioned 'ospitality, is it now? Just you read it for yourself."

The car on its lowest speed had ground its way up a steep, curving ascent. At the corner a notice-board peered over a well-clipped hedge. As Austin said, it was not difficult to read, for the words were few and arresting:—

WARNING.

———

Visitors, Pressmen, and Mendicants
are not encouraged.

G. E. CHALLENGER

"No, it's not what you might call 'earty," said Austin, shaking his head and glancing up at the deplorable placard. "It wouldn't look well in a Christmas card. I beg your pardon, sir, for I haven't spoke as much as this for many a long year, but to-day my feelings seem to 'ave got the better of me. 'E can sack me till 'e's blue in the face, but I ain't going, and that's flat. I'm 'is man and 'e's my master, and so it will be, I expect, to the end of the chapter."

We had passed between the white posts of a gate and up a curving drive, lined with rhododendron bushes. Beyond stood a low brick house, picked out with white woodwork, very comfortable and pretty. Mrs. Challenger, a small, dainty, smiling figure, stood in the open doorway to welcome us.

"Well, my dear," said Challenger, bustling out of the car, "here are our visitors. It is something new for us to have visitors, is it not? No love lost between us and our neighbors, is there? If they could get rat poison into our baker's cart, I expect it would be there."

"It's dreadful—dreadful!" cried the lady, between laughter and tears. "George is always quarreling with everyone. We haven't a friend on the countryside."

"It enables me to concentrate my attention upon my incomparable wife," said Challenger, passing his short, thick arm round her waist. Picture a gorilla and a gazelle, and you have the pair of them. "Come, come, these gentlemen are tired from the journey, and luncheon should be ready. Has Sarah returned?"

The lady shook her head ruefully, and the Professor laughed loudly and stroked his beard in his masterful fashion.

"Austin," he cried, "when you have put up the car you will kindly help your mistress to lay the lunch. Now, gentlemen, will you please step into my study, for there are one or two very urgent things which I am anxious to say to you."

CHAPTER II: THE TIDE OF DEATH

As we crossed the hall the telephone-bell rang, and we were the involuntary auditors of Professor Challenger's end of the ensuing dialogue. I say "we," but no one within a hundred yards could have failed to hear the booming of that monstrous voice, which reverberated through the house. His answers lingered in my mind.

"Yes, yes, of course, it is I.... Yes, certainly, *the* Professor Challenger, the famous Professor, who else?... Of course, every word of it, otherwise I should not have written it.... I shouldn't be surprised.... There is every indication of it.... Within a day or so at the furthest.... Well, I can't help that, can I?... Very unpleasant, no doubt, but I rather fancy it will affect more important people than you. There is no use whining about it.... No, I couldn't possibly. You must take your chance.... That's enough, sir. Nonsense! I have something more important to do than to listen to such twaddle."

He shut off with a crash and led us upstairs into a large airy apartment which formed his study. On the great mahogany desk seven or eight unopened telegrams were lying.

"Really," he said as he gathered them up, "I begin to think that it would save my correspondents' money if I were to adopt a telegraphic address. Possibly 'Noah, Rotherfield,' would be the most appropriate."

As usual when he made an obscure joke, he leaned against the desk and bellowed in a paroxysm of laughter, his hands shaking so that he could hardly open the envelopes.

"Noah! Noah!" he gasped, with a face of beetroot, while Lord John and I smiled in sympathy and Summerlee, like a dyspeptic goat, wagged his head in sardonic disagreement. Finally Challenger, still rumbling and exploding, began to open his telegrams. The three of us stood in the bow window and occupied ourselves in admiring the magnificent view.

It was certainly worth looking at. The road in its gentle curves had really brought us to a considerable elevation—seven hundred feet, as we afterwards discovered. Challenger's house was on the very edge of the hill, and from its southern face, in which was the study window, one looked across the vast stretch of the weald to where the gentle curves of the South Downs formed an undulating horizon. In a cleft of the hills a haze of smoke marked the position of Lewes. Immediately at our feet there lay a rolling plain of heather, with the long, vivid green stretches of the Crowborough golf course, all dotted with the players. A little to the south, through an opening in the woods, we could see a section of the main line from London to Brighton. In the immediate foreground, under our very noses, was a small enclosed yard, in which stood the car which had brought us from the station.

An ejaculation from Challenger caused us to turn. He had read his telegrams and had arranged them in a little methodical pile upon his desk. His broad, rugged face, or as much of it as was visible over the matted beard, was still deeply flushed, and he seemed to be under the influence of some strong excitement.

"Well, gentlemen," he said, in a voice as if he was addressing a public meeting, "this is indeed an interesting reunion, and it takes place under extraordinary—I may say unprecedented—circumstances. May I ask if you have observed anything upon your journey from town?"

"The only thing which I observed," said Summerlee with a sour smile, "was that our young friend here has not improved in his manners during the years that have passed. I am sorry to state that I have had to seriously complain of his conduct in the train, and I should be wanting in frankness if I did not say that it has left a most unpleasant impression in my mind."

"Well, well, we all get a bit prosy sometimes," said Lord John. "The young fellah meant no real harm. After all, he's an International, so if he takes half an hour to describe a game of football he has more right to do it than most folk."

"Half an hour to describe a game!" I cried indignantly. "Why, it was you that took half an hour with some long-winded story about a buffalo. Professor Summerlee will be my witness."

"I can hardly judge which of you was the most utterly wearisome," said Summerlee. "I declare to you, Challenger, that I never wish to hear of football or of buffaloes so long as I live."

"I have never said one word to-day about football," I protested.

Lord John gave a shrill whistle, and Summerlee shook his head sadly.

"So early in the day too," said he. "It is indeed deplorable. As I sat there in sad but thoughtful silence——"

"In silence!" cried Lord John. "Why, you were doin' a music-hall turn of imitations all the way—more like a runaway gramophone than a man."

Summerlee drew himself up in bitter protest.

"You are pleased to be facetious, Lord John," said he with a face of vinegar.

"Why, dash it all, this is clear madness," cried Lord John. "Each of us seems to know what the others did and none of us knows what he did himself. Let's put it all together from the first. We got into a first-class smoker, that's clear, ain't it? Then we began to quarrel over friend Challenger's letter in the *Times.*"

"Oh, you did, did you?" rumbled our host, his eyelids beginning to droop.

"You said, Summerlee, that there was no possible truth in his contention."

"Dear me!" said Challenger, puffing out his chest and stroking his beard. "No possible truth! I seem to have heard the words before. And may I ask with what arguments the great and famous Professor Summerlee proceeded to demolish the humble individual who had ventured to express an opinion upon a matter of scientific possibility? Perhaps before he exterminates that unfortunate nonentity he will condescend to give some reasons for the adverse views which he has formed."

He bowed and shrugged and spread open his hands as he spoke with his elaborate and elephantine sarcasm.

"The reason was simple enough," said the dogged Summerlee. "I contended that if the ether surrounding the earth was so toxic in one quarter that it produced dangerous symptoms, it was hardly likely that we three in the railway carriage should be entirely unaffected."

The explanation only brought uproarious merriment from Challenger. He laughed until everything in the room seemed to rattle and quiver.

"Our worthy Summerlee is, not for the first time, somewhat out of touch with the facts of the situation," said he at last, mopping his heated brow. "Now, gentlemen, I cannot make my point better than by detailing to you what I have myself done this morning. You will the more easily condone any mental aberration upon your own part when you realize that even I have had moments when my balance has been disturbed. We have had for some years in this household a housekeeper—one Sarah, with whose second name I have never attempted to burden my memory. She is a woman of a severe and forbidding aspect, prim and demure in her bearing, very impassive in her nature, and never known within our experience to show signs of any emotion. As I sat alone at my breakfast—Mrs. Challenger is in the habit of keeping her room of a morning—it suddenly entered my head that it would be entertaining and instructive to see whether I could find any limits to this woman's inperturbability. I devised a simple but effective experiment. Having upset a small vase of flowers which stood in the centre of the cloth, I rang the bell and slipped under the table. She entered and, seeing the room empty, imagined that I had withdrawn to the study. As I had expected, she approached and leaned over the table to replace the vase. I had a vision of a cotton stocking and an elastic-sided boot. Protruding my head, I sank my teeth into the calf of her leg. The experiment was successful beyond belief. For some moments she stood paralyzed, staring down at my head. Then with a shriek she tore herself free and rushed from the room. I pursued her with some thoughts of an explanation, but she flew down the drive, and some minutes afterwards I was able to pick her out with my field-glasses traveling very rapidly in a south-westerly direction. I tell you the anecdote for what it is worth. I drop it into your brains and await its germination. Is it illuminative? Has it conveyed anything to your minds? What do *you* think of it, Lord John?"

Lord John shook his head gravely.

"You'll be gettin' into serious trouble some of these days if you don't put a brake on," said he.

"Perhaps you have some observation to make, Summerlee?"

"You should drop all work instantly, Challenger, and take three months in a German watering-place," said he.

"Profound! Profound!" cried Challenger. "Now, my young friend, is it possible that wisdom may come from you where your seniors have so signally failed?"

And it did. I say it with all modesty, but it did. Of course, it all seems obvious enough to you who know what occurred, but it was not so very clear when everything was new. But it came on me suddenly with the full force of absolute conviction.

"Poison!" I cried.

Then, even as I said the word, my mind flashed back over the whole morning's experiences, past Lord John with his buffalo, past my own hysterical tears, past the outrageous conduct of Professor Summerlee, to the queer happenings in London, the row in the park, the driving of the chauffeur, the quarrel at the oxygen warehouse. Everything fitted suddenly into its place.

"Of course," I cried again. "It is poison. We are all poisoned."

"Exactly," said Challenger, rubbing his hands, "we are all poisoned. Our planet has swum into the poison belt of ether, and is now flying deeper into it at the rate of some millions of miles a minute. Our young friend has expressed the cause of all our troubles and perplexities in a single word, 'poison.'"

We looked at each other in amazed silence. No comment seemed to meet the situation.

"There is a mental inhibition by which such symptoms can be checked and controlled," said Challenger. "I cannot expect to find it developed in all of you to the same point which it has reached in me, for I suppose that the strength of our different mental processes bears some proportion to each other. But no doubt it is appreciable even in our young friend here. After the little outburst of high spirits which so alarmed my domestic I sat down and reasoned with myself. I put it to myself that I had never before felt impelled to bite any of my household. The impulse had then been an abnormal one. In an instant I perceived the truth. My pulse upon examination was ten beats above the usual, and my reflexes were increased. I called upon my higher and saner self, the real G. E. C., seated serene and impregnable behind all mere molecular disturbance. I summoned him, I say, to watch the foolish mental tricks which the poison would play. I found that I was indeed the master. I could recognize and control a disordered mind. It was a remarkable exhibition of the victory of mind over matter, for it was a victory over that particular form of matter which is most intimately connected with mind. I might almost say that mind was at fault and that personality controlled it. Thus, when my wife came downstairs and I was impelled to slip behind the door and alarm her by some wild cry as she entered, I was able to stifle the impulse and to greet her with dignity and restraint. An overpowering desire to quack like a duck was met and mastered in the same fashion.

"Later, when I descended to order the car and found Austin bending over it absorbed in repairs, I controlled my open hand even after I had lifted it and refrained from giving him an experience which would possibly have caused him to follow in the steps of the housekeeper. On the contrary, I touched him on the shoulder and ordered the car to be at the door in time to meet your train. At the present instant I am most forcibly tempted to take Professor Summerlee by that silly old beard of his and to shake his head violently backwards and forwards. And yet, as you see, I am perfectly restrained. Let me commend my example to you."

"I'll look out for that buffalo," said Lord John.

"And I for the football match."

"It may be that you are right, Challenger," said Summerlee in a chastened voice. "I am willing to admit that my turn of mind is critical rather than constructive and that I am not a ready convert to any new theory, especially when it happens to be so unusual and fantastic as this one. However, as I cast my mind back over the events of the morning, and as I reconsider the fatuous conduct of my companions, I find it easy to believe that some poison of an exciting kind was responsible for their symptoms."

Challenger slapped his colleague good-humouredly upon the shoulder. "We progress," said he. "Decidedly we progress."

"And pray, sir," asked Summerlee humbly, "what is your opinion as to the present outlook?"

"With your permission I will say a few words upon that subject." He seated himself upon his desk, his short, stumpy legs swinging in front of him. "We are assisting at a tremendous and awful function. It is, in my opinion, the end of the world."

The end of the world! Our eyes turned to the great bow-window and we looked out at the summer beauty of the country-side, the long slopes of heather, the great country-houses, the cozy farms, the pleasure-seekers upon the links.

The end of the world! One had often heard the words, but the idea that they could ever have an immediate practical significance, that it should not be at some vague date, but now, to-day, that was a tremendous, a staggering thought. We were all struck solemn and waited in silence for Challenger to continue. His overpowering presence and appearance lent such force to the solemnity of his words that for a moment all the crudities and absurdities of the man vanished, and he loomed before us as something majestic and beyond the range of ordinary humanity. Then to me, at least, there came back the cheering recollection of how twice since we had entered the room he had roared with laughter. Surely, I thought, there are limits to mental detachment. The crisis cannot be so great or so pressing after all.

"You will conceive a bunch of grapes," said he, "which are covered by some infinitesimal but noxious bacillus. The gardener passes it through a disinfecting medium. It may be that he desires his grapes to be cleaner. It may be that he needs space to breed some fresh bacillus less noxious than the last. He dips it into the poison and they are gone. Our Gardener is, in my opinion, about to dip the solar system, and the human bacillus, the little mortal vibrio which twisted and wriggled upon the outer rind of the earth, will in an instant be sterilized out of existence."

Again there was silence. It was broken by the high trill of the telephone-bell.

"There is one of our bacilli squeaking for help," said he with a grim smile. "They are beginning to realize that their continued existence is not really one of the necessities of the universe."

He was gone from the room for a minute or two. I remember that none of us spoke in his absence. The situation seemed beyond all words or comments.

"The medical officer of health for Brighton," said he when he returned. "The symptoms are for some reason developing more rapidly upon the sea level. Our seven hundred feet of elevation give us an advantage. Folk seem to have learned that I am the first authority upon the question. No doubt it comes from my letter in the Times. That was the mayor of a provincial town with whom I talked when we first arrived. You may have heard me upon the telephone. He seemed to put an entirely inflated value upon his own life. I helped him to readjust his ideas."

Summerlee had risen and was standing by the window. His thin, bony hands were trembling with his emotion.

"Challenger," said he earnestly, "this thing is too serious for mere futile argument. Do not suppose that I desire to irritate you by any question I may ask. But I put it to you whether there may not be some fallacy in your information or in your reasoning. There is the sun shining as brightly as ever in the blue sky. There are the heather and the flowers and the birds. There are the folk enjoying themselves upon the golf-links and the laborers yonder cutting the corn. You tell us that they and we may be upon the very brink of destruction—that this sunlit day may be that day of doom which the human race has so long awaited. So far as we know, you found this tremendous judgment upon what? Upon some abnormal lines in a spectrum—upon rumours from Sumatra—upon some curious personal excitement which we have discerned in each other. This latter symptom is not so marked but that you and we could, by a deliberate effort, control it. You need not stand on ceremony with us, Challenger. We have all faced death together before now. Speak out, and let us know exactly where we stand, and what, in your opinion, are our prospects for our future."

It was a brave, good speech, a speech from that stanch and strong spirit which lay behind all the acidities and angularities of the old zoologist. Lord John rose and shook him by the hand.

"My sentiment to a tick," said he. "Now, Challenger, it's up to you to tell us where we are. We ain't nervous folk, as you know well; but when it comes to makin' a week-end visit and finding you've run full butt into the Day of Judgment, it wants a bit of explainin'. What's the danger, and how much of it is there, and what are we goin' to do to meet it?"

He stood, tall and strong, in the sunshine at the window, with his brown hand upon the shoulder of Summerlee. I was lying back in an armchair, an extinguished cigarette between my lips, in that sort of half-dazed state in which impressions become exceedingly distinct. It may have been a new phase of the poisoning, but the delirious promptings had all passed away and were succeeded by an exceedingly languid and, at the same time, perceptive state of mind. I was a spectator. It did not seem to be any personal concern of mine. But here were three strong men at a great crisis, and it was fascinating to observe them. Challenger bent his heavy brows and stroked his beard before he answered. One could see that he was very carefully weighing his words.

"What was the last news when you left London?" he asked.

"I was at the Gazette office about ten," said I. "There was a Reuter just come in from Singapore to the effect that the sickness seemed to be universal in Sumatra and that the lighthouses had not been lit in consequence."

"Events have been moving somewhat rapidly since then," said Challenger, picking up his pile of telegrams. "I am in close touch both with the authorities and with the press, so that news is converging upon me from all parts. There is, in fact, a general and very insistent demand that I should come to London; but I see no good end to be served. From the accounts the poisonous effect begins with mental excitement; the rioting in Paris this morning is said to have been very violent, and the Welsh colliers are in a state of uproar. So far as the evidence to hand can be trusted, this stimulative stage, which varies much in races and in individuals, is succeeded by a certain exaltation and mental lucidity—I seem to discern some signs of it in our young friend here—which, after an appreciable interval, turns to coma, deepening rapidly into death. I fancy, so far as my toxicology carries me, that there are some vegetable nerve poisons——"

"Datura," suggested Summerlee.

"Excellent!" cried Challenger. "It would make for scientific precision if we named our toxic agent. Let it be daturon. To you, my dear Summerlee, belongs the honour—posthumous, alas, but none the less unique—of having given a name to the universal destroyer, the Great Gardener's disinfectant. The symptoms of daturon, then, may be taken to be such as I indicate. That it will involve the whole world and that no life can possibly remain behind seems to me to be certain, since ether is a universal medium. Up to now it has been capricious in the places which it has attacked, but the difference is only a matter of a few hours, and it is like an advancing tide which covers one strip of sand and then another, running hither and thither in irregular streams, until at last it has submerged it all. There are laws at work in connection with the action and distribution of daturon which would have been of deep interest had the time at our disposal permitted us to study them. So far as I can trace them"—here he glanced over his telegrams—"the less developed races have been the first to respond to its influence. There are deplorable accounts from Africa, and the Australian aborigines appear to have been already exterminated. The Northern races have as yet shown greater resisting power than the Southern. This, you see, is dated from Marseilles at nine-forty-five this morning. I give it to you verbatim:—

"'All night delirious excitement throughout Provence. Tumult of vine growers at Nimes. Socialistic upheaval at Toulon. Sudden illness attended by coma attacked population this morning. *peste foudroyante*. Great numbers of dead in the streets. Paralysis of business and universal chaos.'

"An hour later came the following, from the same source:—

"'We are threatened with utter extermination. Cathedrals and churches full to overflowing. The dead outnumber the living. It is inconceivable and horrible. Decease seems to be painless, but swift and inevitable.'

"There is a similar telegram from Paris, where the development is not yet as acute. India and Persia appear to be utterly wiped out. The Slavonic population of Austria is down, while the Teutonic has hardly been affected. Speaking generally, the dwellers upon the plains and upon the seashore seem, so far as my limited information goes, to have felt the effects more rapidly than those inland or on the heights. Even a little elevation makes a considerable difference, and perhaps if there be a survivor of the human race, he will again be found upon the summit of some Ararat. Even our own little hill may presently prove to be a temporary island amid a sea of disaster. But at the present rate of advance a few short hours will submerge us all."

Lord John Roxton wiped his brow.

"What beats me," said he, "is how you could sit there laughin' with that stack of telegrams under your hand. I've seen death as often as most folk, but universal death—it's awful!"

"As to the laughter," said Challenger, "you will bear in mind that, like yourselves, I have not been exempt from the stimulating cerebral effects of the etheric poison. But as to the horror with which universal death appears to inspire you, I would put it to you that it is somewhat exaggerated. If you were sent to sea alone in an open boat to some unknown destination, your heart might well sink within you. The isolation, the uncertainty, would oppress you. But if your voyage were made in a goodly ship, which bore within it all your relations and your friends, you would feel that, however uncertain your destination might still remain, you would at least have one common and simultaneous experience which would hold you to the end in the same close communion. A lonely death may be terrible, but a universal one, as painless as this would appear to be, is not, in my judgment, a matter for apprehension. Indeed, I could sympathize with the person who took the view that the horror lay in the idea of surviving when all that is learned, famous, and exalted had passed away."

"What, then, do you propose to do?" asked Summerlee, who had for once nodded his assent to the reasoning of his brother scientist.

"To take our lunch," said Challenger as the boom of a gong sounded through the house. "We have a cook whose omelettes are only excelled by her cutlets. We can but trust that no cosmic disturbance has dulled her excellent abilities. My Scharzberger of '96 must also be rescued, so far as our earnest and united efforts can do it, from what would be a deplorable waste of a great vintage." He levered his great bulk off the desk, upon which he had sat while he announced the doom of the planet. "Come," said he. "If there is little time left, there is the more need that we should spend it in sober and reasonable enjoyment."

And, indeed, it proved to be a very merry meal. It is true that we could not forget our awful situation. The full solemnity of the event loomed ever at the back of our minds and tempered our thoughts. But surely it is the soul which has never faced death which shies strongly from it at the end. To each of us men it had, for one great epoch in our lives, been a familiar presence. As to the lady, she leaned upon the strong guidance of her mighty husband and was well content to go whither his path might lead. The future was our fate. The present was our own. We passed it in goodly comradeship and gentle merriment. Our minds were, as I have said, singularly lucid. Even I struck sparks at times. As to Challenger, he was wonderful! Never have I so realized the elemental greatness of the man, the sweep and power of his understanding. Summerlee drew him on with his chorus of subacid criticism, while Lord John and I laughed at the contest and the lady, her hand upon his sleeve, controlled the bellowings of the philosopher. Life, death, fate, the destiny of man—these were the stupendous subjects of that memorable hour, made vital by the fact that as the meal progressed strange, sudden exaltations in my mind and tinglings in my limbs proclaimed that the invisible tide of death was slowly and gently rising around us. Once I saw Lord John put his hand suddenly to his eyes, and once Summerlee dropped back for an instant in his chair. Each breath we breathed was charged with strange forces. And yet our minds were happy and at ease. Presently Austin laid the cigarettes upon the table and was about to withdraw.

"Austin!" said his master.

"Yes, sir?"

"I thank you for your faithful service." A smile stole over the servant's gnarled face.

"I've done my duty, sir."

"I'm expecting the end of the world to-day, Austin."

"Yes, sir. What time, sir?"

"I can't say, Austin. Before evening."

"Very good, sir."

The taciturn Austin saluted and withdrew. Challenger lit a cigarette, and, drawing his chair closer to his wife's, he took her hand in his.

"You know how matters stand, dear," said he. "I have explained it also to our friends here. You're not afraid are you?"

"It won't be painful, George?"

"No more than laughing-gas at the dentist's. Every time you have had it you have practically died."

"But that is a pleasant sensation."

"So may death be. The worn-out bodily machine can't record its impression, but we know the mental pleasure which lies in a dream or a trance. Nature may build a beautiful door and hang it with many a gauzy and shimmering curtain to make an entrance to the new life for our wondering souls. In all my probings of the actual, I have always found wisdom and kindness at the core; and if ever the frightened mortal needs tenderness, it is surely as he makes the passage perilous from life to life. No, Summerlee, I will have none of your materialism, for I, at least, am too great a thing to end in mere physical constituents, a packet of salts and three bucketfuls of water. Here— here"—and he beat his great head with his huge, hairy fist—"there is something which uses matter, but is not of it—something which might destroy death, but which death can never destroy."

"Talkin' of death," said Lord John. "I'm a Christian of sorts, but it seems to me there was somethin' mighty natural in those ancestors of ours who were buried with their axes and bows and arrows and the like, same as if they were livin' on just the same as they used to. I don't know," he added, looking round the table in a shamefaced way, "that I wouldn't feel more homely myself if I was put away with my old .450 Express and the fowlin'-piece, the shorter one with the rubbered stock, and a clip or two of cartridges—just a fool's fancy, of course, but there it is. How does it strike you, Herr Professor?"

"Well," said Summerlee, "since you ask my opinion, it strikes me as an indefensible throwback to the Stone Age or before it. I'm of the twentieth century myself, and would wish to die like a reasonable civilized man. I don't know that I am more afraid of death than the rest of you, for I am an old-ish man, and, come what may, I can't have very much longer to live; but it is all against my nature to sit waiting without a struggle like a sheep for the butcher. Is it quite certain, Challenger, that there is nothing we can do?"

"To save us—nothing," said Challenger. "To prolong our lives a few hours and thus to see the evolution of this mighty tragedy before we are actually involved in it—that may prove to be within my powers. I have taken certain steps——"

"The oxygen?"

"Exactly. The oxygen."

"But what can oxygen effect in the face of a poisoning of the ether? There is not a greater difference in quality between a brick-bat and a gas than there is between oxygen and ether. They are different planes of matter. They cannot impinge upon one another. Come, Challenger, you could not defend such a proposition."

"My good Summerlee, this etheric poison is most certainly influenced by material agents. We see it in the methods and distribution of the outbreak. We should not *a priori* have expected it, but it is undoubtedly a fact. Hence I am strongly of opinion that a gas like oxygen, which increases the vitality and the resisting power of the body, would be extremely likely to delay the action of what you have so happily named the daturon. It may be that I am mistaken, but I have every confidence in the correctness of my reasoning."

"Well," said Lord John, "if we've got to sit suckin' at those tubes like so many babies with their bottles, I'm not takin' any."

"There will be no need for that," Challenger answered. "We have made arrangements—it is to my wife that you chiefly owe it—that her boudoir shall be made as airtight as is practicable. With matting and varnished paper."

"Good heavens, Challenger, you don't suppose you can keep out ether with varnished paper?"

"Really, my worthy friend, you are a trifle perverse in missing the point. It is not to keep out the ether that we have gone to such trouble. It is to keep in the oxygen. I trust that if we can ensure an atmosphere hyper-oxygenated to a certain point, we may be able to retain our senses. I had two tubes of the gas and you have brought me three more. It is not much, but it is something."

"How long will they last?"

"I have not an idea. We will not turn them on until our symptoms become unbearable. Then we shall dole the gas out as it is urgently needed. It may give us some hours, possibly even some days, on which we may look out upon a blasted world. Our own fate is delayed to that extent, and we will have the very singular experience, we five, of being, in all probability, the absolute rear guard of the human race upon its march into the unknown. Perhaps you will be kind enough now to give me a hand with the cylinders. It seems to me that the atmosphere already grows somewhat more oppressive."

CHAPTER III: SUBMERGED

The chamber which was destined to be the scene of our unforgettable experience was a charmingly feminine sitting-room, some fourteen or sixteen feet square. At the end of it, divided by a curtain of red velvet, was a small apartment which formed the Professor's dressing-room. This in turn opened into a large bedroom. The curtain was still hanging, but the boudoir and dressing-room could be taken as one chamber for the purposes of our experiment.

One door and the window frame had been plastered round with varnished paper so as to be practically sealed. Above the other door, which opened on to the landing, there hung a fanlight which could be drawn by a cord when some ventilation became absolutely necessary. A large shrub in a tub stood in each corner.

"How to get rid of our excessive carbon dioxide without unduly wasting our oxygen is a delicate and vital question," said Challenger, looking round him after the five iron tubes had been laid side by side against the wall. "With longer time for preparation I could have brought the whole concentrated force of my intelligence to bear more fully upon the problem, but as it is we must do what we can. The shrubs will be of some small service. Two of the oxygen tubes are ready to be turned on at an instant's notice, so that we cannot be taken unawares. At the same time, it would be well not to go far from the room, as the crisis may be a sudden and urgent one."

There was a broad, low window opening out upon a balcony. The view beyond was the same as that which we had already admired from the study. Looking out, I could see no sign of disorder anywhere. There was a road curving down the side of the hill, under my very eyes. A cab from the station, one of those prehistoric survivals which are only to be found in our country villages, was toiling slowly up the hill. Lower down was a nurse girl wheeling a perambulator and leading a second child by the hand. The blue reeks of smoke from the cottages gave the whole widespread landscape an air of settled order and homely comfort. Nowhere in the blue heaven or on the sunlit earth was there any foreshadowing of a catastrophe. The harvesters were back in the fields once more and the golfers, in pairs and fours, were still streaming round the links. There was so strange a turmoil within my own head, and such a jangling of my overstrung nerves, that the indifference of those people was amazing.

"Those fellows don't seem to feel any ill effects," said I, pointing down at the links.

"Have you played golf?" asked Lord John.

"No, I have not."

"Well, young fellah, when you do you'll learn that once fairly out on a round, it would take the crack of doom to stop a true golfer. Halloa! There's that telephone-bell again."

From time to time during and after lunch the high, insistent ring had summoned the Professor. He gave us the news as it came through to him in a few curt sentences. Such terrific items had never been registered in the world's history before. The great shadow was creeping up from the south like a rising tide of death. Egypt had gone through its delirium and was now comatose. Spain and Portugal, after a wild frenzy in which the Clericals and the Anarchists had fought most desperately, were now fallen silent. No cable messages were received any longer from South America. In North America the southern states, after some terrible racial rioting, had succumbed to the poison. North of Maryland the effect was not yet marked, and in Canada it was hardly perceptible. Belgium, Holland, and Denmark had each in turn been affected. Despairing messages were flashing from every quarter to the great centres of learning, to the chemists and the doctors of world-wide repute, imploring their advice. The astronomers too were deluged with inquiries. Nothing could be done. The thing was universal and beyond our human knowledge or control. It was death—painless but inevitable—death for young and old, for weak and strong, for rich and poor, without hope or possibility of escape. Such was the news which, in scattered, distracted messages, the telephone had brought us. The great cities already knew their fate and so far as we could gather were preparing to meet it with dignity and resignation. Yet here were our golfers and laborers like the lambs who gambol under the shadow of the knife. It seemed amazing. And yet how could they know? It had all come upon us in one giant stride. What was there in the morning paper to alarm them? And now it was but three in the afternoon. Even as we looked some rumour seemed to have spread, for we saw the reapers hurrying from the fields. Some of the golfers were return-ing to the club-house. They were running as if taking refuge from a shower. Their little caddies trailed behind them. Others were continuing their game. The nurse had turned and was pushing her perambulator hurriedly up the hill again. I noticed that she had her hand to her brow. The cab had stopped and the tired horse, with his head sunk to his knees, was resting. Above there was a perfect summer sky—one huge vault of unbroken blue, save for a few fleecy white clouds over the distant downs. If the human race must die to-day, it was at least upon a glorious death-bed. And yet all that gentle loveliness of nature made this terrific and wholesale destruction the more pitiable and awful. Surely it was too goodly a residence that we should be so swiftly, so ruthlessly, evicted from it!

But I have said that the telephone-bell had rung once more. Suddenly I heard Challenger's tremendous voice from the hall.

"Malone!" he cried. "You are wanted."

I rushed down to the instrument. It was McArdle speaking from London.

"That you, Mr. Malone?" cried his familiar voice. "Mr. Malone, there are terrible goings-on in London. For God's sake, see if Professor Challenger can suggest anything that can be done."

"He can suggest nothing, sir," I answered. "He regards the crisis as univer-sal and inevitable. We have some oxygen here, but it can only defer our fate for a few hours."

"Oxygen!" cried the agonized voice. "There is no time to get any. The office has been a perfect pandemonium ever since you left in the morn-ing. Now half of the staff are insensible. I am weighed down with heavi-ness myself. From my window I can see the people lying thick in Fleet Street. The traffic is all held up. Judging by the last telegrams, the whole world——"

His voice had been sinking, and suddenly stopped. An instant later I heard through the telephone a muffled thud, as if his head had fallen forward on the desk.

"Mr. McArdle!" I cried. "Mr. McArdle!"

There was no answer. I knew as I replaced the receiver that I should never hear his voice again.

At that instant, just as I took a step backwards from the telephone, the thing was on us. It was as if we were bathers, up to our shoulders in water, who suddenly are submerged by a rolling wave. An invisible hand seemed to have quietly closed round my throat and to be gently pressing the life from me. I was conscious of immense oppression upon my chest, great tightness within my head, a loud singing in my ears, and bright flashes before my eyes. I staggered to the balustrades of the stair. At the same moment, rushing and snorting like a wounded buffalo, Challenger dashed past me, a terrible vision, with red-purple face, engorged eyes, and bristling hair. His little wife, insensible to all appearance, was slung over his great shoulder, and he blundered and thundered up the stair, scrambling and tripping, but carrying himself and her through sheer will-force through that mephitic atmosphere to the haven of temporary safety. At the sight of his effort I too rushed up the steps, clambering, falling, clutching at the rail, until I tumbled half senseless upon by face on the upper landing. Lord John's fingers of steel were in the collar of my coat, and a moment later I was stretched upon my back, unable to speak or move, on the boudoir carpet. The woman lay beside me, and Summerlee was bunched in a chair by the window, his head nearly touching his knees. As in a dream I saw Challenger, like a monstrous beetle, crawling slowly across the floor, and a moment later I heard the gentle hissing of the escaping oxygen. Challenger breathed two or three times with enormous gulps, his lungs roaring as he drew in the vital gas.

"It works!" he cried exultantly. "My reasoning has been justified!" He was up on his feet again, alert and strong. With a tube in his hand he rushed over to his wife and held it to her face. In a few seconds she moaned, stirred, and sat up. He turned to me, and I felt the tide of life stealing warmly through my arteries. My reason told me that it was but a little respite, and yet, carelessly as we talk of its value, every hour of existence now seemed an inestimable thing. Never have I known such a thrill of sensuous joy as came with that freshet of life. The weight fell away from my lungs, the band loosened from my brow, a sweet feeling of peace and gentle, languid comfort stole over me. I lay watching Summerlee revive under the same remedy, and finally Lord John took his turn. He sprang to his feet and gave me a hand to rise, while Challenger picked up his wife and laid her on the settee.

"Oh, George, I am so sorry you brought me back," she said, holding him by the hand. "The door of death is indeed, as you said, hung with beautiful, shimmering curtains; for, once the choking feeling had passed, it was all unspeakably soothing and beautiful. Why have you dragged me back?"

"Because I wish that we make the passage together. We have been together so many years. It would be sad to fall apart at the supreme moment."

For a moment in his tender voice I caught a glimpse of a new Challenger, something very far from the bullying, ranting, arrogant man who had alternately amazed and offended his generation. Here in the shadow of death was the innermost Challenger, the man who had won and held a woman's love. Suddenly his mood changed and he was our strong captain once again.

"Alone of all mankind I saw and foretold this catastrophe," said he with a ring of exultation and scientific triumph in his voice. "As to you, my good Summerlee, I trust your last doubts have been resolved as to the meaning of the blurring of the lines in the spectrum and that you will no longer contend that my letter in the Times was based upon a delusion."

For once our pugnacious colleague was deaf to a challenge. He could but sit gasping and stretching his long, thin limbs, as if to assure himself that he was still really upon this planet. Challenger walked across to the oxygen tube, and the sound of the loud hissing fell away till it was the most gentle sibilation.

"We must husband our supply of the gas," said he. "The atmosphere of the room is now strongly hyperoxygenated, and I take it that none of us feel any distressing symptoms. We can only determine by actual experiments what amount added to the air will serve to neutralize the poison. Let us see how that will do."

We sat in silent nervous tension for five minutes or more, observing our own sensations. I had just begun to fancy that I felt the constriction round my temples again when Mrs. Challenger called out from the sofa that she was fainting. Her husband turned on more gas.

"In pre-scientific days," said he, "they used to keep a white mouse in every submarine, as its more delicate organization gave signs of a vicious atmosphere before it was perceived by the sailors. You, my dear, will be our white mouse. I have now increased the supply and you are better."

"Yes, I am better."

"Possibly we have hit upon the correct mixture. When we have ascertained exactly how little will serve we shall be able to compute how long we shall be able to exist. Unfortunately, in resuscitating ourselves we have already consumed a considerable proportion of this first tube."

"Does it matter?" asked Lord John, who was standing with his hands in his pockets close to the window. "If we have to go, what is the use of holdin' on? You don't suppose there's any chance for us?"

Challenger smiled and shook his head.

"Well, then, don't you think there is more dignity in takin' the jump and not waitin' to be pushed in? If it must be so, I'm for sayin' our prayers, turnin' off the gas, and openin' the window."

"Why not?" said the lady bravely. "Surely, George, Lord John is right and it is better so."

"I most strongly object," cried Summerlee in a querulous voice. "When we must die let us by all means die, but to deliberately anticipate death seems to me to be a foolish and unjustifiable action."

"What does our young friend say to it?" asked Challenger.

"I think we should see it to the end."

"And I am strongly of the same opinion," said he.

"Then, George, if you say so, I think so too," cried the lady.

"Well, well, I'm only puttin' it as an argument," said Lord John. "If you all want to see it through I am with you. It's dooced interestin', and no mistake about that. I've had my share of adventures in my life, and as many thrills as most folk, but I'm endin' on my top note."

"Granting the continuity of life," said Challenger.

"A large assumption!" cried Summerlee. Challenger stared at him in silent reproof.

"Granting the continuity of life," said he, in his most didactic manner, "none of us can predicate what opportunities of observation one may have from what we may call the spirit plane to the plane of matter. It surely must be evident to the most obtuse person" (here he glared a Summerlee) "that it is while we are ourselves material that we are most fitted to watch and form a judgment upon material phenomena. Therefore it is only by keeping alive for these few extra hours that we can hope to carry on with us to some future existence a clear conception of the most stupendous event that the world, or the universe so far as we know it, has ever encountered. To me it would seem a deplorable thing that we should in any way curtail by so much as a minute so wonderful an experience."

"I am strongly of the same opinion," cried Summerlee.

"Carried without a division," said Lord John. "By George, that poor devil of a chauffeur of yours down in the yard has made his last journey. No use makin' a sally and bringin' him in?"

"It would be absolute madness," cried Summerlee.

"Well, I suppose it would," said Lord John. "It couldn't help him and would scatter our gas all over the house, even if we ever got back alive. My word, look at the little birds under the trees!"

We drew four chairs up to the long, low window, the lady still resting with closed eyes upon the settee. I remember that the monstrous and grotesque idea crossed my mind—the illusion may have been heightened by the heavy stuffiness of the air which we were breathing—that we were in four front seats of the stalls at the last act of the drama of the world.

In the immediate foreground, beneath our very eyes, was the small yard with the half-cleaned motor-car standing in it. Austin, the chauffeur, had received his final notice at last, for he was sprawling beside the wheel, with a great black bruise upon his forehead where it had struck the step or mud-guard in falling. He still held in his hand the nozzle of the hose with which he had been washing down his machine. A couple of small plane trees stood in the corner of the yard, and underneath them lay several pathetic little balls of fluffy feathers, with tiny feet uplifted. The sweep of death's scythe had included everything, great and small, within its swath.

Over the wall of the yard we looked down upon the winding road, which led to the station. A group of the reapers whom we had seen running from the fields were lying all pell-mell, their bodies crossing each other, at the bottom of it. Farther up, the nurse-girl lay with her head and shoulders propped against the slope of the grassy bank. She had taken the baby from the perambulator, and it was a motionless bundle of wraps in her arms. Close behind her a tiny patch upon the roadside showed where the little boy was stretched. Still nearer to us was the dead cab-horse, kneeling between the shafts. The old driver was hanging over the splash-board like some grotesque scarecrow, his arms dangling absurdly in front of him. Through the window we could dimly discern that a young man was seated inside. The door was swinging open and his hand was grasping the handle, as if he had attempted to leap forth at the last instant. In the middle distance lay the golf links, dotted as they had been in the morning with the dark figures of the golfers, lying motionless upon the grass of the course or among the heather which skirted it. On one particular green there were eight bodies stretched where a foursome with its caddies had held to their game to the last. No bird flew in the blue vault of heaven, no man or beast moved upon the vast countryside which lay before us. The evening sun shone its peaceful radiance across it, but there brooded over it all the stillness and the silence of universal death—a death in which we were so soon to join. At the present instant that one frail sheet of glass, by holding in the extra oxygen which counteracted the poisoned ether, shut us off from the fate of all our kind. For a few short hours the knowledge and foresight of one man could preserve our little oasis of life in the vast desert of death and save us from participation in the common catastrophe. Then the gas would run low, we too should lie gasping upon that cherry-coloured boudoir carpet, and the fate of the human race and of all earthly life would be complete. For a long time, in a mood which was too solemn for speech, we looked out at the tragic world.

"There is a house on fire," said Challenger at last, pointing to a column of smoke which rose above the trees. "There will, I expect, be many such—possibly whole cities in flames—when we consider how many folk may have dropped with lights in their hands. The fact of combustion is in itself enough to show that the proportion of oxygen in the atmosphere is normal and that it is the ether which is at fault. Ah, there you see another blaze on the top of Crowborough Hill. It is the golf clubhouse, or I am mistaken. There is the church clock chiming the hour. It would interest our philosophers to know that man-made mechanisms has survived the race who made it."

"By George!" cried Lord John, rising excitedly from his chair. "What's that puff of smoke? It's a train."

We heard the roar of it, and presently it came flying into sight, going at what seemed to me to be a prodigious speed. Whence it had come, or how far, we had no means of knowing. Only by some miracle of luck could it have gone any distance. But now we were to see the terrific end of its career. A train of coal trucks stood motionless upon the line. We held our breath as the express roared along the same track. The crash was horrible. Engine and carriages piled themselves into a hill of splintered wood and twisted iron. Red spurts of flame flickered up from the wreckage until it was all ablaze. For half an hour we sat with hardly a word, stunned by the stupendous sight.

"Poor, poor people!" cried Mrs. Challenger at last, clinging with a whimper to her husband's arm.

"My dear, the passengers on that train were no more animate than the coals into which they crashed or the carbon which they have now become," said Challenger, stroking her hand soothingly. "It was a train of the living when it left Victoria, but it was driven and freighted by the dead long before it reached its fate."

"All over the world the same thing must be going on," said I as a vision of strange happenings rose before me. "Think of the ships at sea—how they will steam on and on, until the furnaces die down or until they run full tilt upon some beach. The sailing ships too—how they will back and fill with their cargoes of dead sailors, while their timbers rot and their joints leak, till one by one they sink below the surface. Perhaps a century hence the Atlantic may still be dotted with the old drifting derelicts."

"And the folk in the coal-mines," said Summerlee with a dismal chuckle. "If ever geologists should by any chance live upon earth again they will have some strange theories of the existence of man in carboniferous strata."

"I don't profess to know about such things," remarked Lord John, "but it seems to me the earth will be 'To let, empty,' after this. When once our human crowd is wiped off it, how will it ever get on again?"

"The world was empty before," Challenger answered gravely. "Under laws which in their inception are beyond and above us, it became peopled. Why may the same process not happen again?"

"My dear Challenger, you can't mean that?"

"I am not in the habit, Professor Summerlee, of saying things which I do not mean. The observation is trivial." Out went the beard and down came the eyelids.

"Well, you lived an obstinate dogmatist, and you mean to die one," said Summerlee sourly.

"And you, sir, have lived an unimaginative obstructionist and never can hope now to emerge from it."

"Your worst critics will never accuse you of lacking imagination," Summerlee retorted.

"Upon my word!" said Lord John. "It would be like you if you used up our last gasp of oxygen in abusing each other. What can it matter whether folk come back or not? It surely won't be in our time."

"In that remark, sir, you betray your own very pronounced limitations," said Challenger severely. "The true scientific mind is not to be tied down by its own conditions of time and space. It builds itself an observatory erected upon the border line of present, which separates the infinite past from the infinite future. From this sure post it makes its sallies even to the beginning and to the end of all things. As to death, the scientific mind dies at its post working in normal and methodic fashion to the end. It disregards so petty a thing as its own physical dissolution as completely as it does all other limitations upon the plane of matter. Am I right, Professor Summerlee?"

Summerlee grumbled an ungracious assent.

"With certain reservations, I agree," said he.

"The ideal scientific mind," continued Challenger—"I put it in the third person rather than appear to be too self-complacent—the ideal scientific mind should be capable of thinking out a point of abstract knowledge in the interval between its owner falling from a balloon and reaching the earth. Men of this strong fibre are needed to form the conquerors of nature and the bodyguard of truth."

"It strikes me nature's on top this time," said Lord John, looking out of the window. "I've read some leadin' articles about you gentlemen controllin' her, but she's gettin' a bit of her own back."

"It is but a temporary setback," said Challenger with conviction. "A few million years, what are they in the great cycle of time? The vegetable world has, as you can see, survived. Look at the leaves of that plane tree. The birds are dead, but the plant flourishes. From this vegetable life in pond and in marsh will come, in time, the tiny crawling microscopic slugs which are the pioneers of that great army of life in which for the instant we five have the extraordinary duty of serving as rear guard. Once the lowest form of life has established itself, the final advent of man is as certain as the growth of the oak from the acorn. The old circle will swing round once more."

"But the poison?" I asked. "Will that not nip life in the bud?"

"The poison may be a mere stratum or layer in the ether—a mephitic Gulf Stream across that mighty ocean in which we float. Or tolerance may be established and life accommodate itself to a new condition. The mere fact that with a comparatively small hyperoxygenation of our blood we can hold out against it is surely a proof in itself that no very great change would be needed to enable animal life to endure it."

The smoking house beyond the trees had burst into flames. We could see the high tongues of fire shooting up into the air.

"It's pretty awful," muttered Lord John, more impressed than I had ever seen him.

"Well, after all, what does it matter?" I remarked. "The world is dead. Cremation is surely the best burial."

"It would shorten us up if this house went ablaze."

"I foresaw the danger," said Challenger, "and asked my wife to guard against it."

"Everything is quite safe, dear. But my head begins to throb again. What a dreadful atmosphere!"

"We must change it," said Challenger. He bent over his cylinder of oxygen.

"It's nearly empty," said he. "It has lasted us some three and a half hours. It is now close on eight o'clock. We shall get through the night comfortably. I should expect the end about nine o'clock to-morrow morning. We shall see one sunrise, which shall be all our own."

He turned on his second tube and opened for half a minute the fanlight over the door. Then as the air became perceptibly better, but our own symptoms more acute, he closed it once again.

"By the way," said he, "man does not live upon oxygen alone. It's dinner time and over. I assure you, gentlemen, that when I invited you to my home and to what I had hoped would be an interesting reunion, I had intended that my kitchen should justify itself. However, we must do what we can. I am sure that you will agree with me that it would be folly to consume our air too rapidly by lighting an oil-stove. I have some small provision of cold meats, bread, and pickles which, with a couple of bottles of claret, may serve our turn. Thank you, my dear—now as ever you are the queen of managers."

It was indeed wonderful how, with the self-respect and sense of propriety of the British housekeeper, the lady had within a few minutes adorned the central table with a snow-white cloth, laid the napkins upon it, and set forth the simple meal with all the elegance of civilization, including an electric torch lamp in the centre. Wonderful also was it to find that our appetites were ravenous.

"It is the measure of our emotion," said Challenger with that air of condescension with which he brought his scientific mind to the explanation of humble facts. "We have gone through a great crisis. That means molecular disturbance. That in turn means the need for repair. Great sorrow or great joy should bring intense hunger—not abstinence from food, as our novelists will have it."

"That's why the country folk have great feasts at funerals," I hazarded.

"Exactly. Our young friend has hit upon an excellent illustration. Let me give you another slice of tongue."

"The same with savages," said Lord John, cutting away at the beef. "I've seen them buryin' a chief up the Aruwimi River, and they ate a hippo that must have weighed as much as a tribe. There are some of them down New Guinea way that eat the late-lamented himself, just by way of a last tidy up. Well, of all the funeral feasts on this earth, I suppose the one we are takin' is the queerest."

"The strange thing is," said Mrs. Challenger, "that I find it impossible to feel grief for those who are gone. There are my father and mother at Bedford. I know that they are dead, and yet in this tremendous universal tragedy I can feel no sharp sorrow for any individuals, even for them."

"And my old mother in her cottage in Ireland," said I. "I can see her in my mind's eye, with her shawl and her lace cap, lying back with closed eyes in the old high-backed chair near the window, her glasses and her book beside her. Why should I mourn her? She has passed and I am passing, and I may be nearer her in some other life than England is to Ireland. Yet I grieve to think that that dear body is no more."

"As to the body," remarked Challenger, "we do not mourn over the parings of our nails nor the cut locks of our hair, though they were once part of ourselves. Neither does a one-legged man yearn sentimentally over his missing member. The physical body has rather been a source of pain and fatigue to us. It is the constant index of our limitations. Why then should we worry about its detachment from our psychical selves?"

"If they can indeed be detached," Summerlee grumbled. "But, anyhow, universal death is dreadful."

"As I have already explained," said Challenger, "a universal death must in its nature be far less terrible than a isolated one."

"Same in a battle," remarked Lord John. "If you saw a single man lying on that floor with his chest knocked in and a hole in his face it would turn you sick. But I've seen ten thousand on their backs in the Soudan, and it gave me no such feelin', for when you are makin' history the life of any man is too small a thing to worry over. When a thousand million pass over together, same as happened to-day, you can't pick your own partic'lar out of the crowd."

"I wish it were well over with us," said the lady wistfully. "Oh, George, I am so frightened."

"You'll be the bravest of us all, little lady, when the time comes. I've been a blusterous old husband to you, dear, but you'll just bear in mind that G. E. C. is as he was made and couldn't help himself. After all, you wouldn't have had anyone else?"

"No one in the whole wide world, dear," said she, and put her arms round his bull neck. We three walked to the window and stood amazed at the sight which met our eyes.

Darkness had fallen and the dead world was shrouded in gloom. But right across the southern horizon was one long vivid scarlet streak, waxing and waning in vivid pulses of life, leaping suddenly to a crimson zenith and then dying down to a glowing line of fire.

"Lewes is ablaze!"

"No, it is Brighton which is burning," said Challenger, stepping across to join us. "You can see the curved back of the downs against the glow. That fire is miles on the farther side of it. The whole town must be alight."

There were several red glares at different points, and the pile of *debris* upon the railway line was still smoldering darkly, but they all seemed mere pin-points of light compared to that monstrous conflagration throbbing beyond the hills. What copy it would have made for the Gazette! Had ever a journalist such an opening and so little chance of using it—the scoop of scoops, and no one to appreciate it? And then, suddenly, the old instinct of recording came over me. If these men of science could be so true to their life's work to the very end, why should not I, in my humble way, be as constant? No human eye might ever rest upon what I had done. But the long night had to be passed somehow, and for me at least, sleep seemed to be out of the question. My notes would help to pass the weary hours and to occupy my thoughts. Thus it is that now I have before me the notebook with its scribbled pages, written confusedly upon my knee in the dim, waning light of our one electric torch. Had I the literary touch, they might have been worthy of the occasion, As it is, they may still serve to bring to other minds the long-drawn emotions and tremors of that awful night.

CHAPTER IV: A DIARY OF THE DYING

How strange the words look scribbled at the top of the empty page of my book! How stranger still that it is I, Edward Malone, who have written them—I who started only some twelve hours ago from my rooms in Streatham without one thought of the marvels which the day was to bring forth! I look back at the chain of incidents, my interview with McArdle, Challenger's first note of alarm in the Times, the absurd journey in the train, the pleasant luncheon, the catastrophe, and now it has come to this—that we linger alone upon an empty planet, and so sure is our fate that I can regard these lines, written from mechanical professional habit and never to be seen by human eyes, as the words of one who is already dead, so closely does he stand to the shadowed borderland over which all outside this one little circle of friends have already gone. I feel how wise and true were the words of Challenger when he said that the real tragedy would be if we were left behind when all that is noble and good and beautiful had passed. But of that there can surely be no danger. Already our second tube of oxygen is drawing to an end. We can count the poor dregs of our lives almost to a minute.

We have just been treated to a lecture, a good quarter of an hour long, from Challenger, who was so excited that he roared and bellowed as if he were addressing his old rows of scientific sceptics in the Queen's Hall. He had certainly a strange audience to harangue: his wife perfectly acquiescent and absolutely ignorant of his meaning, Summerlee seated in the shadow, querulous and critical but interested, Lord John lounging in a corner some-what bored by the whole proceeding, and myself beside the window watching the scene with a kind of detached attention, as if it were all a dream or something in which I had no personal interest whatever. Challenger sat at the centre table with the electric light illuminating the slide under the microscope which he had brought from his dressing room. The small vivid circle of white light from the mirror left half of his rugged, bearded face in brilliant radiance and half in deepest shadow. He had, it seems, been working of late upon the lowest forms of life, and what excited him at the present moment was that in the microscopic slide made up the day before he found the amoeba to be still alive.

"You can see it for yourselves," he kept repeating in great excitement. "Summerlee, will you step across and satisfy yourself upon the point? Malone, will you kindly verify what I say? The little spindle-shaped things in the centre are diatoms and may be disregarded since they are probably vegetable rather than animal. But the right-hand side you will see an undoubted amoeba, moving sluggishly across the field. The upper screw is the fine adjustment. Look at it for yourselves."

Summerlee did so and acquiesced. So did I and perceived a little creature which looked as if it were made of ground glass flowing in a sticky way across the lighted circle. Lord John was prepared to take him on trust.

"I'm not troublin' my head whether he's alive or dead," said he. "We don't so much as know each other by sight, so why should I take it to heart? I don't suppose he's worryin' himself over the state of *our* health."

I laughed at this, and Challenger looked in my direction with his coldest and most supercilious stare. It was a most petrifying experience.

"The flippancy of the half-educated is more obstructive to science than the obtuseness of the ignorant," said he. "If Lord John Roxton would condescend——"

"My dear George, don't be so peppery," said his wife, with her hand on the black mane that drooped over the microscope. "What can it matter whether the amoeba is alive or not?"

"It matters a great deal," said Challenger gruffly.

"Well, let's hear about it," said Lord John with a good-humoured smile. "We may as well talk about that as anything else. If you think I've been too off-hand with the thing, or hurt its feelin's in any way, I'll apologize."

"For my part," remarked Summerlee in his creaky, argumentative voice, "I can't see why you should attach such importance to the creature being alive. It is in the same atmosphere as ourselves, so naturally the poison does not act upon it. If it were outside of this room it would be dead, like all other animal life."

"Your remarks, my good Summerlee," said Challenger with enormous condescension (oh, if I could paint that over-bearing, arrogant face in the vivid circle of reflection from the microscope mirror!)—"your remarks show that you imperfectly appreciate the situation. This specimen was mounted yesterday and is hermetically sealed. None of our oxygen can reach it. But the ether, of course, has penetrated to it, as to every other point upon the universe. Therefore, it has survived the poison. Hence, we may argue that every amoeba outside this room, instead of being dead, as you have erroneously stated, has really survived the catastrophe."

"Well, even now I don't feel inclined to hip-hurrah about it," said Lord John. "What does it matter?"

"It just matters this, that the world is a living instead of a dead one. If you had the scientific imagination, you would cast your mind forward from this one fact, and you would see some few millions of years hence—a mere passing moment in the enormous flux of the ages—the whole world teeming once more with the animal and human life which will spring from this tiny root. You have seen a prairie fire where the flames have swept every trace of grass or plant from the surface of the earth and left only a blackened waste. You would think that it must be forever desert. Yet the roots of growth have been left behind, and when you pass the place a few years hence you can no longer tell where the black scars used to be. Here in this tiny creature are the roots of growth of the animal world, and by its inherent development, and evolution, it will surely in time remove every trace of this incomparable crisis in which we are now involved."

"Dooced interestin'!" said Lord John, lounging across and looking through the microscope. "Funny little chap to hang number one among the family portraits. Got a fine big shirt-stud on him!"

"The dark object is his nucleus," said Challenger with the air of a nurse teaching letters to a baby.

"Well, we needn't feel lonely," said Lord John laughing. "There's somebody livin' besides us on the earth."

"You seem to take it for granted, Challenger," said Summerlee, "that the object for which this world was created was that it should produce and sustain human life."

"Well, sir, and what object do you suggest?" asked Challenger, bristling at the least hint of contradiction.

"Sometimes I think that it is only the monstrous conceit of mankind which makes him think that all this stage was erected for him to strut upon."

"We cannot be dogmatic about it, but at least without what you have ventured to call monstrous conceit we can surely say that we are the highest thing in nature."

"The highest of which we have cognizance."

"That, sir, goes without saying."

"Think of all the millions and possibly billions of years that the earth swung empty through space—or, if not empty, at least without a sign or thought of the human race. Think of it, washed by the rain and scorched by the sun and swept by the wind for those unnumbered ages. Man only came into being yesterday so far as geological times goes. Why, then, should it be taken for granted that all this stupendous preparation was for his benefit?"

"For whose then—or for what?"

Summerlee shrugged his shoulders.

"How can we tell? For some reason altogether beyond our conception—and man may have been a mere accident, a by-product evolved in the process. It is as if the scum upon the surface of the ocean imagined that the ocean was created in order to produce and sustain it or a mouse in a cathedral thought that the building was its own proper ordained residence."

I have jotted down the very words of their argument, but now it degenerates into a mere noisy wrangle with much polysyllabic scientific jargon upon each side. It is no doubt a privilege to hear two such brains discuss the highest questions; but as they are in perpetual disagreement, plain folk like Lord John and I get little that is positive from the exhibition. They neutralize each other and we are left as they found us. Now the hubbub has ceased, and Summerlee is coiled up in his chair, while Challenger, still fingering the screws of his microscope, is keeping up a continual low, deep, inarticulate growl like the sea after a storm. Lord John comes over to me, and we look out together into the night.

There is a pale new moon—the last moon that human eyes will ever rest upon—and the stars are most brilliant. Even in the clear plateau air of South America I have never seen them brighter. Possibly this etheric change has some effect upon light. The funeral pyre of Brighton is still blazing, and there is a very distant patch of scarlet in the western sky, which may mean trouble at Arundel or Chichester, possibly even at Portsmouth. I sit and muse and make an occasional note. There is a sweet melancholy in the air. Youth and beauty and chivalry and love—is this to be the end of it all? The starlit earth looks a dreamland of gentle peace. Who would imagine it as the terrible Golgotha strewn with the bodies of the human race? Suddenly, I find myself laughing.

Halloa, young fellah!" says Lord John, staring at me in surprise. "We could do with a joke in these hard times. What was it, then?"

"I was thinking of all the great unsolved questions," I answer, "the questions that we spent so much labor and thought over. Think of Anglo-German competition, for example—or the Persian Gulf that my old chief was so keen about. Whoever would have guessed, when we fumed and fretted so, how they were to be eventually solved?"

We fall into silence again. I fancy that each of us is thinking of friends that have gone before. Mrs. Challenger is sobbing quietly, and her husband is whispering to her. My mind turns to all the most unlikely people, and I see each of them lying white and rigid as poor Austin does in the yard. There is McArdle, for example, I know exactly where he is, with his face upon his writing desk and his hand on his own telephone, just as I heard him fall. Beaumont, the editor, too—I suppose he is lying upon the blue-and-red Turkey carpet which adorned his sanctum. And the fellows in the reporters' room—Macdona and Murray and Bond. They had certainly died hard at work on their job, with note-books full of vivid impressions and strange happenings in their hands. I could just imagine how this one would have been packed off to the doctors, and that other to Westminster, and yet a third to St.Paul's. What glorious rows of head-lines they must have seen as a last vision beautiful, never destined to materialize in printer's ink! I could see Macdona among the doctors—"Hope in Harley Street"—Mac had always a weakness for alliteration. "Interview with Mr. Soley Wilson." "Famous Specialist says 'Never despair!'" "Our Special Correspondent found the eminent scientist seated upon the roof, whither he had retreated to avoid the crowd of terrified patients who had stormed his dwelling. With a manner which plainly showed his appreciation of the immense gravity of the occasion, the celebrated physician refused to admit that every avenue of hope had been closed." That's how Mac would start. Then there was Bond; he would probably do St. Paul's. He fancied his own literary touch. My word, what a theme for him! "Standing in the little gallery under the dome and looking down upon that packed mass of despairing humanity, groveling at this last instant before a Power which they had so persistently ignored, there rose to my ears from the swaying crowd such a low moan of entreaty and terror, such a shuddering cry for help to the Unknown, that——" and so forth.

Yes, it would be a great end for a reporter, though, like myself, he would die with the treasures still unused. What would Bond not give, poor chap, to see "J. H. B." at the foot of a column like that?

But what drivel I am writing! It is just an attempt to pass the weary time. Mrs. Challenger has gone to the inner dressing-room, and the Professor says that she is asleep. He is making notes and consulting books at the central table, as calmly as if years of placid work lay before him. He writes with a very noisy quill pen which seems to be screeching scorn at all who disagree with him.

Summerlee has dropped off in his chair and gives from time to time a peculiarly exasperating snore. Lord John lies back with his hands in his pockets and his eyes closed. How people can sleep under such conditions is more than I can imagine.

Three-thirty a.m. I have just wakened with a start. It was five minutes past eleven when I made my last entry. I remember winding up my watch and noting the time. So I have wasted some five hours of the little span still left to us. Who would have believed it possible? But I feel very much fresher, and ready for my fate—or try to persuade myself that I am. And yet, the fitter a man is, and the higher his tide of life, the more must he shrink from death. How wise and how merciful is that provision of nature by which his earthly anchor is usually loosened by many little imperceptible tugs, until his consciousness has drifted out of its untenable earthly harbor into the great sea beyond!

Mrs. Challenger is still in the dressing room. Challenger has fallen asleep in his chair. What a picture! His enormous frame leans back, his huge, hairy hands are clasped across his waistcoat, and his head is so tilted that I can see nothing above his collar save a tangled bristle of luxuriant beard. He shakes with the vibration of his own snoring. Summerlee adds his occasional high tenor to Challenger's sonorous bass. Lord John is sleeping also, his long body doubled up sideways in a basket-chair. The first cold light of dawn is just stealing into the room, and everything is grey and mournful.

I look out at the sunrise—that fateful sunrise which will shine upon an unpeopled world. The human race is gone, extinguished in a day, but the planets swing round and the tides rise or fall, and the wind whispers, and all nature goes her way, down, as it would seem, to the very amoeba, with never a sign that he who styled himself the lord of creation had ever blessed or cursed the universe with his presence. Down in the yard lies Austin with sprawling limbs, his face glimmering white in the dawn, and the hose nozzle still projecting from his dead hand. The whole of human kind is typified in that one half-ludicrous and half-pathetic figure, lying so helpless beside the machine which it used to control.

Here end the notes which I made at the time. Henceforward events were too swift and too poignant to allow me to write, but they are too clearly outlined in my memory that any detail could escape me.

Some chokiness in my throat made me look at the oxygen cylinders, and I was startled at what I saw. The sands of our lives were running very low. At some period in the night Challenger had switched the tube from the third to the fourth cylinder. Now it was clear that this also was nearly exhausted. That horrible feeling of constriction was closing in upon me. I ran across and, unscrewing the nozzle, I changed it to our last supply. Even as I did so my conscience pricked me, for I felt that perhaps if I had held my hand all of them might have passed in their sleep. The thought was banished, however, by the voice of the lady from the inner room crying:—

"George, George, I am stifling!"

"It is all right, Mrs. Challenger," I answered as the others started to their feet. "I have just turned on a fresh supply."

Even at such a moment I could not help smiling at Challenger, who with a great hairy fist in each eye was like a huge, bearded baby, new wakened out of sleep. Summerlee was shivering like a man with the ague, human fears, as he realized his position, rising for an instant above the stoicism of the man of science. Lord John, however, was as cool and alert as if he had just been roused on a hunting morning.

"Fifthly and lastly," said he, glancing at the tube. "Say, young fellah, don't tell me you've been writin' up your impressions in that paper on your knee."

"Just a few notes to pass the time."

"Well, I don't believe anyone but an Irishman would have done that. I expect you'll have to wait till little brother amoeba gets grown up before you'll find a reader. He don't seem to take much stock of things just at present. Well, Herr Professor, what are the prospects?"

Challenger was looking out at the great drifts of morning mist which lay over the landscape. Here and there the wooded hills rose like conical islands out of this woolly sea.

"It might be a winding sheet," said Mrs. Challenger, who had entered in her dressing-gown. "There's that song of yours, George, 'Ring out the old, ring in the new.' It was prophetic. But you are shivering, my poor dear friends. I have been warm under a coverlet all night, and you cold in your chairs. But I'll soon set you right."

The brave little creature hurried away, and presently we heard the sizzling of a kettle. She was back soon with five steaming cups of cocoa upon a tray.

"Drink these," said she. "You will feel so much better."

And we did. Summerlee asked if he might light his pipe, and we all had cigarettes. It steadied our nerves, I think, but it was a mistake, for it made a dreadful atmosphere in that stuffy room. Challenger had to open the ventilator.

"How long, Challenger?" asked Lord John.

"Possibly three hours," he answered with a shrug.

"I used to be frightened," said his wife. "But the nearer I get to it, the easier it seems. Don't you think we ought to pray, George?"

"You will pray, dear, if you wish," the big man answered, very gently. "We all have our own ways of praying. Mine is a complete acquiescence in whatever fate may send me—a cheerful acquiescence. The highest religion and the highest science seem to unite on that."

"I cannot truthfully describe my mental attitude as acquiescence and far less cheerful acquiescence," grumbled Summerlee over his pipe. "I submit because I have to. I confess that I should have liked another year of life to finish my classification of the chalk fossils."

"Your unfinished work is a small thing," said Challenger pompously, "when weighed against the fact that my own *magnum opus*, 'The Ladder of Life,' is still in the first stages. My brain, my reading, my experience—in fact, my whole unique equipment—were to be condensed into that epoch-making volume. And yet, as I say, I acquiesce."

"I expect we've all left some loose ends stickin' out," said Lord John. "What are yours, young fellah?"

"I was working at a book of verses," I answered.

"Well, the world has escaped that, anyhow," said Lord John. "There's always compensation somewhere if you grope around."

"What about you?" I asked.

"Well, it just so happens that I was tidied up and ready. I'd promised Merivale to go to Tibet for a snow leopard in the spring. But it's hard on you, Mrs. Challenger, when you have just built up this pretty home."

"Where George is, there is my home. But, oh, what would I not give for one last walk together in the fresh morning air upon those beautiful downs!"

Our hearts re-echoed her words. The sun had burst through the gauzy mists which veiled it, and the whole broad Weald was washed in golden light. Sitting in our dark and poisonous atmosphere that glorious, clean, windswept countryside seemed a very dream of beauty. Mrs. Challenger held her hand stretched out to it in her longing. We drew up chairs and sat in a semicircle in the window. The atmosphere was already very close. It seemed to me that the shadows of death were drawing in upon us—the last of our race. It was like an invisible curtain closing down upon every side.

"That cylinder is not lastin' too well," said Lord John with a long gasp for breath.

"The amount contained is variable," said Challenger, "depending upon the pressure and care with which it has been bottled. I am inclined to agree with you, Roxton, that this one is defective."

"So we are to be cheated out of the last hour of our lives," Summerlee remarked bitterly. "An excellent final illustration of the sordid age in which we have lived. Well, Challenger, now is your time if you wish to study the subjective phenomena of physical dissolution."

"Sit on the stool at my knee and give me your hand," said Challenger to his wife. "I think, my friends, that a further delay in this insufferable atmosphere is hardly advisable. You would not desire it, dear, would you?"

His wife gave a little groan and sank her face against his leg.

"I've seen the folk bathin' in the Serpentine in winter," said Lord John. "When the rest are in, you see one or two shiverin' on the bank, envyin' the others that have taken the plunge. It's the last that have the worst of it. I'm all for a header and have done with it."

"You would open the window and face the ether?"

"Better be poisoned than stifled."

Summerlee nodded his reluctant acquiescence and held out his thin hand to Challenger.

"We've had our quarrels in our time, but that's all over," said he. "We were good friends and had a respect for each other under the surface. Good-by!"

"Good-by, young fellah!" said Lord John. "The window's plastered up. You can't open it."

Challenger stooped and raised his wife, pressing her to his breast, while she threw her arms round his neck.

"Give me that field-glass, Malone," said he gravely.

I handed it to him.

"Into the hands of the Power that made us we render ourselves again!" he shouted in his voice of thunder, and at the words he hurled the field-glass through the window.

Full in our flushed faces, before the last twinkle of falling fragments had died away, there came the wholesome breath of the wind, blowing strong and sweet.

I don't know how long we sat in amazed silence. Then as in a dream, I heard Challenger's voice once more.

"We are back in normal conditions," he cried. "The world has cleared the poison belt, but we alone of all mankind are saved."

CHAPTER V: THE DEAD WORLD

I remember that we all sat gasping in our chairs, with that sweet, wet south-western breeze, fresh from the sea, flapping the muslin curtains and cooling our flushed faces. I wonder how long we sat! None of us afterwards could agree at all on that point. We were bewildered, stunned, semi-conscious. We had all braced our courage for death, but this fearful and sudden new fact—that we must continue to live after we had survived the race to which we belonged—struck us with the shock of a physical blow and left us prostrate. Then gradually the suspended mechanism began to move once more; the shuttles of memory worked; ideas weaved themselves together in our minds. We saw, with vivid, merciless clearness, the relations between the past, the present, and the future—the lives that we had led and the lives which we would have to live. Our eyes turned in silent horror upon those of our companions and found the same answering look in theirs. Instead of the joy which men might have been expected to feel who had so narrowly escaped an imminent death, a terrible wave of darkest depression submerged us. Everything on earth that we loved had been washed away into the great, infinite, unknown ocean, and here were we marooned upon this desert island of a world, without companions, hopes, or aspirations. A few years' skulking like jackals among the graves of the human race and then our belated and lonely end would come.

"It's dreadful, George, dreadful!" the lady cried in an agony of sobs. "If we had only passed with the others! Oh, why did you save us? I feel as if it is we that are dead and everyone else alive."

Challenger's great eyebrows were drawn down in concentrated thought, while his huge, hairy paw closed upon the outstretched hand of his wife. I had observed that she always held out her arms to him in trouble as a child would to its mother.

"Without being a fatalist to the point of nonresistance," said he, "I have always found that the highest wisdom lies in an acquiescence with the actual." He spoke slowly, and there was a vibration of feeling in his sonorous voice.

"I do *not* acquiesce," said Summerlee firmly.

"I don't see that it matters a row of pins whether you acquiesce or whether you don't," remarked Lord John. "You've got to take it, whether you take it fightin' or take it lyin' down, so what's the odds whether you acquiesce or not?

"I can't remember that anyone asked our permission before the thing began, and nobody's likely to ask it now. So what difference can it make what we may think of it?"

"It is just all the difference between happiness and misery," said Challenger with an abstracted face, still patting his wife's hand. "You can swim with the tide and have peace in mind and soul, or you can thrust against it and be bruised and weary. This business is beyond us, so let us accept it as it stands and say no more."

"But what in the world are we to do with our lives?" I asked, appealing in desperation to the blue, empty heaven.

"What am I to do, for example? There are no newspapers, so there's an end of my vocation."

"And there's nothin' left to shoot, and no more soldierin', so there's an end of mine," said Lord John.

"And there are no students, so there's an end of mine," cried Summerlee.

"But I have my husband and my house, so I can thank heaven that there is no end of mine," said the lady.

"Nor is there an end of mine," remarked Challenger, "for science is not dead, and this catastrophe in itself will offer us many most absorbing problems for investigation."

He had now flung open the windows and we were gazing out upon the silent and motionless landscape.

"Let me consider," he continued. "It was about three, or a little after, yesterday afternoon that the world finally entered the poison belt to the extent of being completely submerged. It is now nine o'clock. The question is, at what hour did we pass out from it?"

"The air was very bad at daybreak," said I.

"Later than that," said Mrs. Challenger. "As late as eight o'clock I distinctly felt the same choking at my throat which came at the outset."

"Then we shall say that it passed just after eight o'clock. For seventeen hours the world has been soaked in the poisonous ether. For that length of time the Great Gardener has sterilized the human mold which had grown over the surface of His fruit. Is it possible that the work is incompletely done—that others may have survived besides ourselves?"

"That's what I was wonderin'" said Lord John. "Why should we be the only pebbles on the beach?"

"It is absurd to suppose that anyone besides ourselves can possibly have survived," said Summerlee with conviction. "Consider that the poison was so virulent that even a man who is as strong as an ox and has not a nerve in his body, like Malone here, could hardly get up the stairs before he fell unconscious. Is it likely that anyone could stand seventeen minutes of it, far less hours?"

"Unless someone saw it coming and made preparation, same as old friend Challenger did."

"That, I think, is hardly probable," said Challenger, projecting his beard and sinking his eyelids. "The combination of observation, inference, and anticipatory imagination which enabled me to foresee the danger is what one can hardly expect twice in the same generation."

"Then your conclusion is that everyone is certainly dead?"

"There can be little doubt of that. We have to remember, however, that the poison worked from below upwards and would possibly be less virulent in the higher strata of the atmosphere. It is strange, indeed, that it should be so; but it presents one of those features which will afford us in the future a fascinating field for study. One could imagine, therefore, that if one had to search for survivors one would turn one's eyes with best hopes of success to some Tibetan village or some Alpine farm, many thousands of feet above the sea level."

"Well, considerin' that there are no railroads and no steamers you might as well talk about survivors in the moon," said Lord John. "But what I'm askin' myself is whether it's really over or whether it's only half-time."

Summerlee craned his neck to look round the horizon. "It seems clear and fine," said he in a very dubious voice; "but so it did yesterday. I am by no means assured that it is all over."

Challenger shrugged his shoulders.

"We must come back once more to our fatalism," said he. "If the world has undergone this experience before, which is not outside the range of possibility; it was certainly a very long time ago. Therefore, we may reasonably hope that it will be very long before it occurs again."

"That's all very well," said Lord John, "but if you get an earthquake shock you are mighty likely to have a second one right on the top of it. I think we'd be wise to stretch our legs and have a breath of air while we have the chance. Since our oxygen is exhausted we may just as well be caught outside as in."

It was strange the absolute lethargy which had come upon us as a reaction after our tremendous emotions of the last twenty-four hours. It was both mental and physical, a deep-lying feeling that nothing mattered and that everything was a weariness and a profitless exertion. Even Challenger had succumbed to it, and sat in his chair, with his great head leaning upon his hands and his thoughts far away, until Lord John and I, catching him by each arm, fairly lifted him on to his feet, receiving only the glare and growl of an angry mastiff for our trouble. However, once we had got out of our narrow haven of refuge into the wider atmosphere of everyday life, our normal energy came gradually back to us once more.

But what were we to begin to do in that graveyard of a world? Could ever men have been faced with such a question since the dawn of time? It is true that our own physical needs, and even our luxuries, were assured for the future. All the stores of food, all the vintages of wine, all the treasures of art were ours for the taking. But what were we to *do*? Some few tasks appealed to us at once, since they lay ready to our hands. We descended into the kitchen and laid the two domestics upon their respective beds. They seemed to have died without suffering, one in the chair by the fire, the other upon the scullery floor. Then we carried in poor Austin from the yard. His muscles were set as hard as a board in the most exaggerated rigor mortis, while the contraction of the fibres had drawn his mouth into a hard sardonic grin. This symptom was prevalent among all who had died from the poison. Wherever we went we were confronted by those grinning faces, which seemed to mock at our dreadful position, smiling silently and grimly at the ill-fated survivors of their race.

"Look here," said Lord John, who had paced restlessly about the dining-room whilst we partook of some food, "I don't know how you fellows feel about it, but for my part, I simply *can't* sit here and do nothin'."

"Perhaps," Challenger answered, "you would have the kindness to suggest what you think we ought to do."

"Get a move on us and see all that has happened."

"That is what I should myself propose."

"But not in this little country village. We can see from the window all that this place can teach us."

"Where should we go, then?"

"To London!"

"That's all very well," grumbled Summerlee. "You may be equal to a forty-mile walk, but I'm not so sure about Challenger, with his stumpy legs, and I am perfectly sure about myself." Challenger was very much annoyed.

"If you could see your way, sir, to confining your remarks to your own physical peculiarities, you would find that you had an ample field for comment," he cried.

"I had no intention to offend you, my dear Challenger," cried our tactless friend, "You can't be held responsible for your own physique. If nature has given you a short, heavy body you cannot possibly help having stumpy legs."

Challenger was too furious to answer. He could only growl and blink and bristle. Lord John hastened to intervene before the dispute became more violent.

"You talk of walking. Why should we walk?" said he.

"Do you suggest taking a train?" asked Challenger, still simmering.

"What's the matter with the motor-car? Why should we not go in that?"

"I am not an expert," said Challenger, pulling at his beard reflectively. "At the same time, you are right in supposing that the human intellect in its higher manifestations should be sufficiently flexible to turn itself to anything. Your idea is an excellent one, Lord John. I myself will drive you all to London."

"You will do nothing of the kind," said Summerlee with decision.

"No, indeed, George!" cried his wife. "You only tried once, and you remember how you crashed through the gate of the garage."

"It was a momentary want of concentration," said Challenger complacently. "You can consider the matter settled. I will certainly drive you all to London."

The situation was relieved by Lord John.

"What's the car?" he asked.

"A twenty-horsepower Humber."

"Why, I've driven one for years," said he. "By George!" he added. "I never thought I'd live to take the whole human race in one load. There's just room for five, as I remember it. Get your things on, and I'll be ready at the door by ten o'clock."

Sure enough, at the hour named, the car came purring and crackling from the yard with Lord John at the wheel. I took my seat beside him, while the lady, a useful little buffer state, was squeezed in between the two men of wrath at the back. Then Lord John released his brakes, slid his lever rapidly from first to third, and we sped off upon the strangest drive that ever human beings have taken since man first came upon the earth.

You are to picture the loveliness of nature upon that August day, the freshness of the morning air, the golden glare of the summer sunshine, the cloudless sky, the luxuriant green of the Sussex woods, and the deep purple of heather-clad downs. As you looked round upon the many-coloured beauty of the scene all thought of a vast catastrophe would have passed from your mind had it not been for one sinister sign—the solemn, all-embracing silence. There is a gentle hum of life which pervades a closely-settled country, so deep and constant that one ceases to observe it, as the dweller by the sea loses all sense of the constant murmur of the waves. The twitter of birds, the buzz of insects, the far-off echo of voices, the lowing of cattle, the distant barking of dogs, roar of trains, and rattle of carts—all these form one low, unremitting note, striking unheeded upon the ear. We missed it now. This deadly silence was appalling. So solemn was it, so impressive, that the buzz and rattle of our motor-car seemed an unwarrantable intrusion, an indecent disregard of this reverent stillness which lay like a pall over and round the ruins of humanity. It was this grim hush, and the tall clouds of smoke which rose here and there over the country-side from smoldering buildings, which cast a chill into our hearts as we gazed round at the glorious panorama of the Weald.

And then there were the dead! At first those endless groups of drawn and grinning faces filled us with a shuddering horror. So vivid and mordant was the impression that I can live over again that slow descent of the station hill, the passing by the nurse-girl with the two babes, the sight of the old horse on his knees between the shafts, the cabman twisted across his seat, and the young man inside with his hand upon the open door in the very act of springing out. Lower down were six reapers all in a litter, their limbs crossing, their dead, unwinking eyes gazing upwards at the glare of heaven. These things I see as in a photograph. But soon, by the merciful provision of nature, the over-excited nerve ceased to respond. The very vastness of the horror took away from its personal appeal. Individuals merged into groups, groups into crowds, crowds into a universal phenomenon which one soon accepted as the inevitable detail of every scene. Only here and there, where some particularly brutal or grotesque incident caught the attention, did the mind come back with a sudden shock to the personal and human meaning of it all.

Above all, there was the fate of the children. That, I remember, filled us with the strongest sense of intolerable injustice. We could have wept— Mrs. Challenger did weep—when we passed a great council school and saw the long trail of tiny figures scattered down the road which led from it. They had been dismissed by their terrified teachers and were speeding for their homes when the poison caught them in its net. Great numbers of people were at the open windows of the houses. In Tunbridge Wells there was hardly one which had not its staring, smiling face. At the last instant the need of air, that very craving for oxygen which we alone had been able to satisfy, had sent them flying to the window. The sidewalks too were littered with men and women, hatless and bonnetless, who had rushed out of the houses. Many of them had fallen in the roadway. It was a lucky thing that in Lord John we had found an expert driver, for it was no easy matter to pick one's way. Passing through the villages or towns we could only go at a walking pace, and once, I remember, opposite the school at Tonbridge, we had to halt some time while we carried aside the bodies which blocked our path.

A few small, definite pictures stand out in my memory from amid that long panorama of death upon the Sussex and Kentish high roads. One was that of a great, glittering motor-car standing outside the inn at the village of South-borough. It bore, as I should guess, some pleasure party upon their return from Brighton or from Eastbourne. There were three gaily dressed women, all young and beautiful, one of them with a Peking spaniel upon her lap. With them were a rakish-looking elderly man and a young aristocrat, his eyeglass still in his eye, his cigarette burned down to the stub between the fingers of his begloved hand. Death must have come on them in an instant and fixed them as they sat. Save that the elderly man had at the last moment torn out his collar in an effort to breathe, they might all have been asleep. On one side of the car a waiter with some broken glasses beside a tray was huddled near the step. On the other, two very ragged tramps, a man and a woman, lay where they had fallen, the man with his long, thin arm still outstretched, even as he had asked for alms in his lifetime. One instant of time had put aristocrat, waiter, tramp, and dog upon one common footing of inert and dissolving protoplasm.

I remember another singular picture, some miles on the London side of Sevenoaks. There is a large convent upon the left, with a long, green slope in front of it. Upon this slope were assembled a great number of school children, all kneeling at prayer. In front of them was a fringe of nuns, and higher up the slope, facing towards them, a single figure whom we took to be the Mother Superior. Unlike the pleasure-seekers in the motor-car, these people seemed to have had warning of their danger and to have died beautifully together, the teachers and the taught, assembled for their last common lesson.

My mind is still stunned by that terrific experience, and I grope vainly for means of expression by which I can reproduce the emotions which we felt. Perhaps it is best and wisest not to try, but merely to indicate the facts. Even Summerlee and Challenger were crushed, and we heard nothing of our companions behind us save an occasional whimper from the lady. As to Lord John, he was too intent upon his wheel and the difficult task of threading his way along such roads to have time or inclination for conversation. One phrase he used with such wearisome iteration that it stuck in my memory and at last almost made me laugh as a comment upon the day of doom. "Pretty doin's! What!"

That was his ejaculation as each fresh tremendous combination of death and disaster displayed itself before us. "Pretty doin's! What!" he cried, as we descended the station hill at Rotherfield, and it was still "Pretty doin's! What!" as we picked our way through a wilderness of death in the High Street of Lewisham and the Old Kent Road.

It was here that we received a sudden and amazing shock. Out of the window of a humble corner house there appeared a fluttering handkerchief waving at the end of a long, thin human arm. Never had the sight of unexpected death caused our hearts to stop and then throb so wildly as did this amazing indication of life. Lord John ran the motor to the curb, and in an instant we had rushed through the open door of the house and up the staircase to the second-floor front room from which the signal proceeded.

A very old lady sat in a chair by the open window, and close to her, laid across a second chair, was a cylinder of oxygen, smaller but of the same shape as those which had saved our own lives. She turned her thin, drawn, bespectacled face toward us as we crowded in at the doorway.

"I feared that I was abandoned here forever," said she, "for I am an invalid and cannot stir."

"Well, madam," Challenger answered, "it is a lucky chance that we happened to pass."

"I have one all-important question to ask you," said she. "Gentlemen, I beg that you will be frank with me. What effect will these events have upon London and North-Western Railway shares?"

We should have laughed had it not been for the tragic eagerness with which she listened for our answer. Mrs. Burston, for that was her name, was an aged widow, whose whole income depended upon a small holding of this stock. Her life had been regulated by the rise and fall of the dividend, and she could form no conception of existence save as it was affected by the quotation of her shares. In vain we pointed out to her that all the money in the world was hers for the taking and was useless when taken. Her old mind would not adapt itself to the new idea, and she wept loudly over her vanished stock. "It was all I had," she wailed. "If that is gone I may as well go too."

Amid her lamentations we found out how this frail old plant had lived where the whole great forest had fallen. She was a confirmed invalid and an asthmatic. Oxygen had been prescribed for her malady, and a tube was in her room at the moment of the crisis. She had naturally inhaled some as had been her habit when there was a difficulty with her breathing. It had given her relief, and by doling out her supply she had managed to survive the night. Finally she had fallen asleep and been awakened by the buzz of our motorcar. As it was impossible to take her on with us, we saw that she had all necessaries of life and promised to communicate with her in a couple of days at the latest. So we left her, still weeping bitterly over her vanished stock.

As we approached the Thames the block in the streets became thicker and the obstacles more bewildering. It was with difficulty that we made our way across London Bridge. The approaches to it upon the Middlesex side were choked from end to end with frozen traffic which made all further advance in that direction impossible. A ship was blazing brightly alongside one of the wharves near the bridge, and the air was full of drifting smuts and of a heavy acrid smell of burning. There was a cloud of dense smoke somewhere near the Houses of Parliament, but it was impossible from where we were to see what was on fire.

"I don't know how it strikes you," Lord John remarked as he brought his engine to a standstill, "but it seems to me the country is more cheerful than the town. Dead London is gettin' on my nerves. I'm for a cast round and then gettin' back to Rotherfield."

"I confess that I do not see what we can hope for here," said Professor Summerlee.

"At the same time," said Challenger, his great voice booming strangely amid the silence, "it is difficult for us to conceive that out of seven millions of people there is only this one old woman who by some peculiarity of constitution or some accident of occupation has managed to survive this catastrophe."

"If there should be others, how can we hope to find them, George?" asked the lady. "And yet I agree with you that we cannot go back until we have tried."

Getting out of the car and leaving it by the curb, we walked with some difficulty along the crowded pavement of King William Street and entered the open door of a large insurance office. It was a corner house, and we chose it as commanding a view in every direction. Ascending the stair, we passed through what I suppose to have been the board-room, for eight elderly men were seated round a long table in the centre of it. The high window was open and we all stepped out upon the balcony. From it we could see the crowded city streets radiating in every direction, while below us the road was black from side to side with the tops of the motionless taxis. All, or nearly all, had their heads pointed outwards, showing how the terrified men of the city had at the last moment made a vain endeavor to rejoin their families in the suburbs or the country. Here and there amid the humbler cabs towered the great brass-spangled motor-car of some wealthy magnate, wedged hopelessly among the dammed stream of arrested traffic. Just beneath us there was such a one of great size and luxurious appearance, with its owner, a fat old man, leaning out, half his gross body through the window, and his podgy hand, gleaming with diamonds, outstretched as he urged his chauffeur to make a last effort to break through the press.

A dozen motor-buses towered up like islands in this flood, the passengers who crowded the roofs lying all huddled together and across each others' laps like a child's toys in a nursery. On a broad lamp pedestal in the centre of the roadway, a burly policeman was standing, leaning his back against the post in so natural an attitude that it was hard to realize that he was not alive, while at his feet there lay a ragged newsboy with his bundle of papers on the ground beside him. A paper-cart had got blocked in the crowd, and we could read in large letters, black upon yellow, "Scene at Lord's. County Match Interrupted." This must have been the earliest edition, for there were other placards bearing the legend, "Is It the End? Great Scientist's Warning." And another, "Is Challenger Justified? Ominous Rumours."

Challenger pointed the latter placard out to his wife, as it thrust itself like a banner above the throng. I could see him throw out his chest and stroke his beard as he looked at it. It pleased and flattered that complex mind to think that London had died with his name and his words still present in their thoughts. His feelings were so evident that they aroused the sardonic comment of his colleague.

"In the limelight to the last, Challenger," he remarked.

"So it would appear," he answered complacently. "Well," he added as he looked down the long vista of the radiating streets, all silent and all choked up with death, "I really see no purpose to be served by our staying any longer in London. I suggest that we return at once to Rotherfield and then take counsel as to how we shall most profitably employ the years which lie before us."

Only one other picture shall I give of the scenes which we carried back in our memories from the dead city. It is a glimpse which we had of the interior of the old church of St. Mary's, which is at the very point where our car was awaiting us. Picking our way among the prostrate figures upon the steps, we pushed open the swing door and entered. It was a wonderful sight. The church was crammed from end to end with kneeling figures in every posture of supplication and abasement. At the last dreadful moment, brought suddenly face to face with the realities of life, those terrific realities which hang over us even while we follow the shadows, the terrified people had rushed into those old city churches which for generations had hardly ever held a congregation. There they huddled as close as they could kneel, many of them in their agitation still wearing their hats, while above them in the pulpit a young man in lay dress had apparently been addressing them when he and they had been overwhelmed by the same fate. He lay now, like Punch in his booth, with his head and two limp arms hanging over the ledge of the pulpit. It was a nightmare, the grey, dusty church, the rows of agonized figures, the dimness and silence of it all. We moved about with hushed whispers, walking upon our tip-toes.

And then suddenly I had an idea. At one corner of the church, near the door, stood the ancient font, and behind it a deep recess in which there hung the ropes for the bell-ringers. Why should we not send a message out over London which would attract to us anyone who might still be alive? I ran across, and pulling at the list-covered rope, I was surprised to find how difficult it was to swing the bell. Lord John had followed me.

"By George, young fellah!" said he, pulling off his coat. "You've hit on a dooced good notion. Give me a grip and we'll soon have a move on it."

But, even then, so heavy was the bell that it was not until Challenger and Summerlee had added their weight to ours that we heard the roaring and clanging above our heads which told us that the great clapper was ringing out its music. Far over dead London resounded our message of comradeship and hope to any fellow-man surviving. It cheered our own hearts, that strong, metallic call, and we turned the more earnestly to our work, dragged two feet off the earth with each upward jerk of the rope, but all straining together on the downward heave, Challenger the lowest of all, bending all his great strength to the task and flopping up and down like a monstrous bull-frog, croaking with every pull. It was at that moment that an artist might have taken a picture of the four adventurers, the comrades of many strange perils in the past, whom fate had now chosen for so supreme an experience. For half an hour we worked, the sweat dropping from our faces, our arms and backs aching with the exertion. Then we went out into the portico of the church and looked eagerly up and down the silent, crowded streets. Not a sound, not a motion, in answer to our summons.

"It's no use. No one is left," I cried.

"We can do nothing more," said Mrs. Challenger. "For God's sake, George, let us get back to Rotherfield. Another hour of this dreadful, silent city would drive me mad."

We got into the car without another word. Lord John backed her round and turned her to the south. To us the chapter seemed closed. Little did we foresee the strange new chapter which was to open.

CHAPTER VI: THE GREAT AWAKENING

And now I come to the end of this extraordinary incident, so overshadowing in its importance, not only in our own small, individual lives, but in the general history of the human race. As I said when I began my narrative, when that history comes to be written, this occurrence will surely stand out among all other events like a mountain towering among its foothills. Our generation has been reserved for a very special fate since it has been chosen to experience so wonderful a thing. How long its effect may last—how long mankind may preserve the humility and reverence which this great shock has taught it—can only be shown by the future. I think it is safe to say that things can never be quite the same again. Never can one realize how power-less and ignorant one is, and how one is upheld by an unseen hand, until for an instant that hand has seemed to close and to crush. Death has been imminent upon us. We know that at any moment it may be again. That grim presence shadows our lives, but who can deny that in that shadow the sense of duty, the feeling of sobriety and responsibility, the appreciation of the gravity and of the objects of life, the earnest desire to develop and improve, have grown and become real with us to a degree that has leavened our whole society from end to end? It is something beyond sects and beyond dogmas. It is rather an alteration of perspective, a shifting of our sense of proportion, a vivid realization that we are insignificant and evanescent creatures, exist-ing on sufferance and at the mercy of the first chill wind from the unknown. But if the world has grown graver with this knowledge it is not, I think, a sadder place in consequence. Surely we are agreed that the more sober and restrained pleasures of the present are deeper as well as wiser than the noisy, foolish hustle which passed so often for enjoyment in the days of old—days so recent and yet already so inconceivable. Those empty lives which were wasted in aimless visiting and being visited, in the worry of great and unnecessary households, in the arranging and eating of elaborate and tedious meals, have now found rest and health in the reading, the music, the gentle family communion which comes from a simpler and saner division of their time. With greater health and greater pleasure they are richer than before, even after they have paid those increased contributions to the common fund which have so raised the standard of life in these islands.

There is some clash of opinion as to the exact hour of the great awakening. It is generally agreed that, apart from the difference of clocks, there may have been local causes which influenced the action of the poison. Certainly, in each separate district the resurrection was practically simultaneous. There are numerous witnesses that Big Ben pointed to ten minutes past six at the moment. The Astronomer Royal has fixed the Greenwich time at twelve past six. On the other hand, Laird Johnson, a very capable East Anglia observer, has recorded six-twenty as the hour. In the Hebrides it was as late as seven. In our own case there can be no doubt whatever, for I was seated in Challenger's study with his carefully tested chronometer in front of me at the moment. The hour was a quarter-past six.

An enormous depression was weighing upon my spirits. The cumulative effect of all the dreadful sights which we had seen upon our journey was heavy upon my soul. With my abounding animal health and great physical energy any kind of mental clouding was a rare event. I had the Irish faculty of seeing some gleam of humor in every darkness. But now the obscurity was appalling and unrelieved. The others were downstairs making their plans for the future. I sat by the open window, my chin resting upon my hand and my mind absorbed in the misery of our situation. Could we continue to live? That was the question which I had begun to ask myself. Was it possible to exist upon a dead world? Just as in physics the greater body draws to itself the lesser, would we not feel an overpowering attraction from that vast body of humanity which had passed into the unknown? How would the end come? Would it be from a return of the poison? Or would the earth be uninhabitable from the mephitic products of universal decay? Or, finally, might our awful situation prey upon and unbalance our minds? A group of insane folk upon a dead world! My mind was brooding upon this last dreadful idea when some slight noise caused me to look down upon the road beneath me. The old cab horse was coming up the hill!

I was conscious at the same instant of the twittering of birds, of someone coughing in the yard below, and of a background of movement in the landscape. And yet I remember that it was that absurd, emaciated, superannuated cab-horse which held my gaze. Slowly and wheezily it was climbing the slope. Then my eye traveled to the driver sitting hunched up upon the box and finally to the young man who was leaning out of the window in some excitement and shouting a direction. They were all indubitably, aggressively alive!

Everybody was alive once more! Had it all been a delusion? Was it conceivable that this whole poison belt incident had been an elaborate dream? For an instant my startled brain was really ready to believe it. Then I looked down, and there was the rising blister on my hand where it was frayed by the rope of the city bell. It had really been so, then. And yet here was the world resuscitated—here was life come back in an instant full tide to the planet. Now, as my eyes wandered all over the great landscape, I saw it in every direction—and moving, to my amazement, in the very same groove in which it had halted. There were the golfers. Was it possible that they were going on with their game? Yes, there was a fellow driving off from a tee, and that other group upon the green were surely putting for the hole. The reapers were slowly trooping back to their work. The nurse-girl slapped one of her charges and then began to push the perambulator up the hill. Everyone had unconcernedly taken up the thread at the very point where they had dropped it.

I rushed downstairs, but the hall door was open, and I heard the voices of my companions, loud in astonishment and congratulation, in the yard. How we all shook hands and laughed as we came together, and how Mrs. Challenger kissed us all in her emotion, before she finally threw herself into the bear-hug of her husband.

"But they could not have been asleep!" cried Lord John. "Dash it all, Challenger, you don't mean to believe that those folk were asleep with their staring eyes and stiff limbs and that awful death grin on their faces!"

"It can only have been the condition that is called catalepsy," said Challenger. "It has been a rare phenomenon in the past and has constantly been mistaken for death. While it endures, the temperature falls, the respiration disappears, the heartbeat is indistinguishable—in fact, it *is* death, save that it is evanescent. Even the most comprehensive mind"—here he closed his eyes and simpered—"could hardly conceive a universal outbreak of it in this fashion."

"You may label it catalepsy," remarked Summerlee, "but, after all, that is only a name, and we know as little of the result as we do of the poison which has caused it. The most we can say is that the vitiated ether has produced a temporary death."

Austin was seated all in a heap on the step of the car. It was his coughing which I had heard from above. He had been holding his head in silence, but now he was muttering to himself and running his eyes over the car.

"Young fat-head!" he grumbled. "Can't leave things alone!"

"What's the matter, Austin?"

"Lubricators left running, sir. Someone has been fooling with the car. I expect it's that young garden boy, sir."

Lord John looked guilty.

"I don't know what's amiss with me," continued Austin, staggering to his feet. "I expect I came over queer when I was hosing her down. I seem to remember flopping over by the step. But I'll swear I never left those lubricator taps on."

In a condensed narrative the astonished Austin was told what had happened to himself and the world. The mystery of the dripping lubricators was also explained to him. He listened with an air of deep distrust when told how an amateur had driven his car and with absorbed interest to the few sentences in which our experiences of the sleeping city were recorded. I can remember his comment when the story was concluded.

"Was you outside the Bank of England, sir?"

"Yes, Austin."

"With all them millions inside and everybody asleep?"

"That was so."

"And I not there!" he groaned, and turned dismally once more to the hosing of his car.

There was a sudden grinding of wheels upon gravel. The old cab had actually pulled up at Challenger's door. I saw the young occupant step out from it. An instant later the maid, who looked as tousled and bewildered as if she had that instant been aroused from the deepest sleep, appeared with a card upon a tray. Challenger snorted ferociously as he looked at it, and his thick black hair seemed to bristle up in his wrath.

"A pressman!" he growled. Then with a deprecating smile: "After all, it is natural that the whole world should hasten to know what I think of such an episode."

"That can hardly be his errand," said Summerlee, "for he was on the road in his cab before ever the crisis came."

I looked at the card: "James Baxter, London Correspondent, New York Monitor."

"You'll see him?" said I.

"Not I."

"Oh, George! You should be kinder and more considerate to others. Surely you have learned something from what we have undergone."

He tut-tutted and shook his big, obstinate head.

"A poisonous breed! Eh, Malone? The worst weed in modern civilization, the ready tool of the quack and the hindrance of the self-respecting man! When did they ever say a good word for me?"

"When did you ever say a good word to them?" I answered. "Come, sir, this is a stranger who has made a journey to see you. I am sure that you won't be rude to him."

"Well, well," he grumbled, "you come with me and do the talking. I protest in advance against any such outrageous invasion of my private life." Muttering and mumbling, he came rolling after me like an angry and rather ill-conditioned mastiff.

The dapper young American pulled out his notebook and plunged instantly into his subject.

"I came down, sir," said he, "because our people in America would very much like to hear more about this danger which is, in your opinion, pressing upon the world."

"I know of no danger which is now pressing upon the world," Challenger answered gruffly.

The pressman looked at him in mild surprise.

"I meant, sir, the chances that the world might run into a belt of poisonous ether."

"I do not now apprehend any such danger," said Challenger.

The pressman looked even more perplexed.

"You are Professor Challenger, are you not?" he asked.

"Yes, sir; that is my name."

"I cannot understand, then, how you can say that there is no such danger. I am alluding to your own letter, published above your name in the London Times of this morning."

It was Challenger's turn to look surprised.

"This morning?" said he. "No London Times was published this morning."

"Surely, sir," said the American in mild remonstrance, "you must admit that the London Times is a daily paper." He drew out a copy from his inside pocket. "Here is the letter to which I refer."

Challenger chuckled and rubbed his hands.

"I begin to understand," said he. "So you read this letter this morning?"

"Yes, sir."

"And came at once to interview me?"

"Yes, sir."

"Did you observe anything unusual upon the journey down?"

"Well, to tell the truth, your people seemed more lively and generally human than I have ever seen them. The baggage man set out to tell me a funny story, and that's a new experience for me in this country."

"Nothing else?"

"Why, no, sir, not that I can recall."

"Well, now, what hour did you leave Victoria?"

The American smiled.

"I came here to interview you, Professor, but it seems to be a case of 'Is this nigger fishing, or is this fish niggering?' You're doing most of the work."

"It happens to interest me. Do you recall the hour?"

"Sure. It was half-past twelve."

"And you arrived?"

"At a quarter-past two."

"And you hired a cab?"

"That was so."

"How far do you suppose it is to the station?"

"Well, I should reckon the best part of two miles."

"So how long do you think it took you?"

"Well, half an hour, maybe, with that asthmatic in front."

"So it should be three o'clock?"

"Yes, or a trifle after it."

"Look at your watch."

The American did so and then stared at us in astonishment.

"Say!" he cried. "It's run down. That horse has broken every record, sure. The sun is pretty low, now that I come to look at it. Well, there's something here I don't understand."

"Have you no remembrance of anything remarkable as you came up the hill?"

"Well, I seem to recollect that I was mighty sleepy once. It comes back to me that I wanted to say something to the driver and that I couldn't make him heed me. I guess it was the heat, but I felt swimmy for a moment. That's all."

"So it is with the whole human race," said Challenger to me. "They have all felt swimmy for a moment. None of them have as yet any comprehension of what has occurred. Each will go on with his interrupted job as Austin has snatched up his hose-pipe or the golfer continued his game. Your editor, Malone, will continue the issue of his papers, and very much amazed he will be at finding that an issue is missing. Yes, my young friend," he added to the American reporter, with a sudden mood of amused geniality, "it may interest you to know that the world has swum through the poisonous current which swirls like the Gulf Stream through the ocean of ether. You will also kindly note for your own future convenience that to-day is not Friday, August the twenty-seventh, but Saturday, August the twenty-eighth, and that you sat senseless in your cab for twenty-eight hours upon the Rotherfield hill."

And "right here," as my American colleague would say, I may bring this narrative to an end. It is, as you are probably aware, only a fuller and more detailed version of the account which appeared in the Monday edition of the Daily Gazette—an account which has been universally admitted to be the greatest journalistic scoop of all time, which sold no fewer than three-and-a-half million copies of the paper. Framed upon the wall of my sanctum I retain those magnificent headlines:—

TWENTY-EIGHT HOURS' WORLD COMA
UNPRECEDENTED EXPERIENCE
CHALLENGER JUSTIFIED
OUR CORRESPONDENT ESCAPES
ENTHRALLING NARRATIVE
THE OXYGEN ROOM
WEIRD MOTOR DRIVE
DEAD LONDON
REPLACING THE MISSING PAGE
GREAT FIRES AND LOSS OF LIFE
WILL IT RECUR?

Underneath this glorious scroll came nine and a half columns of narrative, in which appeared the first, last, and only account of the history of the planet, so far as one observer could draw it, during one long day of its existence. Challenger and Summerlee have treated the matter in a joint scientific paper, but to me alone was left the popular account. Surely I can sing "Nunc dimittis." What is left but anti-climax in the life of a journalist after that!

But let me not end on sensational headlines and a merely personal triumph. Rather let me quote the sonorous passages in which the greatest of daily papers ended its admirable leader upon the subject—a leader which might well be filed for reference by every thoughtful man.

"It has been a well-worn truism," said the Times, "that our human race are a feeble folk before the infinite latent forces which surround us. From the prophets of old and from the philosophers of our own time the same message and warning have reached us. But, like all oft-repeated truths, it has in time lost something of its actuality and cogency. A lesson, an actual experience, was needed to bring it home. It is from that salutory but terrible ordeal that we have just emerged, with minds which are still stunned by the suddenness of the blow and with spirits which are chastened by the realization of our own limitations and impotence. The world has paid a fearful price for its schooling. Hardly yet have we learned the full tale of disaster, but the destruction by fire of New York, of Orleans, and of Brighton constitutes in itself one of the greatest tragedies in the history of our race. When the account of the railway and shipping accidents has been completed, it will furnish grim reading, although there is evidence to show that in the vast majority of cases the drivers of trains and engineers of steamers succeeded in shutting off their motive power before succumbing to the poison. But the material damage, enormous as it is both in life and in property, is not the consideration which will be uppermost in our minds to-day. All this may in time be forgotten. But what will not be forgotten, and what will and should continue to obsess our imaginations, is this revelation of the possibilities of the universe, this destruction of our ignorant self-complacency, and this demonstration of how narrow is the path of our material existence and what abysses may lie upon either side of it. Solemnity and humility are at the base of all our emotions to-day. May they be the foundations upon which a more earnest and reverent race may build a more worthy temple."

THE STAR ROVER

Jack London (1915)

AND ABOVE ALL things, next morning Warden Atherton came into my cell on murder intent. With him were Captain Jamie, Doctor Jackson, Pie-Face Jones, and Al Hutchins. Al Hutchins was serving a forty-years' sentence, and was in hopes of being pardoned out. For four years he had been head trusty of San Quentin. That this was a position of great power you will realize when I tell you that the graft alone of the head trusty was estimated at three thousand dollars a year. Wherefore Al Hutchins, in possession of ten or twelve thousand dollars and of the promise of a pardon, could be depended upon to do the Warden's bidding blind.

I have just said that Warden Atherton came into my cell intent on murder. His face showed it. His actions proved it.

"Examine him," he ordered Doctor Jackson.

That wretched apology of a creature stripped from me my dirt encrusted shirt that I had worn since my entrance to solitary, and exposed my poor wasted body, the skin ridged like brown parchment over the ribs and sore-infested from the many bouts with the jacket. The examination was shamelessly perfunctory.

"Will he stand it?" the Warden demanded.

"Yes," Doctor Jackson answered.

"How's the heart?"

"Splendid."

"You think he'll stand ten days of it, Doc.?"

"Sure."

"I don't believe it," the Warden announced savagely. "But we'll try it just the same.—Lie down, Standing."

I obeyed, stretching myself face-downward on the flat-spread jacket. The Warden seemed to debate with himself for a moment.

"Roll over," he commanded.

I made several efforts, but was too weak to succeed, and could only sprawl and squirm in my helplessness.

"Putting it on," was Jackson's comment.

"Well, he won't have to put it on when I'm done with him," said the Warden. "Lend him a hand. I can't waste any more time on him."

So they rolled me over on my back, where I stared up into Warden Atherton's face.

"Standing," he said slowly, "I've given you all the rope I am going to. I am sick and tired of your stubbornness. My patience is exhausted. Doctor Jackson says you are in condition to stand ten days in the jacket. You can figure your chances. But I am going to give you your last chance now. Come across with the dynamite. The moment it is in my hands I'll take you out of here. You can bathe and shave and get clean clothes. I'll let you loaf for six months on hospital grub, and then I'll put you trusty in the library. You can't ask me to be fairer with you than that. Besides, you're not squealing on anybody. You are the only person in San Quentin who knows where the dynamite is. You won't hurt anybody's feelings by giving in, and you'll be all to the good from the moment you do give in. And if you don't—"

He paused and shrugged his shoulders significantly.

"Well, if you don't, you start in the ten days right now."

The prospect was terrifying. So weak was I that I was as certain as the Warden was that it meant death in the jacket. And then I remembered Morrell's trick. Now, if ever, was the need of it; and now, if ever, was the time to practise the faith of it. I smiled up in the face of Warden Atherton. And I put faith in that smile, and faith in the proposition I made to him.

"Warden," I said, "do you see the way I am smiling? Well, if, at the end of the ten days, when you unlace me, I smile up at you in the same way, will you give a sack of Bull Durham and a package of brown papers to Morrell and Oppenheimer?"

"Ain't they the crazy ginks, these college guys," Captain Jamie snorted.

Warden Atherton was a choleric man, and he took my request for insulting braggadocio.

"Just for that you get an extra cinching," he informed me.

"I made you a sporting proposition, Warden," I said quietly. "You can cinch me as tight as you please, but if I smile ten days from now will you give the Bull Durham to Morrell and Oppenheimer?"

"You are mighty sure of yourself," he retorted.

"That's why I made the proposition," I replied.

"Getting religion, eh?" he sneered.

"No," was my answer. "It merely happens that I possess more life than you can ever reach the end of. Make it a hundred days if you want, and I'll smile at you when it's over."

"I guess ten days will more than do you, Standing."

"That's your opinion," I said. "Have you got faith in it? If you have you won't even lose the price of the two five-cents sacks of tobacco. Anyway, what have you got to be afraid of?"

"For two cents I'd kick the face off of you right now," he snarled.

"Don't let me stop you." I was impudently suave. "Kick as hard as you please, and I'll still have enough face left with which to smile. In the meantime, while you are hesitating, suppose you accept my original proposition."

A man must be terribly weak and profoundly desperate to be able, under such circumstances, to beard the Warden in solitary. Or he may be both, and, in addition, he may have faith. I know now that I had the faith and so acted on it. I believed what Morrell had told me. I believed in the lordship of the mind over the body. I believed that not even a hundred days in the jacket could kill me.

Captain Jamie must have sensed this faith that informed me, for he said:

"I remember a Swede that went crazy twenty years ago. That was before your time, Warden. He'd killed a man in a quarrel over twenty-five cents and got life for it. He was a cook. He got religion. He said that a golden chariot was coming to take him to heaven, and he sat down on top the red-hot range and sang hymns and hosannahs while he cooked. They dragged him off, but he croaked two days afterward in hospital. He was cooked to the bone. And to the end he swore he'd never felt the heat. Couldn't get a squeal out of him."

"We'll make Standing squeal," said the Warden.

"Since you are so sure of it, why don't you accept my proposition?" I challenged.

The Warden was so angry that it would have been ludicrous to me had I not been in so desperate plight. His face was convulsed. He clenched his hands, and, for a moment, it seemed that he was about to fall upon me and give me a beating. Then, with an effort, he controlled himself.

"All right, Standing," he snarled. "I'll go you. But you bet your sweet life you'll have to go some to smile ten days from now. Roll him over, boys, and cinch him till you hear his ribs crack. Hutchins, show him you know how to do it."

And they rolled me over and laced me as I had never been laced before. The head trusty certainly demonstrated his ability. I tried to steal what little space I could. Little it was, for I had long since shed my flesh, while my muscles were attenuated to mere strings. I had neither the strength nor bulk to steal more than a little, and the little I stole I swear I managed by sheer expansion at the joints of the bones of my frame. And of this little I was robbed by Hutchins, who, in the old days before he was made head trusty, had learned all the tricks of the jacket from the inside of the jacket.

You see, Hutchins was a cur at heart, or a creature who had once been a man, but who had been broken on the wheel. He possessed ten or twelve thousand dollars, and his freedom was in sight if he obeyed orders. Later, I learned that there was a girl who had remained true to him, and who was even then waiting for him. The woman factor explains many things of men.

If ever a man deliberately committed murder, Al Hutchins did that morning in solitary at the Warden's bidding. He robbed me of the little space I stole. And, having robbed me of that, my body was defenceless, and, with his foot in my back while he drew the lacing light, he constricted me as no man had ever before succeeded in doing. So severe was this constriction of my frail frame upon my vital organs that I felt, there and then, immediately, that death was upon me. And still the miracle of faith was mine. I did not believe that I was going to die. I knew—I say I *knew*—that I was not going to die. My head was swimming, and my heart was pounding from my toenails to the hair-roots in my scalp.

"That's pretty tight," Captain Jamie urged reluctantly.

"The hell it is," said Doctor Jackson. "I tell you nothing can hurt him. He's a wooz. He ought to have been dead long ago."

Warden Atherton, after a hard struggle, managed to insert his forefinger between the lacing and my back. He brought his foot to bear upon me, with the weight of his body added to his foot, and pulled, but failed to get any fraction of an inch of slack.

"I take my hat off to you, Hutchins," he said. "You know your job. Now roll him over and let's look at him."

They rolled me over on my back. I stared up at them with bulging eyes. This I know: Had they laced me in such fashion the first time I went into the jacket, I would surely have died in the first ten minutes. But I was well trained. I had behind me the thousands of hours in the jacket, and, plus that, I had faith in what Morrell had told me.

"Now, laugh, damn you, laugh," said the Warden to me. "Start that smile you've been bragging about."

So, while my lungs panted for a little air, while my heart threatened to burst, while my mind reeled, nevertheless I was able to smile up into the Warden's face.

The door clanged, shutting out all but a little light, and I was left alone on my back. By the tricks I had long since learned in the jacket, I managed to writhe myself across the floor an inch at a time until the edge of the sole of my right shoe touched the door. There was an immense cheer in this. I was not utterly alone. If the need arose, I could at least rap knuckle talk to Morrell.

But Warden Atherton must have left strict injunctions on the guards, for, though I managed to call Morrell and tell him I intended trying the experiment, he was prevented by the guards from replying. Me they could only curse, for, in so far as I was in the jacket for a ten days' bout, I was beyond all threat of punishment.

I remember remarking at the time my serenity of mind. The customary pain of the jacket was in my body, but my mind was so passive that I was no more aware of the pain than was I aware of the floor beneath me or the walls around me. Never was a man in better mental and spiritual condition for such an experiment. Of course, this was largely due to my extreme weakness. But there was more to it. I had long schooled myself to be oblivious to pain. I had neither doubts nor fears. All the content of my mind seemed to be an absolute faith in the over-lordship of the mind. This passivity was almost dream-like, and yet, in its way, it was positive almost to a pitch of exaltation.

I began my concentration of will. Even then my body was numbing and prickling through the loss of circulation. I directed my will to the little toe of my right foot, and I willed that toe to cease to be alive in my consciousness. I willed that toe to die—to die so far as I, its lord, and a different thing entirely from it, was concerned. There was the hard struggle. Morrell had warned me that it would be so. But there was no flicker of doubt to disturb my faith. I knew that that toe would die, and I knew when it was dead. Joint by joint it had died under the compulsion of my will.

The rest was easy, but slow, I will admit. Joint by joint, toe by toe, all the toes of both my feet ceased to be. And joint by joint, the process went on. Came the time when my flesh below the ankles had ceased. Came the time when all below my knees had ceased.

Such was the pitch of my perfect exaltation, that I knew not the slightest prod of rejoicing at my success. I knew nothing save that I was making my body die. All that was I was devoted to that sole task. I performed the work as thoroughly as any mason laying bricks, and I regarded the work as just about as commonplace as would a brick-mason regard his work.

At the end of an hour my body was dead to the hips, and from the hips up, joint by joint, I continued to will the ascending death.

It was when I reached the level of my heart that the first blurring and dizzying of my consciousness' occurred. For fear that I should lose consciousness, I willed to hold the death I had gained, and shifted my concentration to my fingers. My brain cleared again, and the death of my arms to the shoulders was most rapidly accomplished.

At this stage my body was all dead, so far as I was concerned, save my head and a little patch of my chest. No longer did the pound and smash of my compressed heart echo in my brain. My heart was beating steadily but feebly. The joy of it, had I dared joy at such a moment, would have been the cessation of sensations.

At this point my experience differs from Morrell's. Still willing automatically, I began to grow dreamy, as one does in that borderland between sleeping and waking. Also, it seemed as if a prodigious enlargement of my brain was taking place within the skull itself that did not enlarge. There were occasional glintings and flashings of light as if even I, the overlord, had ceased for a moment and the next moment was again myself, still the tenant of the fleshly tenement that I was making to die.

Most perplexing was the seeming enlargement of brain. Without having passed through the wall of skull, nevertheless it seemed to me that the periphery of my brain was already outside my skull and still expanding. Along with this was one of the most remarkable sensations or experiences that I have ever encountered. Time and space, in so far as they were the stuff of my consciousness, underwent an enormous extension. Thus, without opening my eyes to verify, I knew that the walls of my narrow cell had receded until it was like a vast audience-chamber. And while I contemplated the matter, I knew that they continued to recede. The whim struck me for a moment that if a similar expansion were taking place with the whole prison, then the outer walls of San Quentin must be far out in the Pacific Ocean on one side and on the other side must be encroaching on the Nevada desert. A companion whim was that since matter could permeate matter, then the walls of my cell might well permeate the prison walls, pass through the prison walls, and thus put my cell outside the prison and put me at liberty. Of course, this was pure fantastic whim, and I knew it at the time for what it was.

The extension of time was equally remarkable. Only at long intervals did my heart beat. Again a whim came to me, and I counted the seconds, slow and sure, between my heart-beats. At first, as I clearly noted, over a hundred seconds intervened between beats. But as I continued to count the intervals extended so that I was made weary of counting.

And while this illusion of the extension of time and space persisted and grew, I found myself dreamily considering a new and profound problem. Morrell had told me that he had won freedom from his body by killing his body—or by eliminating his body from his consciousness, which, of course, was in effect the same thing. Now, my body was so near to being entirely dead that I knew in all absoluteness that by a quick concentration of will on the yet-alive patch of my torso it, too, would cease to be. But—and here was the problem, and Morrell had not warned me: should I also will my head to be dead? If I did so, no matter what befell the spirit of Darrell Standing, would not the body of Darrell Standing be for ever dead?

I chanced the chest and the slow-beating heart. The quick compulsion of my will was rewarded. I no longer had chest nor heart. I was only a mind, a soul, a consciousness—call it what you will—incorporate in a nebulous brain that, while it still centred inside my skull, was expanded, and was continuing to expand, beyond my skull.

And then, with flashings of light, I was off and away. At a bound I had vaulted prison roof and California sky, and was among the stars. I say "stars" advisedly. I walked among the stars. I was a child. I was clad in frail, fleece-like, delicate-coloured robes that shimmered in the cool starlight. These robes, of course, were based upon my boyhood observance of circus actors and my boyhood conception of the garb of young angels.

Nevertheless, thus clad, I trod interstellar space, exalted by the knowledge that I was bound on vast adventure, where, at the end, I would find all the cosmic formulæ and have made clear to me the ultimate secret of the universe. In my hand I carried a long glass wand. It was borne in upon me that with the tip of this wand I must touch each star in passing. And I knew, in all absoluteness, that did I but miss one star I should be precipitated into some unplummeted abyss of unthinkable and eternal punishment and guilt.

Long I pursued my starry quest. When I say "long," you must bear in mind the enormous extension of time that had occurred in my brain. For centuries I trod space, with the tip of my wand and with unerring eye and hand tapping each star I passed. Ever the way grew brighter. Ever the ineffable goal of infinite wisdom grew nearer. And yet I made no mistake. This was no other self of mine. This was no experience that had once been mine. I was aware all the time that it was I, Darrell Standing, who walked among the stars and tapped them with a wand of glass. In short, I knew that here was nothing real, nothing that had ever been nor could ever be. I knew that it was nothing else than a ridiculous orgy of the imagination, such as men enjoy in drug dreams, in delirium, or in mere ordinary slumber.

And then, as all went merry and well with me on my celestial quest, the tip of my wand missed a star, and on the instant I knew I had been guilty of a great crime. And on the instant a knock, vast and compulsive, inexorable and mandatory as the stamp of the iron hoof of doom, smote me and reverberated across the universe. The whole sidereal system coruscated, reeled and fell in flame.

I was torn by an exquisite and disruptive agony. And on the instant I was Darrell Standing, the life-convict, lying in his strait-jacket in solitary. And I knew the immediate cause of that summons. It was a rap of the knuckle by Ed Morrell, in Cell Five, beginning the spelling of some message.

And now, to give some comprehension of the extension of time and space that I was experiencing. Many days afterwards I asked Morrell what he had tried to convey to me. It was a simple message, namely: "Standing, are you there?" He had tapped it rapidly, while the guard was at the far end of the corridor into which the solitary cells opened. As I say, he had tapped the message very rapidly. And now behold! Between the first tap and the second I was off and away among the stars, clad in fleecy garments, touching each star as I passed in my pursuit of the formulæ that would explain the last mystery of life. And, as before, I pursued the quest for centuries. Then came the summons, the stamp of the hoof of doom, the exquisite disruptive agony, and again I was back in my cell in San Quentin. It was the second tap of Ed Morrell's knuckle. The interval between it and the first tap could have been no more than a fifth of a second. And yet, so unthinkably enormous was the extension of time to me, that in the course of that fifth of a second I had been away star-roving for long ages.

Now I know, my reader, that the foregoing seems all a farrago. I agree with you. It is farrago. It was experience, however. It was just as real to me as is the snake beheld by a man in delirium tremens.

Possibly, by the most liberal estimate, it may have taken Ed Morrell two minutes to tap his question. Yet, to me, æons elapsed between the first tap of his knuckle and the last. No longer could I tread my starry path with that ineffable pristine joy, for my way was beset with dread of the inevitable summons that would rip and tear me as it jerked me back to my strait-jacket hell. Thus my æons of star-wandering were æons of dread.

And all the time I knew it was Ed Morrell's knuckle that thus cruelly held me earth-bound. I tried to speak to him, to ask him to cease. But so thoroughly had I eliminated my body from my consciousness that I was unable to resurrect it. My body lay dead in the jacket, though I still inhabited the skull. In vain I strove to will my foot to tap my message to Morrell. I reasoned I had a foot. And yet, so thoroughly had I carried out the experiment, I had no foot.

Next—and I know now that it was because Morrell had spelled his message quite out—I pursued my way among the stars and was not called back. After that, and in the course of it, I was aware, drowsily, that I was falling asleep, and that it was delicious sleep. From time to time, drowsily, I stirred—please, my reader, don't miss that verb—I STIRRED. I moved my legs, my arms. I was aware of clean, soft bed linen against my skin. I was aware of bodily well-being. Oh, it was delicious! As thirsting men on the desert dream of splashing fountains and flowing wells, so dreamed I of easement from the constriction of the jacket, of cleanliness in the place of filth, of smooth velvety skin of health in place of my poor parchment-crinkled hide. But I dreamed with a difference, as you shall see.

I awoke. Oh, broad and wide awake I was, although I did not open my eyes. And please know that in all that follows I knew no surprise whatever. Everything was the natural and the expected. I was I, be sure of that. *But I was not Darrell Standing.* Darrell Standing had no more to do with the being I was than did Darrell Standing's parchment-crinkled skin have aught to do with the cool, soft skin that was mine. Nor was I aware of any Darrell Standing—as I could not well be, considering that Darrell Standing was as yet unborn and would not be born for centuries. But you shall see.

I lay with closed eyes, lazily listening. From without came the clacking of many hoofs moving orderly on stone flags. From the accompanying jingle of metal bits of man-harness and steed-harness I knew some cavalcade was passing by on the street beneath my windows. Also, I wondered idly who it was. From somewhere—and I knew where, for I knew it was from the inn yard—came the ring and stamp of hoofs and an impatient neigh that I recognized as belonging to my waiting horse.

Came steps and movements—steps openly advertised as suppressed with the intent of silence and that yet were deliberately noisy with the secret intent of rousing me if I still slept. I smiled inwardly at the rascal's trick.

"Pons," I ordered, without opening my eyes, "water, cold water, quick, a deluge. I drank over long last night, and now my gullet scorches."

"And slept over long to-day," he scolded, as he passed me the water, ready in his hand.

I sat up, opened my eyes, and carried the tankard to my lips with both my hands. And as I drank I looked at Pons.

Now note two things. I spoke in French; I was not conscious that I spoke in French. Not until afterward, back in solitary, when I remembered what I am narrating, did I know that I had spoken in French—ay, and spoken well. As for me, Darrell Standing, at present writing these lines in Murderers' Row of Folsom Prison, why, I know only high school French sufficient to enable me to read the language. As for my speaking it—impossible. I can scarcely intelligibly pronounce my way through a menu.

But to return. Pons was a little withered old man. He was born in our house—I know, for it chanced that mention was made of it this very day I am describing. Pons was all of sixty years. He was mostly toothless, and, despite a pronounced limp that compelled him to go slippity-hop, he was very alert and spry in all his movements. Also, he was impudently familiar. This was because he had been in my house sixty years. He had been my father's servant before I could toddle, and after my father's death (Pons and I talked of it this day) he became my servant. The limp he had acquired on a stricken field in Italy, when the horsemen charged across. He had just dragged my father clear of the hoofs when he was lanced through the thigh, overthrown, and trampled. My father, conscious but helpless from his own wounds, witnessed it all. And so, as I say, Pons had earned such a right to impudent familiarity that at least there was no gainsaying him by my father's son.

Pons shook his head as I drained the huge draught.

"Did you hear it boil?" I laughed, as I handed back the empty tankard.

"Like your father," he said hopelessly. "But your father lived to learn better, which I doubt you will do."

"He got a stomach affliction," I deviled, "so that one mouthful of spirits turned it outside in. It were wisdom not to drink when one's tank will not hold the drink."

While we talked Pons was gathering to my bedside my clothes for the day.

"Drink on, my master," he answered. "It won't hurt you. You'll die with a sound stomach."

"You mean mine is an iron-lined stomach?" I wilfully misunderstood him.

"I mean—" he began with a quick peevishness, then broke off as he realized my teasing and with a pout of his withered lips draped my new sable cloak upon a chair-back. "Eight hundred ducats," he sneered. "A thousand goats and a hundred fat oxen in a coat to keep you warm. A score of farms on my gentleman's fine back."

"And in that a hundred fine farms, with a castle or two thrown in, to say nothing, perhaps, of a palace," I said, reaching out my hand and touching the rapier which he was just in the act of depositing on the chair.

"So your father won with his good right arm," Pons retorted. "But what your father won he held."

Here Pons paused to hold up to scorn my new scarlet satin doublet—a wondrous thing of which I had been extravagant.

"Sixty ducats for that," Pons indicted. "Your father'd have seen all the tailors and Jews of Christendom roasting in hell before he'd a-paid such a price."

And while we dressed—that is, while Pons helped me to dress—I continued to quip with him.

"It is quite clear, Pons, that you have not heard the news," I said slyly.

Whereat up pricked his ears like the old gossip he was.

"Late news?" he queried. "Mayhap from the English Court?"

"Nay," I shook my head. "But news perhaps to you, but old news for all of that. Have you not heard? The philosophers of Greece were whispering it nigh two thousand years ago. It is because of that news that I put twenty fat farms on my back, live at Court, and am become a dandy. You see, Pons, the world is a most evil place, life is most sad, all men die, and, being dead . . . well, are dead. Wherefore, to escape the evil and the sadness, men in these days, like me, seek amazement, insensibility, and the madnesses of dalliance."

"But the news, master? What did the philosophers whisper about so long ago?"

"That God was dead, Pons," I replied solemnly. "Didn't you know that? God is dead, and I soon shall be, and I wear twenty fat farms on my back."

"God lives," Pons asserted fervently. "God lives, and his kingdom is at hand. I tell you, master, it is at hand. It may be no later than to-morrow that the earth shall pass away."

"So said they in old Rome, Pons, when Nero made torches of them to light his sports."

Pons regarded me pityingly.

"Too much learning is a sickness," he complained. "I was always opposed to it. But you must have your will and drag my old body about with you—a-studying astronomy and numbers in Venice, poetry and all the Italian *fol-de-rols* in Florence, and astrology in Pisa, and God knows what in that madman country of Germany. Pish for the philosophers! I tell you, master, I, Pons, your servant, a poor old man who knows not a letter from a pike-staff—I tell you God lives, and the time you shall appear before him is short." He paused with sudden recollection, and added: "He is here, the priest you spoke of."

On the instant I remembered my engagement.

"Why did you not tell me before?" I demanded angrily.

"What did it matter?" Pons shrugged his shoulders. "Has he not been waiting two hours as it is?"

"Why didn't you call me?"

He regarded me with a thoughtful, censorious eye.

"And you rolling to bed and shouting like chanticleer, 'Sing cucu, sing cucu, cucu nu nu cucu, sing cucu, sing cucu, sing cucu, sing cucu.'"

He mocked me with the senseless refrain in an ear-jangling falsetto. Without doubt I had bawled the nonsense out on my way to bed.

"You have a good memory," I commented drily, as I essayed a moment to drape my shoulders with the new sable cloak ere I tossed it to Pons to put aside. He shook his head sourly.

"No need of memory when you roared it over and over for the thousandth time till half the inn was a-knock at the door to spit you for the sleep-killer you were. And when I had you decently in the bed, did you not call me to you and command, if the devil called, to tell him my lady slept? And did you not call me back again, and, with a grip on my arm that leaves it bruised and black this day, command me, as I loved life, fat meat, and the warm fire, to call you not of the morning save for one thing?"

"Which was?" I prompted, unable for the life of me to guess what I could have said.

"Which was the heart of one, a black buzzard, you said, by name Martinelli—whoever he may be—for the heart of Martinelli smoking on a gold platter. The platter must be gold, you said; and you said I must call you by singing, 'Sing cucu, sing cucu, sing cucu.' Whereat you began to teach me how to sing, 'Sing cucu, sing cucu, sing cucu.'"

And when Pons had said the name, I knew it at once for the priest, Martinelli, who had been knocking his heels two mortal hours in the room without.

When Martinelli was permitted to enter and as he saluted me by title and name, I knew at once my name and all of it. I was Count Guillaume de Sainte-Maure. (You see, only could I know then, and remember afterward, what was in my conscious mind.)

The priest was Italian, dark and small, lean as with fasting or with a wasting hunger not of this world, and his hands were as small and slender as a woman's. But his eyes! They were cunning and trustless, narrow-slitted and heavy-lidded, at one and the same time as sharp as a ferret's and as indolent as a basking lizard's.

"There has been much delay, Count de Sainte-Maure," he began promptly, when Pons had left the room at a glance from me. "He whom I serve grows impatient."

"Change your tune, priest," I broke in angrily. "Remember, you are not now in Rome."

"My august master—" he began.

"Rules augustly in Rome, mayhap," I again interrupted. "This is France."

Martinelli shrugged his shoulders meekly and patiently, but his eyes, gleaming like a basilisk's, gave his shoulders the lie.

"My august master has some concern with the doings of France," he said quietly. "The lady is not for you. My master has other plans . . ." He moistened his thin lips with his tongue. "Other plans for the lady . . . and for you."

Of course, by the lady I knew he referred to the great Duchess Philippa, widow of Geoffrey, last Duke of Aquitaine. But great duchess, widow, and all, Philippa was a woman, and young, and gay, and beautiful, and, by my faith, fashioned for me.

"What are his plans?" I demanded bluntly.

"They are deep and wide, Count Sainte-Maure—too deep and wide for me to presume to imagine, much less know or discuss with you or any man."

"Oh, I know big things are afoot and slimy worms squirming underground," I said.

"They told me you were stubborn-necked, but I have obeyed commands."

Martinelli arose to leave, and I arose with him.

"I said it was useless," he went on. "But the last chance to change your mind was accorded you. My august master deals more fairly than fair."

"Oh, well, I'll think the matter over," I said airily, as I bowed the priest to the door.

He stopped abruptly at the threshold.

"The time for thinking is past," he said. "It is decision I came for."

"I will think the matter over," I repeated, then added, as afterthought: "If the lady's plans do not accord with mine, then mayhap the plans of your master may fruit as he desires. For remember, priest, he is no master of mine."

"You do not know my master," he said solemnly.

"Nor do I wish to know him," I retorted.

And I listened to the lithe, light step of the little intriguing priest go down the creaking stairs.

Did I go into the minutiæ of detail of all that I saw this half a day and half a night that I was Count Guillaume de Sainte-Maure, not ten books the size of this I am writing could contain the totality of the matter. Much I shall skip; in fact, I shall skip almost all; for never yet have I heard of a condemned man being reprieved in order that he might complete his memoirs—at least, not in California.

When I rode out in Paris that day it was the Paris of centuries agone. The narrow streets were an unsanitary scandal of filth and slime. But I must skip. And skip I shall, all of the afternoon's events, all of the ride outside the walls, of the grand fête given by Hugh de Meung, of the feasting and the drinking in which I took little part. Only of the end of the adventure will I write, which begins with where I stood jesting with Philippa herself—ah, dear God, she was wondrous beautiful. A great lady—ay, but before that, and after that, and always, a woman.

We laughed and jested lightly enough, as about us jostled the merry throng; but under our jesting was the deep earnestness of man and woman well advanced across the threshold of love and yet not too sure each of the other. I shall not describe her. She was small, exquisitely slender—but there, I am describing her. In brief, she was the one woman in the world for me, and little I recked the long arm of that gray old man in Rome could reach out half across Europe between my woman and me.

And the Italian, Fortini, leaned to my shoulder and whispered:

"One who desires to speak."

"One who must wait my pleasure," I answered shortly.

"I wait no man's pleasure," was his equally short reply.

And, while my blood boiled, I remembered the priest, Martinelli, and the gray old man at Rome. The thing was clear. It was deliberate. It was the long arm. Fortini smiled lazily at me while I thus paused for the moment to debate, but in his smile was the essence of all insolence.

This, of all times, was the time I should have been cool. But the old red anger began to kindle in me. This was the work of the priest. This was the Fortini, poverished of all save lineage, reckoned the best sword come up out of Italy in half a score of years. To-night it was Fortini. If he failed the gray old man's command to-morrow it would be another sword, the next day another. And, perchance still failing, then might I expect the common bravo's steel in my back or the common poisoner's philter in my wine, my meat, or bread.

"I am busy," I said. "Begone."

"My business with you presses," was his reply.

Insensibly our voices had slightly risen, so that Philippa heard.

"Begone, you Italian hound," I said. "Take your howling from my door. I shall attend to you presently."

"The moon is up," he said. "The grass is dry and excellent. There is no dew. Beyond the fish-pond, an arrow's flight to the left, is an open space, quiet and private."

"Presently you shall have your desire," I muttered impatiently.

But still he persisted in waiting at my shoulder.

"Presently," I said. "Presently I shall attend to you."

Then spoke Philippa, in all the daring spirit and the iron of her.

"Satisfy the gentleman's desire, Sainte-Maure. Attend to him now. And good fortune go with you." She paused to beckon to her her uncle, Jean de Joinville, who was passing—uncle on her mother's side, of the de Joinvilles of Anjou. "Good fortune go with you," she repeated, and then leaned to me so that she could whisper: "And my heart goes with you, Sainte-Maure. Do not be long. I shall await you in the big hall."

I was in the seventh heaven. I trod on air. It was the first frank admittance of her love. And with such benediction I was made so strong that I knew I could kill a score of Fortinis and snap my fingers at a score of gray old men in Rome.

Jean de Joinville bore Philippa away in the press, and Fortini and I settled our arrangements in a trice. We separated—he to find a friend or so, and I to find a friend or so, and all to meet at the appointed place beyond the fish-pond.

First I found Robert Lanfranc, and, next, Henry Bohemond. But before I found them I encountered a windlestraw which showed which way blew the wind and gave promise of a very gale. I knew the windlestraw, Guy de Villehardouin, a raw young provincial, come up the first time to Court, but a fiery little cockerel for all of that. He was red-haired. His blue eyes, small and pinched close to ether, were likewise red, at least in the whites of them; and his skin, of the sort that goes with such types, was red and freckled. He had quite a parboiled appearance.

As I passed him by a sudden movement he jostled me. Oh, of course, the thing was deliberate. And he flamed at me while his hand dropped to his rapier.

"Faith," thought I, "the gray old man has many and strange tools," while to the cockerel I bowed and murmured, "Your pardon for my clumsiness. The fault was mine. Your pardon, Villehardouin."

But he was not to be appeased thus easily. And while he fumed and strutted I glimpsed Robert Lanfranc, beckoned him to us, and explained the happening.

"Sainte-Maure has accorded you satisfaction," was his judgment. "He has prayed your pardon."

"In truth, yes," I interrupted in my suavest tones. "And I pray your pardon again, Villehardouin, for my very great clumsiness. I pray your pardon a thousand times. The fault was mine, though unintentioned. In my haste to an engagement I was clumsy, most woful clumsy, but without intention."

What could the dolt do but grudgingly accept the amends I so freely proffered him? Yet I knew, as Lanfranc and I hastened on, that ere many days, or hours, the flame-headed youth would see to it that we measured steel together on the grass.

I explained no more to Lanfranc than my need of him, and he was little interested to pry deeper into the matter. He was himself a lively youngster of no more than twenty, but he had been trained to arms, had fought in Spain, and had an honourable record on the grass. Merely his black eyes flashed when he learned what was toward, and such was his eagerness that it was he who gathered Henry Bohemond in to our number.

When the three of us arrived in the open space beyond the fish-pond Fortini and two friends were already waiting us. One was Felix Pasquini, nephew to the Cardinal of that name, and as close in his uncle's confidence as was his uncle close in the confidence of the gray old man. The other was Raoul de Goncourt, whose presence surprised me, he being too good and noble a man for the company he kept.

We saluted properly, and properly went about the business. It was nothing new to any of us. The footing was good, as promised. There was no dew. The moon shone fair, and Fortini's blade and mine were out and at earnest play.

This I knew: good swordsman as they reckoned me in France, Fortini was a better. This, too, I knew: that I carried my lady's heart with me this night, and that this night, because of me, there would be one Italian less in the world. I say I knew it. In my mind the issue could not be in doubt. And as our rapiers played I pondered the manner I should kill him. I was not minded for a long contest. Quick and brilliant had always been my way. And further, what of my past gay months of carousal and of singing "Sing cucu, sing cucu, sing cucu," at ungodly hours, I knew I was not conditioned for a long contest. Quick and brilliant was my decision.

But quick and brilliant was a difficult matter with so consummate a swordsman as Fortini opposed to me. Besides, as luck would have it, Fortini, always the cold one, always the tireless-wristed, always sure and long, as report had it, in going about such business, on this night elected, too, the quick and brilliant.

It was nervous, tingling work, for as surely as I sensed his intention of briefness, just as surely had he sensed mine. I doubt that I could have done the trick had it been broad day instead of moonlight. The dim light aided me. Also was I aided by divining, the moment in advance, what he had in mind. It was the time attack, a common but perilous trick that every novice knows, that has laid on his back many a good man who attempted it, and that is so fraught with danger to the perpetrator that swordsmen are not enamoured of it.

We had been at work barely a minute, when I knew under all his darting, flashing show of offence that Fortini meditated this very time attack. He desired of me a thrust and lunge, not that he might parry it but that he might time it and deflect it by the customary slight turn of the wrist, his rapier point directed to meet me as my body followed in the lunge. A ticklish thing—ay, a ticklish thing in the best of light. Did he deflect a fraction of a second too early, I should be warned and saved. Did he deflect a fraction of a second too late, my thrust would go home to him.

"Quick and brilliant is it?" was my thought. "Very well, my Italian friend, quick and brilliant shall it be, and especially shall it be quick."

In a way, it was time attack against time attack, but I would fool him on the time by being over-quick. And I was quick. As I said, we had been at work scarcely a minute when it happened. Quick? That thrust and lunge of mine were one. A snap of action it was, an explosion, an instantaneousness. I swear my thrust and lunge were a fraction of a second quicker than any man is supposed to thrust and lunge. I won the fraction of a second. By that fraction of a second too late Fortini attempted to deflect my blade and impale me on his. But it was his blade that was deflected. It flashed past my breast, and I was in—inside his weapon, which extended full length in the empty air behind me—and my blade was inside of him, and through him, heart-high, from right side of him to left side of him and outside of him beyond.

It is a strange thing to do, to spit a live man on a length of steel. I sit here in my cell, and cease from writing a space, while I consider the matter. And I have considered it often, that moonlight night in France of long ago, when I taught the Italian hound quick and brilliant. It was so easy a thing, that perforation of a torso. One would have expected more resistance. There would have been resistance had my rapier point touched bone. As it was, it encountered only the softness of flesh. Still it perforated so easily. I have the sensation of it now, in my hand, my brain, as I write. A woman's hat-pin could go through a plum pudding not more easily than did my blade go through the Italian. Oh, there was nothing amazing about it at the time to Guillaume de Sainte-Maure, but amazing it is to me, Darrell Standing, as I recollect and ponder it across the centuries. It is easy, most easy, to kill a strong, live, breathing man with so crude a weapon as a piece of steel. Why, men are like soft-shell crabs, so tender, frail, and vulnerable are they.

But to return to the moonlight on the grass. My thrust made home, there was a perceptible pause. Not at once did Fortini fall. Not at once did I withdraw the blade. For a full second we stood in pause—I, with legs spread, and arched and tense, body thrown forward, right arm horizontal and straight out; Fortini, his blade beyond me so far that hilt and hand just rested lightly against my left breast, his body rigid, his eyes open and shining.

So statuesque were we for that second that I swear those about us were not immediately aware of what had happened. Then Fortini gasped and coughed slightly. The rigidity of his pose slackened. The hilt and hand against my breast wavered, then the arm drooped to his side till the rapier point rested on the lawn. By this time Pasquini and de Goncourt had sprung to him and he was sinking into their arms. In faith, it was harder for me to withdraw the steel than to drive it in. His flesh clung about it as if jealous to let it depart. Oh, believe me, it required a distinct physical effort to get clear of what I had done.

But the pang of the withdrawal must have stung him back to life and purpose, for he shook off his friends, straightened himself, and lifted his rapier into position. I, too, took position, marvelling that it was possible I had spitted him heart-high and yet missed any vital spot. Then, and before his friends could catch him, his legs crumpled under him and he went heavily to grass. They laid him on his back, but he was already dead, his face ghastly still under the moon, his right hand still a-clutch of the rapier.

Yes; it is indeed a marvellous easy thing to kill a man.

We saluted his friends and were about to depart, when Felix Pasquini detained me.

"Pardon me," I said. "Let it be to-morrow."

"We have but to move a step aside," he urged, "where the grass is still dry."

"Let me then wet it for you, Sainte-Maure," Lanfranc asked of me, eager himself to do for an Italian.

I shook my head.

"Pasquini is mine," I answered. "He shall be first to-morrow."

"Are there others?" Lanfranc demanded.

"Ask de Goncourt," I grinned. "I imagine he is already laying claim to the honour of being the third."

At this, de Goncourt showed distressed acquiescence. Lanfranc looked inquiry at him, and de Goncourt nodded.

"And after him I doubt not comes the cockerel," I went on.

And even as I spoke the red-haired Guy de Villehardouin, alone, strode to us across the moonlit grass.

"At least I shall have him," Lanfranc cried, his voice almost wheedling, so great was his desire.

"Ask him," I laughed, then turned to Pasquini. "To-morrow," I said. "Do you name time and place, and I shall be there."

"The grass is most excellent," he teased, "the place is most excellent, and I am minded that Fortini has you for company this night."

"'Twere better he were accompanied by a friend," I quipped. "And now your pardon, for I must go."

But he blocked my path.

"Whoever it be," he said, "let it be now."

For the first time, with him, my anger began to rise.

"You serve your master well," I sneered.

"I serve but my pleasure," was his answer. "Master I have none."

"Pardon me if I presume to tell you the truth," I said.

"Which is?" he queried softly.

"That you are a liar, Pasquini, a liar like all Italians."

He turned immediately to Lanfranc and Bohemond.

"You heard," he said. "And after that you cannot deny me him."

They hesitated and looked to me for counsel of my wishes. But Pasquini did not wait.

"And if you still have any scruples," he hurried on, "then allow me to remove them . . . thus."

And he spat in the grass at my feet. Then my anger seized me and was beyond me. The red wrath I call it—an overwhelming, all-mastering desire to kill and destroy. I forgot that Philippa waited for me in the great hall. All I knew was my wrongs—the unpardonable interference in my affairs by the gray old man, the errand of the priest, the insolence of Fortini, the impudence of Villehardouin, and here Pasquini standing in my way and spitting in the grass. I saw red. I thought red. I looked upon all these creatures as rank and noisome growths that must be hewn out of my path, out of the world. As a netted lion may rage against the meshes, so raged I against these creatures. They were all about me. In truth, I was in the trap. The one way out was to cut them down, to crush them into the earth and stamp upon them.

"Very well," I said, calmly enough, although my passion was such that my frame shook. "You first, Pasquini. And you next, de Goncourt? And at the end, de Villehardouin?"

Each nodded in turn and Pasquini and I prepared to step aside.

"Since you are in haste," Henry Bohemond proposed to me, "and since there are three of them and three of us, why not settle it at the one time?"

"Yes, yes," was Lanfranc's eager cry. "Do you take de Goncourt. De Villehardouin for mine."

But I waved my good friends back.

"They are here by command," I explained. "It is I they desire so strongly that by my faith I have caught the contagion of their desire, so that now I want them and will have them for myself."

I had observed that Pasquini fretted at my delay of speech-making, and I resolved to fret him further.

"You, Pasquini," I announced, "I shall settle with in short account. I would not that you tarried while Fortini waits your companionship. You, Raoul de Goncourt, I shall punish as you deserve for being in such bad company. You are getting fat and wheezy. I shall take my time with you until your fat melts and your lungs pant and wheeze like leaky bellows. You, de Villehardouin, I have not decided in what manner I shall kill."

And then I saluted Pasquini, and we were at it. Oh, I was minded to be rarely devilish this night. Quick and brilliant—that was the thing. Nor was I unmindful of that deceptive moonlight. As with Fortini would I settle with him if he dared the time attack. If he did not, and quickly, then I would dare it.

Despite the fret I had put him in, he was cautious. Nevertheless I compelled the play to be rapid, and in the dim light, depending less than usual on sight and more than usual on feel, our blades were in continual touch.

Barely was the first minute of play past when I did the trick. I feigned a slight slip of the foot, and, in the recovery, feigned loss of touch with Pasquini's blade. He thrust tentatively, and again I feigned, this time making a needlessly wide parry. The consequent exposure of myself was the bait I had purposely dangled to draw him on. And draw him on I did. Like a flash he took advantage of what he deemed an involuntary exposure. Straight and true was his thrust, and all his will and body were heartily in the weight of the lunge he made. And all had been feigned on my part and I was ready for him. Just lightly did my steel meet his as our blades slithered. And just firmly enough and no more did my wrist twist and deflect his blade on my basket hilt. Oh, such a slight deflection, a matter of inches, just barely sufficient to send his point past me so that it pierced a fold of my satin doublet in passing. Of course, his body followed his rapier in the lunge, while, heart-high, right side, my rapier point met his body. And my outstretched arm was stiff and straight as the steel into which it elongated, and behind the arm and the steel my body was braced and solid.

Heart-high, I say, my rapier entered Pasquini's side on the right, but it did not emerge, on the left, for, well-nigh through him, it met a rib (oh, man-killing is butcher's work!) with such a will that the forcing overbalanced him, so that he fell part backward and part sidewise to the ground. And even as he fell, and ere he struck, with jerk and wrench I cleared my weapon of him.

De Goncourt was to him, but he waved de Goncourt to attend on me. Not so swiftly as Fortini did Pasquini pass. He coughed and spat, and, helped by de Villehardouin, propped his elbow under him, rested his head on hand, and coughed and spat again.

"A pleasant journey, Pasquini," I laughed to him in my red anger. "Pray hasten, for the grass where you lie is become suddenly wet and if you linger you will catch your death of cold."

When I made immediately to begin with de Goncourt, Bohemond protested that I should rest a space.

"Nay," I said. "I have not properly warmed up." And to de Goncourt, "Now will we have you dance and wheeze—Salute!"

De Goncourt's heart was not in the work. It was patent that he fought under the compulsion of command. His play was old-fashioned, as any middle-aged man's is apt to be, but he was not an indifferent swordsman. He was cool, determined, dogged. But he was not brilliant, and he was oppressed with foreknowledge of defeat. A score of times, by quick and brilliant, he was mine. But I refrained. I have said that I was devilish-minded. Indeed I was. I wore him down. I backed him away from the moon so that he could see little of me because I fought in my own shadow. And while I wore him down until he began to wheeze as I had predicted, Pasquini, head on hand and watching, coughed and spat out his life.

"Now, de Goncourt," I announced finally. "You see I have you quite helpless. You are mine in any of a dozen ways. Be ready, brace yourself, for this is the way I will."

And, so saying, I merely went from carte to tierce, and as he recovered wildly and parried widely I returned to carte, took the opening, and drove home heart-high and through and through. And at sight of the conclusion Pasquini let go his hold on life, buried his face in the grass, quivered a moment, and lay still.

"Your master will be four servants short this night," I assured de Villehardouin, in the moment just ere we engaged.

And such an engagement! The boy was ridiculous. In what bucolic school of fence he had been taught was beyond imagining. He was downright clownish. "Short work and simple" was my judgment, while his red hair seemed a-bristle with very rage and while he pressed me like a madman.

Alas! It was his clownishness that undid me. When I had played with him and laughed at him for a handful of seconds for the clumsy boor he was, he became so angered that he forgot the worse than little fence he knew. With an arm-wide sweep of his rapier, as though it bore heft and a cutting edge, he whistled it through the air and rapped it down on my crown. I was in amaze. Never had so absurd a thing happened to me. He was wide open, and I could have run him through forthright. But, as I said, I was in amaze, and the next I knew was the pang of the entering steel as this clumsy provincial ran me through and charged forward, bull-like, till his hilt bruised my side and I was borne backward.

As I fell I could see the concern on the faces of Lanfranc and Bohemond and the glut of satisfaction in the face of de Villehardouin as he pressed me.

I was falling, but I never reached the grass. Came a blur of flashing lights, a thunder in my ears, a darkness, a glimmering of dim light slowly dawning, a wrenching, racking pain beyond all describing, and then I heard the voice of one who said:

"I can't feel anything."

I knew the voice. It was Warden Atherton's. And I knew myself for Darrell Standing, just returned across the centuries to the jacket hell of San Quentin. And I knew the touch of finger-tips on my neck was Warden Atherton's. And I knew the finger-tips that displaced his were Doctor Jackson's. And it was Doctor Jackson's voice that said:

"You don't know how to take a man's pulse from the neck. There—right there—put your fingers where mine are. D'ye get it? Ah, I thought so. Heart weak, but steady as a chronometer."

"It's only twenty-four hours," Captain Jamie said, "and he was never in like condition before."

"Putting it on, that's what he's doing, and you can stack on that," Al Hutchins, the head trusty, interjected.

"I don't know," Captain Jamie insisted. "When a man's pulse is that low it takes an expert to find it—"

"Aw, I served my apprenticeship in the jacket," Al Hutchins sneered. "And I've made you unlace me, Captain, when you thought I was croaking, and it was all I could do to keep from snickering in your face."

"What do you think, Doc?" Warden Atherton asked.

"I tell you the heart action is splendid," was the answer. "Of course it is weak. That is only to be expected. I tell you Hutchins is right. The man is feigning."

With his thumb he turned up one of my eyelids, whereat I opened my other eye and gazed up at the group bending over me.

"What did I tell you?" was Doctor Jackson's cry of triumph.

And then, although it seemed the effort must crack my face, I summoned all the will of me and smiled.

They held water to my lips, and I drank greedily. It must be remembered that all this while I lay helpless on my back, my arms pinioned along with my body inside the jacket. When they offered me food—dry prison bread—I shook my head. I closed my eyes in advertisement that I was tired of their presence. The pain of my partial resuscitation was unbearable. I could feel my body coming to life. Down the cords of my neck and into my patch of chest over the heart darting pains were making their way. And in my brain the memory was strong that Philippa waited me in the big hall, and I was desirous to escape away back to the half a day and half a night I had just lived in old France.

So it was, even as they stood about me, that I strove to eliminate the live portion of my body from my consciousness. I was in haste to depart, but Warden Atherton's voice held me back.

"Is there anything you want to complain about?" he asked.

Now I had but one fear, namely, that they would unlace me; so that it must be understood that my reply was not uttered in braggadocio but was meant to forestall any possible unlacing.

"You might make the jacket a little tighter," I whispered. "It's too loose for comfort. I get lost in it. Hutchins is stupid. He is also a fool. He doesn't know the first thing about lacing the jacket. Warden, you ought to put him in charge of the loom-room. He is a more profound master of inefficiency than the present incumbent, who is merely stupid without being a fool as well. Now get out, all of you, unless you can think of worse to do to me. In which case, by all means remain. I invite you heartily to remain, if you think in your feeble imaginings that you have devised fresh torture for me."

"He's a wooz, a true-blue, dyed-in-the-wool wooz," Doctor Jackson chanted, with the medico's delight in a novelty.

"Standing, you *are* a wonder," the Warden said. "You've got an iron will, but I'll break it as sure as God made little apples."

"And you've the heart of a rabbit," I retorted. "One-tenth the jacketing I have received in San Quentin would have squeezed your rabbit heart out of your long ears."

Oh, it was a touch, that, for the Warden did have unusual ears. They would have interested Lombroso, I am sure.

"As for me," I went on, "I laugh at you, and I wish no worse fate to the loom-room than that you should take charge of it yourself. Why, you've got me down and worked your wickedness on me, and still I live and laugh in your face. Inefficient? You can't even kill me. Inefficient? You couldn't kill a cornered rat with a stick of dynamite—*real* dynamite, and not the sort you are deluded into believing I have hidden away."

"Anything more?" he demanded, when I had ceased from my diatribe.

And into my mind flashed what I had told Fortini when he pressed his insolence on me.

"Begone, you prison cur," I said. "Take your yapping from my door."

It must have been a terrible thing for a man of Warden Atherton's stripe to be thus bearded by a helpless prisoner. His face whitened with rage and his voice shook as he threatened:

"By God, Standing, I'll do for you yet."

"There is only one thing you can do," I said. "You can tighten this distressingly loose jacket. If you won't, then get out. And I don't care if you fail to come back for a week or for the whole ten days."

And what can even the Warden of a great prison do in reprisal on a prisoner upon whom the ultimate reprisal has already been wreaked? It may be that Warden Atherton thought of some possible threat, for he began to speak. But my voice had strengthened with the exercise, and I began to sing, "Sing cucu, sing cucu, sing cucu." And sing I did until my door clanged and the bolts and locks squeaked and grated fast.

CITY OF ENDLESS NIGHT

Milo Hastings (1919)

CHAPTER I: THE RED AND BLACK AND GOLD STRUG-GLE FOR SUPREMACY ON THE CHANGING MAP OF THE WORLD

~1~

When but a child of seven my uncle placed me in a private school in which one of the so-called redeemed sub-sailors was a teacher of the German language. As I look back now, in the light of my present knowledge, I better comprehend the docile humility and carefully nurtured ignorance of this man. In his class rooms he used as a text a description of German life, taken from the captured submarine. From this book he had secured his own conception of a civilization of which he really knew practically nothing. I recall how we used to ask Herr Meineke if he had actually seen those strange things of which he taught us. To this he always made answer, "The book is official, man's observation errs."

~2~

"He can talk it," said my playmates who attended the public schools where all teaching of the language of the outcast nation was prohibited. They invariably elected me to be "the Germans," and locked me up in the old garage while they rained a stock of sun-dried clay bombs upon the roof and then came with a rush to "batter down the walls of Berlin" by breaking in the door, while I, muttering strange guttural oaths, would be led forth to be "exterminated."

On rainy days I would sometimes take my favoured playmates into my uncle's library where five great maps hung in ordered sequence on the panelled wall.

The first map was labelled "The Age of Nations—1914," and showed the black spot of Germany, like in size to many of the surrounding countries, the names of which one recited in the history class.

The second map—"Germany's Maximum Expansion of the First World War—1918"—showed the black area trebled in size, crowding into the pale gold of France, thrusting a hungry arm across the Hellespont towards Bagdad, and, from the Balkans to the Baltic, blotting out all else save the flaming red of Bolshevist Russia, which spread over the Eastern half of Europe like a pool of fresh spilled blood.

Third came "The Age of the League of Nations, 1919–1983," with the gold of democracy battling with the spreading red of socialism, for the black of autocracy had erstwhile vanished.

The fourth map was the most fascinating and terrible. Again the black of autocracy appeared, obliterating the red of the Brotherhood of Man, spreading across half of Eurasia and thrusting a broad black shadow to the Yellow Sea and a lesser one to the Persian Gulf. This map was labelled "Maximum German Expansion of the Second World War, 1988," and lines of dotted white retreated in concentric waves till the line of 2041.

This same year was the first date of the fifth map, which was labelled "A Century of the World State," and here, as all the sea was blue, so all the land was gold, save one black blot that might have been made by a single spattered drop of ink, for it was no bigger than the Irish Island. The persistence of this remaining black on the map of the world troubled my boyish mind, as it has troubled three generations of the United World, and strive as I might, I could not comprehend why the great blackness of the fourth map had been erased and this small blot alone remained.

~3~

When I returned from school for my vacation, after I had my first year of physical science, I sought out my uncle in his laboratory and asked him to explain the mystery of the little black island standing adamant in the golden sea of all the world.

"That spot," said my uncle, "would have been erased in two more years if a Leipzig professor had not discovered The Ray. Yet we do not know his name nor how he made his discovery."

"But just what is The Ray?" I asked.

"We do not know that either, nor how it is made. We only know that it destroys the oxygen carrying power of living blood. If it were an emanation from a substance like radium, they could have fired it in projectiles and so conquered the earth. If it were ether waves like electricity, we should have been able to have insulated against it, or they should have been able to project it farther and destroy our aircraft, but The Ray is not destructive beyond two thousand metres in the air and hardly that far in the earth."

"Then why do we not fly over and land an army and great guns and batter down the walls of Berlin and be done with it?"

"That, as you know if you studied your history, has been tried many times and always with disaster. The bomb-torn soil of that black land is speckled white with the bones of World armies who were sent on landing invasions before you or I was born. But it was only heroic folly, one gun popping out of a tunnel mouth can slay a thousand men. To pursue the gunners into their catacombs meant to be gassed; and sometimes our forces were left to land in peace and set up their batteries to fire against Berlin, but the Germans would place Ray generators in the ground beneath them and slay our forces in an hour, as the Angel of Jehovah withered the hosts of the Assyrians."

"But why," I persisted, "do we not tunnel under the Ray generators and dig our way to Berlin and blow it up?"

My uncle smiled indulgently. "And that has been tried too, but they can hear our borings with microphones and cut us off, just as we cut them off when they try to tunnel out and place new generators. It is too slow, too difficult, either way; the line has wavered a little with the years but to no practical avail; the war in our day has become merely a watching game, we to keep the Germans from coming out, they to keep us from penetrating within gunshot of Berlin; but to gain a mile of worthless territory either way means too great a human waste to be worth the price. Things must go on as they are till the Germans tire of their sunless imprisonment or till they exhaust some essential element in their soil. But wars such as you read of in your history, will never happen again. The Germans cannot fight the world in the air, nor in the sea, nor on the surface of the earth; and we cannot fight the Germans in the ground; so the war has become a fixed state of standing guard; the hope of victory, the fear of defeat have vanished; the romance of war is dead."

"But why, then," I asked, "does the World Patrol continue to bomb the roof of Berlin?"

"Politics," replied my uncle, "military politics, just futile display of pyrotechnics to amuse the populace and give heroically inclined young men a chance to strut in uniforms—but after the election this fall such folly will cease."

~4~

My uncle had predicted correctly, for by the time I again came home on my vacation, the newly elected Pacifist Council had reduced the aerial activities to mere watchful patroling over the land of the enemy. Then came the report of an attempt to launch an airplane from the roof of Berlin. The people, in dire panic lest Ray generators were being carried out by German aircraft, had clamoured for the recall of the Pacifist Council, and the bombardment of Berlin was resumed.

During the lull of the bombing activities my uncle, who stood high with the Pacifist Administration, had obtained permission to fly over Europe, and I, most fortunate of boys, accompanied him. The plane in which we travelled bore the emblem of the World Patrol. On a cloudless day we sailed over the pock-marked desert that had once been Germany and came within field-glass range of Berlin itself. On the wasted, bomb-torn land lay the great grey disc—the city of mystery. Three hundred metres high they said it stood, but so vast was its extent that it seemed as flat and thin as a pancake on a griddle.

"More people live in that mass of concrete," said my uncle, "than in the whole of America west of the Rocky Mountains." His statement, I have since learned, fell short of half the truth, but then it seemed appalling. I fancied the city a giant anthill, and searched with my glass as if I expected to see the ants swarming out. But no sign of life was visible upon the monotonous surface of the sand-blanketed roof, and high above the range of naked vision hung the hawk-like watchers of the World Patrol.

The lure of unravelled secrets, the ambition for discovery and exploration stirred my boyish veins. Yes, I would know more of the strange race, the unknown life that surged beneath that grey blanket of mystery. But how? For over a century millions of men had felt that same longing to know. Aviators, landing by accident or intent within the lines, had either returned with nothing to report, or they had not returned. Daring journalists, with baskets of carrier pigeons, had on foggy nights dropped by parachute to the roof of the city; but neither they nor the birds had brought back a single word of what lay beneath the armed and armoured roof.

My own resolution was but a boy's dream and I returned to Chicago to take up my chemical studies.

CHAPTER II: I EXPLORE THE POTASH MINES OF STASSFURT AND FIND A DIARY IN A DEAD MAN'S POCKET

~1~

When I was twenty-four years old, my uncle was killed in a laboratory explosion. He had been a scientist of renown and a chemical inventor who had devoted his life to the unravelling of the secrets of the synthetic foods of Germany. For some years I had been his trusted assistant. In our Chicago laboratory were carefully preserved food samples that had been taken from the captured submarines in years gone by, and what to me was even more fascinating, a collection of German books of like origin, which I had read with avidity. With the exception of those relating to submarine navigation, I found them stupidly childish and decided that they had been prepared to hide the truth and not reveal it.

My uncle had bequeathed me both his work and his fortune, but despairing of my ability worthily to continue his own brilliant researches on synthetic food, I turned my attention to the potash problem, in which I had long been interested. My reading of early chemical works had given me a particular interest in the reclamation of the abandoned potash mines of Stassfurt. These mines, as any student of chemical history will know, were one of the richest properties of the old German state in the days before the endless war began and Germany became isolated from the rest of the world. The mines were captured by the World in the year 2020, and were profitably operated for a couple of decades. Meanwhile the German lines were forced many miles to the rear before the impregnable barrier of the Ray had halted the progress of the World Armies.

A few years after the coming of the Ray defences, occurred what history records as "The Tragedy of the Mines." Six thousand workmen went down into the potash mines of Stassfurt one morning and never came up again. The miners' families in the neighbouring villages died like weevils in fumigated grain. The region became a valley of pestilence and death, and all life withered for miles around. Numerous governmental projects were launched for the recovery of the potash mines but all failed, and for one hundred and eleven years no man had penetrated those accursed shafts.

Knowing these facts, I wasted no time in soliciting government aid for my project, but was content to secure a permit to attempt the recovery with private funds, with which my uncle's fortune supplied me in abundance.

In April, 2151, I set up my laboratory on the edge of the area of death. I had never accepted the orthodox view as to the composition of the gas that issued from the Stassfurt mines. In a few months I was gratified to find my doubts confirmed. A short time after this I made a more unexpected and astonishing discovery. I found that this complex and hitherto misunderstood gas could, under the influence of certain high-frequency electrical discharges, be made to combine with explosive violence with the nitrogen of the atmosphere, leaving only a harmless residue. We wired the surrounding region for the electrical discharge and, with a vast explosion of weird purple flame, cleared the whole area of the century-old curse. Our laboratory was destroyed by the explosion. It was rebuilt nearer the mine shafts from which the gas still slowly issued. Again we set up our electrical machinery and dropped our cables into the shafts, this time clearing the air of the mines.

A hasty exploration revealed the fact that but a single shaft had remained intact. A third time we prepared our electrical machinery. We let down a cable and succeeded in getting but a faint reaction at the bottom of the shaft. After several repeated clearings we risked descent.

Upon arrival at the bottom we were surprised to find it free from water, save for a trickling stream. The second thing we discovered was a pile of huddled skeletons of the workmen who had perished over a century previous. But our third and most important discovery was a boring from which the poisonous gas was slowly issuing. It took but a few hours to provide an apparatus to fire this gas as fast as it issued, and the potash mines of Stassfurt were regained for the world.

My associates were for beginning mining operations at once, but I had been granted a twenty years' franchise on the output of these mines, and I was in no such haste. The boring from which this poisonous vapour issued was clearly man-made; moreover I alone knew the formula of that gas and had convinced myself once for all as to its man-made origin. I sent for microphones and with their aid speedily detected the sound of machinery in other workings beneath.

It is easy now to see that I erred in risking my own life as I did without the precaution of confiding the secret of my discovery to others. But those were days of feverish excitement. Impulsively I decided to make the first attack on the Germans as a private enterprise and then call for military aid. I had my own equipment of poisonous bombs and my sapping and mining experts determined that the German workings were but eighty metres beneath us. Hastily, among the crumbling skeletons, we set up our electrical boring machinery and began sinking a one-metre shaft towards the nearest sound.

After twenty hours of boring, the drill head suddenly came off and rattled down into a cavern. We saw a light and heard guttural shouting below and the cracking of a gun as a few bullets spattered against the roof of our chamber. We heaved down our gas bombs and covered over our shaft. Within a few hours the light below went out and our microphones failed to detect any sound from the rocks beneath us. It was then perhaps that I should have called for military aid, but the uncanny silence of the lower workings proved too much for my eager curiosity. We waited two days and still there was no evidence of life below. I knew there had been ample time for the gas from our bombs to have been dissipated, as it was decomposed by contact with moisture. A light was lowered, but this brought forth no response.

I now called for a volunteer to descend the shaft. None was forthcoming from among my men, and against their protest I insisted on being lowered into the shaft. When I was a few metres from the bottom the cable parted and I fell and lay stunned on the floor below.

~2~

When I recovered consciousness the light had gone out. There was no sound about me. I shouted up the shaft above and could get no answer. The chamber in which I lay was many times my height and I could make nothing out in the dark hole above. For some hours I scarcely stirred and feared to burn my pocket flash both because it might reveal my presence to lurking enemies and because I wished to conserve my battery against graver need.

But no rescue came from my men above. Only recently, after the lapse of years, did I learn the cause of their deserting me. As I lay stunned from my fall, my men, unable to get answer to their shoutings, had given me up for dead. Meanwhile the apparatus which caused the destruction of the German gas had gone wrong. My associates, unable to fix it, had fled from the mine and abandoned the enterprise.

After some hours of waiting I stirred about and found means to erect a rough scaffold and reach the mouth of the shaft above me. I attempted to climb, but, unable to get a hold on the smooth wet rock, I gave up exhausted and despairing. Entombed in the depths of the earth, I was either a prisoner of the German potash miners, if any remained alive, or a prisoner of the earth itself, with dead men for company.

Collecting my courage I set about to explore my surroundings. I found some mining machinery evidently damaged by the explosion of our gas bombs. There was no evidence of men about, living or dead. Stealthily I set out along the little railway track that ran through a passage down a steep incline. As I progressed I felt the air rapidly becoming colder. Presently I stumbled upon the first victim of our gas bombs, fallen headlong as he was fleeing. I hurried on. The air seemed to be blowing in my face and the cold was becoming intense. This puzzled me for at this depth the temperature should have been above that on the surface of the earth.

After a hundred metres or so of going I came into a larger chamber. It was intensely cold. From out another branching passage-way I could hear a sizzling sound as of steam escaping. I started to turn into this passage but was met with such a blast of cold air that I dared not face it for fear of being frozen. Stamping my feet, which were fast becoming numb, I made the rounds of the chamber, and examined the dead miners that were tumbled about. The bodies were frozen.

One side of this chamber was partitioned off with some sort of metal wall. The door stood blown open. It felt a little warmer in here and I entered and closed the door. Exploring the room with my dim light I found one side of it filled with a row of bunks—in each bunk a corpse. Along the other side of the room was a table with eating utensils and back of this were shelves with food packages.

I was in danger of freezing to death and, tumbling several bodies out of the bunks, I took the mattresses and built of them a clumsy enclosure and installed in their midst a battery heater which I found. In this fashion I managed to get fairly warm again. After some hours of huddling I observed that the temperature had moderated.

My fear of freezing abated, I made another survey of my surroundings and discovered something that had escaped my first attention. In the far end of the room was a desk, and seated before it with his head fallen forward on his arms was the form of a man. The miners had all been dressed in a coarse artificial leather, but this man was dressed in a woven fabric of cellulose silk.

The body was frozen. As I tumbled it stiffly back it fell from the chair exposing a ghastly face. I drew away in a creepy horror, for as I looked at the face of the corpse I suffered a sort of waking nightmare in which I imagined that I was gazing at my own dead countenance.

I concluded that my normal mind was slipping out of gear and proceeded to back off and avail myself of a tube of stimulant which I carried in my pocket.

This revived me somewhat, but again, when I tried to look upon the frozen face, the conviction returned that I was looking at my own dead self.

I glanced at my watch and figured out that I had been in the German mine for thirty hours and had not tasted food or drink for nearly forty hours. Clearly I had to get myself in shape to escape hallucinations. I went back to the shelves and proceeded to look for food and drink. Happily, due to my work in my uncle's laboratory, these synthetic foods were not wholly strange to me. I drank copiously of a non-alcoholic chemical liquor and warmed on the heater and partook of some nitrogenous and some starchy porridges. It was an uncanny dining place, but hunger soon conquers mere emotion, and I made out a meal. Then once more I faced the task of confronting this dead likeness of myself.

This time I was clear-headed enough. I even went to the miners' lavatory and, jerking down the metal mirror, scrutinized my own reflection and reassured myself of the closeness of the resemblance. My purpose framed in my mind as I did this. Clearly I was in German quarters and was likely to remain there. Sooner or later there must be a rescuing party.

Without further ado, I set about changing my clothing for that of the German. The fit of the dead man's clothes further emphasized the closeness of the physical likeness. I recalled my excellent command of the German language and began to wonder what manner of man I was supposed to be in this assumed personality. But my most urgent task was speedily to make way with the incriminating corpse. With the aid of the brighter flashlight which I found in my new pockets, I set out to find a place to hide the body.

The cold that had so frightened me had now given way to almost normal temperature. There was no longer the sound of sizzling steam from the unexplored passage-way. I followed this and presently came upon another chamber filled with machinery. In one corner a huge engine, covered with frost, gave off a chill greeting. On the floor was a steaming puddle of liquid, but the breath of this steam cut like a blizzard. At once I guessed it. This was a liquid air engine. The dead engineer in the corner helped reveal the story. With his death from the penetrating gas, something had gone wrong with the engine. The turbine head had blown off, and the conveying pipe of liquid air had poured forth the icy blast that had so nearly frozen me along with the corpses of the Germans. But now the flow of liquid had ceased, and the last remnants were evaporating from the floor. Evidently the supply pipe had been shut off further back on the line, and I had little time to lose for rescuers were probably on the way.

Along one of the corridors running from the engine room I found an open water drain half choked with melting ice. Following this I came upon a grating where the water disappeared. I jerked up the grating and dropped a piece of ice down the well-like shaft. I hastily returned and dragged forth the corpse of my double and with it everything I had myself brought into the mine. Straightening out the stiffened body I plunged it head foremost into the opening. The sound of a splash echoed within the dismal depths.

I now hastened back to the chamber into which I had first fallen and destroyed the scaffolding I had erected there. Returning to the desk where I had found the man whose clothing I wore, I sat down and proceeded to search my abundantly filled pockets. From one of them I pulled out a bulky notebook and a number of loose papers. The freshest of these was an official order from the Imperial Office of Chemical Engineers. The order ran as follows:

Capt. Karl Armstadt
Laboratory 186, E. 58.

Report is received at this office of the sound of sapping operations in potash mine D5. Go at once and verify the same and report of condition of gas generators and make analyses of output of the same.

Evidently I was Karl Armstadt and very happily a chemical engineer by profession. My task of impersonation so far looked feasible—I could talk chemical engineering.

The next paper I proceeded to examine was an identification folder done up in oiled fabric. Thanks to German thoroughness it was amusingly complete. On the first page appeared what I soon discovered to be *my* pedigree for four generations back. The printed form on which all this was minutely filled out made very clear statements from which I determined that my father and mother were both dead.

I, Karl Armstadt, twenty-seven years of age, was the fourteenth child of my mother and was born when she was forty-two years of age. According to the record I was the ninety-seventh child of my father and born when he was fifty-four. As I read this I thought there was something here that I misunderstood, although subsequent discoveries made it plausible enough. There was no further record of my plentiful fraternity, but I took heart that the mere fact of their numerical abundance would make unlikely any great show of brotherly interest, a presumption which proved quite correct.

On the second page of this folder I read the number and location of my living quarters, the sources from which my meals and clothing were issued, as well as the sizes and qualities of my garments and numerous other references to various details of living, all of which seemed painstakingly ridiculous at the time.

I put this elaborate identification paper back into its receptacle and opened the notebook. It proved to be a diary kept likewise in thorough German fashion. I turned to the last pages and perused them hastily.

The notes in Armstadt's diary were concerned almost wholly with his chemical investigations. All this I saw might be useful to me later but what I needed more immediately was information as to his personal life. I scanned back hastily through the pages for a time without finding any such revelations. Then I discovered this entry made some months previously:

"I cannot think of chemistry tonight, for the vision of Katrina dances before me as in a dream. It must be a strange mixture of blood-lines that could produce such wondrous beauty. In no other woman have I seen such a blackness of hair and eyes combined with such a whiteness of skin. I suppose I should not have danced with her—now I see all my resolutions shattered. But I think it was most of all the blackness of her eyes. Well, what care, we live but once!"

I read and re-read this entry and searched feverishly in Armstadt's diary for further evidence of a personal life. But I only found tedious notes on his chemical theories. Perhaps this single reference to a woman was but a passing fancy of a man otherwise engrossed in his science. But if rescuers came and I succeeded in passing for the German chemist the presence of a woman in my new rôle of life would surely undo all my effort. If no personal acquaintance of the dead man came with the rescuing party I saw no reason why I could not for the time pass successfully as Armstadt. I should at least make the effort and I reasoned I could best do this by playing the malingerer and appearing mentally incompetent. Such a ruse, I reasoned, would give me opportunity to hear much and say little, and perhaps so get my bearings in the new rôle that I could continue it successfully.

Then, as I was about to return the notebook to my pocket, my hopes sank as I found this brief entry which I had at first scanning overlooked:

"It is twenty days now since Katrina and I have been united. She does not interfere with my work as much as I feared. She even lets me talk chemistry to her, though I am sure she understands not one word of what I tell her. I think I have made a good selection and it is surely a permanent one. Therefore I must work harder than ever or I shall not get on."

This alarmed me. Yet, if Armstadt had married he made very little fuss about it. Evidently it concerned him chiefly in relation to his work. But whoever and whatever Katrina was, it was clear that her presence would be disastrous to my plans of assuming his place in the German world.

Pondering over the ultimate difficulty of my situation, but with a growing faith in the plan I had evolved for avoiding immediate explanations, I fell into a long-postponed sleep. The last thing I remember was tumbling from my chair and sprawling out upon the floor where I managed to snap out my light before the much needed sleep quite overcame me.

~3~

I was awakened by voices, and opened my eyes to find the place brightly lighted. I closed them again quickly as some one approached and prodded me with the toe of his boot.

"Here is a man alive," said a voice above me.

"He is Captain Armstadt, the chemist," said another voice, approaching; "this is good. We have special orders to search for him."

The newcomer bent over and felt my heart. I was quite aware that it was functioning normally. He shook me and called me by name. After repeated shakings I opened my eyes and stared at him blankly, but I said nothing. Presently he left me and returned with a stretcher. I lay inertly as I was placed thereon and borne out of the chamber. Other stretcher-bearers were walking ahead. We passed through the engine room where mechanics were at work on the damaged liquid air engine. My stretcher was placed on a little car which moved swiftly along the tunnel.

We came into a large subterranean station and I was removed and brought before a bevy of white garbed physicians. They looked at my identification folder and then examined me. Through it all I lay limp and as near lifeless as I could simulate, and they succeeded in getting no speech out of me. The final orders were to forward me post haste to the Imperial Hospital for Complex Gas Cases.

After an eventless journey of many hours I was again unloaded and transferred to an elevator. For several hundred metres we sped upward through a shaft, while about us whistled a blast of cold, crisp air. At last the elevator stopped and I was carried out to an ambulance that stood waiting in a brilliantly lighted passage arched over with grey concrete. I was no longer beneath the surface of the earth but was somewhere in the massive concrete structure of the City of Berlin.

After a short journey our ambulance stopped and attendants came out and carried my litter through an open doorway and down a long hall into the spacious ward of a hospital.

From half closed eyes I glanced about apprehensively for a black-haired woman. With a sigh of relief I saw there were only doctors and male attendants in the room. They treated me most professionally and gave no sign that they suspected I was other than Capt. Karl Armstadt, which fact my papers so eloquently testified. The conclusion of their examination was voiced in my presence. "Physically he is normal," said the head physician, "but his mind seems in a stupor. There is no remedy, as the nature of the gas is unknown. All that can be done is to await the wearing off of the effect."

I was then left alone for some hours and my appetite was troubling me. At last an attendant approached with some savoury soup; he propped me up and proceeded to feed me with a spoon.

I made out from the conversation about me that the other patients were officers from the underground fighting forces. An atmosphere of military discipline pervaded the hospital and I felt reassured in the conclusion that all visiting was forbidden.

Yet my thoughts turned repeatedly to the black-eyed Katrina of Armstadt's diary. No doubt she had been informed of the rescue and was waiting in grief and anxiety to see him. So both she and I were awaiting a tragic moment— she to learn that her husband or lover was dead, I for the inevitable tearing off of my protecting disguise.

After some days the head physician came to my cot and questioned me. I gazed at him and knit my brows as if struggling to think.

"You were gassed in the mine," he kept repeating, "can you remember?"

"Yes," I ventured, "I went to the mine, there was the sound of boring overhead. I set men to watch; I was at the desk, I heard shouting, after that I cannot remember."

"They were all dead but you," said the doctor.

"All dead," I repeated. I liked the sound of this and so kept on mumbling "All dead, all dead."

~4~

My plan was working nicely. But I realized I could not keep up this rôle for ever. Nor did I wish to, for the idleness and suspense were intolerable and I knew that I would rather face whatever problems my recovery involved than to continue in this monotonous and meaningless existence. So I convalesced by degrees and got about the hospital, and was permitted to wait on myself. But I cultivated a slowness and brevity of speech.

One day as I sat reading the attendant announced, "A visitor to see you, sir."

Trembling with excitement and fear I tensely waited the coming of the visitor.

Presently a stolid-faced young man followed the attendant into the room. "You remember Holknecht," said the nurse, "he is your assistant at the laboratory."

I stared stupidly at the man, and cold fear crept over me as he, with puzzled eyes, returned my gaze.

"You are much changed," he said at last. "I hardly recognize you."

"I have been very ill," I replied.

Just then the head physician came into the room and seeing me talking to a stranger walked over to us. As I said nothing, Holknecht introduced himself. The medical man began at once to enlarge upon the peculiarities of my condition. "The unknown gas," he explained, "acted upon the whole nervous system and left profound effects. Never in the records of the hospital has there been so strange a case."

Holknecht seemed quite awed and completely credulous.

"His memory must be revived," continued the head physician, "and that can best be done by recalling the dominating interest of his mind."

"Captain Armstadt was wholly absorbed in his research work in the laboratory," offered Holknecht.

"Then," said the physician, "you must revive the activity of those particular brain cells."

With that command the laboratory assistant was left in charge. He took his new task quite seriously. Turning to me and raising his voice as if to penetrate my dulled mentality, he began, "Do you not remember our work in the laboratory?"

"Yes, the laboratory, the laboratory," I repeated vaguely.

Holknecht described the laboratory in detail and gradually his talk drifted into an account of the chemical research. I listened eagerly to get the threads of the work I must needs do if I were to maintain my rôle as Armstadt.

Knowing now that visitors were permitted me, I again grew apprehensive over the possible advent of Katrina. But no woman appeared, in fact I had not yet seen a woman among the Germans. Always it was Holknecht and, strictly according to his orders, he talked incessant chemistry.

~5~

The day I resumed my normal wearing apparel I was shown into a large lounging room for convalescents. I seated myself a short distance apart from a group of officers and sat eyeing another group of large, hulking fellows at the far end of the room. These I concluded to be common soldiers, for I heard the officers in my ward grumbling at the fact that they were quartered in the same hospital with men of the ranks.

Presently an officer came over and took a seat beside me. "It is very rarely that you men in the professional service are gassed," he said. "You must have a dull life, I do not see how you can stand it."

"But certainly," I replied, "it is not so dangerous."

"And for that reason it must be stupid—I, for one, think that even in the fighting forces there is no longer sufficient danger to keep up the military morale. Danger makes men courageous—without danger courage declines— and without courage what advantage would there be in the military life?"

"Suppose," I suggested, "the war should come to an end?"

"But how can it?" he asked incredulously. "How can there be an end to the war? We cannot prevent the enemy from fighting."

"But what," I ventured, "if the enemy should decide to quit fighting?"

"They have almost quit now," he remarked with apparent disgust; "they are losing the fighting spirit—but no wonder—they say that the World State population is so great that only two per cent of its men are in the fighting forces. What I cannot see is how a people so peaceful can keep from utter degeneration. And they say that the World State soldiers are not even bred for soldiering but are picked from all classes. If they should decide to quit fighting, as you suggest, we also would have to quit—it would intolerable—it is bad enough now."

"But could you not return to industrial life and do something productive?"

"Productive!" sneered the fighter. "I knew that you professional men had no courage—it is not to be expected—but I never before heard even one of your class suggest a thing like that—a military man do something productive! Why don't you suggest that we be changed to women?" And with that my fellow patient rose and, turning sharply on his metal heel, walked away.

The officer's attitude towards his profession set me thinking, and I found myself wondering how far it was shared by the common soldiers. The next day when I came out into the convalescent corridor I walked past the group of officers and went down among the men whose garments bore no medals or insignia. They were unusually large men, evidently from some specially selected regiment. Picking out the most intelligent looking one of the group I sat down beside him.

"Is this the first time you have been gassed?" I inquired.

"Third time," replied the soldier.

"I should think you would have been discharged."

"Discharged," said the soldier, in a perplexed tone, "why I am only forty-four years old, why should I be discharged unless I get in an explosion and lose a leg or something?"

"But you have been gassed three times," I said, "I should think they ought to let you return to civil life and your family."

The soldier looked hard at the insignia of my rank as captain. "You professional officers don't know much, do you? A soldier quit and do common labor, now that's a fine idea. And a family! Do you think I'm a Hohenzollern?" At the thought the soldier chuckled. "Me with a family," he muttered to himself, "now that's a fine idea."

I saw that I was getting on dangerous ground but curiosity prompted a further question: "Then, I suppose, you have nothing to hope for until you reach the age of retirement, unless war should come to an end?"

Again the soldier eyed me carefully. "Now you do have some queer ideas. There was a man in our company who used to talk like that when no officers were around. This fellow, his name was Mannteufel, said he could read books, that he was a forbidden love-child and his father was an officer. I guess he was forbidden all right, for he certainly wasn't right in his head. He said that we would go out on the top of the ground and march over the enemy country and be shot at by the flying planes, like the roof guards, if the officers had heard him they would surely have sent him to the crazy ward—why he said that the war would be over after that, and we would all go to the enemy country and go about as we liked, and own houses and women and flying planes and animals. As if the Royal House would ever let a soldier do things like that."

"Well," I said, "and why not, if the war were over?"

"Now there you go again—how do you mean the war was over, what would all us soldiers do if there was no fighting?"

"You could work," I said, "in the shops."

"But if we worked in the shops, what would the workmen do?"

"They would work too," I suggested.

The soldier was silent for a time. "I think I get your idea," he said. "The Eugenic Staff would cut down the birth rates so that there would only be enough soldiers and workers to fill the working jobs."

"They might do that," I remarked, wishing to lead him on.

"Well," said the soldier, returning to the former thought, "I hope they won't do that until I am dead. I don't care to go up on the ground to get shot at by the fighting planes. At least now we have something over our heads and if we are going to get gassed or blown up we can't see it coming. At least—"

Just then the officer with whom I had talked the day before came up. He stopped before us and scowled at the soldier who saluted in hasty confusion.

"I wish, Captain," said the officer addressing me, "that you would not take advantage of these absurd hospital conditions to disrupt discipline by fraternizing with a private."

At this the soldier looked up and saluted again.

"Well?" said the officer.

"He's not to blame, sir," said the soldier, "he's off his head."

CHAPTER III: IN A BLACK UTOPIA THE BLOND BROOD BREEDS AND SWARMS

~1~

It was with a strange mixture of eagerness and fear that I received the head physician's decision that I would henceforth recover my faculties more rapidly in the familiar environment of my own home.

A wooden-faced male nurse accompanied me in a closed vehicle that ran noiselessly through the vaulted interior streets of the completely roofed-in city. Once our vehicle entered an elevator and was let down a brief distance. We finally alighted in a street very like the one on which the hospital was located, and filed down a narrow passage-way. My companion asked for my keys, which I found in my clothing. I stood by with a palpitating heart as he turned the lock and opened the door.

The place we entered was a comfortably furnished bachelor's apartment. Books and papers were littered about giving evidence of no disturbance since the sudden leaving of the occupant. Immensely relieved I sat down in an upholstered chair while the nurse scurried about and put the place in order.

"You feel quite at home?" he asked as he finished his task.

"Quite," I replied, "things are coming back to me now."

"You should have been sent home sooner," he said. "I wished to tell the chief as much, but I am only a second year interne and it is forbidden me to express an original opinion to him."

"I am sure I will be all right now," I replied.

He turned to go and then paused. "I think," he said, "that you should have some notice on you that when you do go out, if you become confused and make mistakes, the guards will understand. I will speak to Lieut. Forrester, the Third Assistant, and ask that such a card be sent you." With that he took his departure.

When he had gone I breathed joyfully and freely. The rigid face and staring eye that I had cultivated relaxed into a natural smile and then I broke into a laugh. Here I was in the heart of Berlin, unsuspected of being other than a loyal German and free, for the time at least, from problems of personal relations.

I now made an elaborate inspection of my surroundings. I found a wardrobe full of men's clothing, all of a single shade of mauve like the suit I wore. Some suits I guessed to be work clothes from their cheaper texture and some, much finer, were evidently dress apparel.

Having reassured myself that Armstadt had been the only occupant of the apartment, I turned to a pile of papers that the hospital attendant had picked up from the floor where they had dropped from a mail chute. Most of these proved to be the accumulated copies of a daily chemical news bulletin. Others were technical chemical journals. Among the letters I found an invitation to a meeting of a chemical society, and a note from my tailor asking me to call; the third letter was written on a typewriter, an instrument the like of which I had already discovered in my study. This sheet bore a neatly engraved head reading "Katrina, Permit 843 LX, Apartment 57, K Street, Level of the Free Women." The letter ran:

"Dear Karl: For three weeks now you have failed to keep your appointments and sent no explanation. You surely know that I will not tolerate such rude neglect. I have reported to the Supervisor that you are dropped from my list."

So this was Katrina! Here at last was the end of the fears that had haunted me.

~2~

As I was scanning the chemical journal I heard a bell ring and turning about I saw that a metal box had slid forth upon a side board from an opening in the wall. In this box I found my dinner which I proceeded to enjoy in solitude. The food was more varied than in the hospital. Some was liquid and some gelatinous, and some firm like bread or biscuit. But of natural food products there was nothing save a dish of mushrooms and a single sprig of green no longer than my finger, and which, like a feather in a boy's cap, was inserted conspicuously in the top of a synthetic pudding. There was one food that puzzled me, for it was sausage-like in form and sausage-like in flavour, and I was sure contained some real substance of animal origin. Presuming, as I did at that moment, that no animal life existed in Berlin, I ate this sausage with doubts and misgivings.

The dinner finished, I looked for a way to dispose of the dishes. Packing them back in the container I fumbled about and found a switch which set something going in the wall, and my dishes departed to the public dishwasher.

Having cleared the desk I next turned to Armstadt's book shelves. My attention was caught by a ponderous volume. It proved to be an atlas and directory of Berlin. In the front of this was a most revealing diagram which showed Berlin to be a city of sixty levels. The five lowest levels were underground and all were labelled "Mineral Industries." Above these were eight levels of Food, Clothing and Miscellaneous industries. Then came the seven workmen's residence levels, divided by trade groups. Above this were the four "Intellectual Levels," on one of which I, as a chemist had my abode. Directly above these was the "Level of Free Women," and above that the residence level for military officers. The next was the "Royal Level," double in height of the other levels of the city. Then came the "Administrative Level," followed by eight maternity levels, then four levels of female schools and nine levels of male schools. Then, for six levels, and reaching to within five levels of the roof of the city, were soldiers' barracks. Three of the remaining floors were labelled "Swine Levels" and one "Green Gardens." Just beneath the roof was the defence level and above that the open roof itself.

It was a city of some three hundred metres in height with mineral industries at the bottom and the swine levels—I recalled the sausage—at the top. Midway between, remote from possible attack through mines or from the roof, Royalty was sheltered, while the other privileged groups of society were stratified above and below it.

Following the diagram of levels was a most informing chart arranged like a huge multiplication table. It gave after each level the words "permitted," "forbidden," and "permitted as announced," arranged in columns for each of the other levels. From this I traced out that as a chemist I was permitted on all the industrial, workmen's and intellectual levels, and on the Level of Free Women. I was permitted, as announced, on the Administrative and Royal Levels; but forbidden on the levels of military officers and soldiers' barracks, maternity and male and female schools.

I found that as a chemist I was particularly fortunate for many other groups were given even less liberty. As for common workmen and soldiers, they were permitted on no levels except their own.

The most perplexing thing about this system was the apparent segregation of such large groups of men from women. Family life in Germany was evidently wonderfully altered and seemingly greatly restricted, a condition inconsistent with the belief that I had always held—that the German race was rapidly increasing.

Turning to my atlas index I looked up the population statistics of the city, and found that by the last census it was near three hundred million. And except for the few millions in the mines this huge mass of humanity was quartered beneath a single roof. I was greatly surprised, for this population figure was more than double the usual estimates current in the outside world. Coming from a world in which the ancient tendency to congest in cities had long since been overcome, I was staggered by the fact that nearly as many people were living in this one city as existed in the whole of North America.

Yet, when I figured the floor area of the city, which was roughly oval in shape, being eight kilometres in breadth and eleven in length, I found that the population on a given floor area was no greater than it had been in the Island of Manhattan before the reform land laws were put into effect in the latter part of the Twentieth Century. There was, therefore, nothing incredible in these figures of total population, but what I next discovered was a severe strain on credence. It was the German population by sexes; the figures showed that there were nearly two and a half males for every female! According to the usual estimate of war losses the figure should have been at a ratio of six women living to about five men, and here I found them recorded as only two women to five men. Inspection of the birth rate showed an even higher proportion of males. I consulted further tables that gave births by sexes and groups. These varied somewhat but there was this great preponderance of males in every class but one. Only among the seventeen thousand members of Royalty did the proportion of the sexes approach the normal.

Apparently I had found an explanation of the careful segregation of German women—there were not enough to go around!

Turning the further pages of my atlas I came upon an elaborately illustrated directory of the uniforms and insignia of the various military and civil ranks and classes. As I had already anticipated, I found that any citizen in Berlin could immediately be placed in his proper group and rank by his clothing, which was prescribed with military exactness.

Various fabrics and shades indicated the occupational grouping while trimmings and insignia distinguished the ranks within the groups. In all there were many hundreds of distinct uniforms. Two groups alone proved exceptions to this iron clad rule; Royalty and free women were permitted to dress as they chose and were restricted only in that they were forbidden to imitate the particular uniforms of other groups.

I next investigated the contents of Armstadt's desk. My most interesting find was a checkbook, with receipts and expenditures carefully recorded on the stubs. From this I learned that, as Armstadt, I was in receipt of an income of five thousand marks, paid by the Government. I did not know how much purchasing value that would amount to, but from the account book I saw that the expenses had not equalled a third of it, which explained why there was a bank balance of some twenty thousand marks.

Clearly I would need to master the signature of Karl Armstadt so I searched among the papers until I found a bundle of returned decks. Many of the larger checks had been made out to "Katrina," others to the "Master of Games,"—evidently to cover gambling losses. The smaller checks, I found by reference to the stubs, were for ornaments or entertainment that might please a woman. The lack of the more ordinary items of expenditure was presently made clear by the discovery of a number of punch marked cards. For intermittent though necessary expenses, such as tonsorial service, clothing and books. For the more constant necessities of life, such as rent, food, laundry and transportation, there was no record whatever; and I correctly assumed that these were supplied without compensation and were therefore not a matter of personal choice or permissible variation. Of money in its ancient form of metal coins and paper, I found no evidence.

~3~

In my mail the next morning I found a card signed by Lieut. Forrester of the hospital staff. It read:

"The bearer, Karl Armstadt, has recently suffered from gas poisoning while defending the mines beneath enemy territory. This has affected his memory. If he is therefore found disobeying any ruling or straying beyond his permitted bounds, return him to his apartment and call the Hospital for Complex Gas Cases."

It was evidently a very kindly effort to protect a man whose loss of memory might lead him into infractions of the numerous rulings of German life. With this help I became ambitious to try the streets of Berlin alone. The notice from the tailor afforded an excuse.

Consulting my atlas to get my bearings I now ventured forth. The streets were tunnel-like passage-ways closed over with a beamed ceiling of whitish grey concrete studded with glowing light globes. In the residence districts the smooth side walls were broken only by high ventilating gratings and the narrow passage halls from which led the doors of the apartments.

The uncanny quiet of the streets of this city with its three hundred million inhabitants awed and oppressed me. Hurriedly I walked along occasionally passing men dressed like myself. They were pale men, with blanched or sallow faces. But nowhere were there faces of ruddy tan as one sees in a world of sun. The men in the hospital had been pale, but that had seemed less striking for one is used to pale faces in a hospital. It came to me with a sense of something lost that my own countenance blanched in the mine and hospital would so remain colourless like the faces of the men who now stole by me in their felted footwear with a cat-like tread.

At a cross street I turned and came upon a small group of shops with monotonous panelled display windows inserted in the concrete walls. Here I found my tailor and going in I promptly laid down his notice and my clothing card. He glanced casually at the papers, punched the card and then looking up he remarked that my new suit had been waiting some time. I began explaining the incident in the mine and the stay in the hospital; but the tailor was either disinterested or did not comprehend.

"Will you try on your new suit now?" he interrupted, holding forth the garments. The suit proved a trifle tight about the hips, but I hastened to assure the tailor that the fit was perfect. I removed it and watched him do it up in a parcel, open a wall closet, call my house number, and send my suit on its way through one of the numerous carriers that interlaced the city.

As I walked more leisurely back to my apartment by a less direct way, I found my analytical brain puzzling over the refreshing quality of the breezes that blew through those tunnel-like streets. With bits of paper I traced the air flow from the latticed faces of the elevator shafts to the ventilating gratings of the enclosed apartments, and concluded that there must be other shafts to the rear of the apartments for its exit. It occurred to me that it must take an enormous system of ventilating fans to keep this air in motion, and then I remembered the liquid air engine I had seen in the mine, and a realization of the economy and efficiency of the whole scheme dawned upon me. The Germans had solved the power problem by using the heat of the deeper strata of the earth to generate power through the agency of liquid air and the exhaust from their engines had automatically solved their ventilating problem. I recalled with a smile that I had seen no evidence of heating apparatus anywhere except that which the miners had used to warm their food. In this city cooling rather than heating facilities would evidently be needed, even in the dead of winter, since the heat generated by the inhabitants and the industrial processes would exceed the radiation from the exterior walls and roof of the city. Sunshine and "fresh air" they had not, but our own scientists had taught us for generations that heat and humidity and not lack of oxygen or sunshine was the cause of the depression experienced in indoor quarters. The air of Berlin was cool and the excess of vapor had been frozen out of it. Yes, the "climate" of Berlin should be more salubrious to the body, if not to the mind, than the fickle environment of capricious nature. From my reasoning about these ponderous problems of existence I was diverted to a trivial matter. The men I observed on the streets all wore their hair clipped short, while mine, with six weeks' growth, was getting rather long. I had seen several barber's signs but I decided to walk on for quite a distance beyond my apartment. I did not want to confront a barber who had known Karl Armstadt, for barbers deal critically in the matter of heads and faces. At last I picked out a shop. I entered and asked for a haircut.

"But you are not on my list," said the barber, staring at me in a puzzled way, "why do you not go to your own barber?"

Grasping the situation I replied that I did not like my barber.

"Then why do you not apply at the Tonsorial Administrative Office of the level for permission to change?"

Returning to my apartment I looked up the office in my directory, went thither and asked the clerk if I could exchange barbers. He asked for my card and after a deal of clerical activities wrote thereon the name of a new barber. With this official sanction I finally got my hair cut and my card punched, thinking meanwhile that the soundness of my teeth would obviate any amateur detective work on the part of a dentist.

Nothing, it seemed, was left for the individual to decide for himself. His every want was supplied by orderly arrangement and for everything he must have an authoritative permit. Had I not been classed as a research chemist, and therefore a man of some importance, this simple business of getting a hair-cut might have proved my undoing. Indeed, as I afterwards learned, the exclusive privacy of my living quarters was a mark of distinction. Had I been one of lower ranking I should have shared my apartment with another man who would have slept in my bed while I was at work, for in the sunless city was neither night nor day and the whole population worked and slept in prescribed shifts—the vast machinery of industry, like a blind giant in some Plutonic treadmill, toiled ceaselessly.

The next morning I decided to extend my travels to the medical level, which was located just above my own. There were stairs beside the elevator shafts but these were evidently for emergency as they were closed with locked gratings.

The elevator stopped at my ring. Not sure of the proper manner of calling my floor I was carried past the medical level. As we shot up through the three-hundred-metre shaft, the names of levels as I had read them in my atlas flashed by on the blind doors. On the topmost defence level we took on an officer of the roof guard—strangely swarthy of skin—and now the car shot down while the rising air rushed by us with a whistling roar.

On the return trip I called my floor as I had heard others do and was let off at the medical level. It was even more monotonously quiet than the chemical level, save for the hurrying passage of occasional ambulances on their way between the elevators and the various hospitals. The living quarters of the physicians were identical with those on the chemists' level. So, too, were the quiet shops from which the physicians supplied their personal needs.

Standing before one of these I saw in a window a new book entitled "Diseases of Nutrition." I went in and asked to see a copy. The book seller staring at my chemical uniform in amazement reached quickly under the counter and pressed a button. I became alarmed and turned to go out but found the door had been automatically closed and locked. Trying to appear unconcerned I stood idly glancing over the book shelves, while the book seller watched me from the corner of his eye.

In a few minutes the door opened from without and a man in the uniform of the street guard appeared. The book seller motioned toward me.

"Your identification folder," said the guard.

Mechanically I withdrew it and handed it to him. He opened it and discovered the card from the hospital. Smiling on me with an air of condescension, he took me by the arm and led me forth and conducted me to my own apartment on the chemical level. Arriving there he pushed me gently into a chair and stepped toward the switch of the telephone.

"Just a minute," I said, "I remember now. I was not on my level—that was not my book store."

"The card orders me to call up the hospital," said the guard.

"It is unnecessary," I said. "Do not call them."

The guard gazed first at me and then at the card. "It is signed by a Lieutenant and you are a Captain—" his brows knitted as he wrestled with the problem—"I do not know what to do. Does a Captain with an affected memory outrank a Lieutenant?"

"He does," I solemnly assured him.

Still a little puzzled, he returned the card, saluted and was gone. It had been a narrow escape. I got out my atlas and read again the rules that set forth my right to be at large in the city. Clearly I had a right to be found in the medical level—but in trying to buy a book there I had evidently erred most seriously. So I carefully memorized the list of shops set down in my identification folder and on my cards.

For the next few days I lived alone in my apartment unmolested except by an occasional visit from Holknecht, the laboratory assistant, who knew nothing but chemistry, talked nothing but chemistry, and seemed dead to all human emotions and human curiosity. Applying myself diligently to the study of Armstadt's books and notes, I was delighted to find that the Germans, despite their great chemical progress, were ignorant of many things I knew. I saw that my knowledge discreetly used, might enable me to become a great man among them and so learn secrets that would be of immense value to the outer world, should I later contrive to escape from Berlin.

By my discoveries of the German workings in the potash mines I had indeed opened a new road to Berlin. It was up to me by further discoveries to open a road out again, not only for my own escape, but perhaps also to find a way by which the World Armies might enter Berlin as the Greeks entered Troy. Vague ambitious dreams were these that filled and thrilled me, for I was young in years, and the romantic spirit of heroic adventure surged in my blood.

These days of study were quite uneventful, except for a single illuminating incident; a further example of the super-efficiency of the Germans. I found the meals served me at my apartment rather less in quantity than my appetite craved. While there was a reasonable variety, the nutritive value was always the same to a point of scientific exactness, and I had seen no shops where extra food was available. After I had been in my apartment about a week, some one rang at the door. I opened it and a man called out the single word, "Weigher." Just behind him stood a platform scale on small wheels and with handles like a go-cart. The weigher stood, notebook in hand, waiting for me to act. I took the hint and stepped upon the scales. He read the weight and as he recorded it, remarked:

"Three kilograms over."

Without further explanation he pushed the scales toward the next door. The following day I noticed that the portions of food served me were a trifle smaller than they had been previously. The original Karl Armstadt had evidently been of such build that he carried slightly less weight than I, which fact now condemned me to this light diet.

However, I reasoned that a light diet is conducive to good brain work, and as I later learned, the object of this systematic weight control was not alone to save food but to increase mental efficiency, for a fat man is phlegmatic and a lean one too excitable for the best mental output. It would also help my disguise by keeping me the exact weight and build of the original Karl Armstadt.

After a fortnight of study, I felt that I was now ready to take up my work in the laboratory, but I feared my lack of general knowledge of the city and its ways might still betray me. Hence I began further journeyings about the streets and shops of those levels where a man of my class was permitted to go.

~4~

After exhausting the rather barren sport of walking about the monotonous streets of the four professional levels I took a more exciting trip down into the lower levels of the city where the vast mechanical industries held sway. I did not know how much freedom might be allowed me, but I reasoned that I would be out of my supposed normal environment and hence my ignorance would be more excusable and in less danger of betraying me.

Alighting from the elevator, I hurried along past endless rows of heavy columns. I peered into the workrooms, which had no enclosing walls, and discovered with some misgiving that I seemed to have come upon a race of giants. The men at the machines were great hulking fellows with thick, heavy muscles such as one would expect to see in a professional wrestler or weight-lifter. I paused and tried to gauge the size of these men: I decided that they were not giants for I had seen taller men in the outer world. Two officials of some sort, distinguishable by finer garb, walking among them, appeared to be men of average size, and the tops of their heads came about to the workers' chins. That there should be such men among the Germans was not unbelievable, but the strange thing was that there should be so many of them, and that they should be so uniformly large, for there was not a workman in the whole vast factory floor that did not over-top the officials by at least half a head.

"Of course," I reasoned, "this is part of German efficiency";—for the men were feeding large plates through stamping mills—"they have selected all the large men for this heavy work." Then as I continued to gaze it occurred to me that this bright metal these Samsons were handling was aluminum!

I went on and came to a different work hall where men were tending wire winding machinery, making the coils for some light electrical instruments. It was work that girls could easily have done, yet these men were nearly, if not quite, as hulking as their mates in the stamping mill. To select such men for light-fingered work was not efficiency but stupidity,—and then it came to me that I had also thought the soldiers I had seen in the hospital to be men picked for size, and that in a normal population there could not be such an abundance of men of abnormal size. The meaning of it all began to clear in my mind—the pedigree in my own identification folder with the numerous fraternity, the system of social castes which my atlas had revealed, the inexplicable and unnatural proportion of the sexes. These gigantic men were not the mere pick from individual variation in the species, but a distinct breed within a race wherein the laws of nature, that had kept men of equal stature for countless centuries, even as wild animals were equal, had been replaced by the laws of scientific breeding. These heavy and ponderous labourers were the Percherons and Clydesdales of a domesticated and scientifically bred human species. The soldiers, somewhat less bulky and more active, were, no doubt, another distinct breed. The professional classes which had seemed quite normal in physical appearance—were they bred for mental rather than physical qualities? Otherwise why the pedigree, why the rigid castes, the isolation of women? I shuddered as the whole logical, inevitable explanation unfolded. It was uncanny, unearthly, yet perfectly scientific; a thing the world had speculated about for centuries, a thing that every school boy knew could be done, and yet which I, facing the fact that it had been done, could only believe by a strained effort at scientific coolness.

I walked on and on, absorbed, overwhelmed by these assaulting, unbelievable conclusions, yet on either side as I walked was the ever present evidence of the reality of these seemingly wild fancies. There were miles upon miles of these endless workrooms and everywhere the same gross breed of great blond beasts.

The endless shops of Berlin's industrial level were very like those elsewhere in the world, except that they were more vast, more concentrated, and the work more speeded up by super-machines and excessive specialization. Millions upon millions of huge, drab-clad, stolid-faced workmen stood at their posts of duty, performing over and over again their routine movements as the material of their labors shuttled by in endless streams.

Occasionally among the workmen I saw the uniforms of the petty officers who acted as foremen, and still more rarely the administrative offices, where, enclosed in glass panelled rooms, higher officials in more bespangled uniforms poured over charts and plans.

In all this colossal business there was everywhere the atmosphere of perfect order, perfect system, perfect discipline. Go as I might among the electrical works, among the vast factories of chemicals and goods, the lighter labor of the textile mills, or the heavier, noisier business of the mineral works and machine shops the same system of colossal coordinate mechanism of production throbbed ceaselessly. Materials flowed in endless streams, feeding electric furnaces, mills, machines; passing out to packing tables and thence to vast store rooms. Industry here seemed endless and perfect. The bovine humanity fitted to the machinery as the ox to the treadmill. Everywhere was the ceaseless throbbing of the machine. Of the human variation and the free action of man in labour, there was no evidence, and no opportunity for its existence.

Turning from the mere monotonous endlessness of the workshops I made my way to the levels above where the workers lived in those hours when they ceased to be a part of the industrial mechanism of production; and everywhere were drab-coloured men for these shifts of labour were arranged so that no space at any time was wholly idle. I now passed by miles of sleeping dormitories, and other miles of gymnasiums, picture theatres and gaming tables, and, strikingly incongruous with the atmosphere of the place, huge assembly rooms which were labelled "Free Speech Halls." I started to enter one of these, where some kind of a meeting was in progress, but I was thrust back by a great fellow who grinned foolishly and said: "Pardon, Herr Captain, it is forbidden you."

Through half-darkened streets, I again passed by the bunk-shelved sleeping chambers with their cavernous aisles walled with orderly rows of lockers. Again I came to other barracks where the men were not yet asleep but were straggling in and sitting about on the lowest bunks of these sterile makeshift homes.

I then came into a district of mess halls where a meal was being served. Here again was absolute economy and perfect system. The men dined at endless tables and their food like the material for their labours, was served to the workers by the highly efficient device of an endless moving belt that rolled up out of a slot in the floor at the end of the table after the manner of the chained steps of an escalator.

From the moving belts the men took their portions, and, as they finished eating, they cleared away by setting the empty dishes back upon the moving belt. The sight fascinated me, because of the adaptation of this mechanical principle to so strange a use, for the principle is old and, as every engineer knows, was instrumental in founding the house of Detroit Vehicle Kings that once dominated the industrial world. The founder of that illustrious line gave the poorest citizen a motor car and disrupted the wage system of his day by paying his men double the standard wage, yet he failed to realize the full possibilities of efficiency for he permitted his men to eat at round tables and be served by women! Truly we of the free world very narrowly escaped the fetish of efficiency which finally completely enslaved the Germans.

Each of the long tables of this Berlin dining hall, the ends of which faced me, was fenced off from its neighbours. At the entrance gates were signs which read "2600 Calories," "2800 Calories," "3000 Calories"—I followed down the line to the sign which read "Maximum Diet, 4000 Calories." The next one read, "Minimum Diet 2000 Calories," and thence the series was repeated. Farther on I saw that men were assembling before such gates in lines, for the meal there had not begun. Moving to the other side of the street I walked by the lines which curved out and swung down the street. Those before the sign of "Minimum Diet" were not quite so tall as the average, although obviously of the same breed. But they were all gaunt, many of them drooped and old, relatively the inferior specimens and their faces bore a cowering look of fear and shame, of men sullen and dull, beaten in life's battle. Following down the line and noting the improvement in physique as I passed on, I came to the farthest group just as they had begun to pass into the hall. These men, entering the gate labelled "Maximum Diet, 4000 Calories," were obviously the pick of the breed, middle-aged, powerful, Herculean,—and yet not exactly Herculean either, for many of them were overfull of waistline, men better fed than is absolutely essential to physical fitness. Evidently a different principle was at work here than the strict economy of food that required the periodic weighing of the professional classes.

Turning back I now encountered men coming out of the dining hall in which I had first witnessed the meal in progress. I wanted to ask questions and yet was a little afraid. But these big fellows were seemingly quite respectful; except when I started to enter the Free Speech Hall, they had humbly made way for me. Emboldened by their deference I now approached a man whom I had seen come out of a "3800 Calories" gate, and who had crossed the street and stood there picking his teeth with his finger nail.

He ceased this operation as I approached and was about to step aside. But I paused and smiled at him, much, I fear, as one smiles at a dog of unknown disposition, for I could hardly feel that this ungainly creature was exactly human. He smiled back and stood waiting.

"Perhaps, I stammered," you will tell me about your system of eating; it seems very interesting."

"I eat thirty-eight," he grinned, "pretty good, yes? I am twenty-five years old and not so tall either."

I eyed him up—my eyes came just to the top button of his jacket.

"I began thirty," continued the workman, "I came up one almost every year, one year I came up two at once. Pretty good, yes? One more to come."

"What then?" I asked.

The big fellow smiled with a childish pride, and doubling up his arm, as huge as an average man's thigh, he patted his biceps. "I get it all right. I pass examination, no flaws in me, never been to hospital, not one day. Yes, I get it."

"Get what?"

"Paternity," said the man in a lower voice, as he glanced about to see if any of his fellows was listening. "Paternity, you know? Women!"

I thought of many questions but feared to ask them. The worker waited for some men to pass, then he bent over me, grinning sardonically. "Did you see them? You have seen women, yes?"

"Yes," I ventured, "I have seen women."

"Pretty good, beautiful, yes?"

"Yes," I stammered, "they are very beautiful." But I was getting nervous and moved away. The workman, hesitating a little, then followed at my side.

"But tell me," I said, "about these calories. What did you do to get the big meals? Why do some get more to eat than others?"

"Better man," he replied without hesitation.

"But what makes a better man?"

"You don't know; of course, you are an intellectual and don't work. But we work hard. The harder we work the more we eat. I load aluminum pigs on the elevator. One pig is two calories, nineteen hundred pigs a day, pretty good, yes? All kind of work has its calories, so many for each thing to do.

"More work, more food it takes to do it. They say all is alike, that no one can get fat. But all work calories are not alike because some men get fatter than others. I don't get fat; my work is hard. I ought to get two and a half calories for each pig I load. Still I do not get thin, but I do not play hard in gymnasium, see? Those lathe men, they got it too easy and they play hard in gymnasium. I don't care if you do report. I got it mad at them; they got it too easy. One got paternity last year already, and he is not as good a man as I am. I could throw him over my shoulder in wrestling. Do you not think they get it too easy?"

"Do the men like this system," I asked; "the measuring of food by the amount of work one does? Do any of them talk about it and demand that all be fed alike?"

"The skinny minimum eaters do," said the workman with a sneer, "when we let them talk, which isn't often, but when they get a chance they talk Bellamism. But what if they do talk, it does them no good. We have a red flag, we have Imperial Socialism; we have the House of Hohenzollern. Well, then, I say, let them talk if they want to, every man must eat according to his work; that is socialism. We can't have Bellamism when we have socialism."

This speech, so much more informative and evidencing a knowledge I had not anticipated, quite disturbed me. "You talk about these things," I ventured, "in your Free Speech Halls?"

The hitherto pleasant face of the workingman altered to an ugly frown.

"No you don't," he growled, "you don't think because I talk to you, that you can go asking me what is not your right to know, even if you are an officer?"

I remained discreetly silent, but continued to walk at the side of the striding giant. Presently I asked:

"What do you do now, are you going to work?"

"No," he said, looking at me doubtfully, "that was dinner, not breakfast. I am going now to the picture hall."

"And then," I asked, "do you go to bed?"

"No," he said, "we then go to the gymnasium or the gaming tables. Six hours' work, six hours' sleep, and four hours for amusement."

"And what do you do," I asked, "the remainder of the day?"

He turned and stared at me. "That is all we get here, sixteen hours. This is the metal workers' level. Some levels get twenty hours. It depends on the work."

"But," I said, "a real day has twenty-four hours."

"I've heard," he said, "that it does on the upper levels."

"But," I protested, "I mean a real day—a day of the sun. Do you understand that?"

"Oh yes," he said, "we see the pictures of the Place in the Sun. That's a fine show."

"Oh," I said, "then you have pictures of the sun?"

"Of course," he replied, "the sun that shines upon the throne. We all see that."

At the time I could not comprehend this reference, but I made bold to ask if it were forbidden me to go to his picture hall.

"I can't make out," he said, "why you want to see, but I never heard of any order forbidding it.

"I go here," he remarked, as we came to a picture theatre.

I let my Herculean companion enter alone, but followed him shortly and found a seat in a secluded corner. No one disputed my presence.

The music that filled the hall from some hidden horn was loud and, in a rough way, joyous. The pictures—evidently carefully prepared for such an audience—were limited to the life that these men knew. The themes were chiefly of athletic contests, of boxing, wrestling and feats of strength. There were also pictures of working contests, always ending by the awarding of honours by some much bespangled official. But of love and romance, of intrigue and adventure, of pathos and mirth, these pictures were strangely devoid,— there was, in fact, no woman's likeness cast upon the screen and no pictures depicting emotion or sentiment.

As I watched the sterile flittings of the picture screen I decided, despite the glimmering of intelligence that my talking Hercules had shown in reference to socialism and Bellamism and the secrets of the Free Speech Halls, that these men were merely great stupid beasts of burden.

They worked, they fed, they drank, they played exuberantly in their gymnasiums and swimming pools, they played long and eagerly at games of chance. Beyond this their lives were essentially blank. Ambition and curiosity they had none beyond the narrow circle of their round of living. But for all that they were docile, contented and, within their limitations, not unhappy. To me they seemed more and more to be like well cared for domestic animals, and I found myself wondering, as I left the hall, why we of the outer world had not thought to produce pictures in similar vein to entertain our dogs and horses.

~5~

As I returned to my own quarters, I tried to recall the description I had read of the "Children of the Abyss," the dwellers in ancient city slums. There was a certain kinship, no doubt, between those former submerged workers in the democratic world and this labour breed of Berlin. Yet the enslaved and sweated workers of the old regime were always depicted as suffering from poverty, as undersized, ill-nourished and afflicted with disease. The reformers of that day were always talking of sanitary housing, scientific diet and physical efficiency. But here was a race of labourers whose physical welfare was as well taken care of as if they had been prize swine or oxen. There was a paleness of countenance among these labourers of Berlin that to me seemed suggestive of ill health, but I knew that was merely due to lack of sun and did not signify a lack of physical vitality. Mere sun-darkened skin does not mean physiological efficiency, else the negro were the most efficient of races. Men can live without sun, without rain, without contact with the soil, without nature's greenery and the brotherhood of fellow species in wild haunts. The whole climb of civilization had been away from these primitive things. It had merely been an artificial perfecting of the process of giving the living creature that which is needed for sustenance and propagation in the most concentrated and most economical form, the elimination of Nature's superfluities and wastes.

As I thought of these things it came over me that this unholy imprisonment of a race was but the logical culmination of mechanical and material civilization. This development among the Germans had been hastened by the necessities of war and siege, yet it was what the whole world had been driving toward since man first used a tool and built a hut. Our own freer civilization of the outer world had been achieved only by compromises, by a stubborn resistance against the forces to which we ascribed our progress. We were merely not so completely civilized, because we had never been wholly domesticated.

As I now record these thoughts on the true significance of the perfected civilization of the Germans I realize that I was even more right than I then knew, for the sunless city of Berlin is of a truth a civilization gone to seed, its people are a domesticated species, they are the logical outcome of science applied to human affairs, with them the prodigality and waste of Nature have been eliminated, they have stamped out contagious diseases of every kind, they have substituted for the laws of Nature the laws that man may pick by scientific theory and experiment from the multitude of possibilities. Yes, the Germans were civilized. And as I pondered these things I recalled those fairy tales that naturalists tell of the stagnant and fixed society of ants in their subterranean catacombs. These insect species credited for industry and intelligence, have in their lesser world reached a similar perfection of civilization. Ants have a royal house, they have a highly specialized and fixed system of caste, a completely socialized state—yes, a Utopia—even as Berlin was a Utopia, with the light of the sun and the light of the soul, the soul of the wild free man, forever shut out. Yes, I was walking in Utopia, a nightmare at the end of man's long dream—Utopia—Black Utopia—City of Endless Night—diabolically compounded of the three elements of civilization in which the Germans had always been supreme—imperialism, science and socialism.

THE BLIND SPOT

Austin Hall and Homer Eon Flint (1921)

FRIENDS

My name is Harry Wendel.

I am an attorney and until recently boasted of a splendid practice and an excellent prospect for the future. I am still a young man; I have had a good education and still have friends and admirers. Such being the case, you no doubt wonder why I give a past reference to my practice and what the future might have held for me. Listen:

I might as well start 'way back. I shall do it completely and go back to the fast-receding time of childhood.

There is a recollection of childish disaster. I had been making strenuous efforts to pull the tail out of the cat that I might use it for a feather duster. My desire was supreme logic. I could not understand objection; the cat resisted for certain utilitarian reasons of its own and my mother through humane sympathy. I had been scratched and spanked in addition: it was the first storm centre that I remember. I had been punished but not subdued. At the first opportunity, I stole out of the house and onto the lawn that stretched out to the pavement.

I remember the day. The sun was shining, the sky was clear, and everything was green with springtime. For a minute I stood still and blinked in the sunlight. It was beautiful and soft and balmy, the world at full exuberance; the buds upon the trees, the flowers, and the songbirds singing. I could not understand it. It was so beautiful and soft. My heart was still beating fiercely, still black with perversity and stricken rancour. The world had no right to be so. I hated with the full rush of childish anger.

And then I saw.

Across the street coming over to meet me was a child of my age. He was fat and chubby, a mass of yellow curls and laughter; when he walked he held his feet out at angles as is the manner of fat boys and his arms away from his body. I slid off the porch quietly. Here was something that could suffer for the cat and my mother. At my rush he stopped in wonder. I remember his smiling face and my anger. In an instant I had him by the hair and was biting with all the fury of vindictiveness.

At first he set up a great bawl for assistance. He could not understand; he screamed and held his hands aloft to keep them out of my reach. Then he tried to run away. But I had learned from the cat that had scratched me. I clung on, biting, tearing. The shrill of his scream was music: it was conflict, sweet and delicious; it was strife, swift as instinct.

At last I stopped him; he ceased trying to get away and began to struggle. It was better still; it was resistance. But he was stronger than I; though I was quicker he managed to get my by the shoulders, to force me back, and finally to upset me. Then in the stolid way, and after the manner of fat boys, he sat upon my chest. When our startled mothers came upon the scene they so found us—I upon my back, clinching my teeth and threatening all the dire fates of childhood, and he waiting either for assistance or until my ire should retire sufficiently to allow him to release me in safety.

"Who did it? Who started it?"

That I remember plainly.

"Hobart, did you do this?" The fat boy backed off quietly and clung to his mother; but he did not answer.

"Hobart, did you start this?"

Still no answer.

"Harry, this was you; you started it. Didn't you try to hurt Hobart?"

I nodded.

My mother took me by the hand and drew me away.

"He is a rascal, Mrs. Fenton, and has a temper like sin; but he will tell the truth, thank goodness."

I am telling this not for the mere relation, but by way of introduction. It was my first meeting with Hobart Fenton. It is necessary that you know us both and our characters. Our lives are so entwined and so related that without it you could not get the gist of the story. In the afternoon I came across the street to play with Hobart. He met me smiling. It was not in his healthy little soul to hold resentment. I was either all smiles or anger. I forgot as quickly as I battled. That night there were two happy youngsters tucked into the bed and covers.

So we grew up; one with the other. We played as children do and fought as boys have done from the beginning. I shall say right now that the fights were mostly my fault. I started them one and all; and if every battle had the same beginning it likewise had the same ending. The first fight was but the forerunner of all the others.

Please do not think hardly of Hobart. He is the kindest soul in the world; there never was a truer lad nor a kinder heart. He was strong, healthy, fat, and, like fat boys, forever laughing. He followed me into trouble and when I was retreating he valiantly defended the rear. Stronger, sturdier, and slower, he has been a sort of protector from the beginning. I have called him the Rear Guard; and he does not resent it.

I have always been in mischief, restless, and eager for anything that would bring quick action; and when I got into deep water Hobart would come along, pluck me out and pull me to shore and safety. Did you ever see a great mastiff and a fox terrier running together? It is a homely illustration; but an apt one.

We were boys together, with our delights and troubles, joys and sorrows. I thought so much of Hobart that I did not shirk stooping to help him take care of his baby sister. That is about the supreme sacrifice of a boy's devotion. In after years, of course, he has laughed at me and swears I did it on purpose. I do not know, but I am willing to admit that I think a whole lot of that sister.

Side by side we grew up and into manhood. We went to school and into college. Even as we were at odds in our physical builds and our dispositions, so were we in our studies. From the beginning Hobart has had a mania for screws, bolts, nuts, and pistons. He is practical; he likes mathematics; he can talk to you from the binomial theorem up into Calculus; he is never so happy as when the air is buzzing with a conversation charged with induction coils, alternating currents, or atomic energy. The whole swing and force of popular science is his kingdom. I will say for Hobart that he is just about in line to be king of it all. Today he is in South America, one of our greatest engineers. He is bringing the water down from the Andes; and it is just about like those strong shoulders and that good head to restore the land of the Incas.

About myself? I went into the law. I enjoy an atmosphere of strife and contention. I liked books and discussion and I thought that I would like the law. On the advice of my elders I entered law college, and in due time was admitted to practice. It was while studying to qualify that I first ran into philosophy. I was a lad to enjoy quick, pithy, epigrammatic statements. I have always favoured a man who hits from the shoulder. Professor Holcomb was a man of terse, heavy thinking; he spoke what he thought and he did not quibble. He favoured no one.

I must confess that the old white-haired professor left his stamp upon me. I loved him like all the rest; though I was not above playing a trick on the old fellow occasionally. Still he had a wit of his own and seldom came out second best, and when he lost out he could laugh like the next one. I was deeply impressed by him. As I took course after course under him I was convinced that for all of his dry philosophy the old fellow had a trick up his sleeve; he had a way of expounding that was rather startling; likewise, he had a scarcely concealed contempt for some of the demigods of our old philosophy.

What this trick was I could never uncover. I hung on and dug into great tomes of wisdom. I became interested and gradually took up with his speculation; for all my love of action I found that I had a strong subcurrent for the philosophical.

Now I roomed with Hobart. When I would come home with some dry tome and would lose myself in it by the hour he could not understand it. I was preparing for the law. He could see no advantage to be derived from this digging into speculation. He was practical and unless he could drive a nail into a thing or at least dig into its chemical elements it was hard to get him interested.

"Of what use is it, Harry? Why waste your brains? These old fogies have been pounding on the question for three thousand years. What have they got? You could read all their literature from the pyramids down to the present sky-scrapers and you wouldn't get enough practical wisdom to drive a dump-cart."

"That's just it," I answered. "I'm not hankering for a dump-cart. You have an idea that all the wisdom in the world is locked up in the concrete; unless a thing has wheels, pistons, some sort of combustion, or a chemical action you are not interested. What gives you the control over your machinery? Brains! But what makes the mind go?"

Hobart blinked. "Fine," he answered. "Go on."

"Well," I answered, "that's what I am after."

He laughed. "Great. Well, keep at it. It's your funeral, Harry. When you have found, it let me know and I'll beat you to the patent."

With that he turned to his desk and dug into one of his everlasting formulas. Just the same, next day when I entered Holcomb's lecture-room I was in for a surprise. My husky room-mate was in the seat beside me.

"What's the big idea?" I asked. "Big idea is right, Harry," he grinned. "Just thought I would beat you to it. Had a dickens of a time with Dan Clark, of the engineering department. Told him I wanted to study philosophy. The old boy put up a beautiful holler. Couldn't understand what an engineer would want with psychology or ethics. Neither could I until I got to thinking last night when I went to roost. Because a thing has never been done is no reason why it never will be; is it, Harry?"

"Certainly not. I don't know just what you are driving at. Perhaps you intend to take your notes over to the machine shop and hammer out the Secret of the Absolute."

He grinned.

"Pretty wise head at that, Harry. What did you call it? The Secret of the Absolute. Will remember that. I'm not much on phrases; but I'm sure the strong boy with the hammer. You don't object to my sitting here beside you; so that I, too, may drink in the little drops of wisdom?"

It was in this way that Hobart entered into the study of philosophy. When the class was over and we were going down the steps he patted me on the shoulder.

"That's not so bad, Harry. Not so bad. The old doctor is there; he's got them going. Likewise little Hobart has got a big idea."

Now it happened that this was just about six weeks before Dr. Holcomb announced his great lecture on the Blind Spot. It was not more than a week after registration. In the time ensuing Fenton became just as great an enthusiast as myself. His idea, of course, was chimerical and a blind; his main purpose was to get in with me where he could argue me out of my folly.

He wound up by being a convert of the professor.

Then came the great day. The night of the announcement we had a long discussion. It was a deep question. For all of my faith in the professor I was hardly prepared for a thing like this. Strange to say I was the sceptic; and stranger still, it was Hobart who took the side of the doctor.

"Why not?" he said. "It merely comes down to this: you grant that a thing is possible and then you deny the possibility of a proof—outside of your abstract. That's good paradox, Harry; but almighty poor logic. If it is so it certainly can be proven. There's not one reason in the world why we can't have something concrete. The professor is right. I am with him. He's the only professor in all the ages."

Well, it turned out as it did. It was a terrible blow to us all. Most of the world took it as a great murder or an equally great case of abduction. There were but few, even in the university, who embraced the side of the doctor. It was a case of villainy, of a couple of remarkably clever rogues and a trusting scholar.

But there was one whose faith was not diminished. He had been one of the last to come under the influence of the doctor. He was practical and concrete, and not at all attuned to philosophy; he had not the training for deep dry thinking. He would not recede one whit. One day I caught him sitting down with his head between his hands. I touched him on the shoulder.

"What's the deep study?" I asked him.

He looked up. By his eyes I could see that his thoughts had been far away.

"What's the deep study?" I repeated.

"I was just thinking, Harry; just thinking."

"What?"

"I was just thinking, Harry, that I would like to have about one hundred thousand dollars and about ten years' leisure."

"That's a nice thought," I answered; "I could think that myself. What would you do with it?"

"Do? Why, there is just one thing that I would do if I had that much money. I would solve the Blind Spot."

This happened years ago while we were still in college. Many things have occurred since then. I am writing this on the verge of disaster. How little do we know! What was the idea that buzzed in the head of Hobart Fenton? He is concrete, physical, fearless. He is in South America. I have cabled to him and expect him as fast as steam can bring him. The great idea and discovery of the professor is a fact, not fiction. What is it? That I cannot answer. I have found it and I am a witness to its potency.

Some law has been missed through the ages. It is inexorable and insidious; it is concrete. Out of the unknown comes terror. Through the love for the great professor I have pitted myself against it. From the beginning it has been almost hopeless. I remember that last digression in ethics. "The mystery of the occult may be solved. We are five-sensed. When we bring the thing down to the concrete we may understand."

Sometimes I wonder at the Rhamda. Is he a man or a phantom? Does he control the Blind Spot? Is he the substance and the proof that was promised by Dr. Holcomb? Through what process and what laws did the professor acquire even his partial control over the phenomena? Where did the Rhamda and his beautiful companion come from? Who are they? And lastly—what was the idea that buzzed in the head of Hobart Fenton?

When I look back now I wonder. I have never believed in fate. I do not believe in it now. Man is the master of his own destiny. We are cowards else. Whatever is to be known we should know it. One's duty is ever to one's fellows. Heads up and onward. I am not a brave man, perhaps, under close analysis; but once I have given my word I shall keep it. I have done my bit; my simple duty. Perhaps I have failed. In holding myself against the Blind Spot I have done no more than would have been done by a million others. I have only one regret. Failure is seldom rewarded. I had hoped that my life would be the last; I have a dim hope still. If I fail in the end, there must be still one more to follow.

Understand I do not expect to die. It is the unknown that I am afraid of. I who thought that we knew so much have found it still so little. There are so many laws in the weave of Cosmos that are still unguessed. What is this death that we are afraid of? What is life? Can we solve it? Is it permissible? What is the Blind Spot? If Hobart Fenton is right it has nothing to do with death. If so, what is it?

My pen is weak. I am weary. I am waiting for Hobart. Perhaps I shall not last. When he comes I want him to know my story. What he knows already will not hurt repeating. It is well that man shall have it; it may be that we shall both fail-there is no telling; but if we do the world can profit by our blunders and guide itself—perhaps to the mastery of the phenomenon that controls the Blind Spot.

I ask you to bear with me. If I make a few mistakes or I am a bit loose, remember the stress under which I am writing. I shall try to be plain so that all may follow.

CHICK WATSON

Now to go back.

In due time we were both of us graduated from college. I went into the law and Hobart into engineering. We were both successful. There was not a thing to foreshadow that either of us was to be jerked from his profession. There was no adventure, but lots of work and reward in proportion.

Perhaps I was a bit more fortunate. I was in love and Hobart was still a confirmed bachelor. It was a subject over which he was never done joking. It was not my fault. I was innocent. If the blame ran anywhere it would have to be placed upon that baby sister of his.

It happened as it happened since God first made the maiden. One autumn Hobart and I started off for college. We left Charlotte at the gate a girl of fifteen years and ten times as many angles. I pulled one of her pigtails, kissed her, and told her I wanted her to get pretty. When we came home next summer I went over to pull the other pigtail. I did not pull it. I was met by the fairest young woman I had ever looked on. And I could not kiss her. Seriously, was I to blame?

Now to the incident.

It was a night in September. Hobart had completed his affairs and had booked passage to South America. He was to sail next morning. We had dinner that day with his family, and then came up to San Francisco for a last and farewell bachelor night. We could take in the opera together, have supper at our favourite cafe, and then turn in. It was a long hark back to our childhood; but for all that we were still boys together.

I remember that night. It was our favourite opera—"Faust." It was the one piece that we could agree on. Looking back since, I have wondered at the coincidence. The old myth of age to youth and the subcurrent of sin with its stalking, laughing, subtle Mephistopheles. It is strange that we should have gone to this one opera on this one evening. I recall our coming out of the theatre; our minds thrilling to the music and the subtle weirdness of the theme.

A fog had fallen—one of those thick, heavy, grey mists that sometimes come upon us in September. Into its sombre depths the crowd disappeared like shadows. The lights upon the streets blurred yellow. At the cold sheer contact we hesitated upon the pavement.

I had on a light overcoat. Hobart, bound for the tropics, had no such protection. It was cold and miserable, a chill wind stirring from the north was unusually cutting. Hobart raised his collar and dug his hands into his pockets.

"Brr," he muttered; "brr, some coffee or some wine. Something."

The sidewalks were wet and slippery, the mists settling under the lights had the effect of drizzle. I touched Hobart's arm and we started across the street.

"Brr is right," I answered, "and some wine. Notice the shadows, like ghosts."

We were half across the street before he answered; then he stopped.

"Ghosts! Did you say ghosts, Harry?" I noted a strange inflection in his voice. He stood still and peered into the fog bank. His stop was sudden and suggestive. Just then a passing taxicab almost caught us and we were compelled to dodge quickly. Hobart ducked out of the way and I side-stepped in another direction. We came up on the sidewalk. Again he peered into the shadow.

"Confound that cab," he was saying, "now we have gone and missed him."

He took off his hat and then put it back on his head. His favourite trick when bewildered. I looked up and down the street.

"Didn't you see him? Harry! Didn't you see him? It was Rhamda Avec!"

I had seen no one; that is to notice; I did not know the Rhamda. Neither did he.

"The Rhamda? You don't know him."

Hobart was puzzled.

"No," he said; "I do not; but it was he, just as sure as I am a fat man."

I whistled. I recalled the tale that was now a legend. The man had an affinity for the fog mist. To come out of "Faust" and to run into the Rhamda! What was the connection? For a moment we both stood still and waited.

"I wonder—" said Hobart. "I was just thinking about that fellow tonight. Strange! Well, let's get something hot—some coffee."

But it had given us something for discussion. Certainly it was unusual. During the past few days I had been thinking of Dr. Holcomb; and for the last few hours the tale had clung with reiterating persistence. Perhaps it was the weirdness and the tremulous intoxication of the music. I was one of the vast majority who disbelieved it. Was it possible that it was, after all, other than the film of fancy? There are times when we are receptive; at that moment I could have believed it.

We entered the cafe and chose a table slightly to the rear. It was a contrast to the cold outside; the lights so bright, the glasses clinking, laughter and music. A few young people were dancing. I sat down; in a moment the lightness and jollity had stirred my blood. Hobart took a chair opposite. The place was full of beauty. In the back of my mind blurred the image of Rhamda. I had never seen him; but I had read the description. I wondered absently at the persistence.

I have said that I do not believe in fate. I repeat it. Man should control his own destiny. A great man does. Perhaps that is it. I am not great. Certainly it was circumstance.

In the back part of the room at one of the tables was a young man sitting alone. Something caught my attention. Perhaps it was his listlessness or the dreamy unconcern with which he watched the dancers; or it may have been the utter forlornness of his expression. I noted his unusual pallor and his cast of dissipation, also the continual working of his long, lean fingers. There are certain set fixtures in the night life of any city. But this was not one. He was not an habitue. There was a certain greatness to his loneliness and his isolation. I wondered.

Just then he looked up. By a mere coincidence our eyes met. He smiled, a weak smile and a forlorn one, and it seemed to me rather pitiful. Then as suddenly his glance wandered to the door behind me. Perhaps there was something in my expression that caught Hobart's attention. He turned about.

"Say, Harry, who is that fellow? I know that face, I'm certain."

"Come to think I have seen him myself. I wonder—"

The young man looked up again. The same weary smile. He nodded. And again he glanced over my shoulder toward the door. His face suddenly hardened.

"He knows us at any rate," I ventured.

Now Hobart was sitting with his face toward the entrance. He could see anyone coming or going. Following the young man's glance he looked over my shoulder. He suddenly reached over and took me by the forearm.

"Don't look round," he warned; "take it easy. As I said—on my honour as a fat man."

The very words foretold. I could not but risk a glance. Across the room a man was coming down the aisle—a tall man, dark, and of a very decided manner. I had read his description many times; I had seen his likeness drawn by certain sketch artists of the city. They did not do him justice. He had a wonderful way and presence—you might say, magnetism. I noticed the furtive wondering glances that were cast, especially by the women. He was a handsome man beyond denying, about the handsomest I had ever seen. The same elusiveness.

At first I would have sworn him to be near sixty; the next minute I was just as certain of his youth. There was something about him that could not be put to paper, be it strength, force or vitality; he was subtle. His step was prim and distinctive, light as shadow, in one hand he carried the red case that was so often mentioned. I breathed an exclamation.

Hobart nodded.

"Am I a fat man? The famous Rhamda! What say! Ah, ha! He has business with our wan friend yonder. See!"

And it was so. He took a chair opposite the wan one. The young man straightened. His face was even more familiar, but I could not place him. His lips were set; in their grim line—determination; whatever his exhaustion there was still a will. Somehow one had a respect for this weak one; he was not a mere weakling. Yet I was not so sure that he was not afraid of the Rhamda. He spoke to the waiter. The Rhamda began talking. I noted the poise in his manner; it was not evil, rather was it calm—and calculating. He made an indication. The young man drew back. He smiled; it was feeble and weary, but for all of that disdainful. Though one had a pity for his forlornness, there was still an admiration. The waiter brought glasses.

The young man swallowed his drink at a gulp, the other picked his up and sipped it. Again he made the indication. The youth dropped his hand upon the table, a pale blue light followed the movement of his fingers. The older man pointed. So that was their contention? A jewel? After all our phantom was material enough to desire possession; his solicitude was calmness, but for all that aggression. I could sense a battle, but the young man turned the jewel to the palm side of his fingers; he shook his head.

The Rhamda drew up. For a moment he waited. Was it for surrender? Once he started to speak, but was cut short by the other. For all of his weakness there was spirit to the young man. He even laughed. The Rhamda drew out a watch. He held up two fingers. I heard Hobart mumble.

"'Two minutes. Well, I'm betting on the young one. Too much soul. He's not dead; just weary.'"

He was right. At exactly one hundred and twenty seconds the Rhamda closed his watch. He spoke something. Again the young man laughed. He lit a cigarette; from the flicker and jerk of the flame he was trembling. But he was still emphatic. The other rose from the table, walked down the aisle and out of the building. The youth spread out both arms and dropped his head upon the table.

It was a little drama enacted almost in silence. Hobart and I exchanged glances. The mere glimpse of the Rhamda had brought us both back to the Blind Spot. Was there any connection? Who was the young man with the life sapped out? I had a recollection of a face strangely familiar. Hobart interrupted my thoughts.

"I'd give just about one leg for the gist of that conversation. That was the Rhamda; but who is the other ghost?"

"Do you think it has to do with the Blind Spot?"

"I don't think," averred Hobart. "I know. Wonder what's the time." He glanced at his watch. "Eleven thirty."

Just here the young man at the table raised up his head. The cigarette was still between his fingers; he puffed lamely for a minute, taking a dull note of his surroundings. In the well of gaiety and laughter coming from all parts of the room his actions were out of place. He seemed dazed; unable to pull himself together. Suddenly he looked at us. He started.

"He certainly knows us," I said. "I wonder—by George, he's coming over."

Even his step was feeble. There was exertion about every move of his body, the wanness and effort of vanished vitality; he balanced himself carefully. Slowly, slowly, line by line his features became familiar, the underlines of another, the ghost of one departed. At first I could not place him. He held himself up for breath. Who was he? Then it suddenly came to me—back to the old days at college—an athlete, one of the best of fellows, one of the sturdiest of men! He had come to this!

Hobart was before me.

"By all the things that are holy!" he exclaimed. "Chick Watson! Here, have a seat. In the name of Heavens, Chick! What on earth—"

The other dropped feebly into the chair. The body that had once been so powerful was a skeleton. His coat was a disguise of padding.

"Hello, Hobart; hello, Harry," he spoke in a whisper. "Not much like the old Chick, am I? First thing, I'll take some brandy."

It was almost tragic. I glanced at Hobart and nodded to the waiter. Could it be Chick Watson? I had seen him a year before, hale, healthy, prosperous. And here he was—a wreck!

"No," he muttered, "I'm not sick—not sick. Lord, boys, it's good to meet you. I just thought I would come out for this one last night, hear some music, see a pretty face, perhaps meet a friend. But I am afraid—" He dropped off like one suddenly drifting into slumber.

"Hustle that waiter," I said to Hobart. "Hurry that brandy."

The stimulant seemed to revive him. He lifted up suddenly. There was fear in his eyes; then on seeing himself among friends—relief. He turned to me.

"Think I'm sick, don't you?" he asked.

"You certainly are," I answered.

"Well, I'm not."

For a moment silence. I glanced at Hobart. Hobart nodded.

"You're just about in line for a doctor, Chick, old boy," I said. "I'm going to see that you have one. Bed for you, and the care of mother—"

He started; he seemed to jerk himself together.

"That's it, Harry; that's what I wanted. It's so hard for me to think. Mother, mother! That's why I came downtown. I wanted a friend. I have something for you to give to mother."

"Rats," I said. "I'll take you to her. What are you talking about?"

But he shook his head.

"I wish that you were telling the truth, Harry. But it's no use—not after tonight. All the doctors in the world could not save me. I'm not sick, boys, far from it."

Hobart spoke up.

"What is it, Chick? I have a suspicion. Am I right?"

Chick looked up; he closed his eyes.

"All right, Hobart, what's your suspicion?"

Fenton leaned over. It seemed to me that he was peering into the other's soul. He touched his forearm.

"Chick, old boy, I think I know. But tell me. Am I right? It's the Blind Spot."

At the words Watson opened his eyes; they were full of hope and wonder, for a moment, and then, as suddenly of a great despair. His body went to a heap. His voice was feeble.

"Yes," he answered, "I am dying—of the Blind Spot"

THE RING

It was a terrible thing; death stalking out of the Blind Spot. We had almost forgotten. It had been a story hitherto—a wonderful one to be sure, and one to arouse conjecture. I had never thought that we were to be brought to its shivering contact. It was out of the occult; it had been so pronounced by the professor; a great secret of life holding out a guerdon of death to its votaries. Witness Chick Watson, the type of healthy, fighting manhood—come to this. He opened his eyes feebly; one could see the light; the old spirit was there— fighting for life. What was this struggle of soul and flesh? Why had the soul hung on? He made another effort.

"More drink," he asked; "more drink. Anything to hold me together. I must tell you. You must take my place and—and—fight the Blind Spot! Promise that—"

"Order the drinks," I told Hobart. "I see Dr. Hansen over there. Even if we cannot save him we must hold him until we get his story."

I went and fetched Hansen over.

"A strange case," he murmured. "Pulse normal; not a trace of fever. Not sick, you say—" Hobart pointed to his head. "Ah, I see! I would suggest home and a bed."

Just here Watson opened his eyes again. They rested first upon the doctor, then upon myself, and finally upon the brandy. He took it up and drank it with eagerness. It was his third one; it gave him a bit more life.

"Didn't I tell you, boys, that there is not a doctor on earth that can save me? Excuse me, doc. I am not sick. I told them. I am far past physic; I have gone beyond medicine. All I ask is stimulant and life enough to tell my story."

"My boy," asked the doctor kindly, "what ails you?"

Watson smiled. He touched himself on the forehead.

"Up here, doc. There are things in the world with which we may not tamper. I tried it. Somebody had to do it and somebody has to do it yet. You remember Dr. Holcomb; he was a great man; he was after the secret of life. He began it."

Dr. Hansen started.

"Lord!" he exclaimed, looking at us all; "you don't mean this man is mixed up in the Blind Spot?"

We nodded. Watson smiled; again he dropped back into inertia; the speech he had made was his longest yet; the brandy was coming into effect.

"Give him brandy," the doctor said; "it's as good as anything. It will hold him together and give him life for a while. Here." He reached into his pocket and flicked something into the glass. "That will help him. Gentlemen, do you know what it means? I had always thought! I knew Dr. Holcomb! Crossing over the border! It may not be done! The secret of life is impossible. Yet—"

Watson opened his eyes again; his spirit seemed suddenly to flicker into defiance.

"Who said it was impossible? Who said it? Gentlemen, it IS possible. Dr. Holcomb—pardon me. I do not wish to appear a sot; but this brandy is about the only thing to hold me together. I have only a few hours left."

He took the glass, and at one gulp downed the contents. I do not know what the doctor had dropped into it. Chick revived suddenly, and a strange light blazed up in his eyes, like life rekindled.

"Ah, now I am better. So?"

He turned to us all; then to the doctor.

"So you say the secret of life is impossible?"

Chick smiled wanly. "May I ask you: what it is that has just flared up within me? I am weak, anaemic, fallen to pieces; my muscles have lost the power to function, my blood runs cold, I have been more than two feet over the border. And yet—a few drinks of brandy, of stimulants, and you have drawn me back, my heart beats strongly, for an hour. By means of drugs you have infused a new life—which of course is the old—and driven the material components of my body into correlation. You are successful for a time; so long as nature is with you; but all the while you are held aghast by the knowledge that the least flaw, the least disarrangement, and you are beaten.

"It is your business to hold this life or what you may. When it has gone your structures, your anatomy, your wonderful human machine is worthless. Where has it come from? Where has it gone? I have drunk four glasses of brandy; I have a lease of four short hours. Ordinarily it would bring reaction; it is poison, to be sure; but it is driving back my spirit, giving me life and strength enough to tell my story—in the morning I shall be no more. By sequence I am a dead man already. Four glasses of brandy; they are speaking. Whence comes this affinity of substance and of shadow?"

We all of us listened, the doctor most of all. "Go on," he said.

"Can't you see?" repeated Watson. "There is affinity between substance and shadow; and therefore your spirit or shadow or what you will is concrete, is in itself a substance. It is material just as much as you are. Because you do not see it is no proof that it is not substance. That pot palm yonder does not see you; it is not blessed with eyes."

The doctor looked at Watson; he spoke gently.

"This is very old stuff, my boy, out of your abstract philosophy. No man knows the secret of life. Not even yourself."

The light in Watson's eyes grew brighter, he straightened; he began slipping the ring from his finger.

"No," he answered. "I don't. I have tried and it was like playing with lightning. I sought for life and it is giving me death. But there is one man living who has found it."

"And this man?"

"Is Dr. Holcomb!"

We all of us started. We had every one given the doctor up as dead. The very presence of Watson was tragedy. We did not doubt that he had been through some terrible experience. There are things in the world that may not be unriddled. Some power, some sinister thing was reaching for his vitality. What did he know about the professor? Dr. Holcomb had been a long time dead.

"Gentlemen. You must hear my story; I haven't long to tell it. However, before I start here is a proof for a beginning."

He tossed the ring upon the table.

It was Hobart who picked it up. A beautiful stone, like a sapphire; blue but uncut and of a strange pellucid transparency—a jewel undoubtedly; but of a kind we have never seen. We all of us examined it, and were all, I am afraid, a bit disappointed. It was a stone and nothing else.

Watson watched us. The waiter had brought more brandy, and Watson was sipping it, not because he liked it, he said, but just to keep himself at the proper lift.

"You don't understand it, eh? You see nothing? Hobart, have you a match? There, that's it; now give me the ring. See—" He struck the match and held the flame against the jewel. "Gentlemen, there is no need for me to speak. The stone will give you a volume. It's not trickery, I assure you, but fact. There, now, perfect. Doctor, you are the sceptic. Take a look at the stone."

The doctor picked it up casually and held it up before his eyes. At first he frowned; then came a look of incredulity; his chin dropped and he rose in his chair.

"My God," he exclaimed, "the man's living! It—he—"

But Hobart and I had crowded over. The doctor held the ring so we could see it. Inside the stone was Dr. Holcomb!

It was a strenuous moment, and the most incredible. We all of us knew the doctor. It was not a photograph, nor a likeness; but the man himself. It was beyond all reason that he could be in the jewel; indeed there was only the head visible; one could catch the expression of life, the movements of the eyelids. Yet how could it be? What was it? It was Hobart who spoke first.

"Chick," he asked, "what's the meaning? Were it not for my own eyes I would call it impossible. It's absurd on the face. The doctor! Yet I can see him—living. Where is he?"

Chick nodded.

"That's the whole question. Where is he? I know and yet I know nothing. You are now looking into the Blind Spot. The doctor sought the secret of life—and found it. He was trapped by his own wisdom!"

TANKS

Murray Leinster (1923)

Two miles of American front had gone dead. And on two lone infantrymen, lost in the menace of the fog-gas and the tanks, depended the outcome of the war of 1932.

THE PERSISTENT, OILY smell of fog-gas was everywhere, even in the little pill-box. Outside, all the world was blotted out by the thick gray mist that went rolling slowly across country with the breeze. The noises that came through it were curiously muted—fog-gas mutes all noises somewhat—but somewhere to the right artillery was pounding something with H E shell, and there were those little spitting under-current explosions that told of tanks in action. To the right there was a distant rolling of machine-gun fire. In between was an utter, solemn silence.

Sergeant Coffee, disreputable to look at and disrespectful of mien, was sprawling over one of the gunners' seats and talking into a field telephone while mud dripped from him. Corporal Wallis, equally muddy and still more disreputable, was painstakingly manufacturing one complete cigarette from the pinched-out butts of four others. Both were rifle-infantry. Neither had any right or reason to be occupying a definitely machine-gun-section post. The fact that the machine-gun crew was all dead did not seem to make much difference to sector H.Q. at the other end of the telephone wire, judging from the questions that were being asked.

"I tell you," drawled Sergeant Coffee, "they're dead.... Yeah, all dead. Just as dead as when I told you the firs' time, maybe even deader.... Gas, o'course. I don't know what kind.... Yeh. They got their masks on."

He waited, looking speculatively at the cigarette Corporal Wallis had in manufacture. It began to look imposing. Corporal Wallis regarded it affectionately. Sergeant Coffee put his hand over the mouthpiece, and looked intently at his companion.

"Gimme a drag o' that, Pete," he suggested. "I'll slip y' some butts in a minute."

Corporal Wallis nodded, and proceeded to light the cigarette with infinite artistry. He puffed delicately upon it, inhaled it with the care a man learns when he has just so much tobacco and never expects to get any more, and reluctantly handed it to Sergeant Coffee.

Sergeant Coffee emptied his lungs in a sigh of anticipation. He put the cigarette to his lips. It burned brightly as he drew upon it. Its tip became brighter and brighter until it was white-hot, and the paper crackled as the line of fire crept up the tube.

"Hey!" said Corporal Wallis in alarm.

Sergeant Coffee waved him aside, and his chest expanded to the fullest limit of his blouse. When his lungs could hold no more he ceased to draw, grandly returned about one-fourth of the cigarette to Corporal Wallis, and blew out a cloud of smoke in small driblets until he had to gasp for breath.

"When y' ain't got much time," said Sergeant Coffee amiably, "that's a quick smoke."

Corporal Wallis regarded the ruins of his cigarette with a woeful air.

"Hell!" said Corporal Wallis gloomily. But he smoked what was left.

"Yeah," said Sergeant Coffee suddenly, into the field telephone, "I'm still here, an' they're still dead.... Listen, Mr. Officer, I got me a black eye an' numerous contusions. Also my gas-mask is busted. I called y'up to do y' a favor. I aim to head for distant parts.... Hell's bells! Ain't there anybody else in the army—" He stopped, and resentment died out in wide-eyed amazement. "Yeh.... Yeh.... Yeh.... I gotcha, Loot. A'right, I'll see what I c'n do. Yeh.... Wish y'd see my insurance gets paid. Yeh."

He hung up, gloomily, and turned to Corporal Wallis.

"We' got to be heroes," he announced bitterly. "Sit out here in th' stinkin' fog an' wait for a tank t' come along an' wipe us out. We' the only listenin' post in two miles of front. That new gas o' theirs wiped out all the rest without report."

He surveyed the crumpled figures, which had been the original occupants of the pill-box. They wore the same uniform as himself and when he took the gas-mask off of one of them the man's face was strangely peaceful.

"Hell of a war," said Sergeant Coffee bitterly. "Here our gang gets wiped out by a helicopter. I ain't seen sunlight in a week, an' I got just four butts left. Lucky I started savin' 'em." He rummaged shrewdly. "This guy's got half a sack o' makin's. Say, that was Loot'n't Madison on the line, then. Transferred from our gang a coupla months back. They cut him in the line to listen in on me an' make sure I was who I said I was. He recognized my voice."

Corporal Wallis, after smoking to the last and ultimate puff, pinched out his cigarette and put the fragments of a butt back in his pocket.

"What we got to do?" he asked, watching as Sergeant Coffee divided the treasure-trove into two scrupulously exact portions.

"Nothin'," said Coffee bitterly, "except find out how this gang got wiped out, an' a few little things like that. Half th' front line is in th' air, the planes can't see anything, o'course, an' nobody dares cut th' fog-gas to look. He didn't say much, but he said for Gawd's sake find out somethin'."

Corporal Wallis gloated over one-fourth of a sack of tobacco and stowed it away.

"Th' infantry always gets th' dirty end of the stick," he said gloomily. "I'm goin' to roll me a whole one, pre-war, an' smoke it, presently."

"Hell yes," said Coffee. He examined his gas-mask from force of habit before stepping out into the fog once more, then contemptuously threw it aside. "Gas-masks, hell! Ain't worth havin'. Come on."

Corporal Wallis followed as he emerged from the little round cone of the pill-box.

The gray mist that was fog-gas hung over everything. There was a definite breeze blowing, but the mist was so dense that it did not seem to move. It was far enough from the fog-flares for the last least trace of striation to have vanished. Fifteen miles to the north the fog-flares were placed, ranged by hundreds and by thousands, burning one after another as the fog service set them off, and sending out their incredible masses of thick gray vapor in long threads that spread out before the wind, coalesced, and made a smoke-screen to which the puny efforts of the last war—the war that was to make the world safe for democracy—were as nothing.

Here, fifteen miles down wind from the flares, it was possible to see clearly in a circle approximately five feet in diameter. At the edge of that circle out-lines began to blur. At ten feet all shapes were the faintest of bulks, the dim-mest of outlines. At fifteen feet all was invisible, hidden behind a screen of mist.

"Cast around," said Coffee gloomily. "Maybe we'll find a shell, or tracks of a tank or somethin' that chucked the gas here."

It was rather ludicrous to go searching for anything in that mass of vapor. At three yards distance they could make each other out as dim outlines, no more. But it did not even occur to them to deplore the mist. The war which had already been christened, by the politicians at home, the last war, was always fought in a mist. Infantry could not stand against tanks, tanks could not live under aircraft-directed artillery fire—not when forty guns fired sal-vos for the aircraft to spot—and neither artillery nor aircraft could take any advantage of a victory which either, under special conditions, might win. The general staffs of both the United States and the prominent nation—let us say the Yellow Empire—at war with it had come to a single conclusion. Tanks or infantry were needed for the use of victories. Infantry could be destroyed by tanks. But tanks could be hidden from aerial spotters by smoke-screens.

The result was fog-gas, which was being used by both sides in the most modern fashion when, their own unit wiped out and themselves wandering aimlessly in the general direction of the American rear, Sergeant Coffee and Corporal Wallis stumbled upon an American pill-box with its small garrison lying dead. For forty miles in one direction and perhaps thirty in the other, the vapor lay upon the earth. It was being blown by the wind, of course, but it was sufficiently heavier than air to cling to the ground level, and the industries of two nations were straining every nerve to supply the demands of their respective armies for its material.

The fog-bank was nowhere less than a hundred feet thick—a cloud of impalpable particles impenetrable to any eye or any camera, however shrewdly filtered. And under that mattress of pale opacity the tanks crawled heavily. They lurched and rumbled upon their deadly errands, uncouth and barbarous, listening for each other by a myriad of devices, locked in desperate, short-range conflict when they came upon each other, and emitting clouds of deadly vapor, against which gas-masks were no protection, when they came upon opposing infantry.

The infantrymen, though, were few. Their principal purpose was the reporting of the approach or passage of tanks, and trenches were of no service to them. They occupied unarmed little listening-posts with field telephones, small wireless or ground buzzer sets for reporting the enemy before he overwhelmed them. They held small pill-boxes, fitted with anti-tank guns which sometimes—if rarely—managed to get home a shell, aimed largely by sound, before the tank rolled over gun and gunners alike.

And now Sergeant Coffee and Corporal Wallis groped about in that blinding mist. There had been two systems of listening-posts hidden in it, each of admittedly little fighting value, but each one deep and composed of an infinity of little pin-point posts where two or three men were stationed. The American posts, by their reports, had assured the command that all enemy tanks were on the other side of a certain definite line. Their own tanks, receiving recognition signals, passed and repassed among them, prowling in quest of invaders. The enemy tanks crawled upon the same grisly patrol on their own side.

But two miles of the American front had suddenly gone silent. A hundred telephones had ceased to make reports along the line nearest the enemy. As Coffee and Wallis stumbled about the little pill-box, looking for some inkling of the way in which the original occupants of the small strong-point had been wiped out, the second line of observation-posts began to go dead.

Now one, now another abruptly ceased to communicate. Half a dozen were in actual conversation with their sector headquarters, and broke off between words. The wires remained intact. But in fifteen nerve-racking minutes a second hundred posts ceased to make reports and ceased to answer the inquiry-signal. G.H.Q. was demanding explanations in crisp accents that told the matter was being taken very seriously indeed. And then, as the officer in command of the second-line sector headquarters was explaining frenziedly that he was doing all any man could do, he stopped short between two words and thereafter he, also, ceased to communicate.

Front-line sector headquarters seemed inexplicably to have escaped whatever fate had overtaken all its posts, but it could only report that they had apparently gone out of existence without warning. American tanks, prowling in the area that had gone dead, announced that no enemy tanks had been seen. G-81, stumbling on a pill-box no more than ten minutes after it had gone silent, offered to investigate. A member of her crew, in a gas-mask, stepped out of the port doorway. Immediately thereafter G-81's wireless reports stopped coming in.

The situation was clearly shown in the huge tank that had been built to serve as G.H.Q. That tank was seventy feet long, and lay hidden in the mist with a brood of other, smaller tanks clustered near it, from each of which a cable ran to the telephones and instruments of the greater monster. Farther off in the fog, of course, were other tanks, hundreds of them, fighting machines all, silent and motionless now, but infinitely ready to protect the brain of the army.

The G.H.Q. maneuver-board showed the battle as no single observer could ever have seen it. A map lay spread out on a monster board, under a pitiless white light. It was a map of the whole battlefield. Tiny sparks crawled here and there under the map, and there were hundreds of little pins with different-colored heads to mark the position of this thing and that. The crawling sparks were the reported positions of American tanks, made visible as positions of moving trains had been made visible for years on the electric charts of railroads in dispatcher's offices. Where the tiny bulbs glowed under the map, there a tank crawled under the fog. As the tank moved, the first bulb went out and another flashed into light.

The general watched broodingly as the crawling sparks moved from this place to that place, as varicolored lights flashed up and vanished, as a steady hand reached down to shift tiny pins and place new ones. The general moved rarely, and spoke hardly at all. His whole air was that of a man absorbed in a game of chess—a game on which the fate of a nation depended.

He was thus absorbed. The great board, illuminated from above by the glaring bulb, and speckled with little white sparks from below by the tiny bulbs beneath, showed the situation clearly at every instant. The crawling white sparks were his own tanks, each in its present position. Flashing blue sparks noted the last report of enemy tanks. Two staff officers stood behind the general, and each spoke from time to time into a strapped-on telephone transmitter. They were giving routine orders, heading the nearest American patrol-tanks toward the location of the latest reported enemies.

The general reached out his hand suddenly and marked off an area with his fingers. They were long fingers, and slender ones: an artist's fingers.

"Our outposts are dead in this space," he observed meditatively. The use of the word "outposts" dated him many years back as a soldier, back to the old days of open warfare, which had only now come about again. "Penetration of two miles—"

"Tank, sir," said the man of the steady fingers, putting a black pin in position within that area, "let a man out in a gas-mask to examine a pill-box. The tank does not report or reply, sir."

"Gas," said the general, noting the spot. "Their new gas, of course. It must go through masks or sag-paste, or both."

He looked up to one of a row of officers seated opposite him, each man with headphones strapped to his ears and a transmitter before his lips, and each man with a map-pad on his knees, on which from time to time he made notations and shifted pins absorbedly.

"Captain Harvey," said the general, "you are sure that dead spot has not been bombarded with gas-shells?"

"Yes, General. There has been no artillery fire heavy enough to put more than a fraction of those posts out of action, and all that fire, sir, has been accounted for elsewhere."

The officer looked up, saw the general's eyes shift, and bent to his map again, on which he was marking areas from which spotting aircraft reported flashes as of heavy guns beneath the mist.

"Their aircraft have not been dropping bombs, positively?"

A second officer glanced up from his own map.

"Our planes cover all that space, sir, and have for some time."

"They either have a noiseless tank," observed the general meditatively, "or...."

The steady fingers placed a red pin at a certain spot.

"One observation-post, sir, has reopened communication. Two infantry-men, separated from their command, came upon it and found the machine-gun crew dead, with gas-masks adjusted. No tanks or tracks. They are identified, sir, and are now looking for tank tracks or shells."

The general nodded emotionlessly.

"Let me know immediately."

He fell back to the ceaseless study of the board with its crawling sparks and sudden flashes of light. Over at the left, there were four white sparks crawl-ing toward a spot where a blue flash had showed a little while since. A red light glowed suddenly where one of the white sparks crawled. One of the two officers behind the general spoke crisply. Instantly, it seemed, the other three white sparks changed their direction of movement. They swung toward the red flash—the point where a wireless from the tank represented by the first white flash had reported, contact with the enemy.

"Enemy tank destroyed here, sir," said the voice above the steady fingers.

"Wiped out three of our observation posts," murmured the general, "His side knows it. That's an opportunity. Have those posts reoccupied."

"Orders given, sir," said a staff officer from behind. "No reports as yet."

The general's eyes went back to the space two miles wide and two miles deep in which there was only a single observation-post functioning, and that in charge of two strayed infantrymen. The battle in the fog was in a forma-tive stage, now, and the general himself had to watch the whole, because it was by small and trivial indications that the enemy's plans would be dis-closed. The dead area was no triviality, however. Half a dozen tanks were crawling through it, reporting monotonously that no sign of the enemy could be found. One of the little sparks representing those tanks abruptly went out.

"Tank here, sir, no longer reports."

The general watched with lack-luster eyes, his mind withdrawn in thought.

"Send four helicopters," he said slowly, "to sweep that space. We'll see what the enemy does."

One of the seated officers opposite him spoke swiftly. Far away a roaring set up and was stilled. The helicopters were taking off.

They would rush across the blanket of fog, their vertical propellers sending blasts of air straight downward. For most of their sweep they would keep a good height, but above the questionable ground they would swoop down to barely above the fog-blanket. There their monstrous screws would blow holes in the fog until the ground below was visible. If any tanks crawled there, in the spaces the helicopters swept clear, they would be visible at once and would be shelled by batteries miles away, batteries invisible under the artificial cloud-bank.

No other noises came through the walls of the monster tank. There was a faint, monotonous murmur of the electric generator. There were the quiet, crisp orders of the officers behind the general, giving the routine commands that kept the fighting a stalemate.

The aircraft officer lifted his head, pressing his headphones tightly against his ears, as if to hear mores clearly.

"The enemy, sir, has sent sixty fighting machines to attack our helicopters. We sent forty single-seaters as escort."

"Let them fight enough," said the general absently, "to cause the enemy to think us desperate for information. Then draw them off."

There was silence again. The steady fingers put pins here and there. An enemy tank destroyed here. An American tank encountered an enemy and ceased to report further. The enemy sent four helicopters in a wide sweep behind the American lines, escorted by fifty fighting planes. They uncovered a squadron of four tanks, which scattered like insects disturbed by the over-turning of a stone. Instantly after their disclosure a hundred and fifty guns, four miles away, were pouring shells about the place where they had been seen. Two of the tanks ceased to report.

The general's attention was called to a telephone instrument with its call-light glowing.

"Ah," said the general absently. "They want publicity matter."

The telephone was connected to the rear, and from there to the Capital. A much-worried cabinet waited for news, and arrangements were made and had been used, to broadcast suitably arranged reports from the front, the voice of the commander-in-chief in the field going to every workshop, every gathering-place, and even being bellowed by loud-speakers in the city streets.

The general took the phone. The President of the United States was at the other end of the wire, this time.

"General?"

"Still in a preliminary stage, sir," said the general, without haste. "The enemy is preparing a break-through effort, possibly aimed at our machine-shops and supplies. Of course, if he gets them we will have to retreat. An hour ago he paralyzed our radios, not being aware, I suppose, of our tuned earth-induction wireless sets. I daresay he is puzzled that our communications have not fallen to pieces."

"But what are our chances?" The voice of the President was steady, but it was strained.

"His tanks outnumber ours two to one, of course, sir," said the general calmly. "Unless we can divide his fleet and destroy a part of it, of course we will be crushed in a general combat. But we are naturally trying to make sure that any such action will take place within point-blank range of our artillery, which may help a little. We will cut the fog to secure that help, risking everything, if a general engagement occurs."

There was silence.

The President's voice, when it came, was more strained still.

"Will you speak to the public, General?"

"Three sentences. I have no time for more."

There were little clickings on the line, while the general's eyes returned to the board that was the battlefield in miniature. He indicated a spot with his finger.

"Concentrate our reserve-tanks here," he said meditatively. "Our fighting aircraft here. At once."

The two spots were at nearly opposite ends of the battle field. The chief of staff, checking the general's judgment with the alert suspicion that was the latest addition to his duties, protested sharply.

"But sir, our tanks will have no protection against helicopters!"

"I am quite aware of it," said the general mildly.

He turned to the transmitter. A thin voice had just announced at the other end of the wire, "The commander-in-chief of the army in the field will make a statement."

The general spoke unhurriedly.

"We are in contact with the enemy, have been for some hours. We have lost forty tanks and the enemy, we think, sixty or more. No general engagement has yet taken place, but we think decisive action on the enemy's part will be attempted within two hours. The tanks in the field need now, as always, ammunition, spare tanks, and the special supplies for modern warfare. In particular, we require ever-increasing quantities of fog-gas. I appeal to your patriotism for reinforcements of material and men."

He hung up the receiver and returned to his survey of the board.

"Those three listening-posts," he said abruptly, indicating a place near where an enemy tank had been destroyed. "Have they been reoccupied?"

"Yes, sir. Just reported. The tank they reported rolled over them, destroying the placement. They are digging in."

"Tell me," said the general, "when they cease to report again. They will."

He watched the board again and without lifting his eyes from it, spoke again.

"That listening-post in the dead sector, with the two strayed infantrymen in it. Was it reported?"

"Not yet, sir."

"Tell me immediately it does."

The general leaned back in his chair and deliberately relaxed. He lighted a cigar and puffed at it, his hands quite steady. Other officers, scenting the smoke, glanced up enviously. But the general was the only man who might smoke. The enemy's gases, like the American ones, could go through any gas-mask if in sufficient concentration. The tanks were sealed like so many submarines, and opened their interiors to the outer air only after that air had been thoroughly tested and proven safe. Only the general might use up more than a man's allowance for breathing.

The general gazed about him, letting his mind rest from its intense strain against the greater strain that would come on it in a few minutes. He looked at a tall blond man who was surveying the board intently, moving away, and returning again, his forehead creased in thought.

The general smiled quizzically. That man was the officer appointed to I. I. duty—interpretative intelligence—chosen from a thousand officers because the most exhaustive psychological tests had proven that his brain worked as nearly as possible like that of the enemy commander. His task was to take the place of the enemy commander, to reconstruct from the enemy movements reported and the enemy movements known as nearly as possible the enemy plans.

"Well, Harlin," said the general, "Where will he strike?"

"He's tricky, sir," said Harlin. "That gap in our listening-posts looks, of course, like preparation for a massing of his tanks inside our lines. And it would be logical that he fought off our helicopters to keep them from discovering his tanks massing in that area."

The general nodded.

"Quite true," he admitted. "Quite true."

"But," said Harlin eagerly. "He'd know we could figure that out. And he may have wiped out listening posts to make us think he was planning just so. He may have fought off our helicopters, not to keep them from discovering his tanks in there, but to keep them from discovering that there were no tanks in there!"

"My own idea exactly," said the general meditatively. "But again, it looks so much like a feint that it may be a serious blow. I dare not risk assuming it to be a feint only."

He turned back to the board.

"Have those two strayed infantrymen reported yet?" he asked sharply.

"Not yet, sir."

The general drummed on the table. There were four red flashes glowing at different points of the board—four points where American tanks or groups of tanks were locked in conflict with the enemy. Somewhere off in the enveloping fog that made all the world a gray chaos, lumbering, crawling monsters rammed and battered at each other at infinitely short range. They fought blindly, their guns swinging menacingly and belching lurid flames into the semi-darkness, while from all about them dropped the liquids that meant death to any man who breathed their vapor. Those gases penetrated any gas-mask, and would even strike through the sag-pastes that had made the vesica-tory gases of 1918 futile.

With tanks by thousands hidden in the fog, four small combats were kept up, four only. Battles fought with tanks as the main arm are necessarily battles of movement, more nearly akin to cavalry battles than any other unless it be fleet actions. When the main bodies come into contact, the issue is decided quickly. There can be no long drawn-out stalemates such as infantry trenches produced in years past. The fighting that had taken place so far, both under the fog and aloft in the air, was outpost skirmishing only. When the main body of the enemy came into action it would be like a whirlwind, and the bat-tle would be won or lost in a matter of minutes only.

The general paid no attention to those four conflicts, or their possible meaning.

"I want to hear from those two strayed infantrymen," he said quietly, "I must base my orders on what they report. The whole battle, I believe, hinges on what they have to say."

He fell silent, watching the board without the tense preoccupation he had shown before. He knew the moves he had to make in any of three eventualities. He watched the board to make sure he would not have to make those moves before he was ready. His whole air was that of waiting: the commander-in-chief of the army of the United States, waiting to hear what he would be told by two strayed infantrymen, lost in the fog that covered a battlefield.

The fog was neither more dense nor any lighter where Corporal Wallis paused to roll his pre-war cigarette. The tobacco came from the gassed machine-gunner in the pill-box a few yards off. Sergeant Coffee, three yards distant, was a blurred figure. Corporal Wallis put his cigarette into his mouth, struck his match, and puffed delicately.

"Ah!" said Corporal Wallis, and cheered considerably. He thought he saw Sergeant Coffee moving toward him and ungenerously hid his cigarette's glow.

Overhead, a machine-gun suddenly burst into a rattling roar, the sound sweeping above them with incredible speed. Another gun answered it. Abruptly, the whole sky above them was an inferno of such tearing noises and immediately after they began a multitudinous bellowing set up. Airplanes on patrol ordinarily kept their engines muffled, in hopes of locating a tank below them by its noise. But in actual fighting there was too much power to be gained by cutting out the muffler for any minor motive to take effect. A hundred aircraft above the heads of the two strayed infantrymen were fighting madly about five helicopters. Two hundred yards away, one fell to the earth with a crash, and immediately afterward there was a hollow boom. For an instant even the mist was tinged with yellow from the exploded gasoline tank. But the roaring above continued—not mounting, as in a battle between opposing patrols of fighting planes, when each side finds height a decisive advantage, but keeping nearly to the same level, little above the bank of cloud.

Something came down, roaring, and struck the earth no more than fifty yards away. The impact was terrific, but after it there was dead silence while the thunder above kept on.

Sergeant Coffee came leaping to Corporal Wallis' side.

"Helicopters!" he barked. "Huntin' tanks an' pill-boxes! Lay down!"

He flung himself down to the earth.

Wind beat on them suddenly, then an outrageous blast of icy air from above. For an instant the sky lightened. They saw a hole in the mist, saw the little pill-box clearly, saw a huge framework of supporting screws sweeping swiftly overhead with figures in it watching the ground through wind-angle glasses, and machine-gunners firing madly at dancing things in the air. Then it was gone.

"One o' ours," shouted Coffee in Wallis' ear. "They' tryin' to find th' Yellows' tanks!"

The center of the roaring seemed to shift, perhaps to the north. Then a roaring drowned out all the other roarings. This one was lower down and approaching in a rush. Something swooped from the south, a dark blotch in the lighter mist above. It was an airplane flying in the mist, a plane that had dived into the fog as into oblivion. It appeared, was gone—and there was a terrific crash. A shattering roar drowned out even the droning tumult of a hundred aircraft engines. A sheet of flame flashed up, and a thunderous detonation.

"Hit a tree," panted Coffee, scrambling to his feet again. "Suicide club, aimin' for our helicopter."

Corporal Wallis was pointing, his lips drawn back in a snarl.

"Shut up!" he whispered. "I saw a shadow against that flash! Yeller infantryman! Le's get 'im!"

"Y'crazy," said Sergeant Coffee, but he strained his eyes and more especially his ears.

It was Coffee who clutched Corporal Wallis' wrist and pointed. Wallis could see nothing, but he followed as Coffee moved silently through the gray mist. Presently he too, straining his eyes, saw an indistinct movement.

The roaring of motors died away suddenly. The fighting had stopped, a long way off, apparently because the helicopters had been withdrawn. Except for the booming of artillery a very long distance away, firing unseen at an unseen target, there was no noise at all.

"Aimin' for our pill-box," whispered Coffee.

They saw the dim shape, moving noiselessly, halt. The dim figure seemed to be casting about for something. It went down on hands and knees and crawled forward. The two infantrymen crept after it. It stopped, and turned around. The two dodged to one side in haste. The enemy infantryman crawled off in another direction, the two Americans following him as closely as they dared.

He halted once more, a dim and grotesque figure in the fog. They saw him fumbling in his belt. He threw something, suddenly. There was a little tap as of a fountain pen dropped upon concrete. Then a hissing sound. That was all, but the enemy infantryman waited, as if listening....

The two Americans fell upon him as one individual. They bore him to the earth and Coffee dragged at his gas-mask, good tactics in a battle where every man carries gas-grenades. He gasped and fought desperately, in a seeming frenzy of terror.

They squatted over him, finally, having taken away his automatics, and Coffee worked painstakingly to get off his gas-mask while Wallis went poking about in quest of tobacco.

"Dawggone!" said Coffee. "This mask is intricate."

"He ain't got any pockets," mourned Wallis.

Then they examined him more closely.

"It's a whole suit," explained Coffee. "H-m.... He don't have to bother with sag-paste. He's got him on a land diving-suit."

"S-s-say," gasped the prisoner, his language utterly colloquial in spite of the beady eyes and coarse black hair that marked him racially as of the enemy, "say, don't take off my mask! Don't take off my mask!"

"He talks an' everything," observed Coffee in mild amazement. He inspected the mask again and painstakingly smashed the goggles. "Now, big boy, you take your chance with th' rest of us. What' you doin' around here?"

The prisoner set his teeth, though deathly pale, and did not reply.

"H'm-m...." said Coffee meditatively. "Let's take him in the pill-box an' let Loot'n't Madison tell us what to do with him."

They picked him up.

"No! No! For Gawd's sake, no!" cried the prisoner shrilly. "I just gassed it!"

The two halted. Coffee scratched his nose.

"Reckon he's lyin', Pete?" he asked.

Corporal Wallis shrugged gloomily.

"He ain't got any tobacco," he said morosely. "Let's chuck him in first an' see."

The prisoner wriggled until Coffee put his own automatic in the small of his back.

"How long does that gas last?" he asked, frowning. "Loot'n't Madison wants us to report. There's some fellers in there, all gassed up, but we were in there a while back an' it didn't hurt us. How long does it last?"

"Fur-fifteen minutes, maybe twenty," chattered the prisoner. "Don't put me in there!"

Coffee scratched his nose again and looked at his wrist-watch.

"A'right," he conceded, "we give you twenty minutes. Then we chuck you down inside. That is, if you act real agreeable until then. Got anything to smoke?"

The prisoner agonizedly opened a zipper slip in his costume and brought out tobacco, even tailor-made cigarettes. Coffee pounced on them one second before Wallis. Then he divided them with absorbed and scrupulous fairness.

"Right," said Sergeant Coffee comfortably. He lighted up. "Say, you, if y' want to smoke, here's one o' your pills. Let's see the gas stuff. How' y' use it?"

Wallis had stripped off a heavy belt about the prisoner's waist and it was trailing over his arm. He inspected it now. There were twenty or thirty little sticks in it, each one barely larger than a lead pencil, of dirty gray color, and each one securely nested in a tube of flannel-lined papier-mache.

"These things?" asked Wallis contentedly. He was inhaling deeply with that luxurious enjoyment a tailor-made cigarette can give a man who had been remaking butts into smokes for days past.

"Don't touch 'em," warned the prisoner nervously. "You broke my goggles. You throw 'em, and they light and catch fire, and that scatters the gas."

Coffee touched the prisoner, indicating the ground, and sat down, comfortably smoking one of the prisoner's cigarettes. By his air, he began to approve of his captive.

"Say, you," he said curiously, "you talk English pretty good. How'd you learn it?"

"I was a waiter," the prisoner explained. "New York. Corner Forty-eighth and Sixth."

"My Gawd!" said Coffee. "Me, I used to be a movie operator along there. Forty-ninth. Projection room stuff, you know. Say, you know Heine's place?"

"Sure," said the prisoner. "I used to buy Scotch from that blond feller in the back room. With a benzine label for a prescription?"

Coffee lay back and slapped his knee.

"Ain't it a small world?" he demanded. "Pete, here, he ain't never been in any town bigger than Chicago. Ever in Chicago?"

"Hell," said Wallis, morose yet comfortable with a tailor-made cigarette. "If you guys want to start a extra war, go to knockin' Chicago. That's all."

Coffee looked at his wrist-watch again.

"Got ten minutes yet," he observed. "Say, you must know Pete Hanfry—"

"Sure I know him," said the enemy prisoner, scornfully. "I waited on him. Onc day, just before us reserves were called back home...."

In the monster tank that was headquarters the general tapped his fingers on his knees. The pale white light flickered a little as it shone on the board where the bright sparks crawled. White sparks were American tanks. Blue flashes were for enemy tanks sighted and reported, usually in the three-second interval between their identification and the annihilation of the observation-post that had reported them. Red glows showed encounters between American and enemy tanks. There were a dozen red glows visible, with from one to a dozen white sparks hovering about them. It seemed as if the whole front line were about to burst into a glare of red, were about to become one long lane of conflicts in impenetrable obscurity, where metal monsters roared and rumbled and clanked one against the other, bellowing and belching flame and ramming each other savagely, while from them dripped the liquids that made their breath mean death. There were nightmarish conflicts in progress under the blanket of fog, unparalleled save perhaps in the undersea battles between submarines in the previous European war.

The chief of staff looked up; his face drawn.

"General," he said harshly, "it looks like a frontal attack all along our line."

The general's cigar had gone out. He was pale, but calm with an iron composure.

"Yes," he conceded. "But you forget that blank spot in our line. We do not know what is happening there."

"I am not forgetting it. But the enemy outnumbers us two to one—"

"I am waiting," said the general, "to hear from those two infantrymen who reported some time ago from a listen-post in the dead area."

The chief of staff pointed to the outline formed by the red glows where tanks were battling.

"Those fights are keeping up too long!" he said sharply. "General, don't you see, they're driving back our line, but they aren't driving it back as fast as if they were throwing their whole weight on it! If they were making a frontal attack there, they'd wipe out the tanks we have facing them; they'd roll right over them! That's a feint! They're concentrating in the dead space—"

"I am waiting," said the general softly, "to hear from those two infantrymen." He looked at the board again and said quietly, "Have the call-signal sent them. They may answer."

He struck a match to relight his dead cigar. His fingers barely quivered as they held the match. It might have been excitement—but it might have been foreboding, too.

"By the way," he said, holding the match clear, "have our machine-shops and supply-tanks ready to move. Every plane is, of course, ready to take the air on signal. But get the aircraft ground personnel in their traveling tanks immediately."

Voices began to murmur orders as the general puffed. He watched the board steadily.

"Let me know if anything is heard from these infantrymen...."

There was a definite air of strain within the tank that was headquarters. It was a sort of tensity that seemed to emanate from the general himself.

Where Coffee and Wallis and the prisoner squatted on the ground, however, there was no sign of strain at all. There was a steady gabble of voices.

"What kinda rations they give you?" asked Coffee interestedly.

The enemy prisoner listed them, with profane side-comments.

"Hell," said Wallis gloomily. "Y'ought to see what we get! Las' week they fed us worse'n dogs. An' th' canteen stuff—"

"Your tank men, they get treated fancy?" asked the prisoner.

Coffee made a reply consisting almost exclusively of high powered expletives.

"—and the infantry gets it in the neck every time," he finished savagely. "We do the work—"

Guns began to boom, far away. Wallis cocked his ears.

"Tanks gettin' together," he judged, gloomily. "If they'd all blow each other to hell an' let us infantry fight this battle—"

"Damn the tanks!" said the enemy prisoner viciously. "Look here, you fellers. Look at me. They sent a battalion of us out, in two waves. We hike along by compass through the fog, supposed to be five paces apart. We come on a pill-box or listenin' post, we gas it an' go on. We try not to make a noise. We try not to get seen before we use our gas. We go on, deep in your lines as we can. We hear one of your tanks, we dodge it if we can, so we don't get seen at all. O'course we give it a dose of gas in passing, just in case. But we don't get any orders about how far to go or how to come back. We ask for recognition signals for our own tanks, an' they grin an' say we won't see none of our tanks till the battle's over. They say 'Re-form an' march back when the fog is out.' Ain't that pretty for you?"

"You second wave?" asked Coffee, with interest.

The prisoner nodded.

"Mopping up," he said bitterly, "what the first wave left. No fun in that! We go along gassin' dead men, an' all the time your tanks is ravin' around to find out what's happenin' to their listenin'-posts. They run into us—"

Coffee nodded sympathetically.

"The infantry always gets the dirty end of the stick," said Wallis morosely.

Somewhere, something blew up with a violent explosion. The noise of battle in the distance became heavier and heavier.

"Goin' it strong," said the prisoner, listening.

"Yeh," said Coffee. He looked at his wrist-watch. "Say, that twenty minutes is up. You go down in there first, big boy."

They stood beside the little pill-box. The prisoner's knees shook.

"Say, fellers," he said pleadingly, "they told us that stuff would scatter in twenty minutes, but you busted my mask. Yours ain't any good against this gas. I'll have to go down in there if you fellers make me, but—"

Coffee lighted another of the prisoner's tailor-made cigarettes.

"Give you five minutes more," he said graciously. "I don't suppose it'll ruin the war."

They sat down relievedly again, while the fog-gas made all the earth invisible behind a pall of grayness, a grayness from which the noises of battle came.

In the tank that was headquarters, the air of strain was pronounced. The maneuver-board showed the situation as close to desperation, now. The reserve-tank positions had been switched on the board, dim orange glows, massed in curiously precise blocks. And little squares of green showed there that the supply and machine-shop tanks were massed. They were moving slowly across the maneuver-board. But the principal change lay in the front-line indications.

The red glows that showed where tank battles were in progress formed an irregularly curved line, now. There were twenty or more such isolated battles in progress, varying from single combats between single tanks to greater conflicts where twenty to thirty tanks to a side were engaged. And the positions of those conflicts were changing constantly, and invariably the American tanks were being pushed back.

The two staff officers behind the general were nearly silent. There were few sparks crawling within the American lines now. Nearly every one had been diverted into the front-line battles. The two men watched the board with feverish intensity, watching the red glows moving back, and back....

The chief of staff was shaking like a leaf, watching the American line stretched, and stretched....

The general looked at him with a twisted smile.

"I know my opponent," he said suddenly. "I had lunch with him once in Vienna. We were attending a disarmament conference." He seemed to be amused at the ironic statement. "We talked war and battles, of course. And he showed me, drawing on the tablecloth, the tactical scheme that should have been used at Cambrai, back in 1917. It was a singularly perfect plan. It was a beautiful one."

"General," burst out one of the two staff officers behind him. "I need twenty tanks from the reserves."

"Take them," said the general. He went on, addressing his chief of staff. "It was an utterly flawless plan. I talked to other men. We were all pretty busy estimating each other there, we soldiers. We discussed each other with some freedom, I may say. And I formed the opinion that the man who is in command of the enemy is an artist: a soldier with the spirit of an amateur. He's a very skilful fencer, by the way. Doesn't that suggest anything?"

The chief of staff had his eyes glued to the board.

"That is a feint, sir. A strong feint, yes, but he has his force concentrated in the dead area."

"You are not listening, sir," said the general, reprovingly. "I am saying that my opponent is an artist, an amateur, the sort of person who delights in the delicate work of fencing. I, sir, would thank God for the chance to defeat my enemy. He has twice my force, but he will not be content merely to defeat me. He will want to defeat me by a plan of consummate artistry, which will arouse admiration among soldiers for years to come."

"But General, every minute, every second—"

"We are losing men, of whom we have plenty, and tanks, of which we have not enough. True, very true," conceded the general. "But I am waiting to hear from two strayed infantrymen. When they report, I will speak to them myself."

"But, sir," cried the chief of staff, withheld only by the iron habit of discipline from violent action and the taking over of command himself, "they may be dead! You can't risk this battle waiting for them! You can't risk it, sir! You can't!"

"They are not dead," said the general coolly. "They cannot be dead. Sometimes, sir, we must obey the motto on our coins. Our country needs this battle to be won. We have got to win it, sir! And the only way to win it—"

The signal-light at his telephone glowed. The general snatched it up, his hands quivering. But his voice, was steady and deliberate as he spoke.

"Hello, Sergeant—Sergeant Coffee, is it?... Very well, Sergeant. Tell me what you've found out.... Your prisoner objects to his rations, eh? Very well, go on.... How did he gas our listening-posts?... He did, eh? He got turned around and you caught him wandering about?... Oh, he was second wave! They weren't taking any chances on any of our listening-posts reporting their tanks, eh?... Say that again, Sergeant Coffee!" The general's tone had changed indescribably. "Your prisoner has no recognition signals for his own tanks? They told him he wouldn't see any of them until the battle was over?... Thank you, Sergeant. One of our tanks will stop for you. This is the commanding general speaking."

He rang off, his eyes blazing. Relaxation was gone. He was a dynamo, snapping orders.

"Supply tanks, machine-shop tanks, ground forces of the air service, concentrate here!" His finger rested on a spot in the middle of the dead area. "Reserve tanks take position behind them. Draw off every tank we've got—take 'em out of action!—and mass them in front, on a line with our former first line of outposts. Every airplane and helicopter take the air and engage in general combat with the enemy, wherever the enemy may be found and in whatever force. And our tanks move straight through here!"

Orders were snapping into telephone transmitters. The commands had been relayed before their import was fully realized. Then there was a gasp.

"General!" cried the chief of staff. "If the enemy is massed there, he'll destroy our forces in detail as they take position!"

"He isn't massed there," said the general, his eyes blazing. "The infantrymen who were gassing our listening-posts were given no recognition signals for their tanks. Sergeant Coffee's prisoner has his gas-mask broken and is in deadly fear. The enemy commander is foolish in many ways, perhaps, but not foolish enough to break down morale by refusing recognition signals to his own men who will need them. And look at the beautiful plan he's got."

He sketched half a dozen lines with his fingers, moving them in lightning gestures as his orders took effect.

"His main force is here, behind those skirmishes that look like a feint. As fast as we reinforce our skirmishing-line, he reinforces his—just enough to drive our tanks back slowly. It looks like a strong feint, but it's a trap! This dead space is empty. He thinks we are concentrating to face it. When he is sure of it—his helicopters will sweep across any minute, now, to see—he'll throw his whole force on our front line. It'll crumple up. His whole fighting force will smash through to take us, facing the dead space, in the rear! With twice our numbers, he'll drive us before him."

"But general! You're ordering a concentration there! You're falling in with his plans!"

The general laughed.

"I had lunch with the general in command over there, once upon a time. He is an artist. He won't be content with a defeat like that! He'll want to make his battle a masterpiece, a work of art! There's just one touch he can add. He has to have reserves to protect his supply-tanks and machine-shops. They're fixed. The ideal touch, the perfect tactical fillip, will be—Here! Look. He expects to smash in our rear, here. The heaviest blow will fall here. He will swing around our right wing, drive us out of the dead area into his own lines—and drive us on his reserves! Do you see it? He'll use every tank he's got in one beautiful final blow. We'll be outwitted, out-numbered, out-flanked and finally caught between his main body and his reserves and pounded to bits. It is a perfect, a masterly bit of work!"

He watched the board, hawklike.

"We'll concentrate, but our machine-shops and supplies will concentrate with us. Before he has time to take us in rear we'll drive ahead, in just the line he plans for us! We don't wait to be driven into his reserves. We roll into them and over them! We smash his supplies! We destroy his shops! And then we can advance along his line of communication and destroy it, our own depots being blown up—give the orders when necessary—and leaving him stranded with motor-driven tanks, motorized artillery, and nothing to run his motors with! He'll be marooned beyond help in the middle of our country, and we will have him at our mercy when his tanks run out of fuel. As a matter of fact, I shall expect him to surrender in three days."

The little blocks of green and yellow that had showed the position of the reserve and supply-tanks, changed abruptly to white, and began to crawl across the maneuver-board. Other little white sparks turned about. Every white spark upon the maneuver-board suddenly took to itself a new direction.

"Disconnect cables," said the general, crisply. "We move with our tanks, in the lead!"

The monotonous humming of the electric generator was drowned out in a thunderous uproar that was muffled as an air-tight door was shut abruptly. Fifteen seconds later there was a violent lurch, and the colossal tank was on the move in the midst of a crawling, thundering horde of metal monsters whose lumbering progress shook the earth.

Sergeant Coffee, still blinking his amazement, absent-mindedly lighted the last of his share of the cigarettes looted from the prisoner.

"The big guy himself!" he said, still stunned. "My Gawd! The big guy himself!"

A distant thunder began, a deep-toned rumbling that seemed to come from the rear. It came nearer and grew louder. A peculiar quivering seemed to set up in the earth. The noise was tanks moving through the fog, not one tank or two tanks, or twenty tanks, but all the tanks in creation rumbling and lurching at their topmost speed in serried array.

Corporal Wallis heard, and turned pale. The prisoner heard, and his knees caved in.

"Hell," said Corporal Wallis dispairingly. "They can't see us, an' they couldn't dodge us if they did!"

The prisoner wailed, and slumped to the floor.

Coffee picked him up by the collar and jerked him out of the pill-box.

"C'mon Pete," he ordered briefly. "They ain't givin' us a infantryman's chance, but maybe we can do some dodgin'!"

Then the roar of engines, of metal treads crushing upon earth and clinking upon their joints, drowned out all possible other sounds. Before the three men beside the pill-box could have moved a muscle, monster shapes loomed up, rushing, rolling, lurching, squeaking. They thundered past, and the hot fumes of their exhausts enveloped the trio.

Coffee growled and put himself in a position of defiance, his feet braced against the concrete of the pill-box dome. His expression was snarling and angry but, surreptitiously, he crossed himself. He heard the fellows of the two tanks that had roared by him, thundering along in alignment to right and left. A twenty-yard space, and a second row of the monsters came hurtling on, gun muzzles gaping, gas-tubes elevated, spitting smoke from their exhausts that was even thicker than the fog. A third row, a fourth, a fifth....

The universe was a monster uproar. One could not think in this volume of sound. It seemed that there was fighting overhead. Crackling noises came feebly through the reverberating uproar that was the army of the United States in full charge. Something came whirling down through the overhanging mist and exploded in a lurid flare that for a second or two cast the grotesque shadows of a row of tanks clearly before the trio of shaken infantrymen.

Still the tanks came on and roared past. Twenty tanks, twenty-one ... twenty-two.... Coffee lost count, dazed and almost stunned by the sheer noise. It rose from the earth and seemed to be echoed back from the topmost limit of the skies. It was a colossal din, an incredible uproar, a sustained thunder that beat at the eardrums like the reiterated concussions of a thousand guns that fired without ceasing. There was no intermission, no cessation of the tumult. Row after row after row of the monsters roared by, beaked and armed, going greedily with hungry guns into battle.

And then, for a space of seconds, no tanks passed. Through the pandemonium of their going, however, the sound of firing somehow seemed to creep. It was gunfire of incredible intensity, and it came from the direction in which the front-rank tanks were heading.

"Forty-eight, forty-nine, forty-ten, forty-'leven," muttered Coffee dazedly, his senses beaten down almost to unconsciousness by the ordeal of sound. "Gawd! The whole army went by!"

The roaring of the fighting-tanks was less, but it was still a monstrous din. Through it, however, came now a series of concussions that were so close together that they were inseparable, and so violent that they were like slaps upon the chest.

Then came other noises, louder only because nearer. These were different noises, too, from those the fighting-tanks had made. Lighter noises. The curious, misshapen service tanks began to rush by, of all sizes and all shapes. Fuel-carrier tanks. Machine-shop tanks, huge ones, these. Commissary tanks....

Something enormous and glistening stopped short. A door opened. A voice roared an order. The three men, beaten and whipped by noise, stared dumbly.

"Sergeant Coffee!" roared the voice. "Bring your men! Quick!"

Coffee dragged himself back to a semblance of life. Corporal Wallis moved forward, sagging. The two of them loaded their prisoner into the door and tumbled in. They were instantly sent into a heap as the tank took up its progress again with a sudden sharp leap.

"Good man," grinned a sooty-faced officer, clinging to a handhold. "The general sent special orders you were to be picked up. Said you'd won the battle. It isn't finished yet, but when the general says that—"

"Battle?" said Coffee dully. "This ain't my battle. It's a parade of a lot of damn tanks!"

There was a howl of joy from somewhere above. Discipline in the machine-shop tanks was strict enough, but vastly different in kind from the formality of the fighting-machines.

"Contact!" roared the voice again. "General wireless is going again! Our fellows have rolled over their reserves and are smashing their machine-shops and supplies!"

Yells reverberated deafeningly inside the steel walls, already filled with tumult from the running motors and rumbling treads.

"Smashed 'em up!" shrieked the voice above, insane with joy. "Smashed 'em! Smashed 'em! Smashed 'em! We've wiped out their whole reserve and—" A series of detonations came through even the steel shell of the lurching tank. Detonations so violent, so monstrous, that even through the springs and treads of the tank the earth-concussion could be felt. "There goes their ammunition! We set off all their dumps!"

There was sheer pandemonium inside the service-tank, speeding behind the fighting force with only a thin skin of reserve-tanks between it and a panic-stricken, mechanically pursuing enemy.

"Yell, you birds!" screamed the voice. "The general says we've won the battle! Thanks to the fighting force! We're to go on and wipe out the enemy line of communications, letting him chase us till his gas gives out! Then we come back and pound him to bits! Our tanks have wiped him out!"

Coffee managed to find something to hold on to. He struggled to his feet. Corporal Wallis, recovering from the certainty of death and the torture of sound, was being very sea-sick from the tank's motion. The prisoner moved away from him on the steel floor. He looked gloomily up at Coffee.

"Listen to 'em," said Coffee bitterly. "Tanks! Tanks! Tanks! Hell! If they'd given us infantry a chance—"

"You said it," said the prisoner savagely. "This is a hell of a way to fight a war."

Corporal Wallis turned a greenish face to them.

"The infantry always gets the dirty end of the stick," he gasped. "Now they—now they' makin' infantry ride in tanks! Hell!"

THE MAN WHO SAVED THE EARTH

Austin Hall (1926)

CHAPTER I: THE BEGINNING

Even the beginning. From the start the whole thing has the precision of machine work. Fate and its working—and the wonderful Providence which watches over Man and his future. The whole thing unerring: the incident, the work, the calamity, and the martyr. In the retrospect of disaster we may all of us grow strong in wisdom. Let us go into history.

A hot July day. A sun of scant pity, and a staggering street; panting thousands dragging along, hatless; fans and parasols; the sultry vengeance of a real day of summer. A day of bursting tires; hot pavements, and wrecked endeavor, heartaches for the seashore, for leafy bowers beside rippling water, a day of broken hopes and listless ambition.

Perhaps Fate chose the day because of its heat and because of its natural benefit on fecundity. We have no way of knowing. But we do know this: the date, the time, the meeting; the boy with the burning glass and the old doctor. So commonplace, so trivial and hidden in obscurity! Who would have guessed it? Yet it is—after the creation—one of the most important dates in the world's history.

This is saying a whole lot. Let us go into it and see what it amounts to. Let us trace the thing out in history, weigh it up and balance it with sequence.

Of Charley Huyck we know nothing up to this day. It is a thing which, for some reason, he has always kept hidden. Recent investigation as to his previous life and antecedents have availed us nothing. Perhaps he could have told us; but as he has gone down as the world's great martyr, there is no hope of gaining from his lips what we would so like to know.

After all, it does not matter. We have the day—the incident, and its purport, and its climax of sequence to the day of the great disaster. Also we have the blasted mountains and the lake of blue water which will ever live with his memory. His greatness is not of warfare, nor personal ambition; but of all mankind. The wreaths that we bestow upon him have no doubtful color. The man who saved the earth!

From such a beginning, Charley Huyck, lean and frail of body, with, even then, the wistfulness of the idealist, and the eyes of a poet. Charley Huyck, the boy, crossing the hot pavement with his pack of papers; the much treasured piece of glass in his pocket, and the sun which only he should master burning down upon him. A moment out of the ages; the turning of a straw destined to out-balance all the previous accumulation of man's history.

The sun was hot and burning, and the child—he could not have been more than ten—cast a glance over his shoulder. It was in the way of calculation. In the heyday of childhood he was not dragged down by the heat and weather: he had the enthusiasm of his half-score of years and the joy of the plaything. We will not presume to call it the spirit of the scientist, though it was, perhaps, the spark of latent investigation that was destined to lead so far.

A moment picked out of destiny! A boy and a plaything. Uncounted millions of boys have played with glass and the sun rays. Who cannot remember the little, round-burning dot in the palm of the hand and the subsequent exclamation? Charley Huyck had found a new toy, it was a simple thing and as old as glass. Fate will ever be so in her working.

And the doctor? Why should he have been waiting? If it was not destiny, it was at least an accumulation of moment. In the heavy eye-glasses, the square, close-cut beard; and his uncompromising fact-seeking expression. Those who knew Dr. Robold are strong in the affirmation that he was the antithesis of all emotion. He was the sternest product of science: unbending, hardened by experiment, and caustic in his condemnation of the frailness of human nature.

It had been his one function to topple over the castles of the foolish; with his hard-seeing wisdom he had spotted sophistry where we thought it not. Even into the castles of science he had gone like a juggernaut. It is hard to have one's theories derided—yea, even for a scientist—and to be called a fool! Dr. Robold knew no middle language; he was not relished by science.

His memory, as we have it, is that of an eccentric. A man of slight compassion, abrupt of manner and with no tact in speaking. Genius is often so; it is a strange fact that many of the greatest of men have been denied by their follows. A great man and laughter. He was not accepted.

None of us know today what it cost Dr. Robold. He was not the man to tell us. Perhaps Charley Huyck might; but his lips are sealed forever. We only know that he retired to the mountain, and of the subsequent flood of benefits that rained upon mankind. And we still denied him. The great cynic on the mountain. Of the secrets of the place we know little. He was not the man to accept the investigator; he despised the curious. He had been laughed at—let be—he would work alone on the great moment of the future.

In the light of the past we may well bend knee to the doctor and his protégé, Charley Huyck. Two men and destiny! What would we be without them? One shudders to think. A little thing, and yet one of the greatest moments in the world's history. It must have been Fate, Why was it that this stern man, who hated all emotion, should so have unbended at this moment? That we cannot answer. But we can conjecture. Mayhap it is this: We were all wrong; we accepted the man's exterior and profession as the fact of his marrow.

No man can lose all emotion. The doctor, was, after all, even as ourselves—he was human. Whatever may be said, we have the certainty of that moment—and of Charley Huyck.

The sun's rays were hot; they were burning; the pavements were intolerable; the baked air in the canyoned street was dancing like that of an oven; a day of dog-days. The boy crossing the street; his arms full of papers, and the glass bulging in his little hip-pocket.

At the curb he stopped. With such a sun it was impossible to long forget his plaything. He drew it carefully out of his pocket, lay down a paper and began distancing his glass for the focus. He did not notice the man beside him. Why should he? The round dot, the brownish smoke, the red spark and the flash of flame! He stamped upon it. A moment out of boyhood; an experimental miracle as old as the age of glass, and just as delightful. The boy had spoiled the name of a great Governor of a great Stata; but the paper was still salable. He had had his moment. Mark that moment.

A hand touched his shoulder. The lad lsaped up.

"Yessir. *Star* or *Bulletin*?"

"I'll take one of each," said the man. "There now. I was just watching you. Do you know what you were doing?"

"Yessir. Burning paper. Startin' fire. That's the way the Indians did it."

The man smiled at the perversion of fact. There is not such a distance between sticks and glass in the age of childhood.

"I know," he said—"the Indians. But do you know how it was done; the why—why the paper began to blaze?"

"Yessir."

"All right, explain."

The boy looked up at him. He was a city boy and used to the streets. Here was some old highbrow challenging his wisdom. Of course he knew.

"It's the sun."

"There," laughed the man. "Of course. You said you knew, but you don't. Why doesn't the sun, without the glass, burn the paper? Tell me that."

The boy was still looking up at him; he saw that the man was not like the others on the street. It may be that the strange intimacy kindled into being at that moment. Certainly it was a strange unbending for the doctor.

"It would if it was hot enough or you could get enough of it together."

"Ah! Then tbat is whet the glass is for, is it?"

"Yessir."

"Concentration?"

"Con——I don't know, sir. But it's the sun. She's sure some bot. I know a lot about the sun, sir. I've studied it with the glass. The glass picks up all the rays and puts them in one hole and that's what burns the paper.

"It's lots of fun. I'd like to have a bigger one; but it's all I've got. Why, do you know, if I had a glass big enough and a place to stand, I'd burn up the earth?"

The old man laughed. "Why, Archimides! I thought you were dead."

"My name ain't Archimedes. It's Charley Huyck."

Again the old man laughed.

"Oh, is it? Well, that's a good name, too. And if you keep on you'll make it famous as the name of the other." Wherein he was foretelling history. "Where do you live?"

The boy was still looking. Ordinarily he would not have told, but he motioned back with his thumb.

"I don't live; I room over on Brennan Street."

"Oh, I see. You room. Where's your mother?"

"Search me; I never saw her."

"I see; and your father?"

"How do I know. He went floating when I was four years old."

"Floating?"

"Yes sir—to sea."

"So your mother's gone and your father's floating. Archimedes is adrift. You go to school?"

"Yessir."

"What reader?"

"No reader. Sixth grade."

"I see. What school?"

"School Twenty-six. Say, it's hot. I can't stand here all day. I've got to sell my papers."

The man pulled out a purse.

"I'll take the lot," he said. Then kindly: "My boy, I would like to have you go with me."

It was a strange moment. A little thing with the fates looking on. When destiny plays she picks strange moments. This was one. Charley Huyck went with Dr. Bobold.

CHAPTER II: THE POISON PALL

We all of us remember that fatal day when the news startled all of Oakland. No one can forget it. At first it read like a newspaper hoax, in spite of the oft-proclaimed veracity of the press, and we were inclined to laughter. 'Twixt wonder at the story and its impossibilities we were not a little enthused at the nerve of the man who put it over.

It was in the days of dry reading. The world had grown populous and of well-fed content. Our soap-box artists had come to the point at last where they preached, not disaster, but a full-bellied thanks for the millennium that was here. A period of Utopian quietness—no villain around the corner; no man to covet the ox of his neighbor.

Quiet reading, you'll admit. Those were the days of the millennium. Nothing ever happened. Here's hoping they never come again. And then:

Honestly, we were not to blame for bestowing blessing out of our hearts upon that newspaperman. Even if it were a hoax, it was at least something.

At high noon. The clock in the city hall had just struck the hour that held the post 'twixt a.m. and p.m., a hot day with a sky that was clear and azure; a quiet day of serene peace and contentment. A strange and a portent moment. Looking back and over the miracle we may conjecture that it was the clearness of the atmospbere and the brightness of the sun that helped to the impact of the disaster. Knowing what we know now we can appreciate the impulse of natural phenomena. It was *not* a miracle.

The spot: Fourteenth and Broadway, Oakland, California.

Fortunately the thousands of employees in the stores about had not yet come out for their luncheons. The lapse that it takes to put a hat on, or to pat a ribbon, saved a thousand lives. One shudders to think of what would have happened had the spot been crowded. Even so, it was too impossible and too terrible to be true. Such things could not happen.

At high noon: Two street-cars crossing Fourteenth on Broadway—two cars with the-same joggle and bump and the same aspect of any of a hundred thousand at a traffic corner. The wonder is—there were so few people. A Telegraph car outgoing, and a Broadway car coming in. The traffic policeman at his post had just given his signal. Two automobiles were passing and a single pedestrian, so it is said, was working his way diagonally across the corner. Of this we are not certain.

It was a moment that impinged on miracle. Even as we recount it, knowing, as we do, the explanation, we sense the impossibility of the event. A phenomenon that holds out and, in spite of our findings, lingers into the miraculous. To be and not to be. One moment life and action, an ordinary scene of existent monotony; and the next moment nothing. The spot, the intersection of the street, the passing street-cars, the two automobiles, pedestrian, the policeman—non-existent! When events are instantaneous reports are apt to be misleading. This is what we find.

Some of those who beheld it, report a flash of bluish white light; others that it was of a greenish or even a violet hue; and others, no doubt of stronger vision, that it was not only of a predominant color but that it was shot and sparkled with a myriad specks of flame and burning.

It gave no warning and it made no sound; not even a whir. Like a hot breath out of the void. Whatever the forces that had focused, they were destruction. There was no Fourteenth and Broadway. The two automobiles, the two street-cars, the pedestrian, the policeman had been whiffed away as if they had never existed. In place of the intersection of the thoroughfares was a yawning gulf that looked down into the center of the earth to a depth of nausea.

It was instantaneous; it was without sound; no warning. A tremendous force of unlimited potentiality had been loosed to kinetic violence. It was the suddenness and the silence that belied credence. We were accustomed to associate all disaster with confusion; calamity has an affinity with pandemonium, all things of terror climax into sound. In this case there was no sound. Hence the wonder.

A hole or bore forty feet in diameter. Without a particle of warning and without a bit of confusion. The spectators one and all aver that at first they took it for nothing more than the effect of startled eyesight. Almost subtle. It was not until after a full minute's reflection that they became aware that a miracle had been wrought before their faces. Then the crowd rushed up and with awe and now awakened terror gazed down into that terrible pit.

We say "terrible" because in this case it is an exact adjective. The strangest hole that man ever looked into. It was so deep that at first it appeared to have no bottom; not even the strongest eyesight could penetrate the smoldering blackness that shrouded the depths descending. It took a stout heart and courage to stand and hold one's head on the brink for even a minute.

It was straight and precipitous; a perfect circle in shape; with sides as smooth as the effect of machine work, the pavement and stone curb had been cut as if by a razor. Of the two street cars, two automobiles and their occupants there was nothing. The whole thing so silent and complete. Not even the spectators could really believe it.

It was a hard thing to believe. The newspapers themselves, when the news came clamoring, accepted it with reluctance. It was too much like a hoax. Not until the most trusted reporters had gone and had wired in their reports would they even consider it. Then the whole world sat up and took notice.

A miracle! Like Oakland's *Press* we all of us doubted that hole. We had attained almost everything that was worth the knowing; we were the masters of the earth and its secrets and we were proud of our wisdom; naturally we refused such reports all out of reason. It must be a hoax.

But the wires were persistent. Came corroboration. A reliable news-gathering organization soon was coming through with elaborate and detailed accounts of just what was happening. We had the news from the highest and most reputable authority.

And still we doubted. It was the story itself that brought the doubting; its touch on miracle. It was too easy to pick on the reporter. There might be a hole, and all that; but this thing of no explanation! A bomb perhaps? No noise? Some new explosive? No such thing? Well, how did we know? It was better than a miracle.

Then came the scientists. As soon as could be men of great minds had been hustled to the scene. The world had long been accustomed to accept without quibble the dictum of these great specialists of fact. With their train of accomplishments behind them we would hardly be consistent were we to doubt them.

We know the scientist and his habits. He is the one man who will believe nothing until it is proved. It is his profession, and for that we pay him. He can catch the smallest bug that ever crawled out of an atom and give it a name so long that a Polish wrestler, if he had to bear it, would break under the burden. It is his very knack of getting in under that has given us our civilization. You don't baffle a scientist in our Utopia. It can't be done. Which is one of the very reasons why we began to believe in the miracle.

In a few moments a crowd of many thousands had gathered about the spot; the throng grew so dense that there was peril of some of them being crowded into the pit at the center. It took all the spare policemen of the city to beat them back far enough to string ropes from the corners. For blocks the streets were packed with wondering thousands. Street traffic was impossible. It was necessary to divert the cars to a roundabout route to keep the arteries open to the suburbs.

Wild rumors spread over the city. No one knew how many passengers had been upon the street cars. The officials of the company, from the schedule, could pick the numbers of the cars and their crews; but who could tell of the occupants?

Telephones rang with tearful pleadings. When the first rumors of the horror leaked out every wife and mother felt the clutch of panic at her heartstrings. It was a moment of historical psychology. Out of our books we had read of this strange phase of human nature that was wont to rise like a mad screeching thing out of disaster. We had never had it in Utopia.

It was rumbling at first and out of exaggeration; as the tale passed farther back to the waiting thousands it gained with the repetition. Grim and terrible enough in fact, it ratioed up with reiteration. Perhaps after all it was not psychology. The average impulse of the human mind does not even up so exactly. In the light of what we now know it may have been the poison that had leaked into the air; the new element that was permeating the atmosphere of the city.

At first it was spasmodic. The nearest witnesses of the disaster were the first victims. A strange malady began to spot out among those of the crowd who had been at the spot of contact. This is to be noticed. A strange affliction which from the virulence and rapidity of action was quite puzzling to the doctors.

Those among the physicians who would consent to statement gave it out that it was breaking down of tissue. Which of course it was; the new element that was radiating through the atmosphere of the city. They did not know it then.

The pity of it! The subtle, odorless pall was silently shrouding out over the city. In a short time the hospitals were full and it was necessary to call in medical aid from San Francisco. They had not even time for diagnosis. The new plague was fatal almost at conception. Happily the scientists made the discovery.

It was the pall. At the end of three hours it was known that the death sheet was spreading out over Oakland. We may thank our stars that it was learned so early. Had the real warning come a few hours later the death list would have been appalling.

A new element had been discovered; or if not a new element, at least something which was tipping over all the laws of the atmospheric envelope. A new combination that was fatal. When the news and the warning went out, panic fell upon the bay shore.

But some men stuck. In the face of such terror there were those who stayed and with grimness and sacrifice hung to their posts for mankind. There are some who had said that the stuff of heroes had passed away. Let them then consider the case of John Robinson.

Robinson was a telegraph operator. Until that day he was a poor unknown; not a whit better than his fellows. Now he has a name that will run in history. In the face of what he knew he remained under the blanket. The last words out of Oakland—his last message:

"Whole city of Oakland in grip of strange madness. Keep out of Oakland,"—following which came a haphazard personal commentary:

"I can feel it coming on myself. It is like what our ancestors must have felt when they were getting drunk—alternating desires of fight and singing—a strange sensation, light, and ecstatic with a spasmodic twitching over the forehead. Terribly thirsty. Will stick it out if I can get enough water. Never so dry in my life."

Followed a lapse of silence. Then the last words:

"I guess we're done for. There is some poison in the atmosphere—something. It has leaked, of course, out of this thing at Fourteenth and Broadway. Dr. Manson of the American Institute says it is something new that is forming a fatal combination; but he cannot understand a new element; the quantity is too enormous.

"Populace has been warned out of the city. All roads are packed with refugees. The Berkeley Hills are covered as with flies—north, east, and south and on the boats to Frisco. The poison, whatever it is, is advancing in a ring from Fourteenth and Broadway. You have got to pass it to these old boys of science. They are staying with that ring. Already they have calculated the rate of its advance and have given warning. They don't know what it is, but they have figured just how fast it is moving. They have saved the city.

"I am one of the few men now inside the wave. Out of curiosity I have stuck. I have a jug and as long as it lasts I shall stay. Strange feeling. Dry, dry, dry, as if the juice of one's life cells was turning into dust. Water evaporating almost instantly. It cannot pass through glass. Whatever the poison it has an affinity for moisture. Do not understand it. I have had enough—"

That was all. After that there was no more news out of Oakland. It is the only word that we have out of the pall itself. It was short and disconnected and a bit slangy; but for all that a basis from which to conjecture.

It is a strange and glorious thing how some men will stick to the post of danger. This operator knew that it meant death; but he held with duty. Had he been a man of scientific training his information might have been of incalculable value. However, may God bless his heroic soul!

What we know is thirst! The word that came from the experts confirmed it. Some new element of force was stealing or sapping the humidity out of the atmosphere. Whether this was combining and entering into a poison could not be determined.

Chemists worked frantically at the outposts of the advancing ring. In four hours it had covered the city; in six it had reached San Leandro, and was advancing on toward Haywards.

It was a strange story and incredible from the beginning. No wonder the world doubted. Such a thing had never happened. We had accepted the the law of judging the future by the past; by deduction; we were used to sequence and to law; to the laws of Nature. This thing did look like a miracle; which was merely because—as usually it is with "miracles"—we could not understand it. Happily, we can look back now and still place our faith in Nature.

The world doubted and was afraid. Was this peril to spread slowly over the whole state of California and then on to the—world. Doubt always precedes terror. A tense world waited. Then came the word of reassurance—from the scientists:

"Danger past; vigor of the ring is abating. Calculation has deduced that the wave is slowly decreasing in potentiality. It is too early yet to say that there will be recessions, as the wave is just reaching its zenith. What it is we cannot say; but it cannot be inexplicable. After a little time it will all be explained. Say to the world there is no cause for alarm."

But the world was now aroused; as it doubted the truth before, it doubted now the reassurance. Did the scientists know? Could they have only seen the future! We know now that they did not. There was but one man in all the world great enough to foresee disaster. That man was Charley Huyck.

CHAPTER III: THE MOUNTAIN THAT WAS

On the same day on which all this happened, a young man, Pizzozi by name and of Italian parentage, left the little town of Ione in Amador County, California, with a small truck-load of salt. He was one of the cattlemen whose headquarters or home-farms are clustered about the foot-hills of the Sierras. In the wet season they stay with their home-land in the valley; in the summer they penetrate into the mountains. Pizzozi had driven in from the mountains the night before, after salt. He had been on the road since midnight.

Two thousand salt-hungry cattle do not allow time for gossip. With the thrift of his race, Joe had loaded up his truck and after a running snatch at breakfast was headed back into the mountains. When the news out of Oakland was thrilling around the world he was far into the Sierras.

The summer quarters of Pizzozi were close to Mt. Heckla, whose looming shoulders rose square in the center of the pasture of the three brothers. It was not a noted mountain—that is, until this day—and had no reason for a name other than that it was a peak outstanding from the range; like a thousand others; rugged, pine clad, coated with deer-brush, red soil, and mountain miserie,

It was the deer-brush that gave it value to the Pizzozis—a succulent feed richer than alfalfa. In the early summer they would come up with bony cattle. When they returned in the fall they went out driving beef-steaks. But inland cattle must have more than forage. Salt is the tincture that makes them healthy.

It was far past the time of the regular salting. Pizzozi was in a hurry. It was nine o'clock when he passed through the mining town of Jackson; and by twelve o'clock—the minute of the disaster—he was well beyond the last little hamlet that linked up with civilization. It was four o'clock when he drew up at the little pine-sheltered cabin that was his headquarters for the summer.

He had been on the road since midnight. He was tired. The long weary hours of driving, the grades, the unvaried stress though the deep red dust, the heat, the stretch of a night and day had worn both mind and muscle. It had been his turn to go after salt; now that he was here, he could lie in for a bit of rest while his brothers did the salting.

It was a peaceful spot! this cabin of the Pizzozis; nestled among the virgin shade trees, great tall feathery sugar-pines with a mountain live-oak spreading over the door yard. To the east the rising heights of the Sierras, misty, gray-green, undulating into the distance to the pink-white snow crests of Little Alpine. Below in the canyon, the waters of the Mokolumne; to the west the heavy dark masses of Mt. Heckla, deep verdant in the cool of coming evening.

Joe drew up under the shade of the live oak. The air was full of cool, sweet scent of the afternoon. No moment could have been more peaceful; the blue clear sky overhead, the breath of summer, and the soothing spice of the pine trees. A shepherd dog came bounding from the doorway to meet him.

It was his favorite cow dog. Usually when Joe came back the dog would be far down the road to forestall him. He had wondered, absently, coming up, at the dog's delay. A dog is most of all a creature of habit; only something unusual would detain him. However the dog was here; as the man drew up he rushed out to greet him. A rush, a circle, a bark, and a whine of welcome. Perhaps the dog had been asleep.

But Joe noticed that whine; he was wise in the ways of dogs; when Ponto whined like that there was something unusual. It was not effusive or spontaneous; but rather of the delight of succor. After scarce a minute of patting, the dog squatted and faced to the westward. His whine was startling; almost fearful.

Pizzozi knew that something was wrong. The dog drew up, his stub tail erect, and his hair all bristled; one look was for his master and the other whining and alert to Mt. Heckla. Puzzled, Joe gazed at the mountain. But he saw nothing.

Was it the canine instinct, or was it coincidence? We have the account from Pizzozi. From the words of the Italian, the dog was afraid. It was not the way of Ponto; usually in the face of danger he was alert and eager; now he drew away to the cabin. Joe wondered.

Inside the shack he found nothing but evidence of departure. There was no sign of his brothers. It was his turn to go to sleep; he was wearied almost to numbness, for forty-eight hours he had not closed an eyelid. On the table were a few unwashed dishes and crumbs of eating. One of the three rifles that hung usually on the wall was missing; the coffee pot was on the floor with the lid open. On the bed the coverlets were mussed up. It was a temptation to go to sleep. Back of him the open door and Ponto. The whine of the dog drew his will and his consciousness into correlation. A faint rustle in the sugar-pines soughed from the canyon.

Joe watched the dog. The sun was just glowing over the crest of the mountain; on the western line the deep lacy silhouettes of the pine trees and the bare bald head of Heckla. What was it? His brothers should be on hand for the salting; it was not their custom to put things off for the morrow. Shading his eyes he stepped out of the doorway.

The dog rose stealthily and walked behind him, uneasily, with the same insistent whine and ruffled hair. Joe listened. Only the mountain murmurs, the sweet breath of the forest, and in the lapse of bated breath the rippling melody of the river far below him.

"What you see, Ponto? What you see?"

At the words the dog sniffed and advanced slightly—a growl and then a sudden scurry to the heels of his master. Ponto was afraid. It puzzled Pizzozi. But whatever it was that roused his fear, it was on Mt. Heckla.

This is one of the strange parts of the story—the part the dog played, and what came after. Although it is a trivial thing it is one of the most inexplicable. Did the dog sense it? We have no measure for the range of instinct, but we do have it that before the destruction of Pompeii the beasts roared in their cages. Still, knowing what we now know, it is hard to accept the analogy. It may, after all have been coincidence.

Nevertheless it decided Pizzozi. The cattle needed salt. He would catch up his pinto and ride over to the salt logs.

There is no moment in the cattle industry quite like the salting on the range. It is not the most spectacular perhaps, but surely it is not lacking in intenseness. The way of Pizzozi was musical even if not operatic. He had a long-range call, a rising rhythm that for depth and tone had a peculiar effect on the shattered stillness. It echoed and reverberated, and peeled from the top to the bottom of the mountain. The salt call is the talisman of the mountains.

"*Alleewahoo!*"

Two thousand cattle augmented by a thousand strays held up their heads in answer. The sniff of the welcome salt call! Through the whole range of the man's voice the stock stopped in their leafy pasture and listened.

"*Alleewahoo!*"

An old cow bellowed. It was the beginning of bedlam. From the bottom of the mountain to the top and for milse beyond went forth the salt call. Three thousand head bellowed to the delight of salting.

Pizzozi rode along. Each lope of his pinto through the tall tangled miserie was accented. "*Alleewahoo! Alleewahoo!*" The rending of brush, the confusion, and pandemonium spread to the very bottom of the leafy gulches. It is no place for a pedestrian. Heads and tails erect, the cattle were stampeding toward the logs.

A few head had beat him to it. These he quickly drove away and cut the sack open. With haste he poured it upon the logs; then he rode out of the dust that for yards about the place was tramped to the finest powder. The center of a herd of salting range stock is no place for comfort. The man rode away; to the left he ascended a low knob where he would be safe from the stampede; but close enough to distinguish the brands.

In no time the place was alive with milling stock. Old cows, heifers, bulls, calves, steers rushed out of the crashing brush into the clearing. There is no moment exactly like it. What before had been a broad clearing of brownish reddish dust was trampled into a vast cloud of bellowing blur, a thousand cattle, and still coming. From the farthest height came the echoing call. Pizzozi glanced up at the top of the mountain.

And then a strange thing happened.

From what we gathered from the excited accounts of Pizzozi it was instantaneous; and yet by the same words it was of such a peculiar and beautiful effect as never to be forgotten. A bluish azure shot though with a myriad flecks of crimson, a peculiar vividness of opalescence; the whole world scintillating; the sky, the air, the mountain, a vast flame of color so wide and so intense that there seemed not a thing beside it. And instantaneous—it was over almost before it was started. No noise or warning, and no subsequent detonation: as silent as winking and much, indeed, like the queer blur of color induced by defective vision. All in the fraction of a second. Pizzozi had been gazing at the mountain. There was no mountain!

Neither were there cattle. Where before had been the shade of the towering peak was now the rays of the western sun. Where had been the blur of the milling herd and its deafening pandemonium was now a strange silence. The transparency of the air was unbroken into the distance. Far off lay a peaceful range in the sunset. There was no mountain! Neither were there cattle!

For a moment the man had enough to do with his plunging mustang. In the blur of the subsequent second Pizzozi remembers nothing but a convulsion of fighting horseflesh bucking, twisting, plunging, the gentle pinto suddenly maddened into a demon. It required all the skill of the cowman to retain his saddle.

He did not know that he was riding on the rim of Eternity. In his mind was the dim subconscious realization of a thing that had happened. In spite of all his efforts the horse fought backward. It was some moments before he conquered. Then he looked.

It was a slow, hesitant moment. One cannot account for what he will do in the open face of a miracle. What the Italian beheld was enough for terror. The sheer immensity of the thing was too much for thinking.

At the first sight his simplex mind went numb from sheer impotence; his terror to a degree frozen. The whole of Mt. Heckla had been shorn away; in the place of its darkened shadow the sinking sun was blinking in his face; the whole western sky all golden. There was no vestige of the flat salt-clearing at the base of the mountain. Of the two thousand cattle milling in the dust not a one remained. The man crossed himself in stupor. Mechanically he put the spurs to the pinto.

But the mustang would not. Another struggle with bucking, fighting, maddened horseflesh. The cow-man must needs bring in all the skill of his training; but by the time he had conquered his mind had settled within some scope of comprehension.

The pony had good reasons for his terror. This time though the man's mind reeled it did not go dumb at the clash of immensity. Not only had the whole mountain been torn away, but its roots as well. The whole thing was up-side down; the world torn to its entrails. In place of what had been the height was a gulf so deep that its depths were blackness.

He was standing on the brink. He was a cool man, was Pizzozi; but it was hard in the confusion of such a miracle to think clearly; much less to reason. The prancing mustang was snorting with terror. The man glanced down.

The very dizziness of the gulf, sheer, losing itself into shadows and chaos overpowered him, his mind now clear enough for perception reeled at the distance. The depth was nauseating. His whole body succumbed to a sudden qualm of weakness: the sickness that comes just before falling. He went limp in the saddle.

But the horse fought backward; warned by instinct it drew back from the sheer banks of the gulf. It had no reason but its nature. At the instant it sensed the snapping of the iron will of its master. In a moment it had turned and was racing on its wild way out of the mountains. At supreme moments a cattle horse will always hit for home. The pinto and its limp rider were fleeing on the road to Jackson.

Pizzozi had no knowledge of what had occurred in Oakland. To him the whole thing had been but a flash of miracle; he could not reason. He did not curb his horse. That he was still in the saddle was due moreto the near-instinct of his training than to his volition.

He did not even draw up at the cabin. That he could make better time with his motor than with his pinto did not occur to him; his mind was far too busy; and, now that the thing was passed, too full of terror. It was forty-four miles to town; it was night and the stars were shining when he rode into Jackson.

CHAPTER IV: "MAN—A GREAT LITTLE BUG"

And what of Charley Huyck? It was his anticipation, and his training which leaves us here to tell the story. Were it not for the strange manner of his rearing, and the keen faith and appreciation of Dr. Hobold there would be to-day no tale to tell. The little incident of the burning-glass had grown. If there is no such thing as Fate there is at least something that comes very close to being Destiny.

On this night we find Charley at the observatory in Arizona. He is a grown man and a great one, and though mature not so very far drawn from the lad we met on the street selling papers. Tall, slender, very slightly stooped and with the same idealistic, dreaming eyes of the poet. Surely no one at first glance would have taken him for a scientist. Which he was and was not.

Indeed, there is something vastly different about the science of Charley Huyck. Science to be sure, but not prosaic. He was the first and perhaps the last of the school of Dr. Robold, a peculiar combination of poetry and fact, a man of vision, of vast, far-seeing faith and idealism linked and based on the coldest and sternest truths of materialism. A peculiar tenet of the theory of Robold: "True science to be itself should be half poetry." Which any of us who have read or been at school know it is not. It is a peculiar theory and though rather wild still with some points in favor.

We all of us know our schoolmasters; especially those of science and what they stand for. Facts, facts, nothing but facts; no dreams or romance. Looking back we can grant them just about the emotions of cucumbers. We remember their cold, hard features, the prodding after fact, the accumulation of data. Surely there is no poetry in them.

Yet we must not deny that they have been by far the most potent of all men in the progress of civilzation. Not even Robold would deny it.

The point is this:

The doctor maintained that from the beginning the progress of material civilization had been along three distinct channels; science, invention, and administration. It was simply his theory that the first two should be one; that the scientist deal not alone with dry fact but with invention, and that the inventor, unless he is a scientist, has mastered but half his trade. "The really great scientist should be a visionary," said Robold, "and an inventor is merely a poet, with tools."

Which is where we get Charley Huyck. He was a visionary, a scientist, a poet with tools, the protégé of Dr. Robold. He dreamed things that no scientist had thought of. And we are thankful for his dreaming.

The one great friend of Huyck was Professor Williams, a man from Charley's home city, who had known him even back in the days of selling papers. They had been cronies in boyhood, in their teens, and again at College. In after years, when Huyck had become the visionary, the mysterious Man of the Mountain, and Williams a great professor of astronomy, the friendship was as strong as ever.

But there was a difference between them. Williams was exact to acuteness, with not a whit of vision beyond pure science. He had been reared in the old stone-cold theory of exactness; he lived in figures. He could not understand Huyck or his reasoning. Perfectly willing to follow as far as facts permitted he refused to step off into speculation.

Which was the point between them. Charley Huyck had vision; although exact as any man, he had ever one part of his mind soaring out into speculation. What is, and what might be, and the gulf between. To bridge the gulf was the life work of Charley Huyck.

In the snug little office in Arizona we find them; Charley with his feet poised on the desk and Williams precise and punctilious, true to his training, defending the exactness of his philosophy. It was the cool of the evening; the sun was just mellowing the heat of the desert. Through the open door and windows a cool wind was blowing. Charley was smoking; the same old pipe had been the bane of Williams's life at college.

"Then we know?" he was asking.

"Yes," spoke the professor, "what we know, Charley, we know; though of course it is not much. It is very hard, nay impossible, to deny figures. We have not only the proofs of geology but of astronomical calculation, we have facts and figures plus our sidereal relations all about us.

"The world must come to an end. It is a hard thing to say it, but it is a fact of science. Slowly, inevitably, ruthlessly, the end will come. A mere question of arithmetic."

Huyck nodded. It was his special function in life to differ with his former roommate. He had come down from his own mountain in Colorado just for the delight of difference.

"I see. Your old calculations of tidal retardation. Or if that doesn't work the loss of oxygen and the water."

"Either one or the other; a matter of figures; the earth is being drawn every day by the sun: its rotation is slowing up; when the time comes it will act to the sun in exactly the same manner as the moon acts to the earth to-day."

"I understand. It will be a case of eternal night for one side of the earth, and eternal day for the other. A case of burn up or freeze up."

"Exactly. Or if it doesn't reach to that, the water gas will gradually lose out into sidereal space and we will go to desert. Merely a question of the old dynamical theory of gases; of the molecules to be in motion, to be forever colliding and shooting out into variance.

"Each minute, each hour, each day we are losing part of our atmospheric envelope. In course of time it will all be gone; when it is we shall be all desert. For intance, take a look outside. This is Arizona. Once it was the bottom of a deep blue sea. Why deny when we can already behold the beginning."

The other laughed.

"Pretty good mathematics at that, professor. Only—"

"Only?"

"That it is merely mathematics."

"Merely mathematics?" The professor frowned slightly. "Mathematics do not lie, Charlie, you cannot get away from them. What sort of fanciful argument are you bringing up now?"

"Simply this," returned the other, "that you depend too much on figures. They are material and in the nature of things can only be employed in a calculation of what *may* happen in the future. You must have premises to stand on, facts. Your figures are rigid: they have no elasticity; unless your foundations are permanent and faultless your deductions will lead you only into error."

"Granted; just the point: we know where we stand. Wherein are we in error?"

It was the old point of difference. Huyck was ever crashing down the idols of pure materialism. Williams was of the world-wide school.

"You are in error, my dear professor, in a very little thing and a very large one."

"What is that?"

"Man."

"Man?"

"Yes. He's a great little bug. You have left him out of your calculation—which he will upset."

The professor smiled indulgently. "I'll allow; he is at least a conceited bug; but you surely cannot grant him much when pitted against the Universe."

"No? Did it ever occur to you, Professor, what the Universe is? The stars for instance? Space, the immeasurable distance of Infinity. Have you never dreamed?"

Williams could not quite grasp him. Huyck had a habit that had grown out of childhood. Always he would allow his opponent to commit himself. The professor did not answer. But the other spoke.

"Ether. You know it. Whether mind or granite. For instance, your desert." He placed his finger to his forehead. "Your mind, my mind—localized ether."

"What are you driving at?"

"Merely this. Your universe has intelligence. It has mind as well as matter. The little knot called the earth is becoming conscious. Your deductions are incompetent unless they embrace mind as well as matter, and they cannot do it. Your mathematics are worthless."

The professor bit his lip.

"Always fanciful.." he commented, "and visionary. Your argument is beautiful, Charley, and hopeful. I would that it were true. But all things must mature. Even an earth must die."

"Not our earth. You look into the past, professor, for your proof, and I look into the future. Give a planet long enough time in maturing and it will develop life; give it still longer and it will produce intelligence. Our own earth is just coming into consciousness; it has thirty million years, at least, to run."

"You mean?"

"This. That man is a great little bug. Mind: the intelligence of the earth."

This of course is a bit dry. The conversation of such men very often is to those who do not care to follow them. But it is very pertinent to what came after. We know now, everyone knows, that Charley Huyck was right. Even Professor Williams admits it. Our earth is conscious. In leas than twenty-four hours it had to employ its consciousness to save itself from destruction.

A bell rang. It was the private wire that connected the office with the residence. The professor picked up the receiver. "Just a minute. Yes? All right." Then to his companion: "I must go over to the house, Charley. We have plenty of time. Then we can go up to the observatory."

Which shows how little we know about ourselves. Poor Professor Williams! Little did he think that those casual words were the last he would ever speak to Charley Huyck.

The whole world seething! The beginning of the end! Charley Huyck in the vortex. The next few hours were to be the most strenuous of the planet's history.

CHAPTER V: APPROACHING DISASTER

It was night. The stars which had just been coming out were spotted by millions over the sleeping desert. One of the nights that are peculiar to the country, which we all of us know so well, if not from experience, at least from hearsay; mellow, soft, sprinkled like salted fire, twinkling.

Each little light a message out of infinity. Cosmic grandeur; mind: chaos, eternity—a night for dreaming. Whoever had chosen the spot in the desert had picked full well. Charley had spoken of consciousness. On that night when he gazed up at the stars he was its personification. Surely a good spirit was watching over the earth.

A cool wind was blowing; on its breath floated the murmurs from the village; laughter, the song of children, the purring of motors and the startled barking of a dog; the confused drone of man and his civilization. From the eminence the observatory looked down upon the town and the sheen of light, spotting like jewels in the dim glow of the desert. To the east the mellow moon just tipping over the mountain. Charley stepped to the window.

He could see it all. The subtle beauty that was so akin to poetry: the stretch of desert, the mountains, the light in the eastern sky; the dull level shadow that marked the plain to the northward. To the west the mountains looming black to the star line. A beautiful night; sweetened with the breath of desert and tuned to its slumber.

Across the lawn he watched the professor descending the pathway under the acacias. An automobile was coming up the driveway; as it drove up under the arcs he noticed its powerful lines and its driver; one of those splendid pleasure cars that have returned to favor during the last decade; the soft purr of its motor, the great heavy tires and its coating of dust. There is a lure about a great car coming in from the desert. The car stopped, Charley noted. Doubtless some one for Williams. If it were, he would go into the observatory alone.

In the strict sense of the word Huyck was not an astronomer. He had not made it his profession. But for all that he knew things about the stars that the more exact professors had not dreamed of. Charley was a dreamer. He had a code all his own and a manner of reasoning. Between him and the stars lay a secret.

He had not divulged it, or if he had, it was in such an open way that it was laughed at. It was not cold enough in calculation or, even if so, was too far from their deduction. Huyck had imagination; his universe was alive and potent; it had intelligence. Matter could not live without it. Man was its manifestation; just come to consciousness. The universe teemed with intelligence. Charley looked at the stars.

He crossed the office, passed through the reception-room and thence to the stairs that led to the observatory. In the time that would lapse before the coming of his friend he would have ample time for observation. Somehow he felt that there was time for discovery. He had come down to Arizona to employ the lens of his friend the astronomer. The instrument that he had erected on his own mountain in Colorado had not given him the full satisfaction that he expected. Here in Arizona, in the dry clear air, which had hitherto given such splendid results, he hoped to find what he was after. But little did he expect to discover the terrible thing he did.

It is one of the strangest parts of the story that he should be here at the very moment when Fate and the world's safety would have had him. For years he and Dr. Robold had been at work on their visionary projects. They were both dreamers. While others had scoffed they had silently been at their great work on kinetics.

The boy and the burning glass had grown under the tutelage of Dr. Robold: the time was about at hand when he could out-rival the saying of Archimedes. Though the world knew it not, Charley Huyck had arrived at the point where he could literally burn up the earth.

But he was not sinister; though he had the power he had of course not the slightest intention. He was a dreamer and it was part of his dream that man break his thraldom to the earth and reach out into the universe. It was a great conception and were it not for the terrible event which took his life we have no doubt but that he would have succeeded.

It was ten-thirty when he mounted the steps and seated himself. He glanced at his watch: he had a good ten minutes. He had computed before just the time for the observation. For months he had waited for just this moment; he had not hoped to be alone and now that he was in solitary possession he counted himself fortunate. Only the stars and Charley Huyck knew the secret; and not even he dreamed what it would amount to.

From his pocket he drew a number of papers; most of them covered with notations; some with drawings; and a good sized map in colors. This he spread before him, and with his pencil began to draw right across its face a net of lines and cross lines. A number of figures and a rapid computation. He nodded and then he made the observation.

It would have been interesting to study the face of Charley Huyck during the next few moments. At first he was merely receptive, his face placid but with the studious intentness of one who has come to the moment: and as he began to find what he was after—an eagerness of satisfaction. Then a queer blankness; the slight movement of his body stopped, and the tapping of his feet ceased entirely.

For a full five minutes an absolute intentness. During that time he was out among the stars beholding what not even he had dreamed of. It was more than a secret: and what it was only Charley Huyck of all the millions of men could have recognized. Yet it was more than even he had expected. When he at last drew away his face was chalk-like; great drops of sweat stood on his forehead: and the terrible truth in his eyes made him look ten years older.

"My God!"

For a moment indecision and strange impotence. The truth he had beheld numbed action; from his lips the mumbled words:

"This world; my world; our great and splendid mankind!"

A sentence that was despair and a benediction.

Then mechanically he turned back to confirm his observation. This time, knowing what he would see, he was not so horrified: his mind was cleared by the plain fact of what he was beholding. When at last he drew away his face was settled.

He was a man who thought quickly—thank the stars for that—and, once he thought, quick to spring to action. There was a peril poising over the earth. If it were to be voided there was not a second to lose in weighing up the possibilities.

He had been dreaming all his life. He had never thought that the climax was to be the very opposite of what he hoped for. In his under mind he prayed for Dr. Robold—dead and gone forever. Were he only here to help him!

He seized a piece of paper. Over its white face he ran a mass of computations. He worked like lightning; his fingers plying and his mind keyed to the pin-point of genius. Not one thing did he overlook in his calculation. If the earth had a chance he would find it.

There are always possibilities. He was working out the odds of the greatest race since creation. While the whole world slept, while the uncounted millions lay down in fond security, Charley Huyck there in the lonely room on the desert drew out their figured odds to the point of infinity.

"Just one chance in a million."

He was going to take it. The words were not out of his mouth before his long legs were leaping down the stairway. In the flash of seconds his mind was rushing into clear action. He had had years of dreaming; all his years of study and tutelage under Robold gave him just the training for such a disaster.

But he needed time. Time! Time! Why was it so precious? He must get to his own mountain. In six jumps he was in the office.

It was empty. The professor had not returned. He thought rather grimly and fleetingly of their conversation a few minutes before; what would Williams think now of science and consciousness? He picked up the telephone receiver. While he waited he saw out of the corner of his eye the car in the driveway. It was—

"Hello. The professor? What? Gone down to town? No! Well, say, this is Charley"—he was watching the car in front of the building, "Say, hello—tell him I have gone home, home! H-o-m-e to Colorado—to Colorado, yes—to the mountain—the m-o-u-n-t-a-i-n. Oh, never mind—I'll leave a note."

He clamped down the receiver. On the desk he scrawled on a piece of paper:

Ed:
"Look these up. I'm bound for the mountain. No time to explain. There's a car outside. Stay with the lens. Don't leave it. If the earth goes up you will know that I have not reached the mountain."

Beside the note he placed one of the maps that he had in his pocket—with his pencil drew a black cross just above the center. Under the map were a number of computations.

It is interesting to note that in the stress of the great critical moment he forgot the professor's title. It was a good thing. When Williams read it he recognized the significance. All through their life in crucial moments he had been "Ed" to Charley.

But the note was all he was destined to find. A brisk wind was blowing. By a strange balance of fate the same movement that let Huyck out of the building ushered in the wind and upset calculation.

It was a little thing, but it was enough to keep all the world in ignorance and despair. The eddy whisking in through the door picked up the precious map, poised it like a tiny plane, and dropped it neatly behind a bookcase.

CHAPTER VI: A RACE TO SAVE THE WORLD

Huyck was working in a straight line. Almost before his last words on the phone were spoken he had requisitioned that automobile outside; whether money or talk, faith or force, he was going to have it. The hum of the motor sounded in his ears as he ran down the steps. He was hatless and in his shirtsleeves. The driver was just putting some tools in the car. With one jump Charley had him by the collar.

"Five thousand dollars if you can get me to Robold Mountain in twenty hours."

The very suddenness of the rush caught the man by surprise and lurched him against the car, turning him half around. Charley found himself gazing into dull brown eyes and sardonic laughter: a long, thin nose and lips drooped at the corners, then as suddenly tipping up—a queer creature, half devil, half laughter, and all fun.

"Easy, Charley, easy! How much did you say? Whisper it."

It was Bob Winters. Bob Winters and his car. And waiting. Surely no twist of fortune could nave been greater. He was a college chum of Huyck's and of the professor's. If there was one man that could make the run in the time allotted, Bob was he. But Huyck was impersonal. With the burden on his mind he thought of naught but his destination.

"Ten thousand!" he shouted.

The man held back his head. Huyck was far too serious to appreciate mischief. But not the man.

"Charley Huyck, of all men. Did young Lochinvar come out of the West? How much did you say? This desert air and the dust, 'tis hard on the hearing. She must be a young, fair maiden. Ten thousand."

"Twenty thousand. Thirty thousand. Damnation, man, you can have the mountain. Into the car."

By sheer subjective strength he forced the other into the machine. It was not until they were shooting out of the grounds on two wheels that he realized that the man was Bob Winters. Still the workings of fate.

The madcap and wild Bob of the races! Surely Destiny was on the job. The challenge of speed and the premium. At the opportune moment before disaster the two men were brought together. Minutes weighed up with centuries and hours out-balanced millenniums. The whole world slept; little did it dream that its very life was riding north with these two men into the midnight.

Into the midnight! The great car, the pride of Winter's heart, leaped between the pillars. At the very outset, madcap that he was, he sent her into seventy miles an hour; they fairly jumped off the hill into the village. At a full seventy-five he took the curve; she skidded, sheered half around and swept on.

For an instant Charley held his breath. But the master hand held her; she steadied, straightened, and shot out into the desert. Above the whir of the motor, flying dust and blurring what-not, Charley got the tones of his companion's voice. He had heard the words somewhere in history.

"Keep your seat, Mr. Greely. Keep your seat!"

The moon was now far up over the mountain, the whole desert was bathed in a mellow twilight; in the distance the mountains brooded like an uncertain slumbering cloud bank. They were headed straight to the northward; though there was a better road round about, Winters had chosen the hard, rocky bee-line to the mountain.

He knew Huyck and his reputation; when Charley offered thirty thousand for a twenty-hour drive it was not mere byplay. He had happened in at the observatory to drop in on Williams on his way to the coast. They had been classmates; likewise he and Charley.

When the excited man out of the observatory had seized him by the collar, Winters merely had laughed. He was the speed king. The three boys who had gone to school were now playing with the destiny of the earth. But only Huyck knew it.

Winters wondered. Through miles and miles of fleeting sagebrush, cacti and sand and desolation, he rolled over the problem. Steady as a rock, slightly stooped, grim and as certain as steel he held to the north. Charley Huyck by his side, hatless, coatless, his hair dancing to the wind, all impatience. Why was it? Surely a man even for death would have time to get his hat.

The whole thing spelled speed to Bob Winters; perhaps it was the infusion of spirit or the intensity of his companion; but the thrill ran into his vitals. Thirty thousand dollars—for a stake like that—what was the balance? He had been called Wild Bob for his daring; some had called him insane; on this night his insanity was enchantment.

It was wild; the lee of the giant roadster a whirring shower of gravel: into the darkness, into the night the car fought over the distance. The terrific momentum and the friction of the air fought in their faces; Huyck's face was unprotected: in no time his lips were cracked, and long before they had crossed the level his whole face was bleeding.

But he heeded it not. He only knew that they were moving; that slowly, minute by minute, they were cutting down the odds that bore disaster. In his mind a maze of figures; the terrible sight he had seen in the telescope and the thing impending. Why had he kept his secret?

Over and again he impeached himself and Dr. Robold. It had come to this. The whole world sleeping and only himself to save it. Oh, for a few minutes, for one short moment! Would he get it?

At last they reached the mountains. A rough, rocky road, and but little traveled. Happily Winters had made it once before, and knew it. He took it with every bit of speed they could stand, but even at that it was diminished to a minimum.

For hours they fought over grades and gulches, dry washouts and boulders. It was dawn, and the sky was growing pink when they rode down again upon the level. It was here that they ran across their first trouble; and it was here that Winters began to realize vaguely what a race they might be running.

The particular level which they had entered was an elbow of the desert projecting into the mountains just below a massive, newly constructed dam. The reservoir had but lately been filled, and all was being put in readiness for the dedication.

An immense sheet of water extending far back into the mountains—it was intended before long to transform the desert into a garden. Below, in the valley, was a town, already the center of a prosperous irrigation settlement; but soon, with the added area, to become a flourishing city. The elbow, where they struck it, was perhaps twenty miles across. Their northward path would take them just outside the tip where the foothills of the opposite mountain chain melted into the desert. Without ado Winters put on all speed and plunged across the sands. And then:

It was much like winking; but for all that something far more impressive. To Winters, on the left hand of the car and with the east on the right hand, it was much as if the sun had suddenly leaped up and as suddenly plumped down behind the horizon—a vast vividness of scintillating opalescence: an azure, naming diamond shot by a million fire points.

Instantaneous and beautiful. In the pale dawn of the desert air its wonder and color were beyond all beauty. Winters caught it out of the corner of his eye; it was so instantaneous and so illusive that he was not certain. Instinctively he looked to his companion.

But Charley, too, had seen it. His attitude of waiting and hoping was vigorized into vivid action. He knew just what it was. With one hand he clutched Winters and fairly shouted.

"On, on, Bob! On, as you value your life. Put into her every bit of speed you have got."

At the same instant, at the same breath came a roar that was not to be forgotten; crunching, rolling, terrible—like the mountain moving.

Bob knew it. It was the dam. Something had broken it. To the east the great wall of water fallout of the mountains! A beautiful sight and terrible; a relentless glassy roller fringed along its base by a lace of racing foam. The upper part was as smooth as crystal; the stored-up waters of the mountain moving out compactly. The man thought of the little town below and its peril. But Huyck thought also. He shouted in Winter's ear:

"Never mind the town. Keep straight north. Over yonder to the point of the water. The town will have to drown."

It was inexorable; there was no pity; the very strength and purpose of the command drove into the other's understanding. Dimly now he realized that they were really running a race against time. Winters was a daredevil; the very catastrophe sent a thrill of exultation through him. It was the climax, the great moment of his life, to be driving at a hundred miles an hour under that wall of water.

The roar was terrible, Before they were half across it seemed to the two men that the very sound would drown them. There was nothing in the world but pandemonium. The strange flash was forgotten in the terror of the living wall that was reaching out to engulf them. Like insects they whizzed in the open face of the deluge. When they had reached the tip they were so close that the outrunning fringe of the surf was at their wheels.

Around the point with the wide open plain before them. With the flood behind them it was nothing to outrun it. The waters with a wider stretch spread out. In a few moments they had left all behind them.

But Winters wondered; what was the strange flash of evanescent beauty? He knew this dam and its construction; to outlast the centuries. It had been whiffed in a second. It was not lightning. He had heard no sound other than the rush of the waters. He looked to his companion.

Hueyk nodded.

"That's the thing we are racing. We have only a few hours. Can we make it?"

Bob had thought that he was getting all the speed possible out of his motor. What it yielded from that moment on was a revelation.

It is not safe and hardly possible to be driving at such speed on the desert. Only the best car and a firm roadway can stand it. A sudden rut, squirrel hole, or pocket of sand is as good as destruction. They rushed on till noon.

Not even Winters, with all his alertness, could avoid it. Perhaps he was weary. The tedious hours, the racking speed had worn him to exhaustion. They had ceased to individualize, their way a blur, a nightmare of speed and distance.

It came suddenly, a blind barranca—one of those sunken, useless channels that are death to the unwary. No warning.

It was over just that quickly. A mere flash of consciousness plus a sensation of flying. Two men broken on the sands and the great, beautiful roadster a twisted ruin.

CHAPTER VII: A RIVEN CONTINENT

But back to the world. No one knew about Charley Huyck nor what was occurring on the desert. Even if we had it would have been impossible to construe connection.

After the news out of Oakland, and the destruction of Mt. Heckla, we were far too appalled. The whole thing was beyond us. Not even the scientists with all their data could find one thing to work on. The wires of the world buzzed with wonder and with panic. We were civilized. It is really strange how quickly, in spite of our boasted powers, we revert to the primitive.

Superstition cannot die. Where was no explanation must be miracle. The thing had been repeated. When would it strike again. And where?

There was not long to wait. But this time the stroke was of far more consequence and of far more terror. The sheer might of the thing shook the earth. Not a man or government that would not resign in the face of such destruction.

It was omnipotent. A whole continent had been riven. It would be impossible to give description of such catastrophe; no pen can tell it any more than it could describe the creation. We can only follow in its path.

On the morning after the first catastrophe, at eight o'clock, just south of the little city of Santa Cruz, on the north shore of the Bay of Monterey, the same light and the same, though not quite the same, instantaneousness. Those who beheld it report a vast ball of azure blue and opalescent fire and motion; a strange sensation of vitalized vibration; of personified living force. In shape like a marble, as round as a full moon in its glory, but of infinitely more beauty.

It came from nowhere; neither from above the earth nor below it. Seeming to leap out of nothing, it glided or rather vanished to the eastward. Still the effect of winking, though this time, perhaps from a distanced focus, more vivid. A dot or marble, like a full moon, burning, opal, soaring to the eastward.

And instantaneous. Gone as soon as it was come; noiseless and of phantom beauty; like a finger of the Omnipotent tracing across the world, and as terrible. The human mind had never conceived a thing so vast.

Beginning at the sands of the ocean the whole country had vanished; a chasm twelve miles wide and of unknown depth running straight to the eastward. Where had been farms and homes was nothing; the mountains had been seared like butter. Straight as an arrow.

Then the roar of the deluge. The waters of the Pacific breaking through its sands and rolling into the Gulf of Mexico. That there was no heat was evidenced by the fact that there was no steam. The thing could not be internal. Yet what was it?

One can only conceive in figures. From the shores of Santa Cruz to the Atlantic—a few seconds; then out into the eastern ocean straight out into the Sea of the Sargasso. A great gulf riven straight across the face of North America.

The path seemed to follow the sun; it bore to the eastward with a slight southern deviation. The mountains it cut like cheese. Passing just north of Fresno it seared through the gigantic Sierras halfway between the Yosemite and Mt. Whitney, through the great desert to southern Nevada, thence across northern Arizona, New Mexico, Texas, Arkansas, Mississippi, Alabama, and Georgia, entering the Atlantic at a point half-way between Brunswick and Jacksonville. A great canal twelve miles in width linking the oceans. A cataclysmic blessing. Today, with thousands of ships bearing freight over its water, we can bless that part of the disaster.

But there was more to come. So far the miracle had been sporadic. Whatever had been its force it had been fatal only on point and occasion. In a way it had been local. The deadly atmospheric combination of its aftermath was invariable in its recession. There was no suffering. The death that it dealt was the death of obliteration. But now it entered on another stage.

The world is one vast ball, and, though large, still a very small place to live in. There are few of us, perhaps, who look upon it, or even stop to think of it, as a living being. Yet it is just that. It has its currents, life, pulse, and its fevers; it is coordinate; a million things such as the great streams of the ocean, the swirls of the atmosphere, make it a place to live in. And we are conscious only, or mostly, through disaster.

A strange thing happened.

The great opal like a mountain of fire had riven across the continent. From the beginning and with each succession the thing was magnified. But it was not until it had struck the waters of the Atlantic that we became aware of its full potency and its fatality.

The earth quivered at the shock, and man stood on his toes in terror. In twenty-four hours our civilization was literally falling to pieces. We were powerful with the forces that we understood; but against this that had been literally ripped from the unknown we were insignificant. The whole world was frozen. Let us see.

Into the Atlantic! The transition. Hitherto silence. But now the roar of ten thousand million Niagaras, the waters of the ocean rolling, catapulting, roaring into the gulf that had been seared in its bosom. The Gulf Stream cut in two, the currents that tempered our civilization sheared in a second. Straight into the Sargasso Sea. The great opal, liquid fire, luminiscent, a ball like the setting sun, lay poised upon the ocean. It was the end of the earth!

What was this thing? The whole world knew of it in a second. And not a one could tell. In less than forty hours after its first appearance in Oakland it had consumed a mountain, riven a continent, and was drinking up an ocean. The tangled sea of the Sargasso, dead calm for ages, was a cataract; a swirling torrent of maddened waters rushed to the opal—and disappeared.

It was hellish and out of madness; as beautiful as it was uncanny. The opal high as the Himalayas brooding upon the water; its myriad colors blending, winking in a phantasm of iridescence. The beauty of its light could be seen a thousand miles. A thing out of mystery and out of forces. We had discovered many things and knew much; but had guessed no such thing as this. It was vampirish, and it was literally drinking up the earth.

Consequences were immediate. The point of contact was fifty miles across, the waters of the Atlantic with one accord turned to the magnet. The Gulf Stream veered straight from its course and out across the Atlantic. The icy currents from the poles freed from the warmer barrier descended along the coasts and thence out into the Sargasso Sea. The temperature of the temperate zone dipped below the point of a blizzard.

The first word come out of London. Freezing! And in July! The fruit and entire harvest of northern Europe destroyed. Olympic games at Copenhagen postponed by a foot of snow. The river Seine frozen. Snow falling in New York. Crops nipped with frost as far south as Cape Hatteras.

A fleet of airplanes was despatched from the United States and another from the west coast of Africa. Not half of them returned. Those that did reported even more disaster. The reports that were handed in were appalling. They had sailed straight on. It was like flying into the sun; the vividness of the opalescence was blinding, rising for miles above them alluring, drawing and unholy, and of a beauty that was terror.

Only the tardy had escaped. It even drew their motors, it was like gravity suddenly become vitalized and conscious. Thousands of machines vaulted into the opalescence. From those ahead hopelessly drawn and powerless came back the warning. But hundreds could not escape.

"Back," came the wireless. "Do not come too close. The thing is a magnet. Turn back before too late. Against this man is insignificant."

Then like gnats flitting into fire they vanished into the opalescence.

The others turned back. The whole world freezing shuddered in horror. A great vampire was brooding over the earth. The greatness that man had attained to was nothing. Civilization was tottering in a day. We were hopeless.

Then came the last revelation; the truth and verity of the disaster and the threatened climax. The water level of all the coast had gone down. Vast ebb tides had gone out not to return. Stretches of sand where had been surf extended far out into the sea. Then the truth! The thing, whatever it was, was drinking up the ocean.

CHAPTER VIII: THE MAN WHO SAVED THE EARTH

It was tragic; grim, terrible, cosmic. Out of nowhere had come this thing that was eating up the earth. Not a thing out of all our science had there been to warn us; not a word from all our wise men. We who had built up our civilization, piece by piece, were after all but insects.

We were going out in a maze of beauty into the infinity whence we came. Hour by hour the great orb of opalescence grew in splendor; the effect and the beauty of its lure spread about the earth; thrilling, vibrant like suppressed music. The old earth helpless. Was it possible that out of her bosom she could not pluck one intelligence to save her? Was there not one law—no answer?

Out on the desert with his face to the sun lay the answer. Though almost hopeless there was still some time and enough of near-miracle to save us. A limping fate in the shape of two Indians and a battered runabout at the last moment.

Little did the two red men know the value of the two men found that day on the desert. To them the debris of the mighty car and the prone bodies told enough of the story. They were Samaritans; but there are many ages to bless them.

As it was there were many hours lost. Without this loss there would have been thousands spared and an almost immeasurable amount of disaster. But we have still to be thankful. Charley Huyck was still living.

He had been stunned; battered, bruised, and unconscious; but he had not been injured vitally. There was still enough left of him to drag himself to the old runabout and call for Winters. His companion, as it happened, was in even better shape than himself, and waiting. We do not know how they talked the red men out of their relic—whether by coaxing, by threat, or by force.

Straight north. Two men battered, worn, bruised, but steadfast, bearing in that limping old motor-car the destiny of the earth. Fate was still on the job, but badly crippled.

They had lost many precious hours. Winters had forfeited his right to the thirty thousand. He did not care. He understood vaguely that there was a stake over and above all money. Huyck said nothing; he was too maimed and too much below will-power to think of speaking. What had occurred during the many hours of their unconsciousness was unknown to them. It was not until they came sheer upon the gulf that had been riven straight across the continent that the awful truth dawned on them.

To Winters it was terrible. The mere glimpse of that blackened chasm was terror. It was bottomless; so deep that its depths were cloudy; the misty haze of its uncertain shadows was akin to chaos. He understood vaguely that it was related to that terrible thing they had beheld in the morning. It was not the power of man. Some force had been loosened which was ripping the earth to its vitals. Across the terror of the chasm he made out the dim outlines of the opposite wall. A full twelve miles across.

For a moment the sight overcame even Huyck himself. Full well he knew; but knowing, as he did, the full fact of the miracle was even more than he expected. His long years under Robold, his scientific imagination had given him comprehension. Not puny steam, nor weird electricity, but force, kinetics—out of the universe.

He knew. But knowing as he did, he was overcome by the horror. Such a thing turned loose upon the earth! He had lost many hours; he had but a few hours remaining. The thought gave him sudden energy. He seized Winters by the arm.

"To the first town, Bob. To the first town—an aerodome."

There was speed in that motor for all its decades. Winters turned about and shot out in a lateral course parallel to the great chasm. But for all his speed he could not keep back his question.

"In the name of Heaven, Charley, what did it? What is it?"

Came the answer; and it drove the lust of all speed through Winters:

"Bob," said Charley, "it is the end of the world—if we don't make it. But a few hours left. We must have an airplane. I must make the mountain."

It was enough for Wild Bob. He settled down. It was only an old runabout; but he could get speed out of a wheelbarrow. He had never driven a race like this. Just once did he speak. The words were characteristic.

"A world's record, Charley. And we're going to win. Just watch us."

And they did.

There was no time lost in the change. The mere fact of Huyck's name, his appearance and the manner of his arrival was enough. For the last hours messages had been pouring in at every post in the Rocky Mountains for Charley Huyck. After the failure of all others many thousands had thought of him.

Even the government, unappreciative before, had awakened to a belated and almost frantic eagerness. Orders were out that everything, no matter what, was to be at his disposal. He had been regarded as visionary; but in the face of what had occurred, visions were now the most practical things for mankind. Besides, Professor Williams had sent out to the world the strange portent of Huyck's note. For years there had been mystery on that mountain. Could it be?

Unfortunately we cannot give it the description we would like to give. Few men outside of the regular employees have ever been to the Mountain of Robold. From the very first, owing perhaps to the great forces stored, and the danger of carelessness, strangers and visitors had been barred. Then, too, the secrecy of Dr. Robold—and the respect of his successor. But we do know that the burning glass had grown into the mountain.

Bob Winters and the aviator are the only ones to tell us; the employees, one and all, chose to remain. The cataclysm that followed destroyed the work of Huyck and Robold—but not until it had served the greatest deed that ever came out of the minds of men. And had it not been for Huyck's insistence we would not have even the account that we are giving.

It was he who insisted, nay, begged, that his companions return while there was yet a chance. Full well he knew. Out of the universe, out of space he had coaxed the forces that would burn up the earth. The great ball of luminous opalescence, and the diminishing ocean!

There was but one answer. Through the imaginative genius of Robold and Huyck, fate had worked up to the moment. The lad and the burning glass had grown to Archimedes.

What happened?

The plane neared the Mountain of Robold. The great bald summit and the four enormous globes of crystal. At least we so assume. We have Winter's word and that of the aviator that they were of the appearance of glass. Perhaps they were not; but we can assume it for description. So enormous that were they set upon a plain they would have overtopped the highest building ever constructed; though on the height of the mountain, and in its contrast, they were not much more than golf balls.

It was not their size but their effect that was startling. They were alive. At least that is what we have from Winters. Living, luminous, burning, twisting within with a thousand blending, iridescent beautiful colors. Not like electricity but something infinitely more powerful. Great mysterious magnets that Huyck had charged out of chaos. Glowing with the softest light; the whole mountain brightened as in a dream, and the town of Robold at its base lit up with a beauty that was past beholding.

It was new to Winters. The great buildings and the enormous machinery. Engines of strangest pattern, driven by forces that the rest of the world had not thought of. Not a sound; the whole works a complicated mass covering a hundred acres, driving with a silence that was magic. Not a whir nor friction. Like a living composite body pulsing and breathing the strange and mysterious force that had been evolved from Huyck's theory of kinetics. The four great steel conduits running from the globes down the side of the mountain. In the center, at a point midway between the globes, a massive steel needle hung on a pivot and pointed directly at the sun.

Winters and the aviator noted it and wondered. From the lower end of the needle was pouring a luminous stream of pale-blue opalescence, a stream much like a liquid, and of an unholy, radiance. But it was not a liquid, nor fire, nor anything seen by man before.

It was force. We have no better description than the apt phrase of Winters. Charley Huyck was milking the sun, as it dropped from the end of the four living streams to the four globes that took it into storage. The four great, wonderful living globes; the four batteries; the very sight of their imprisoned beauty and power was magnetic.

The genius of Huyck and Robold! Nobody but the wildest dreamers would have conceived it. The life of the sun. And captive to man; at his will and volition. And in the next few minutes we were to lose it all! But in losing it we were to save ourselves. It was fate and nothing else. There was but one thing more upon the mountain—the observatory and another needle apparently idle; but with a point much like a gigantic phonograph needle. It rose square out of the observatory, and to Winters it gave an impression of a strange gun, or some implement for sighting.

That was all. Coming with the speed that they were making, the airmen had no time for further investigation. But even this is comprehensive. Minus the force. If we only knew more about that or even its theory we might perhaps reconstruct the work of Charley Huyck and Dr. Robold.

They made the landing. Winters, with his nature, would be in at the finish; but Charley would not have it.

"It is death, Bob," he said. "You have a wife and babies. Go back to the world. Go back with all the speed you can get out of your motors. Get as far away as you can before the end comes."

With that he bade them a sad farewell. It was the last spoken word that the outside world had from Charley Huyck.

The last seen of him he was running up the steps of his office. As they soared away and looked back they could see men, the employees, scurrying about in frantic haste to their respective posts and stations. What was it all about? Little did the two aviators know. Little did they dream that it was the deciding stroke.

CHAPTER IX: THE MOST TERRIFIC MOMENT IN HISTORY

Still the great ball of Opalescence brooding over the Sargasso. Europe now was frozen, and though it was midsummer had gone into winter quarters. The Straits of Dover were no more. The waters had receded and one could walk, if careful, dry-shod from the shores of France to the chalk cliffs of England. The Straits of Gibraltar had dried up. The Mediterranean completely land-locked, was cut off forever from the tides of the mother ocean.

The whole world going dry; not in ethics, but in reality. The great Vampire, luminous, beautiful beyond all ken and thinking, drinking up our life-blood. The Atlantic a vast whirlpool.

A strange frenzy had fallen over mankind: men fought in the streets and died in madness. It was fear of the Great Unknown, and hysteria. At such a moment the veil of civilization was torn to tatters. Man was reverting to the primeval.

Then came the word from Charley Huyck; flashing and repeating to every clime and nation. In its assurance it was almost as miraculous as the Vampire itself. For man had surrendered.

To the People of the World:

The strange and terrible Opalescence which, for the past seventy hours, has been playing havoc with the world, is not miracle, nor of the supernatural, but a mere manifestation and result of the application of celestial kinetics. Such a thing always was and always will be possible where there is intelligence to control and harness the forces that lie about us. Space is not space exactly, but an infinite cistern of unknown laws and forces. We may control certain laws on earth, but until we reach out farther we are but playthings.

Man is the intelligence of the earth. The time will come when he must be the intelligence of a great deal of space as well. At the present time you are merely fortunate and a victim of a kind fate. That I am the instrument of the earth's salvation is merely chance. The real man is Dr. Robold. When he picked me up on the streets I had no idea that the sequence of time would drift to this moment. He took me into his work and taught me.

Because he was sensitive and was laughed at, we worked in secret. And since his death, and out of respect to his memory, I have continued in the same manner. But I have written down everything, all the laws, computations, formulas—everything; and I am now willing it to mankind.

Robold had a theory on kinetics. It was strange at first and a thing to laugh at; but he reduced it to laws as potent and as inexorable as the laws of gravitation.

The luminous Opalescence that has almost destroyed us is but one of its minor manifestations. It is a message of sinister intelligence; for back of it all is an Intelligence. Yet it is not all sinister. It is self-preservation. The time is coming when eons of ages from now our own man will be forced to employ just such a weapon for his own preservation. Either that or we shall die of thirst and agony.

Let me ask you to remember now, that whatever you have suffered, you have saved a world. I shall now save you and the earth.

In the vaults you will find everything. All the knowledge and discoveries of the great Dr. Robold, plus a few minor findings by myself.

"And now I bid you farewell. You shall soon be free."

Charley Huyck.

A strange message. Spoken over the wireless and flashed to every clime, it roused and revived the hope of mankind. Who was this Charley Huyck? Uncounted millions of men had never heard his name; there were but few, very few who had.

A message out of nowhere and of very dubious and doubtful explanation. Celestial kinetics! Undoubtedly. But the words explained nothing. However, man was ready to accept anything, so long as it saved him.

For a more lucid explanation we must go back to the Arizona observatory and Professor Ed. Williams. And a strange one it was truly; a certain proof that consciousness is more potent, far more so than mere material; also that many laws of our astronomers are very apt to be overturned in spite of their mathematics.

Charley Huyck was right. You cannot measure intelligence with a yard-stick. Mathematics do not lie; but when applied to consciousness they are very likely to kick backward. That is precisely what had happened.

The suddenness of Huyck's departure had puzzled Professor Williams; that, and the note which he found upon the table. It was not like Charley to go off so in the stress of a moment. He had not even taken the time to get his hat and coat. Surely something was amiss.

He read the note carefully, and with a deal of wonder.

"Look these up. Keep by the lens. If the world goes up you will know I have not reached the mountain."

What did he mean? Besides, there was no data for him to work on. He did not know that an errant breeze, had plumped the information behind the bookcase. Nevertheless he went into the observatory, and for the balance of the night stuck by the lens.

Now there are uncounted millions of stars in the sky. Williams had nothing to go by. A needle in the hay-stack were an easy task compared with the one that he was allotted. The flaming mystery, whatever it was that Huyck had seen, was not caught by the professor. Still, he wondered. "If the world goes up you will know I have not reached the mountain." What was the meaning?

But he was not worried. The professor loved Huyck as a visionary and smiled not a little at his delightful fancies. Doubtless this was one of them. It was not until the news came flashing out of Oakland that he began to take it seriously. Then followed the disappearance of Mount Heckla. "If the world goes up"—it began to look as if the words had meaning.

There was a frantic professor during the next few days. When he was not with the lens he was flashing out messages to the world for Charley Huyck. He did not know that Huyck was lying unconscious and almost dead upon the desert. That the world was coming to catastrophe he knew full well; but where was the man to save it? And most of all, what had his friend meant by the words, "look these up"?

Surely there must be some further information. Through the long, long hours he stayed with the lens and waited. And he found nothing.

It was three days. Who will ever forget them? Surely not Professor Williams. He was sweating blood. The whole world was going to pieces without the trace of an explanation. All the mathematics, all the accumulations of the ages had availed for nothing. Charley Huyck held the secret. It was in the stars, and not an astronomer could find it. But with the seventeenth hour came the turn of fortune. The professor was passing through the office. The door was open, and the same fitful wind which had played the original prank was now just as fitfully performing restitution. Williams noticed a piece of paper protruding from the back of the bookcase and fluttering in the breeze. He picked it up. The first words that he saw were in the handwriting of Charley Huyck. He read:

"In the last extremity—in the last phase when there is no longer any water on the earth; when even the oxygen of the atmospheric envelope has been reduced to a minimum—man, or whatever form of intelligence is then upon the earth, must go back to the laws which governed his forebears. Necessity must ever be the law of evolution. There will be no water upon the earth, but there will be an unlimited quantity elsewhere.

"By that time, for instance, the great planet, Jupiter, will be in just a convenient state for exploitation. Gaseous now, it will be, by that time, in just about the stage when the steam and water are condensing into ocean. Eons of millions of years away in the days of dire necessity. By that time the intelligence and consciousness of the earth will have grown equal to the task.

"It is a thing to laugh at (perhaps) just at present. But when we consider the ratio of man's advance in the last hundred years, what will it be in a billion? Not all the laws of the universe have been discovered, by any means. At present we know nothing. Who can tell?

"Aye, who can tell? Perhaps we ourselves have in store the fate we would mete out to another. We have a very dangerous neighbor close beside us. Mars is in dire straits for water. And we know there is life on Mars and intelligence!

The very fact on its face proclaims it. The oceans have dried up; the only way they have of holding life is by bringing their water from the polar snow-caps. Their canals pronounce an advanced state of cooperative intelligence; there is life upon Mars and in an advanced stage of evolution.

"But how far advanced? It is a small planet, and consequently eons of ages in advance of the earth's evolution. In the nature of things Mars cooled off quickly, and life was possible there while the earth was yet a gaseous mass. She has gone to her maturity and into her retrogression; she is approaching her end. She has had less time to produce intelligence than intelligence will have—in the end—upon the earth.

"How far has this intelligence progressed? That is the question. Nature is a slow worker. It took eons of ages to put life upon the earth; it took eons of more ages to make this life conscious. How far will it go? How far has it gone on Mars?"

That was as far the the comments went. The professor dropped his eyes to the rest of the paper. It was a map of the face of Mars, and across its center was a black cross scratched by the dull point of a soft pencil.

He knew the face of Mars. It was the Ascræus Lucus. The oasis at the juncture of a series of canals running much like the spokes of a wheel. The great Uranian and Alander Canals coming in at about right angles.

In two jumps the professor was in the observatory with the great lens swung to focus. It was the great moment out of his lifetime, and the strangest and most eager moment, perhaps, ever lived by any astronomer. His fingers fairly twitched with tension. There before his view was the full face of our Martian neighbor!

But was it? He gasped out a breath of startled exclamation. Was it Mars that he gazed at; the whole face, the whole thing had been changed before him.

Mars has ever been red. Viewed through the telescope it has had the most beautiful tinge imaginable, red ochre, the weird tinge of the desert in sunset. The color of enchantment and of hell!

For it is so. We know that for ages and ages the planet has been burning up; that life was possible only in the dry sea-bottoms and under irrigation. The rest, where the continents once were, was blazing desert. The redness, the beauty, the enchantment that we so admired was burning hell.

All this had changed.

Instead of this was a beautiful shade of iridescent green. The red was gone forever. The great planet standing in the heavens had grown into infinite glory. Like the great Dog Star transplanted.

The professor sought out the Ascræus Lucus. It was hard to find. The whole face had been transfigured; where had been canals was now the beautiful sheen of green and verdure. He realized what he was beholding and what he had never dreamed of seeing; the seas of Mars filled up.

With the stolen oceans our grim neighbor had come back to youth. But how had it been done. It was horror for our world. The great luminescent ball of Opalescence! Europe frozen and New York a mass of ice. It was the earth's destruction. How long could the thing keep up; and whence did it come? What was it?

He sought for the Ascræus Lucus. And he beheld a strange sight. At the very spot where should have been the juncture of the canals he caught what at first looked like a pin-point flame, a strange twinkling light with flitting glow of Opalescence. He watched it, and he wondered. It seemed to the professor to grow; and he noticed that the green about it was of different color. It was winking, like a great force, and much as if alive; baneful.

It was what Charley Huyck had seen. The professor thought of Charley. He had hurried to the mountain. What could Huyck, a mere man, do against a thing like this? There was naught to do but sit and watch it drink of our life-blood. And then—

It was the message, the strange assurance that Huyck was flashing over the world. There was no lack of confidence in the words he was speaking. "Celestial Kinetics," so that was the answer! Certainly it must be so with the truth before him. Williams was a doubter no longer. And Charley Huyck could save them. The man he had humored. Eagerly he waited and stuck by the lens. The whole world waited.

It was perhaps the most terrific moment since creation. To describe it would be like describing doomsday. We all of us went through it, and we all of us thought the end had come; that the earth was torn to atoms and to chaos.

The State of Colorado was lurid with a red light of terror; for a thousand miles the flame shot above the earth and into space. If ever spirit went out in glory that spirit was Charley Huyck! He had come to the moment and to Archimedes. The whole world rocked to the recoil. Compared to it the mightiest earthquake was but a tender shiver. The consciousness of the earth had spoken!

The professor was knocked upon the floor. He knew not what had happened. Out of the windows and to the north the flame of Colorado, like the whole world going up. It was the last moment. But he was a scientist to the end. He had sprained his ankle and his face was bleeding; but for all that he struggled, fought his way to the telescope. And he saw:

The great planet with its sinister, baleful, wicked light in the center, and another light vastly larger covering up half of Mars. What was it? It was moving. The truth set him almost to shouting.

It was the answer of Charley Huyck and of the world. The light grew smaller, smaller, and almost to a pin-point on its way to Mars.

The real climax was in silence. And of all the world only Professor Williams beheld it. The two lights coalesced and spread out; what it was on Mars, of course, we do not know.

But in a few moments all was gone. Only the green of the Martian Sea winked in the sunlight. The luminous opal was gone from the Sargasso. The ocean lay in peace.

It was a terrible three days. Had it not been for the work of Robold and Huyck life would have been destroyed. The pity of it that all of their discoveries have gone with them. Not even Charley realized how terrific the force he was about to loosen.

He had carefully locked everything in vaults for a safe delivery to man. He had expected death, but not the cataclysm. The whole of Mount Robold was shorn away; in its place we have a lake fifty miles in diameter.

So much for celestial kinetics.

And we look to a green and beautiful Mars. We hold no enmity. It was but the law of self-preservation. Let us hope they have enough water; and that their seas will hold. We don't blame them, and we don't blame ourselves, either for that matter. We need what we have, and we hope to keep it.

THE MOON METAL

Garrett P. Serviss (1926)

SOUTH POLAR GOLD

When the news came of the discovery of gold at the south pole, nobody suspected that the beginning had been reached of a new era in the world's history. The newsboys cried "Extra!" as they had done a thousand times for murders, battles, fires, and Wall Street panics, but nobody was excited. In fact, the reports at first seemed so exaggerated and improbable that hardly anybody believed a word of them. Who could have been expected to credit a despatch, forwarded by cable from New Zealand, and signed by an unknown name, which contained such a statement as this:

"A seam of gold which can be cut with a knife has been found within ten miles of the south pole."

The discovery of the pole itself had been announced three years before, and several scientific parties were known to be exploring the remarkable continent that surrounds it. But while they had sent home many highly interesting reports, there had been nothing to suggest the possibility of such an amazing discovery as that which was now announced. Accordingly, most sensible people looked upon the New Zealand despatch as a hoax.

But within a week, and from a different source, flashed another despatch which more than confirmed the first. It declared that gold existed near the South Pole in practically unlimited quantity. Some geologists said this accounted for the greater depth of the Antarctic Ocean. It had always been noticed that the southern hemisphere appeared to be a little overweighted. People now began to prick up their ears, and many letters of inquiry appeared in the newspapers concerning the wonderful tidings from the south. Some asked for information about the shortest route to the new goldfields.

In a little while several additional reports came, some *via* New Zealand, others *via* South America, and all confirming in every respect what had been sent before. Then a New York newspaper sent a swift steamer to the Antarctic, and when this enterprising journal published a four-page cable describing the discoveries in detail, all doubt vanished and the rush began.

Some time I may undertake a description of the wild scenes that occurred when, at last, the inhabitants of the northern hemisphere were convinced that boundless stores of gold existed in the unclaimed and uninhabited wastes surrounding the South Pole. But at present I have something more wonderful to relate.

Let me briefly depict the situation.

For many years silver had been absent from the coinage of the world. Its increasing abundance rendered it unsuitable for money, especially when contrasted with gold. The "silver craze," which had raged in the closing decade of the nineteenth century, was already a forgotten incident of financial history. The gold standard had become universal, and business all over the earth had adjusted itself to that condition. The wheels of industry ran smoothly, and there seemed to be no possibility of any disturbance or interruption. The common monetary system prevailing in every land fostered trade and facilitated the exchange of products. Travelers never had to bother their heads about the currency of money; any coin that passed in New York would pass for its face value in London, Paris, Berlin, Rome, Madrid, St. Petersburg, Constantinople, Cairo, Khartoum, Jerusalem, Peking, or Yeddo. It was indeed the "Golden Age," and the world had never been so free from financial storms.

Upon this peaceful scene the south polar gold discoveries burst like an unheralded tempest.

I happened to be in the company of a famous bank president when the confirmation of those discoveries suddenly filled the streets with yelling newsboys. "Get me one of those 'extras'!" he said, and an office-boy ran out to obey him. As he perused the sheet his face darkened.

"I'm afraid it's too true," he said, at length. "Yes, there seems to be no getting around it. Gold is going to be as plentiful as iron. If there were not such a flood of it, we might manage, but when they begin to make trousers buttons out of the same metal that is now locked and guarded in steel vaults, where will be our standard of worth? My dear fellow," he continued, impulsively laying his hand on my arm, "I would as willingly face the end of the world as this that's coming!"

"You think it so bad, then?" I asked. "But most people will not agree with you. They will regard it as very good news."

"How can it be good?" he burst out. "What have we got to take the place of gold? Can we go back to the age of barter? Can we substitute cattle-pens and wheat-bins for the strong boxes of the Treasury? Can commerce exist with no common measure of exchange?"

"It does indeed look serious," I assented.

"Serious! I tell you, it is the deluge!"

Thereat he clapped on his hat and hurried across the street to the office of another celebrated banker.

His premonitions of disaster turned out to be but too well grounded. The deposits of gold at the south pole were richer than the wildest reports had represented them. The shipments of the precious metal to America and Europe soon became enormous—so enormous that the metal was no longer precious. The price of gold dropped like a falling stone, with accelerated velocity, and within a year every money centre in the world had been swept by a panic. Gold was more common than iron. Every government was compelled to demonetize it, for when once gold had fallen into contempt it was less valuable in the eyes of the public than stamped paper. For once the world had thoroughly learned the lesson that too much of a good thing is worse than none of it.

Then somebody found a new use for gold by inventing a process by which it could be hardened and tempered, assuming a wonderful toughness and elasticity without losing its non-corrosive property, and in this form it rapidly took the place of steel.

In the mean time every effort was made to bolster up credit. Endless were the attempts to find a substitute for gold. The chemists sought it in their laboratories and the mineralogists in the mountains and deserts. Platinum might have served, but it, too, had become a drug in the market through the discovery of immense deposits. Out of the twenty odd elements which had been rarer and more valuable than gold, such as uranium, gallium, etc., not one was found to answer the purpose. In short, it was evident that since both gold and silver had become too abundant to serve any longer for a money standard, the planet held no metal suitable to take their place.

The entire monetary system of the world must be readjusted, but in the readjustment it was certain to fall to pieces. In fact, it had already fallen to pieces; the only recourse was to paper money, but whether this was based upon agriculture or mining or manufacture, it gave varying standards, not only among the different nations, but in successive years in the same country. Exports and imports practically ceased. Credit was discredited, commerce perished, and the world, at a bound, seemed to have gone back, financially and industrially, to the dark ages.

One final effort was made. A great financial congress was assembled at New York. Representatives of all the nations took part in it. The ablest financiers of Europe and America united the efforts of their genius and the results of their experience to solve the great problem. The various governments all solemnly stipulated to abide by the decision of the congress.

But, after spending months in hard but fruitless labor, that body was no nearer the end of its undertaking than when it first assembled. The entire world awaited its decision with bated breath, and yet the decision was not formed.

At this paralyzing crisis a most unexpected event suddenly opened the way.

THE MAGICIAN OF SCIENCE

An attendant entered the room where the perplexed financiers were in session and presented a peculiar-looking card to the president, Mr. Boon. The president took the card in his hand and instantly fell into a brown study. So complete was his absorption that Herr Finster, the celebrated Berlin banker, who had been addressing the chair for the last two hours from the opposite end of the long table, got confused, entirely lost track of his verb, and suddenly dropped into his seat, very red in the face and wearing a most injured expression.

But President Boon paid no attention except to the singular card, which he continued to turn over and over, balancing it on his fingers and holding it now at arm's-length and then near his nose, with one eye squinted as if he were trying to look through a hole in the card.

At length this odd conduct of the presiding officer drew all eyes upon the card, and then everybody shared the interest of Mr. Boon. In shape and size the card was not extraordinary, but it was composed of metal. What metal? That question had immediately arisen in Mr. Boon's mind when the card came into his hand, and now it exercised the wits of all the others. Plainly it was not tin, brass, copper, bronze, silver, aluminum—although its lightness might have suggested that metal—nor even base gold.

The president, although a skilled metallurgist, confessed his inability to say what it was. So intent had he become in examining the curious bit of metal that he forgot it was a visitor's card of introduction, and did not even look for the name which it presumably bore.

As he held the card up to get a better light upon it a stray sunbeam from the window fell across the metal and instantly it bloomed with exquisite colors! The president's chair being in the darker end of the room, the radiant card suffused the atmosphere about him with a faint rose tint, playing with surprising liveliness into alternate canary color and violet.

The effect upon the company of clear-headed financiers was extremely remarkable. The unknown metal appeared to exercise a kind of mesmeric influence, its soft hues blending together in a chromatic harmony which captivated the sense of vision as the ears are charmed by a perfectly rendered song. Gradually all gathered in an eager group around the president's chair.

"What can it be?" was repeated from lip to lip.

"Did you ever see anything like it?" asked Mr. Boon for the twentieth time.

None of them had ever seen the like of it. A spell fell upon the assemblage. For five minutes no one spoke, while Mr. Boon continued to chase the flickering sunbeam with the wonderful card. Suddenly the silence was broken by a voice which had a touch of awe in it:

"It must be the metal!"

The speaker was an English financier, First Lord of the Treasury, Hon. James Hampton-Jones, K.C.B. Immediately everybody echoed his remark, and the strain being thus relieved, the spell dropped from them and several laughed loudly over their momentary aberration.

President Boon recollected himself, and, coloring slightly, placed the card flat on the table, in order more clearly to see the name. In plain red letters it stood forth with such surprising distinctness that Mr. Boon wondered why he had so long overlooked it.

"DR. MAX SYX."

"Tell the gentleman to come in," said the president, and thereupon the attendant threw open the door.

The owner of the mysterious card fixed every eye as he entered. He was several inches more than six feet in height. His complexion was very dark, his eyes were intensely black, bright, and deep-set, his eyebrows were bushy and up-curled at the ends, his sable hair was close-trimmed, and his ears were narrow, pointed at the top, and prominent. He wore black mustaches, covering only half the width of his lip and drawn into projecting needles on each side, while a spiked black beard adorned the middle of his chin.

He smiled as he stepped confidently forward, with a courtly bow, but it was a very disconcerting smile, because it more than half resembled a sneer. This uncommon person did not wait to be addressed.

"I have come to solve your problem," he said, facing President Boon, who had swung round on his pivoted chair.

"The metal!" exclaimed everybody in a breath, and with a unanimity and excitement which would have astonished them if they had been spectators instead of actors of the scene. The tall stranger bowed and smiled again:

"Just so," he said. "What do you think of it?"

"It is beautiful!"

Again the reply came from every mouth simultaneously, and again if the speakers could have been listeners they would have wondered not only at their earnestness, but at their words, for why should they instantly and unanimously pronounce that beautiful which they had not even seen? But every man knew he had seen it, for instinctively their minds reverted to the card and recognized in it the metal referred to. The mesmeric spell seemed once more to fall upon the assemblage, for the financiers noticed nothing remarkable in the next act of the stranger, which was to take a chair, uninvited, at the table, and the moment he sat down he became the presiding officer as naturally as if he had just been elected to that post. They all waited for him to speak, and when he opened his mouth they listened with breathless attention.

His words were of the best English, but there was some peculiarity, which they had already noticed, either in his voice or his manner of enunciation, which struck all of the listeners as denoting a foreigner. But none of them could satisfactorily place him. Neither the Americans, the Englishmen, the Germans, the Frenchmen, the Russians, the Austrians, the Italians, the Spaniards, the Turks, the Japanese, or the Chinese at the board could decide to what race or nationality the stranger belonged.

"This metal," he began, taking the card from Mr. Boon's hand, "I have discovered and named. I call it 'artemisium.' I can produce it, in the pure form, abundantly enough to replace gold, giving it the same relative value that gold possessed when it was the universal standard."

As Dr. Syx spoke he snapped the card with his thumb-nail and it fluttered with quivering hues like a humming-bird hovering over a flower. He seemed to await a reply, and President Boon asked:

"What guarantee can you give that the supply would be adequate and continuous?"

"I will conduct a committee of this congress to my mine in the Rocky Mountains, where, in anticipation of the event, I have accumulated enough refined artemisium to provide every civilized land with an amount of coin equivalent to that which it formerly held in gold. I can there satisfy you of my ability to maintain the production."

"But how do we know that this metal of yours will answer the purpose?"

"Try it," was the laconic reply.

"There is another difficulty," pursued the president. "People will not accept a new metal in place of gold unless they are convinced that it possesses equal intrinsic value. They must first become familiar with it, and it must be abundant enough and desirable enough to be used sparingly in the arts, just as gold was."

"I have provided for all that," said the stranger, with one of his disconcerting smiles. "I assure you that there will be no trouble with the people. They will be only too eager to get and to use the metal. Let me show you."

He stepped to the door and immediately returned with two black attendants bearing a large tray filled with articles shaped from the same metal as that of which the card was composed. The financiers all jumped to their feet with exclamations of surprise and admiration, and gathered around the tray, whose dazzling contents lighted up the corner of the room where it had been placed as if the moon were shining there.

There were elegantly formed vases, adorned with artistic figures, embossed and incised, and glowing with delicate colors which shimmered in tiny waves with the slightest motion of the tray. Cups, pins, finger-rings, earrings, watch-chains, combs, studs, lockets, medals, tableware, models of coins—in brief, almost every article in the fabrication of which precious metals have been employed was to be seen there in profusion, and all composed of the strange new metal which everybody on the spot declared was far more splendid than gold.

"Do you think it will answer?" asked Dr. Syx.

"We do," was the unanimous reply.

All then resumed their seats at the table, the tray with its magnificent array having been placed in the centre of the board. This display had a remarkable influence. Confidence awoke in the breasts of the financiers. The dark clouds that had oppressed them rolled off, and the prospect grew decidedly brighter.

"What terms do you demand?" at length asked Mr. Boon, cheerfully rubbing his hands.

"I must have military protection for my mine and reducing works," replied Dr. Syx. "Then I shall ask the return of one per cent, on the circulating medium, together with the privilege of disposing of a certain amount of the metal—to be limited by agreement—to the public for use in the arts. Of the proceeds of this sale I will pay ten per cent. to the government in consideration of its protection."

"But," exclaimed President Boon, "that will make you the richest man who ever lived!"

"Undoubtedly," was the reply.

"Why," added Mr. Boon, opening his eyes wider as the facts continued to dawn upon him, "you will become the financial dictator of the whole earth!"

"Undoubtedly," again responded Dr. Syx, unmoved. "That is what I purpose to become. My discovery entitles me to no less. But, remember, I place myself under government inspection and restriction. I should not be allowed to flood the market, even if I were disposed to do so. But my own interest would restrain me. It is to my advantage that artemisium, once adopted, shall remain stable in value."

A shadow of doubt suddenly crossed the president's face.

"Suppose your secret is discovered," he said. "Surely your mine will not remain the only one. If you, in so short a time, have been able to accumulate an immense quantity of the new metal, it must be extremely abundant. Others will discover it, and then where shall we be?"

While Mr. Boon uttered these words, those who were watching Dr. Syx (as the president was not) resembled persons whose startled eyes are fixed upon a wild beast preparing to spring. As Mr. Boon ceased speaking he turned towards the visitor, and instantly his lips fell apart and his face paled.

Dr. Syx had drawn himself up to his full stature, and his features were distorted with that peculiar mocking smile which had now returned with a concentrated expression of mingled self-confidence and disdain.

"Will you have relief, or not?" he asked in a dry, hard voice. "What can you do? I alone possess the secret which can restore industry and commerce. If you reject my offer, do you think a second one will come?"

President Boon found voice to reply, stammeringly:

"I did not mean to suggest a rejection of the offer. I only wished to inquire if you thought it probable that there would be no repetition of what occurred after gold was found at the south pole?"

"The earth may be full of my metal," returned Dr. Syx, almost fiercely, "but so long as I alone possess the knowledge how to extract it, is it of any more worth than common dirt? But come," he added, after a pause and softening his manner, "I have other schemes. Will you, as representatives of the leading nations, undertake the introduction of artemisium as a substitute for gold, or will you not?"

"Can we not have time for deliberation?" asked President Boon.

"Yes, one hour. Within that time I shall return to learn your decision," replied Dr. Syx, rising and preparing to depart. "I leave these things," pointing to the tray, "in your keeping, and," significantly, "I trust your decision will be a wise one."

His curious smile again curved his lips and shot the ends of his mustache upward, and the influence of that smile remained in the room when he had closed the door behind him. The financiers gazed at one another for several minutes in silence, then they turned towards the coruscating metal that filled the tray.

THE GRAND TETON MINE

Away on the western border of Wyoming, in the all but inaccessible heart of the Rocky Mountains, three mighty brothers, "The Big Tetons," look perpendicularly into the blue eye of Jenny's Lake, lying at the bottom of the profound depression among the mountains called Jackson's Hole. Bracing against one another for support, these remarkable peaks lift their granite spires from 12,000 to nearly 14,000 feet into the blue dome that arches the crest of the continent. Their sides, and especially those of their chief, the Grand Teton, are streaked with glaciers, which shine like silver trappings when the morning sun comes up above the wilderness of mountains stretching away eastward from the hole.

When the first white men penetrated this wonderful region, and one of them bestowed his wife's name upon Jenny's Lake, they were intimidated by the Grand Teton. It made their flesh creep, accustomed though they were to rough scrambling among mountain gorges and on the brows of immense precipices, when they glanced up the face of the peak, where the cliffs fall, one below another, in a series of breathless descents, and imagined themselves clinging for dear life to those skyey battlements.

But when, in 1872, Messrs. Stevenson and Langford finally reached the top of the Grand Teton—the only successful members of a party of nine practised climbers who had started together from the bottom—they found there a little rectangular enclosure, made by piling up rocks, six or seven feet across and three feet in height, bearing evidences of great age, and indicating that the red Indians had, for some unknown purpose, resorted to the summit of this tremendous peak long before the white men invaded their mountains. Yet neither the Indians nor the whites ever really conquered the Teton, for above the highest point that they attained rises a granite buttress, whose smooth vertical sides seemed to them to defy everything but wings.

Winding across the sage-covered floor of Jackson's Hole runs the Shoshone, or Snake River, which takes its rise from Jackson's Lake at the northern end of the basin, and then, as if shrinking from the threatening brows of the Tetons, whose fall would block its progress, makes a détour of one hundred miles around the buttressed heights of the range before it finds a clear way across Idaho, and so on to the Columbia River and the Pacific Ocean.

On a July morning, about a month after the visit of Dr. Max Syx to the assembled financiers in New York, a party of twenty horsemen, following a mountain-trail, arrived on the eastern margin of Jackson's Hole, and pausing upon a commanding eminence, with exclamations of wonder, glanced across the great depression, where lay the shining coils of the Snake River, at the towering forms of the Tetons, whose ice-striped cliffs flashed lightnings in the sunshine. Even the impassive broncos that the party rode lifted their heads inquiringly, and snorted as if in equine astonishment at the magnificent spectacle.

One familiar with the place would have noticed something, which, to his mind, would have seemed more surprising than the pageantry of the mountains in their morning sun-bath. Curling above one of the wild gorges that cut the lower slopes of the Tetons was a thick black smoke, which, when lifted by a passing breeze, obscured the precipices half-way to the summit of the peak.

Had the Grand Teton become a volcano? Certainly no hunting or exploring party could make a smoke like that. But a word from the leader of the party of horsemen explained the mystery.

"There is my mill, and the mine is underneath it."

The speaker was Dr. Syx, and his companions were members of the financial congress. When he quitted their presence in New York, with the promise to return within an hour for their reply, he had no doubt in his own mind what that reply would be. He knew they would accept his proposition, and they did. No time was then lost in communicating with the various governments, and arrangements were quickly perfected whereby, in case the inspection of Dr. Syx's mine and its resources proved satisfactory, America and Europe should unite in adopting the new metal as the basis of their coinage. As soon as this stage in the negotiations was reached, it only remained to send a committee of financiers and metallurgists, in company with Dr. Syx, to the Rocky Mountains. They started under the doctor's guidance, completing the last stage of their journey on horseback.

"An inspection of the records at Washington," Dr. Syx continued, addressing the horsemen, "will show that I have filed a claim covering ten acres of ground around the mouth of my mine. This was done as soon as I had discovered the metal. The filing of the claim and the subsequent proceedings which perfected my ownership attracted no attention, because everybody was thinking of the south pole and its gold-fields."

The party gathered closer around Dr. Syx and listened to his words with silent attention, while their horses rubbed noses and jingled their gold-mounted trappings.

"As soon as I had legally protected myself," he continued, "I employed a force of men, transported my machinery and material across the mountains, erected my furnaces, and opened the mine. I was safe from intrusion, and even from idle curiosity, for the reason I have just mentioned. In fact, so exclusive was the attraction of the new gold-fields that I had difficulty in obtaining workmen, and finally I sent to Africa and engaged negroes, whom I placed in charge of trustworthy foremen. Accordingly, with half a dozen exceptions, you will see only black men at the mine."

"And with their aid you have mined enough metal to supply the mints of the world?" asked President Boon.

"Exactly so," was the reply. "But I no longer employ the large force which I needed at first."

"How much metal have you on hand? I am aware that you have already answered this question during our preliminary negotiations, but I ask it again for the benefit of some members of our party who were not present then."

"I shall show you to-day," said Dr. Syx, with his curious smile, "2500 tons of refined artemisium, stacked in rock-cut vaults under the Grand Teton."

"And you have dared to collect such inconceivable wealth in one place?"

"You forget that it is not wealth until the people have learned to value it, and the governments have put their stamp upon it."

"True, but how did you arrive at the proper moment?"

"Easily. I first ascertained that before the Antarctic discoveries the world contained altogether about 16,000 tons of gold, valued at $450,000 per ton, or $7,200,000,000 worth all told. Now my metal weighs, bulk for bulk, one-quarter as much as gold. It might be reckoned at the same intrinsic value per ton, but I have considered it preferable to take advantage of the smaller weight of the new metal, which permits us to make coins of the same size as the old ones, but only one-quarter as heavy, by giving to artemisium four times the value per ton that gold had. Thus only 4000 tons of the new metal are required to supply the place of the 16,000 tons of gold. The 2500 tons which I already have on hand are more than enough for coinage. The rest I can supply as fast as needed."

The party did not wait for further explanations. They were eager to see the wonderful mine and the store of treasure. Spurs were applied, and they galloped down the steep trail, forded the Snake River, and, skirting the shore of Jenny's Lake, soon found themselves gazing up the headlong slopes and dizzy parapets of the Grand Teton. Dr. Syx led them by a steep ascent to the mouth of the canyon, above one of whose walls stood his mill, and where the "Champ! Champ!" of a powerful engine saluted their ears.

THE WEALTH OF THE WORLD

An electric light shot its penetrating rays into a gallery cut through virgin rock and running straight towards the heart of the Teton. The centre of the gallery was occupied by a narrow railway, on which a few flat cars, propelled by electric power, passed to and fro. Black-skinned and silent workmen rode on the cars, both when they came laden with broken masses of rock from the farther end of the tunnel and when they returned empty.

Suddenly, to an eye situated a little way within the gallery, appeared at the entrance the dark face of Dr. Syx, wearing its most discomposing smile, and a moment later the broader countenance of President Boon loomed in the electric glare beside the doctor's black framework of eyebrows and mustache. Behind them were grouped the other visiting financiers.

"This tunnel," said Dr. Syx, "leads to the mine head, where the ore-bearing rock is blasted."

As he spoke a hollow roar issued from the depths of the mountain, followed in a short time by a gust of foul air.

"You probably will not care to go in there," said the doctor, "and, in fact, it is very uncomfortable. But we shall follow the next car-load to the smelter, and you can witness the reduction of the ore."

Accordingly when another car came rumbling out of the tunnel, with its load of cracked rock, they all accompanied it into an adjoining apartment, where it was cast into a metallic shute, through which, they were informed, it reached the furnace.

"While it is melting," explained Dr. Syx, "certain elements, the nature of which I must beg to keep secret, are mixed with the ore, causing chemical action which results in the extraction of the metal. Now let me show you pure artemisium issuing from the furnace."

He led the visitors through two apartments into a third, one side of which was walled by the front of a furnace. From this projected two or three small spouts, and iridescent streams of molten metal fell from the spouts into earthen receptacles from which the blazing liquid was led, like flowing iron, into a system of molds, where it was allowed to cool and harden.

The financiers looked on wondering, and their astonishment grew when they were conducted into the rock-cut store-rooms beneath, where they saw metallic ingots glowing like gigantic opals in the light which Dr. Syx turned on. They were piled in rows along the walls as high as a man could reach. A very brief inspection sufficed to convince the visitors that Dr. Syx was able to perform all that he promised. Although they had not penetrated the secret of his process of reducing the ore, yet they had seen the metal flowing from the furnace, and the piles of ingots proved conclusively that he had uttered no vain boast when he said he could give the world a new coinage.

But President Boon, being himself a metallurgist, desired to inspect the mysterious ore a little more closely. Possibly he was thinking that if another mine was destined to be discovered he might as well be the discoverer as anybody. Dr. Syx attempted no concealment, but his smile became more than usually scornful as he stopped a laden car and invited the visitors to help themselves.

"I think," he said, "that I have struck the only lode of this ore in the Teton, or possibly in this part of the world, but I don't know for certain. There may be plenty of it only waiting to be found. That, however, doesn't trouble me. The great point is that nobody except myself knows how to extract the metal."

Mr. Boon closely examined the chunk of rock which he had taken from the car. Then he pulled a lens from his pocket, with a deprecatory glance at Dr. Syx.

"Oh, that's all right," said the latter, with a laugh, the first that these gentlemen had ever heard from his lips, and it almost made them shudder; "put it to every test, examine it with the microscope, with fire, with electricity, with the spectroscope—in every way you can think of! I assure you it is worth your while!"

Again Dr. Syx uttered his freezing laugh, passing into the familiar smile, which had now become an undisguised mock.

"Upon my word," said Mr. Boon, taking his eye from the lens, "I see no sign of any metal here!"

"Look at the green specks!" cried the doctor, snatching the specimen from the president's hand. "That's it! That's artemisium! But it's of no use unless you can get it out and purify it, which is my secret!"

For the third time Dr. Syx laughed, and his merriment affected the visitors so disagreeably that they showed impatience to be gone. Immediately he changed his manner.

"Come into my office," he said, with a return to the graciousness which had characterized him ever since the party started from New York.

When they were all seated, and the doctor had handed round a box of cigars, he resumed the conversation in his most amiable manner.

"You see, gentlemen," he said, turning a piece of ore in his fingers, "artemisium is like aluminum. It can only be obtained in the metallic form by a special process. While these greenish particles, which you may perhaps mistake for chrysolite, or some similar unisilicate, really contain the precious metal, they are not entirely composed of it. The process by which I separate out the metallic element while the ore is passing through the furnace is, in truth, quite simple, and its very simplicity guards my secret. Make your minds easy as to over-production. A man is as likely to jump over the moon as to find me out."

"But," he continued, again changing his manner, "we have had business enough for one day; now for a little recreation." While speaking the doctor pressed a button on his desk, and the room, which was illuminated by electric lamps—for there were no windows in the building—suddenly became dark, except part of one wall, where a broad area of light appeared. Dr. Syx's voice had become very soothing when next he spoke: "I am fond of amusing myself with a peculiar form of the magic-lantern, which I invented some years ago, and which I have never exhibited except for the entertainment of my friends. The pictures will appear upon the wall, the apparatus being concealed."

He had hardly ceased speaking when the illuminated space seemed to melt away, leaving a great opening, through which the spectators looked as if into another world on the opposite side of the wall. For a minute or two they could not clearly discern what was presented; then, gradually, the flitting scenes and figures became more distinct until the lifelikeness of the spectacle absorbed their whole attention.

Before them passed, in panoramic review, a sunny land, filled with brilliant-hued vegetation, and dotted with villages and cities which were bright with light-colored buildings. People appeared moving through the scenes, as in a cinematograph exhibition, but with infinitely more semblance of reality. In fact, the pictures, blending one into another, seemed to be life itself. Yet it was not an earth-like scene. The colors of the passing landscape were such as no man in the room had ever beheld; and the people, tall, round-limbed, with florid complexion, golden hair, and brilliant eyes and lips, were indescribably beautiful and graceful in all their movements.

From the land the view passed out to sea, and bright blue waves, edged with creaming foam, ran swiftly under the spectator's eyes, and occasionally, driven before light winds, appeared fleets of daintily shaped vessels, which reminded the beholder, by their flashing wings, of the feigned "ship of pearl."

After the fairy ships and breezy sea views came a long, curving line of coast, brilliant with coral sands, and indented by frequent bays, along whose enchanting shores lay pleasant towns, the landscapes behind them splendid with groves, meadows, and streams.

Presently the shifting photographic tape, or whatever the mechanism may have been, appeared to have settled upon a chosen scene, and there it rested. A broad champaign reached away to distant sapphire mountains, while the foreground was occupied by a magnificent house, resembling a large country villa, fronted with a garden, shaded by bowers and festoons of huge, brilliant flowers. Birds of radiant plumage flitted among the trees and blossoms, and then appeared a company of gayly attired people, including many young girls, who joined hands and danced in a ring, apparently with shouts of laughter, while a group of musicians standing near thrummed and blew upon curiously shaped instruments.

Suddenly the shadow of a dense cloud flitted across the scene; whereupon the brilliant birds flew away with screams of terror which almost seemed to reach the ears of the onlookers through the wall. An expression of horror came over the faces of the people. The children broke from their merry circle and ran for protection to their elders. The utmost confusing and whelming terror were evidenced for a moment—then the ground split asunder, and the house and the garden, with all their living occupants were swallowed by an awful chasm which opened just where they had stood. The great rent ran in a widening line across the sunlit landscape until it reached the horizon, when the distant mountains crumbled, clouds poured in from all sides at once, and billows of flame burst through them as they veiled the scene.

But in another instant the commotion was over, and the world whose curious spectacles had been enacted as if on the other side of a window, seemed to retreat swiftly into space, until at last, emerging from a fleecy cloud, it reappeared in the form of the full moon hanging in the sky, but larger than is its wont, with its dry ocean-beds, its keen-spired peaks, its ragged mountain ranges, its gaping chasms, its immense crater rings, and Tycho, the chief of them all, shooting raylike streaks across the scarred face of the abandoned lunar globe. The show was ended, and Dr. Syx, turning on only a partial illumination in the room, rose slowly to his feet, his tall form appearing strangely magnified in the gloom, and invited his bewildered guests to accompany him to his house, outside the mill, where he said dinner awaited them. As they emerged into daylight they acted like persons just aroused from an opiate dream.

WONDERS OF THE NEW METAL

Within a twelvemonth after the visit of President Boon and his fellow financiers to the mine in the Grand Teton a railway had been constructed from Jackson's Hole, connecting with one of the Pacific lines, and the distribution of the new metal was begun. All of Dr. Syx's terms had been accepted. United States troops occupied a permanent encampment on the upper waters of the Snake River, to afford protection, and as the consignments of precious ingots were hurried east and west on guarded trains, the mints all over the world resumed their activity. Once more a common monetary standard prevailed, and commerce revived as if touched by a magic wand.

Artemisium quickly won its way in popular favor. Its matchless beauty alone was enough. Not only was it gladly accepted in the form of money, but its success was instantaneous in the arts. Dr. Syx and the inspectors representing the various nations found it difficult to limit the output to the agreed upon amount. The demand was incessant.

Goldsmiths and jewellers continually discovered new excellences in the wonderful metal. Its properties of translucence and refraction enabled skilful artists to perform marvels. By suitable management a chain of artemisium could be made to resemble a string of vari-colored gems, each separate link having a tint of its own, while, as the wearer moved, delicate complementary colors chased one another, in rapid undulation, from end to end.

A fresh charm was added by the new metal to the personal adornment of women, and an enhanced splendor to the pageants of society. Gold in its palmiest days had never enjoyed such a vogue. A crowded reception room or a dinner party where artemisium abounded possessed an indescribable atmosphere of luxury and richness, refined in quality, yet captivating to every sense. Imaginative persons went so far as to aver that the sight and presence of the metal exercised a strangely soothing and dreamy power over the mind, like the influence of moonlight streaming through the tree-tops on a still, balmy night.

The public curiosity in regard to the origin of artemisium was boundless. The various nations published official bulletins in which the general facts— omitting, of course, such incidents as the singular exhibition seen by the visiting financiers on the wall of Dr. Syx's office—were detailed to gratify the universal desire for information.

President Boon not only submitted the specimens of ore-bearing rock which he had brought from the mine to careful analysis, but also appealed to several of the greatest living chemists and mineralogists to aid him; but they were all equally mystified. The green substance contained in the ore, although differing slightly from ordinary chrysolite, answered all the known tests of that mineral. It was remembered, however, that Dr. Syx had said that they would be likely to mistake the substance for chrysolite, and the result of their experiments justified his prediction. Evidently the doctor had gone a stone's-cast beyond the chemistry of the day, and, just as evidently, he did not mean to reveal his discovery for the benefit of science, nor for the benefit of any pockets except his own.

Notwithstanding the failure of the chemists to extract anything from Dr. Syx's ore, the public at large never doubted that the secret would be discovered in good time, and thousands of prospectors flocked to the Teton Mountains in search of the ore. And without much difficulty they found it. Evidently the doctor had been mistaken in thinking that his mine might be the only one. The new miners hurried specimens of the green-speckled rock to the chemical laboratories for experimentation, and meanwhile began to lay up stores of the ore in anticipation of the time when the proper way to extract the metal should be discovered.

But, alas! that time did not come. The fresh ore proved to be as refractory as that which had been obtained from Dr. Syx. But in the midst of the universal disappointment there came a new sensation.

One morning the newspapers glared with a despatch from Grand Teton station announcing that the metal itself had been discovered by prospectors on the eastern slope of the main peak.

"It outcrops in many places," ran the despatch, "and many small nuggets have been picked out of crevices in the rocks."

The excitement produced by this news was even greater than when gold was discovered at the south pole. Again a mad rush was made for the Tetons. The heights around Jackson's Hole and the shores of Jackson's and Jenny's lakes were quickly dotted with camps, and the military force had to be doubled to keep off the curious, and occasionally menacing, crowds which gathered in the vicinity and seemed bent on unearthing the great secret locked behind the windowless walls of the mill, where the column of black smoke and the roar of the engine served as reminders of the incredible wealth which the sole possessor of that secret was rolling up.

This time no mistake had been made. It was a fact that the metal, in virgin purity, had been discovered scattered in various places on the ledges of the Grand Teton. In a little while thousands had obtained specimens with their own hands. The quantity was distressingly small, considering the number and the eagerness of the seekers, but that it was genuine artemisium not even Dr. Syx could have denied. He, however, made no attempt to deny it.

"Yes," he said, when questioned, "I find that I have been deceived. At first I thought the metal existed only in the form of the green ore, but of late I have come upon veins of pure artemisium in my mine. I am glad for your sakes, but sorry for my own. Still, it may turn out that there is no great amount of free artemisium after all."

While the doctor talked in this manner close observers detected a lurking sneer which his acquaintances had not noticed since artemisium was first adopted as the money basis of the world.

The crowd that swarmed upon the mountain quickly exhausted all of the visible supply of the metal. Sometimes they found it in a thin stratum at the bottom of crevices, where it could be detached in opalescent plates and leaves of the thickness of paper. These superficial deposits evidently might have been formed from water holding the metal in solution. Occasionally, deep cracks contained nuggets and wiry masses which looked as if they had run together when molten.

The most promising spots were soon staked out in miners' claims, machinery was procured, stock companies were formed, and borings were begun. The enthusiasm arising from the earlier finds and the flattering surface indications caused everybody to work with feverish haste and energy, and within two months one hundred tunnels were piercing the mountain.

For a long time nobody was willing to admit the truth which gradually forced itself upon the attention of the miners. The deeper they went the scarcer became the indications of artemisium! In fact, such deposits as were found were confined to fissures near the surface. But Dr. Syx continued to report a surprising increase in the amount of free metal in his mine, and this encouraged all who had not exhausted their capital to push on their tunnels in the hope of finally striking a vein. At length, however, the smaller operators gave up in despair, until only one heavily capitalized company remained at work.

A STRANGE DISCOVERY

"It is my belief that Dr. Max Syx is a deceiver."

The person who uttered this opinion was a young engineer, Andrew Hall, who had charge of the operations of one of the mining companies which were driving tunnels into the Grand Teton.

"What do you mean by that?" asked President Boon, who was the principal backer of the enterprise.

"I mean," replied Hall, "that there is no free metal in this mountain, and Dr. Syx knows there is none."

"But he is getting it himself from his mine," retorted President Boon.

"So he says, but who has seen it? No one is admitted into the Syx mine, his foremen are forbidden to talk, and his workmen are specially imported negroes who do not understand the English language."

"But," persisted Mr. Boon, "how, then, do you account for the nuggets scattered over the mountain? And, beside, what object could Dr. Syx have in pretending that there is free metal to be had for the digging?"

"He may have salted the mountain, for all I know," said Hall. "As for his object, I confess I am entirely in the dark; but, for all that, I am convinced that we shall find no more metal if we dig ten miles for it."

"Nonsense," said the president; "if we keep on we shall strike it. Did not Dr. Syx himself admit that he found no free artemisium until his tunnel had reached the core of the peak? We must go as deep as he has gone before we give up."

"I fear the depths he attains are beyond most people's reach," was Hall's answer, while a thoughtful look crossed his clear-cut brow, "but since you desire it, of course the work shall go on. I should like, however, to change the direction of the tunnel."

"Certainly," replied Mr. Boon; "bore in whatever direction you think proper, only don't despair."

About a month after this conversation Andrew Hall, with whom a community of tastes in many things had made me intimately acquainted, asked me one morning to accompany him into his tunnel.

"I want to have a trusty friend at my elbow," he said, "for, unless I am a dreamer, something remarkable will happen within the next hour, and two witnesses are better than one."

I knew Hall was not the person to make such a remark carelessly, and my curiosity was intensely excited, but, knowing his peculiarities, I did not press him for an explanation. When we arrived at the head of the tunnel I was surprised at finding no workmen there.

"I stopped blasting some time ago," said Hall, in explanation, "for a reason which, I hope, will become evident to you very soon. Lately I have been boring very slowly, and yesterday I paid off the men and dismissed them with the announcement, which, I am confident, President Boon will sanction after he hears my report of this morning's work, that the tunnel is abandoned. You see, I am now using a drill which I can manage without assistance. I believe the work is almost completed, and I want you to witness the end of it."

He then carefully applied the drill, which noiselessly screwed its nose into the rock. When it had sunk to a depth of a few inches he withdrew it, and, taking a hand-drill capable of making a hole not more than an eighth of an inch in diameter, cautiously began boring in the centre of the larger cavity. He had made hardly a hundred turns of the handle when the drill shot through the rock! A gratified smile illuminated his features, and he said in a suppressed voice:

"Don't be alarmed; I'm going to put out the light."

Instantly we were in complete darkness, but being close at Hall's side I could detect his movements. He pulled out the drill, and for half a minute remained motionless as if listening. There was no sound.

"I must enlarge the opening," he whispered, and immediately the faint grating of a sharp tool cutting through the rock informed me of his progress.

"There," at last he said, "I think that will do; now for a look."

I could tell that he had placed his eye at the hole and was gazing with breathless attention. Presently he pulled my sleeve.

"Put your eye here," he whispered, pushing me into the proper position for looking through the hole.

At first I could discern nothing except a smoky blue glow. But soon my vision cleared a little, and then I perceived that I was gazing into a narrow tunnel which met ours directly end to end. Glancing along the axis of this gallery I saw, some two hundred yards away, a faint light which evidently indicated the mouth of the tunnel.

At the end where we had met it the mysterious tunnel was considerably widened at one side, as if the excavators had started to change direction and then abandoned the work, and in this elbow I could just see the outlines of two or three flat cars loaded with broken stone, while a heap of the same material lay near them. Through the centre of the tunnel ran a railway track.

"Do you know what you are looking at?" asked Hall in my ear.

"I begin to suspect," I replied, "that you have accidentally run into Dr. Syx's mine."

"If Dr. Syx had been on his guard this accident wouldn't have happened," replied Hall, with an almost inaudible chuckle.

"I heard you remark a month ago," I said, "that you were changing the direction of your tunnel. Has this been the aim of your labors ever since?"

"You have hit it," he replied. "Long ago I became convinced that my company was throwing away its money in a vain attempt to strike a lode of pure artemisium. But President Boon has great faith in Dr. Syx, and would not give up the work. So I adopted what I regarded as the only practicable method of proving the truth of my opinion and saving the company's funds. An electric indicator, of my invention, enabled me to locate the Syx tunnel when I got near it, and I have met it end on, and opened this peep-hole in order to observe the doctor's operations. I feel that such spying is entirely justified in the circumstances. Although I cannot yet explain just how or why I feel sure that Dr. Syx was the cause of the sudden discovery of the surface nuggets, and that he has encouraged the miners for his own ends, until he has brought ruin to thousands who have spent their last cent in driving useless tunnels into this mountain. It is a righteous thing to expose him."

"But," I interposed, "I do not see that you have exposed anything yet except the interior of a tunnel."

"You will see more clearly after a while," was the reply.

Hall now placed his eye again at the aperture, and was unable entirely to repress the exclamation that rose to his lips. He remained staring through the hole for several minutes without uttering a word. Presently I noticed that the lenses of his eye were illuminated by a ray of light coming through the hole, but he did not stir.

After a long inspection he suddenly applied his ear to the hole and listened intently for at least five minutes. Not a sound was audible to me, but, by an occasional pressure of the hand, Hall signified that some important disclosure was reaching his sense of hearing. At length he removed his ear.

"Pardon me," he whispered, "for keeping you so long in waiting, but what I have just seen and overheard was of a nature to admit of no interruption. He is still talking, and by pressing your ear against the hole you may be able to catch what he says."

"Who is 'he'?"

"Look for yourself."

I placed my eye at the aperture, and almost recoiled with the violence of my surprise. The tunnel before me was brilliantly illuminated, and within three feet of the wall of rock behind which we crouched stood Dr. Syx. Well, they've spent a pretty lot of money for their experience, and I rather think we shall not be troubled again by artemisium-seekers for some time to come."

The doctor's voice ceased, and instantly I clapped my eye to the hole. He had changed his position so that his black eyes now looked straight at the aperture. My heart was in my mouth, for at first I believed from his expression that he had detected the gleam of my eyeball. But if so, he probably mistook it for a bit of mica in the rock, and paid no further attention. Then his lips moved, and I put my ear again to the hole. He seemed to be replying to a question that the foreman had asked.

"If they do," he said, "they will never guess the real secret."

Thereupon he turned on his heel, kicked a bit of rock off the track, and strode away towards the entrance. The foreman paused long enough to turn out the electric lamp, and then followed the doctor.

"Well," asked Hall, "what have you heard?"

I told him everything.

"It fully corroborates the evidence of my own eyes and ears," he remarked, "and we may count ourselves extremely lucky. It is not likely that Dr. Syx will be heard a second time proclaiming his deception with his own lips. It is plain that he was led to talk as he did to the foreman on account of the latter's having informed him of the sudden discharge of my men this morning. Their presence within ear-shot of our hiding-place during their conversation was, of course, pure accident, and so you can see how kind fortune has been to us. I expected to have to watch and listen and form deductions for a week, at least, before getting the information which five lucky minutes have placed in our hands."

While he was speaking my companion busied himself in carefully plugging up the hole in the rock. When it was closed to his satisfaction he turned on the light in our tunnel.

"Did you observe," he asked, "that there was a second tunnel?"

"What do you say?"

"When the light was on in there I saw the mouth of a smaller tunnel entering the main one behind the cars on the right. Did you notice it?"

"Oh yes," I replied. "I did observe some kind of a dark hole there, but I paid no attention to it because I was so absorbed in the doctor."

"Well," rejoined Hall, smiling, "it was worth considerably more than a glance. As a subject of thought I find it even more absorbing than Dr. Syx. Did you see the track in it?"

"No," I had to acknowledge, "I did not notice that. But," I continued, a little piqued by his manner, "being a branch of the main tunnel, I don't see anything remarkable in its having a track also."

"It was rather dim in that hole," said Hall, still smiling in a somewhat provoking way, "but the railroad track was there plain enough. And, whether you think it remarkable or not, I should like to lay you a wager that that track leads to a secret worth a dozen of the one we have just overheard."

"My good friend," I retorted, still smarting a little, "I shall not presume to match my stupidity against your perspicacity. I haven't cat's eyes in the dark."

Hall immediately broke out laughing, and, slapping me good-naturedly on the shoulder, exclaimed:

"Come, come now! If you go to kicking back at a fellow like that, I shall be sorry I ever undertook this adventure."

A MYSTERY INDEED!

When President Boon had heard our story he promptly approved Hall's dismissal of the men. He expressed great surprise that Dr. Syx should have resorted to a deception which had been so disastrous to innocent people, and at first he talked of legal proceedings. But, after thinking the matter over, he concluded that Syx was too powerful to be attacked with success, especially when the only evidence against him was that he had claimed to find artemisium in his mine at a time when, as everybody knew, artemisium actually was found outside the mine. There was no apparent motive for the deception, and no proof of malicious intent. In short, Mr. Boon decided that the best thing for him and his stockholders to do was to keep silent about their losses and await events. And, at Hall's suggestion, he also determined to say nothing to anybody about the discovery we had made.

"It could do no good," said Hall, in making the suggestion, "and it might spoil a plan I have in mind."

"What plan?" asked the president.

"I prefer not to tell just yet," was the reply.

I observed that, in our interview with Mr. Boon, Hall made no reference to the side tunnel to which he had appeared to attach so much importance, and I concluded that he now regarded it as lacking significance. In this I was mistaken.

A few days afterwards I received an invitation from Hall to accompany him once more into the abandoned tunnel.

"I have found out what that sidetrack means," he said, "and it has plunged me into another mystery so dark and profound that I cannot see my way through it. I must beg you to say no word to any one concerning the things I am about to show you."

I gave the required promise, and we entered the tunnel, which nobody had visited since our former adventure. Having extinguished our lamp, my companion opened the peep-hole, and a thin ray of light streamed through from the tunnel on the opposite side of the wall. He applied his eye to the hole.

"Yes," he said, quickly stepping back and pushing me into his place, "they are still at it. Look, and tell me what you see."

"I see," I replied, after placing my eye at the aperture, "a gang of men unloading a car which has just come out of the side tunnel, and putting its contents upon another car standing on the track of the main tunnel."

"Yes, and what are they handling?"

"Why, ore, of course."

"And do you see nothing significant in that?"

"To be sure!" I exclaimed. "Why, that ore—"

"Hush! hush!" admonished Hall, putting his hand over my mouth; "don't talk so loud. Now go on, in a whisper."

"The ore," I resumed, "may have come back from the furnace-room, because the side tunnel turns off so as to run parallel with the other."

"It not only may have come back, it actually has come back," said Hall.

"How can you be sure?"

"Because I have been over the track, and know that it leads to a secret apartment directly under the furnace in which Dr. Syx pretends to melt the ore!"

For a minute after hearing this avowal I was speechless.

"Are you serious?" I asked at length.

"Perfectly serious. Run your finger along the rock here. Do you perceive a seam? Two days ago, after seeing what you have just witnessed in the Syx tunnel, I carefully cut out a section of the wall, making an aperture large enough to crawl through, and, when I knew the workmen were asleep, I crept in there and examined both tunnels from end to end. But in solving one mystery I have run myself into another infinitely more perplexing."

"How is that?"

"Why does Dr. Syx take such elaborate pains to deceive his visitors, and also the government officers? It is now plain that he conducts no mining operations whatever. This mine of his is a gigantic blind. Whenever inspectors or scientific curiosity seekers visit his mill his mute workmen assume the air of being very busy, the cars laden with his so-called 'ore' rumble out of the tunnel, and their contents are ostentatiously poured into the furnace, or appear to be poured into it, really dropping into a receptacle beneath, to be carried back into the mine again. And then the doctor leads his gulled visitors around to the other side of the furnace and shows them the molten metal coming out in streams. Now what does it all mean? That's what I'd like to find out. What's his game? For, mark you, if he doesn't get artemisium from this pretended ore, he gets it from some other source, and right on this spot, too. There is no doubt about that. The whole world is supplied by Syx's furnace, and Syx feeds his furnace with something that comes from his ten acres of Grand Teton rock. What is that something? How does he get it, and where does he hide it? These are the things I should like to find out."

"Well," I replied, "I fear I can't help you."

"But the difference between you and me," he retorted, "is that you can go to sleep over it, while I shall never get another good night's rest so long as this black mystery remains unsolved."

"What will you do?"

"I don't know exactly what. But I've got a dim idea which may take shape after a while."

Hall was silent for some time; then he suddenly asked:

"Did you ever hear of that queer magic-lantern show with which Dr. Syx entertained Mr. Boon and the members of the financial commission in the early days of the artemisium business?"

"Yes, I've heard the story, but I don't think it was ever made public. The newspapers never got hold of it."

"No, I believe not. Odd thing, wasn't it?"

"Why, yes, very odd, but just like the doctor's eccentric ways, though. He's always doing something to astonish somebody, without any apparent earthly reason. But what put you in mind of that?"

"Free artemisium put me in mind of it," replied Hall, quizzically.

"I don't see the connection."

"I'm not sure that I do either, but when you are dealing with Dr. Syx nothing is too improbable to be thought of."

Hall thereupon fell to musing again, while we returned to the entrance of the tunnel. After he had made everything secure, and slipped the key into his pocket, my companion remarked:

"Don't you think it would be best to keep this latest discovery to ourselves?"

"Certainly."

"Because," he continued, "nobody would be benefited just now by knowing what we know, and to expose the worthlessness of the 'ore' might cause a panic. The public is a queer animal, and never gets scared at just the thing you expect will alarm it, but always at something else."

We had shaken hands and were separating when Hall stopped me.

"Do you believe in alchemy?" he asked.

"That's an odd question from you," I replied. "I thought alchemy was exploded long ago."

"Well," he said, slowly, "I suppose it has been exploded, but then, you know, an explosion may sometimes be a kind of instantaneous education, breaking up old things but revealing new ones."

MORE OF DR. SYX'S MAGIC

Important business called me East soon after the meeting with Hall described in the foregoing chapter, and before I again saw the Grand Teton very stirring events had taken place.

As the reader is aware, Dr. Syx's agreement with the various governments limited the output of his mine. An international commission, continually in session in New York, adjusted the differences arising among the nations concerning financial affairs, and allotted to each the proper amount of artemisium for coinage. Of course, this amount varied from time to time, but a fair average could easily be maintained. The gradual increase of wealth, in houses, machinery, manufactured and artistic products called for a corresponding increase in the circulating medium; but this, too, was easily provided for. An equally painstaking supervision was exercised over the amount of the precious metal which Dr. Syx was permitted to supply to the markets for use in the arts. On this side, also, the demand gradually increased; but the wonderful Teton mine seemed equal to all calls upon its resources.

After the failure of the mining operations there was a moderate revival of the efforts to reduce the Teton ore, but no success cheered the experimenters. Prospectors also wandered all over the earth looking for pure artemisium, but in vain. The general public, knowing nothing of what Hall had discovered, and still believing Syx's story that he also had found pure artemisium in his mine, accounted for the failure of the tunneling operations on the supposition that the metal, in a free state, was excessively rare, and that Dr. Syx had had the luck to strike the only vein of it that the Grand Teton contained. As if to give countenance to this opinion, Dr. Syx now announced, in the most public manner, that he had been deceived again, and that the vein of free metal he had struck being exhausted, no other had appeared. Accordingly, he said, he must henceforth rely exclusively, as in the beginning, upon reduction of the ore.

Artemisium had proved itself an immense boon to mankind, and the new era of commercial prosperity which it had ushered in already exceeded everything that the world had known in the past. School-children learned that human civilization had taken five great strides, known respectively, beginning at the bottom, as the "age of stone," the "age of bronze," the "age of iron," the "age of gold," and the "age of artemisium."

Nevertheless, sources of dissatisfaction finally began to appear, and, after the nature of such things, they developed with marvellous rapidity. People began to grumble about "contraction of the currency." In every country there arose a party which demanded "free money." Demagogues pointed to the brief reign of paper money after the demonetization of gold as a happy period, when the people had enjoyed their rights, and the "money barons"— borrowing a term from nineteenth-century history—were kept at bay.

Then came denunciations of the international commission for restricting the coinage. Dr. Syx was described as "a devil-fish sucking the veins of the planet and holding it helpless in the grasp of his tentacular billions." In the United States meetings of agitators passed furious resolutions, denouncing the government, assailing the rich, cursing Dr. Syx, and calling upon "the oppressed" to rise and "take their own." The final outcome was, of course, violence. Mobs had to be suppressed by military force. But the most dramatic scene in the tragedy occurred at the Grand Teton. Excited by inflammatory speeches and printed documents, several thousand armed men assembled in the neighborhood of Jenny's Lake and prepared to attack the Syx mine. For some reason the military guard had been depleted, and the mob, under the leadership of a man named Bings, who showed no little talent as a commander and strategist, surprised the small force of soldiers and locked them up in their own guard-house.

Telegraphic communication having been cut off by the astute Bings, a fierce attack was made on the mine. The assailants swarmed up the sides of the canyon, and attempted to break in through the foundation of the buildings. But the masonry was stronger than they had anticipated, and the attack failed. Sharp-shooters then climbed the neighboring heights, and kept up an incessant peppering of the walls with conical bullets driven at four thousand feet per second.

No reply came from the gloomy structure. The huge column of black smoke rose uninterruptedly into the sky, and the noise of the great engine never ceased for an instant. The mob gathered closer on all sides and redoubled the fire of the rifles, to which was now added the belching of several machine-guns. Ragged holes began to appear in the walls, and at the sight of these the assailants yelled with delight. It was evident that, the mill could not long withstand so destructive a bombardment. If the besiegers had possessed artillery they would have knocked the buildings into splinters within twenty minutes. As it was, they would need a whole day to win their victory.

Suddenly it became evident that the besieged were about to take a hand in the fight. Thus far they had not shown themselves or fired a shot, but now a movement was perceived on the roof, and the projecting arms of some kind of machinery became visible. Many marksmen concentrated their fire upon the mysterious objects, but apparently with little effect. Bings, mounted on a rock, so as to command a clear view of the field, was on the point, of ordering a party to rush forward with axes and beat down the formidable doors, when there came a blinding flash from the roof, something swished through the air, and a gust of heat met the assailants in the face. Bings dropped dead from his perch, and then, as if the scythe of the Destroyer had swung downward, and to right and left in quick succession, the close-packed mob was levelled, rank after rank, until the few survivors crept behind rocks for refuge.

Instantly the atmospheric broom swept up and down the canyon and across the mountain's flanks, and the marksmen fell in bunches like shaken grapes. Nine-tenths of the besiegers were destroyed within ten minutes after the first movement had been noticed on the roof. Those who survived owed their escape to the rocks which concealed them, and they lost no time in crawling off into neighboring chasms, and, as soon as they were beyond eye-shot from the mill, they fled with panic speed.

Then the towering form of Dr. Syx appeared at the door. Emerging without sign of fear or excitement, he picked his way among his fallen enemies, and, approaching the military guard-house, undid the fastening and set the imprisoned soldiers free.

"I think I am paying rather dear for my whistle," he said, with a characteristic sneer, to Captain Carter, the commander of the troop. "It seems that I must not only defend my own people and property when attacked by mob force, but must also come to the rescue of the soldiers whose pay-rolls are met from my pocket."

The captain made no reply, and Dr. Syx strode back to the works. When the released soldiers saw what had occurred their amazement had no bounds. It was necessary at once to dispose of the dead, and this was no easy undertaking for their small force. However, they accomplished it, and at the beginning of their work made a most surprising discovery.

"How's this, Jim?" said one of the men to his comrade, as they stooped to lift the nearest victim of Dr. Syx's withering fire. "What's this fellow got all over him?"

"Artemisium! 'pon my soul!" responded "Jim," staring at the body. "He's all coated over with it."

Immediately from all sides came similar exclamations. Every man who had fallen was covered with a film of the precious metal, as if he had been dipped into an electrolytic bath. Clothing seemed to have been charred, and the metallic atoms had penetrated the flesh of the victims. The rocks all round the battle-field were similarly veneered. "It looks to me," said Captain Carter, "as if old Syx had turned one of his spouts of artemisium into a hose-pipe and soaked 'em with it."

"That's it," chimed in a lieutenant, "that's exactly what he's done."

"Well," returned the captain, "if he can do that, I don't see what use he's got for us here."

"Probably he don't want to waste the stuff," said the lieutenant. "What do you suppose it cost him to plate this crowd?"

"I guess a month's pay for the whole troop wouldn't cover the expense. It's costly, but then—gracious! Wouldn't I have given something for the doctor's hose when I was a youngster campaigning in the Philippines in '99?"

The story of the marvellous way in which Dr. Syx defended his mill became the sensation of the world for many days. The hose-pipe theory, struck off on the spot by Captain Carter, seized the popular fancy, and was generally accepted without further question. There was an element of the ludicrous which robbed the tragedy of some of its horror. Moreover, no one could deny that Dr. Syx was well within his rights in defending himself by any means when so savagely attacked, and his triumphant success, no less than the ingenuity which was supposed to underlie it, placed him in an heroic light which he had not hitherto enjoyed.

As to the demagogues who were responsible for the outbreak and its terrible consequences, they slunk out of the public eye, and the result of the battle at the mine seemed to have been a clearing up of the atmosphere, such as a thunderstorm effects at the close of a season of foul weather.

But now, little as men guessed it, the beginning of the end was close at hand.

THE DETECTIVE OF SCIENCE

The morning of my arrival at Grand Teton station, on my return from the East, Andrew Hall met me with a warm greeting.

"I have been anxiously expecting you," he said, "for I have made some progress towards solving the great mystery. I have not yet reached a conclusion, but I hope soon to let you into the entire secret. In the meantime you can aid me with your companionship, if in no other way, for, since the defeat of the mob, this place has been mighty lonesome. The Grand Teton is a spot that people who have no particular business out here carefully avoid. I am on speaking terms with Dr. Syx, and occasionally, when there is a party to be shown around, I visit his works, and make the best possible use of my eyes. Captain Carter of the military is a capital fellow, and I like to hear his stories of the war in Luzon forty years ago, but I want somebody to whom I can occasionally confide things, and so you are as welcome as moonlight in harvest-time."

"Tell me something about that wonderful fight with the mob. Did you see it?"

"I did. I had got wind of what Bings intended to do while I was down at Pocotello, and I hurried up here to warn the soldiers, but unfortunately I came too late. Finding the military cooped up in the guard-house and the mob masters of the situation, I kept out of sight on the side of the Teton, and watched the siege with my binocular. I think there was very little of the spectacle that I missed."

"What of the mysterious force that the doctor employed to sweep off the assailants?"

"Of course, Captain Carter's suggestion that Syx turned molten artemisium from his furnace into a hose-pipe and sprayed the enemy with it is ridiculous. But it is much easier to dismiss Carter's theory than to substitute a better one. I saw the doctor on the roof with a gang of black workmen, and I noticed the flash of polished metal turned rapidly this way and that, but there was some intervening obstacle which prevented me from getting a good view of the mechanism employed. It certainly bore no resemblance to a hose-pipe, or anything of that kind. No emanation was visible from the machine, but it was stupefying to see the mob melt down."

"How about the coating of the bodies with artemisium?"

"There you are back on the hose-pipe again," laughed Hall. "But, to tell you the truth, I'd rather be excused from expressing an opinion on that operation in wholesale electro-plating just at present. I've the ghost of an idea what it means, but let me test my theory a little before I formulate it. In the meanwhile, won't you take a stroll with me?"

"Certainly; nothing could please me better," I replied. "Which way shall we go?"

"To the top of the Grand Teton."

"What! are you seized with the mountain-climbing fever?"

"Not exactly, but I have a particular reason for wishing to take a look from that pinnacle."

"I suppose you know the real apex of the peak has never been trodden by man?"

"I do know it, but it is just that apex that I am determined to have under my feet for ten minutes. The failure of others is no argument for us."

"Just as you say," I rejoined. "But I suppose there is no indiscretion in asking whether this little climb has any relation to the mystery?"

"If it didn't have an important relation to the clearing up of that dark thing I wouldn't risk my neck in such an undertaking," was the reply.

Accordingly, the next morning we set out for the peak. All previous climbers, as we were aware, had attacked it from the west. That seemed the obvious thing to do, because the westward slopes of the mountain, while very steep, are less abrupt than those which face the rising sun. In fact, the eastern side of the Grand Teton appears to be absolutely unclimbable. But both Hall and I had had experience with rock climbing in the Alps and the Dolomites, and we knew that what looked like the hardest places sometimes turn out to be next to the easiest. Accordingly we decided—the more particularly because it would save time, but also because we yielded to the common desire to outdo our predecessors—to try to scale the giant right up his face.

We carried a very light but exceedingly strong rope, about five hundred feet long, wore nail-shod shoes, and had each a metal-pointed staff and a small hatchet in lieu of the regular mountaineer's axe. Advancing at first along the broken ridge between two gorges we gradually approached the steeper part of the Teton, where the cliffs looked so sheer and smooth that it seemed no wonder that nobody had ever tried to scale them. The air was deliciously clear and the sky wonderfully blue above the mountains, and the moon, a few days past its last quarter, was visible in the southwest, its pale crescent face slightly blued by the atmosphere, as it always appears when seen in daylight.

"Slow westering, a phantom sail—
The lonely soul of yesterday."

Behind us, somewhat north of east, lay the Syx works, with their black smoke rising almost vertically in the still air. Suddenly, as we stumbled along on the rough surface, something whizzed past my face and fell on the rock at my feet. I looked at the strange missile, that had come like a meteor out of open space, with astonishment.

It was a bird, a beautiful specimen of the scarlet tanagers, which I remembered the early explorers had found inhabiting the Teton canyons, their brilliant plumage borrowing splendor from contrast with the gloomy surroundings. It lay motionless, its outstretched wings having a curious shrivelled aspect, while the flaming color of the breast was half obliterated with smutty patches. Stooping to pick it up, I noticed a slight bronzing, which instantly recalled to my mind the peculiar appearance of the victims of the attack on the mine.

"Look here!" I called to Hall, who was several yards in advance. He turned, and I held up the bird by a wing.

"Where did you get that?" he asked.

"It fell at my feet a moment ago."

Hall glanced in a startled manner at the sky, and then down the slope of the mountain.

"Did you notice in what direction it was flying?" he asked.

"No, it dropped so close that it almost grazed my nose. I saw nothing of it until it made me blink."

"I have been heedless," muttered Hall under his breath. At the time I did not notice the singularity of his remark, my attention being absorbed in contemplating the unfortunate tanager.

"Look how its feathers are scorched," I said.

"I know it," Hall replied, without glancing at the bird.

"And it is covered with a film of artemisium," I added, a little piqued by his abstraction.

"I know that, too."

"See here, Hall," I exclaimed, "are you trying to make game of me?"

"Not at all, my dear fellow," he replied, dropping his cogitation. "Pray forgive me. But this is no new phenomenon to me. I have picked up birds in that condition on this mountain before. There is a terrible mystery here, but I am slowly letting light into it, and if we succeed in reaching the top of the peak I have good hope that the illumination will increase."

"Here now," he added a moment later, sitting down upon a rock and thrusting the blade of his penknife into a crevice, "what do you think of this?"

He held up a little nugget of pure artemisium, and then went on:

"You know that all this slope was swept as clean as a Dutch housewife's kitchen floor by the thousands of miners and prospectors who swarmed over it a year or two ago, and do you suppose they would have missed such a tidbit if it had been here then?"

"Dr. Syx must have been salting the mountain again," I suggested.

"Well," replied Hall, with a significant smile, "if the doctor hasn't salted it somebody else has, that's plain enough. But perhaps you would like to know precisely what I expect to find out when we get on the topknot of the Teton."

"I should certainly be delighted to learn the object of our journey," I said. "Of course, I'm only going along for company and for the fun of the thing; but you know you can count on me for substantial aid whenever you need it."

"It is because you are so willing to let me keep my own counsel," he rejoined, "and to wait for things to ripen before compelling me to disclose them, that I like to have you with me at critical times. Now, as to the object of this break-neck expedition, whose risks you understand as fully as I do, I need not assure you that it is of supreme importance to the success of my plans. In a word, I hope to be able to look down into a part of Dr. Syx's mill which, if I am not mistaken, no human eye except his and those of his most trustworthy helpers has ever been permitted to see. And if I see there what I fully expect to see, I shall have got a long step nearer to a great fortune."

"Good!" I cried. "*En avant*, then! We are losing time."

THE TOP OF THE GRAND TETON

The climbing soon became difficult, until at length we were going up hand over hand, taking advantage of crevices and knobs which an inexperienced eye would have regarded as incapable of affording a grip for the fingers or a support for the toes. Presently we arrived at the foot of a stupendous precipice, which was absolutely insurmountable by any ordinary method of ascent. Parts of it overhung, and everywhere the face of the rock was too free from irregularities to afford any footing, except to a fly.

"Now, to borrow the expression of old Bunyan, we are hard put to it," I remarked. "If you will go to the left I will take the right and see if there is any chance of getting up."

"I don't believe we could find any place easier than this," Hall replied, "and so up we go where we are."

"Have you a pair of wings concealed about you?" I asked, laughing at his folly.

"Well, something nearly as good," he responded, unstrapping his knapsack. He produced a silken bag, which he unfolded on the rock.

"A balloon!" I exclaimed. "But how are you going to inflate it?"

For reply Hall showed me a receptacle which, he said, contained liquid hydrogen, and which was furnished with a device for retarding the volatilization of the liquid so that it could be carried with little loss.

"You remember I have a small laboratory in the abandoned mine," he explained, "where we used to manufacture liquid air for blasting. This balloon I made for our present purpose. It will just suffice to carry up our rope, and a small but practically unbreakable grapple of hardened gold. I calculate to send the grapple to the top of the precipice with the balloon, and when it has obtained a firm hold in the riven rock there we can ascend, sailor fashion. You see the rope has knots, and I know your muscles are as trustworthy in such work as my own."

There was a slight breeze from the eastward, and the current of air slanting up the face of the peak assisted the balloon in mounting with its burden, and favored us by promptly swinging the little airship, with the grapple swaying beneath it, over the brow of the cliff into the atmospheric eddy above. As soon as we saw that the grapple was well over the edge we pulled upon the rope. The balloon instantly shot into view with the anchor dancing, but, under the influence of the wind, quickly returned to its former position behind the projecting brink. The grapple had failed to take hold.

"'Try, try again' must be our motto now," muttered Hall.

We tried several times with the same result, although each time we slightly shifted our position. At last the grapple caught.

"Now, all together!" cried my companion, and simultaneously we threw our weight upon the slender rope. The anchor apparently did not give an inch.

"Let me go first," said Hall, pushing me aside as I caught the first knot above my head. "It's my device, and it's only fair that I should have the first try."

In a minute he was many feet up the wall, climbing swiftly hand over hand, but occasionally stopping and twisting his leg around the rope while he took breath.

"It's easier than I expected," he called down, when he had ascended about one hundred feet. "Here and there the rock offers a little hold for the knees."

I watched him, breathless with anxiety, and, as he got higher, my imagination pictured the little gold grapple, invisible above the brow of the precipice, with perhaps a single thin prong wedged into a crevice, and slowly ploughing its way towards the edge with each impulse of the climber, until but another pull was needed to set it flying! So vivid was my fancy that I tried to banish it by noticing that a certain knot in the rope remained just at the level of my eyes, where it had been from the start. Hall was now fully two hundred feet above the ledge on which I stood, and was rapidly nearing the top of the precipice. In a minute more he would be safe.

Suddenly he shouted, and, glancing up with a leap of the heart, I saw that he was falling! He kept his face to the rock, and came down feet foremost. It would be useless to attempt any description of my feelings; I would not go through that experience again for the price of a battleship. Yet it lasted less than a second. He had dropped not more than ten feet when the fall was arrested.

"All right!" he called, cheerily. "No harm done! It was only a slip."

But what a slip! If the balloon had not carried the anchor several yards back from the edge it would have had no opportunity to catch another hold as it shot forward. And how could we know that the second hold would prove more secure than the first? Hall did not hesitate, however, for one instant. Up he went again. But, in fact, his best chance was in going up, for he was within four yards of the top when the mishap occurred. With a sigh of relief I saw him at last throw his arm over the verge and then wriggle his body upon the ledge. A few seconds later he was lying on his stomach, with his face over the edge, looking down at me.

"Come on!" he shouted. "It's all right."

When I had pulled myself over the brink at his side I grasped his hand and pressed it without a word. We understood one another.

"It was pretty close to a miracle," he remarked at last. "Look at this."

The rock over which the grapple had slipped was deeply scored by the unyielding point of the metal, and exactly at the verge of the precipice the prong had wedged itself into a narrow crack, so firmly that we had to chip away the stone in order to release it. If it had slipped a single inch farther before taking hold it would have been all over with my friend.

Such experiences shake the strongest nerves, and we sat on the shelf we had attained for fully a quarter of an hour before we ventured to attack the next precipice which hung beetling directly above us. It was not as lofty as the one we had just ascended, but it impended to such a degree that we saw we should have to climb our rope while it swung free in the air!

Luckily we had little difficulty in getting a grip for the prongs, and we took every precaution to test the security of the anchorage, not only putting our combined weight repeatedly upon the rope, but flipping and jerking it with all our strength. The grapple resisted every effort to dislodge it, and finally I started up, insisting on my turn as leader.

The height I had to ascend did not exceed one hundred feet, but that is a very great distance to climb on a swinging rope, without a wall within reach to assist by its friction and occasional friendly projections. In a little while my movements, together with the effect of the slight wind, had imparted a most distressing oscillation to the rope. This sometimes carried me with a nerve-shaking bang against a prominent point of the precipice, where I would dislodge loose fragments that kept Hall dodging for his life, and then I would swing out, apparently beyond the brow of the cliff below, so that, as I involuntarily glanced downward, I seemed to be hanging in free space, while the steep mountain-side, looking ten times steeper than it really was, resembled the vertical wall of an absolutely bottomless abyss, as if I were suspended over the edge of the world.

I avoided thinking of what the grapple might be about, and in my haste to get through with the awful experience I worked myself fairly out of breath, so that, when at last I reached the rounded brow of the cliff, I had to stop and cling there for fully a minute before I could summon strength enough to lift myself over it.

When I was assured that the grapple was still securely fastened I signalled to Hall, and he soon stood at my side, exclaiming, as he wiped the perspiration from his face:

"I think I'll try wings next time!"

But our difficulties had only begun. As we had foreseen, it was a case of Alp above Alp, to the very limit of human strength and patience. However, it would have been impossible to go back. In order to descend the two precipices we had surmounted it would have been necessary to leave our life-lines clinging to the rocks, and we had not rope enough to do that. If we could not reach the top we were lost.

Having refreshed ourselves with a bite to eat and a little stimulant, we resumed the climb. After several hours of the most exhausting work I have ever performed we pulled our weary limbs upon the narrow ridge, but a few square yards in area, which constitutes the apex of the Grand Teton. A little below, on the opposite side of a steep-walled gap which divides the top of the mountain into two parts, we saw the singular enclosure of stones which the early white explorers found there, and which they ascribed to the Indians, although nobody has ever known who built it or what purpose it served.

The view was, of course, superb, but while I was admiring it in all its wonderful extent and variety, Hall, who had immediately pulled out his binocular, was busy inspecting the Syx works, the top of whose great tufted smoke column was thousands of feet beneath our level. Jackson's Lake, Jenny's Lake, Leigh's Lake, and several lakelets glittered in the sunlight amid the pale grays and greens of Jackson's Hole, while many a bending reach of the Snake River shone amid the wastes of sage-brush and rock.

"There!" suddenly exclaimed Hall, "I thought I should find it."

"What?"

"Take a look through my glass at the roof of Syx's mill. Look just in the centre."

"Why, it's open in the middle!" I cried as soon as I had put the glass to my eyes. "There's a big circular hole in the centre of the roof."

"Look inside! Look inside!" repeated Hall, impatiently.

"I see nothing there except something bright."

"Do you call it nothing because it is bright?"

"Well, no," I replied, laughing. "What I mean is that I see nothing that I can make anything of except a shining object, and all I can make of that is that it is bright."

"You've been in the Syx works many times, haven't you?"

"Yes."

"Did you ever see the opening in the roof?"

"Never."

"Did you ever hear of it?"

"Never."

"Then Dr. Syx doesn't show his visitors everything that is to be seen."

"Evidently not since, as we know, he concealed the double tunnel and the room under the furnace."

"Dr. Syx has concealed a bigger secret than that," Hall responded, "and the Grand Teton has helped me to a glimpse of it."

For several minutes my friend was absorbed in thought. Then he broke out:

"I tell you he's the most wonderful man in the world!"

"Who, Dr. Syx? Well, I've long thought that."

"Yes, but I mean in a different way from what you are thinking of. Do you remember my asking you once if you believed in alchemy?"

"I remember being greatly surprised by your question to that effect."

"Well, now," said Hall, rubbing his hands with a satisfied air, while his eyes glanced keen and bright with the reflection of some passing thought, "Max Syx is greater than any alchemist that ever lived. If those old fellows in the dark ages had accomplished everything they set out to do, they would have been of no more consequence in comparison with our black-browed friend down yonder than—than my head is of consequence in comparison with the moon."

"I fear you flatter the man in the moon," was my laughing reply.

"No, I don't," returned Hall, "and some day you'll admit it."

"Well, what about that something that shines down there? You seem to see more in it than I can."

But my companion had fallen into a reverie and didn't hear my question. He was gazing abstractedly at the faint image of the waning moon, now nearing the distant mountain-top over in Idaho. Presently his mind seemed to return to the old magnet, and he whirled about and glanced down at the Syx mill. The column of smoke was diminishing in volume, an indication that the engine was about to enjoy one of its periodical rests. The irregularity of these stoppages had always been a subject of remark among practical engineers. The hours of labor were exceedingly erratic, but the engine had never been known to work at night, except on one occasion, and then only for a few minutes, when it was suddenly stopped on account of a fire.

Just as Hall resumed his inspection two huge quarter spheres, which had been resting wide apart on the roof, moved towards one another until their arched sections met over the circular aperture which they covered like the dome of an observatory.

"I expected it," Hall remarked. "But come, it is mid-afternoon, and we shall need all of our time to get safely down before the light fades."

As I have already explained, it would not have been possible for us to return the way we came. We determined to descend the comparatively easy western slopes of the peak, and pass the night on that side of the mountain. Letting ourselves down with the rope into the hollow way that divides the summit of the Teton into two pinnacles, we had no difficulty in descending by the route followed by all previous climbers. The weather was fine, and, having found good shelter among the rocks, we passed the night in comfort. The next day we succeeded in swinging round upon the eastern flank of the Teton, below the more formidable cliffs, and, just at nightfall, we arrived at the station. As we passed the Syx mine the doctor himself confronted us. There was a very displeasing look on his dark countenance, and his sneer was strongly marked.

"So you have been on top of the Teton?" he said.

"Yes," replied Hall, very blandly, "and if you have a taste for that sort of thing I should advise you to go up. The view is immense, as fine as the best in the Alps."

"Pretty ingenious plan, that balloon of yours," continued the doctor, still looking black.

"Thank you," Hall replied, more suavely than ever. "I've been planning that a long time. You probably don't know that mountaineering used to be my chief amusement."

The doctor turned away without pursuing the conversation.

"I could kick myself," Hall muttered as soon as Dr. Syx was out of earshot. "If my absurd wish to outdo others had not blinded me, I should have known that he would see us going up this side of the peak, particularly with the balloon to give us away. However, what's done can't be undone. He may not really suspect the truth, and if he does he can't help himself, even though he is the richest man in the world."

STRANGE FATE OF A KITE

"Are you ready for another tramp?" was Andrew Hall's greeting when we met early on the morning following our return from the peak.

"Certainly I am. What is your program for to-day?"

"I wish to test the flying qualities of a kite which I have constructed since our return last night."

"You don't allow the calls of sleep to interfere very much with your activity."

"I haven't much time for sleep just now," replied Hall, without smiling. "The kite test will carry us up the flanks of the Teton, but I am not going to try for the top this time. If you will come along I'll ask you to help me by carrying and operating a light transit I shall carry another myself. I am desirous to get the elevation that the kite attains and certain other data that will be of use to me. We will make a détour towards the south, for I don't want old Syx's suspicions to be prodded any more."

"What interest can he have in your kite-flying?"

"The same interest that a burglar has in the rap of a policeman's night-stick."

"Then your experiment to-day has some connection with the solution of the great mystery?"

"My dear fellow," said Hall, laying his hand on my shoulder, "until I see the end of that mystery I shall think of nothing else."

In a few hours we were clambering over the broken rocks on the south-eastern flank of the Teton at an elevation of about three thousand feet above the level of Jackson's Hole. Finally Hall paused and began to put his kite together. It was a small box-shaped affair, very light in construction, with paper sides.

"In order to diminish the chances of Dr. Syx noticing what we are about," he said, as he worked away, "I have covered the kite with sky-blue paper. This, together with distance, will probably insure us against his notice."

In a few minutes the kite was ready. Having ascertained the direction of the wind with much attention, he stationed me with my transit on a commanding rock, and sought another post for himself at a distance of two hundred yards, which he carefully measured with a gold tape. My instructions were to keep the telescope on the kite as soon as it had attained a considerable height, and to note the angle of elevation and the horizontal angle with the base line joining our points of observation.

"Be particularly careful," was Hall's injunction, "and if anything happens to the kite by all means note the angles at that instant."

As soon as we had fixed our stations Hall began to pay out the string, and the kite rose very swiftly. As it sped away into the blue it was soon practically invisible to the naked eye, although the telescope of the transit enabled me to follow it with ease.

Glancing across now and then at my companion, I noticed that he was having considerable difficulty in, at the same time, managing the kite and manipulating his transit. But as the kite continued to rise and steadied in position his task became easier, until at length he ceased to remove his eye from the telescope while holding the string with outstretched hand.

"Don't lose sight of it now for an instant!" he shouted.

For at least half an hour he continued to manipulate the string, sending the kite now high towards the zenith with a sudden pull, and then letting it drift off. It seemed at last to become almost a fixed point. Very slowly the angles changed, when, suddenly, there was a flash, and to my amazement I saw the paper of the kite shrivel and disappear in a momentary flame, and then the bare sticks came tumbling out of the sky.

"Did you get the angles?" yelled Hall, excitedly.

"Yes; the telescope is yet pointed on the spot where the kite disappeared."

"Read them off," he called, "and then get your angle with the Syx works."

"All right," I replied, doing as he had requested, and noticing at the same time that he was in the act of putting his watch in his pocket. "Is there anything else?" I asked.

"No, that will do, thank you."

Hall came running over, his face beaming, and with the air of a man who has just hooked a particularly cunning old trout.

"Ah!" he exclaimed, "this has been a great success! I could almost dispense with the calculation, but it is best to be sure."

"What are you about, anyhow?" I asked, "and what was it that happened to the kite?"

"Don't interrupt me just now, please," was the only reply I received.

Thereupon my friend sat down on a rock, pulled out a pad of paper, noted the angles which I had read on the transit, and fell to figuring with feverish haste. In the course of his work he consulted a pocket almanac, then glanced up at the sky, muttered approvingly, and finally leaped to his feet with a half-suppressed "Hurrah!" If I had not known him so well I should have thought that he had gone daft.

"Will you kindly tell me," I asked, "how you managed to set the kite afire?"

Hall laughed heartily. "You though it was a trick, did you?" said he. "Well, it was no trick, but a very beautiful demonstration. You surely haven't forgotten the scarlet tanager that gave you such a surprise the day before yesterday."

"Do you mean," I exclaimed, startled at the suggestion, "that the fate of the bird had any connection with the accident to your kite?"

"Accident isn't precisely the right word," replied Hall. "The two things are as intimately related as own brothers. If you should care to hunt up the kite sticks, you would find that they, too, are now artemisium plated."

"This is getting too deep for me," was all that I could say.

"I am not absolutely confident that I have touched bottom myself," said Hall, "but I'm going to make another dive, and if I don't bring up treasures greater than Vanderdecken found at the bottom of the sea, then Dr. Syx is even a more wonderful human mystery than I have thought him to be."

"What do you propose to do next?"

"To shake the dust of the Grand Teton from my shoes and go to San Francisco, where I have an extensive laboratory."

"So you are going to try a little alchemy yourself, are you?"

"Perhaps; who knows? At any rate, my good friend, I am forever indebted to you for your assistance, and even more for your discretion, and if I succeed you shall be the first person in the world to hear the news

BETTER THAN ALCHEMY

I come now to a part of my narrative which would have been deemed altogether incredible in those closing years of the nineteenth century that witnessed the first steps towards the solution of the deepest mysteries of the ether, although men even then held in their hands, without knowing it, powers which, after they had been mastered and before use had made them familiar, seemed no less than godlike.

For six months after Hall's departure for San Francisco I heard nothing from him. Notwithstanding my intense desire to know what he was doing, I did not seek to disturb him in his retirement. In the meantime things ran on as usual in the world, only a ripple being caused by renewed discoveries of small nuggets of artemisium on the Tetons, a fact which recalled to my mind the remark of my friend when he dislodged a flake of the metal from a crevice during our ascent of the peak. At last one day I received this telegram at my office in New York:

"SAN FRANCISCO, May 16, 1940.
"Come at once. The mystery is solved.
"(Signed) HALL."

As soon as I could pack a grip I was flying westward one hundred miles an hour. On reaching San Francisco, which had made enormous strides since the opening of the twentieth century, owing to the extension of our Oriental possessions, and which already ranked with New York and Chicago among the financial capitals of the world, I hastened to Hall's laboratory. He was there expecting me, and, after a hearty greeting, during which his elation over his success was manifest, he said:

"I am compelled to ask you to make a little journey. I found it impossible to secure the necessary privacy here, and, before opening my experiments, I selected a site for a new laboratory in an unfrequented spot among the mountains this side of Lake Tahoe. You will be the first man, with the exception of my two devoted assistants, to see my apparatus, and you shall share the sensation of the critical experiment."

"Then you have not yet completed your solution of the secret?"

"Yes, I have; for I am as certain of the result as if I had seen it, but I thought you were entitled to be in with me at the death."

From the nearest railway station we took horses to the laboratory, which occupied a secluded but most beautiful site at an elevation of about six thousand feet above sea-level. With considerable surprise I noticed a building surmounted with a dome, recalling what we had seen from the Grand Teton on the roof of Dr. Syx's mill. Hall, observing my look, smiled significantly, but said nothing. The laboratory proper occupied a smaller building adjoining the domed structure. Hall led the way into an apartment having but a single door and illuminated by a skylight.

"This is my sanctum sanctorum," he said, "and you are the first outsider to enter it. Seat yourself comfortably while I proceed to unveil a little corner of the artemisium mystery."

Near one end of the room, which was about thirty feet in length, was a table, on which lay a glass tube about two inches in diameter and thirty inches long. In the farther end of the tube gleamed a lump of yellow metal, which I took to be gold. Hall and I were seated near another table about twenty-five feet distant from the tube, and on this table was an apparatus furnished with a concave mirror, whose optical axis was directed towards the tube. It occurred to me at once that this apparatus would be suitable for experimenting with electric waves. Wires ran from it to the floor, and in the cellar beneath was audible the beating of an engine. My companion made an adjustment or two, and then remarked:

"Now, keep your eyes on the lump of gold in the farther end of the tube yonder. The tube is exhausted of air, and I am about to concentrate upon the gold an intense electric influence, which will have the effect of making it a kind of kathode pole. I only use this term for the sake of illustration. You will recall that as long ago as the days of Crookes it was known that a kathode in an exhausted tube would project particles, or atoms, of its substance away in straight lines. Now watch!"

I fixed my attention upon the gold, and presently saw it enveloped in a most beautiful violet light. This grew more intense, until, at times, it was blinding, while, at the same moment, the interior of the tube seemed to have become charged with a luminous vapor of a delicate pinkish hue.

"Watch! Watch!" said Hall. "Look at the nearer end of the tube!"

"Why, it is becoming coated with gold!" I exclaimed.

He smiled, but made no reply. Still the strange process continued. The pink vapor became so dense that the lump of gold was no longer visible, although the eye of violet light glared piercingly through the colored fog. Every second the deposit of metal, shining like a mirror, increased, until suddenly there came a curious whistling sound. Hall, who had been adjusting the mirror, jerked away his hand and gave it a flip, as if hot water had spattered it, and then the light in the tube quickly died away, the vapor escaped, filling the room with a peculiar stimulating odor, and I perceived that the end of the glass tube had been melted through, and the molten gold was slowly dripping from it.

"I carried it a little too far," said Hall, ruefully rubbing the back of his hand, "and when the glass gave way under the atomic bombardment a few atoms of gold visited my bones. But there is no harm done. You observed that the instant the air reached the kathode, as I for convenience call the electrified mass of gold, the action ceased."

"But your anode, to continue your simile," I said, "is constantly exposed to the air."

"True," he replied, "but in the first place, of course, this is not really an anode, just as the other is not actually a kathode. As science advances we are compelled, for a time, to use old terms in a new sense until a fresh nomenclature can be invented. But we are now dealing with a form of electric action more subtile in its effects than any at present described in the text-books and the transactions of learned societies. I have not yet even attempted to work out the theory of it. I am only concerned with its facts."

"But wonderful as the exhibition you have given is, I do not see," I said, "how it concerns Dr. Syx and his artemisium."

"Listen," replied Hall, settling back in his chair after disconnecting his apparatus. "You no doubt have been told how one night the Syx engine was heard working for a few minutes, the first and only night work it was ever known to have done, and how, hardly had it started up when a fire broke out in the mill, and the engine was instantly stopped. Now there is a very remarkable story connected with that, and it will show you how I got my first clew to the mystery, although it was rather a mere suspicion than a clew, for at first I could make nothing out of it. The alleged fire occurred about a fortnight after our discovery of the double tunnel. My mind was then full of suspicions concerning Syx, because I thought that a man who would fool people with one hand was not likely to deal fairly with the other.

"It was a glorious night, with a full moon, whose face was so clear in the limpid air that, having found a snug place at the foot of a yellow-pine-tree, where the ground was carpeted with odoriferous needles, I lay on my back and renewed my early acquaintance with the romantically named mountains and 'seas' of the Lunar globe. With my binocular I could trace those long white streaks which radiate from the crater ring, called 'Tycho,' and run hundreds of miles in all directions over the moon. As I gazed at these singular objects I recalled the various theories which astronomers, puzzled by their enigmatical aspect, have offered to a more or less confiding public concerning them.

"In the midst of my meditation and moon gazing I was startled by hearing the engine in the Syx works suddenly begin to run. Immediately a queer light, shaped like the beam of a ship's searchlight, but reddish in color, rose high in the moonlit heavens above the mill. It did not last more than a minute or two, for almost instantly the engine was stopped, and with its stoppage the light faded and soon disappeared. The next day Dr. Syx gave it out that on starting up his engine in the night something had caught fire, which compelled him immediately to shut down again. The few who had seen the light, with the exception of your humble servant, accepted the doctor's explanation without a question. But I knew there had been no fire, and Syx's anxiety to spread the lie led me to believe that he had narrowly escaped giving away a vital secret. I said nothing about my suspicions, but upon inquiry I found out that an extra and pressing order for metal had arrived from the Austrian government the very day of the pretended fire, and I drew the inference that Syx, in his haste to fill the order—his supply having been drawn low—had started to work, contrary to his custom, at night, and had immediately found reason to repent his rashness. Of course, I connected the strange light with this sudden change of mind.

"My suspicion having been thus stimulated, and having been directed in a certain way, I began, from that moment to notice closely the hours during which the engine labored. At night it was always quiet, except on that one brief occasion. Sometimes it began early in the morning and stopped about noon. At other times the work was done entirely in the afternoon, beginning sometimes as late as three or four o'clock, and ceasing invariably at sundown. Then again it would start at sunrise and continue the whole day through.

"For a long time I was unable to account for these eccentricities, and the problem was not rendered much clearer, although a startling suggestiveness was added to it, when, at length, I noticed that the periods of activity of the engine had a definite relation to the age of the moon. Then I discovered, with the aid of an almanac, that I could predict the hours when the engine would be busy. At the time of new moon it worked all day; at full moon, it was idle; between full moon and last quarter, it labored in the forenoon, the length of its working hours increasing as the quarter was approached; between last quarter and new moon, the hours of work lengthened, until, as I have said, at new moon they lasted all day; between new moon and first quarter, work began later and later in the forenoon as the quarter was approached, and between first quarter and full moon the laboring hours rapidly shortened, being confined to the latter part of the afternoon, until at full moon complete silence reigned in the mill."

"Well! well!" I broke in, greatly astonished by Hall's singular recital, "you must have thought Dr. Syx was a cross between an alchemist and an astrologer."

"Note this," said Hall, disregarding my interruption, "the hours when the engine worked were invariably the hours during which the moon was above the horizon!"

"What did you infer from that?" "Of course, I inferred that the moon was directly concerned in the mystery; but how? That bothered me for a long time, but a little light broke into my mind when I picked up, on the mountainside, a dead bird, whose scorched feathers were bronzed with artemisium, and sometime later another similar victim of a mysterious form of death. Then came the attack on the mine and its tragic finish. I have already told you what I observed on that occasion. But, instead of helping to clear up the mystery, it rather complicated it for a time. At length, however, I reasoned my way partly out of the difficulty. Certain things which I had noticed in the Syx mill convinced me that there was a part of the building whose existence no visitor suspected, and, putting one thing with another, I inferred that the roof must be open above that secret part of the structure, and that if I could get upon a sufficiently elevated place I could see something of what was hidden there.

"At this point in the investigation I proposed to you the trip to the top of the Teton, the result of which you remember. I had calculated the angles with great care, and I felt certain that from the apex of the mountain I should be able to get a view into the concealed chamber, and into just that side of it which I wished particularly to inspect. You remember that I called your attention to a shining object underneath the circular opening in the roof. You could not make out what it was, but I saw enough to convince me that it was a gigantic parabolic mirror. I'll show you a smaller one of the same kind presently.

"Now, at last, I began to perceive the real truth, but it was so wildly incredible, so infinitely remote from all human experience, that I hardly ventured to formulate it, even in my own secret mind. But I was bound to see the thing through to the end. It occurred to me that I could prove the accuracy of my theory with the aid of a kite. You were kind enough to lend your assistance in that experiment, and it gave me irrefragable evidence of the existence of a shaft of flying atoms extending in a direct line between Dr. Syx's pretended mine and the moon!"

"Hall!" I exclaimed, "you are mad!" My friend smiled good-naturedly, and went on with his story.

"The instant the kite shrivelled and disappeared I understood why the works were idle when the moon was not above the horizon, why birds flying across that fatal beam fell dead upon the rocks, and whence the terrible master of that mysterious mill derived the power of destruction that could wither an army as the Assyrian host in Byron's poem

"Melted like snow in the glance of the Lord."

"But how did Dr. Syx turn the flying atoms against his enemies?" I asked.

"In a very simple manner. He had a mirror mounted so that it could be turned in any direction, and would shunt the stream of metallic atoms, heated by their friction with the air, towards any desired point. When the attack came he raised this machine above the level of the roof and swept the mob to a lustrous, if expensive, death."

"And the light at night—"

"Was the shining of the heated atoms, not luminous enough to be visible in broad day, for which reason the engine never worked at night, and the stream of volatilized artemisium was never set flowing at full moon, when the lunar globe is above the horizon only during the hours of darkness."

"I see," I said, "whence came the nuggets on the mountain. Some of the atoms, owing to the resistance of the air, fell short and settled in the form of impalpable dust until the winds and rains collected and compacted them in the cracks and crevices of the rocks."

"That was it, of course."

"And now," I added, my amazement at the success of Hall's experiments and the accuracy of his deductions increasing every moment, "do you say that you have also discovered the means employed by Dr. Syx to obtain artemisium from the moon?"

"Not only that," replied my friend, "but within the next few minutes I shall have the pleasure of presenting to you a button of moon metal, fresh from the veins of Artemis herself."

THE LOOTING OF THE MOON

I shall spare the reader a recital of the tireless efforts, continuing through many almost sleepless weeks, whereby Andrew Hall obtained his clew to Dr. Syx's method. It was manifest from the beginning that the agent concerned must be some form of etheric, or so-called electric, energy; but how to set it in operation was the problem. Finally he hit upon the apparatus for his initial experiments which I have already described.

"Recurring to what had been done more than half a century ago by Hertz, when he concentrated electric waves upon a focal point by means of a concave mirror," said Hall, "I saw that the key I wanted lay in an extension of these experiments. At last I found that I could transform the energy of an engine into undulations of the ether, which, when they had been concentrated upon a metallic object, like a chunk of gold, imparted to it an intense charge of an apparently electric nature. Upon thus charging a metallic body enclosed in a vacuum, I observed that the energy imparted to it possessed the remarkable power of disrupting its atoms and projecting them off in straight lines, very much as occurs with a kathode in a Crookes's tube. But—and this was of supreme importance—I found that the line of projection was directly towards the apparatus from which the impulse producing the charge had come. In other words, I could produce two poles between which a marvellous interaction occurred. My transformer, with its concentrating mirror, acted as one pole, from which energy was transferred to the other pole, and that other pole immediately flung off atoms of its own substance in the direction of the transformer. But these atoms were stopped by the glass wall of the vacuum tube; and when I tried the experiment with the metal removed from the vacuum, and surrounded with air, it failed utterly.

"This at first completely discouraged me, until I suddenly remembered that the moon is in a vacuum, the great vacuum of interplanetary space, and that it possesses no perceptible atmosphere of its own. At this a great light broke around me, and I shouted 'Eureka!' Without hesitation I constructed a transformer of great power, furnished with a large parabolic mirror to transmit the waves in parallel lines, erected the machinery and buildings here, and when all was ready for the final experiment I telegraphed for you." Prepared by these explanations I was all on fire to see the thing tried. Hall was no less eager, and, calling in his two faithful assistants to make the final adjustments, he led the way into what he facetiously named "the lunar chamber."

"If we fail," he remarked with a smile that had an element of worriment in it, "it will become the 'lunatic chamber'—but no danger of that. You observe this polished silver knob, supported by a metallic rod curved over at the top like a crane. That constitutes the pole from which I propose to transmit the energy to the moon, and upon which I expect the storm of atoms to be centred by reflection from the mirror at whose focus it is placed."

"One moment," I said. "Am I to understand that you think that the moon is a solid mass of artemisium, and that no matter where your radiant force strikes it a 'kathodic pole' will be formed there from which atoms will be projected to the earth?"

"No," said Hall, "I must carefully choose the point on the lunar surface where to operate. But that will present no difficulty. I made up my mind as soon as I had penetrated Syx's secret that he obtained the metal from those mystic white streaks which radiate from Tycho, and which have puzzled the astronomers ever since the invention of telescopes. I now believe those streaks to be composed of immense veins of the metal that Syx has most appropriately named artemisium, which you, of course, recognize as being derived from the name of the Greek goddess of the moon, Artemis, whom the Romans called Diana. But now to work!"

It was less than a day past the time of new moon, and the earth's satellite was too near the sun to be visible in broad daylight. Accordingly, the mirror had to be directed by means of knowledge of the moon's place in the sky. Driven by accurate clockwork, it could be depended upon to retain the proper direction when once set.

With breathless interest I watched the proceedings of my friend and his assistants. The strain upon the nerves of all of us was such as could not have been borne for many hours at a stretch. When everything had been adjusted to his satisfaction, Hall stepped back, not without betraying his excitement in flushed cheeks and flashing eyes, and pressed a lever. The powerful engine underneath the floor instantly responded. The experiment was begun.

"I have set it upon a point about a hundred miles north of Tycho, where the Yerkes photographs show a great abundance of the white substance," said Hall.

Then we waited. A minute elapsed. A bird, fluttering in the opening above, for a second or two, wrenched our strained nerves. Hall's face turned pale.

"They had better keep away from here," he whispered, with a ghastly smile.

Two minutes! I could hear the beating of my heart. The engine shook the floor.

Three minutes! Hall's face was wet with perspiration. The bird blundered in and startled us again.

Four minutes! We were like statues, with all eyes fixed on the polished ball of silver, which shone in the brilliant light concentrated upon it by the mirror.

Five minutes! The shining ball had become a confused blue, and I violently winked to clear my vision.

"At last! Thank God! Look! There it is!"

It was Hall who spoke, trembling like an aspen. The silver knob had changed color. What seemed a miniature rainbow surrounded it, with concentric circles of blinding brilliance.

Then something dropped flashing into an earthen dish set beneath the ball! Another glittering drop followed, and, at a shorter interval, another!

Almost before a word could be uttered the drops had coalesced and become a tiny stream, which, as it fell, twisted itself into a bright spiral, gleaming with a hundred shifting hues, and forming on the bottom of the dish a glowing, interlacing maze of viscid rings and circlets, which turned and twined about and over one another, until they had blended and settled into a button-shaped mass of hot metallic jelly. Hall snatched the dish away, and placed another in its stead.

"This will be about right for a watch charm when it cools," he said, with a return of his customary self-command. "I promised you the first specimen. I'll catch another for myself."

"But can it be possible that we are not dreaming?" I exclaimed. "Do you really believe that this comes from the moon?"

"Just as surely as rain comes from the clouds," cried Hall, with all his old impatience. "Haven't I just showed you the whole process?"

"Then I congratulate you. You will be as rich as Dr. Syx."

"Perhaps," was the unperturbed reply, "but not until I have enlarged my apparatus. At present I shall hardly do more than supply mementoes to my friends. But since the principle is established, the rest is mere detail."

Six weeks later the financial centres of the earth were shaken by the news that a new supply of artemisium was being marketed from a mill which had been secretly opened in the Sierras of California. For a time there was almost a panic. If Hall had chosen to do so, he might have precipitated serious trouble. But he immediately entered into negotiations with government representatives, and the inevitable result was that, to preserve the monetary system of the world from upheaval, Dr. Syx had to consent that Hall's mill should share equally with his in the production of artemisium. During the negotiations the doctor paid a visit to Hall's establishment. The meeting between them was most dramatic. Syx tried to blast his rival with a glance, but knowledge is power, and my friend faced his mysterious antagonist, whose deepest secrets he had penetrated, with an unflinching eye. It was remarked that Dr. Syx became a changed man from that moment. His masterful air seemed to have deserted him, and it was with something resembling humility that he assented to the arrangement which required him to share his enormous gains with his conqueror.

Of course, Hall's success led to an immediate recrudescence of the efforts to extract artemisium from the Syx ore, and, equally of course, every such attempt failed. Hall, while keeping his own secret, did all he could to discourage the experiments, but they naturally believed that he must have made the very discovery which was the subject of their dreams, and he could not, without betraying himself, and upsetting the finances of the planet, directly undeceive them. The consequence was that fortunes were wasted in hopeless experimentation, and, with Hall's achievement dazzling their eyes, the deluded fortune-seekers kept on in the face of endless disappointments and disaster.

And presently there came another tragedy. The Syx mill was blown up! The accident—although many people refused to regard it as an accident, and asserted that the doctor himself, in his chagrin, had applied the match—the explosion, then, occurred about sundown, and its effects were awful. The great works, with everything pertaining to them, and every rail that they contained, were blown to atoms. They disappeared as if they had never existed. Even the twin tunnels were involved in the ruin, a vast cavity being left in the mountain-side where Syx's ten acres had been. The force of the explosion was so great that the shattered rock was reduced to dust. To this fact was owing the escape of the troops camped near. While the mountain was shaken to its core, and enormous parapets of living rock were hurled down the precipices of the Teton, no missiles of appreciable size traversed the air, and not a man at the camp was injured. But Jackson's Hole, filled with red dust, looked for days afterwards like the mouth of a tremendous volcano just after an eruption. Dr. Syx had been seen entering the mill a few minutes before the catastrophe by a sentinel who was stationed about a quarter of a mile away, and who, although he was felled like an ox by the shock, and had his eyes, ears, and nostrils filled with flying dust, miraculously escaped with his life.

After this a new arrangement was made whereby Andrew Hall became the sole producer of artemisium, and his wealth began to mount by leaps of millions towards the starry heights of the billions.

About a year after the explosion of the Syx mill a strange rumor got about. It came first from Budapest, in Hungary, where it was averred several persons of credibility had seen Dr. Max Syx. Millions had been familiar with his face and his personal peculiarities, through actually meeting him, as well as through photographs and descriptions, and, unless there was an intention to deceive, it did not seem possible that a mistake could be made in identification. There surely never was another man who looked just like Dr. Syx. And, besides, was it not demonstrable that he must have perished in the awful destruction of his mill?

Soon after came a report that Dr. Syx had been seen again; this time at Ekaterinburg, in the Urals. Next he was said to have paid a visit to Batang, in the mountainous district of southwestern China, and finally, according to rumor, he was seen in Sicily, at Nicolosi, among the volcanic pimples on the southern slope of Mount Etna.

Next followed something of more curious and even startling interest. A chemist at Budapest, where the first rumors of Syx's reappearance had placed the mysterious doctor, announced that he could produce artemisium, and proved it, although he kept his process secret. Hardly had the sensation caused by this news partially subsided when a similar report arrived from Ekaterinburg; then another from Batang; after that a fourth from Nicolosi!

Nobody could fail to notice the coincidence; wherever the doctor—or was it his ghost?—appeared, there, shortly afterwards, somebody discovered the much-sought secret.

After this Syx's apparitions rapidly increased in frequency, followed in each instance by the announcement of another productive artemisium mill. He appeared in Germany, Italy, France, England, and finally at many places in the United States.

"It is the old doctor's revenge," said Hall to me one day, trying to smile, although the matter was too serious to be taken humorously. "Yes, it is his revenge, and I must admit that it is complete. The price of artemisium has fallen one-half within six months. All the efforts we have made to hold back the flood have proved useless. The secret itself is becoming public property. We shall inevitably be overwhelmed with artemisium, just as we were with gold, and the last condition of the financial world will be worse than the first."

My friend's gloomy prognostications came near being fulfilled to the letter. Ten thousand artemisium mills shot their etheric rays upon the moon, and our unfortunate satellite's metal ribs were stripped by atomic force. Some of the great white rays that had been one of the telescopic wonders of the lunar landscapes disappeared, and the face of the moon, which had remained unchanged before the eyes of the children of Adam from the beginning of their race, now looked as if the blast of a furnace had swept it. At night, on the moonward side, the earth was studded with brilliant spikes, all pointed at the heart of its child in the sky.

But the looting of the moon brought disaster to the robber planet. So mad were the efforts to get the precious metal that the surface of our globe was fairly showered with it, productive fields were, in some cases, almost smothered under a metallic coating, the air was filled with shining dust, until finally famine and pestilence joined hands with financial disaster to punish the grasping world.

Then, at last, the various governments took effective measures to protect themselves and their people. Another combined effort resulted in an international agreement whereby the production of the precious moon metal was once more rigidly controlled. But the existence of a monopoly, such as Dr. Syx had so long enjoyed, and in the enjoyment of which Andrew Hall had for a brief period succeeded him, was henceforth rendered impossible.

THE LAST OF DR. SYX

Many years after the events last recorded I sat, at the close of a brilliant autumn day, side by side with my old friend Andrew Hall, on a broad, vine-shaded piazza which faced the east, where the full moon was just rising above the rim of the Sierra, and replacing the rosy counter-glow of sunset with its silvery radiance. The sight was calculated to carry the minds of both back to the events of former years. But I noticed that Hall quickly changed the position of his chair, and sat down again with his back to the rising moon. He had managed to save some millions from the wreck of his vast fortune when artemisium started to go to the dogs, and I was now paying him one of my annual visits at his palatial home in California.

"Did I ever tell you of my last trip to the Teton?" he asked, as I continued to gaze contemplatively at the broad lunar disk which slowly detached itself from the horizon and began to swim in the clear evening sky.

"No," I replied, "but I should like to hear about it."

"Or of my last sight of Dr. Syx?"

"Indeed! I did not suppose that you ever saw him after that conference in your mill, when he had to surrender half of the world to you."

"Once only I saw him again," said Hall, with a peculiar intonation.

"Pray go ahead, and tell me the whole story."

My friend lighted a fresh cigar, tipped his chair into a more comfortable position, and began:

"It was about seven years ago. I had long felt an unconquerable desire to have another look at the Teton and the scenes amid which so many strange events in my life had occurred. I thought of sending for you to go with me, but I knew you were abroad much of your time, and I could not be certain of catching you. Finally I decided to go alone. I travelled on horseback by way of the Snake River canyon, and arrived early one morning in Jackson's Hole. I can tell you it was a gloomy place, as barren and deserted as some of those Arabian wadies that you have been describing to me. The railroad had long ago been abandoned, and the site of the military camp could scarcely be recognized. An immense cavity with ragged walls showed where Dr. Syx's mill used to send up its plume of black smoke.

"As I stared up the gaunt form of the Teton, whose beetling precipices had been smashed and split by the great explosion, I was seized with a resistless impulse to climb it. I thought I should like to peer off again from that pinnacle which had once formed so fateful a watch-tower for me. Turning my horse loose to graze in the grassy river bottom, and carrying my rope tether along as a possible aid in climbing, I set out for the ascent. I knew I could not get up the precipices on the eastern side, which we were able to master with the aid of our balloon, and so I bore round, when I reached the steepest cliffs, until I was on the southwestern side of the peak, where the climbing was easier.

"But it took me a long time, and I did not reach the rift in the summit until just before sundown. Knowing that it would be impossible for me to descend at night, I bethought me of the enclosure of rocks, supposed to have been made by Indians, on the western pinnacle, and decided that I could pass the night there.

"The perpendicular buttress forming the easternmost and highest point of the Teton's head would have baffled me but for the fact that I found a long crack, probably an effect of the tremendous explosion, extending from bottom to top of the rock. Driving my toes and fingers into this rift, I managed, with a good deal of trouble, and no little peril, to reach the top. As I lifted myself over the edge and rose to my feet, imagine my amazement at seeing Dr. Syx standing within arm's-length of me!

"My breath seemed pent in my lungs, and I could not even utter the exclamation that rose to my lips. It was like meeting a ghost. Notwithstanding the many reports of his having been seen in various parts of the world, it had always been my conviction that he had perished in the explosion.

"Yet there he stood in the twilight, for the sun was hidden by the time I reached the summit, his tall form erect, and his black eyes gleaming under the heavy brows as he fixed them sternly upon my face. You know I never was given to losing my nerve, but I am afraid I lost it on that occasion. Again and again I strove to speak, but it was impossible to move my tongue. So powerless seemed my lungs that I wondered how I could continue breathing.

"The doctor remained silent, but his curious smile, which, as you know, was a thing of terror to most people, overspread his black-rimmed face and was broad enough to reveal the gleam of his teeth. I felt that he was looking me through and through. The sensation was as if he had transfixed me with an ice-cold blade. There was a gleam of devilish pleasure in his eyes, as though my evident suffering was a delight to him and a gratification of his vengeance. At length I succeeded in overcoming the feeling which oppressed me, and, making a step forward, I shouted in a strained voice,

"'You black Satan!'

"I cannot clearly explain the psychological process which led me to utter those words. I had never entertained any enmity towards Dr. Syx, although I had always regarded him as a heartless person, who had purposely led thousands to their ruin for his selfish gain, but I knew that he could not help hating me, and I felt now that, in some inexplicable manner, a struggle, not physical, but spiritual, was taking place between us, and my exclamation, uttered with surprising intensity, produced upon me, and apparently upon him, the effect of a desperate sword thrust which attains its mark.

"Immediately the doctor's form seemed to recede, as if he had passed the verge of the precipice behind him. At the same time it became dim, and then dimmer, until only the dark outlines, and particularly the jet-black eyes, glaring fiercely, remained visible. And still he receded, as though floating in the air, which was now silvered with the evening light, until he appeared to cross the immense atmospheric gulf over Jackson's Hole and paused on the rim of the horizon in the east.

"Then, suddenly, I became aware that the full moon had risen at the very place on the distant mountain-brow where the spectre rested, and as I continued to gaze, as if entranced, the face and figure of the doctor seemed slowly to frame themselves within the lunar disk, until at last he appeared to have quitted the air and the earth and to be frowning at me from the circle of the moon."

While Hall was pronouncing his closing words I had begun to stare at the moon with swiftly increasing interest, until, as his voice stopped, I exclaimed,

"Why, there he is now! Funny I never noticed it before. There's Dr. Syx's face in the moon, as plain as day."

"Yes," replied Hall, without turning round, "and I never like to look at it."

THE COMING OF THE ICE

G. Peyton Wertenbaker (1926)

IT IS STRANGE to be alone, and so cold. To be the last man on earth....

The snow drives silently about me, ceaselessly, drearily. And I am isolated in this tiny white, indistinguishable corner of a blurred world, surely the loneliest creature in the universe. How many thousands of years is it since I last knew the true companionship? For a long time I have been lonely, but there were people, creatures of flesh and blood. Now they are gone. Now I have not even the stars to keep me company, for they are all lost in an infinity of snow and twilight here below.

If only I could know how long it has been since first I was imprisoned upon the earth. It cannot matter now. And yet some vague dissatisfaction, some faint instinct, asks over and over in my throbbing ears: What year? What year?

It was in the year 1930 that the great thing began in my life. There was then a very great man who performed operations on his fellows to compose their vitals—we called such men surgeons. John Granden wore the title "Sir" before his name, in indication of nobility by birth according to the prevailing standards in England. But surgery was only a hobby of Sir John's, if I must be precise, for, while he had achieved an enormous reputation as a surgeon, he always felt that his real work lay in the experimental end of his profession. He was, in a way, a dreamer, but a dreamer who could make his dreams come true.

I was a very close friend of Sir John's. In fact, we shared the same apartments in London. I have never forgotten that day when he first mentioned to me his momentous discovery. I had just come in from a long sleigh-ride in the country with Alice, and I was seated drowsily in the window-seat, writing idly in my mind a description of the wind and the snow and the grey twilight of the evening. It is strange, is it not, that my tale should begin and end with the snow and the twilight.

Sir John opened suddenly a door at one end of the room and came hurrying across to another door. He looked at me, grinning rather like a triumphant maniac.

"It's coming!" he cried, without pausing, "I've almost got it!" I smiled at him: he looked very ludicrous at that moment.

"What have you got?" I asked.

"Good Lord, man, the Secret—the Secret!" And then he was gone again, the door closing upon his victorious cry, "The Secret!"

I was, of course, amused. But I was also very much interested. I knew Sir John well enough to realize that, however amazing his appearance might be, there would be nothing absurd about his "Secret"—whatever it was. But it was useless to speculate. I could only hope for enlightenment at dinner. So I immersed myself in one of the surgeon's volumes from his fine Library of Imagination, and waited.

I think the book was one of Mr. H. G. Wells', probably "The Sleeper Awakes," or some other of his brilliant fantasies and predictions, for I was in a mood conducive to belief in almost anything when, later, we sat down together across the table. I only wish I could give some idea of the atmosphere that permeated our apartments, the reality it lent to whatever was vast and amazing and strange. You could then, whoever you are, understand a little the ease with which I accepted Sir John's new discovery.

He began to explain it to me at once, as though he could keep it to himself no longer.

"Did you think I had gone mad, Dennell?" he asked. "I quite wonder that I haven't. Why, I have been studying for many years—for most of my life—on this problem. And, suddenly, I have solved it! Or, rather, I am afraid I have solved another one much greater."

"Tell me about it, but for God's sake don't be technical."

"Right," he said. Then he paused. "Dennell, it's *magnificent*! It will change everything that is in the world." His eyes held mine suddenly with the fatality of a hypnotist's. "Dennell, it is the Secret of Eternal Life," he said.

"Good Lord, Sir John!" I cried, half inclined to laugh.

"I mean it," he said. "You know I have spent most of my life studying the processes of birth, trying to find out precisely what went on in the whole history of conception."

"You have found out?"

"No, that is just what amuses me. I have discovered something else without knowing yet what causes either process.

"I don't want to be technical, and I know very little of what actually takes place myself. But I can try to give you some idea of it."

IT is thousands, perhaps millions of years since Sir John explained to me. What little I understood at the time I may have forgotten, yet I try to reproduce what I can of his theory.

"In my study of the processes of birth," he began, "I discovered the rudiments of an action which takes place in the bodies of both men and women. There are certain properties in the foods we eat that remain in the body for the reproduction of life, two distinct Essences, so to speak, of which one is

retained by the woman, another by the man. It is the union of these two properties that, of course, creates the child.

"Now, I made a slight mistake one day in experimenting with a guinea-pig,
and I re-arranged certain organs which I need not describe so that I thought
I had completely messed up the poor creature's abdomen. It lived, however,
and I laid it aside. It was some years later that I happened to notice it again.
It had not given birth to any young, but I was amazed to note that it had
apparently grown no older: it seemed precisely in the same state of growth in
which I had left it.

"From that I built up. I re-examined the guinea-pig, and observed it carefully. I need not detail my studies. But in the end I found that my 'mistake'
had in reality been a momentous discovery. I found that I had only to close
certain organs, to re-arrange certain ducts, and to open certain dormant
organs, and, *mirabile dictu*, the whole process of reproduction was changed.

"You have heard, of course, that our bodies are continually changing, hour
by hour, minute by minute, so that every few years we have been literally
reborn. Some such principle as this seems to operate in reproduction, except
that, instead of the old body being replaced by the new, and in its form,
approximately, the new body is created apart from it. It is the creation of
children that causes us to die, it would seem, because if this activity is, so
to speak, dammed up or turned aside into new channels, the reproduction
operates on the old body, renewing it continually. It is very obscure and very
absurd, is it not? But the most absurd part of it is that it is true. Whatever the
true explanation may be, the fact remains that the operation can be done, that
it actually prolongs life indefinitely, and that I alone know the secret."

Sir John told me a very great deal more, but, after all, I think it amounted to
little more than this. It would be impossible for me to express the great hold
his discovery took upon my mind the moment he recounted it. From the very
first, under the spell of his personality, I believed, and I knew he was speaking the truth. And it opened up before me new vistas. I began to see myself
become suddenly eternal, never again to know the fear of death. I could see
myself storing up, century after century, an amplitude of wisdom and experience that would make me truly a god.

"Sir John!" I cried, long before he was finished. "You must perform that
operation on me!"

"But, Dennell, you are too hasty. You must not put yourself so rashly into
my hands."

"You have perfected the operation, haven't you?"

"That is true," he said.

"You must try it out on somebody, must you not?"

"Yes, of course. And yet—somehow, Dennell, I am afraid. I cannot help
feeling that man is not yet prepared for such a vast thing. There are sacrifices.
One must give up love and all sensual pleasure. This operation not only takes
away the mere fact of reproduction, but it deprives one of all the things that

go with sex, all love, all sense of beauty, all feeling for poetry and the arts. It leaves only the few emotions, selfish emotions, that are necessary to self-preservation. Do you not see? One becomes an intellect, nothing more—a cold apotheosis of reason. And I, for one, cannot face such a thing calmly."

"But, Sir John, like many fears, it is largely horrible in the foresight. After you have changed your nature you cannot regret it. What you are would be as horrible an idea to you afterwards as the thought of what you will be seems now."

"True, true. I know it. But it is hard to face, nevertheless."

"I am not afraid to face it."

"You do not understand it, Dennell, I am afraid. And I wonder whether you or I or any of us on this earth are ready for such a step. After all, to make a race deathless, one should be sure it is a perfect race."

"Sir John," I said, "it is not you who have to face this, nor any one else in the world till you are ready. But I am firmly resolved, and I demand it of you as my friend."

Well, we argued much further, but in the end I won. Sir John promised to perform the operation three days later.

... But do you perceive now what I had forgotten during all that discussion, the one thing I had thought I could never forget so long as I lived, not even for an instant? It was my love for Alice—I had forgotten that!

I CANNOT write here all the infinity of emotions I experienced later, when, with Alice in my arms, it suddenly came upon me what I had done. Ages ago—I have forgotten how to feel. I could name now a thousand feelings I used to have, but I can no longer even understand them. For only the heart can understand the heart, and the intellect only the intellect.

With Alice in my arms, I told the whole story. It was she who, with her quick instinct, grasped what I had never noticed.

"But Carl!" she cried, "Don't you see?—It will mean that we can never be married!" And, for the first time, I understood. If only I could re-capture some conception of that love! I have always known, since the last shred of comprehension slipped from me, that I lost something very wonderful when I lost love. But what does it matter? I lost Alice too, and I could not have known love again without her.

We were very sad and very tragic that night. For hours and hours we argued the question over. But I felt somewhat that I was inextricably caught in my fate, that I could not retreat now from my resolve. I was perhaps, very school-boyish, but I felt that it would be cowardice to back out now. But it was Alice again who perceived a final aspect of the matter.

"Carl," she said to me, her lips very close to mine, "it need not come between our love. After all, ours would be a poor sort of love if it were not more of the mind than of the flesh. We shall remain lovers, but we shall forget mere carnal desire. I shall submit to that operation too!"

And I could not shake her from her resolve. I would speak of danger that I could not let her face. But, after the fashion of women, she disarmed me with the accusation that I did not love her, that I did not want her love, that I was trying to escape from love. What answer had I for that, but that I loved her and would do anything in the world not to lose her?

I have wondered sometimes since whether we might have known the love of the mind. Is love something entirely of the flesh, something created by an ironic God merely to propagate His race? Or can there be love without emotion, love without passion—love between two cold intellects? I do not know. I did not ask then. I accepted anything that would make our way more easy.

There is no need to draw out the tale. Already my hand wavers, and my time grows short. Soon there will be no more of me, no more of my tale—no more of Mankind. There will be only the snow, and the ice, and the cold ...

THREE days later I entered John's Hospital with Alice on my arm. All my affairs—and they were few enough—were in order. I had insisted that Alice wait until I had come safely through the operation, before she submitted to it. I had been carefully starved for two days, and I was lost in an unreal world of white walls and white clothes and white lights, drunk with my dreams of the future. When I was wheeled into the operating room on the long, hard table, for a moment it shone with brilliant distinctness, a neat, methodical white chamber, tall and more or less circular. Then I was beneath the glare of soft white lights, and the room faded into a misty vagueness from which little steel rays flashed and quivered from silvery cold instruments. For a moment our hands, Sir John's and mine, gripped, and we were saying good-bye—for a little while—in the way men say these things. Then I felt the warm touch of Alice's lips upon mine, and I felt sudden painful things I cannot describe, that I could not have described then. For a moment I felt that I must rise and cry out that I could not do it. But the feeling passed, and I was passive.

Something was pressed about my mouth and nose, something with an ethereal smell. Staring eyes swam about me from behind their white masks. I struggled instinctively, but in vain—I was held securely. Infinitesimal points of light began to wave back and forth on a pitch-black background; a great hollow buzzing echoed in my head. My head seemed suddenly to have become all throat, a great, cavernous, empty throat in which sounds and lights were mingled together, in a swift rhythm, approaching, receding eternally. Then, I think, there were dreams. But I have forgotten them....

I began to emerge from the effect of the ether. Everything was dim, but I could perceive Alice beside me, and Sir John.

"Bravely done!" Sir John was saying, and Alice, too, was saying something, but I cannot remember what. For a long while we talked, I speaking the nonsense of those who are coming out from under ether, they teasing me a little solemnly. But after a little while I became aware of the fact that they were about to leave. Suddenly, God knows why, I knew that they must not leave. Something cried in the back of my head that they *must* stay—one cannot explain these things, except by after events. I began to press them to remain, but they smiled and said they must get their dinner. I commanded them not to go; but they spoke kindly and said they would be back before long. I think I even wept a little, like a child, but Sir John said something to the nurse, who began to reason with me firmly, and then they were gone, and somehow I was asleep....

WHEN I awoke again, my head was fairly clear, but there was an abominable reek of ether all about me. The moment I opened my eyes, I felt that something had happened. I asked for Sir John and for Alice. I saw a swift, curious look that I could not interpret come over the face of the nurse, then she was calm again, her countenance impassive. She reassured me in quick meaningless phrases, and told me to sleep. But I could not sleep: I was absolutely sure that something had happened to them, to my friend and to the woman I loved. Yet all my insistence profited me nothing, for the nurses were a silent lot. Finally, I think, they must have given me a sleeping potion of some sort, for I fell asleep again.

For two endless, chaotic days, I saw nothing of either of them, Alice or Sir John. I became more and more agitated, the nurse more and more taciturn. She would only say that they had gone away for a day or two.

And then, on the third day, I found out. They thought I was asleep. The night nurse had just come in to relieve the other.

"Has he been asking about them again?" she asked.

"Yes, poor fellow. I have hardly managed to keep him quiet."

"We will have to keep it from him until he is recovered fully." There was a long pause, and I could hardly control my labored breathing.

"How sudden it was!" one of them said. "To be killed like that—" I heard no more, for I leapt suddenly up in bed, crying out.

"Quick! For God's sake, tell me what has happened!" I jumped to the floor and seized one of them by the collar. She was horrified. I shook her with a superhuman strength.

"Tell me!" I shouted, "Tell me—Or I'll—!" She told me—what else could she do.

"They were killed in an accident," she gasped, "in a taxi—a collision—the Strand—!" And at that moment a crowd of nurses and attendants arrived, called by the other frantic woman, and they put me to bed again.

I have no memory of the next few days. I was in delirium, and I was never told what I said during my ravings. Nor can I express the feelings I was saturated with when at last I regained my mind again. Between my old emotions and any attempt to put them into words, or even to remember them, lies always that insurmountable wall of my Change. I cannot understand what I must have felt, I cannot express it.

I only know that for weeks I was sunk in a misery beyond any misery I had ever imagined before. The only two friends I had on earth were gone to me. I was left alone. And, for the first time, I began to see before me all these end-less years that would be the same, dull, lonely.

Yet I recovered. I could feel each day the growth of a strange new vigor in my limbs, a vast force that was something tangibly expressive to eternal life. Slowly my anguish began to die. After a week more, I began to understand how my emotions were leaving me, how love and beauty and everything of which poetry was made—how all this was going. I could not bear the thought at first. I would look at the golden sunlight and the blue shadow of the wind, and I would say,

"God! How beautiful!" And the words would echo meaninglessly in my ears. Or I would remember Alice's face, that face I had once loved so inex-tinguishably, and I would weep and clutch my forehead, and clench my fists, crying,

"O God, how can I live without her!" Yet there would be a little strange fancy in my head at the same moment, saying,

"Who is this Alice? You know no such person." And truly I would wonder whether she had ever existed.

So, slowly, the old emotions were shed away from me, and I began to joy in a corresponding growth of my mental perceptions. I began to toy idly with mathematical formulae I had forgotten years ago, in the same fashion that a poet toys with a word and its shades of meaning. I would look at everything with new, seeing eyes, new perception, and I would understand things I had never understood before, because formerly my emotions had always occu-pied me more than my thoughts.

And so the weeks went by, until, one day, I was well.

...What, after all, is the use of this chronicle? Surely there will never be men to read it. I have heard them say that the snow will never go. I will be buried, it will be buried with me; and it will be the end of us both. Yet, somehow, it eases my weary soul a little to write....

Need I say that I lived, thereafter, many thousands of thousands of years, until this day? I cannot detail that life. It is a long round of new, fantastic impressions, coming dream-like, one after another, melting into each other. In looking back, as in looking back upon dreams, I seem to recall only a few isolated periods clearly; and it seems that my imagination must have filled in the swift movement between episodes. I think now, of necessity, in terms of centuries and millenniums, rather than days and months.... The snow blows terribly about my little fire, and I know it will soon gather courage to quench us both ...

YEARS passed, at first with a sort of clear wonder. I watched things that took place everywhere in the world. I studied. The other students were much amazed to see me, a man of thirty odd, coming back to college.

"But Judas, Dennell, you've already got your Ph.D! What more do you want?" So they would all ask me. And I would reply;

"I want an M.D. and an F.R.C.S." I didn't tell them that I wanted degrees in Law, too, and in Biology and Chemistry, in Architecture and Engineering, in Psychology and Philosophy. Even so, I believe they thought me mad. But poor fools! I would think. They can hardly realize that I have all of eternity before me to study.

I went to school for many decades. I would pass from University to University, leisurely gathering all the fruits of every subject I took up, eveling in study as no student reveled ever before. There was no need of hurry in my life, no fear of death too soon. There was a magnificence of vigor in my body, and a magnificence of vision and clarity in my brain. I felt myself a superman. I had only to go on storing up wisdom until the day should come when all knowledge of the world was mine, and then I could command the world. I had no need for hurry. O vast life! How I gloried in my eternity! And how little good it has ever done me, by the irony of God.

For several centuries, changing my name and passing from place to place, I continued my studies. I had no consciousness of monotony, for, to the intellect, monotony cannot exist: it was one of those emotions I had left behind. One day, however, in the year 2132, a great discovery was made by a man called Zarentzov. It had to do with the curvature of space, quite changing the conceptions that we had all followed since Einstein. I had long ago mastered the last detail of Einstein's theory, as had, in time, the rest of the world. I threw myself immediately into the study of this new, epoch-making conception.

To my amazement, it all seemed to me curiously dim and elusive. I could not quite grasp what Zarentzov was trying to formulate.

"Why," I cried, "the thing is a monstrous fraud!" I went to the professor of Physics in the University I then attended, and I told him it was a fraud, a huge book of mere nonsense. He looked at me rather pityingly.

"I am afraid, Modevski," he said, addressing me by the name I was at the time using, "I am afraid you do not understand it, that is all. When your mind has broadened, you will. You should apply yourself more carefully to your Physics." But that angered me, for I had mastered my Physics before he was ever born. I challenged him to explain the theory. And he did! He put it, obviously, in the clearest language he could. Yet I understood nothing. I stared at him dumbly, until he shook his head impatiently, saying that it was useless, that if I could not grasp it I would simply have to keep on studying. I was stunned. I wandered away in a daze.

For do you see what happened? During all those years I had studied ceaselessly, and my mind had been clear and quick as the day I first had left the hospital. But all that time I had been able only to remain what I was—an extraordinarily intelligent man of the twentieth century. And the rest of the race had been progressing! It had been swiftly gathering knowledge and power and ability all that time, faster and faster, while I had been only remaining still. And now here was Zarentzov and the teachers of the Universities, and, probably, a hundred intelligent men, who had all outstripped me! I was being left behind.

And that is what happened. I need not dilate further upon it. By the end of that century I had been left behind by all the students of the world, and I never did understand Zarentzov. Other men came with other theories, and these theories were accepted by the world. But I could not understand them. My intellectual life was at an end. I had nothing more to understand. I knew everything I was capable of knowing, and, thenceforth, I could only play wearily with the old ideas.

MANY things happened in the world. A time came when the East and West, two mighty unified hemispheres, rose up in arms: the civil war of a planet. I recall only chaotic visions of fire and thunder and hell. It was all incomprehensible to me: like a bizarre dream, things happened, people rushed about, but I never knew what they were doing. I lurked during all that time in a tiny shuddering hole under the city of Yokohama, and by a miracle I survived. And the East won. But it seems to have mattered little who did win, for all the world had become, in all except its few remaining prejudices, a single race, and nothing was changed when it was all rebuilt again, under a single government.

I saw the first of the strange creatures who appeared among us in the year 6371, men who were later known to be from the planet Venus. But they were repulsed, for they were savages compared with the Earthmen, although they were about equal to the people of my own century, 1900. Those of them who did not perish of the cold after the intense warmth of their world, and those who were not killed by our hands, those few returned silently home again. And I have always regretted that I had not the courage to go with them.

I watched a time when the world reached perfection in mechanics, when men could accomplish anything with a touch of the finger. Strange men, these creatures of the hundredth century, men with huge brains and tiny shriveled bodies, atrophied limbs, and slow, ponderous movements on their little conveyances. It was I, with my ancient compunctions, who shuddered when at last they put to death all the perverts, the criminals, and the insane, ridding the world of the scum for which they had no more need. It was then that I was forced to produce my tattered old papers, proving my identity and my story. They knew it was true, in some strange fashion of theirs, and, thereafter, I was kept on exhibition as an archaic survival.

I saw the world made immortal through the new invention of a man called Kathol, who used somewhat the same method "legend" decreed had been used upon me. I observed the end of speech, of all perceptions except one, when men learned to communicate directly by thought, and to receive directly into the brain all the myriad vibrations of the universe.

All these things I saw, and more, until that time when there was no more discovery, but a Perfect World in which there was no need for anything but memory. Men ceased to count time at last. Several hundred years after the 154th Dynasty from the Last War, or, as we would have counted in my time, about 200,000 A.D., official records of time were no longer kept carefully. They fell into disuse. Men began to forget years, to forget time at all. Of what significance was time when one was immortal?

AFTER long, long uncounted centuries, a time came when the days grew noticeably colder. Slowly the winters became longer, and the summers diminished to but a month or two. Fierce storms raged endlessly in winter, and in summer sometimes there was severe frost, sometimes there was only frost. In the high places and in the north and the sub-equatorial south, the snow came and would not go.

Men died by the thousands in the higher latitudes. New York became, after awhile, the furthest habitable city north, an arctic city, where warmth seldom penetrated. And great fields of ice began to make their way southward, grinding before them the brittle remains of civilizations, covering over relentlessly all of man's proud work.

Snow appeared in Florida and Italy one summer. In the end, snow was there always. Men left New York, Chicago, Paris, Yokohama, and everywhere they traveled by the millions southward, perishing as they went, pursued by the snow and the cold, and that inevitable field of ice. They were feeble creatures when the Cold first came upon them, but I speak in terms of thousands of years; and they turned every weapon of science to the recovery of their physical power, for they foresaw that the only chance for survival lay in a hard, strong body. As for me, at last I had found a use for my few powers, for my physique was the finest in that world. It was but little comfort, however, for we were all united in our awful fear of that Cold and that grinding field of Ice. All the great cities were deserted. We would catch silent, fearful glimpses of them as we sped on in our machines over the snow—great hungry, haggard skeletons of cities, shrouded in banks of snow, snow that the wind rustled through desolate streets where the cream of human life once had passed in calm security. Yet still the Ice pursued. For men had forgotten about that Last Ice Age when they ceased to reckon time, when they lost sight of the future and steeped themselves in memories. They had not remembered that a time must come when Ice would lie white and smooth over all the earth, when the sun would shine bleakly between unending intervals of dim, twilight snow and sleet.

Slowly the Ice pursued us down the earth, until all the feeble remains of civilization were gathered in Egypt and India and South America. The deserts flowered again, but the frost would come always to bite the tiny crops. For still the Ice came. All the world now, but for a narrow strip about the equator, was one great silent desolate vista of stark ice-plains, ice that brooded above the hidden ruins of cities that had endured for hundreds of thousands of years. It was terrible to imagine the awful solitude and the endless twilight that lay on these places, and the grim snow, sailing in silence over all....

It surrounded us on all sides, until life remained only in a few scattered clearings all about that equator of the globe, with an eternal fire going to hold away the hungry Ice. Perpetual winter reigned now; and we were becoming terror-stricken beasts that preyed on each other for a life already doomed. Ah, but I, I the archaic survival, I had my revenge then, with my great physique and strong jaws—God! Let me think of something else. Those men who lived upon each other—it was horrible. And I was one.

SO inevitably the Ice closed in.... One day the men of our tiny clearing were but a score. We huddled about our dying fire of bones and stray logs. We said nothing. We just sat, in deep, wordless, thoughtless silence. We were the last outpost of Mankind.

I think suddenly something very noble must have transformed these creatures to a semblance of what they had been of old. I saw, in their eyes, the question they sent from one to another, and in every eye I saw that the answer was, Yes. With one accord they rose before my eyes and, ignoring me as a baser creature, they stripped away their load of tattered rags and, one by one, they stalked with their tiny shrivelled limbs into the shivering gale of swirling, gusting snow, and disappeared. And I was alone....

So am I alone now. I have written this last fantastic history of myself and of Mankind upon a substance that will, I know, outlast even the snow and the Ice—as it has outlasted Mankind that made it. It is the only thing with which I have never parted. For is it not irony that I should be the historian of this race—I, a savage, an "archaic survival?" Why do I write? God knows, but some instinct prompts me, although there will never be men to read.

I have been sitting here, waiting, and I have thought often of Sir John and Alice, whom I loved. Can it be that I am feeling again, after all these ages, some tiny portion of that emotion, that great passion I once knew? I see her face before me, the face I have lost from my thoughts for eons, and something is in it that stirs my blood again. Her eyes are half-closed and deep, her lips are parted as though I could crush them with an infinity of wonder and discovery. O God! It is love again, love that I thought was lost! They have often smiled upon me when I spoke of God, and muttered about my foolish, primitive superstitions. But they are gone, and I am left who believe in God, and surely there is purpose in it.

I am cold, I have written. Ah, I am frozen. My breath freezes as it mingles with the air, and I can hardly move my numbed fingers. The Ice is closing over me, and I cannot break it any longer. The storm cries weirdly all about me in the twilight, and I know this is the end. The end of the world. And I—I, the last man....

The last man....

... I am cold—cold....

But is it you, Alice? Is it you?

THE NEW ACCELERATOR

H. G. Wells (1926)

CERTAINLY, IF EVER a man found a guinea when he was looking for a pin it is my good friend Professor Gibberne. I have heard before of investigators overshooting the mark, but never quite to the extent that he has done. He has really, this time at any rate, without any touch of exaggeration in the phrase, found something to revolutionise human life. And that when he was simply seeking an all-round nervous stimulant to bring languid people up to the stresses of these pushful days. I have tasted the stuff now several times, and I cannot do better than describe the effect the thing had on me. That there are astonishing experiences in store for all in search of new sensations will become apparent enough.

Professor Gibberne, as many people know, is my neighbour in Folkestone. Unless my memory plays me a trick, his portrait at various ages has already appeared in The Strand Magazine—I think late in 1899; but I am unable to look it up because I have lent that volume to some one who has never sent it back. The reader may, perhaps, recall the high forehead and the singularly long black eyebrows that give such a Mephistophelian touch to his face. He occupies one of those pleasant little detached houses in the mixed style that make the western end of the Upper Sandgate Road so interesting. His is the one with the Flemish gables and the Moorish portico, and it is in the little room with the mullioned bay window that he works when he is down here, and in which of an evening we have so often smoked and talked together. He is a mighty jester, but, besides, he likes to talk to me about his work; he is one of those men who find a help and stimulus in talking, and so I have been able to follow the conception of the New Accelerator right up from a very early stage. Of course, the greater portion of his experimental work is not done in Folkestone, but in Gower Street, in the fine new laboratory next to the hospital that he has been the first to use.

As every one knows, or at least as all intelligent people know, the special department in which Gibberne has gained so great and deserved a reputation among physiologists is the action of drugs upon the nervous system. Upon soporifics, sedatives, and anaesthetics he is, I am told, unequalled. He is also a chemist of considerable eminence, and I suppose in the subtle and complex jungle of riddles that centres about the ganglion cell and the axis fibre there are little cleared places of his making, little glades of illumination, that, until he sees fit to publish his results, are still inaccessible to every other living man. And in the last few years he has been particularly assiduous upon this question of nervous stimulants, and already, before the discovery of the New Accelerator, very successful with them. Medical science has to thank him for at least three distinct and absolutely safe invigorators of unrivalled value to practising men. In cases of exhaustion the preparation known as Gibberne's B Syrup has, I suppose, saved more lives already than any lifeboat round the coast.

"But none of these little things begin to satisfy me yet," he told me nearly a year ago. "Either they increase the central energy without affecting the nerves or they simply increase the available energy by lowering the nervous conductivity; and all of them are unequal and local in their operation. One wakes up the heart and viscera and leaves the brain stupefied, one gets at the brain champagne fashion and does nothing good for the solar plexus, and what I want—and what, if it's an earthly possibility, I mean to have—is a stimulant that stimulates all round, that wakes you up for a time from the crown of your head to the tip of your great toe, and makes you go two—or even three—to everybody else's one. Eh? That's the thing I'm after."

"It would tire a man," I said.

"Not a doubt of it. And you'd eat double or treble—and all that. But just think what the thing would mean. Imagine yourself with a little phial like this"—he held up a little bottle of green glass and marked his points with it—"and in this precious phial is the power to think twice as fast, move twice as quickly, do twice as much work in a given time as you could otherwise do."

"But is such a thing possible?"

"I believe so. If it isn't, I've wasted my time for a year. These various preparations of the hypophosphites, for example, seem to show that something of the sort... Even if it was only one and a half times as fast it would do."

"It WOULD do," I said.

"If you were a statesman in a corner, for example, time rushing up against you, something urgent to be done, eh?"

"He could dose his private secretary," I said.

"And gain—double time. And think if YOU, for example, wanted to finish a book."

"Usually," I said, "I wish I'd never begun 'em."

"Or a doctor, driven to death, wants to sit down and think out a case. Or a barrister—or a man cramming for an examination."

"Worth a guinea a drop," said I, "and more to men like that."

"And in a duel, again," said Gibberne, "where it all depends on your quickness in pulling the trigger."

"Or in fencing," I echoed.

"You see," said Gibberne, "if I get it as an all-round thing it will really do you no harm at all—except perhaps to an infinitesimal degree it brings you nearer old age. You will just have lived twice to other people's once—"

"I suppose," I meditated, "in a duel—it would be fair?"

"That's a question for the seconds," said Gibberne.

I harked back further. "And you really think such a thing IS possible?" I said.

"As possible," said Gibberne, and glanced at something that went throbbing by the window, "as a motor-bus. As a matter of fact—"

He paused and smiled at me deeply, and tapped slowly on the edge of his desk with the green phial. "I think I know the stuff.... Already I've got something coming." The nervous smile upon his face betrayed the gravity of his revelation. He rarely talked of his actual experimental work unless things were very near the end. "And it may be, it may be—I shouldn't be surprised—it may even do the thing at a greater rate than twice."

"It will be rather a big thing," I hazarded.

"It will be, I think, rather a big thing."

But I don't think he quite knew what a big thing it was to be, for all that.

I remember we had several talks about the stuff after that. "The New Accelerator" he called it, and his tone about it grew more confident on each occasion. Sometimes he talked nervously of unexpected physiological results its use might have, and then he would get a little unhappy; at others he was frankly mercenary, and we debated long and anxiously how the preparation might be turned to commercial account. "It's a good thing," said Gibberne, "a tremendous thing. I know I'm giving the world something, and I think it only reasonable we should expect the world to pay. The dignity of science is all very well, but I think somehow I must have the monopoly of the stuff for, say, ten years. I don't see why ALL the fun in life should go to the dealers in ham."

My own interest in the coming drug certainly did not wane in the time. I have always had a queer little twist towards metaphysics in my mind. I have always been given to paradoxes about space and time, and it seemed to me that Gibberne was really preparing no less than the absolute acceleration of life. Suppose a man repeatedly dosed with such a preparation: he would live an active and record life indeed, but he would be an adult at eleven, middle-aged at twenty-five, and by thirty well on the road to senile decay. It seemed to me that so far Gibberne was only going to do for any one who took his drug exactly what Nature has done for the Jews and Orientals, who are men in their teens and aged by fifty, and quicker in thought and act than we are all the time. The marvel of drugs has always been great to my mind; you can madden a man, calm a man, make him incredibly strong and alert or a helpless log, quicken this passion and allay that, all by means of drugs, and here was a new miracle to be added to this strange armoury of phials the doctors use! But Gibberne was far too eager upon his technical points to enter very keenly into my aspect of the question.

It was the 7th or 8th of August when he told me the distillation that would decide his failure or success for a time was going forward as we talked, and it was on the 10th that he told me the thing was done and the New Accelerator a tangible reality in the world. I met him as I was going up the Sandgate Hill towards Folkestone—I think I was going to get my hair cut, and he came hurrying down to meet me—I suppose he was coming to my house to tell me at once of his success. I remember that his eyes were unusually bright and his face flushed, and I noted even then the swift alacrity of his step.

"It's done," he cried, and gripped my hand, speaking very fast; "it's more than done. Come up to my house and see."

"Really?"

"Really!" he shouted. "Incredibly! Come up and see."

"And it does—twice?

"It does more, much more. It scares me. Come up and see the stuff. Taste it! Try it! It's the most amazing stuff on earth." He gripped my arm and, walking at such a pace that he forced me into a trot, went shouting with me up the hill. A whole char-a-banc-ful of people turned and stared at us in unison after the manner of people in chars-a-banc. It was one of those hot, clear days that Folkestone sees so much of, every colour incredibly bright and every outline hard. There was a breeze, of course, but not so much breeze as sufficed under these conditions to keep me cool and dry. I panted for mercy.

"I'm not walking fast, am I?" cried Gibberne, and slackened his pace to a quick march.

"You've been taking some of this stuff," I puffed.

"No," he said. "At the utmost a drop of water that stood in a beaker from which I had washed out the last traces of the stuff. I took some last night, you know. But that is ancient history, now."

"And it goes twice?" I said, nearing his doorway in a grateful perspiration.

"It goes a thousand times, many thousand times!" cried Gibberne, with a dramatic gesture, flinging open his Early English carved oak gate.

"Phew!" said I, and followed him to the door.

"I don't know how many times it goes," he said, with his latch-key in his hand.

"And you—"

"It throws all sorts of light on nervous physiology, it kicks the theory of vision into a perfectly new shape!... Heaven knows how many thousand times. We'll try all that after—The thing is to try the stuff now."

"Try the stuff?" I said, as we went along the passage.

"Rather," said Gibberne, turning on me in his study. "There it is in that little green phial there! Unless you happen to be afraid?"

I am a careful man by nature, and only theoretically adventurous. I WAS afraid. But on the other hand there is pride.

"Well," I haggled. "You say you've tried it?"

"I've tried it," he said, "and I don't look hurt by it, do I? I don't even look livery and I FEEL—"

I sat down. "Give me the potion," I said. "If the worst comes to the worst it will save having my hair cut, and that I think is one of the most hateful duties of a civilised man. How do you take the mixture?"

"With water," said Gibberne, whacking down a carafe.

He stood up in front of his desk and regarded me in his easy chair; his manner was suddenly affected by a touch of the Harley Street specialist. "It's rum stuff, you know," he said.

I made a gesture with my hand.

"I must warn you in the first place as soon as you've got it down to shut your eyes, and open them very cautiously in a minute or so's time. One still sees. The sense of vision is a question of length of vibration, and not of multitude of impacts; but there's a kind of shock to the retina, a nasty giddy confusion just at the time, if the eyes are open. Keep 'em shut."

"Shut," I said. "Good!"

"And the next thing is, keep still. Don't begin to whack about. You may fetch something a nasty rap if you do. Remember you will be going several thousand times faster than you ever did before, heart, lungs, muscles, brain—everything—and you will hit hard without knowing it. You won't know it, you know. You'll feel just as you do now. Only everything in the world will seem to be going ever so many thousand times slower than it ever went before. That's what makes it so deuced queer."

"Lor'," I said. "And you mean—"

"You'll see," said he, and took up a little measure. He glanced at the material on his desk. "Glasses," he said, "water. All here. Mustn't take too much for the first attempt."

The little phial glucked out its precious contents.

"Don't forget what I told you," he said, turning the contents of the measure into a glass in the manner of an Italian waiter measuring whisky. "Sit with the eyes tightly shut and in absolute stillness for two minutes," he said. "Then you will hear me speak."

He added an inch or so of water to the little dose in each glass.

"By-the-by," he said, "don't put your glass down. Keep it in your hand and rest your hand on your knee. Yes—so. And now—"

He raised his glass.

"The New Accelerator," I said.

"The New Accelerator," he answered, and we touched glasses and drank, and instantly I closed my eyes.

You know that blank non-existence into which one drops when one has taken "gas." For an indefinite interval it was like that. Then I heard Gibberne telling me to wake up, and I stirred and opened my eyes. There he stood as he had been standing, glass still in hand. It was empty, that was all the difference.

"Well?" said I.

"Nothing out of the way?"

"Nothing. A slight feeling of exhilaration, perhaps. Nothing more."

"Sounds?"

"Things are still," I said. "By Jove! yes! They ARE still. Except the sort of faint pat, patter, like rain falling on different things. What is it?"

"Analysed sounds," I think he said, but I am not sure. He glanced at the window. "Have you ever seen a curtain before a window fixed in that way before?"

I followed his eyes, and there was the end of the curtain, frozen, as it were, corner high, in the act of flapping briskly in the breeze.

"No," said I; "that's odd."

"And here," he said, and opened the hand that held the glass. Naturally I winced, expecting the glass to smash. But so far from smashing it did not even seem to stir; it hung in mid-air—motionless.

"Roughly speaking," said Gibberne, "an object in these latitudes falls 16 feet in the first second. This glass is falling 16 feet in a second now. Only, you see, it hasn't been falling yet for the hundredth part of a second. That gives you some idea of the pace of my Accelerator." And he waved his hand round and round, over and under the slowly sinking glass. Finally, he took it by the bottom, pulled it down, and placed it very carefully on the table. "Eh?" he said to me, and laughed.

"That seems all right," I said, and began very gingerly to raise myself from my chair. I felt perfectly well, very light and comfortable, and quite confident in my mind. I was going fast all over. My heart, for example, was beating a thousand times a second, but that caused me no discomfort at all. I looked out of the window. An immovable cyclist, head down and with a frozen puff of dust behind his driving-wheel, scorched to overtake a galloping char-a-banc that did not stir. I gaped in amazement at this incredible spectacle. "Gibberne," I cried, "how long will this confounded stuff last?"

"Heaven knows!" he answered. "Last time I took it I went to bed and slept it off. I tell you, I was frightened. It must have lasted some minutes, I think—it seemed like hours. But after a bit it slows down rather suddenly, I believe."

I was proud to observe that I did not feel frightened—I suppose because there were two of us. "Why shouldn't we go out?" I asked.

"Why not?"

"They'll see us."

"Not they. Goodness, no! Why, we shall be going a thousand times faster than the quickest conjuring trick that was ever done. Come along! Which way shall we go? Window, or door?"

And out by the window we went.

Assuredly of all the strange experiences that I have ever had, or imagined, or read of other people having or imagining, that little raid I made with Gibberne on the Folkestone Leas, under the influence of the New Accelerator, was the strangest and maddest of all. We went out by his gate into the road, and there we made a minute examination of the statuesque passing traffic. The tops of the wheels and some of the legs of the horses of this char-a-banc, the end of the whip-lash and the lower jaw of the conductor—who was just beginning to yawn—were perceptibly in motion, but all the rest of the lumbering conveyance seemed still. And quite noiseless except for a faint rattling that came from one man's throat! And as parts of this frozen edifice there were a driver, you know, and a conductor, and eleven people! The effect as we walked about the thing began by being madly queer, and ended by being disagreeable. There they were, people like ourselves and yet not like ourselves, frozen in careless attitudes, caught in mid-gesture. A girl and a man smiled at one another, a leering smile that threatened to last for evermore; a woman in a floppy capelline rested her arm on the rail and stared at Gibberne's house with the unwinking stare of eternity; a man stroked his moustache like a figure of wax, and another stretched a tiresome stiff hand with extended fingers towards his loosened hat. We stared at them, we laughed at them, we made faces at them, and then a sort of disgust of them came upon us, and we turned away and walked round in front of the cyclist towards the Leas.

"Goodness!" cried Gibberne, suddenly; "look there!"

He pointed, and there at the tip of his finger and sliding down the air with wings flapping slowly and at the speed of an exceptionally languid snail—was a bee.

And so we came out upon the Leas. There the thing seemed madder than ever. The band was playing in the upper stand, though all the sound it made for us was a low-pitched, wheezy rattle, a sort of prolonged last sigh that passed at times into a sound like the slow, muffled ticking of some monstrous clock. Frozen people stood erect, strange, silent, self-conscious-looking dummies hung unstably in mid-stride, promenading upon the grass. I passed close to a little poodle dog suspended in the act of leaping, and watched the slow movement of his legs as he sank to earth. "Lord, look here!" cried Gibberne, and we halted for a moment before a magnificent person in white faint-striped flannels, white shoes, and a Panama hat, who turned back to wink at two gaily dressed ladies he had passed. A wink, studied with such leisurely deliberation as we could afford, is an unattractive thing. It loses any quality of alert gaiety, and one remarks that the winking eye does not completely close, that under its drooping lid appears the lower edge of an eyeball and a little line of white. "Heaven give me memory," said I, "and I will never wink again."

"Or smile," said Gibberne, with his eye on the lady's answering teeth.

"It's infernally hot, somehow," said I. "Let's go slower."

"Oh, come along!" said Gibberne.

We picked our way among the bath-chairs in the path. Many of the people sitting in the chairs seemed almost natural in their passive poses, but the contorted scarlet of the bandsmen was not a restful thing to see. A purple-faced little gentleman was frozen in the midst of a violent struggle to refold his newspaper against the wind; there were many evidences that all these people in their sluggish way were exposed to a considerable breeze, a breeze that had no existence so far as our sensations went. We came out and walked a little way from the crowd, and turned and regarded it. To see all that multitude changed, to a picture, smitten rigid, as it were, into the semblance of realistic wax, was impossibly wonderful. It was absurd, of course; but it filled me with an irrational, an exultant sense of superior advantage. Consider the wonder of it! All that I had said, and thought, and done since the stuff had begun to work in my veins had happened, so far as those people, so far as the world in general went, in the twinkling of an eye. "The New Accelerator—" I began, but Gibberne interrupted me.

"There's that infernal old woman!" he said.

"What old woman?"

"Lives next door to me," said Gibberne. "Has a lapdog that yaps. Gods! The temptation is strong!"

There is something very boyish and impulsive about Gibberne at times. Before I could expostulate with him he had dashed forward, snatched the unfortunate animal out of visible existence, and was running violently with it towards the cliff of the Leas. It was most extraordinary. The little brute, you know, didn't bark or wriggle or make the slightest sign of vitality. It kept quite stiffly in an attitude of somnolent repose, and Gibberne held it by the neck. It was like running about with a dog of wood. "Gibberne," I cried, "put it down!" Then I said something else. "If you run like that, Gibberne," I cried, "you'll set your clothes on fire. Your linen trousers are going brown as it is!"

He clapped his hand on his thigh and stood hesitating on the verge. "Gibberne," I cried, coming up, "put it down. This heat is too much! It's our running so! Two or three miles a second! Friction of the air!"

"What?" he said, glancing at the dog.

"Friction of the air," I shouted. "Friction of the air. Going too fast. Like meteorites and things. Too hot. And, Gibberne! Gibberne! I'm all over pricking and a sort of perspiration. You can see people stirring slightly. I believe the stuff's working off! Put that dog down."

"Eh?" he said.

"It's working off," I repeated. "We're too hot and the stuff's working off! I'm wet through."

He stared at me. Then at the band, the wheezy rattle of whose performance was certainly going faster. Then with a tremendous sweep of the arm he hurled the dog away from him and it went spinning upward, still inanimate, and hung at last over the grouped parasols of a knot of chattering people. Gibberne was gripping my elbow. "By Jove!" he cried. "I believe—it is! A sort of hot pricking and—yes. That man's moving his pocket-handkerchief! Perceptibly. We must get out of this sharp."

But we could not get out of it sharply enough. Luckily, perhaps! For we might have run, and if we had run we should, I believe, have burst into flames.

Almost certainly we should have burst into flames! You know we had neither of us thought of that.... But before we could even begin to run the action of the drug had ceased. It was the business of a minute fraction of a second. The effect of the New Accelerator passed like the drawing of a curtain, vanished in the movement of a hand. I heard Gibberne's voice in infinite alarm. "Sit down," he said, and flop, down upon the turf at the edge of the Leas I sat—scorching as I sat. There is a patch of burnt grass there still where I sat down. The whole stagnation seemed to wake up as I did so, the disarticulated vibration of the band rushed together into a blast of music, the promenaders put their feet down and walked their ways, the papers and flags began flapping, smiles passed into words, the winker finished his wink and went on his way complacently, and all the seated people moved and spoke.

The whole world had come alive again, was going as fast as we were, or rather we were going no faster than the rest of the world. It was like slowing down as one comes into a railway station. Everything seemed to spin round for a second or two, I had the most transient feeling of nausea, and that was all. And the little dog which had seemed to hang for a moment when the force of Gibberne's arm was expended fell with a swift acceleration clean through a lady's parasol!

That was the saving of us. Unless it was for one corpulent old gentleman in a bath-chair, who certainly did start at the sight of us and afterwards regarded us at intervals with a darkly suspicious eye, and, finally, I believe, said something to his nurse about us, I doubt if a solitary person remarked our sudden appearance among them. Plop! We must have appeared abruptly. We ceased to smoulder almost at once, though the turf beneath me was uncomfortably hot. The attention of every one—including even the Amusements' Association band, which on this occasion, for the only time in its history, got out of tune—was arrested by the amazing fact, and the still more amazing yapping and uproar caused by the fact that a respectable, over-fed lap-dog sleeping quietly to the east of the bandstand should suddenly fall through the parasol of a lady on the west—in a slightly singed condition due to the extreme velocity of its movements through the air. In these absurd days, too, when we are all trying to be as psychic, and silly, and superstitious as possible! People got up and trod on other people, chairs were overturned, the Leas policeman ran. How the matter settled itself I do not know—we were much too anxious to disentangle ourselves from the affair and get out of range of the eye of the old gentleman in the bath-chair to make minute inquiries. As soon as we were sufficiently cool and sufficiently recovered from our giddiness and nausea and confusion of mind to do so we stood up and, skirting the crowd, directed our steps back along the road below the Metropole towards Gibberne's house. But amidst the din I heard very distinctly the gentleman who had been sitting beside the lady of the ruptured sunshade using quite unjustifiable threats and language to one of those chair-attendants who have "Inspector" written on their caps. "If you didn't throw the dog," he said, "who DID?"

The sudden return of movement and familiar noises, and our natural anxiety about ourselves (our clothe's were still dreadfully hot, and the fronts of the thighs of Gibberne's white trousers were scorched a drabbish brown), prevented the minute observations I should have liked to make on all these things. Indeed, I really made no observations of any scientific value on that return. The bee, of course, had gone. I looked for that cyclist, but he was already out of sight as we came into the Upper Sandgate Road or hidden from us by traffic; the char-a-banc, however, with its people now all alive and stirring, was clattering along at a spanking pace almost abreast of the nearer church.

We noted, however, that the window-sill on which we had stepped in getting out of the house was slightly singed, and that the impressions of our feet on the gravel of the path were unusually deep.

So it was I had my first experience of the New Accelerator. Practically we had been running about and saying and doing all sorts of things in the space of a second or so of time. We had lived half an hour while the band had played, perhaps, two bars. But the effect it had upon us was that the whole world had stopped for our convenient inspection. Considering all things, and particularly considering our rashness in venturing out of the house, the experience might certainly have been much more disagreeable than it was. It showed, no doubt, that Gibberne has still much to learn before his preparation is a manageable convenience, but its practicability it certainly demonstrated beyond all cavil.

Since that adventure he has been steadily bringing its use under control, and I have several times, and without the slightest bad result, taken measured doses under his direction; though I must confess I have not yet ventured abroad again while under its influence. I may mention, for example, that this story has been written at one sitting and without interruption, except for the nibbling of some chocolate, by its means. I began at 6.25, and my watch is now very nearly at the minute past the half-hour. The convenience of securing a long, uninterrupted spell of work in the midst of a day full of engagements cannot be exaggerated. Gibberne is now working at the quantitative handling of his preparation, with especial reference to its distinctive effects upon different types of constitution. He then hopes to find a Retarder with which to dilute its present rather excessive potency. The Retarder will, of course, have the reverse effect to the Accelerator; used alone it should enable the patient to spread a few seconds over many hours of ordinary time,—and so to maintain an apathetic inaction, a glacier-like absence of alacrity, amidst the most animated or irritating surroundings. The two things together must necessarily work an entire revolution in civilised existence. It is the beginning of our escape from that Time Garment of which Carlyle speaks. While this Accelerator will enable us to concentrate ourselves with tremendous impact upon any moment or occasion that demands our utmost sense and vigour, the Retarder will enable us to pass in passive tranquillity through infinite hardship and tedium. Perhaps I am a little optimistic about the Retarder, which has indeed still to be discovered, but about the Accelerator there is no possible sort of doubt whatever. Its appearance upon the market in a convenient, controllable, and assimilable form is a matter of the next few months. It will be obtainable of all chemists and druggists, in small green bottles, at a high but, considering its extraordinary qualities, by no means excessive price. Gibberne's Nervous Accelerator it will be called, and he hopes to be able to supply it in three strengths: one in 200, one in 900, and one in 2000, distinguished by yellow, pink, and white labels respectively.

No doubt its use renders a great number of very extraordinary things possible; for, of course, the most remarkable and, possibly, even criminal proceedings may be effected with impunity by thus dodging, as it were, into the interstices of time. Like all potent preparations it will be liable to abuse. We have, however, discussed this aspect of the question very thoroughly, and we have decided that this is purely a matter of medical jurisprudence and altogether outside our province. We shall manufacture and sell the Accelerator, and, as for the consequences—we shall see.

THE STOLEN MIND

M. L. Staley (1930)

The structure, pivoting downward, plunged Quest to his waist in the osmotic solution.

WHAT WOULD YOU do, if, like Quest, you were tricked, and your very Mind and Will stolen from your body?

"What caused you to answer our advertisement?" Owen Quest felt the steel of the quick gray eyes that jabbed like gimlets across the office table.

"Why does any man apply for a job?" he bristled.

Keane Clason gave an impatient smile.

"Come!" he said. "I'm not trying to snare you. But there were unusual features to my ad, and they were put there to attract an unusual type of man. To judge your qualifications, I must know just why this proposition appeals to you."

"I can tell you that," nodded Quest, "but there's nothing unusual about it. In the first place, I knew that the Clason Research Corporation is the leading concern of its kind in the country. In the second place, this seemed to offer a way to obtain a substantial sum of money quickly."

"Good," said Clason. "And you feel that you have all the necessary qualifications?"

"Decidedly. I am 24 years old, athletic, and of an earnest and determined nature. Moreover, I have no family ties, and I'm willing to run any reasonable risk in order to improve the condition of my fellow men."

Clason smiled his approval.

"You say you need money. How much immediately?"

Quest was unprepared for the question.

"A thousand dollars," he ventured.

Without hesitation Clason counted out ten one-hundred-dollar notes from his wallet and laid them on the table.

"There's your advance fee. You're ready to go to work immediately, I hope?"

"Certainly," stammered Quest.

Stunned by the swiftness of the transaction, he sat staring at the money that lay untouched before him.

To accept it would be like signing an unread contract. But he had asked for it; to refuse it was impossible. Even to delay about picking it up might arouse Clason's suspicion. Already the latter had turned away and was opening the door of a steel cabinet. Quest had one second in which to reach a decision.... He crammed the currency into his pocket.

With delicate care Clason set two objects on the table. One looked to Quest like a miniature broadcasting tower or a mooring mast for lighter than air craft. The other was a circular vat of some black material, probably carbon. Within it a series of concentric tissues were suspended from metal rings, and in a trough outside ranged four stoppered flasks containing liquids of as many different colors.

"Look at these models carefully," said Clason. "They represent two of the most remarkable discoveries of all time. The one on your left is the most *de*structive weapon known to man. The other I consider the most *con*structive discovery in the history of science. It may even lead to an understanding of the nature of life, and of the future of the spirit after death.

"Both of these were developed by my brother Philip and me together—but we have disagreed about the use to which they shall be put.

"Philip"—the inventor dropped his voice to a whisper—"wants to sell the secret of the Death Projector—the tower, there—as an instrument of war. If I should permit him to do that, it might lead to the destruction of whole nations!"

"How?" demanded Quest "I've heard of a device called the Death Ray. Is this it?"

"No, no," said Clason contemptuously. "Even in a perfected state the Ray would be a child's toy compared to the Projector. This is based on our discovery that invisible light rays of a certain wave-length, if highly concentrated, destroy life—and our additional discovery that if these are synchronized with short radio waves the effect is absolutely devastating.

"We obtain the desired concentration of invisible light by using a tellurium current-filter under the influence of alternate flashes of red and blue light. The projector can literally blanket vast areas with death, up to a top range of at least five hundred miles.

"Just picture to yourself what this means! In a space of ten minutes two men can lay down a circle of destruction a thousand miles in diameter; or they can cut a swath five hundred miles long in any desired direction."

"Have you ever proved it?" demanded Quest skeptically.

"Yes, young man, we have," snapped Clason. "Right here in the laboratory—but on a minute scale, of course. However, there's no time to demonstrate now. The point is that my brother is determined to sell if he can obtain his price for the invention. He argues that instead of bringing disaster upon the world, this machine will forever discourage war by making it too terrible for any civilized nation to consider. In spite of my opposition he has opened negotiations with an ambitious Balkan power. He may actually close the sale at any moment!

"However," Clason drew a deep breath "you see this other device? Simple as it appears, it is the key to the whole situation. We can use it—you and I—to overcome Philip's will and prevent this unthinkable transaction. The two of us can do it. Alone I would be virtually helpless."

"Why not have the Projector confiscated or destroyed by our own Government?" suggested Quest. "That seems to me the only safe and sure way out of the difficulty."

"You simply do not understand," frowned Clason impatiently. "Philip is selling the plans and descriptions of the machine, not the machine itself. Even if this model and the larger test machine that we have built were destroyed—even if I were willing to have Philip sent to Leavenworth for life—he could still sell the Projector.

"But this other invention, our Osmotic Liberator, makes it possible for me to gain control of Philip and actually *change his mind*, through the medium of an agent. I have hired you to act as my Agent, Quest, because I can see that you are a young man of unusual character and vitality. And by way of reward I can promise you both money and a brilliant future."

The inventor poised in a tense attitude on the edge of his chair as though his body were charged with electricity. His eyes seemed to dart out emanations that set Quest's blood to tingling. Then for a moment the latter lost consciousness of his physical self. It was as though he had opened a door and found himself suddenly on the brink of a new and totally strange world. He dispelled this fancy by a quick effort of the will, for he knew that he had a delicate problem on his hands and that it must be solved within a very few minutes. However he proceeded, he must act without disloyalty to his Government, and at the same time without injustice to Keane Clason.

"Tell me," he said in a husky voice, "how do you intend to use me? I do not believe in Spiritualism. I would be a poor medium."

Clason gave a short laugh.

"You are not to be a medium in that sense at all. Spiritualism as practiced is just a blind sort of groping and hoping. Osmotic Liberation, on the other hand, is an exact and opposite physico-chemical science. Here—I will show you."

Into the outer cell of the Liberator he emptied the purple vial, and so on to the innermost, which he filled with a golden-green liquid like old Chartreuse.

"The separating membranes, you understand, are permeable by these complicated solutions. Each liquid has a different osmotic pressure and therefore should, under normal conditions, interchange with the others through the membranes until all pressures are equalized. I prevent such interchange, however, by maintaining an anti-electrolysis which retards ionization and thus builds up what might be called osmotic potential.

"Now if an Agent—yourself for instance—submerges himself in the central cell, at the same time maintaining a physical contact with his Control at the surface of the liquid, and if then the osmotic potential is suddenly released by throwing the electrolytic switch, the host of ions thus turned loose in the outer compartments make one grand rush for the center solution, which contains the cathode.

"Under these conditions your body becomes a sort of sixth cell, and your skin another membrane in the series. Properly speaking, however, you are not a part of the electrolytic circuit but are merely present in the action. Your body acts as a catalyser, hastening the chemical action without itself being affected in any way. Physically you undergo no change whatever; but in some strange way which is, like life, beyond analysis, your mind flows out into the solution, while your unaltered body remains at the bottom of the tank in a state of suspended animation.

"If no Control is present, all that is needed to return your mind into your body is a throw of the electrolytic switch back to negative, whereupon you emerge from the tank exactly as you entered it. But with your Control present and in contact with your submerged body, your mind, instead of remaining suspended in the solution, flows instantly into his body and resides there subject to his will.

"This can not be done, however, unless the wills of Control and Agent have first been brought into accord. To accomplish that, we clasp hands"—Quest grasped Clason's extended hand—"and look steadily into each other's eyes.

"Now, it is well known that the vibrations of an individual's will are as distinctive as the sworls of his finger-prints. What is not so well known is that the frequency of vibration in one person can be brought into accord with that in another.

"You consciously retract your will by concentrating your mind upon the thing which you know I wish to accomplish. Gradually while we continue in this position your vibrations speed up or slow down until they acquire exactly the same frequency as my own. We are then in accord, and when your mind is liberated in the tank it is in a state which admits absorption into my body. And it is subject to my will because you have purposely attuned it to my peculiar frequency. Immediately after the transfer there will be a brief conflict, due to the instinctive desire of your will to obtain the ascendancy. But of course mine will gain the upper hand at once, since both wills will be in my frequency."

Quest felt, rather than saw, a wall of alarm closing in on him. He tried to avert his eyes, to withdraw his hand from Clason's grasp. With a nostalgic pang in the pit of his stomach he suddenly realized that he could not do so. He had gone too far—farther than any man in his position had a right to go. Having deliberately weakened his will, it seemed now to have deserted him entirely. A prickling sensation coursed up his spine, his extended arm went numb, his hand trembled violently.

"Splendid!" said Clason, suddenly releasing both eye and hand. "Just as I foresaw, you will be able to attune yourself to my vibration-frequency with hardly an effort. Now please remain seated; I'll be back in a moment."

For a second after the door closed, Quest remained slumped in his chair. Then he was on his feet, shaking himself like a wet dog to free himself from the spell under which he had fallen. Something about Clason attracted and at the same time repelled him, fraying his nerves like an irritant drug and confusing his mind at the moment when he needed the full alertness of every faculty.

Invisible light—disembodied minds—will vibrations! Nothing there to get hold of. Were these things real or imaginary? Was Keane Clason a great inventor, or a madman? Would Philip prove to be a real or an imaginary scoundrel? Should he summon help, or go on alone?

Professional pride said: wait, don't be an alarmist! With his knuckles Quest tapped the table, half expecting it to melt under his fingers. The feeling and sound of the contact gave him a peculiar start. On the farther end of the table stood a letter-box—an invitation. From his pocket Quest snatched a slip of paper, and wrote:

6 stroke 4—9:45A—Hired. If no report in 48 hours, clamp down hard.

To address a stamped envelope and slip it in with the outgoing mail was the work of seconds. But he was none too quick. He had just dropped back into a lounging attitude when the door burst open and Clason flew into the room?

"We must act instantly," hissed the inventor. "Philip plans to close the transaction within a day."

In spite of himself, Quest jumped upright in his chair. Clason tapped him on the shoulder reassuringly.

"It's all right," he smiled, "I'm ready for him. We'll make our move this afternoon and beat him by eighteen hours.

"Let's see." He paused. "Oh! yes. I was about to explain to you that as soon as the will of the Agent enters the body of his Control, the latter can again transfer it into the body of still another person.

"Now you understand why I advertised for a man of exceptional character? As my Agent, I want you to enter the body of Philip, and your will must be strong enough to conquer his in the battle for mastery which will begin the instant you intrude into his body. You will still be under my control, but your will must be strong enough on its own merits to overcome his. I can direct you, but your strength must be your own. That's clear, isn't it?"

"I think so," said Quest slowly. "But what becomes of me after you have frustrated Philip's plot?"

"That's the easy part of the process," smiled Clason; "but naturally you feel some anxiety about it. I simply withdraw your will from Philip, return it to your own body, and pay you a reward of ten thousand dollars."

"You're sure you can?"

"Perfectly. I have merely to touch Philip's hand to recapture your will. Then I immerse myself in the tank with the switch at plus. The osmotic action will extract both wills momentarily from my body. But the presence of two bodies and two wills in the solution together forces a balance, and each will seeks out and enters its own body. Then you and I climb out of the tank exactly as we are this minute."

"If it weren't for my belief that anything is possible," Quest shook his head, "I'd say that your claims for this invention were ridiculous."

"And you couldn't be blamed," admitted Clason readily. "This toy of a model is hardly convincing. But come along with me and I'll show you how the Liberator looks in actual operation."

The office rug concealed a trap door which gave upon a spiral stair. Below, Clason unlocked another door and led the way through a narrow and tremendously long passage lighted at intervals by small electric bulbs. Presently another door yielded to the inventor's deft touch and closed behind them with a portentous chug. Here the darkness was so utter and intense that Quest imagined he could feel the weight of it on his shoulders. From the slope of the passageway and the muffled beat of machinery that had come to his ears on the way along, he guessed that he was below ground in some chamber at the rear of the factory.

He gave a low exclamation as Clason switched on the toplight. No wonder the darkness had seemed of almost supernatural quality! Even the hard white glare of the daylight arc was grisly. Its rays rebounded from the liquids of the great circular tank in a blinding dazzle of color, while the dull black walls and ceiling were so perfectly absorptive that beyond arm's length they became to all effects invisible. Even the ledge on which he stood—the shoulder of the vat—gave Quest the feeling that to move would be to step off into a bottomless pit.

But Clason took his attention at once, pointing here and there in his quick, nervous way to indicate how faithfully the Liberator had been reproduced from the model. In all respects the arrangements were the same, with the addition that here a long plank like a spring-board extended out from a wall-mount as far as the central compartment of the tank, and that from its end a narrow ladder hung down to the surface of the Chartreuse liquid. A double-throw switch fixed to the wall above the base of the plank was evidently the source of electrolytic control.

"When you throw the switch to plus," said Clason, pointing to the chalk-marked sign above, "you produce the violent electrolytic action needed to bring about a liberation. All the rest of the time it should be closed at minus, in order to maintain the anti-action which I explained to you.

"Now let's rehearse, so that when the time for the real performance arrives we can be sure of running it off without a hitch."

"All right, sir," nodded Quest, so dazed by the glittering light that he was hardly conscious of what he said.

"First," said Clason, running lightly up the steps to the plank, "you walk out to the end, like this, and start down the ladder. Then you lower yourself into the tank. The liquid is at body temperature; it's neither strongly acid nor caustic; it will cause you no injury or discomfort whatever.

"Meanwhile I keep in contact with your hand until the instant that you become submerged. Now your mind is in me, see?—ready for transfer into Philip, where it will act as my Agent. That's how simple it is! Come on up and we'll go through the motions."

Quest experienced a shiver as he mounted the bridge. Annoyed with himself, he shrugged the feeling off. There was no risk here. Moreover, it was a part of his daily work to take chances; he had done so a hundred times without hesitation. Now he moved all the more quickly, as if to belie the squeamishness that possessed him in spite of himself.

Swinging past Clason on the plank, he lowered himself without a pause to the bottom rung of the ladder, while the inventor, hanging head down, maintained contact with him.

"No need to stay here," he said in sudden irritation. "I understand perfectly what I am to do."

"I'm testing my own acrobatic ability," grunted Clason amiably. "Just a minute now."

He wriggled as if trying to adjust himself to a better balance, but in reality to mask the motion of his free hand with which he reached up and pressed a button in the side of the plank. Instantly the structure, pivoting downward on its wall-socket, plunged Quest to his waist in the osmotic solution.

"For God's sake get out of the way!" he shouted, trying to wrench his hand out of Clason's sinewy grip. "Let go, I tell you!"

But Clason clung like a leech, his teeth gritted under the strain. Again the plank lurched downward, and with a violent splash Quest vanished below the surface.

Quick as a cat, Clason scrambled up the ladder and back to the base of the plank, where he erased and interchanged the chalk-marked signs with which he had misled Quest. Then with a sinister twist of a smile he threw the switch to minus, and turned to watch as the plank slowly righted itself and the vacant ladder came clear of the liquid.

For some time he stood staring at the gleaming colored rings of his dissociation-vat like some witch over her cauldron, his lips working, his hands clasping and unclasping like the tentacles of some sub-sea monster. Then, as if the spell had suddenly broken, he turned on his heel and switched off the light. As he hastened down the passageway toward his office, the airlock sucked the door against its jamb with an ominous whistle.

In a twinkling, as Quest's shackled spirit writhed in its new housing, he knew that he was in bondage to a scoundrel. Formless and voiceless, he still fought madly for the freedom which the instinct of ten thousand generations made necessary to him.

At the same time he was furious at himself for having been tricked like an innocent schoolboy. The plank socket, the button which had tripped the supporting spring, the fake rehearsal, the tuning of his will to that of Clason—step by step the whole cunning scheme unfolded itself to him now.

But what could be the purpose behind this villainy? Only one answer seemed possible. Keane must be the one bent on selling the Death Projector, Philip the one who wished to frustrate the fiendish transaction! And Quest of the Secret Service—he was to be the tool to force the sale.

With the soundless scream of rage Quest's will hurled itself against Keane's. The two met like infuriated bulls, and for an instant too brief to be pictured as a lapse of time they poised immovable. But two wills can not exist on equal terms in a single body, and in this case the vibration of both was that of Clason. Quest had challenged the Master Will. He could do no more. It hurled him back, crushed him like foam, compressed him to the proportions of an atom in the background of his consciousness. So brief and unequal was the conflict that in the next breath Clason had all but forgotten the presence of the stolen will within him. When he was ready to use his Agent, that would be time enough to summon him!

Despite this suppression, Quest began to see dimly through strange eyes, and to hear vaguely with ears that were not his own. Feelers, tentacles, some intangible kind of conduits carried thought impulses to him from the Master Will. He received these impressions vividly, but those which he gave off in return were so weak, due to the subjection of his will, that Clason was entirely unconscious of any response. Quest was not enough of a scientist to be astonished at the ability of a disembodied mind to experience sense impressions in the body of another. He was only glad that the darkness and silence were growing less. Very, very slowly he was awakening to a new kind of consciousness—the consciousness of another person's Self. He hated and loathed that Self, yet it was better than the awful blankness that had gone before.

Suddenly, as light grew brighter and sound more clear and definite, a new element entered—the element of hope. At first it was feeble: its only suggestion was that sometime, somehow, he might escape this prison. But it was like water to a parched plant. It caused his will to expand, to extend its feelers, to press up a little more bravely against the crushing pile of the Master Will.

Now another surprise sprang upon him. He was moving! That is, Clason's body was moving in some kind of a conveyance, which was threading its way through crowded streets. Stores, buildings, buses, people—Quest remembered them all distantly as things he had known thousands of years ago. The driver turned his head, and his profile seemed vaguely familiar.

Now a rush of foreign thoughts drowned out his own. They were a sort of overflow from the mind of Clason. They thronged along the conduits that bound the two wills together, but only Quest was conscious of the movement.

Keane's mind was on his brother Philip: that much was particularly clear. And there was something about a telephone call. Yes, Keane had telephoned to the police, disguising his voice, refusing to divulge his name. He had said that a man by the name of Philip Clason was in trouble and had told them where to find him. Then the police had telephoned the factory, and Keane had pretended astonishment and alarm at the news. That's why he was here now—he was on the way to confer with the police. And he was chuckling— chuckling because he had fooled Quest and the police, and because now the hundred million dollars was almost in his grasp.

Cutting in close, the car turned a corner and drew up before one of a row of loft buildings in a section of the city which Quest failed to recognize. As Clason stepped to the sidewalk, Quest was more painfully aware than ever of his powerlessness to influence by so much as the twitch of a muscle the behavior of this hostile body in which he had permitted himself to be trapped. In his weakness he felt himself shrinking, contracting almost to nothingness under the careless pressure of the Master Will.

Clason glanced casually at his watch, and three men converged toward him from as many directions. There was nothing to distinguish them from anyone else in the street, but along the conduits it came to Quest that they were detectives and that they were there by appointment with Keane Clason.

"What floor?" asked the latter, with an excitement which Quest felt instantly was pure pretense. "Are you sure they haven't spirited him away?"

"Don't worry," replied the leader of the detectives. "The alley and roof are covered. We'll take care of the rest ourselves."

On tiptoe they climbed three long flights of stairs in the half-light. Clason held back as if in fear. He was a good actor, and Quest felt the shrinking and hesitation of his body as he crouched and slunk along in the wake of the detectives, pretending terror at what was about to happen, though he knew— and Quest knew he knew—that there would be no resistance up there—that Philip would be found alone exactly as he had been left by Keane's hired thugs.

On the top landing Burke, the leader, paused to count the doors from front to rear.

"This is it," he whispered to the bull-necked fellow just behind him.

The other nodded, and crouched back against the opposite wall while his companions placed themselves in position to cross-fire into the room the moment the door gave way.

Quest longed for the power to kick his hypocrite of a master as he still held back, cowering on the stairs, playing his fake to the limit. Then the door flew in with a splintering shriek under the charge of the human battering ram, and across it hurtled the other two detectives in a cloud of ancient dust.

"Here he is!" someone shouted.

"Phil! Phil!" Keane Clason's voice fairly quavered with sham emotion as he ran into the room and threw himself at a man tightly bound to an upholstered chair, which in turn was wedged in among other articles of stored furniture.

But Philip was too securely gagged to reply, and as Burke slashed the ropes from across his chest he dropped forward in a state of collapse. Stretched on a couch, he soon gave signs of response as a brisk massage began to restore the circulation to his cramped limbs. Suddenly he sat up and thrust his rescuers aside.

"What time is it?" he demanded with an air of alarm.

"One o'clock," replied Keane before anyone else could answer, patting his brother affectionately on the shoulder while within him Quest writhed with indignation. "By Jove! Phil, it's wonderful that we got to you in time. Really, how—you're not injured?"

"No," grunted Philip, "just lamed up. I'll be as fit as ever by to-morrow."

"If you feel equal to it," suggested Burke, "I wish you'd tell me briefly how you arrived here. Do you know the motive behind this affair? Did you recognize any of the body-snatchers?"

Philip frowned and shook his head.

"Yesterday noon," he said slowly, "I took the eight-passenger Airline Express to Cleveland on business. There were three other passengers in the cabin—two men and a woman. Right away I got out a correspondence file and was running over some letters. The next thing I knew I was approaching the ground in the strangest state of mind I ever experienced. My head was splitting, and everything looked unreal to me. Seemed as if I was coming down on some new planet."

"You mean the ship was gliding down to land?"

"No, no. I was dangling from a parachute.... By the way, where am I now?"

"In a Munson Avenue loft."

"In Chicago?"

Burke nodded.

"I guessed as much," frowned Philip. "You see, I came down in a field, and then before I could free myself from my trappings I was pounced on—trussed up and blindfolded—by a gang of men. I knew they had taken me a long distance by automobile, but I saw nothing more until they tore the blindfold from my eyes when they left me here."

"And they were all strangers to you?"

"Yes—those that I saw."

"Isn't this enough for just now, Burke?" interrupted Keane, and Quest received an impression of uneasiness that was not apparent in the inventor's tone. "After a good rest he's sure to recall things that escape him now."

"Just one minute," nodded the detective, turning back to Philip. "Can you think of no plausible reason for this attack? Is there no one who might possibly benefit by putting you temporarily out of the way?"

Philip gave a frightened start. Then he was on his feet, clutching at his brother's arm.

"Keane!" he pleaded, "Keane! What's happened? I know, I know! It's the Projector."

"Water!" roared Keane, and Quest felt the panic that coursed through him as he tried to drown out his brother. "Somebody bring water! He needs it!"

At the same time he snatched up Philip's hand in a grip of steel. Instantly the latter's wild eyes became calm, the flush passed from his relaxing face, and he slumped down weakly on the couch.

In that fleeting moment Quest surged into the body of Philip and confronted his will with a fierce and triumphant ardor. For now his will would have command of a body with which to fight his fiend of a Control.

With a sensation of contempt he met Philip's resistance and buffeted him ruthlessly backward, crushed down and compressed his feebly struggling will. And as Philip yielded, Quest felt his own will expanding to normal, taking possession of the borrowed body with hungry greed, and flashing from its faded eyes the spark of youth.

Burke stared in amazement at the kaleidoscopic rapidity of the changes in the rescued man's expression. Strange lights and shadows continued to flit across Philip's face as Quest's invasion of him proceeded, but with a diminishing frequency which soon assured Keane that his Agent was tightening his command.

The younger of Burke's aides stood fascinated, his mouth agape. The other spoke guardedly to his superior:

"Dope, eh!"

"Nah!" replied Burke, shrugging himself out of his trance. "Shock."

The actual duration of the conflict in Philip was something less than three seconds. It would have been more brief if Quest had exerted himself to the utmost. But his sensations as he first surged into this new habitat under Keane's propulsion were so weird and unearthly that for the moment he was lost in the wonder of the experience. For that short time, therefore, Philip was able to fight back against the onrush of the invading will.

In the next second Quest became conscious of the resistance. Urged on by his Control, he must push Philip back and quell him; but his sympathy for his opponent and his hatred of Keane roused him to sudden revolt. He wanted to disobey the Master Will, retreat, leave Philip in command of himself. But he could only go on, unwillingly thrusting back Philip's will despite the indescribable torment and confusion in his own. Then, with the feeling that he was ten times worse than the most inhuman ghoul, he took full possession of his borrowed body.

"I'll take him home now," said Keane composedly to Burke. "As you see, he needs a little extra sleep. Meanwhile, if you have any occasion to call me, I will be at the factory."

To the youthful mind of the Agent, used to the lightness of an athletic physique, the body in which it moved down the stairs to the limousine seemed strangely heavy and awkward.

"I'm badly done up, Keane," he said with Philip's lips as the car got under way.

"Bah!" snorted Keane, "you've had a scare, that's all. Go to bed when you get home and sleep till nine this evening. At ten a man named Dr. Nukharin will call for you. He will drive you to a garage, leave the car, and transfer to another one a few blocks away.

"Out near Marbleton you will find an airplane staked in an open field. Nukharin is a capable pilot. He will fly back southeast along the lakeshore to the meeting place. You should arrive about twelve-thirty. The test is set for one o'clock."

Quest listened in a state of abject rage. Lacking the power to resist his Control, he could only boil away in Philip's body like a wild creature hemmed in by bars of steel.

"Bring with you," continued Keane venomously, "the set of papers that you took from the safe in my office. Hold the other set in readiness to deliver to Nukharin to-morrow, after he has studied the results of the test and has notified Paris to release a hundred million dollars in cash for delivery at your Loop office at 3 p.m."

The murderous greed of the man maddened Quest. He tried to revolt, his will squirming like a physical thing, threshing the ether like a wounded shark in the sea. For a moment he felt that he was about to burst the bonds that his demon of a Control had woven around him. So violently did he resist that the immured and sporelike will of Philip forged up fitfully out of the blackness and joined his in the hopeless struggle. But along the attenuated conduits that still chained Quest to the Master Will Keane caught the impulse of the mutiny, and his eyes darted flame as he countered with a will-shock that paralyzed his unruly Agent.

"Listen! you whimpering dog," he snarled. "Think as I tell you—and nothing more! You are going to apologize to Dr. Nukharin for your previous unwillingness to sell the Projector. You are going to tell him that I am at fault—that I held out—but that you found a way to force my compliance. You understand?"

Quest could find no words. With Philip's head he nodded meekly. Just then the car stopped and the chauffeur threw open the door.

Dr. Nukharin flew high despite the masses of cumulus cloud which frequently reduced visibility to zero. He had merely to follow the rim of the lake to his destination, and an occasional glimpse of the water was sufficient to hold him on his course.

In the back seat hunched Philip, his body crumbling under the weight of Quest's despair. For hours the latter had gone on vaguely, hoping somehow to thwart this horrible transaction that was rushing the world to its doom, thinking he might grow strong enough to wrench himself free and so liberate Philip from the dominance of his conscienceless brother. Even though such a move should leave his own will forever separate from his body, he was ready and anxious to make the sacrifice.

Suddenly the crash of the motor ceased and Nukharin banked the ship up in a spiral glide. Quest had never been in the air before, and the long whirl down into the darkness on this devil's errand was to him as eery as a ride to perdition in a white-hot projectile.

His mind seemed to trail out in a great nebular helix behind the descending ship. He felt that he had suddenly crossed some cosmic meridian into a new plane of existence, where he was changed to a gas, yet continued capable of thought. But even here his obsession remained the same. Keane Clason—trickster, traitor, arch-criminal—must be destroyed!

"I'll get him!" vowed Quest in words that were no less real for being soundless. "I'll trail him to the end of space and bring him to account!"

Then wheels touched earth and the cold, bare facts of his destiny rushed in on him with redoubled force. He felt the nearness of his Control seconds before he perceived him through the eyes of Philip. With a sensation like a stab he realized that now he must speak, play his part, be any bloodless hypocrite that Keane Clason chose to make him. The silent order surged down the conduits promptly enough; he responded as an automaton obeys the pressure of a button.

"Well, Doctor," chuckled Philip with a cunning leer, "here's the magic tower, just as I promised you. We'll run it up in a jiffy. This test is going to be so vivid and conclusive that not even a hard-headed skeptic like you can raise a question."

"You misunderstand me," returned Nukharin in an injured tone. "So far as I am concerned this procedure is only a formality, but it is none the less necessary. Suppose that I should spend a hundred million of my government's money and the purchase prove worthless? You may guess that my folly would cost me dear."

Keane Clason was waiting on the platform of a giant truck, the motor of which was idling. All the apparatus was in readiness except that the three demountable sections of the tower had yet to be run up into position.

"One of the beauties of the D. P.," said Philip gleefully to the Doctor, while Keane smiled slyly to himself, "is that this pint-size dynamo provides all the current needed for the test. We pick the power for our radio right out of the air by means of a wave trap and mensurator invented by this bright little brother of mine," and he clapped Keane patronizingly on the back.

"Yes, ah—Dr. Nukharin," ventured Keane timidly, and at that moment Quest experienced the raging red hatred that causes men to murder. "Philip has promised me that you will employ this device only as a threat to hold the ambitions of the larger powers in check."

"Of course, of course!" replied the Doctor heartily. "But now let's have the test. Even at night I'm not too fond of these open-air performances."

The height of the tower as they ran the upper sections into place was forty feet. When all connections had been inspected, first by Keane, then by Philip, the former led Nukharin aloft.

As the climax of his plot approached, Keane's excitement bordered on a cataleptic state, hints of which came confusedly through the conduits to Quest. With a peculiar satisfaction he felt that Keane was suffering. The inventor's jaws became rigid, as though his blood had changed to liquid air and frozen him, and he had difficulty in controlling the movements of his arms.

Now he was afraid! Genuinely afraid, this time. Quest caught the impulse too clearly to doubt its meaning. This was no sham! Keane was doubting his own machine, fearing that in the crisis some element in the finely calculated mechanism might fail to operate, thus cheating him of the blood-money on which his heart was set. Then he was speaking, and even Nukharin noticed the tremor in his voice:

"These nine tubes, which look like a row of gun barrels, are molded from silicon paste. Each shoots a beam of invisible light and a radio dart of precisely the same wave length. The destructive effect depends chiefly upon this exactness of synchronization."

"A question occurs to me," said the Doctor: "will others be able to manipulate the machine as successfully as you can?"

"It's fool-proof," chattered Keane, almost losing control of his voice, "absolutely fool-proof. Surely you have scientists in your country who can follow written directions! Nothing more is necessary."

"Very well," shrugged Nukharin. "I only want to be sure that no unforeseen difficulties may arise in an emergency."

"See this range-setter?" continued Keane. "The thread on the vertical shaft enables us not only to limit the range by angling the beams into the ground, but it can also be disengaged and the Projector revolved in a flat circle for maximum ranges."

"And is there no danger of the machine going wrong—of destroying itself and us?" suggested Nukharin.

"None whatever, Doctor. There is no explosive force and no great electrical voltage involved. As long as we stand back of the muzzles we have nothing to fear.

"Now look. I have set the micrometer at three hundred yards, which will just about cover the stretch between ourselves and the lake. I will cut a swath for you—and every bush, every blade of grass, every insect in this swath will be withered to ash in the twinkling of an eye. The destruction will be absolute."

"Please proceed," said Nukharin grimly.

Keane pulled a lever in its slot, then pressed it down into its lock as his projection battery swung lakeward at the desired angle. Then with one hand poised on another lever, he pressed an electric button.

At the controls below, a bulb flashed on and off. The signal was superfluous, for already Quest had received his silent command from the Master Will. An icy dread fastened on him. He must obey the unspoken command; he had no will of his own with which to resist. The test would be a success; the

Projector would be sold; the world would be turned into a shambles. And he, Owen Quest, would be the destroyer, the murderer, the weak fool who made this horror possible.

All this flashed through the Agent's mind in the fraction of a second that it took him to extend Philip's hand, close the switch of the dynamo, and snap on the alternating lights in the housing over the tellurium filter.

For an interminable five seconds he waited, in a ferment of revolt which the paralysis of his will made it impossible to put into action. Then again the command pulsed within him, the signal bulb flashed, and he reversed his motions of the moment before.

Cold sweat cascaded down Philip's face as Quest felt the ladder vibrating under descending feet. He longed for the power to hurl Keane Clason to the ground and turn the Projector upon him. But with an awful irony the Master Will forced him to his feet, and to speak in a tone that withered the manhood within him.

"Come," said Philip in a triumphant tone to Nukharin, "and I will show you that Clason inventions perform as well as they sound."

Flashlight in hand, he started toward the lake with Nukharin and his brother close behind him. Twenty paces, and the long meadow grass suddenly vanished from beneath their feet.

"See that!" whispered Philip excitedly, waving the light from side to side to show the forty-foot swath that stretched away before them. "Not a trace of life left, not a blade of grass—nothing but dust!"

The only response was a gurgling sound that issued from Nukharin's throat.

"Look!" Quest formed the word with Philip's lips under the urge of the Master Will. "Here was a tall bush. What do you see now? Just a teaspoonful of ash. When you examine the remains by daylight, you will find that even the root has disintegrated to a depth of two feet."

"Enough of this," croaked Nukharin in horror. "The deal is closed."

His face was convulsed with fear. Without another word he whirled about and fled toward his airplane. Philip gave a start as if to follow.

"Halt! you slob," growled Keane, whose composure had returned with the successful outcome of the test. "I have use for your company, even though you are as great a coward as our Slavic friend."

Coward! The epithet stung Quest like a flaming goad. One of the fine, intangible lines that bound him under the will of Keane Clason severed, and his own will exploded into action like a thunderbolt. With startling agility he whirled Philip about, the flashlight clubbed in his hand. But Keane was quicker still. A clip on the wrist sent the weapon flying. Then Philip reeled backward from a kick in the stomach, and his clutching hands beat the air as he sank unconscious in the dust.

With a violent tug, Quest lifted Philip's body to a sitting posture. The phone was ringing, and by the pull on the will-fibers he knew that Keane was at the other end of the wire. Philip's body was failing under the strain of the part it was forced to play, and the blow of the night before had further weakened it. Now he sat rocking his head painfully between his hands. But Quest lifted him to his feet by sheer will, and he staggered across the room.

"Hello!", he said in a hoarse voice.

"Get the hell out here to the factory!" rasped Keane, and the crash of the receiver emphasized the command.

It was one o'clock as Philip whirled his sedan into Olmstead Avenue. At three, reflected Quest as the car scorched over the pavements, he must be at the downtown office to deliver the papers and receive the money.

Then he was face to face with Keane, reeling dizzily at the hatred that blazed from the latter's accusing eyes.

"Double-crossed me, eh!" The voice was a low snarl, and as he spoke Keane thumped the extra outspread on his desk. "But you're not going to get away with it—neither of you!"

Dismay, hope, dread, wonder robbed Quest of the power to speak. But he whirled around behind the desk with such unexpected violence that Keane staggered back in alarm. Then he was devouring the screaming headlines of the newspaper. Three seconds, like a slow exposure, and every word of the Record's great scoop was etched upon his mind as if with caustic:

DOOM LAUNCH ADRIFT ON LAKE
Physician Baffled by Condition of Five Bodies Found in Craft
Blighted Area on Shore Said to Have Bearing on Tragedy
THAW HARBOR, IND., June 6.—Five Chicago sportsmen, most of them prominent in business and society, perished in the early hours this morning while returning in the launch of A. Gaston Andrews from a weekend camping party near Hook Spit on the Michigan shore.

The boat was towed into this port at daybreak by the Interlake Tug Mordecai after being found adrift less than a mile off shore. According to Captain Goff of the Mordecai the death craft carried no lights and he barely avoided running her down. The weather along the Indiana shore was perfect throughout the night and there is nothing to indicate that the launch was in trouble at any time. The bodies are unmarked, and this little community is agog with rumors ranging all the way from murder and suicide to the supernatural.

Dr. J. M. Addis of Thaw Harbor, the first physician to examine the bodies, says that they appear to have suffered some violent electro-chemical action the nature of which cannot be determined at the moment. This statement is considered significant in view of the reported discovery ashore of a large blighted area almost directly opposite the point where the launch was found. Joseph Sleichert, a farmer who lives in that vicinity, reports that this patch of ground extending back from the lakeshore was completely stripped of vegetation overnight. He ascribes the damage to some unknown insect pest.

Others say that the condition of the ground indicates that it has been burned at incinerator temperatures. Nothing is left of the soil but a blue powder.

Philip faced his brother with eyes that were dull with agony.

"You have made me a murderer!" Quest forced out the words in painful gasps.

But Keane snapped back at him like a rabid dog.

"You did it—you did it yourself! You tampered with the Projector. You tried to spoil the test. You changed the range. You tried to kill me, and instead you killed these others. And you're going to pay—both of you. You hear me?—you're going to pay!"

His voice mounted the scale to a scream. It was a wail of unreasoning terror, of the dread of exposure, of the fear that he would fail to collect the fortune now so nearly in his grasp. The accident that had jarred his well-laid plans had unnerved him.

Frantically Quest strove to answer him, to explain his utter subjection, as Agent, to say that if he had possessed the will to oppose or trick him he would have turned him over to the police, or might even have killed him, at the very outset. But in his frenzy, Keane had so tightened his control that Quest was speechless. Now he tried to substitute gesture for words, but Philip was rooted to the spot like a statue; even his hands were immovable.

He might have remained in this state indefinitely had not Keane's fears withdrawn his mind from his immediate surroundings. Momentarily he forgot Quest, Philip—everything but himself and his predicament. And in the instant that his vigilance relaxed, Quest's enslaved will experienced a sudden lease of strength and hope. Independently of his Control, he found that he could move Philip's hand, could take a faltering step.

But now, what to do? How might he fan this feeble spark of volition to sufficient strength for decisive resistance? The idea came to him: if only he could place distance between himself and Keane, perhaps with one titanic effort he might launch himself against the Master Will, take him by surprise, crush him down, and reverse him to the status of Agent instead of Control.

With infinite effort Quest forced Philip's body step by step across the room. He must reach that window, get a signal of distress to someone in the street.

But Keane began to sense a mutiny. He followed. He crossed the floor with slinking, tigerish steps and snaking body. His wet lips writhed back over his teeth, and his contorted features wove the leer of the abyss. Now as his Control drew physically near, Quest felt his mite of strength ebbing fast. Slowly Keane reached up with his clawed fingers and grasped his Agent by the arm.

"Remember!" he hissed, "if these deaths are traced to us, you break down—you confess—you take the blame—you paint me lily white—you describe the cowardly means by which you moulded me to your will—you plead only for a quick trial and the full penalty of the law. You understand?"

Quest made no reply, but he understood all too well the hideous intention of his betrayer. What a fool he had been to imagine that Keane Clason would ever restore him to his body! Philip to the chair, Quest a homeless spirit wandering in space, and for the body at the bottom of the tank, the brief regrets of the Department!

A sudden rushing sound filled the air with a sense of action and alarm.

Two—three—four speeding automobiles swung in recklessly to the curb and shrieked to a standstill under smoking brakes. Men leaped out and deployed on the run to surround the factory. Keane darted to the door and twisted the key.

"Come on!" he spat at Philip as he snatched back the rug and threw open the trap door.

The command galvanized Quest to action. In two bounds he had Philip on the stairs. A heavy impact rattled the office door just as he dropped the trap into place over his head. Then, infected with Keane's panic, he was running down the passageway like mad.

Inside the tank chamber the brilliantly colored rings of liquid flashed back the rays of the arclight. Half crazed with anxiety, Keane danced on the black ledge like a monkey on a griddle. His face was ashen, drool ran from his twisted mouth, his eyes were two black pools of terror.

Again Quest experienced the peculiar sensation which came with the slackening of control. New hope sprang up in his agonized being as heavy blows boomed against the air-locked door. Great waves of fear poured along the conduits, betraying to the Agent the state of mind of his Control. Now what would Keane do? What could he do? Why, of all places, had he fled down into this blind burrow?

Thud, thud! Then came a series of sharp reports. Outside, they were trying to shoot away the deep-sunk disk hinges.

Still the door stood fast, but the fury of the assault on it whipped the faltering Keane to action. In a bound he was on the platform. With a lightning hand he threw the switch to plus, starting electrolytic action in the tank. Then he pressed a button concealed under the edge of the switch-mount and a panel slid silently aside in the wall, revealing a narrow outlet.

To Quest everything went a flaming red. He might have known that this fox would have something in reserve—a way of escape when danger threatened!

But his Control gave him no time for independent thought. He forced Quest to turn Philip's eyes up to his own. Without disconnecting that grip of his glittering eyes, Keane leaped back to the ledge. Quest felt the silent order:

"Get up on that plank! Dive into the tank! Get back into your own body, let Philip have his! Then come up—the two of you—and face the music. For I'll be gone, and your story will sound like the ravings of a maniac."

Quest took an obedient step toward the platform. But at the same instant a tremendous crash shivered the door. It seemed to unnerve Keane Clason.

With a gasp he sank down upon the steps, his body doubled in pain, his hand clutching at his heart. Another crash followed, and he shuddered and cried out.

Instantly Quest felt an expansion of the will. Keane's sudden physical weakness had loosened his control. Philip's lips worked painfully as Quest forced him to pause, to disobey the command of the Master Will. In a spasm of will he fought to wrench himself free from the countless clinging tentacles of his Control. In great surges, Quest's reviving volition pounded against the walls of his borrowed body. Now he sought to force this sluggish body back to the wall, so that he might release the airlock and spring the door. But Philip seemed to ossify, every cord and muscle of his body frozen to stone by the conflict that raged within him.

Braced against the wall, Keane was rising slowly to his feet. His seizure was easing, and so he was able to exert a better pressure upon his rebellious Agent.

"Come!" he gasped, realizing that he lacked the strength to escape alone and must therefore change his plan. "Lift me—quick! Carry me out! Slide the panel back into place. We will escape together!"

The spoken command turned the balance against Quest. His will yielded to the master. At the same instant Philip's body relaxed like an object relieved of a great excess of electrical potential. Suddenly strong and supple, he lifted the trembling Keane and tossed him across his shoulder.

For a moment there had been a lull in the assault on the door. Now the battering resumed with a fury that jarred the whole chamber and sent ripples dancing across the varicolored liquids in the osmotic tank.

"Quick!" gasped Keane. "Move! I say. Carry me out."

But he was in a fainting condition. Crash after crash rocked the chamber, and with every blow Quest's will felt a stimulation that enabled him to stand off the commands of his Control. Then a wave of nausea swept over him and left him reeling. It seemed that Philip's blood had turned to boiling oil. A dazzling mist swallowed him up, and with a weird sense of inflation he felt full strength returning to his will.

A booming blow that bulged the door inward acted upon him like a stage player's cue. He leaped to the platform. The gurgling sound of remonstrance rattled from Keane's throat. But Quest paid no heed. Philip was walking the plank—away from the open panel—out over the tank.

Rapidly he dropped down the ladder to the bottom rung, snatched Keane's wrist in a gorillalike grip, and hurled him down into the vat.

Then Philip was clinging desperately to the ladder, his strength gone, his body shivering as if with ague.

"Go on up!" came a strange, impatient voice from below him. "For heaven's sake let me out of here!"

A downward glance, and with a shout of alarm Philip was scrambling up the ladder, for there was a head down there, and a pair of naked shoulders, and the face of a man he had never seen before. Hand over hand Quest followed. Philip had collapsed and lay prone on the plank. Quest lifted him to his feet and shook him anxiously.

"Philip!" he urged. "Philip! Can you walk?"

The tattoo on the battered door helped to revive the older man.

"Quick!" whispered Quest, kneading Philip's arms. "There's barely an hour left. Get to your office. Burn the papers. Refuse the money. Do you hear me?"

Philip nodded dazedly.

"Hurry!" puffed Quest, thrusting him through the opening that Keane had reserved for his own escape, and sliding the panel back into place.

Quest was himself now—young, strong, free. Instantly he threw the electrolytic switch to minus. For Keane had failed to emerge from the tank, and since he was submerged alone, he could not escape until electrolysis was halted.

Just as Quest leaped from the platform to release the airlock, the door burst in and three men with drawn guns rushed into the chamber.

The leader stopped with a startled oath and stood blinking his unbelieving eyes. Quest was poised like a statue, his naked body gleaming an unearthly white against the lusterless black of the wall.

"Quest," came from the three in chorus. Then a rush of questions: "What's the matter? What's happened to you? Where are the Clasons?"

Quest turned toward the platform, expecting to see Keane.

"Something's wrong!" he shouted. "Quick! Somebody get Philip. He's gone to his Loop office. Keane Clason's at the bottom of this tank. I'm not sure how this thing works, but Philip can get him out! I'm sure of it!"

Despite the confident predictions of both Quest and Philip Clason, osmotic association failed to restore Keane to life, and at last the coroner ordered the removal of the body. The autopsy revealed heart disease as the cause of his death.

For reasons best understood at Washington, the cause of the five launch deaths was withheld from the public. Quest's punishment for his part in the crime consisted of a promotion and a warm personal letter from the President of the United States.

A SCIENTIST RISES

D. W. Hall (1932)

"The face of the giant was indeed that of a god...."
All gazed, transfixed, at the vast form that
towered above them.

ON THAT SUMMER day the sky over New York was unflecked by clouds, and the air hung motionless, the waves of heat undisturbed. The city was a vast oven where even the sounds of the coiling traffic in its streets seemed heavy and weary under the press of heat that poured down from above. In Washington Square, the urchins of the neighborhood splashed in the fountain, and the usual midday assortment of mothers, tramps and out-of-works lounged listlessly on the hot park benches.

As a bowl, the Square was filled by the torrid sun, and the trees and grass drooped like the people on its walks. In the surrounding city, men worked in sweltering offices and the streets rumbled with the never-ceasing tide of business—but Washington Square rested.

And then a man walked out of one of the houses lining the square, and all this was changed.

He came with a calm, steady stride down the steps of a house on the north side, and those who happened to see him gazed with surprised interest. For he was a giant in size. He measured at least eleven feet in height, and his body was well-formed and in perfect proportion. He crossed the street and stepped over the railing into the nearest patch of grass, and there stood with arms folded and legs a little apart. The expression on his face was preoccupied and strangely apart, nor did it change when, almost immediately from the park bench nearest him, a woman's excited voice cried:

"Look! Look! Oh, look!"

The people around her craned their necks and stared, and from them grew a startled murmur. Others from farther away came to see who had cried out, and remained to gaze fascinated at the man on the grass. Quickly the murmur spread across the Square, and from its every part men and women and children streamed towards the center of interest—and then, when they saw, backed away slowly and fearfully, with staring eyes, from where the lone figure stood.

THERE was about that figure something uncanny and terrible. There, in the hot midday hush, something was happening to it which men would say could not happen; and men, seeing it, backed away in alarm. Quickly they dispersed. Soon there were only white, frightened faces peering from behind buildings and trees.

Before their very eyes the giant was growing.

When he had first emerged, he had been around eleven feet tall, and now, within three minutes, he had risen close to sixteen feet.

His great body maintained its perfect proportions. It was that of an elderly man clad simply in a gray business suit. The face was kind, its clear-chiselled features indicating fine spiritual strength; on the white forehead beneath the sparse gray hair were deep-sunken lines which spoke of years of concentrated work.

No thought of malevolence could come from that head with its gentle blue eyes that showed the peace within, but fear struck ever stronger into those who watched him, and in one place a woman fainted; for the great body continued to grow, and grow ever faster, until it was twenty feet high, then swiftly twenty-five, and the feet, still separated, were as long as the body of a normal boy. Clothes and body grew effortlessly, the latter apparently without pain, as if the terrifying process were wholly natural.

The cars coming into Washington Square had stopped as their drivers sighted what was rising there, and by now the bordering streets were tangled with traffic. A distant crowd of milling people heightened the turmoil. The northern edge was deserted, but in a large semicircle was spread a fear-struck, panicky mob. A single policeman, his face white and his eyes wide, tried to straighten out the tangle of vehicles, but it was infinitely beyond him and he sent in a riot call; and as the giant with the kind, dignified face loomed silently higher than the trees in the Square, and ever higher, a dozen blue-coated figures appeared, and saw, and knew fear too, and hung back awe-stricken, at a loss what to do. For by now the rapidly mounting body had risen to the height of forty feet.

AN excited voice raised itself above the general hubbub.

"Why, I know him! I know him! It's Edgar Wesley! Doctor Edgar Wesley!"

A police sergeant turned to the man who had spoken.

"And it—he knows you? Then go closer to him, and—and—ask him what it means."

But the man looked fearfully at the giant and hung back. Even as they talked, his gigantic body had grown as high as the four-storied buildings lining the Square, and his feet were becoming too large for the place where they had first been put. And now a faint smile could be seen on the giant's face, an enigmatic smile, with something ironic and bitter in it.

"Then shout to him from here," pressed the sergeant nervously. "We've got to find out something! This is crazy—impossible! My God! Higher yet—and faster!"

Summoning his courage, the other man cupped his hands about his mouth and shouted:

"Dr. Wesley! Can you speak and tell us? Can we help you stop it?"

The ring of people looked up breathless at the towering figure, and a wave of fear passed over them and several hysterical shrieks rose up as, very slowly, the huge head shook from side to side. But the smile on its lips became stronger, and kinder, and the bitterness seemed to leave it.

There was fear at that motion of the enormous head, but a roar of panic sounded from the watchers when, with marked caution, the growing giant moved one foot from the grass into the street behind and the other into the nearby base of Fifth Avenue, just above the Arch. Fearing harm, they were gripped by terror, and they fought back while the trembling policemen tried vainly to control them; but the panic soon ended when they saw that the leviathan's arms remained crossed and his smile kinder yet. By now he dwarfed the houses, his body looming a hundred and fifty feet into the sky. At this moment a woman back of the semicircle slumped to her knees and prayed hysterically.

"Someone's coming out of his house!" shouted one of the closest onlookers.

THE door of the house from which the giant had first appeared had opened, and the figure of a middle-aged, normal-sized man emerged. For a second he crouched on the steps, gaping up at the monstrous shape in the sky, and then he scurried down and made at a desperate run for the nearest group of policemen.

He gripped the sergeant and cried frantically:

"That's Dr. Wesley! Why don't you do something? Why don't—"

"Who are you?" the officer asked, with some return of an authoritative manner.

"I work for him. I'm his janitor. But—can't you do anything? Look at him! Look!"

The crowd pressed closer. "What do you know about this?" went on the sergeant.

The man gulped and stared around wildly. "He's been working on something—many years—I don't know what, for he kept it a close secret. All I knew is that an hour ago I was in my room upstairs, when I heard some disturbance in his laboratory, on the ground floor. I came down and knocked on the door, and he answered from inside and said that everything was all right—"

"You didn't go in?"

"No. I went back up, and everything was quiet for a long time. Then I heard a lot of noise down below—a smashing—as if things were being broken. But I thought he was just destroying something he didn't need, and I didn't investigate: he hated to be disturbed. And then, a little later, I heard them shouting out here in the Square, and I looked out and saw. I saw him—

just as I knew him—but a giant! Look at his face! Why, he has the face of—of a god! He's—as if he were looking down on us—and—pitying us...."

For a moment all were silent as they gazed, transfixed, at the vast form that towered two hundred feet above them. Almost as awe-inspiring as the astounding growth was the fine, dignified calmness of the face. The sergeant broke in:

"The explanation of this must be in his laboratory. We've got to have a look. You lead us there."

THE other man nodded; but just then the giant moved again, and they waited and watched.

With the utmost caution the titanic shape changed position. Gradually, one great foot, over thirty feet in length, soared up from the street and lowered farther away, and then the other distant foot changed its position; and the leviathan came gently to rest against the tallest building bordering the Square, and once more folded his arms and stood quiet. The enormous body appeared to waver slightly as a breath of wind washed against it: obviously it was not gaining weight as it grew. Almost, now, it appeared to float in the air. Swiftly it grew another twenty-five feet, and the gray expanse of its clothes shimmered strangely as a ripple ran over its colossal bulk.

A change of feeling came gradually over the watching multitude. The face of the giant was indeed that of a god in the noble, irony-tinged serenity of his calm features. It was if a further world had opened, and one of divinity had stepped down; a further world of kindness and fellow-love, where were none of the discords that bring conflicts and slaughterings to the weary people of Earth. Spiritual peace radiated from the enormous face under the silvery hair, peace with an undertone of sadness, as if the giant knew of the sorrows of the swarm of dwarfs beneath him, and pitied them.

From all the roofs and the towers of the city, for miles and miles around, men saw the mammoth shape and the kindly smile grow more and more tenuous against the clear blue sky. The figure remained quietly in the same position, his feet filling two empty streets, and under the spell of his smile all fear seemed to leave the nearer watchers, and they became more quiet and controlled.

THE group of policemen and the janitor made a dash for the house from which the giant had come. They ascended the steps, went in, and found the door of the laboratory locked. They broke the door down. The sergeant looked in.

"Anyone in here?" he cried. Nothing disturbed the silence, and he entered, the others following.

A long, wide, dimly-lit room met their eyes, and in its middle the remains of a great mass of apparatus that had dominated it.

The apparatus was now completely destroyed. Its dozen rows of tubes were shattered, its intricate coils of wire and machinery hopelessly smashed. Fragments lay scattered all over the floor. No longer was there the least shape of meaning to anything in the room; there remained merely a litter of glass and stone and scrap metal.

Conspicuous on the floor was a large hammer. The sergeant walked over to pick it up, but, instead, paused and stared at what lay beyond it.

"A body!" he said.

A sprawled out dead man lay on the floor, his dark face twisted up, his sightless eyes staring at the ceiling, his temple crushed as with a hammer. Clutched tight in one stiff hand was an automatic. On his chest was a sheet of paper.

The captain reached down and grasped the paper. He read what was written on it, and then he read it to the others:

THERE was a fool who dreamed the high dream of the pure scientist, and who lived only to ferret out the secrets of nature, and harness them for his fellow men. He studied and worked and thought, and in time came to concentrate on the manipulation of the atom, especially the possibility of contracting and expanding it—a thing of greatest potential value. For nine years he worked along this line, hoping to succeed and give new power, new happiness, a new horizon to mankind. Hermetically sealed in his laboratory, self-exiled from human contacts, he labored hard.

There came a day when the device into which the fool had poured his life stood completed and a success. And on that very day an agent for a certain government entered his laboratory to steal the device. And in that moment the fool realized what he had done: that, from the apparatus he had invented, not happiness and new freedom would come to his fellow men, but instead slaughter and carnage and drunken power increased a hundredfold. He realized, suddenly, that men had not yet learned to use fruitfully the precious, powerful things given to them, but as yet could only play with them like greedy children—and kill as they played. Already his invention had brought death. And he realized—even on this day of his triumph—that it and its secret must be destroyed, and with them he who had fashioned so blindly.

For the scientist was old, his whole life was the invention, and with its going there would be nothing more.

And so he used the device's great powers on his own body; and then, with those powers working on him, he destroyed the device and all the papers that held its secrets.

Was the fool also mad? Perhaps. But I do not think so. Into his lonely laboratory, with this marauder, had come the wisdom that men must wait, that the time is not yet for such power as he was about to offer. A gesture, his strange death, which you who read this have seen? Yes, but a useful one, for with it he and his invention and its hurtful secrets go from you; and a fitting one, for he dies through his achievement, through his very life.

But, in a better sense, he will not die, for the power of his achievement will dissolve his very body among you infinitely; you will breathe him in your air; and in you he will live incarnate until that later time when another will give you the knowledge he now destroys, and he will see it used as he wished it used.—E. W.

THE sergeant's voice ceased, and wordlessly the men in the laboratory looked at each other. No comment was needed. They went out.

They watched from the steps of Edgar Wesley's house. At first sight of the figure in the sky, a new awe struck them, for now the shape of the giant towered a full five hundred feet into the sun, and it seemed almost a mirage, for definite outline was gone from it. It shimmered and wavered against the bright blue like a mist, and the blue shone through it, for it was quite transparent. And yet still they imagined they could discern the slight ironic smile on the face, and the peaceful, understanding light in the serene eyes; and their hearts swelled at the knowledge of the spirit, of the courage, of the fine, far-seeing mind of that outflung titanic martyr to the happiness of men.

The end came quickly. The great misty body rose; it floated over the city like a wraith, and then it swiftly dispersed, even as steam dissolves in the air. They felt a silence over the thousands of watching people in the Square, a hush broken at last by a deep, low murmur of awe and wonderment as the final misty fragments of the vast sky-held figure wavered and melted imperceptibly—melted and were gone from sight in the air that was breathed by the men whom Edgar Wesley loved.

THE WORLD BEYOND

Ray Cummings (1942)

THE OLD WOMAN was dying. There could be no doubt of it now. Surely she would not last through the night. In the dim quiet bedroom he sat watching her, his young face grim and awed. Pathetic business, this ending of earthly life, this passing on. In the silence, from the living room downstairs the gay laughter of the young people at the birthday party came floating up. His birthday—Lee Anthony, twenty-one years old today. He had thought he would feel very different, becoming—legally—a man. But the only difference now, was that old Anna Green who had been always so good to him, who had taken care of him almost all his life, now was dying.

Terrible business. But old age is queer. Anna knew what was happening. The doctor, who had given Lee the medicines and said he would be back in the morning, hadn't fooled her. And she had only smiled.

Lee tensed as he saw that she was smiling now; and she opened her eyes. His hand went to hers where it lay, so white, blue-veined on the white bedspread.

"I'm here, Anna. Feel better?"

"Oh, yes. I'm all right." Her faint voice, gently tired, mingled with the sounds from the party downstairs. She heard the laughter. "You should be down there, Lee. I'm all right."

"I should have postponed it," he said. "And what you did, preparing for it—"

She interrupted him, raising her thin arm, which must have seemed so heavy that at once she let it fall again. "Lee—I guess I am glad you're here—want to talk to you—and I guess it better be now."

"Tomorrow—you're too tired now—"

"For me," she said with her gentle smile, "there may not be any tomorrow—not here. Your grandfather, Lee—you really don't remember him?"

"I was only four or five."

"Yes. That was when your father and mother died in the aero accident and your grandfather brought you to me."

Very vaguely he could remember it. He had always understood that Anna Green had loved his grandfather, who had died that same year.

"What I want to tell you, Lee—" She seemed summoning all her last remaining strength. "Your grandfather didn't die. He just went away. What you've never known—he was a scientist. But he was a lot more than that. He had—dreams. Dreams of what we mortals might be—what we ought to be—but are not. And so he—went away."

This dying old woman; her mind was wandering?...

"Oh—yes," Lee said. "But you're much too tired now, Anna dear—"

"Please let me tell you. He had—some scientific apparatus. I didn't see it—I don't know where he went. I think he didn't know either, where he was going. But he was a very good man, Lee. I think he had an intuition—an inspiration. Yes, it must have been that. A man—inspired. And so he went. I've never seen or heard from him since. Yet—what he promised me—if he could accomplish it—tonight—almost now, Lee, would be the time—"

Just a desperately sick old woman whose blurred mind was seeing visions. The thin wrinkled face, like crumpled white parchment, was transfigured as though by a vision. Her sunken eyes were bright with it. A wonderment stirred within Lee Anthony. Why was his heart pounding? It seemed suddenly as though he must be sharing this unknown thing of science—and mysticism. As though something within him—his grandfather's blood perhaps—was responding.... He felt suddenly wildly excited.

"Tonight?" he murmured.

"Your grandfather was a very good man, Lee—"

"And you, Anna—all my life I have known how good you are. Not like most women—you're just all gentleness—just kindness—"

"That was maybe—just an inspiration from him." Her face was bright with it. "I've tried to bring you up—the way he told me. And what I must tell you now—about tonight, I mean—because I may not live to see it—"

Her breath gave out so that her faint tired voice trailed away.

"What?" he urged. "What is it, Anna? About tonight—"

What a tumult of weird excitement was within him! Surely this was something momentous. His twenty-first birthday. Different, surely, for Lee Anthony than any similar event had ever been for anyone else.

"He promised me—when you were twenty-one—just then—at this time, if he could manage it—that he would come back—"

"Come back, Anna? Here?"

"Yes. To you and me. Because you would be a man—brought up, the best I could do to make you be—like him—because you would be a man who would know the value of love—and kindness—those things that ought to rule this world—but really do not."

This wild, unreasoning excitement within him...! "You think he will come—tonight, Anna?"

"I really do. I want to live to see him. But now—I don't know—"

He could only sit in silence, gripping her hand. And again the gay voices of his guests downstairs came up like a roar of intrusion. They didn't know that she was more than indisposed. She had made him promise not to tell them.

Her eyes had closed, and now she opened them again. "They're having a good time, aren't they, Lee? That's what I wanted—for you and them both. You see, I've had to be careful—not to isolate you from life—life as it is. Because your grandfather wanted you to be normal—a healthy, happy—regular young man. Not queer—even though I've tried to show you—"

"If he—he's coming tonight, Anna—we shouldn't have guests here."

"When they have had their fun—"

"They have. We're about finished down there. I'll get rid of them—tell them you're not very well—"

She nodded. "Perhaps that's best—now—"

He was hardly aware of how he broke up the party and sent them away. Then in the sudden heavy silence of the little cottage, here in the grove of trees near the edge of the town, he went quietly back upstairs.

Her eyes were closed. Her white face was placid. Her faint breath was barely discernible. Failing fast now. Quietly he sat beside her. There was nothing that he could do. The doctor had said that very probably she could not live through the night. Poor old Anna. His mind rehearsed the life that she had given him. Always she had been so gentle, so wise, ruling him with kindness.

He remembered some of the things she had reiterated so often that his childish mind had come to realize their inevitable truth. The greatest instinctive desire of every living creature is happiness. And the way to get it was not by depriving others of it. It seemed now as though this old woman had had something of goodness inherent to her—as though she were inspired? And tonight she had said, with her gentle smile as she lay dying, that if that were so—it had been an inspiration from his grandfather.

Something of science which his grandfather had devised, and which had enabled him to—go away. What could that mean? Go where? And why had he gone? To seek an ideal? Because he was dissatisfied with life here? Her half incoherent words had seemed to imply that. And now, because Lee was twenty-one—a man—his grandfather was coming back. Because he had thought that Lee would be able to help him?... Help him to do—what?

He stirred in his chair. It was nearly midnight now. The little cottage—this little second floor bedroom where death was hovering—was heavy with brooding silence. It was awesome; almost frightening. He bent closer to the bed. Was she dead? No, there was still a faint fluttering breath, but it seemed now that there would be no strength for her to speak to him again.

Mysterious business, this passing on. Her eyelids were closed, a symbol of drawn blinds of the crumbling old house in which she had lived for so long. It was almost a tenantless house now. And yet she was somewhere down there behind those drawn blinds. Reluctant perhaps to leave, still she lingered, with the fires going out so that it must be cold ... cold and silent where she huddled. Or was she hearing now the great organ of the Beyond with its sweep of harmonies summoning her to come—welcoming her....

A shiver ran through young Lee Anthony as he saw that the pallid bloodless lips of the white wrinkled face had stirred into a smile. Down there somewhere her spirit—awed and a little frightened doubtless—had opened some door to let the sound of the organ in—and to let in the great riot of color which must have been outside.... And then she had not been frightened, but eager....

He realized suddenly that he was staring at an empty shell and that old Anna Green had gone....

A sound abruptly brought Lee out of his awed thoughts. It was outside the house—the crunching of wheels in the gravel of the driveway—the squeal of grinding brakes. A car had stopped. He sat erect in his chair, stiffened, listening, with his heart pounding so that the beat of it seemed to shake his tense body. His grandfather—returning?

An automobile horn honked. Footsteps sounded on the verandah. The front doorbell rang.

There were voices outside as he crossed the living room—a man's voice, and then a girl's laugh. He flung open the door. It was a young man in dinner clothes and a tall blonde girl. Tom Franklin, and a vivid, theatrical-looking girl, whom Lee had never seen before. She was inches taller than her companion. She stood clinging to his arm; her beautiful face, with beaded lashes and heavily rouged lips, was laughing. She was swaying; her companion steadied her, but he was swaying himself.

"Easy, Viv," he warned. "We made it—tol' you we would.... Hello there, Lee ol' man—your birthday—think I'd forget a thing like that, not on your life. So we come t'celebrate—meet Vivian Lamotte—frien' o' mine. Nice kid, Viv—you'll like her."

"Hello," the girl said. She stared up at Lee. He towered above her, and beside him the undersized and stoop-shouldered Franklin was swaying happily. Admiration leaped into the girl's eyes.

"Say," she murmured, "you sure are a swell looker for a fact. He said you were—but my Gawd—"

"And his birthday too," Frank agreed, "so we're gonna celebrate—" His slack-jawed, weak-chinned face radiated happiness and triumph. "Came fas' to get here in time. I tol' Viv I could make it—we never hit a thing—"

"Why, yes—come in," Lee agreed awkwardly. He had only met young Tom Franklin once or twice, a year ago now, and Lee had completely forgotten it. The son of a rich man, with more money than was good for him.... With old Anna lying there upstairs—surely he did not want these happy inebriated guests here now....

He stood with them just inside the threshold. "I—I'm awfully sorry," he began. "My birthday—yes, but you see—old Mrs. Green—my guardian—just all the family I've got—she died, just a few minutes ago—upstairs here—I've been here alone with her—"

It sobered them. They stared blankly. "Say, my Gawd, that's tough," the girl murmured. "Your birthday too. Tommy listen, we gotta get goin'—can't celebrate—"

It seemed that there was just a shadow out on the dark verandah. A tall figure in a dark cloak.

"Why—what the hell," Franklin muttered.

A group of gliding soundless figures were out there in the darkness. And across the living room the window sash went up with a thump. A black shape was there, huddled in a great loose cloak which was over the head so that the thing inside was shapeless.

For an instant Lee and his two companions stood stricken. The shapes seemed babbling with weird unintelligible words. Then from the window came words of English:

"*We—want—*" Slow words, strangely intoned. Young Tom Franklin broke in on them.

"Say—what the devil—who do you people think you are, comin' in here—" He took a swaying step over the threshold. There was a sudden sharp command from one of the shapes. Lee jumped in front of the girl. On the verandah the gliding figures were engulfing Franklin; he had fallen.

Lee went through the door with a leap, his fist driving at the cowled head of one of the figures—a solid shape that staggered backward from his blow. But the others were on him, dropping down before his rush, gripping his legs and ankles. He went down, fighting. And then something struck his face—something that was like a hand, or a paw with claws that scratched him. His head suddenly was reeling; his senses fading....

How long he fought Lee did not know. He was aware that the girl was screaming—and that he was hurling clutching figures away—figures that came pouncing back. Then the roaring in his head was a vast uproar. The fighting, scrambling dark shapes all seemed dwindling until they were tiny points of white light—like stars in the great abyss of nothingness....

He knew—as though it were a blurred dream—that he was lying inert on the verandah, with Franklin and the girl lying beside him.... The house was being searched.... Then the muttering shapes were standing here. Lee felt himself being picked up. And then he was carried silently out into the darkness. The motion seemed to waft him off so that he knew nothing more.

The Flight Into Size and Space

Lee came back to consciousness with the feeling that some great length of time must have elapsed. He was on a couch in a small, weird-looking metal room—metal of a dull, grey-white substance like nothing he had ever seen before. With his head still swimming he got up dizzily on one elbow, trying to remember what had happened to him. That fingernail, or claw, had scratched his face. He had been drugged. It seemed obvious. He could remember his roaring senses as he had tried to fight, with the drug gradually overcoming him....

The room had a small door, and a single round window, like a bullseye pane of thick lens. Outside there was darkness, with points of stars. His head was still humming from the remaining effect of the drug. Or was the humming an outside noise? He was aware as he got to his feet and staggered to the door, that the humming was distantly outside the room. The door was locked; its lever resisted his efforts to turn it.

There he saw the inert figures of the girl, and Tom Franklin. They were lying uninjured on two other small couches against the room's metal wall. The girl stirred a little as he touched her dank forehead. Her dyed blonde hair had fallen disheveled to her shoulders. Franklin lay sprawled, his stiff white shirt bosom dirty and rumpled, his thin sandy hair dangling over his flushed face. His slack mouth was open. He was breathing heavily.

At the lens-window Lee stood gasping, his mind still confused and blurred, trying to encompass what was out there. This was a spaceship! A small globular thing of white metal. He could see a rim of it, like a flat ring some ten feet beneath him. A spaceship, and obviously it had left the Earth! There was a black firmament—dead-black monstrous abyss with white blazing points of stars. And then, down below and to one side there was just an edge of a great globe visible. The Earth, with the sunlight edging its sweeping crescent limb—the Earth, down there with a familiar coastline and a huge spread of ocean like a giant map in monochrome.

Back on the couch Lee sat numbed. There was the sound of scraping metal; a doorslide in the wall opened. A face was there—a man with a blur of opalescent light behind him.

"You are all right now?" a voice said.

"Yes. I guess so. Let me out of here—"

Let him out of here? To do what? To make them head this thing back to Earth.... To Lee Anthony as he sat confused, the very thoughts were a fantasy.... Off the Earth! Out in Space! So often he had read of it, as a future scientific possibility—but with this actuality now his mind seemed hardly to grasp it....

The man's voice said gently, "We cannot trust you. There must be no fighting—"

"I won't fight. What good could it do me?"

"You did fight. That was bad—that was frightening. We must not harm you—"

"Where are we going?" Lee murmured. "Why in the devil are you—"

"We think now it is best to say nothing. We will give you food through here. And over there—behind you—a little doorslide to another room. You and these other two can be comfortable—"

"For how long?" Lee demanded.

"It should not seem many days. Soon we shall go fast. Please watch it at the window—he would want that. You have been taught some science?"

"Yes. I guess so."

To Lee it was a weird, unnatural exchange between captor and captive. The voice, intoning the English words so slowly, so carefully, seemed gentle, concerned with his welfare ... and afraid of him.

Abruptly the doorslide closed again, and then at once it reopened.

"He would want you to understand what you see," the man said. "You will find it very wonderful—we did, coming down here. This was his room—so long ago when he used it. His dials are there—you can watch them and try to understand. Dials to mark our distance and our size. The size-change will start soon."

Size-change? Lee's numbed mind turned over the words and found them almost meaningless.

"From the window there—what you can see will be very wonderful," the man said again. "He would want you to study it. Please do that."

The doorslide closed....

What you can see from the window will be very wonderful. No one, during the days that followed could adequately describe what Lee Anthony and Thomas Franklin and Vivian saw through that lens-window. A vast panorama in monochrome ... a soundless drama of the stars, so immense, so awesome that the human mind could grasp only an infinitesimal fragment of its wonders....

They found the little door which led into another apartment. There were tables and chairs of earth-style, quaintly old-fashioned. Food and drink were shoved through the doorslide; the necessities of life and a fair comfort of living were provided. But their questions, even as the time passed and lengthened into what on Earth might have been a week or more, remained unanswered. There was only that gentle but firm negation:

"We have decided that he would want us to say nothing. We do not know about this girl and this smaller man. We brought them so that they could not remain on Earth to talk of having seen us. We are sorry about that. He probably won't like it."

"He? Who the devil are you talking about?" Franklin demanded. "See here, if I had you fellows back on Earth now I'd slam you into jail. Damned brigands. You can't do this to me! My—my father's one of the most important men in New York—"

But now the doorslide quietly closed.

A week? It could have been that, or more. In a wall recess of the room Lee found a line of tiny dials with moving pointers. Miles—thousands of miles. A million; ten millions; a hundred million. A light-year; tens, thousands. And, for the size-change, a normal diameter, Unit 1—and then up into thousands.

For hours at a time, silent, awed beyond what he had ever conceived the emotion of awe could mean, he sat at the lens-window, staring out and trying to understand.

The globe-ship was some five-hundred thousand miles out from Earth when the size-change of the weird little vehicle began. It came to Lee with a sudden shock to his senses, his head reeling, and a tingling within him as though every fibre of his being were suddenly stimulated into a new activity.

"Well, my Gawd," Vivian gasped. "What're they doin' to us now?"

The three of them had been warned by a voice through the doorslide, so that they sat together on one of the couches, waiting for what would happen.

"This—I wish they wouldn't do it," Franklin muttered. "Damn them—I want to get out of here."

Fear seemed to be Franklin's chief emotion now—fear and a petty sense of personal outrage that all this could be done to him against his will. Often, when Lee and the girl were at the window, Franklin had sat brooding, staring at his feet.

"Easy," Lee said. "It evidently won't hurt us. We're started in size-change. The globe, and everything in it, is getting larger."

Weird. The grey metal walls of the room were glowing now with some strange current which suffused them. The starlight from the window-lens mingled with an opalescent sheen from the glowing walls. It was like an aura, bathing the room—an aura which seemed to penetrate every smallest cell-particle of Lee's body—stimulating it....

Size-change! Vaguely, Lee could fathom how it was accomplished; his mind went back to many scientific articles he had read on the theory of it—only theory, those imaginative scientific pedants had considered it; and now it was a reality upon him! He recalled the learned phrases the writers had used.... The *state of matter*. In all the Universe, the inherent factors which govern the state of matter yield most readily to a change. An electronic charge—a current perhaps akin to, but certainly not identical with electricity, would change the state of all organic and inorganic substances ... a rapid duplication of the fundamental entities within the electrons—and electrons themselves, so unsubstantial—mere whirlpools of nothingness!

A rapid duplication of the fundamental whirlpools—that would add size. The complete substance—with shape unaltered—would grow larger.

All just theory, but here, now, it was brought to an accomplished fact. Within himself, Lee could feel it. But as yet, he could not see it. The glowing room and everything in it was so weirdly luminous, there was no alteration in shape. These objects, the figure of Vivian beside him, and the pallid frightened Franklin, relative to each other they were no different from before. And the vast panorama of starry Universe beyond the lens-window, the immense distances out there, made any size-change as yet unperceivable.

But the size-change had begun, there was no question of it. With his senses steadying, Lee crossed the room. A weird feeling of lightness was upon him; he swayed as he stood before the little line of dials in the wall-recess. Five hundred thousand miles from Earth. More than twice the distance of the Moon. The globe had gone that far with accelerating velocity so that now the pointers marked a hundred thousand miles an hour—out beyond the Moon, heading for the orbit-line of Mars. Now the size-change pointers were stirring. Unit One, the size this globe had been as it rested on Earth, fifty feet in height, and some thirty feet at its mid-section bulge. Already that unit was two, a globe—which, if it were on Earth, would be a hundred feet high. And Lee himself? He would be a giant more than twelve feet tall now.... He stood staring at the dials for a moment or two. That little pointer of the first of the size-change dials was creeping around. An acceleration! Another moment and it had touched Unit four. A two hundred foot globe. And Lee, if he had been on Earth, would already be a towering human nearly twenty-five feet in height!

Behind him, he heard Franklin suddenly muttering, "If only I could change without everything else changing! Damn them all—what I could do—"

"You're nuts," Vivian said. "I don't see anything growing bigger—everything here—jus' the same." Her laugh was abruptly hysterical. "This room—you two—you look like ghosts. Say, maybe we're all dead an' don't know it."

Queerly her words sent a shiver through Lee. He turned, stared blankly at her. This weird thing! The electronic light streaming from these walls had a stroboscopic quality. The girl's face was greenish, putty-colored, and her teeth shone phosphorescent.

Maybe we're all dead and don't know it.... Lee knew that this thing was a matter of cold, precise, logical science....Yet who shall say but what mysticism is not mingled with science? A thing, which if we understood it thoroughly, would be as logical, as precise as the mathematics of science itself? Death? Who shall say what, of actuality, Death may be. A leaving of the mortal shell? A departure from earthly substance? A new state of being? Surely some of those elements were here now. And, logically, why could there not be a state of being not all Death, but only with some of its elements?

"I—I don't like this," Franklin suddenly squealed. On the couch he sat hunched, trembling. "Something wrong here—Lee—damn you Lee—don't you feel it?"

Lee tried to smile calmly. "Feel what?"

"We're not—not alone here," Franklin stammered. "Not just you and Vivian and me—something else is here—something you can't see, but you can almost feel. An' I don't like it—"

A presence. Was there indeed something else here, of which now in this new state of being they were vaguely aware? Something—like a fellow voyager—making this weird journey with them? Lee's heart was so wildly beating that it seemed smothering him.

Unit Ten ... Twenty ... a Hundred.... With steady acceleration, the lowest size-change pointer was whirling, and the one above it was moving. The globe was five thousand feet high now. And on Earth Lee would have been a monstrous Titan over six hundred feet tall. A globe, and humans in that tremendous size—the very weight of them—in a moment more of this growth—would disarrange the rotation of the Earth on its axis!...

And then abruptly Lee found himself envisaging the monstrous globe out here in Space. A thing to disarrange the mechanics of all the Celestial Universe! In an hour or two, with this acceleration of growth, the globe would be a huge meteorite—then an asteroid....

He stared at the distance dials. With the growth had come an immense augmentation of velocity. A hundred thousand miles an hour—that had been accelerated a hundred fold now. Ten million miles an hour.... Through the window-lens Lee gazed, mute with awe. The size-change was beginning to show! Far down, and to one side the crescent Earth was dwindling ... Mars was far away in another portion of its orbit—the Moon was behind the Earth. There were just the myriad blazing giant worlds of the stars—infinitely remote, with vast distances of inky void between them. And now there was a visible movement to the stars! A sort of shifting movement....

An hour.... A day.... A week.... Who shall try and describe what Lee Anthony beheld during that weird outward journey?... For a brief time, after they swept past the orbit of Mars, the great planets of Jupiter and Saturn were almost in a line ahead of the plunging, expanding globe. A monstrous thing now—with electronically charged gravity-plates so that it plunged onward by its own repellant force—the repellant force of the great star-field beneath it.

Lee stared at Jupiter, a lead-colored world with its red spot like a monster's single glaring eye. With the speed of light Jupiter was advancing, swinging off to one side with a visible flow of movement, and dropping down into the lower void as the globe went past it. Yet, as it approached, visually it had not grown larger. Instead, there was only a steady dwindling. A dwindling of great Saturn, with its gorgeous, luminous rings came next. These approaching planets, seeming to shrink! Because, with Lee's expanding viewpoint, everything in the vast scene was shrinking! Great distances here, in relation to the giant globe, were dwindling! These millions of miles between Saturn and Jupiter had shrunk into thousands. And then were shrinking to hundreds.

Abruptly, with a startled shock to his senses, Lee's viewpoint changed. Always before he had instinctively conceived himself to be his normal six foot earthly size. The starry Universe was vast beyond his conception. And in a second now, that abruptly was altered. He conceived the vehicle as of actuality it was—a globe as large as the ball of Saturn itself! And simultaneously he envisaged the present reality of Saturn. Out in the inky blackness it hung— not a giant ringed world millions of miles away, but only a little ringed ball no bigger than the spaceship—a ringed ball only eight or ten times as big as Lee himself. It hung there for an instant beside them—only a mile or so away perhaps. And as it went past, with both distance and size-change combining now, it shrank with amazing rapidity! A ball only as big as this room.... Then no larger than Lee it hung, still seemingly no further away than before. And then in a few minutes more, a mile out there in the shrinking distance, it was a tiny luminous point, vanishing beyond his vision.

Uranus, little Neptune—Pluto, almost too far away in its orbit to be seen—
all of them presently were dwindled and gone. Lee had a glimpse of the Solar
system, a mere bunch of lights. The Sun was a tiny spot of light, holding its
little family of tiny planets—a mother hen with her brood. It was gone in a
moment, lost like a speck of star-dust among the giant starry worlds.

Another day—that is a day as it would have been on Earth. But here was
merely a progressing of human existence—a streaming forward of human
consciousness. The Light-year dial pointers were all in movement. By Earth
standards of size and velocity, long since had the globe's velocity reached and
passed the speed of light. Lee had been taught—his book-learning colored by
the Einstein postulates—that there could be no speed greater than the speed
of light—by Earth standards—perhaps, yes. The globe—by comparison with
its original fifty-foot earth-size—might still be traveling no more than a few
hundred thousand miles an hour. But this monster—a thing now as big as
the whole Solar System doubtless—was speeding through a light-year in a
moment!

Futile figures! The human mind can grasp nothing of the vastness of inter-
stellar space. To Lee it was only a shrinking inky void—an emptiness crowded
with whirling little worlds all dwindling.... This crowded space! Often little
points of star-dust had come whirling at the globe—colliding, bursting into
pin-points of fire. Each of them might have been bigger than the Earth.

There was a time when it seemed that beneath the globe all the tiny stars
were shrinking into one lens-shaped cluster. The Inter-stellar Universe—all
congealed down there into a blob, and everywhere else there was just nothingness.... But then little distant glowing nebulae were visible—luminous,
floating rings, alone in the emptiness.... Distant? One of them drifted past,
seemingly only a few hundred feet away—a luminous little ring of star-dust.
The passage of the monstrous globe seemed to hurl it so that like a blown
smoke ring it went into chaos, lost its shape, and vanished.

Then at last all the blobs—each of them, to Earth-size conception, a monstrous Universe—all were dwindled into one blob down to one side of Lee's
window. And then they were gone....

Just darkness now. Darkness and soundless emptiness. But as he stared
at intervals through another long night of his human consciousness, Lee
seemed to feel that the emptiness out there was dwindling—a finite emptiness. He noticed, presently, that the size-change pointers had stopped their
movement; the ultimate size of the globe had been reached. The figures of
the Light-year dials were meaningless to his comprehension. The velocity
was meaningless. And now another little set of dials were in operation. A
thousand—something—of distance. There was a meaningless word which
named the unit. A thousand Earth-miles, if he had been in his former size?
The pointer marked nine hundred in a moment. Was it, perhaps, the distance
now from their destination?

Vivian was beside him. "Lee, what's gonna happen to us? Won't this come to an end some time? Lee—you won't let anybody hurt me?"

She was like a child, almost always clinging to him now. And suddenly she said a very strange thing. "Lee, I been thinkin'—back there on Earth I was doin' a lot of things that maybe were pretty rotten—anglin' for his money for instance—an' not carin' much what I had to do to get it." She gestured at the sullen Franklin who was sitting on the couch. "You know—things like that. An' I been thinkin'—you suppose, when we get where we're goin' now, that'll be held against me?"

What a queer thing to say! She was like a child—and so often a child has an insight into that which is hidden from those more mature!

"I—don't know," Lee muttered.

From the couch, Franklin looked up moodily. "Whispering about me again? I know you are—damn you both. You and everybody else here."

"We're not interested in you," Vivian said.

"Oh, you're not? Well you were, back on Earth. I'm not good enough for you now, eh? He's better—because he's big—big and strong—that the idea? Well if I ever had the chance—"

"Don't be silly," Lee said.

The sullen Franklin was working himself into a rage. Lee seemed to understand Franklin better now. A weakling. Inherently, with a complex of inferiority, the vague consciousness of it lashing him into baffled anger.

"You, Anthony," Franklin burst out, "don't think you've been fooling me. You can put it over that fool girl, but not me. I'm onto you."

"Put what over?" Lee said mildly.

"That you don't know anything about this affair or these men who've got us—you don't know who they are, do you?"

"No. Do you?" Lee asked.

Franklin jumped to his feet. "Don't fence with me. By God, if I was bigger I'd smash your head in. They abducted us, because they wanted you. That fellow said as much near the start of this damned trip. They won't talk—afraid I'll find out. And you can't guess what it's all about! The hell you can't."

Lee said nothing. But there was a little truth in what Franklin was saying, of course.... Those things that the dying old Anna Green had told him—surely this weird voyage had some connection.

He turned away; went back to the window. There was a sheen now. A vague outline of something vast, as though the darkness were ending at a great wall that glowed a little.

It seemed, during the next time-interval, as though the globe might have turned over, so that now it was dropping down upon something tangible. Dropping—floating down—with steadily decreasing velocity, descending to a Surface. The sheen of glow had expanded until now it filled all the lower hemisphere of darkness—a great spread of surface visually coming up. Then there were things to see, illumined by a faint half-light to which color was coming; a faint, pastel color that seemed a rose-glow.

"Why—why," Vivian murmured, "say, it's beautiful, ain't it? It looks like fairyland—or Heaven. It does—don't it, Lee?"

"Yes," Lee murmured. "Like—like—"

The wall-slide rasped. The voice of one of their captors said, "We will arrive soon. We can trust you—there must be no fighting?"

"You can trust us," Lee said.

It was dark in the little curving corridor of the globe, where with silent robed figures around them, they stood while the globe gently landed. Then they were pushed forward, out through the exit port.

The new realm. The World Beyond. What was it? To Lee Anthony then came the feeling that there was a precise scientific explanation of it, of course. And yet, beyond all that pedantry of science, he seemed to know that it was something else, perhaps a place that a man might mould by his dreams. A place that would be what a man made of it, from that which was within himself.

Solemn with awe he went with his companions slowly down the incline.

Realm of Mystery

"We wish nothing of you," the man said, "save that you accept from us what we have to offer. You are hungry. You will let us bring you food."

It was a simple rustic room to which they had been brought—a room in a house seemingly of plaited straw. Crude furnishings were here—table and chairs of Earth fashion, padded with stuffed mats. Woven matting was on the floor. Through a broad latticed window the faint rose-light outside—like a soft pastel twilight—filtered in, tinting the room with a gentle glow. Thin drapes at the window stirred in a breath of breeze—a warm wind from the hills, scented with the vivid blooms which were everywhere.

It had been a brief walk from the space-globe. Lee had seen what seemed a little village stretching off among the trees. There had been people crowding to see the strangers—men, women and children, in simple crude peasant garb—brief garments that revealed their pink-white bodies. They babbled with strange unintelligible words, crowding forward until the robed men from the globe shoved them away.

It was a pastoral, peaceful scene—a little country-side drowsing in the warm rosy twilight. Out by the river there were fields where men stood at their simple agricultural implements—stood at rest, staring curiously at the commotion in the village.

And still Lee's captors would say nothing, merely drew them forward, into this room. Then all of them left, save one. He had doffed his robe now. He was an old man, with long grey-white hair to the base of his neck. He stood smiling. His voice, with the English words queerly pronounced, was gentle, but with a firm finality of command.

"My name is Arkoh," he said. "I am to see that you are made comfortable. This house is yours. There are several rooms, so that you may do in them as you wish."

"Thank you," Lee said. "But you can certainly understand—I have asked many questions and never had any answers. If you wish to talk to me alone—"

"That will come presently. There is no reason for you to be worried—"

"We're not worried," Franklin burst out. "We're fed up with this high-handed stuff. You'll answer questions now. What I demand to know is why—"

"Take it easy," Lee warned.

Franklin had jumped to his feet. He flung off Lee's hand. "Don't make me laugh. I know you're one of them—everything about you is a fake. You got us into this—"

"So? You would bring strife here from your Earth?" Arkoh's voice cut in, like a knife-blade cleaving through Franklin's bluster. "That is not permissible. Please do not make it necessary that there should be violence here." He stood motionless. But before his gaze Franklin relaxed into an incoherent muttering.

"Thank you," Arkoh said. "I shall send you the food." He turned and left the room.

Vivian collapsed into a chair. She was trembling. "Well—my Gawd—what is all this? Lee—that old man with his gentle voice—he looked like if you crossed him you'd be dead. Not that he'd hurt you—it would be—would be something else—"

"You talk like an ass," Franklin said. "You've gone crazy—and I don't blame you—this damned weird thing. For all that old man's smooth talk, we're just prisoners here. Look outside that window—"

It was a little garden, drowsing in the twilight. A man stood watching the window. And as Lee went to the lattice, he could see others, like guards outside.

The man who brought their simple food was a stalwart fellow in a draped garment of brown plaited fibre. His black hair hung thick about his ears. He laid out the food in silence.

"What's *your* name?" Franklin demanded.

"I am Groff."

"And you won't talk either, I suppose? Look here, I can make it worth your while to talk."

"Everyone has all he needs here. There is nothing that you need give us."

"Isn't there? You just give me a chance and I'll show you. No one has all he needs—or all he wants."

Groff did not answer. But as he finished placing the food, and left the room, it seemed to Lee that he shot a queer look back at Franklin. A look so utterly incongruous that it was startling. Franklin saw it and chuckled.

"Well, at least there's one person here who's not so damn weird that it gives you the creeps."

"You don't know what you're talking about," Lee said. With sudden impulse he lowered his voice. "Franklin, listen—there are a few things that perhaps I can tell you. Things that I can guess—that Vivian senses—"

"I don't want to hear your explanation. It would be just a lot of damn lies anyway."

"All right. Perhaps it would. We'll soon know, I imagine."

"Let's eat," Vivian said. "I'm hungry, even if I am scared."

To Lee it seemed that the weird mystery here was crowding upon them. As though, here in this dim room, momentous things were waiting to reveal themselves. A strange emotion was upon Lee Anthony. A sort of tense eagerness. Certainly it was not fear. Certainly it seemed impossible that there could be anything here of which he should be afraid. Again his mind went back to old Anna Green and what she had told him of his grandfather. How far away—how long ago that had been.... And yet, was Anna Green far away now? Something of her had seemed always to be with him on that long, weird voyage, from the infinite smallness and pettiness of Earth to this realm out beyond the stars. And more than ever now, somehow Lee seemed aware of her presence here in this quiet room. Occultism? He had always told himself that surely he was no mystic. A practical fellow, who could understand science when it was taught him, but certainly never could give credence to mysticism. The dead are dead, and the living are alive; and between them is a gulf—an abyss of nothingness.

Now he found himself wondering. Were all those people on Earth who claimed to feel the presence of dead loved ones near them? Were those people just straining their fancy—just comforting themselves with what they wished to believe? Or was the scoffer himself the fool? And if that could be so, on Earth, why could not this strange realm be of such a quality that an awareness of those who have passed from life would be the normal thing? Who shall say that the mysteries of life and death are unscientific? Was it not rather that they embraced those gaps of science not yet understood? Mysteries which, if only we could understand them, would be mysteries no longer?

Lee had left the table and again was standing at the latticed window, beyond which the drowsing little garden lay silent, and empty now. The guard who had been out here had moved further away; his figure was a blob near a flowered thicket at the house corner. And suddenly Lee was aware of another figure. There was a little splashing fountain near the garden's center—a rill of water which came down a little embankment and splashed into a pool where the rose light shimmered on the ripples.

The figure was sitting at the edge of the pool—a slim young girl in a brief dress like a drape upon her. She sat, half reclining on the bank by the shimmering water, with her long hair flowing down over her shoulders and a lock of it trailing in the pool. For a moment he thought that she was gazing into the water. Then as the light which tinted her graceful form seemed to intensify, he saw that she was staring at him.

It seemed as though both of them, for that moment, were breathless with a strange emotion awakened in them by the sight of each other. And then slowly the girl rose to her feet. Still gazing at Lee, she came slowly forward with her hair dangling, framing her small oval face. The glow in the night-air tinted her features. It was a face of girlhood, almost mature—a face with wonderment on it now.

He knew that he was smiling; then, a few feet from the window she stopped and said shyly:

"You are Lee Anthony?"

"Yes."

"I am Aura. When you have finished eating, I am to take you to him."

"To him?"

"Yes. The One of Our Guidance. He bade me bring you." Her soft voice was musical; to her, quite obviously, the English was a foreign tongue.

"I'm ready," Lee said. "I'm finished."

One of her slim bare arms went up with a gesture. From the corner of the little house the guard there turned, came inside. Lee turned to the room. The guard entered. "You are to come," he said.

"So we just stay here, prisoners," Franklin muttered. He and Vivian were blankly staring as Lee was led away.

Then in a moment he was alone beside the girl who had come for him. Silently they walked out into the glowing twilight, along a little woodland path with the staring people and the rustic, nestling dwellings blurring in the distance behind them. A little line of wooded hills lay ahead. The sky was like a dark vault—empty. The pastel light on the ground seemed inherent to the trees and the rocks; it streamed out like a faint radiation from everywhere. And then, as Lee gazed up into the abyss of the heavens, suddenly it seemed as though very faintly he could make out a tiny patch of stars. Just one small cluster, high overhead.

"The Universe you came from," Aura said.

"Yes." The crown of her tresses as she walked beside him was at his shoulder. He gazed down at her. "To whom are you taking me? It seems that I could guess—"

"I was told not to talk of that."

"Well, all right. Is it far?"

"No. A little walk—just to that nearest hill."

Again they were silent. "My Earth," he said presently, "do you know much about it?"

"A little. I have been told."

"It seems so far away to me now."

She gazed up at him. She was smiling. "Is it? To me it seems quite close." She gestured. "Just up there. It seemed far to you, I suppose—that was because you were so small, for so long, coming here."

Like a man the size of an ant, trying to walk ten miles. Of course, it would be a monstrous trip. But if that man were steadily to grow larger, as he progressed he would cover the distance very quickly.

"Well," Lee said, "I suppose I can understand that. You were born here, Aura?"

"Yes. Of course."

"Your world here—what is it like?"

She gazed up at him as though surprised. "You have seen it. It is just a simple little place. We have not so many people here in the village, and about that many more—those who live in the hills close around here."

"You mean that's all? Just this village? Just a few thousand people?"

"Oh there are others, of course. Other groups—like ours, I guess—out in the forests—everywhere in all the forests, maybe." Her gesture toward the distant, glowing, wooded horizons was vague. "We have never tried to find out. Why should we? Wherever they are, they have all that they need or want. So have we."

The thing was so utterly simple. He pondered it. "And you—you're very happy here?"

Her wide eyes were childlike. "Why yes. Of course. Why not? Why should not everyone be happy?"

"Well," he said, "there are things—"

"Yes. I have heard of them. Things on your Earth—which the humans create for themselves—but that is very silly. We do not have them here."

Surely he could think of no retort to such childlike faith. Her faith. How horribly criminal it would be to destroy it. A priceless thing—human happiness to be created out of the faith that it was the normal thing. He realized that his heart was pounding, as though now things which had been dormant within him all his life were coming out—clamoring now for recognition.

And then, out of another silence he murmured, "Aura—you're taking me to my grandfather, aren't you? He came here from Earth—and then he sent back there to get me?"

"Yes," she admitted. "So you know it? But I was instructed to—"

"All right. We won't talk of it. And he's told you about me?"

"Yes," she agreed shyly. She caught her breath as she added, "I have been—waiting for you—a long time." Shyly she gazed up at him. The night-breeze had blown her hair partly over her face. Her hand brushed it away so that her gaze met his. "I hoped you would be, well, like you are," she added.

"Oh," he said awkwardly. "Well—thanks."

"And you," she murmured out of another little silence, "you—I hope I haven't disappointed you. I am the way you want—like you wished—"

What a weird thing to say! He smiled. "Not ever having heard of you, Aura, I can't exactly say that I—"

He checked himself. Was she what he had wished? Why yes—surely he had been thinking of her—in his dreams, all his life vaguely picturing something like this for Lee Anthony....

"I guess I have been thinking of you," he agreed. "No, you haven't disappointed me, Aura. You—you are—"

He could find no words to say it. "We are almost there," she said. "He will be very happy to have you come. He is a very good man, Lee. The one, we think, of the most goodness—and wiseness, to guide us all—"

The path had led them up a rocky defile, with gnarled little trees growing between the crags. Ahead, the hillside rose up in a broken, rocky cliff. There was a door, like a small tunnel entrance. A woman in a long white robe was by the door.

"He is here," Aura said. "Young Anthony."

"You go in."

Silently they passed her. The tunnel entrance glowed with the pastel radiance from the rocks. The radiance was a soft blob of color ahead of them.

"You will find that he cannot move now," Aura whispered. "You will sit by his bed. And talk softly."

"You mean—he's ill?"

"Well—what you would call paralysis. He cannot move. Only his lips—his eyes. He will be gone from us soon, so that then he can only be unseen. A Visitor—"

Her whisper trailed off. Lee's heart was pounding, seeming to thump in his throat as Aura led him silently forward. It was a draped, cave-like little room. Breathless, Lee stared at a couch—a thin old figure lying there—a frail man with white hair that framed his wrinkled face. It was a face that was smiling, its sunken, burning eyes glowing with a new intensity. The lips moved; a faint old voice murmured:

"And you—you are Lee?"

"Yes—grandfather—"

He went slowly forward and sat on the bedside.

Mad Giant

To Lee, after a moment, his grandfather seemed not awe-inspiring, but just a frail old man, paralyzed into almost complete immobility, lying here almost pathetically happy to have his grandson at last with him. An old man, with nothing of the mystic about him—an old man who had been—unknown to the savants of his Earth—perhaps the greatest scientist among them. Quietly, with pride welling in him, Lee held the wasted, numbed hand of his grandfather and listened....

Phineas Anthony, the scientist. After many years of research, spending his own private fortune, he had evolved the secret of size-change—solved the intricate problems of anti-gravitational spaceflight; and combining the two, had produced that little vehicle.

A man of science; and perhaps more than that. As old Anna Green had said, perhaps he was a man inspired—a man, following his dreams, his convictions, convinced that somewhere in God's great creation of things that are, there must be an existence freed of those things by which Man himself so often makes human life a tortured hell.

"And Something led me here, Lee," the gentle old voice was saying. "Perhaps not such a coincidence. On this great Inner Surface of gentle light and gentle warmth—with Nature offering nothing against which one must strive—there must be many groups of simple people like these. They have no thought of evil—there is nothing—no one, to teach it to them. If I had not landed here, I think I would have found much the same thing almost anywhere else on the Inner Surface."

"The Inner Surface? I don't understand, grandfather."

A conception—a reality here—that was numbing in its vastness. This was the concave, inner surface, doubtless deep within the atom of some material substance. A little empty Space here, surrounded by solidity.

"And that—" Lee murmured, "then that little space is our Inter-Stellar abyss?"

"Yes. Of course. The stars, as we call them—from here you could call them tiny particles—like electrons whirling. All of them in this little void. With good eyesight, you can sometimes see them there—"

"I did."

And to this viewpoint which Lee had now—so gigantic, compared to Earth—all the Inter-Stellar universe was a void here of what old Anthony considered would be perhaps eight or ten thousand miles. A void, to Lee now, was itself of no greater volume than the Earth had been to him before!

Silently he pondered it. This Inner Surface—not much bigger, to him now, than the surface of the Earth is to its humans.... Suddenly he felt small—infinitely tiny. Out here beyond the stars, he was only within the atom of something larger, a human, partly on his way—emerging—outward—

It gave him a new vague conception. As though now, because he was partly emerged, the all-wise Creator was giving him a new insight. Surely in this simple form of existence humans were totally unaware of what evil could be. Was not this a higher form of life than down there on his tiny Earth?

The conception numbed him with awe....

"You see, Lee, I have been looking forward to having you become a man—to having you here," old Anthony was saying. As he lay, so utterly motionless, only his voice, his face, his eyes, seemed alive. It was an amazingly expressive old face, radiant, transfigured. "I shall not be here long. You see? And when I have—gone on—when I can only come back here as a Visitor—like Anna Green, you have been aware of her, Lee?"

"Yes, grandfather. Yes, I think I have."

"The awareness is more acute, here, than it was back on Earth. A very comforting thing, Lee. I was saying—I want you here. These people, so simple—you might almost think them childlike—they need someone to guide them. The one who did that—just as I came, was dying. Maybe—maybe that is what led me here. So now I need you."

It welled in Lee with an awe, and a feeling suddenly of humbleness—and of his own inadequacy, so that he murmured,

"But grandfather—I would do my best—but surely—"

"I think it will be given you—the ability—and I've been thinking, Lee, if only some time it might be possible to show them on Earth—"

Lee had been aware that he and old Anthony were alone here. When Lee entered, Aura had at once withdrawn. Now, interrupting his grandfather's faint, gentle voice there was a commotion outside the underground apartment. The sound of women's startled cries, and Aura's voice.

Then Aura burst in, breathless, pale, with her hair flying and on her face and in her eyes a terror so incongruous that Lee's heart went cold.

He gasped, "Aura! Aura, what is it?"

"This terrible thing—that man who came with you—that man, Franklin—he talked with Groff. Some evil spell to put upon Groff—it could only have been that—"

Lee seized her. "What do you mean? Talk slower. Groff? The man who served us that meal—"

"Yes, Groff. And two of the men who were to guard there. What that man said to them—did to them—and when old Arkoh found it out he opposed them—" Her voice was drab with stark horror—so new an emotion that it must have confused her, so that now she just stood trembling.

"Child, come here—come here over to me—" Old Anthony's voice summoned her. "Now—talk more slowly—try and think what you want to tell us.... What happened?"

"Oh—I saw old Arkoh—him whom I love so much—who always has been so good to me—to us all—I saw him lying there on the floor—"

Words so unnatural here that they seemed to reverberate through the little cave-room with echoes that jostled and muttered like alien, menacing things which had no right here—and yet, were here.

"You saw him—lying there?" Lee prompted.

"Yes. His throat, with red blood running out of it where they had cut him—and he was dying—he died while I stood there—"

The first murder. A thing so unnatural. Old Anthony stared for an instant mute at the girl who now had covered her face with her hands as she trembled against Lee.

"Killed him?" Lee murmured.

On Anthony's face there was wonderment—disillusion, and then bitterness. "So? This is what comes to us, from Earth?"

Lying so helpless, old Anthony could only murmur that now Lee must do what he could.

"Your own judgement, my son—do what you can to meet this." The sunken, burning eyes of the old man flashed. "If there must be violence here, let it be so. Violence for that which is right."

"Grandfather—yes! That miserable cowardly murderer—"

To meet force, with force. Surely, even in a world of ideals, there is no other way.

With his fists clenched, Lee ran from the cave-room. Frightened women scattered before him at its entrance. Where had Franklin gone? That fellow Groff, and two or three of the guards had gone with him. Cynicism swept Lee; he remembered the look Groff had flung at Franklin. Even here in this realm—because it was peopled by humans—evil passions could brood. Groff indeed must have been planning something, and he had seen in Franklin a ready helper—a man from Earth, whom Groff very well may have thought would be more resourceful, more experienced in the ways of violence than himself.

This realm where everyone had all of happiness that he could want! Human perfection of existence. A savage laugh of irony was within Lee as he thought of it. No one had ever held out the offer of more than perfection to these people. But Franklin evidently had done it—playing upon the evil which must lie within every living thing, no matter how latent it may be. Awakening in those guards the passion of cupidity—desire for something better than they had now.

What had happened to Vivian? Out in the rose-light dimness, a little way down the path, Lee found himself staring off toward the forest where the village lay nestled. Voices of the frightened people came wafting through the night silence.

"Lee—Lee—"

It was Aura behind him, running after him. "Lee—wait—I belong with you. You know that—"

He gripped her. "That girl from Earth—that Vivian—she was with Franklin. What happened to her?"

"She went. He took her—"

"She went—voluntarily?"

"Yes. The people saw her running out with Franklin, and Groff and the other men. Oh, Lee—what—what are you going to do?"

"I don't know." He stood for a moment dazed, confused—panting, his fingers twitching. If only he could get a grip on Franklin's throat. And so Vivian went too! That was a laugh—girl of the streets, pretty worthless, on Earth. But here—she had seemed to sense what this realm could mean.

"Aura, where would Groff be likely to go?"

"Go? Why—why I do remember, Groff often went up into the hills. He never said why?"

"Would they have any weapons?"

"Weapons?" Her eyes widened as though for a second she did not comprehend. "Weapons? You mean—instruments with which to kill people? No—how could there be? But a knife can kill. A knife cut old Arkoh's throat. We have knives—in the houses—and knives that are used for the harvests—"

She had turned to gaze out toward the glowing hills.... "Oh, Lee—look—"

Numbed, with their breath catching in their throats, they stared. Out by the hills a man's figure rose up—monstrous, gigantic figure.

Franklin! He stood beside the little hill, with a hand on its top, his huge bulk dwarfing it! Franklin, a titan, his head and shoulders looming monstrously against the inky blackness of the sky!

Combat of Titans

"Aura, you think you know where Groff may have gone—those times he went out into the hills?"

"Yes. I think so. Lee—that giant, I think now I understand what must have happened."

The giant shape of Franklin, a mile or two from them, had stood for a moment and then had receded, vanished momentarily as he moved backward behind the hills. Lee and Aura, stunned, still stood beside the little rocky path. Lee's mind was a turmoil of confusion, with only the knowledge that he must do something now, quickly. There were no weapons here in this peaceful little realm. Four or five of these madmen villains—what need had they of weapons? The monstrous power of size. The thought of it struck at Lee with a chill that seemed turning his blood to ice. The monster that Franklin had become—with a size like that he could scatter death with his naked hands.

"I remember now," Aura was gasping. "There was a time when your grandfather was working on his science. Groff was helping him then. Your grandfather taught Groff much."

"Working at what?"

"It was never said. Then your grandfather gave it up—he had decided it would not be wise here."

Some individual apparatus, with the size-change principle of the space-globe? And Groff had gotten the secret. An abnormality here—Groff with the power of evil latent within him, tempted by this opportunity. What could he have hoped to accomplish? Of what use to him would it be to devastate this little realm? Bitter irony swept Lee. Of what use was vast personal power to anyone? Those madmen of Earth's history, with their lust for conquest—of what use could the conquest be to them? And yet they had plunged on.

He realized that with Groff there could have been a wider field of conquest. Groff had heard much of Earth. With the power of size here, he could master this realm; then seize the space-globe. Go with it to Earth. Why, in a gigantic size there, he and a few villainous companions could master the Earth-world. A mad dream indeed, but Lee knew it was a lustful possibility matched by many in Earth's history.

And then Franklin had come here. Franklin, with his knowledge of Earth which Groff would need. Franklin, with his inherent feeling of inferiority—his groping desire for the strength and power of size. What an opportunity for Franklin!

Lee heard himself saying out of the turmoil of his thoughts: "Then, Aura—out there in the hills they've got some apparatus, of course, which—"

His words were stricken away. From somewhere in the glowing dimness near at hand there was a groan. A gasping, choking groan; and the sound of something falling.

"Lee—over there—" Aura's whispered words were drab with horror.

A figure which had been staggering among the rocks near them, had fallen. They rushed to it. Vivian! She was trying to drag herself forward. Her hair, streaming down in a sodden mass, was matted with blood. Her pallid face was blood-smeared. Her neck and throat were a welter of crimson horror. Beside her on the ground lay a strange-looking apparatus of grids and wires—a metal belt—a skeleton helmet.... She was gripping it with a blood-smeared hand, dragging it with her.

"Vivian—Vivian—"

"Oh—you, Lee? Thank Gawd I got to you—"

Her elbows gave way; her head and shoulders sank to the rock. Faintly gasping, with blood-foam at her livid lips, she lay motionless. But her glazing eyes gazed up at Lee, and she was trying to smile.

"I went with them—that damned Franklin—he thought I was as bad as him—" Her faint words were barely audible as he bent down to her. "Just want to tell you, Lee—you're perfectly swell—I guess I fell for you, didn't I? That's over now—just wanted you to know it anyway. There's one of the damned mechanisms they've got—"

"Where are they, Vivian?"

"A cave, not very far from here—down that little ravine—just ahead—they're in there—four or five of them, getting ready to—" Blood was rattling in her throat, choking her. She tried, horribly, to cough. And then she gasped:

"I stole this mechanism. He—Franklin—he caught me—slashed me. He thought I was dead, I guess—but—when he had gone, I got this mechanism—trying to get to you—"

Her choking, rattling breath again gave out. For a moment she lay with a paroxysm of death twitching her. And then, very faintly she gasped:

"Sort of nice—I was able to do one good thing—anyhow. I'm glad of that—"

The paroxysm ended in a moment. Her white lips were still trying to smile as the light went out of her eyes and she was gone. Trembling, Lee stood up, with the mute, white-faced Aura clinging to him. It was fairly obvious how the weird mechanism should be adjusted—anklets, the skeleton helmet of electrodes, the belt around his waist, with its grids, tiny dials and curved battery box. In a moment he stood with the wires strung from his head, to wrist, ankles and waist. There seemed but one little control switch that would slide over a metal arc of intensity contacts.

"Oh, Lee—what—what are you going to do—?" Aura stood white with terror.

"She said—four or five of them in a cave near here—perhaps they haven't yet gotten large—"

Down in a little ravine Lee found himself running forward in the luminous darkness. He called back, "Aura—you stay where you are—you hide, until it's over—"

Then, in the turmoil of his mind, there was no thought of the girl. There was only the vision of old Anthony lying back there so helpless—his burning eyes bitter with this thing which had so horribly come to his little realm. To meet force with force was the only answer.

It was not Lee's plan to increase his size for a moment now. By doing that, almost at once he would be discovered. And perhaps there were still four or five of the murderers, still not giants, in a cave nearby.

The dim rocky ravine, heavy with shadows, led downward. He came to a tunnel opening, advancing more cautiously now. And then, as he turned an angle ahead of him, down a little subterranean declivity a luminous cave was visible. Groff's hideout. At one of its entrances here Lee stood for an instant gasping. The five men were here—Groff and four of his villainous companions.

The five bodies lay strewn—horribly mangled. And the wreckage of their size-change mechanisms was strewn among them.

So obvious, what had happened! Franklin had been the first to get large. And at once he had turned on them. Franklin, the weakling who dared not have any rivalry! And now Franklin was outside, out in the hills, a raging, murderous monster. For a moment, in the grisly shambles of the little cave Lee stood transfixed. Then his hand was fumbling at his belt. He shoved the small switch-lever.

There was a shock—a humming—a reeling of his senses. It was akin to what he had felt on the space-globe, but stronger, more intense now. For an instant he staggered, confused. The wires strung on him were glowing; he could feel their heat. Weird luminous opalescence streamed from them—it bathed him—strange electrolite radiance that permeated every minute fibre of his being.

With his head steadying, Lee suddenly was aware of movement all about him. The dim outlines of the cave-room were shrinking with a creeping, crawling movement. Cave-walls and roof all shrinking, dwindling, drawing down upon him. Under his feet the rocky ground seemed hitching forward.

This little cave! In a moment while he stood shocked into immobility, the cave was a tiny cell. Down by his feet the gruesome mangled corpses were the size of children. The cave-roof bumped his head. He must get out of here! The realization stabbed him. Why, in another moment or two these dark walls would close upon him! Then with instant changing viewpoint he saw the true actuality. He was a growing giant, crouching here underground—a giant who would be crushed, mangled by his own monstrous growth.

Lee turned, staggered into the little tunnel, shoved his way out. The walls pressed him; they seemed in a moment to close after him as he gained the outer glowing darkness.... There was only a narrow slit in the dwindling cliff to mark the tunnel entrance. Lee had the wits to crouch in a fairly open space as he stared at the dwindling trees, the little hills, all shrinking. Franklin must be around here somewhere. Franklin doubtless would see him in a moment.

And then as Lee rose up, Franklin saw him. Lee put a hand on one of the little hills at his waist, vaulted it so that he faced Franklin with what seemed no more than a hundred feet between them. For that second Franklin was transfixed. Amazement swept his face. His muttering was audible:

"Why—why—what's this—"

An adversary had come to challenge his power. As Lee bounded forward, on Franklin's face while he stood transfixed, there was wonderment—disappointment—sudden instinctive fear—and then wild rage. He stooped; seized a boulder, hurled it at the oncoming Lee. It missed; and then Lee was on him, seizing him.

Franklin's body had not been enlarging, but as he saw Lee coming, his hand had flung his switch. They gripped each other now, swaying, locked together, staggering. Franklin still was more than head and shoulders above Lee. His huge arms, with amazing power in them, bent Lee backward. He stumbled, went down with Franklin on him. "Got you! Damn you," he said.

His giant hands gripped Lee's throat, but Lee was aware that his own body was enlarging faster than Franklin's, upon which the size-current had only now started to act. If Lee could only resist—just a little bit longer! His groping hands beside him on the ground seized a rock. Monstrous strangling fingers were at this throat—his breath was gone, his head roaring. Then he was aware that he had seized a rock and struck it up into Franklin's face. For a second the hands at Lee's throat relaxed. He gulped in air, desperately broke free and staggered to his feet.

But Franklin was up as quickly. The tiny forest trees crackled under Lee's tread as again he hurled himself viciously on his antagonist....

At the head of the distant ravine, the numbed Aura crouched alone, staring out at the hills with mute horror—staring at the two monstrous giants slugging it out. Franklin was the larger. She saw Lee rise up, and with a hand on one of the hills, vault over it. Giants that loomed against the sky as they fronted each other and then crashed together, went down.

Lee was underneath! Dear God—

Two monstrous bodies—Lee was lying with a ridge of crags under his shoulders.... Franklin's voice was a blurred roar of triumph in the distance. Then she saw Lee's groping hand come up with a monstrous fifty foot boulder. He crashed it home.

They were up again. Their giant staggering lunges had carried them five miles from her. They were almost the size of fighting titans. The blurred distant shapes of them were silhouettes against the glow of the sky. The forest out there was crackling under their tread ... a blurred roar of breaking, mangled trees....

It was just a few seconds while Aura stared, but each second was an eternity of horror. Then one of the monstrous figures was toppling. A great boulder had crashed on Franklin's head; he had broken loose, staggering while Lee jumped backward and crouched.

For just a second the towering shape of the stricken Franklin loomed up in the sky. And then it fell crashing forward. A swift-flowing stream was there, and the body fell across it—blocking the water which dammed up, then turned aside and went roaring off through the mangled forest.

Lee, again in his former size, sat at old Anthony's bedside, with Aura behind him. The news of the combat out there against the sky had come to Anthony—the excitement of it, too much for his faltering old heart....

"But you will be all right, grandfather. The thing is over now."

"Yes. All right—of course, Lee. Just a visitor here—and you will take my place—"

He lay now—as old Anna Green had been that night—just on the brink. "Lee, listen to me—those mechanisms—the space-globe—Lee, I realize now there is no possibility that we could help Earth—and surely it could only bring us evil here. What we have found here—don't you see, back on Earth each man must create it for himself. Within himself: He could do that, if he chose. And so you—you must disconnect us—forever—"

"Yes, grandfather—"

"And I—guess that is all—"

For some time he seemed to hover on the brink, while Lee and Aura, sitting hand in hand, silently watched him. And then he was gone.

The last of the mechanisms irrevocably was smashed. The little line of vacuums and tubes of the space-globe's mechanisms went up into a burst of opalescent light under Lee's grim smashing blows.

Then silently he went outside and joined Aura. Behind them, down the declivity toward the village, the people were gathering. He was silent, his heart pounding with emotion, as he faced them from a little eminence—faced them and heard their shouts, and saw their arms go up to welcome him.

Slowly he and Aura walked down the slope toward his waiting people. And with her by his side, her hand in his, Lee Anthony knew then that he had found fulfillment—the attainment of that which is within every man's heart—man's heritage—those things for which he must never cease to strive.